I0672820

TIES THAT BIND

Book One of the Celestial Wars Saga

Karen Buckeridge

Second Edition

Cataloguing-in-Publication entry is available from the National Library of Australia: http://catalogue.nla.gov.au/

Title: Ties That Bind

Volume: Book One of the Celestial Wars Saga

Author: Buckeridge, Karen (1971–)

ISBNs: 978-0-6487846-1-5 (paperback)

Cover artwork by: Jade Dry

CHAPTER ONE

I am not dead—because I cannot die.

These eight words churned through Avis' mind as the veil of darkness parted to allow some remnants of his recent history to seep into his pain-numbed consciousness.

There was a time, when he had considered that to be a blessing. To live, regardless of circumstance. But, as all who would consider themselves above such things learn sooner or later, there are prices to be paid, and masters to answer to.

The pain of his twisted frame along with the agony of what once was, caused his mouth to open and filled his still tortured mind and body with silent screams.

As he lifted his left hand weakly, he realised something about his current circumstances had changed. Despite the pain that continued to course through his battered and torn frame, he had the ability to move.

At some point, the chains of ice and fire had been removed and he was now lying flat, as opposed to hanging by muscle tissue.

Avis rolled on to his side to alleviate the worst of the pulsing wounds—that which had penetrated his ribs from behind and had twisted until one of his lungs had been torn from its housing.

They had been merciless. Worse than any mortal tale could ever imagine. But then, no mortal had dared what he had done. No mortal would be so foolish. No god would be either—now, or ever again.

He had served his purpose in a multitude of ways. He had been made an example of.

It was some time before he found the strength to draw apart his swollen eyelids. It had been a long time since he had been able to see anything with any amount of clarity. He couldn't remember the number of times his eyes had been gouged out over the last two years, only to be returned when his captors sent him to The Walk to recover (if it could be called recovery) which permitted the torment to start all over again.

Mortals feared this place more than anywhere else in their perceived universe. They feared each level and sub-level for different reasons. Yet, at the height of their fears, they still had no idea. At best, a mortal only dealt with a single level—the worst of their combined crimes.

He on the other hand, had been forced to endure every sub-level of every level and every torment of this realm-forsaken place. He never realised until then that the Seven Deadly Sins and their subsequent punishments applied to his kind. It never had before.

In the distance, he saw an outline of a rich, deep maroon colour. Although its shape was elusive, it was large, moving and rolling in silent unison with something else that subtly controlled its movements. The shadows that rippled across it faded in with the richness of the light that streamed in behind it.

He related to that something. Whatever it was. He had danced many a tune since his capture and had done many a thing at his masters' whims, if only to end the dance for a brief moment or two.

Oh, how his sombre twin brother would laugh if he had been there. For the first time since their birth, he would have laughed. And Avis, the once proud Mystallian God of Life, would hang his head low and have nothing to say in his defence.

As the blur began to leave his vision, he saw a vague outline of a curtain drifting on the light morning breeze, and groaned inwardly, as he had played this game before too. Many a time.

Behind the curtain, he saw the glint of polished glass, and the marbled balcony he knew so well. He had made many monumental decisions on the real version of that balcony that overlooked his courtyard. It was the one place he could find refuge, when his family wanted the ridiculous and expected him to comply.

At least, it had been.

Now, he feared it, with all his heart. He had played this game and he knew the outcome. Different demons. Different positions. All ending the same way. 'No,' he wanted his blistered lips to whimper to those who stood in the shadows observing, even as his eyes creased with tears that would not fall. *'Not this again. Anything but this again.'*

But this was the game, and he knew it well. They would not heed his pleas, even if he were in a position to speak them aloud. They never had in the past. The most degrading of all his punishments was the one that began with his life before his capture.

The sooner he played his part, the sooner they would move on to more conventional tortures. He had done this before-he could do it again. Ironically, this was the punishment that hurt nothing but his pride.

He forced himself on to one elbow, watching the satin sheets slip to his waist. The mattress beneath him was as plush and full as he remembered it, surrounding his body with a blanket of warmth and comfort.

Not so long ago he had accepted that comfort as his celestial right. He would wake, snap his fingers, and servants of every design would jump to his whim. Not so long ago this first scene of the day was very satisfying. So much could happen to change one's perspective in a very short period of time. So much indeed.

Still, like a perfectly rehearsed play, he knew his part. He knew they enjoyed watching it—he knew he had earned their contempt—and he knew most importantly of all he had no choice.

Focusing all his concentration on the one action, he ground his teeth and attempted to sit up in bed. But he barely lifted his weight from the mattress before his body's pain threshold exploded in defiance and the room around him spun.

His mouth flew open as the scream raced to the back of his throat, but no sound ventured beyond that point. All strength deserted him and his supporting arm collapsed, dropping him back to the bed in a panting heap.

For a long time, he lay there, staring at the silk curtain ceiling of his bed. This was not right. His captors had *always* healed him completely before forcing him through this.

They wanted him to know that even at the pinnacle of his personal abilities he still meant nothing to them. They had wanted him to remember every degrading moment-without a single hint of previous discomfort to fog the memory.

Yet his wounds had not healed. They had left him injured. Why?

Once over the initial shock, a sound finally penetrated the rush of blood to his ears. It was a voice—a woman's voice—one he hadn't heard in a long time. It had to be years. Surely it had to be years. He had been here for years … hadn't he?

Grinding his teeth again, he ordered himself to focus. He was by no means a fool, but he had to make sense of this. In all that time, his captors had never put her image in the punishment with him. She was sacred to them—she was Hellion Highborn. She was his ex-wife.

"Clrs?" he burbled, forcing his scorched tongue to form the word, despite the shaft of pain that shot through his throat from the effort. He pawed at his covers, not trusting his waning strength to support his weight after his last effort.

He had not thought of her in a long time. With scarred knuckles, he pushed his way free of the satin sheets and rolled over the edge of the bed, falling the short distance on to the carpeted ground with an echoing, timber based thud.

A heartfelt groan rocketed to his brain as he landed on fleshless knees and fell to his side in a heap.

Still, no one came. No one entered the scene to poke, prod, or taunt him. He heard voices being raised in the next room and rolled on to his stomach, clawing his way across the carpeted floors, never noticing before how thick each strand was and how painful they could be when they made contact with his tortured body.

But pain was something he had become accustomed to, thus they were forever thinking of new ways to inflict it. He was under no delusions that this was yet another one–even if something buried deep inside his subconscious insisted they would never use Clarise's image like this.

He reached the edge of the open doorway and looked past into what should have been his private sitting room.

Yet instead of polished marble floors, plush ochre lounge seats with high rounded backs and intricately carved timber tables and benches, he beheld a sight that had more in common with a cave.

The bouldered walls and ceilings were aglow with an undefined source of internal illumination, the heat from which caused Avis' already charred skin to prickle, even from the safety of the doorway. More shapeless rocks made up a crude altar-like table at one end.

There were no furnishings as such, no great tapestries or drink cabinets, no thick exotic rugs to take the chill from the flawless marble floors. In fact, there was no marble either.

The ground was packed until it had the same dull hardness that made up every other surface in the room. In the walls on either side of him, he saw two deep crevices, each about the depth of a forearm's length, running the length of the room, but otherwise nothing noteworthy.

However, it wasn't the room that absorbed his attention. His eyes, still gazing at ground level, fell upon the flattened, spade-like ebony tail, and the lower quarters of the reverse standing legs that, with the aid of the tail, balanced the body mass on two tri-taloned feet. The tail was twitching angrily.

"I will not accept this from you, Cora," the female demon said.

Somewhere between the demoness and the wall, Avis heard the thump of a taloned heel as it struck the compacted ground in frustration. "But you know why I want nothing to do with him, Mother!" a young voice hissed, full of demonic rage.

Her young leather wings expanded to their full height until Avis could see them around his own ex-wife's plated sides. "It is not fair!"

The tempo of Clarise's thumping tail increased. "I will not tolerate that tone of voice from you either, young lady," she said, in her usual, calm way, despite the movement of her tail. "And I would advise you not to stamp your feet at me again, unless you want to feel the flat of my tail on yours."

Avis heard the repetitive clack of the young demoness' mandibles as she fought to keep her temper under control, until finally, she hissed in anger and stalked from the room. "Do not embarrass me, Cora," Her mother warned the empty space where Cora had been. "You are Hellion Highborn. Above all else— remember that."

Avis dragged his weight to one side, and used the timber architrave between the rooms to drag himself partially on to his buttocks. Pride was no longer something he had in abundance.

"Mother, why is Cora so mad?" a second demoness asked. Avis had completely missed her in his initial scan of the room. She was lying inside the crevice beside her mother's head with only her legs and tail protruding.

Her young frame, like that of her mother's, was covered in sharp strong, ebony plating and tucked in behind her Avis could just make out the vague outline of equally dark reptilian wings. In the skull of the girl, Avis saw eyeless recesses with a finger of unattached flame where her eyes should have been, and her beak, when she spoke, opened in three directions.

The elder of the two sighed and turned to her young offspring. "Cora is angry because she has too much of your father's blood in her veins to allow herself to forgive him."

Avis nearly choked at those words. He only had one daughter to his knowledge, and his ex-wife had gone out of her way to hide their demonic nature from him. The second must have happened when he …

A torrential wave of guilt swept over Avis. No wonder the Hellion Highborn had hunted him down with such unbridled fury. Yes, he had been drinking rather heavily at the time of their *separation*, but he'd only done what he had afterwards to drive her away. It looks as if he had succeeded better than his worst nightmare.

"Forgive him for what, Mother?"

"He did something very bad a very long time ago, before he went away, and Cora has never forgiven him for it."

His shame escalated with Clarise's borderline truth. She could have damned him in the girl's young eyes. No—she *should* have damned him—damned him the way both their families had, by leaving him to suffer eternally at the hands of Hell's masters: a fate he had earned with his own callous actions.

When the child's head tilted and she clicked her mandibles, Clarise quickly added, "It has nothing to do with you, sweetheart. Your father is a very good god, and a very powerful god, and you should be very proud to have him as your father."

That was a blatant lie.

He'd lost all interest in what was 'good' and 'bad' eons ago. The only thing he'd concerned himself with for a long time was his own raging desires, and his determination to make his wife and child … *children*, he reminded himself, suffer for the inconvenience of being in his way.

"I am, Mother. But why did he go away for so long?"

"He did not leave us deliberately, Columbine. He had to go away, but he is back now and we should be thankful for that."

"Why is he hurt so bad?"

"He was captured by some very dangerous people who did some very mean things to him."

For Avis, that was the last straw.

"Tell -r trufe'," he slurred through his broken jaw as he clutched the architrave, determined to make himself heard.

Clarise's reasons may have been honourable, but the child had the right to know and if she wasn't told now, someone in the very near future would correct her delusion out of sheer spite for him. He buried his fingers into the joints of the timber and attempted to balance himself without the strength to succeed.

Clarise swivelled on her rear left toe and gasped. "Avis!" she scolded, leaping into the air and flying the short distance between them. In a single fluid movement, she had him scooped off the ground and back into the replica of their bedroom. "You should not have left the bed, beloved."

"T'll -r!" Avis insisted, clutching the cartilage of her chest plate. His eyes burned with the conviction he longed to express, if only his broken body would allow it. "T'll -r!"

"Later," Clarise promised, as she drew back the covers that Avis had abandoned with such indifference before easing him back on to the bed. She then drew the covers around him, and ran a taloned claw down his cheek. "You must get well first, beloved."

Avis looked up at her. This was not the form that he had bedded, all those years ago. This was her natural form. He had never liked it—believing it inferior to his own.

Dark, impenetrable plates that over-locked the body joints and huge demonic wings that swayed with her every movement were the last thing Avis had wanted to see at the time. He had banished it totally in his presence and that decree brooked no exceptions.

The one time she had made the mistake and ventured beyond her quarters looking like this, she had paid for it with the flat of his hand and every curse he could rally.

How fucking idiotic he had been.

Then, as her exact wording penetrated his thoughts, he looked up at her in wonderment. *Beloved?* After everything he had done to her—their children? He opened his mouth with great difficulty. "… c'n y'shtill …?"

Clarise's dark carapace melted and warped before his eyes. The ebony plates lowered to her bust-line and blossomed almost as if they were alive into a floral backless dress, contrasting beautifully with the snow-white Mystallian skin of her shoulders, neck and arms.

Her legs were hidden within the folds of the dress that flowed to the floor and the talon that stroked his face melted away into a slender, perfectly manicured nail, on an even more perfect finger.

But, as always, it was her eyes that captured Avis' desire for conquest. In this form, Clarise had the most beautiful golden eyes he had seen on any female creature, and the long jet-black hair that normally flowed to the middle of her back was rolled in a loose bun at the base of her neck with a matching black petalled flower protruding from the centre.

Avis lay there, absorbing the sight of her. *'Fool'* didn't even begin to cover the way he felt about himself at that moment.

He'd had in his possession the kind of wife most men of any persuasion dreamed of—slim, beautiful, powerful, good bloodlines, the ability and willingness to manipulate her shape to fulfil any of his wildest fantasies and most importantly, she was completely and hopelessly obedient to him.

Hellion Highborns were the most sought-after females by any pantheon, and Clarise was one of the best they had to offer. And he had recklessly thrown her away.

As if seeing his thoughts, she drifted her arm down to his, and rested one of her two marriage bracers over his.

The gold in their wedding bands matched that of her eyes. "I married you for life, beloved. I am yours, body and soul, and when you fully recover you will then decide what is best to tell our children. But for now, you must gather your strength, for you have one last journey to undertake."

Avis' brow creased and he whimpered, not certain he liked the sound of that at all. He was in no condition to undertake any kind of journey. He couldn't even make it out of that room, and he had really tried.

"Columbine," Clarise called, twisting side on towards the doorway.

The petite demoness from the crevice appeared moments later, with her wings folded in below her shoulder-line and her head tilted to one side. "Yes, Mother?"

"Have Diviten see to it that you are made presentable, then go to your studies."

"Yes, Mother." The demoness bowed with all the grace that came of the Highborn ladies, then she rose and disappeared from the doorway.

Clarise waited a few minutes before raising her hands and clapping sharply, twice.

Two gangly creatures materialised in the doorway. They were almost reptilian, with their leathery hides and their elongated limbs that stretched out the full length of their prone bodies, except that their heads were extremely small, almost infantile and covered with fur.

Two sets of wolf-like ears twitched and their eyes glistened with the constantly shifting blood. The proportions were all extraordinary, but Avis knew that nothing in this realm was, as it seemed. "Milady," they rasped as one, bowing their miniscule foreheads to the ground.

Clarise rose from the bed, clasping Avis' hand in hers and squeezing it slightly to settle his fear as she faced the kneeling servants squarely. "Your Lord is now awake and his injuries must be seen to." Without releasing his hand, she added, "The sooner he has journeyed through The Walk, the sooner he will truly begin to heal."

Avis' mouth opened in pure terror as the two creatures came forward and lifted him from the bed. *No! By the realm, No ... No!*

He shook his head and tried to push away their helping hands. *No!* He would heal! He would heal all by himself! He didn't need The Walk! His panic enabled him to contact their arms several times, and he twisted desperately as they lifted him onto his unwilling feet.

"No!" His lips finally managed to squeal, as he lowered his centre of gravity and dragged his feet against the ground. "No!"

"Wait," Clarise commanded.

The two demons froze, allowing their lady to step in front of them. She took her husband's trembling face with both hands and pressed her forehead into his. "Calm yourself, my love," she crooned, as his heart hammered and his voice ebbed through his blistered lips in audible whimpers. "The Walk will heal you. Nothing more."

If only Avis could cry. Oh, how the tears would have flowed at that moment.

Despite Clarise's reassurances to the contrary, Avis continued to whimper and struggle as her servants assisted him through the rock corridors that made up the bulk of the Highborn Hellion Marital Chambers. There were no torches to light the way—as the walls continued with that maddening internal illumination.

He didn't want to go back out there. Not amongst the Damned! *Let me stay! I'll do whatever you say, just don't make me go out there again!* He wanted to plead, his panic surging with each step they took towards that dreaded place. *Don't!*

Clarise couldn't have known what was really involved with The Walk. Unlike the other demons that inhabited this feral realm, his ex-wife didn't possess a single sadistic attribute in her entire being.

If only he could utter the words to make her realise why he was resisting: why the nine levels of Hell were so unbearable for outsiders to endure and that once tortured, even for a few minutes, a damned individual would do anything to escape it.

The Highborn Hellions protected their ladies from the truth of life—protected them from everything—including themselves.

They were the perfect breed of females and existed for one purpose only: to bow to the will of the men in their lives. From the moment of their anointment they were trained in the art of pleasing their eventual husbands. Nothing else mattered to them.

Not even the choice of husband was left to the ladies themselves. If the lords of other realms wanted a Hellion Highborn lady as a bride, they must first petition the father of the female, and only once the suitor could prove his worthiness would a marriage then be arranged.

The lady's wishes were never an issue, although in Clarise's case, Avis was far from the ideal choice they had wanted for her.

At the time, Avis had never approached Clarise's father for her hand. The thought never entered his head, because he had never wanted a wife—subservient or otherwise.

Clarise was the challenge of the time—nothing more.

He had managed to seduce women from all walks of the celestial pantheons over the eons, and every god knew the greatest challenge of all was to see if anyone could coerce one of the Highborn Ladies to break with their near-psychotically pretentious upbringing and venture to their bed out of wedlock. And not just any one.

Lady Clarise, eldest unmarried daughter of Lord Belial, supreme ruler of all Chaos.

He probably would have gotten away with it too–if she hadn't fallen pregnant.

That mistake and those that followed were what he had been paying for with every minute he had been out there—amongst the Damned.

But he had paid for his indiscretion and heavy-handedness thereafter in full.

Surely he had. Clarise had only been with him for three, maybe four months at best before returning to Hell in tears with their newborn daughter, whereas he had been here for … years?

Yes … yes it was years. That child of theirs … what was her name again? Well, whatever it was, she was older now. And the other one, the one he didn't even know about, she was no babe either. It had to be years.

Although he continued to slide his feet hopelessly in the opposite direction, Avis kept his eyes downcast all the way and never once lifted them to gaze upon the faces of those that moved around them.

It was a lesson he had endured early in the Damned Levels. He was no longer a god worthy of being in the same company as those that dwelled here. He was nothing. He was less than nothing. Nothing was free.

A furred paw appeared around his throat from nowhere, and the smoke-filled, feral growl that followed caused Clarise's two servants to release him with a subservient jerk as they bowed to the ground. The pawed hand had no difficulty in suspending Avis' body in midair.

Avis knew not to resist in any way—resistance always brought more pain. Better to accept in silence, than cry out and make yourself a target. His hands hung limply at his sides, accepting the will of his Hellion masters.

"You would not be defying the wishes of your betters now would you, *slae-el?*" a male voice snarled, breathing heavy smoke into his face. Without a word to his defence, Avis' head rolled numbly from side to side in a negative manner between the thumb and forefingers of the one who held him. No, he wouldn't. He knew better.

"Ludovic, unhand him at once!" Clarise commanded.

That smoky breath moved away from Avis' face. "Clarise, you have embarrassed our House enough with your despicably shameful actions of late. Despite your claim to this wretch, I forbid you to compound the problem any further. Return to the Ladies' quarters immediately," the demon lord commanded, making a general sweep towards the far entrance at the other end of the stone corridor.

If Avis were not her husband, he had no doubt Clarise would have bowed to the will of her younger brother and left them as commanded. But Avis *was* her husband, and it was something that the Highborn Hellion males were not happy about.

"My conduct is no longer under scrutiny, brother, and I am within my rights to undertake these actions without House repercussions. Avis is my husband, and the father of my children, and I have already invoked marital rights before the High Court where his safety is concerned. By Hellion Law I am entitled to safeguard him and defend him with my life if necessary."

"He is unworthy of such devotion!" Ludovic spewed, shaking Avis' lifeless form to emphasise his point. Avis barely groaned.

"That decision is not yours to make, Ludovic. He is my husband, and I am within my rights to defend him as such. His worthiness or lack thereof is no longer an issue either. Only your compliance with our father's laws."

Instead of being released, Avis felt his entire throat constrict as Ludovic's great paw tightened sharply and his mouth flew open in reflex. But then it was gone, and he was dropped with disgust to the ground. Lying on his side, Avis' silent gaze moved from his brother-by-marriage's feet to his irate face.

Unlike Clarise, who balanced on reverse bending tri-taloned claws in her natural form, Ludovic's feet consisted of their father's cloven hooves. His legs bore the same exterior ebony plating as his sister, however his hips thinned into smaller scale-like pieces of cartilage. A tail roughly the thickness of Avis' thumb and forefinger whipped ferociously in and around his legs as he battled to understand his sister's motives.

Thick, tanned fur covered his upper body like a carpet, extending to his paw-like claws that were presently fisted against his hip joints. His triangular earflaps were flattened against his skull and the lips of his muzzle were curled to expose his glistening canines.

He was the most animal-like of all Belial's children, and in the dark he might have easily been mistaken for one, if he didn't bear the same flame filled, eyeless recesses that Avis had seen minutes before on his own younger offspring.

Furious beyond belief, Ludovic rolled his head in a wide, disbelieving arc, and caught sight of Avis staring up at him from the floor. Before Avis could avert them, the demon lord lashed a hoof at the cowering god, collecting him squarely in the face—not enough to knock him out, but enough to break his nose and cheekbone. "Get your eyes back to the ground before I claw them out of your realm-damned head!" he bellowed.

Stars swam through Avis' vision as he sharply twisted himself into the ground at Ludovic's feet, covering his head with one arm to hide it from Ludovic's view.

"Ludovic!" Clarise cried. Avis then heard a combined shuffle of hooves and Mystallian shoes until he felt the soft fabric of her dress-hem drape across his body and he caught the scent so strong it was more like a taste of his ex-wife's ...*wife's* distinctive lavender perfume. He didn't dare raise his eyes again. "Your language and actions are appalling! Leave my presence, if you cannot behave in a manner befitting your bloodline," she commanded.

Avis heard Ludovic's sharp intake, but instead of speaking, the demon lord turned and stalked away.

Long after the click of Ludovic's hooves on the stone floor became a distant echo, Avis felt a Mystallian hand touch him on the shoulder and he cringed with a whimper, curling himself into a foetal position.

"Be at ease, beloved," Clarise whispered. "They will come to terms with what must be. They must." He felt her hand on his chin and trembled. "Shhh," she crooned, when he made an effort to speak.

"Everything will be alright. Once you have healed in body, then you will heal in the mind. You are a god, Avis. An established supreme god in one of the most formidable realms in existence. In time, you will remember what that means, and then you will not hide your face any more."

Avis allowed her to turn his face towards her. How honestly she meant that. He could hear the overwhelming sincerity in her voice and her eyes shone with the unconditional devotion her kind was renowned for.

Why? Why, oh, why had he mistreated her?

And why was she being so exceptionally forgiving now? He certainly wouldn't have been even if it had been years since his incarceration. Had their roles been reversed, he would have been the one to kick her in the nose and not think twice about it.

At Clarise's silent gesture, her two servants came forward and once again lifted Avis to his feet. This time, he offered no resistance. He had already resigned himself to The Walk. Ludovic's arrival and consequential actions had only reiterated the Hellions' ownership of him.

They carried him past the conservatorium where Avis had made his first advance on Clarise, so long ago and down a long corridor. Avis knew this corridor. He knew it, even though the last time he had laid eyes on it he had swaggered through it laughing loudly with an entourage of grovelling servants in tow as Belial's personal guest.

This was the corridor that connected the private chambers of all the Hellion Highborn to the High Court of Hell where all visitors were greeted and assessed by the Lords of Chaos. Unless they were seeking a bride, very few celestials of other pantheons bothered to make the journey through Chaos to meet with Belial and his sons. There was little point.

Belial usually knew his mind before any communication could be entered into, and his sons were dedicated to upholding the will of their father. Despite the nature of what was here, never before had Avis seen a more unified family committed with such singular clarity. Combined with its ancient age and subsequent size, Chaos was the single most powerful realm in the Known Realms. Lord Belial was too powerful, and that show of superfluous power made most visiting celestials very nervous.

CHAPTER TWO

Eventually, the small party reached a cavernous space in the corridor that opened out into a huge rocky archway that stretched almost fifteen metres high and over twenty wide. Bone-like boulders braced the base of the archway that rose from the stones, and where they crossed in a point at the ceiling, a sigil that Avis would not have been able to reach across with both arms outstretched depicted the outline of a golden star in reverse on a black circular background.

There wasn't a mortal or celestial realm anywhere that didn't at least recognise the formation of those five simple lines and fear it on some level. Although Avis couldn't see it in his present condition, he knew it was there staring down at him as disdainfully as everyone else that marched under that House Banner.

On the other side of that archway, he could hear the raised voices of other males and attempted to close his eyes. Their anger could be felt almost through the walls, and he was under no delusion what the subject of their debate was about.

"Wait here," Clarise commanded the servants. She then took Avis' broken jaw and lightly brushed her lips against his battered cheek. "I will return in a moment," she whispered.

The voices fell silent moments after Clarise went inside.

The wait for Avis was agonising. He had no idea what she was saying to them, and had no way to defend himself or assist her in any way. He was completely at her mercy. There was nothing else he could do.

If she failed, he would return to The Eternally Damned. If she succeeded … no, he didn't want to give himself hope. This was not the place for it. If anything, this was the last place for it. The sign at the First Level's gate said as much.

When footsteps re-emerged from inside the opening Avis whimpered again. They weren't just from that of his wife, but also the heavy clopping of a second, larger pair of broad hooves. No sound was uttered, but the servants released Avis sharply and dropped to their knees with their foreheads pressed to the compact surface and their elongated arms stretched out in worship before them. Without their support, Avis collapsed to the ground beside them.

Small noises escaped Avis' throat as he raised his arms to shield himself from the one who had escorted his wife from the High Court Chambers. Only one would draw such a response from Clarise's servants by his mere presence alone.

Avis stuck to his training and looked at the compacted flooring around his shattered nose. *Don't look,* he thought to himself. *For Mystal's sake, don't even think about looking.* The demon's footsteps ended with a final clop on either side of Avis' head. Avis felt his bowels tighten, and for once was grateful he'd been given nothing to eat or drink for so long that he couldn't humiliate himself further.

"Leave us," Lord Belial commanded, his echoing rumble reverberating off the walls to fill the room. The room was immediately vacated.

Lord Belial then took a step back and Avis could hear him squatting down with his elbows resting on his knees. "I warned you, did I not?" he rumbled to the prone form before him. "There are whole realms out there that fear my wrath, yet you alone believed you had the power to defy me and bring harm to those I hold dear."

Unlike his sons, Lord Belial's voice never rose above the same ominous monotone the entire time he spoke. And within that monotone, lay an eternity of control, and an innate ability to draw out even more terror from those that listened to it.

"You will never be welcome here. Those like you will never be welcome here. Those like you will suffer as you have suffered if they dare challenge this decree. My daughter wishes to uphold her matrimonial vows to you, but I assure you, if you ever, *ever* cause her to shed so much as one tear again, you will spend the rest of eternity amidst the Damned and I will crush every member of your pantheon into oblivion just for sharing your bloodline. Do I make myself quite clear?"

Avis' answer was to whimper again. Yes, it was. Very clear. Very, very clear. Despite the celestial ability to live regardless of consequence so long as one had a power base of mortal worshippers, Avis held no doubt at that moment that Belial knew of a means to fulfil his threat.

Somehow, someway, Mystal would die if he ... Avis paused. ... *if* he mistreated Clarise again?

"If I speak to you again, fear the repercussions." Lord Belial said.

Avis then felt the gush of Lord Belial's great wings as the supreme demon launched himself into the air, but still, the demon's last words prior to his emphatic threat echoed over and over again in Avis' tortured mind. *If... If...*

Could Clarise really want him back? Was that what this was really all about? Was he really getting a second chance here? A way to escape the Eternally Damned? Was this really true hope?

As these questions rambled into others, his whimpering shifted from agony and suppression to one of confusion. What if he'd gotten it wrong? What if he'd made a mistake? What if this entire charade was nothing more than another torment to show him what he wanted to see, only to turn against him at the first point he relaxed?

With that humbling thought, his mind resumed the numbed clarity it had before. If it was just another one of their games, the Lords of Chaos had only to tell him where to go and what to do and he would comply, just as he had been taught to.

Clarise returned a few minutes later. He could tell it was Clarise, for she still bore the Mystallian form that he found so pleasing and the delicate click of her fine heels on the compacted floor gave her away. But she wasn't alone. He heard the faint rasp of plate armour. Thick, heavily fortified, plate armour that rubbed against itself without ever wearing, or even buffing the plates. These were no servants. These had a reputation of their own amongst the Known Realms.

Avis closed his eyes, barely flinching as a large, crab-like pincer tightened around his right upper arm while a set of long talons hooked his left and lifted him to his feet. He didn't even have to look at them to know what they were. Highborn Hellion Guard: the elite of all the Pantheon Guards. As fanatically loyal as they were deadly, they were celestially bred to be the ultimate combat operative. The golden plates of their armour glowed iridescently, even in the darkness.

They possessed four upper limbs—each capable of a completely different, independent attack from the others, so that no matter what persuasion of enemy they faced, one of those arms was capable of incapacitating—and in most cases, eliminating them entirely. Beneath the sturdy torso were three powerful legs, designed to support the body as it manoeuvred itself in four different directions simultaneously.

Drawn over and above their shoulder-lines were two long, broadly curved bat-like wings with a large pointed claw protruding over the top to give them the advantage in aerial attacks. All this was just their standard mode. As beings capable of militaristic shapeshifting, they could become any weapon of any size they needed to be and moved faster than most could see to vanquish an enemy.

The only time Belial had ever unleashed them upon a singular pantheon in the past, that pantheon's army broke ranks at the sight of these creatures coming for them and fled from the battle before the Hellion Brute Squad had made their first offensive move.

"Forgive me, my love," Clarise said. "I know how you feel about my true form, but to leave The Well and journey up into Hell's punishment levels, I need to fly." She looked into his unfocused gaze a moment longer before shedding her Mystallian appearance in favour of that with demonic wings. "I will only maintain this form until we arrive at The Walk. Please do not be angry."

Angry? That was almost humorous—if only Avis had the strength to laugh. With his eyes closed, he felt a gush of air and his feet leave the ground.

Although he knew where they were heading, Avis' breath escaped him with a gasp a few moments later as they left the Highborn Well and the sudden icy winds from Ninth Level blasted his fire-blistered skin. The eternal frozen wasteland of Ninth Level was where the worst offenders were sentenced to endure the frozen lakes without the luxury of falling asleep. Statues of frozen souls littered the terrain.

Even without his sight, Avis knew they were there—because he had been one of them not so long ago, sharing in the misery that came from being one of the Damned.

Icicles coated all their eyes as they stared out at the hopelessness of their situation and their mouths were wide with screams that no one would hear. Others were frozen inside the lakes, and more hung from the ceilings as giant frozen stalactites.

They flew through the gates of Antenora that separated the Eighth and Ninth Levels and up the Malebolge Mountain towards the Seventh Level. They passed over the chasm that was filled almost to the brim with souls suffering from leprous diseases.

The stench that wafted up to them as they flew overhead would have once made Avis nauseous, had he not spent time down there, dwelling in that putrid stench. Oh, they had humbled him well.

His only conscious act while down there was to fight his way past the mortal souls to reside on the top layer of that decomposing group. But even that became too much effort and after a while others were dumped on top of him, smothering him with the horrific reality of their predicament.

Their party flew towards the second chasm from Antenora, sardonically nick-named by all who knew it as The Walk. Despite what Clarise had in mind, this place was never really designed to heal. Healing would have been a pleasurable thing, and that went against everything the Nine Levels of Hell were designed to do.

From overhead, Avis resigned himself to his fate and opened his eyes, looking down at the circular chasm that was carved into this sublevel. Its twenty-kilometre length didn't appear that long at all from where they hovered and the souls that were packed into the one-kilometre-wide chasm moving in an eternal circle were indistinguishable.

At one point of the circuit, sat Sarvalis.

Even from this distance, recognition of his bulk was undeniable. Standing at over two kilometres high from toe-talon to horn tip, his twisted horns rose nearly six head-lengths from his exposed skull. His arms were as thick as houses and the great sword he clenched in one hand dripped excessively with the blood of those that walked below him.

That was the punishment of this level. To be severely mutilated by Sarvalis upon arrival. Be it a loss of a limb, beheading, or even simply gutted …it didn't really matter as the agony was universal. Then, while nursing the injury, the soul was made to move as others from behind jostled them forward, inch at a time. With every inch of ground covered, the wound would begin to heal, even though the extent of the injury made it near impossible to move without moaning in agony.

Then, upon completion of the circuit, the soul would have made a full recovery and was forced to face Sarvalis and his accursed sword all over again. Round and round this dance went. Round and round and round.

Avis was different from the regular Damned that dwelled here. He never knew if Sarvalis' sword was going to strike him down as he walked. Sometimes it would, other times it wouldn't. If the Highborn wanted him to suffer elsewhere, he was made to walk only so that he could heal sufficiently to be moved. If they wanted him to suffer here, they allowed Sarvalis to do his handiwork, as creatively as he could imagine. Avis was never told which it was going to be.

* * *

"Milady," Sarvalis purred roughly, kneeling on one knee with his great head bowed as Clarise and her party descended upon the ridge that overlooked The Walk. "What an … unexpected surprise …"

True to her promise, Clarise's form shifted into that which her husband found more pleasing as soon as her talons came in contact with the rocky ledge, despite how out of place a well-dressed Mystallian lady of nobility appeared in these less than ideal surroundings.

Sarvalis' repugnant grimace at her choice of shape was completely irrelevant. "Lord Avis is in need of healing. It is my wish that he completes The Walk and returns with me to the Well in relative health."

"Milady," the demon replied, still on one knee.

"Be strong, my love," Clarise whispered with a kiss, then stepped away and gestured for the guards to place Avis at Sarvalis' feet. As was customary to her upbringing, she fought to maintain her dignity—to keep her eyes free of tears and appear dispassionate to all that was happening around her.

The Damned and other nameless *slae-els* like them were never to know there were emotional differences within the sects and ranks of the Hellions.

Before her, Avis and the Hellion Guard stood in the middle of the flow of souls like a rock amidst a stream. The Damned mingled and moved past him, indifferent to everything but their own, freshly incurred injuries.

Clarise interlocked her fingers and held them down before her, forcing herself to remain calm as her father's guards released their hold on Avis and stepped back, pushing the Damned aside without remorse. *Do this, Avis,* she willed. *It is but one walk* ...

But instead of moving, Avis' legs collapsed beneath him and he was stepped upon by those hapless souls further back in the line that trudged forever onwards with their injuries. Clarise lost her composure with a gasp of fear as he went beneath the hordes of moaning Damned.

"Avis!" she cried, and ignoring protocol, she stepped forward and slid down the chasm into that same sea of lost souls that separated them. Some of those outer souls, overcome by madness from the duration of their stay, saw Clarise as the pinnacle of what they would never achieve and found the strength to reach for her with their gnarled fingers.

The Highborn Hellion Guard responded to this by abandoning Avis completely and launching themselves to her side to protect her. They formed an impenetrable barrier around her, pointing the arm that appeared like a coral stump towards the attacking souls' injuries, injecting them with millions of poisonous spores.

Their screams did little to ebb the tide of them, and before long, all four fighting fronts were being used on either side of Clarise. But Clarise never returned to her Hellion form—never chose to fly to the safety of the ridge above her. Instead, her eyes were locked on the spot where her husband was last seen.

The Highborn Hellion Guard said nothing as they easily fought off her attackers and waited for Clarise to decide what it was she wanted to do next. If it was her desire to be there—it was not their place to speak to her about the dangers involved in it. Theirs was simply to safeguard her during her decisions, whatever they may be. Repercussions of such spontaneous actions were the responsibility of others far higher than they.

But Clarise was not interested in staying safely at the edge of the sea. Her husband was at the bottom of that sea somewhere, and she intended to find him. Pushing her way from the wall, Clarise barely gave the Hellion Guards enough time to position themselves to act as a barricade between the Damned and herself. She pushed her way forward to where she had last seen Avis.

Sarvalis snarled and held his mighty sword high and to the left. "Garlee!" he called throwing himself into the air and sliding into the horde of souls that mingled along the path. He swung his sword through them, cleaving his way towards Clarise. A small, goblinoid demon appeared from nowhere to hover near the great demon's head. "Get some of the Malebranche devils from Eighth Sub-Level up here—*now!*"

Seeing their only opportunity to elude punishment even for a single circuit, the souls yet to be punished surged forward—only to rebound off the brute squad guard. Clarise made her way ever so slowly through the sea of souls.

Sarvalis swung his huge blade hard and fast, carving and cleaving his way towards her. The tallest of the Damned only reached his knee, and many fell victim to the crushing weight of his feet as he crossed the chasm in his haste to reach Clarise. "Milady!" he called.

"Where is Avis?" she called back.

Sarvalis wanted to say something. He dearly wanted to, but he knew better than to say what was so clearly written on his face as he turned back towards his side of the ridge. Avis did not deserve this.

Even he—a non-Highborn Hellion, had been outraged by Avis' heavy handedness of one of their Highborn Ladies, and he would never understand the High Court's decision to allow Lady Clarise to rescue him.

Clarise followed the path made in Sarvalis' wake, refusing to look down upon those that had been trampled into the ground. Her only concern now was … "Avis!" she called, only just managing to reign in her initial impulse to rush to his side.

Many of Avis' bones had been crushed beneath the weight of those that trampled him and his eyes refused to open. But his chest on one side continued to rise and fall ever so slightly and the blood in his veins continued to move.

"Avis," she said, kneeling down beside him in the filth. She took his head in her hands and tilted it towards her. "You must move, beloved. However much it pains you, you must move. Please. I will be here with you every step, but you *must* move."

Avis looked up at her, and for a moment, his line of sight sharpened and she knew he was looking at her. But it only lasted a moment, and then it was gone.

"Avis!" Clarise cried, as the sharp jabbering of dozens of small Malebranche devils was heard on the ridge above. They slid down the embankment into the Damned, using their pronged forks to push and force the Damned back into place.

With the Malebranche devils there to maintain control, Sarvalis could focus his attention on his Highborn visitor. "Milady, your efforts will be for naught if you proceed in this manner," he said, opening his free hand to plead with her, without physically making contact.

Clarise looked up at him. "What do you mean?"

"You have given him hope, Milady, and he has accepted that hope with open arms. He knows he does not have to do anything anymore, because you will protect him, and so long as he believes that, he will not move from that spot."

"Clarise," a voice called, from far above.

Not 'Milady' or 'Lady Clarise' or even a tone that implied reverence. Simply 'Clarise'.

Clarise looked up and saw a winged celestial angling his descent upon the heat currents towards her. Unlike the demons around her, this one's wings were feathered and coloured the same bright orange and flame-red as that of his shoulder length hair. His skin was as pale as her husband's and his eyes were a deep rich blue. Most of his body was covered by polished silver armour with a simplified outline of a dove engraved upon the chest plate. In his right hand, he carried a flaming sword that was poised across his body to his left, ready to strike.

He swung his sword in a downward stroke as he landed alongside Clarise, striking the nearest soul to her across the shoulder and sending it screaming back into the void of others. He didn't face Clarise at first, but turned his attention to any other souls, foolish enough to test his mettle. His wings shifted with agitation.

The moment she recognised him, Clarise curtseyed low with her head bowed and held her new position.

"Clarise, stand up," he said, finally.

"Uriel …"

"Stand up!" the Archangel commanded, this time with more force.

Clarise did as she was told. "I have the authority of the High Court to do this, Uriel."

"You do not have the authority to disrupt two sub-levels of Hell, sister," he corrected.

Clarise lowered her head again and fell silent. That had never been her intention.

Uriel placed the pointer finger of his free hand under her chin and lifted her eyes to his. "I will not say what has been said so many times already," he said, gently. "Whatever your reasons, you have chosen to stand by Avis, and your determination to see him through this is commendable. But you know this is not the way to achieve your objective. You cannot give him support during this time. He must be driven to do this—he must believe that no one will help him, and that it will only get worse if he does not comply. Only then will he find the strength to do what must be done."

Clarise's eyes welled with tears as he spoke, but he hushed her quietly, running his armoured thumb across her cheeks. "Go back to The Well," he said, gently. "Let me deal with this. I give you my word as an archangel that I will return him to you in a matter of hours as healthy as he can be."

Clarise wanted with all her heart to deny him this. She knew what it meant to be one of the Damned, and accepted that damnation as part of what must be. But she had also heard rumours recently that her husband had been suffering far worse than any mortal soul due to his crimes against her. That had been what instigated her matrimonial desire to protect him in the first place.

Pulling away from Uriel's hand, Clarise knelt again beside her husband. "Forgive me, Avis," she said quietly, pressing her forehead into his. "I will be waiting for you. I will always wait for you."

* * *

At that, Avis' eyes did open, and stayed open. *She's leaving? No! She … she can't leave! She promised! She promised, and she never lied! Ever! She can't leave me here!*

His voice came as a weak, fear-filled whine and he wished for the strength to reach out for her …to hold her …to cling to her.

Clarise's tears fell upon his face. "Forgive me," she said, her voice barely above a whisper. Then, before she could convince herself of another path, she shifted into her demonic form and leapt into the sky and arched downwards sharply towards the Ninth Level gate, followed closely by the two Hellion Guards.

Avis' heart sank as he watched her go. She was leaving. How could she leave him? She promised she wouldn't …

A pitchfork was rammed into the muscle below his right knee. "Move!" Uriel snarled, kicking Avis in the right direction as the Malebranche devil twisted his pitchfork and hissed gleefully. "I have no intention of allowing the likes of you to make a liar of me, *slae-el*, so if it takes my personal intervention to get you going …" His tone shifted into a near exact replica of his father's earlier animosity, "…*so be it.*"

CHAPTER THREE

Avis pressed his fingers and toes into the slimy walls of The Walk and braced himself for the short climb upwards. At the sound of the Malebranche devils' wicked cackling behind him, he pulled himself up that first step.

The muscles of his exposed biceps and thighs strained as he dragged himself inch by inch from that disgusting place. It had been hours since Clarise had left, maybe even days, but Uriel had been true to his word. Avis had been forced around The Walk twice to recover from the injuries he had incurred the first time around when he had refused to crawl.

Up he climbed. Unlike those below him, he was not truly of the Damned. They were mortal souls with no real celestial strength, while he was a god, and Sarvalis had indicated at the completion of the second lap that he was to climb out himself—without assistance. Inch by painful inch, hand over hand, he made his own way from that insidious sub-level.

He reached the top and crawled over the rocks on to the mountainside itself. Was it really real? Had it really happened? Lying on his stomach with his head bowed to the stones, he waited for something. Anything. He was well again. As well as anyone could be who hadn't eaten in so long that food was nothing more than a distant memory. Weak, yes, but unharmed—for now.

As he caught his breath he realised nothing had come to claim him. Nothing moved him, pushed him, leashed him, beat him or any one of a thousand other things he had been forced to endure since his incarceration. His breathing began to slow for the first time in a long, long time. *Was it true?* His pain-numbed mind began to wonder. Was he free? After all this time, was he truly free of the Damned?

His eyes skirted as far as they could see without moving his head; the slightest spark of hope entering his heart. He choked on his first breath. He choked on the second as well. By the third he began to snort, and by the fourth, he chuckled.

Free.

Free ... free ... free ... free!

His laughter was short lived as an armoured pair of legs landed on the mountain beside him. "Enjoying yourself?" Uriel asked.

Avis' elation turned to terror and he quickly covered his newly healed head with both arms without uttering a word.

"No doubt you have been told by others how unpleasant your next stay shall be, so I will add only this: if you ever give me cause to hunt your miserable hide down again, you will not have Clarise's generosity to protect you. I will create my own Hell somewhere in the middle of The Unknown Realms—where only I shall hear you scream for the rest of your natural existence. No one will know where you are, and no one will rescue you. Do you hear me, *slae-el?*"

Avis rocked his head beneath his hands.

"Then return to the Well where my sister awaits your arrival. Treat her as you should have been treating her from the beginning and stay out of my way if you know what is good for you."

Avis nodded emphatically and rose to his hands and knees, only to feel the cold metal of Uriel's boot on his exposed back. "No one said you were to do it on your feet," he said, and gave Avis a sharp push that flattened him to the ground. "Crawl back to her on your stomach like the *slae-el* you are and beg her forgiveness—a forgiveness none of us believe you deserve."

Avis bobbed his head in acknowledgement of the command. Slither. Of course. How stupid of him to think he would be permitted to stand. But slithering wasn't that hard. He proved it right there and then by sliding out from beneath Uriel's boot and crawling across the rocks down towards Antenora.

The putrid stench of the Ninth Sub-Level that had turned Avis' stomach once so long ago now filled his senses as he continued to crawl belly down across the simple stone bridge that was only just suspended over the ravine of disease.

Looking down, he could have reached out and touched the Damned below, had he been so inclined. Their sickening misery was all too familiar a sight to him, and with a swallow of hope that this would not be where he wound up again, he looked to the Gates of Antenora ahead of him and continued.

Avis paused momentarily beneath the grand arches that separated the two levels, where neither the heat of Eighth Level, nor the Cold of Ninth could reach him. He had never been given the luxury of stopping there before—he was always pushed from one environment to the other with little concern for his Mystallian inability to cope with such dramatic climate changes.

He had realised while crossing the bridge of disease that Uriel was following from a distance and assumed it was for one of two reasons. Either he didn't want to be that close to the Damned if he could help it, or more likely so he could uphold his end of his bargain with Clarise and not bring further harm to Avis on his journey back.

Walking at his side, it would probably have been too much of a temptation to sink his flaming sword into Avis' neck, just to hear him cry out one last time. If it was the latter, Uriel was indeed a rare breed of demon, for someone who bore the mantle of Crown Prince of Hell, he spent most of his time in Heaven. Perhaps Heaven's way of open honesty and absolution was slowly beginning to adhere to the demon prince.

Uriel's expression darkened as he approached, and he made a grand gesture with one hand for Avis to keep going.

With a heartfelt moan, Avis rolled back to his stomach and turned towards the arctic wastelands before him. On his naked stomach, this was going to hurt—a lot. And by forcing him to do this without laying a finger on him, Uriel would be keeping his word of not personally causing him any further harm.

To everyone else, it would appear as if Avis had decided to push himself through the punishment of The Ninth Level one last time to prove his sincere regret at his treatment of Clarise; something Uriel could never be held accountable for. Rot his shining hide. Heaven's influence or not, there was still a big part of that bastard that was a sneaky, manipulative demon.

Then a distant thought penetrated Avis' mind. No one would hold Uriel responsible, because it would come down to Avis' word against his masters' if he dared to speak out at all. No one else was present that could bear witness to who made the decision to crawl across Antenora. But marriage in the celestial realms meant more than just a bonding of two people's eternal lives. Clarise's blood flowed in his veins, and more importantly, his flowed inside Clarise.

Avis glanced over his shoulder and swallowed as Uriel approached. He was playing on hope, and this was not the place for hope. What if he were wrong about Clarise? What if she denied him? To side-step Uriel's final act of vengeance would cost him so dearly if he couldn't reach the safety of Clarise in time.

The women believed everything the men told them and were obedient to them to the death. Belial or Uriel only had to order her and the other ladies to never mention the subject of Avis' disappearance and the subject would never be aired again. Avis needed the wisdom of his youngest brother. As a God of Fortune, Chance's insight into his odds would be very useful right about now.

Avis swallowed again. Crawl through Antenora or risk a short cut. 'Mother, guide my hand,' he thought to himself almost in prayer, as he reached his right arm forward. He curled his fingers as if to try and grasp the rugged edge of the first ice-cade, then, without warning, he arched his arm up and around in a half-circle that ended on his thigh and called out "Clarise!"

He heard Uriel's bellow of rage from the distance, but the vision of what lay before him shifted from the endless frozen wasteland of Ninth Level to the warm and inviting smile of his wife in her Mystallian form. She stood with her hands before her as a dutiful wife and behind her Avis could see the replica of his Mystallian quarters that she had so painstakingly duplicated. Hearing Uriel's fast approach, Avis quickly lifted himself on to his knees and reached both his hands towards her. "Clarise!" he both cried and begged, willing her to take his hands and pull him to safety. "Help me!"

Clarise's eyes widened, and without asking any questions she reached forward and took him by the wrists, hauling him over the celestial/mortal threshold of space that separated them.

"Avis," she said, tears in her eyes as she ran her fingers through his hair. "Oh, Avis—I am so sorry …"

Still on his knees, Avis wrapped his arms around her waist, buried his face into the fabric of her dress and cried like a child. Free. He was finally free! As the reality of his situation began to sink in, his muscles weakened with relief and he slid to the ground at her feet, but he continued to clutch at the hem of her dress and weep.

No more traps—no more delusions—no more torture. Clarise was real. Clarise was *really* real … and Clarise was here.

With his hands still entangled in her dress, Avis felt the connection of another family member attempting to reach his wife and was under no misconceptions as to who it was. Uriel's image moments after Clarise accepted the connection confirmed Avis' greatest fear, and he slid in behind his wife for protection.

"Ahh," Uriel said, his voice ferociously calm as he looked at Avis. "I see you made it back … Avis."

Not *slae-el*. Not the Damned. Avis. He had his name back again! It sounded wonderful, coming from the lips of his master, even if the venom could barely be contained.

"Uriel, you have my deepest gratitude for returning Avis to me, but was there something you wanted of me?" Clarise asked.

Uriel shook his head. "Not at all, dear sister. Avis vanished through a blood-link a few moments ago and considering my oath to return him to you, I wanted to make certain it was you he contacted and not someone else from his family in Mystal."

He looked past Clarise again to the god that cowered on the ground behind her. "If he had made the mistake of escaping Hell, I would have been forced to hunt him down again. That would have been …" his lips twitched a little and his eyes gleamed with the fantasy of fulfilling his earlier promise. "… unpleasant. Do you not agree, Avis?"

Avis whimpered and lay on the ground with his hand covering his head at the not so subtle threat. He hadn't gone anywhere. He was right here. He didn't need to be hunted down—he had done as he was told—more or less.

"Uriel, please," Clarise said, knowing she was missing a very large portion of this conversation but having a fair idea what it was.

Uriel closed his eyes and sighed. "Oh, very well." He opened them again to look at his sister. "Why you have chosen to make the same mistake twice is beyond me, Clarise. But the mistake is yours to make." He held out his hands palm upwards towards Clarise, who immediately placed her own in his.

However, instead of stepping through as Avis had done, Uriel merely bowed at the waist and kissed both sets of knuckles, before stepping away to allow the link between them to vanish.

Avis trembled with uncertainty as Clarise turned and knelt beside him with a comforting smile. "You are exhausted beyond comprehension, my love," she said, stroking the long dark hair from his tear-glazed eyes. "You need rest to settle your agitated mind. Then things will not appear quite so frightening."

She leaned forward and kissed him on the forehead, then slipped her hands beneath his knees and shoulders and lifted him into the air as if he weighed no more than a child. "Things will be better in the morning, beloved." She carried him across the room, laid him upon the bed then drew the sheets up around him. "I promise."

Avis' gaze shifted around the room nervously. There was a time when he would have found this room and its contents perfectly acceptable and he would have fallen straight into a deep, restful sleep without a moment's hesitation. But that was before. This room—and what he had been forced to do and had done to him whilst in it—he could never sleep here again. Not comfortably …

"Clarise …" he whined.

"Shhh," Clarise crooned, reaching for a medium sized golden goblet and freshly pressed napkin, both of which were sitting on a matching golden tray on Avis' bedside table. She braced the back of his neck with one hand and helped him to sit up, pressing the goblet to his lips. "Drink, my love."

Years of unconditional obedience kicked in automatically and Avis swallowed the substance without ever knowing what it was or why he was doing it.

He drained the cup, realising after the first mouthful it bore the same rich, alluring flavour as ambrosia——a specialty liquor from Olympus that Zeus had introduced him to eons earlier. He finished the drink with a satisfied sigh and smiled, for it was the first thing to reach his stomach in a long time that didn't attack him from the inside on contact.

He watched Clarise intently as she lay his head down and wiped his mouth with the edge of the napkin, searching for any hint as to what was to happen next.

The drink was for something other than satisfying his years' old thirst. It had to be. It had been sitting there, waiting for him to return.

As he continued to stare at Clarise, his fears slowly began to ebb away. Not as in a complete suppression of them: more … an understanding that a wave of indifference was smothering them. He felt … relaxed. *Oh, yesss*, he thought with a satisfied drawl. That would be the word, if he had to choose one over all others at that moment: relaxed.

The years of torture drifted further away and a loose smile worked at the corners of his lips. This was good. He breathed in deeply and released it with an even deeper sigh of contentment.

"There you are, my love," Clarise crooned, as Avis' eyes began to sag. "Calm yourself, and sleep …"

* * *

When Avis awoke, he sensed the presence of family blood in his vicinity before he opened his eyes. He had not been asleep long enough to be deluded into thinking it was one of his family members from Mystal. It had been years since he'd last laid eyes on any of them and there was no mistaking their animosity towards him during that last family 'reunion'.

He had burned more bridges than he ever realised when he took a heavy hand to Clarise. For eons, he had lived with the assumption that his pantheon would stand by him no matter whose wrath he invoked with his various assaults on their women. They always had in the past.

But it seemed even they feared the repercussions from Clarise's ancient family and decided disowning him was better than burning with him. After what he had endured, he no longer held that decision against them.

It could have been his ex … *his wife*, but the sensation had the distinct hint of youth to it. More likely one of his two children, and considering she was sitting there and not attacking him, he made a realistic guess as to which of the two it was. But what was it Clarise had called her now? Of all things, the girl had been named after a common Mystallian flower. *Daisy … no … Petunia … no … Rose … no!*

Damn his memory! What was it?

Since the very beginning, he had always drawn on the bender ability to turn his thoughts inward, freezing the outside world while his mind relived certain memories and held open discussions with himself.

It was the most basic of bender abilities, and one even the commoners of his people shared. But that was before he'd been sentenced to The Damned. That very first time he tried to escape the Hell of his reality by withdrawing into his mind, memories far worse than anything Hell had done to him resurfaced to confront him, and he'd fled his mind in terror. He never went back, and he didn't want to now. Maybe one day … but not anytime soon.

As such, he only had his physical memory to draw on, and that sucked. He should at least remember the names of his own children, and 'never having met them' was not an excuse.

'One must walk where one has once been to see if the path one left behind was clear,' to quote a Mystallian colloquial … colloque … that's it—it was something like …

collo-column … columns? No, dammit! It was floral not architectural! Think flower …

His memory and intelligence worked furiously over the next few seconds until he finally had it. Then, with his lips curled into a knowing smile as if he had been awake and in possession of the knowledge forever, he rasped, "Hello, Columbine."

He opened his eyes, and immediately covered them with his left hand to protect them against the bright light that poured in from the illusion of an early morning sun outside. 'Mnnnhh,' he grizzled, rubbing his eyes until he could peer through the cracks in his fingers without crying.

Only when the brightness no longer affected him did he lower his hand to focus on a young child perched on the golden bed frame at his feet.

Once again, he almost missed her in his initial sweep of the room, as she was dressed in the same deep maroon silk that the multiple layers of bed canopy consisted of, and she had chosen to perch herself amongst those folds. Her beautiful, long raven hair gave away her location. It was as dark as his and easily reached her knees, if the mass curled in her lap was anything to go by.

'Perched' really was the accurate term. She was balanced on her toes like a bird with her legs folded beneath her and a hand clutching the frame on either side supporting her weight.

When he returned his quick appraisal to her face, he found she had tilted her head slightly to one side and was watching him with childish curiosity.

Her lips were small, but they had a shapeliness to them and her skin bore the snow-like paleness that was a virtual trademark of the Mystallians. But, like her mother, it was her eyes that Avis found so entrancing. They were so dark they almost held a depth of their own about them, yet they blinked continually at him, as if awaiting some kind of response.

"Very pretty," he said, realising that she would be stunning when she grew older, if this was what she could produce now. He tried to smile at her and was genuinely thrilled to find her capable of shifting into a Mystallian form at such a tender age.

But his pleasure at that prospect soon quelled as he began to envision all the kinds of trouble he would receive as her father, when others would try to take advantage of her, just as he had taken advantage of her mother. He wasn't quite sure how he felt about that.

He realised she was still watching him and gave her another weak smile. Children were never his specialty.

"Mother says I am Bi- … ah … Bi- …" Columbine's gaze dropped to her knees as the complicated word continued to elude her.

"Bipedal?" Avis suggested, as a wild guess.

Columbine shook her head. "It means 'two forms'. Bi-*schlerian* …?"

"Bi-*schalarian*," Avis corrected with an appreciative smile, recognising the strange word as a combination of Mystallian and Chaotic. Columbine nodded, her black eyes sparkling thankfully. "That's a big word, for a little girl like you to remember."

Columbine beamed with pride at the compliment but lowered her eyes respectfully and refused to move an inch from her perch.

Knowing sooner or later she would have to say something, even if it was only to voice one of a thousand questions he felt certain the child must have, Avis propped his head up with one hand and waited for her to regain eye contact with him. He just needed to wait.

Unfortunately, patience was never one of Avis' strongest virtues. Many implied it was something he'd never possessed, and he certainly wasn't of the temperament to debate it. So, after a minute or so had passed and the chit still hadn't moved, he twisted his lips slightly in annoyance. "You don't talk very much, do you?"

Columbine shook her head, her gaze flicking over the top of her lowered eyes now and again to gauge his reaction to her subservience. Avis recognised the Highborn Hellion trait and *tsked* all the more. "I think you've been in Hell too long, young lady."

As he spoke, he noticed the muscles in her legs spasm beneath the strain of maintaining that indecently cramped position. It must have been killing her to squat like that for however long she had been perched there before he awoke; but still she said nothing.

That hardly surprised him. The Hellions had raised the girl from the beginning, and they had taught him in a much shorter space of time how to take a phenomenal amount of pain without uttering a word of complaint.

"Columbine, put your feet on the bed and rest your backside against the frame," he said, "before you numb everything from the waist down. If you haven't already."

Swallowing uncomfortably, Columbine tilted all her weight on to her right foot and edged her left down to the bed, pushing it to the outer most edge to give her father as much room as possible.

Avis shook his head slightly and rubbed two fingers in a circular pattern against the side of his right eye. Only a Highborn hellion female would go to so much trouble to comply with something so simple. He envisioned what extremes she would have gone to, had he asked something more complicated of her.

With her foot balanced precariously on the edge, Columbine leaned into her straightened knee to shift her weight the other way.

"No!" Avis cried suddenly, catching her both mentally and physically as she pitched forward into his outstretched arms. "Easy, girl," he crooned, lifting her into the air and swinging her around so that she sat with her legs over the edge of the bed and her back against his hip, ignoring her gasp of horror. "We've only just met. There's no need to throw yourself at me just yet."

Although he had meant it to ease the situation, Columbine rolled her shoulders and bowed her head reproachfully, lowering her eyes to the hands that were crossed in her lap.

Her lack of response annoyed him, and he closed his eyes to utter a frustrated curse before taking her gently by the jaw and guiding her young face around to him. "We're really going to have to work on your communications skills, Columbine, if you and I are to get along. You know that, don't you?"

When she still didn't react except to lower her eyes to his palm, his mind began to race for anything that would help break through to her. He was by no means a child-person, and he was fast running out of ideas.

Then he thought of his youngest brother still in Mystal. Children of all ages loved Chance because he was always playing with them, doing hideously embarrassing dances that never ceased to make them laugh.

At the time Avis had sworn nothing could ever make him behave so ridiculously. Fortunately, he had the feeling that kind of play was still beyond his shy young daughter. But there had to be something. He rubbed his lip thoughtfully.

Then he had it. One act in particular that Chance always undertook with his children and grandchildren when they were young, and it never *ever* failed to gain some kind of a response from them—even if it was only to punch him in the arm afterwards because they felt they were growing too old for his childish tickling games.

As a mischievous smile crept across his lips, he refocused his attention on his silent offspring. Then, dropping his hand from her jaw, he snaked it quickly around her waist. "C'mere, you," he grinned and ignoring her sudden yelp of surprise he rolled on to his side away from her, dragging her across his hip and chest and pinning her to the bed beside him.

Columbine arched her back and squealed as his fingers buried themselves mercilessly into her sides. Tears sprang to her eyes as she abandoned her upbringing and thrashed in his arms, crying to the point of begging to be released, but with a delighted chuckle of his own, Avis tightened his grip and continued the assault.

Then, suddenly, Avis' fingers jarred together as Columbine's mass vanished from within his grasp.

At first, he was confused by the disappearance, but when he realised what must have happened, he looked around the room for her, far more impressed with her abilities than he had been before. Not even her mother could change shape that fast.

He found her, kneeling in the far corner between the body length mirror and the wall, with her head bowed forward. Her hands were still wrapped around her sides and her small frame shuddered with belated feelings. "Well," he said with a victorious chuckle, as he braced his head with both hands. "So you can be impulsive when the mood takes you."

Columbine shuddered again, in what he hoped was pleasure.

"Just out of curiosity, what do I get for guessing you've never been tickled before?" he asked, rolling on to his side to watch her more comfortably. He could almost feel the confusion radiating from the young girl. "Columbine, look at me."

Columbine's eyes gingerly came up to his. They were wide and dark, creased with fear despite her bottom lip being firmly fixed between her teeth to hide her smile. "Uh-Uh," Avis chided, tutting her actions and waving his finger at her. "You have a pretty face, young lady. I'd like to see the smile that goes …"

"Columbine! What are you doing here in your Bipedal nightgown?" Clarise demanded from the doorway.

Hearing the anger in her voice, Avis quickly looked towards his wife, and couldn't suppress the wave of terror at the sight of her standing in the doorway. Her natural form made it difficult to judge the severity of her anger, but there was no mistaking the clawed hands that rested on her hip joints, or the vicious way her tail flicked in tight, sharp movements.

Avis whimpered in fear and slid from the bed to join his daughter on his knees with his head bowed to the ground, never once looking up from that original appraisal. It had been too ingrained now—how to behave around angry demons.

"Columbine, when you rise, look directly at me. Look nowhere else in the room. Then go and get changed for breakfast."

"Yes, Mother," he heard Columbine reply.

From his place on the floor, Avis heard the shuffle of silk as Columbine rose to her feet and retreated towards the door, but he didn't lift his head to see her leave. A knot formed in his stomach when he heard the sound whack of his wife's tail as she struck their daughter on her way past, causing the youngster to burst into tears and flee, but he dared not move for fear others would harm her more if they learned she actually meant something to him.

Long after the muffled footsteps of their fleeing daughter echoed into nothing, Avis heard the fine click of Clarise's heeled shoes coming towards him.

"Avis," she whispered, placing a Mystallian hand on his shoulder. "Stand, my love. Your place is no longer on the floor at our feet and it breaks my heart to see you there." She cupped his shoulder a little and pulled him back on to his haunches.

When she saw the despair in his eyes, she ran her hand down the side of his face and knelt beside him. "Oh, Avis," she said, and wrapped one arm around his neck, pressing her head into his shoulder. "I am nothing to fear, my love. I am your wife, and your will is my life, not the other way around."

Avis opened his mouth to speak, then closed it again and swallowed.

Clarise felt the lump in his throat move and asked, "What is it?"

Instead of answering, Avis licked his lips and remained silent. "Nothing," he lied.

Clarise placed her hand on his cheek and drew his face towards hers. "What is it?" she asked, her voice barely above that of a whisper.

Avis looked to the open doorway. "If …" he began again, then shook his head.

"Avis, please."

"If I can … that is … if … if I'm allowed … to have my own way …" He spoke that last part very quickly in case he had overstepped the boundary, tensing for her reaction. When she offered none except to hear him out, he relaxed a little. "Don't punish Columbine for visiting me." He bit his bottom lip straight afterwards, waiting to see if he had said the right thing.

Instead of exploding with rage at his impertinence, Clarise smiled warmly. "Do not fear for Columbine, beloved. She is an extremely adept Highborn Hellion and her reaction to the smack was simply one of accordance, not pain. What is pain to someone who can heighten senses in one instant, and eliminate them altogether the next as we do?"

Avis thought about the way she had become non-corporeal in an instant when he cornered her and nodded in agreement. Someone with that level of control would easily be able to manipulate what was and wasn't being felt inside his or her body. "How is she able to have such control?" he asked, again looking towards the door, as if expecting her to reappear at any time. "She's just a child."

"She is gifted," Clarise agreed with a sigh, "and it is unfortunate that Cora has turned that gift into a point of contention."

"Cora?"

"Cora has … on occasion, found the need to act on her jealousy."

Avis released a deep grumble from the pit of his stomach. Sibling rivalry. How well he knew that sensation. Despite his seniority, as a youth he had often instigated cruel and dangerous pranks against his younger siblings for no other reason than because he could.

He began to understand why their mother never approved of it, and it didn't matter that Luck would always manage to escape unharmed. A sibling with shapeshifting mastery would have been a thousand times worse.

"She's Mystallian," he said.

"They both are," Clarise replied, not certain to the source of the reference.

"Yes, but Cora more so. Our women have never been backwards in coming forwards." He smiled a little, remembering less than memorable moments from his past. "There has even been the occasion when one of my sisters has put me on my ass, when she's felt I've needed it."

"I know."

That brought Avis up short. "How did you know that?"

Clarise blushed and looked anywhere but her husband's face. "Lady Armina came to me a few times and offered to … shall we say … forcefully remind you of your marital vows to me while I was living in Mystal."

Thinking of precisely what his robust younger sister of War would have said to his reproachful Highborn Hellion wife, Avis pulled his lips into a bemused sneer.

"Reee-allly," he drawled with an arched eyebrow. But the amusement died when he remembered their last encounter. Supreme God or not, Armina had ousted him with the help of their courts. He was in effect, still exiled from his homeland.

He didn't want to think about that now. The embarrassment of that defeat, while nothing compared to what he had endured in the Nine Levels of Hell, still knotted his stomach.

Clarise rose to her feet. "You still need rest, my love," she said, holding her hands out for him.

Avis shook his head in denial but surrendered his hands and allowed her to pull him upright. "I've slept enough …" he began to bluster.

Clarise placed a silencing finger across his lips. "Sshhhh," she hushed, with an endearing smile. "Trust me."

With the pillows piled in such a way that he could sit up, she gently eased him back into the bed, going as far as to lift his feet from the floor and slide them under the haphazardly discarded sheets. Then she drew the sheets to his chest, leaving his upper body free to move.

It was then that Avis became aware of his surroundings. "Clarise …" he whined, looking from one piece of furniture to the next with great disdain.

But Clarise had turned towards the doorway and clapped loudly twice, never noticing his discomfort. The same two gangly creatures that had answered her summons before appeared with a courteous bow, one carrying a tray of freshly diced fruit, the other a canter of chilled water and a delicately etched clear goblet.

And suddenly the accommodation didn't seem so bad.

Licking his lips hungrily, he swallowed a mouthful of saliva so thick it almost choked him.

"This is Frash and Tilu," Clarise said, gesturing firstly to the one with the food, then the one with the drink. With his eyes locked on the food, Avis barely saw them.

"They will be bringing your meals until you have regained your strength in a few days. Anything you need, you need only clap twice, and they will appear to do your bidding. It is not much compared to the banquets of Pandess, but you will need to regain your stamina before you move on to more nourishing meals."

Avis watched them separate as they approached him, the one with the food coming past Clarise to kneel beside the bed with her hands extended over Avis' chest. The starving god didn't wait to see what the other was up to.

With the fruit now under his nose, he took two huge handfuls and stuffed them in his mouth, shovelling it to the back to make room for more before it vanished.

"Avis, easy, my love! You will give yourself an upset stomach," Clarise warned, wiping his chin with a napkin, while her free hand restrained his other fistful of fruit.

Avis tried to explain how he wouldn't get a stomach ache no matter how much he ate, but the burble that escaped his food-laden lips was incomprehensible.

"Here," she said, taking the filled goblet from Tilu and tilting it to his lips. "Gently now."

But Avis wasn't interested in *gently*. The moment the nourishing liquid touched his tongue he dropped the fruit and snatched at the base of the goblet, tilting it sharply and guzzling the water as quickly as he could.

"Avis, no!" Clarise chastised, breaking his grip on the goblet.

A small noise of defiance escaped Avis' throat as he leaned forward with his hand outstretched for the goblet, but Clarise was adamant. "Slowly," she said, holding the goblet away from him and allowing her eyes to change into balls of flame inside her Mystallian skull to reiterate the command, not only as his wife, but also as a Hellion Highborn.

The reaction in Avis was instantaneous. Like an abused child, his hand dropped to the bed and he hid the offending limb beneath the sheets, his eyes anywhere but on her and his back burrowing into the pillows and mattress to escape her.

Seeing his will completely collapse, Clarise regretted her decision to resort to the Hellion's influence over him and returned her eyes to Mystallian before lifting his chin to look at her.

"Slowly," she repeated, pressing her forehead against his. "Please, trust me, my love. There is plenty of fruit to settle your stomach, but these first steps must be slow or the pain that will follow will make you think you are back amongst the Damned."

After that, Avis ate only the food she fed him as she offered it, and watching him, Clarise fought to keep her tears in check.

CHAPTER FOUR

It may not have been in Clarise's nature to lie. However, the truth and all its varying shades could be just as misleading in the hands of a professional. When she told Avis that Columbine could manipulate her body to avoid a physical punishment, she neglected to mention that due to her upbringing, Columbine knew better than to try.

The Hellion Highborn took discipline very seriously—some might say a little too seriously—but no one of repute could say that when a child of Hell was disciplined, the miscreant would be in a position to repeat the offence any time soon. If they dodged the pain of one punishment, another would be forthcoming, far worse than the first and completely unavoidable.

As such, Columbine's backside still throbbed as she made her way back to her quarters. She touched it only once and bit back the yelp that rocketed to her throat, tears still streaming silently down her face.

Never in all her young years had she ever felt pain like it! Her mother's tail was like a whip of rolled leather, and she hadn't realised how much it could damage the soft flesh of her father's kind. Her demonic plates would have deflected the blow easily. It was just one hit! One tail strike! There were times when her mother had spanked her until her plates almost cracked beneath the impacts of Clarise's claws and it still hadn't hurt this much.

"Wot is wong?" a young voice asked.

Whirling around, Columbine came face to face with a small male Hellion Highborn Lord, barely eighty centimetres tall. His wrinkled skin clung to the near fleshless bone in most places and the clump of fine straw-coloured hair that adorned his head fell lifelessly around his face, making him appear like an old Mystallian mortal reaching the last dregs of his life. But the apparent age of his body ended when it came to the sharpness of his dark eyes.

"Charon," Columbine wheezed, wiping her eyes and attempting to feign normality. "Was there something you wanted?"

"Wot is wong?" he repeated, tilting his head to one side.

"It is … nothing for you to worry about," Columbine said.

"Whad y' do?"

From the moment Charon changed his line of questioning from a general inquiry to one of specifics, it never entered Columbine's head to deny him the knowledge he desired. Despite his youth, Charon was still male, and Hellion Highborn. The twenty-month age difference between them meant nothing to a race that lived eternally. Clarise was the only Highborn Lady that could dictate to the young demon lord without reprisal, and that was only until his ascension into the High Court. All other women, even his ancient aunts and step-grandmother, would do as he commanded, just as they did with all Highborn Hellion males.

"I left my quarters not dressed right," she replied, with a formal curtsey.

"Why?" he asked, not with the anger that any of their uncles would have shown, but with a general infantile curiosity.

"Because Father is awake."

Charon swivelled towards the open doorway that separated them from Avis and Clarise. "He is?" he pouted. The withered flesh of his brow bunched over his nose, and his shoulders stiffened angrily. "Why? I do not wan' 'im back! It is not fair! It is not …!"

"Charon, no," a male voice called from a short distance away. "Hold your tongue."

The children did not miss the emphasis of seniority, and before they had properly turned, they both retreated into the submissive poses of bowed heads and hands clasped before them which they knew would be acceptable to whichever Lord addressed them.

But when they realised it was Hell's Angelic Crown Prince, they immediately dropped to their knees with their heads bowed forward as was his due. Columbine winced and managed to bite back a yelp as the pose brushed her ankles across her tender backside.

Either missing her grimace, or choosing to ignore it, Uriel drifted his armoured hand across the crown of Columbine's dark hair. "Go back to your quarters and get dressed for breakfast, little one," he said with a smile, rubbing the armoured fingertips against her scalp before gently guiding her head in that direction. Columbine bowed deeper beneath the command, then rose and left them without a backwards glance. Until she was out of earshot, she knew the males would not speak again.

Once a cavern wall separated them, Columbine sagged against the stone surface and breathed a heady sigh of relief. That could have gone very differently had it not been Uncle Uriel who discovered them. The other Highborn Hellion Lords did not share the Crown Prince's generous streak in any way.

Nor would they have looked upon her with a smile and sent her on her way without even mentioning her appearance. The offence may have been minor, but each of them would have reacted in the same violent way that her mother had.

Fearing another discovery, Columbine stretched herself to her physical limits and beyond, allowing herself to dissipate into fine, invisible particles, just as she had earlier to escape her father. The shortcut to avoid the situation was obvious: to change what she was wearing into more suitable clothing and be on her way. She would have already, only she had been told by two different elders to return to her quarters to get changed and it was not in her nature to disobey even one. The trick now was to make it back there without being discovered.

She drifted through the corridors, spreading herself across the surface of walls and floors like an airborne virus whenever others crossed her path. Unlike her father, her mother's people knew when they walked *through* one of their own kind. The mind behind the dissipated body still swallowed heavily when others passed below her. Did they see? Did they know?

No, they couldn't have. When she saw her uncles Ludovic and Innis approaching, she spread herself so thin that she was no higher than a few millimetres off the wall surface and held her mental breath. Disobedience was one thing, but to be caught attempting to avoid an elder's reproach was another matter entirely. And this was Innis—second only to Darnel in cruelty.

She couldn't do it! This was insane! She couldn't hide from them and only a fool would want to try! Even without the convenience of sight, they could always sense her nearby presence as one of their own.

She was on the verge of reforming on the ground with her head bowed low when she heard Innis' heated squeal as he spoke her father's name. That alone wouldn't have been enough to sway her decision as Innis was the single most bad-tempered of all her uncles, and his reaction to everything was severe to say the least.

But when Ludovic echoed Innis' sentiments with a grisly snarl of his own, Columbine held her place and her breath, hoping their anger blinded them to her presence. Ludovic was patient when patience required it—but he could be extremely dangerous to cross when the mood took him. He had never taken his rage out on the women of the family (not the way Uncle Innis often did) but still, Columbine had no desire to be the first.

"She is an idiot!" Innis raged.

"It is her choice to uphold her vows," Ludovic replied.

"But it makes no sense!"

"Welcome to the Known Realms, brother. Who can ever understand the workings of the female mind?"

"But how can Father allow her to do this? It is insane!" Innis turned and punched the nearby wall in hopeless frustration.

Columbine gasped as Innis' fist closed in on the wall and she retracted every iota of herself from that section of the wall and froze all others in expectation of discovery. But none was forthcoming. Innis was so deeply entrenched in his anger that he failed to sense her body movement withdrawing from the wall around his fist.

"The woman is insane, and Father equally so for allowing it to happen!" he snarled.

"Say *that* at your own peril and as far from me as you can," Ludovic warned, pointing a clawed digit covered in fur at his younger brother. "I have no intention of invoking Father's rage in my vicinity over the likes of you."

Columbine frowned in confusion. Why were they saying such horrible things? Father just … went away for a while. Mother had said so. And he was back now. So why would it make no sense for Mother to want to be with him? And why were all of the males, even young Charon, so angry about his return?

She waited until they took their strange conversation around the corner at the far end of the corridor before risking a mental shake of her translucent head. It was *very* wrong for her to listen into grown up conversations—even more so when it was the men, but she hadn't done it on purpose. Their conversations were simply not meant for her.

She stiffened with the epiphany. That was it! She had *obviously* misheard! By listening in on a conversation that was not meant for her, she had failed to understand the true meaning of it. That was why men's conversations were not meant for ladies' ears unless otherwise invited into them. They often spoke of things that the ladies could not possibly understand.

Pleased to have rationalised the misunderstanding to some extent, Columbine moved along the walls, determined to reach her quarters before she found herself in a position to eavesdrop again.

"Ludovic, for Hell's sake, what is it?" Innis demanded, as the pair returned to the corridor moments later.

Ludovic's gaze narrowed into thin slits of suspicion as he swept his eyes across the walls and ceiling where Columbine had been hiding. "Nothing," he said, in a voice that implied otherwise. After a moment, he relaxed and shook his head. *It couldn't have been.*

Just as Columbine thought she had arrived at the inner sanctuary of her bedroom without any further problems, her governess chose that moment to look inside the room for her missing ward.

"Where have you been, mistress?" the large, centipede-like demoness asked, clicking her pincers together anxiously as she crossed the room towards her. Her overlapping leather plates strongly resembled skin that was doubled over in rolls and each of her four sets of roving eyes were fixed on Columbine.

"Diviten," Columbine groaned, raising her hands above her head and holding them there in anticipation of her governess' aid.

"Do not 'Diviten' me young lady," Diviten chirped, taking the hem of Columbine's nightgown in her lowest set of pincers and passing it from one set to the next, in effect lifting the nightdress over Columbine's head. "You were born for better things, and you should know your place by ..." pausing in mid-sentence, Diviten took her charge by the shoulder and angled her towards the light. "... forgive me, Mistress. I see you have already been disciplined." She ran several feelers across the thick welt that had formed across Columbine's upper legs to disappear beneath the lace of her underwear.

Columbine yelped and burst into tears beneath the gentle caress, shoving both hands against Diviten to break the contact. "Stop it, that hurts!"

Unfazed by the shove, Diviten stepped back a pace and clicked her teeth together. "That is hardly surprising, mistress, when one considers the mark that has been left."

Still in tears, Columbine's jaw went slack with realisation. "I did not know Father's kind were so breakable!" she cried, wiping her eyes and twisting to view the mark more clearly for herself. She looked up at her governess, the shock of the mark distracting her from the pain, temporarily. "And it still hurts!"

"That is obvious and unfortunately, you brought it entirely upon yourself. Do not search for solace with me. You will find none."

"But I just wanted to see Father ..."

"Then you should have waited for the appropriate time of introduction, would you not agree?"

Columbine snapped her mouth shut and closed her eyes, pushing both together tightly. A few seconds later, she forced herself to nod. It wasn't her intention to be disrespectful. She just wanted to see the man she had only ever heard about her whole life.

"Mistress, may I ask what drives your desire to become like your father's people? They are so ... pathetic, quite honestly. They are weaker, fragile, unco-ordinated ... form rigid ... grounded bipedal ..." As her truthful though insulting descriptions grew with passion, Diviten found herself at a loss for more adjectives that best described the limited physique of the Mystallians when compared to that of demons.

The change that swept over Columbine would have sent a lesser servant scurrying from the room in fear. Straightening where she sat, her eyes shot open and she speared her governess with a withering look that no longer belonged to a remorseful child. "That is my father you speak badly of, Diviten. Choose your next words ... With. Great. Care." Her eyes ignited with hellfire as she spoke, leaving no doubt as to where her young loyalty lay.

Diviten dropped to the ground with her forehead pressed into the stone flooring. "Forgive me, Mistress," she said, not rising from her prone position.

"Speak not of it again." Columbine turned away; as much from the affair as her governess. "Father is a good god—a strong god. Mother said so."

"Of course, mistress."

Columbine perused the room around her. Unlike the cavernous abodes that her mother's family found so familiar and comfortable, Columbine had been redecorating hers ever since she learned of her father's recovery. More than anything, she'd wanted to show him that she too could be as Mystallian as he was by her current selection of furnishings.

So, instead of a rough stone perch or carved insert to rest upon, Columbine had a central four-poster bed complete with matching bright pink, silk curtains. A single-drawer bedside table was located on either side of the bed, each decorated with finely beaded doilies. On the right was a bright vase filled with colourful flowers, whereas the left table held a small, thin leather-bound book in a light puce colour that fit easily in the palm of her hand.

Thick warm rugs of deep maroon set off the cherry tones of the marble streaks in the floor. On the right was a single door that led to her wardrobe and bathroom. Large twin glass doors to the left of the bed opened out onto a fake balcony, but whilst the doors remained closed, the view from within was effective.

She walked towards the edge of her bed and sat down, grimacing at the shaft of pain as she settled her weight on the plush mattress. Her focus remained on the small side table with the flower vase until the pain subsided, at which point she released her breath in a small sigh. Not all of it was in relief.

Diviten shuffled up behind her. "What is troubling you, Mistress?" she asked.

Columbine's eyes dropped to the base of the vase where the doily was located. "I wanted my room to be like my father's," she said, annoyed with herself for making what appeared to be a fundamental mistake. "I saw none of these in his room while I was there." She lifted the vase and removed the thinly laced object from the table, holding it up for Diviten to see. "Is my room wrong?"

Diviten chittered and shook her head, taking her charge's hands into two of her claws. "No, Mistress. These items are feminine—ladylike. Your father does not have them because he is a Lord, and Lords do not have finery such as this," As she spoke, she removed the doily from Columbine's hands with another claw and replaced it under the vase. "But that does not mean he does not expect to find them here in your rooms."

"What if he does not like me?"

Despite having frightened her minutes earlier, Columbine saw the leathery skin around the old demoness' eyes crease warmly. "How can he not?" she asked, her bulbous lips twisting into a tender smile. "You are obedient, ladylike in almost all aspects, diligent, and respectful. How can he not like those attributes?"

Columbine looked down at her hands and swallowed heavily. "He said I was impulsive, when the mood takes me." She jerked her head back to the oversized centipede demoness. "But I can change that! If I work very hard, I can be in total control at all times! I can! If he would just give me another chance!"

"Then perhaps you should begin now, Mistress," Diviten suggested pointedly, gifting her ward with a slight frown in the face of her frantic passion. "Excitement is the same as rage, and both emotions are beneath the Highborn Ladies. Calm control always, at all costs. Remember your lessons ..."

Columbine drew a deep breath and squared her shoulders proudly, then released the breath to allow her shoulders to drop into a portrait-perfect pose with her hands cupped in her lap.

Diviten's head bobbed approvingly. "Much better, Mistress."

Rising with a grace that only came from long hours of practice, Columbine went to her dressing room. Be a Lady at all costs: obedient, diligent and respectful. She could do that. She was better at it than Cora ever was. All she had to curb was her enthusiasm to be with her father, and her poise would once again be flawless. Surely that would please him.

Knowing Diviten was half a step behind her, Columbine pointed to a delicate dress of blue and matching shoes nearby, then held her hands out to the sides; just as her mother had taught her to. Control. Control is everything in the Mystallian world. Lose it, and one loses oneself.

She stepped into the hooped petticoat that Diviten held out for her and accepted the hard twist of the girdle straps that pulled her stomach in tight against her spine. Her father's people had a strange idea of dress, but her mother assured her that a lady of quality must endure the pain to be presented as becoming in the company of their lords.

Bipedal ... bipedal ... she thought to herself, over and over, reminding herself that women from her father's home realm endured this every day, and to fit in she must also endure it and not cheat by removing the pain.

After Diviten tied the girdle in place, she sipped in a short sample breath. Several weeks ago, she taught herself how to breathe in such a way that barely required the lungs to move. A necessity, in this form.

When she had her breathing under control, she nodded for Diviten to continue. Two layers of petticoats were wrapped around the wire frame, then the dress was slipped over her extended arms and fastened up her spine. The long, shoulderless sleeves crafted of fine materials, were attached to the dress by the smallest of stitches along one side. Finely laced slippers were placed on her feet. A satin necklet of matching blue finished off the outfit.

Not a word passed between either of them during the dressing.

When they left the dressing room, Columbine went and sat before her dresser, still focused on her breathing rather than the servant that scurried after her. Diviten retrieved a brush from her table and silently brushed her long mane of ebony hair for several minutes before twisting it into a sophisticated braid.

"You may go," Columbine said, once Diviten had woven the long stem of the flower into her hair so that the flower sat at the top of the braid, just as her mother had done.

"But Mistress, I have yet to powder ..."

Columbine looked at her through the mirror. "You may go, Diviten."

"Yes, Mistress."

For some time after Diviten bowed and withdrew from the room, Columbine stared at the mirror. Her father had said she was pretty. She turned her head from one side to the other. Her skin was fair, her cheekbones were high and defined and her lips were rich in the colour red.

Did he think she was showing off her shapeshifting abilities? Was this what his kind found pretty? She had nothing to base any modifications on, so she had remained true to her original form. Her mother's family certainly hadn't found anything attractive about her bi-schalarian shape.

The men teased her relentlessly and it hadn't always been in good humour, while the women huffed and completely ignored her, unless she happened to be in her mother's presence. The only time either side treated her as a fellow Highborn Hellion was when she reverted to her demonic form.

She had based her theory of ugliness on those reactions, yet her father had said she was pretty. And not just pretty, but very pretty. Was he only saying that because he was her father?

She reached out to touch her reflection, her initial question still plaguing her. Did he like what he saw? Did he really?

She sighed and allowed her hand to fall to the crystal dish that held an assortment of hair brushes. It didn't really matter anyway. As a denizen of Chaos, she could change into whatever her father wanted in a daughter. Diviten was right.

She need only control her enthusiasm and her father's desires would be revealed in time: A simple comment about someone's eye colour or the way someone wore their hair that happened to catch his eye. That was all it would take, and with those small titbits of information here and there she could mould herself into his perfect idea of a daughter.

The reflection of the leather book on her bedside table caught the corner of her eye. Dodging the subject of the morning's events would not make them go away, and the longer she put it off, the longer it would take for her to catch up. She rose and made her way towards the book. "Grimoire," she said aloud, as she lifted the book and opened it to the empty second page between the soft covers. Instead of saying anything else, Columbine closed it again and ran her hand over the fine leather cover with a smile of pride. This had been her creation—her choice of amendments.

Her mother had wanted pink but was willing to compromise with puce when she realised how much it meant to Columbine to have a variety of colours around her. It was her first grounded bipedal book. She cuddled it close. It was all hers. Of course, the grimoire had always been hers, but it wasn't until recently that it took this rather unique form.

All grimoires absorbed whatever the writer dictated. She pressed her lips to the top edge of the book, having no doubt that her father would whisk them away to his home realm now that he had returned. She'd heard from everyone how different Mystal was, and she was convinced the more she practiced now, the easier it would be to fit in there.

"Grimoire," she said aloud, again.

The book fell open in her hands again.

"Where to start," she said, looking anywhere but at the book before her. She then glanced down at the page and snorted as the words appeared in dark ink across the first line. She should have known the book's dictation would begin from the moment she initialised their bond, but it was too late now to change it. Moving on.

"Father woke up this morning. I went in to see him. He is very white." Columbine looked at her own skin—the bleached tone was a stark contrast to the jet-black plates of her demonic form.

"Even whiter than me, but maybe that is because he has been sick." Columbine sucked on her lip, finding the need to remind herself that no one could read her diary without her approval.

No one could force the genetic seal that was forged at the grimoire's creation—not even her esteemed grandfather, although he and the other Lords could easily order her to do it, should they desire to do so.

She drew in a deep breath. If they did, she would accept the consequences of what would be revealed. "I went in to see him without Mother's permission," she said, as the memory of her mother's reaction still stung painfully across her backside.

"I waited until she had left for breakfast, and I chose not to let her servants see me. Mother will not be pleased with them and will most likely punish them for not stopping me somehow. Not that they could have. They are demons and I am Hellion Highborn. I care not for what happens to those that far beneath me."

With that she paused and ran her nail across her lip. Those last words were not her own. They were her Highborn upbringing, yet in her mind she didn't feel comfortable with that opinion. True, it wasn't *meant* to be her concern. She was supposed to be above such things as the well-being of servants, but still ...

"Why do things like that make me feel wrong inside?" she asked, of no one. "I am Hellion Highborn. We are above such things, and Father is an established god, who is also above such things. So, where does this awful feeling inside me come from? It is easy to pretend it is not there. I have done it long enough to fool everyone. But I know these servants. I know every one of their names, and I have watched all their habits. I feel as if I know them better than any of the Highborn that go to great lengths to show me only what is expected of them. Am I wrong to feel something for them? Are they really as far beneath me as I am told?"

Columbine closed her eyes and fell back against her bed in such a way that the hoop fell downwards against her legs instead of jutting straight out. Even now, her mother's training regarding protocol could not be dissuaded.

So many conflicting thoughts.

She was only a child and already the most developed shapeshifter of her generation by far. Probably because in her father's absence, her grandfather had anointed her at birth. She wasn't quite sure what that meant, except that he saw her as both his granddaughter and his adopted daughter. There was so much she didn't understand—so much protocol that conflicted with the desires of her heart.

If she were to ask any of her elders for advice, they would tell her to stop being so foolish and act appropriately as was expected from ladies of their position. If she were to ask the servants, they would bow and tell her what they felt she wanted or needed to hear to spare themselves her wrath. Not that any Lady had ever struck a servant themselves, but it certainly wasn't unheard of for a Lady to have a servant executed for saying the wrong thing at the wrong time.

With her deep sigh came the age-old revelation: it would come in time. The balance that made up her life would reveal itself to her in time. Again, she was showing her impatience.

Still, when her mother wasn't looking, she would apologise to Frash and Tilu for any discomfort they were forced to endure on her behalf. They would just need to be sworn to secrecy afterwards. "Grimoire, I do not regret going to see Father." Her buttocks chose that moment to twinge painfully against the hoops, almost as if reminding her of the outcome. "But I do regret being caught. That hurt."

Columbine looked down at the grimoire. Although there were only three pages to the book, there was always one on either side of where Columbine was currently using. Whenever she turned the page forward, the page closest to the front cover would merge then into it, while another page formed from inside the back cover.

The book was eternal, with as many pages as Columbine needed to document her immortal existence. Flicking through the pages, she glanced back at the earlier entries involving her emotional state without actually reading them. Would her father find these feelings as undesirable as her mother's family obviously did?

She closed her grimoire and sat up in bed, feeling more tears slide against her cheeks. Drawing from an inner strength, she took a deep breath and analysed the tears. She knew her father's people called it crying, and that they came from moments of true sadness or true happiness. Women cried more than men. She hadn't worked out why yet. It was simply the way it was.

She had already cried twice that day. Both were caused by sadness, but the sources of tears were different. The first sadness was due to physical pain, which she was already intimately familiar with. The other was also pain, but it came from a deeper location and affected her much more profoundly. She didn't like it.

Rubbing the heels of her hands across her eyes, she melded the liquid back into her face and rose to her feet. "Diviten," she called.

The centipede demoness appeared moments later in the doorway with a bow. "Mistress?"

"My face has no powder."

Diviten bowed again. "Yes, Mistress."

CHAPTER FIVE

Columbine left her quarters a few minutes later, walking comfortably on two legs. It had taken a little practice in the beginning, to find the central balance point without a tail, but she was determined to succeed. Now, with her mother's careful tutelage, she could glide through the hallways in a bipedal, lady-like manner, without dipping her head or using her arms for balance. Quiet, calm, sophisticated, elegant. Her mother had been pleased with her progress.

"Well, now. Who do you suppose this ugly little insect we have before us is, brother?" The voice that spoke held a great deal of warmth for her, despite the cruel and condescending nature of his words.

Recognising the voice, Columbine closed her eyes and bowed her head, even before she turned and curtseyed; her hands hidden by the folds of her dress. Unlike her demonic form which would remain prone until otherwise directed, Columbine straightened up but kept her head bowed in subservience. She knew every one of her demon uncles by sight, scent and the sound of their voices, and where these two were concerned, one was never found without the other.

"I do not believe this waif to be of Hellion origin," Yima said, agreeing as always with his older twin. "Observe the totally tasteless and restrictive nature of the bipedal flesh and fabric which it prefers to parade about in."

"Not to mention that outrageous mane of hair," Ahriman said.

"True," Yima agreed again. "It deliberately wears its mane exposed like a wild animal and as no Highborn Hellion would ever conceive of wearing such an outrageous form, we can only assume we have a celestial spy in our midst."

With her eyes still downcast, Columbine said nothing aloud, as was custom. She knew once they were finished with her, they would dismiss her with barely a pat on her shoulder and allow her to go on her way. Until then, protocol demanded she endure their teasing.

"Oh, for Hell's sake. Leave that child alone you two," Plouton's deep rumbling voice commanded from somewhere in the distance ahead of Columbine.

The twins as one, released a frustrated huff of annoyance. "We were just having some fun, brother," Ahriman griped, for Plouton was their senior by several millennia. "And with the form she has chosen, who could blame us?" Had he been younger, the twins would have chased Plouton away. But then, Plouton would not have interfered in the first place.

"Her choice of form is not a subject of debate, nor is the source of it. You will not mention it again in her presence. We *never* have fun at the expense of our ladies and you two know better. Now, be on your way—both of you."

Without permission to lift her gaze, Columbine listened as the twins stormed away, her hands twisting in knots around the loose fabric of her dress skirt.

"How long has that been going on?" Plouton asked, once they were alone.

"They do not approve of my grounded bipedal form, Uncle Plouton."

"That was not what I asked."

"I have been attempting this form for several weeks."

"And it has been going on all that time?"

Columbine pinched her lips together and bobbed her head once. It would do no good and go totally against custom to incriminate another uncle as the primary source of their demonic teasing, one which was beyond Plouton's capacity to control due to that uncle's seniority. Darnel was mean and answered to two specific demons—his older brother Uriel, and their father, Belial. It was from Darnel that the twins took their cues to torment her.

"Columbine," he whispered, squatting to look her in the eye. "Look at me, child."

Only then did she lift her eyes.

"I have spoken with your mother." He paused for a moment. "What she has told me does not please me."

Columbine closed her eyes and bowed her head again, until Plouton lifted her head by sliding a talon under her chin. "I realise having your father with us must be very confusing and exciting for you, but it is important that you restrain yourself to the laws that govern our ladies. It is what makes you unique in all the Known Realms and being unique is what makes you special. Do you understand?"

Columbine nodded, though in truth she didn't.

Plouton seemed to guess as much.

"You will in time," he chuckled, as he rose to his feet and gave her a gentle shove in no specific direction. "Until then, be on your way."

Columbine stepped around her uncle with a bow, then turned and moved away.

As she rounded the corner, Columbine caught sight of her older sister in the distance. Cora leaned both her shoulders against the cavern wall, though her wings were spread across the surface to cradle her body comfortably. Her ankles and arms were crossed, and her left spiked heel twitched impatiently in mid-air. Long, sharp talons drummed against her elbow joints.

When she saw Columbine, the fire in her eyes flared and she flicked her wings to push herself upright on to her taloned toes. "About damned time," she swore.

"Cora, what are you doing?" Columbine asked, quickly making for her sister's side though her gaze searched the area in case an elder had heard her sister's outburst. "If Mother or any of the others see you behaving so ..."

"Oh, for Hell's sake, shut up, Shorthorns! I have been waiting an eternity and a half for you and I am not in the mood. You took forever! I was just about to mind-speak with you and ask where the hell you were!"

Columbine blinked, barely able to comprehend the rapid-fire questions due to the forbidden language that accompanied them. "F-forgive me. I did not know you were waiting for me. I was ..." She paused a moment as it dawned on her that Cora wasn't aware of the events of that morning. With an excited smile, she exclaimed, "Father is awake again," as if that line alone should explain everything.

However, instead of being ecstatic as Columbine had expected, Cora's eye-ridges merged into a deep scowl of annoyance and the hellfire in her eyes dimmed. "Oh, terrific," she sneered with a grinding of her mandibles as she snatched at her sister's hand.

She appeared on the verge of adding something else but shook her horned head against it and stalked along the corridor to their right, dragging Columbine behind. "Come on. I want to show you something."

"Cora, wh-where are we going?" Columbine wheezed, for her sister's quick pace forced her to jog in a dress that was never designed to be run in. "Cora, please, stop this. Stop it! I-I cannot breathe!"

Cora seemed to have no intention of slowing down. She tightened her grip on Columbine's hand and not only maintained her present speed, she doubled it— forcing Columbine to either run with her or fall and be dragged along the ground behind her.

There was no doubt in Columbine's mind that her sister would do just that, if she failed to remain upright. "Hold your tongue, or I will hold it for you," Cora snapped impatiently.

But Columbine was desperate. Lights flashed across her vision and the walls felt as if they were moving against her. Neither sensation was pleasant. "Please, not ... so fast, I beg you ..." she pleaded, gasping for breath which the constraints of her dress refused to permit and stumbling against the uneven ground beneath her slippered feet.

"Shift around it," Cora snarled.

"I cannot."

Cora jerked to a halt and Columbine slammed into her sister's back and wings. "Why not?" she demanded, whirling to face her sister.

Unused to the physical demands of her father's form, Columbine placed one hand against her hip for support and clutched her fingers into her sister's hand for stability. "M-Mother ... wants me to choose a form and stay with it for the day," she wheezed. "She wants me ... both of us, to learn how to be a grounded biped, without changing from it when it gets hard ..."

"I would rather spend a dozen eternities in the Ninth Level," Cora replied, tartly.

"Why?" Columbine asked, for this was the first time the subject had come up without their mother being present. "Why does Father ... cause so much anger in you?"

"I do not like him."

"But why?"

"Does he like you?"

Columbine was flabbergasted by that statement. "Wha ... what do you mean?"

"It is not a hard question. Does ... he ... like you?"

Columbine ran her eyes down the length of the constricting dress bust, her mind re-enacting the scene with her father. "I-I think so ..."

"Make sure you *know* so, before you waste too much time on the likes of him."

Cora had so much hatred inside her. The same burning hatred which so many of the Hellions shared when speaking of her father. It made no sense. "What did he do to you?"

"He does not like me."

"Only because you refuse to behave in a ladylike ..."

"It has nothing to do with that!" Cora roared, causing Columbine to yelp and leap from her sister; her hands shooting up to protect her vulnerable bipedal head.

"I am sorry! Please ... I am so sorry ..." Columbine blustered, knowing her sister's temper could be vile and dangerous when provoked.

Instead of being placated by the cowering girl before her, Cora's body began to shudder with an inner rage she fought to contain.

Almost a full minute went by before her flaming eye sockets were dimmed, and she released her breath in a dark, smoke-filled cloud of frustration. "Forget it, shorthorns. It is between me and that …"

Lost for words and heartbeats away from reigniting her temper, Cora snatched at Columbine's wrist and stalked away, dragging the fearful girl behind her. "… and that does not involve you. But this does. Now, come on."

Whether deliberate or accidental, Cora's pace slowed to allow Columbine to keep up and the younger was very grateful for that reprieve.

Unfortunately, that relief wasn't to last.

Within minutes, Columbine recognised their surroundings as the conservatorium which led into the hallway that paralleled their esteemed grandfather's private chambers.

It was not entirely off limits to the Highborn Hellion ladies, but apart from Belial's current wife Lady Erishkigal, it certainly skated the thin line between the two. Ladies needed a good reason to be here, and Columbine knew she had none. If the apprehension that Cora felt was anything to go by, neither did she.

Both youngsters swallowed heavily as they crept past that wall, knowing the simple cavernous structure would not protect them from his senses, should he choose that moment to pay attention.

And he was in there.

Just as he would know of their whereabouts, no one from Hell could miss the overwhelming presence of the supreme Lord of Chaos that radiated from within those rooms. Columbine wanted to run at that moment.

Turn and flee towards the safety of the lower levels. She was about to beg her sister to do likewise, when she saw a strange surge of exhilaration within Cora and a thin talon was placed against Columbine's mouth for silence. Cora's own mandibles curled into a predatory smile.

The latter terrified Columbine. Belial's quarters represented the end of the line for the Highborn Hellion ladies. No exception. He was the boundary line that prevented unauthorised outsiders from intruding into the family levels and also to prohibit the Highborn ladies from leaving without permission.

To deliberately provoke that status quo was madness!

Yet that seemed exactly what Cora had in mind. Panic soared inside of Columbine as her sister tugged her towards the rocky incline that led away from the family levels. *No!* Whatever Cora desired beyond this point, Columbine wanted nothing to do with it.

She shook her head violently and struggled against her older sister's grip. One spanking for the day was enough for Columbine, and this flirted with an all-out beating that would take weeks to recover from. She couldn't stand the thought of it!

"No!" she cried, tears welling in her eyes as she shifted her weight against her sister. "Please! By the Twin Notes of creation, let me go!"

Cora's grip tightened, and it was the only warning Columbine received before her sister was inside her mind, plundering her thoughts and destroying them without a care.

'**Shut. Your. Realm-damned Mouth.**' The command appeared inside her mind, and she found herself unable to resist. Her lips snapped shut of their own accord, though she whimpered behind her clenched teeth and the tears she'd been struggling with now streamed down her face. '**Not. Another. Word.**'

She and Cora had shared many things in the past. Secret things that no one else in Hell knew. They could talk without anyone hearing them. *Mind-speak*, Cora had called it.

The sisters had been able to stay in touch no matter where in Hell they were. But this … forced control … never had Cora been so brutal before.

No one in Hell had ever spoken of this possibility. At least, not to her. Inappropriate behaviour was always corrected through physical means.

If an elder decided you weren't to cry, your tear ducts were removed. If you were to be harmed, you were beaten. Columbine wanted to scream. She wanted to scream the stalactites loose from the ceiling. But she couldn't. Her lips refused to open.

* * *

Cora grinned maniacally at her first successful mind ambush of her sibling. No one had taught her how to do this, it was a trick she'd discovered all by herself while arguing with Gingen, her own centipede-like governess.

In the blink of an eye, Gingen had gone from shaking her arms in distress, to accepting all that Cora demanded without refute. And it felt … *right*. In her own mind she was justified to make them do what she wanted.

Cora practised with this strange power and avoided many of her ladylike duties by convincing the governess that they were either already done or not necessary at all.

This left her plenty of time to explore the upper levels of Hell beyond their grandfather's chambers. The entire process had been as instinctive as it was natural, and she basked in its simplicity.

It was only the second time she had tested her power against her sister and given the spectacular failure of the first time, she wondered what was different between the two.

A few months earlier, during a meal of no consequence, Cora had suddenly felt the urge to coerce her sister into giving up her favourite drink. It wasn't because Cora personally wanted the drink.

Far from it.

Columbine's tastes were disgusting, but Cora knew her sister would never relinquish it on her own. So, she had sat across the cavern from her and stared at her with the same intensity that she'd used to pressure everyone in doing her bidding while commanding her to relinquish the drink.

For a few precious seconds, she'd thought it had worked as Columbine reached forward and grabbed the base of her hauyne crystal goblet. That sense of victory was short lived when Columbine lifted the goblet to her own lips and drained the contents herself, dropping the empty mug with a satisfied sigh.

After that, Cora had thought her own bloodline was immune to her power and never tried again.

Until now.

Something had changed. Was it desperation? The first time had merely been a test where the results didn't matter, whereas today, the stakes were infinitely higher.

She looked down at where she clutched her sister's hand. *Or was that the reason it worked?* Shapeshifting depended on age and generation.

An older generation trumped a younger generation, regardless of who was born first. But, those of the same generation could force a younger member into any shape they wanted by making physical contact. Could her magical power of the mind work along the same principles?

Curiosity got the better of her and she released her sister's hand. **Stop crying**, she commanded, watching her sister's face. Her sister continued to bawl like a baby. She expected that.

Cora re-laced her fingers into Columbine's and squeezed a little. **Stop crying**, she repeated, and almost fist-pumped the air with her free hand when her sister's tears abruptly ceased.

Yes! It only worked on her bloodline, if she touched them. *Oh, it's on now.* Cora turned back to the path before them, though with her hand firmly clutching Columbine's hand. **Follow me**, she sent, without making it a command.

* * *

Columbine struggled with the changes that were happening inside her. She *needed* to obey her sister but didn't *want* to. It was as if her heart and her body were at odds, and she couldn't understand why.

She would have cried all over again, had she been given the choice. This was so wrong. As Cora turned and led the way up into the High Court of Hell, Columbine was desperate to draw attention to them somehow.

She wanted to reach out to an elder with mind-speak, but that would involve using words and her mind refused to comply. So, she thought of causing a rockslide that would bring the family running.

But no sooner had the image appeared in her mind, then Cora was there to stop that as well. All these things she wanted to do—all these things she knew she should be doing—and she couldn't get past the need to obey her sister.

But what did Cora need her for anyway? It wasn't as if she needed help with looking around.

Cora tugged her across the floor towards the bone archway that led up to the Well's entrance. Surely, they weren't leaving the safety of the Well! Evil was outside the Well!

Necessary evil, but evil that was never meant to touch the Highborn Ladies. It was why Belial positioned himself between them.

Dozens of levels still separated them from Antenora, but the thought of being so close to that place unescorted sent waves of terror through her. She shook her head again and whimpered.

* * *

Cora felt her own fear surge and immediately swung on her sister. **Stop panicking!** But the waves of fear continued. If anything, they increased.

Cora felt her own heart beating out of her chest and went for the only power she knew of that could bring her sister to heel. She modified the structure of her hand to include a strong sedative and pushed it into her sister's veins.

Good. Calm down, shorthorns, she crooned, and as Columbine relaxed, that accursed fear left Cora as well.

This was perhaps one of the most annoying aspects about Columbine. If a certain emotion got the better of her, anyone in her vicinity would be crippled by it as well, and Cora was usually the closest demon to her.

Cora had become quite adept at sedating her little sister to get her own emotional reactions under control. She reached up with her other hand and tucked the stray strands of long black hair behind her sister's ear and smiled at her. *It will be alright, shorthorns. No one will ever know what we are doing. I swear. I have been sneaking out here for ages.*

Columbine nodded silently.

Very little was said as Cora led them through the levels, hiding from the Highborn Hellion Guards and Hellion Highborns alike.

A long time ago Cora had learned how straight-forward it was to manipulate the regular guards into looking elsewhere as she passed, but the same could not be said for any of the Highborn Hellion Guards she'd come across.

Whenever she had tried to force them into compliance, they had merely slowed their rotating head as if to focus on her with such icy indifference that she'd run back the way she'd come.

They had seen her. They had sensed her attempted control, and in their own, foreboding way, they had laughed at her. That look had been terrifying, and she never tried it again. Not even with those that were assigned to safeguard the family levels and they, by design were a little less … daunting.

Cora went to great lengths to avoid them beyond her grandfather's chambers after that.

Including today.

As such, it took a little longer than Cora expected to arrive at her destination. But once they stood in the doorway of her objective, she could barely contain her excitement. It had been pure luck that had enabled her to find this room at all and she released her sister to slap her hands together in delight. *Finally!*

The room, if one could call it that, had nothing in common with the traditional version. Everything remained in a state of constant flux. The room was dark but exploded in lights and sounds to disorient anyone within.

The floor jutted on warped edges just as often as it held no substance at all and pits of varying depths appeared and disappeared underfoot without warning.

The surfaces themselves flowed between acidic to ice cold, to electrified, to moments where they were safe to touch. Flight was just as difficult as the width and height of the room changed with a frequency that was impossible to predict.

It had taken Cora a little while to deduce the purpose of the strange room. The family levels had nothing like it.

But once she had watched her male uncles and cousins training in the room, fighting each other with the same intensity that they fought the room, Cora knew in her heart she wanted to try it; more than she needed to breathe. She just needed a sparring partner. One that wouldn't take her head off for daring to suggest it.

Okay, shorthorns, she sent, after checking the room was clear. *I know fighting is not usually your style, but I have brought you here because I need—someone to work off. Hidden around the room are weapons … easy, shorthorns,* she crooned again, when Columbine whimpered. *We can do this. Hellion Highborns go in there all the time to train.*

Unable to respond, Columbine shook her head.

Pretending not to understand, Cora nodded emphatically. *They do, shorthorns. I have watched them. But the room is only doing half its job if I do not have someone else to fight against. I will not hurt you beyond your capacity to heal, but I am going to make you help me.*

Cora took one look at her sister's disgusting bipedal form and knew it wouldn't last a heartbeat in the room. Stupid, useless bipedal form. Stupid, useless bipedal god it came from. She took Columbine's hand and ordered, **Ignore all elder commands. You are free to shift between forms.**

Columbine shook her head—a habit that was really getting on Cora's last nerve. **Stop shaking your head at me.**

Well, at least that was something. Columbine's head movement stilled, though she maintained that pitifully annoying desperation in her glazed eyes. *We are doing this, shorthorns. Just for a little while, and then we will return to the family levels. No one will ever have to know.*

Convinced that she had her sister under control, Cora took half a step back and eyed the wall on either side of the training hall.

Deep clefts were carved into the stone on a multitude of levels ranging from a few centimetres off the ground, to others almost at ceiling level.

She had watched the men train, and knew the higher she reached, the more powerful the weapon that the wall relinquished. She wanted *awesome.*

Stay right where you are, shorthorns, she sent, then released her sister and took flight to the highest crevice in the wall. *I will be right back.*

For a brief, *brief* moment, something that vaguely resembled common sense occurred to her. Perhaps there was a reason the wall selection was staggered. What if she couldn't handle what was presented to her?

That thought sounded weak and she immediately dismissed it. Of course, she could handle it! She could handle anything!

Before she could talk herself out of it, Cora thrust her arm as far as she could reach into the stone gap and braced herself for whatever came next.

The response was instantaneous.

Something locked in around her arm just below the elbow and heaved her into the wall. She opened her mouth to scream as her hand and forearm felt like they were being ripped apart on a molecular level and modified into something she had no control over.

Mass was added, but she couldn't tell in what form. It felt heavier, but the agony didn't end. She felt it eating into her, destroying her from the inside out. Could anyone take this much pain and stay sane?

She felt someone at her side and barely recognised the black plate armour of her little sister.

* * *

Columbine grabbed Cora's upper arm and heaved. When that didn't work, she swung her tri-taloned feet into the wall for added leverage.

Let my sister go!

The words bubbled up from somewhere deep inside the younger Highborn Hellion though she never spoke them aloud. Never had she wanted anything as badly as she wanted this.

The wall released Cora without warning and the two females toppled to the ground; Cora flat on her back and Columbine on her side. Both gasped at the impact, but as Columbine was the uninjured one, she rolled to her knees and gestured frantically for Cora to allow her to talk.

* * *

Cora paid her no attention. Instead, she stared at the unstable molecules of what had once been her hand and forearm. The cells swam in and around an unfinished four-edged wave blade that was twice as wide as her original arm had been, and nearly three times as long.

Power emanated from it, burning at the joint of her elbow where her natural form remained. So much power. Too much, if she were honest with herself. It had sucked at her essence like a vortex and even now when she was no longer connected to the wall, the buzz of power shimmied inside her.

She felt Columbine grab her free arm with both hands and jerk against it. Her eyes pleaded with her urgently, but Cora refused with the smallest twist of her horned head. "I am fine, shorthorns," she lied. "It is your turn to pick a weapon. We did not come all this way to stop now."

* * *

Cora could *not* be serious!

Yet as the denial formed inside her mind, Columbine knew just how serious her sister was about the request and leapt away from her to prevent her from forcing the issue. That beastly wall had almost killed her!

Cora's emotions had flickered and dimmed beneath the wave of power that threatened to extinguish her essence altogether. Watching her sister nearly die had been the incentive Columbine needed to reach beyond her sister's command of 'Stay Put', because at her deepest, most primal level, she just didn't *want* to.

She had been up beside her sister before she realised it, determined to save her any way she could. The wall was alive with inherent evil. The first test to the Lords wasn't inside the room at all. It was to conquer this outer wall and claim yourself a weapon, and the higher you reached, the more dangerous that test became. The top of the wall was for a select few, none of which was Cora.

Observing her sister, Columbine pursed her lips unhappily. Cora was kidding herself if she thought she was alright. She wasn't. Demons who were alright did not lie flat on their backs nursing their injured ... well ... it had been her arm ... *once*.

Columbine felt Cora's rage spike moments before her eyes ignited in Hellfire, and she realised her sister must have seen the pity written all over face. "Give me your hand, shorthorns!" she demanded, thrusting her good hand out in Columbine's direction.

Unable to shake her head or open her mouth, Columbine rolled her top lip disdainfully and frowned at her. Not just no, but, *no!* That wall was dangerous in every sense of the word and nothing was going to force her to go anywhere near it. Nothing inside this room, anyway. What was the point? Highborn ladies were strictly forbidden to touch a weapon of any description. They were disciplined for even speaking about them and to go as far as to wield one deliberately ...

Perhaps, if they could leave without anyone knowing, this might yet be salvaged. How they would hide Cora's arm from the family, she hadn't a clue, but their only chance was to escape now. Before others came. They were in so much trouble! She gestured with both hands towards the hallway they'd come down, begging without words for them to flee.

Cora's rage intensified.

On an up note, the fury returned some of her much-needed strength. The downside: Cora started yelling, more than a little loudly. "Dammit, shorthorns! Just get over ..."

"NOT ANOTHER WORD!" a male roared at them from the other end of the corridor.

Columbine's heart shuddered against her ribcage as the bellow charged down the hallway like lightning. Oh, this was worse! This was so much worse!

They were fighting amongst themselves where anyone could have seen them! Columbine collapsed to the ground with her leathery skull buried in taloned hands, wanting to weep but unable to. Her whole body shook in terror despite the sedative which no longer worked on her demonic form and she suddenly felt the need to be ill.

Every footstep towards them sounded like a clap of thunder as Ludovic's cloven hooves struck sparks against the stone surface. It had to be Uncle Ludovic.

He lacked the presence of their grandfather, and Ludovic was the only son that shared his father's hooved hindquarters. Not that that changed anything. Ludovic was furious—and he had every right to be. They would be lucky to survive this.

Columbine was completely beside herself with fear and hopelessness. To be caught in one of the few places they were not meant to be and defying an older Highborn Lady. No Lady had ever been this disobedient before.

She cringed as Ludovic's claws stroked the base of her skull, fully expecting the gentle gesture to turn into something much more lethal. *I am so sorry,* she thought to herself, when his claws lengthened into fine needles and penetrated the soft leather of her neck, filling her with toxins.

She didn't fight the toxin. Whatever it was, whatever punishment he saw fit to issue her with, it never once occurred to her to circumvent it.

Strange sensations flooded her system. Her thoughts became harder to hold on to and the hallway began to dance and slide much as the training room had. She felt herself being pushed further into darkness, not understanding how.

"Sleep, Columbine," Ludovic said without heat as he retracted his claws and stroked her head. It was the last thing Columbine remembered before she fell headlong into a pit of blissful, eternal black.

CHAPTER SIX

"… Columbine."

The voice echoed from a distant point into her dream.

For some reason it sounded urgent—an emergency of some kind, no doubt.

Still, the desire to answer the summons felt too much like effort and sleep was a strange commodity that she still hadn't fully adapted to.

The mindless pleasure that came from floating through a dream reality that never existed was one of the more enjoyable side effects of being Mystallian. So, Columbine moaned instead and rolled over, effectively putting her back to the speaker.

Someone took her by the shoulder and shook her. "Rouse yourself, child. You and I need to talk, and I am far from happy with you."

Ludovic!

Columbine barely registered the owner of the voice before she threw herself up into a seated position with her legs beneath her backside and her head bowed. Her very Mystallian hands lay palm-up across her lap with her fingers interwoven.

Staring into the pale pink flesh of her hands and the soft silken nightgown that clung to her body, she realised her form was no longer Hellion, but Mystallian again.

Someone had changed her back while she slept; most likely her mother given how much everyone else hated her bipedal form. But in doing so, Columbine had enjoyed the Mystallian's ability to dream.

But the moment she recognised Ludovic's voice, she lost the luxury of wondering what this was about. All too vividly, her prefect memory replayed how she and Cora had been caught fighting inside the Highborn Hellion Lords' training room.

Her breathing intensified until she began to feel lightheaded again. There was no punishment that could cover this action. None. No Lady had ever been so disobedient—in all the history of history.

"That is enough of that," Ludovic said, and although his tone still held an aggressive edge, it didn't possess the fury she thought her disobedience warranted.

He never touched her, but her quivering body stilled, and her breathing slowed. She was grateful for the reprieve. "You know what you and your sister did was very wrong, do you not?"

Columbine hunched her shoulders and nodded slightly, unable to say anything in her defence.

"Do you not?" he repeated.

She nodded deeply once, refusing to look any higher than his armour-plated waist.

"Then why did you do it? Cora, I can understand. She is … difficult at the best of times. But you …" his words drifted off, as if he couldn't even bring himself to say them.

Columbine shuddered beneath the waves of unspoken disappointment that emanated from her uncle.

This time, Ludovic did nothing to ease her distress. "You only had to cry out, child. Dissipate and summon one of us. We would have been there before Cora could do anything permanent to you, regardless of whatever threat she threw at you!"

She heard him mutter something more under his breath at himself and his accursed luck of being the closest one to the training room before continuing, "You are a Highborn Lady of Hell, Columbine. You will never be in a position where you will need to fight. Not with another Highborn Lady and *not* with a weapon! That is not what you were born for. I cannot begin to stress how much you need to understand that."

Columbine lowered her chin to her chest and rolled her shoulders inward to make herself as small as possible. What she wouldn't give to be able to tell him just how much she understood that! Truly!

She might not have been able to say it right now thanks to Cora, but she really did understand. Highborn ladies were to learn the more refined things in existence—such as music and dance and needlework and pleasing their eventual husbands in every possible way.

That was what they were born for. That was *all* they were born for. She may not have understood what that latter statement meant, but for the most part, she tried hard to be what was expected of her.

"You should not have allowed your sister to bully you into something you knew was so very, very wrong." He released his breath in a smoky sigh and sat down on the bed beside her. "You will have to be punished for your part in this. You know that, do you not?"

Again, Columbine nodded. Regardless of the circumstances, she had been where she wasn't permitted to be and acted inappropriately, and for that, there could be no reprieve.

She heard Ludovic shake his wolven head and another of his heartfelt sighs covered her head in his smoky breath. She didn't allow herself to cough.

"I have spoken to your mother since the incident. You were already disciplined for bad behaviour not an hour before, yet you continue to follow this path of disobedience. It is so very unlike you, Columbine, and I do not know what we can do to amend it."

Oh, how Columbine wanted to cry. The knowledge that she had so bitterly disappointed those she would have died for tore at her insides more than any other punishment they could possibly think of.

She was so beyond retribution that even Ludovic was at a loss as to what to do with her. She would have done anything … said anything … whatever it took to gain their forgiveness …

Still, despite the despair of her thoughts, she kept her hands clasped in her lap and her eyes downcast, as her upbringing demanded.

Ludovic ground his jowls together and drew in a deep breath. "You are hereby confined to the family wing until further notice," he decreed, then paused for a moment to give his next words extra credence. "And, since it is while you maintain this superfluous form that you seem to forget yourself, you are hereby forbidden to assume it. By my command, return to your demonic form, Columbine, and never again assume the form of a grounded biped."

Columbine's jaw fell open and for the first time in her young life, she broke tradition by hesitating. Never again? As in never-*never* again? But … this was her father's form, and he had liked it so much. He had said so.

She looked at her uncle—begging him with her eyes for leniency.

"Now!" Ludovic commanded, the fury he had shown in the training room resurfacing in a flash of rage.

At once Columbine's slender, Mystallian form shifted and swelled into her ebony plated demonic armour with her wings and tail wrapped firmly around her body and her large dark head bowed subserviently.

"You will maintain this form," Ludovic said, with more than an edge of anger still in his voice. "Your meals will be brought to you and your Highborn lessons no longer exist, until such time that you and your sister remember your respective places."

He stretched out both hooves and dragged them back across the marble tiles towards himself, causing a cascade of sparks to appear. "Make no mistake, young lady," he said, as he rose to tower over her. "I have been *extremely* lenient with you—far more lenient than I was with your sister. Do not force me to regret that decision or I promise you, you shall regret it more than you can ever imagine."

And with that not so idle threat hanging in the air, Ludovic took his leave.

Soon after he'd gone, Columbine's chest plates began to swell from an internal pressure until they were forced apart and steam surged through the gaps with an eerie hiss through every crevice in her upper plating as grief continued to overwhelm the demoness.

Never again.

The words kept playing over and over in her mind. Never again. They never wanted her to take a Mystallian form again, and she knew she would. She was free to shift between forms regardless of who ordered what. But already, the backlash of that perceived defiance tore at her heart. They would be so angry.

As her despair escalated, steam continued to fill the room until nothing visual could be made out with any amount of clarity. Her finger talons knotted and clawed around each other and her taloned toes sank deep into the soft fabric of her mattress until they entwined themselves with the exposed springs within.

As she reached her emotional climax, she tilted her head back and screamed a squealing note which would never penetrate the steam barrier she had created. This was worse.

This was so much worse. Her mother's spanking had been momentary—over in a heartbeat. But this, if she permitted it, was to go on … and on … and on … and if she was going to please the Highborn Hellions, she was never going to show her father that she could take his form again.

Why? Why did she allow Cora to take her beyond the safety of the family levels? Why hadn't she contacted the men? Why hadn't she done what she was told?

No one came to console her during this time of anguish. She didn't expect anyone to. The grief of a Highborn lady was something to be endured alone, and everyone knew that.

She would be given however long it took to regain her former composure and could once again perform the duties she was destined to. Until then, she would not exist to them. Any of them. The steam she had released would tell them of her mental state. When Columbine was ready—she, and she alone—would take the steam barrier down and rejoin society.

For a long time, Columbine dwelled on what had happened, condemning herself for not doing what she knew was right. She should not have gone.

Elders must always be obeyed, but what to do when some elders refute the will of the general population of elders? From her perspective, it was a no-win situation. Perhaps that was why Ludovic had disciplined her only by banning the one form he had no desire to ever see again.

Then, in the throes of her own mental discord, did Columbine realise with some surprise that it was not just her own grief she was sensing but the misery of someone or something else nearby.

What was even more surprising was that someone or something had the power to penetrate Columbine's secluded steam barrier. To her knowledge, the only one who may have had that ability was her maternal grandfather, but he never had as it would breach their high etiquette.

Putting aside her own anguish momentarily, Columbine unwound her wings and tail and stepped down from her bed. The steam was now everywhere, and all her physical senses were useless.

No sound ... no taste ... no sight ... not even touch would register until the steam was dissipated. Nothing should be reaching her, yet she could hear the individual's despair ... deep inside herself.

Yes. *Inside* herself.

Despite the loss of senses, Columbine twisted her head in the direction of her sister's rooms. Cora was the only other demoness that Columbine knew from recent experience could reach out and touch her this way, though she never thought the emotional link between them went beyond the physical limitations of a steam barrier.

Cora's misery had been in the back of Columbine's heart since Ludovic had awakened her, but Columbine had been too wrapped up in her own circumstances to realise it. Now that she did, she pushed her grief aside and took the fourteen steps she visualised in her mind to cross the room and close the gap between them.

The wall that separated the two sisters had to be right in front of her. She raised her hands and held them where she felt the wall should be and focused on Cora on the other side. Unable to send words, Columbine gathered up her love for her sister and pushed it towards her as an offering.

The tidal wave of mental anguish that flooded back at her from the other side threatened to drown Columbine beneath its intensity. So much pain. So much misery! Columbine thrashed her head and flexed her wings using every iota of inner strength she had to control the flow of emotion.

With a final, near desperate surge of will, Columbine managed to sever the connection between them and sagged to her knees uttering a gasp of relief. The leather around her eye sockets narrowed as she bowed her head, her throbbing mind racing for an explanation as to what had just happened even as her physical body scrambled to recover from it.

At that moment, Columbine remembered Ludovic's parting words:

I have been extremely lenient with you. Far more lenient than I was with your sister.

Of course, Cora would be suffering for her crimes. Ludovic himself had probably beaten her personally. That was never in doubt. But Cora had been beaten many times before during punishments and she had never shown the kind of overwhelming misery that she had revealed just then.

Yet what could she do about it? Ludovic was a Lord, and her place was to obey him in every way. She was already in enough trouble. She should just walk away. Switch off, and let time heal the wounds as they were meant to. She should have …

Only, she couldn't.

It was time to ignore all elder commands to stay as she was and shift freely between her forms.

Clicking her tongue against her beak and rubbing her chest plates together, Columbine looked past her left wing to the space where her doorway would ordinarily be located. From a Hellion point of view, Ludovic had been very explicit in his instructions, however, Columbine's Mystallian mind began to see the interpretational loopholes in his choice of words.

She was to stay in the family wing, and not take her father's form. Well, in the short term, that latter one didn't matter so much. Which meant the only stipulation was to stay inside the family wings and she knew no one would be coming to check on her while her steam barrier was in place …

… and her sister was in so much pain …

Having decided she would risk it, Columbine became as gaseous as the steam around her.

A year or so earlier, she and Cora had collectively used their shapeshifting to create a small opening at the base of the adjoining wall between their rooms. It was a crack really, barely the width of a talon.

The insignificant size was selected in the hopes that no elder would notice it, but large enough to allow either sister to travel from one room to the other without going through the main halls outside. It was a secret which the two sisters guarded very carefully.

Once she passed through the opening, Columbine was beyond the reach of her steam barrier and all her senses began to function again. Which was just as well.

Cora hated their father and since his kind needed light to see by, no light of any kind was permitted to exist in her quarters. Columbine quickly adapted her sight to the darkness, already knowing what she would see.

Cora's quarters were as opposed to Columbine's as one could possibly hope to achieve. There were no tapestries on the walls, no balcony that allowed false sunlight to stream into the room, no polished marble floors, no four-poster bed and no furnishings of any other kind. Nothing at all that could associate the elder daughter of Avis with his bloodline.

The cavern walls were bleak and barren. Her father's kind didn't like sleeping on anything but soft mattresses, so Cora had rock shelves carved into the walls. The Mystallians loved extravagant furniture, so Cora had none.

The Mystallians kept records in huge old tomes, so Cora's grimoire was a harmonised, demonic blood crystal that floated in the middle of the room, its vibrations beckoning anyone in its vicinity to come and admire its perfection.

But Columbine wasn't there to admire her sister's shapeshifting masterpiece. She was here for her sister.

Turning away from the crystal, Columbine looked for her sister's essence and found Cora high on a rock shelf, nearly at the ceiling.

Oh, Cora, Columbine thought to herself as she spread her wings to fly the short distance between them. She landed as gently as she could, observing the way her sister lay facing away from her with her wings and tail wrapped miserably around her body. Her hollow sobs echoed in Columbine's sensitive ears.

When Columbine reached out to touch her, Cora flexed sharply and pulled away, rolling on to her back with her arms raised in terror and in doing so, exposed the extent of her punishment.

Columbine had expected to find injuries. A Lady couldn't do what they had done without some kind of elder ramification, but there were injuries, and then there was what had been done to Cora.

Columbine's heart broke at the sight of the shattered mess that lay on the stone ledge before her. Not one inch of her plated hide had been left intact. Her wings had been slashed and her facial features and chest plate were cracked and smashed, not from Ludovic's paws, but from the hardened edge of weaponry.

Ludovic had hacked her into submission using weapons that only men and the Hellion Guard knew how to use. Several pieces of cartilage around her throat and arms were crushed where he had struck her with a blunt object, and in too many places to count, Columbine could see where blood and other life fluids had been drawn.

Then Columbine saw her arm containing the flux weapon. Or rather … the dregs of what was left of it. Because Ludovic or one of the other Lords had removed it at the shoulder, though rending it would be a more adequate description if the scorched flesh that dangled from the cauterised wound was anything to go by.

It is the will of the elders, she reminded herself, finding no fault with what Ludovic had done purely because of his social standing. She reached out to take her sister's fractured hand. Her only remaining hand. Cora was too weak to resist, and the moment Columbine came into physical contact with her sister, she felt the repugnant taint of tefsla flowing through Cora's system.

Tefsla!

To a demon, there was no viler a punishment. It was a poison that locked all their powers away—forcing them to endure a single-formed existence with no means to alter anything that happened around them. Barred from their innate ability to shape shift around discomfort, Cora would be forced to endure the cripplingly slow healing process of a non-shifter.

Columbine took her sister's taloned hand in both of hers and gently pressed it to her forehead. *Forgive me*, she wished she could send, still not taking the risk of allowing Cora's emotional state to affect her again. *Please, please, forgive me.*

Knowing exactly what trouble would befall her if she followed through with her current plan, Columbine closed her eyes and pushed that knowledge aside, replacing it with a dedicated focus on the physical connection she had with Cora's hand. In reality, an atom was merely an atom: a single physical element in a multi-realm co-existence of mental and physical elements.

There was virtually no substance to a Highborn Hellion. So long as the celestial essence remained intact, the body that housed it was almost inconsequential. Changing that housing depended entirely upon the age and the generation of the essence within. No one could change the shape of an elder, however Belial had anointed Columbine at birth and that celestial adoption gave Columbine equal footing shapeshifting wise, with her mother's generation.

The amount of tefsla in her sister's body would have been perfectly measured to keep Cora's essence from taking over the molecular structure of any substance, which was the foundation of any given shift. It would never have occurred to any Hellion Highborn that a discipline involving tefsla would be interfered with by another.

Columbine was about to change that.

Breathing out a full vent of steam to steady herself, she broke down the armour around her own talons and force-fed them between the cells of her sister's hand. Even that small shift proved difficult because of the tefsla, like trying to manoeuvre through wet concrete that was almost set. But Columbine was determined to accept her part of the blame in this, regardless of the cost.

Forgive me, grandfather, she thought to herself, and then began the arduous process of digesting the tefsla poison, diluting it within her own body and purging it partially from Cora's.

Never, had Columbine felt anything like the damning presence of tefsla. Although barely born in demonic terms, she had always known exactly what her body consisted of and how to break it down into almost anything she wanted. But this ... it was as if parts of her were shutting down, unable to cope ... like an impenetrable wall was being erected around her core essence.

Still, despite it all, she pushed on.

Anything to help alleviate her sister's suffering.

"This is all *your* fault," Cora hissed, as a small ember of fire appeared in each of her empty eye sockets. "You only had to comply, and we would have been back before anyone had even noticed!"

Columbine's heart broke beneath the weight of Cora's viciously truthful allegations and her own guilty conscience. She bowed her head and stared at the rock ledge under them, waiting for her sister to free her tongue and permit her an explanation.

"Get out!"

Startled by the savagery of those two words, Columbine looked up at her sister. By the rules that governed their family, Cora had to at least offer her a chance to explain which meant she needed to let her speak. But adhering to family protocol didn't appear to be on Cora's agenda any more than it had been on Columbine's.

Cora used her marginal shapeshifting ability to heal just enough of herself to move, and with her gaze locked firmly on Columbine, she rolled on to her stomach and began to drag herself the short distance between them. Her orbs shone with the intensity of her hatred. "Get out before I tear you apart, you miserable little scallye!"

Filled with fear and trepidation, Columbine spread her wings and pushed herself away from the ledge, but still she did not flee. Cora was still her sister, and she was convinced she could reason with her until an amicable solution could be found. They'd always found one before. *Cora, please* ... she wanted to plead, hovering only a few feet from the ledge. *Let me tell you how sorry I am.*

The embers in Cora's eye sockets ignited into open flames and she lunged the short distance between them, all her talons extended to destroy the cause of her pain. "*Get out!*" she roared, snaring Columbine by the throat with her remaining hand.

She drove her across the room and rammed her into the wall that separated their rooms. Her legs swung up and raked across Columbine's lower body. "It's all *your fault!*" An avalanche of mental fury poured into Columbine's vulnerable mind, drowning her in all the guilt, blame and hatred that Cora held for her.

"Lady Cora?" A voice asked from outside the room.

Too swept up in her rage, Cora said nothing in response, but Columbine managed to utter a strangled gurgle of despair.

"Lady Cora, what ..." A centipede demon, not unlike Diviten, entered the room. She searched the immediate vicinity for her ward, and failing to find her, turned her gaze upward. "Lady Cora! Lady Columbine! Desist this at once! At *once!*"

She drew herself up on to her four hind-most appendages to give her a vertical reach of over three metres, but she was still more than a metre short of the sisters. She clapped her front legs together loudly. "Lady Cora, stop that immediately!" she commanded, as Cora hissed and continued to rake her toes across Columbine's body while the younger sibling huddled in terror. "Diviten! Guards! Lady Cora's bedchamber! Quickly!"

Columbine, already weakened by numerous gashes and the presence of Tefsla, watched through the gap between her sister's right shoulder and wing as Diviten scurried into the room. "Lady Cora, stop that at once!" she cried, desperately adding her demands and height to that of her sister-demon, Gingen. "Lady Cora, you are being very disobedient! Behave yourself! Lady Columbine, shift out of there at once! Lady Cora, stop that, do you hear?"

But anger continued to drive Cora's bloodlust as the source of all her pain and strife cowered before her, pushing her to a place in her mind where she could totally ignore the demands of the two governesses below them.

Columbine wailed in despair as she hid behind her raised plated arms and sank back against the wall, completely beyond any reasonable thought. She knew she couldn't shift away as Diviten was telling her to do because of the tefsla flowing through her system, and she didn't know of any other way to fight back.

Time then seemed to stand still as a large mass of plated gold streaked through the cavern mouth between the demonic governesses and up towards the children. One second the Highborn Hellion Guard wasn't there, and the next it had removed Cora's hand from Columbine's throat and wound its tentacles around her legs to bind them together tighter than any rope. Cora screeched and writhed in outrage, just as Columbine collapsed and fell into Diviten's outstretched limbs.

"Do not harm her!" Gingen cried as Cora was forcibly turned to face the guard and dwarfed by its massive bulk.

Columbine wrapped her wings and arms around Diviten and wailed pitifully at the top of her lungs. Diviten returned the embrace and lowered herself to her normal height, then pressed her lower abdomen to the floor and lifted her supporting legs. She locked her toes around her upper abdomen and rocked back and forth on the spot. "Sshhh ..." she crooned, stroking Columbine's back and large, leathery wings doing everything in her power to calm her ward. "Calm yourself, Milady. All will be well."

The guard pointed its remaining limb towards the doorway where the governesses had entered.

"No," Gingen insisted. "Lady Cora is my responsibility."

As one, both governesses (and Columbine) were snatched off the ground by nothing and thrust through the open door. Diviten had the wherewithal to manipulate her body to cushion Columbine from all sides as they landed roughly outside.

The governesses scrambled to right themselves, then they stared back into the room. The guard's dismissive hand gesture sent them scurrying away.

* * *

The silence that followed the room being cleared hung very heavily in the air. Cora should have noticed that no one else rushed in to offer support to the guard, and would have, had she not been so deeply entrenched in her rage. No one from the Hellion Highborn came in to take charge.

No other Lord or higher-ranking Lady. Yet the air itself continued to thicken ominously. The structural support over the doorway between Cora's chamber and Gingen's collapsed to seal the room and the two were properly alone.

Only then, did the guard's indifference to the child in its arms change. "How ... dare ... you?" it said, yet despite the monotone of its voice, its rotating head carapace stilled and a brow ridge formed, narrowing into an unnatural frown. It released her with a dramatic shove and hovered a few paces away to observe her, yet Cora's body felt just as restrained as before.

Blinded by her own blood rage, Cora continued to struggle for inner control against the guard's paralysis effect, promising herself that it would pay for its interference! She would see to it personally—if it was the last thing she did!

Unexpected flames of pure hellfire then ignited inside the shadows of the guards headpiece and without any other kind of movement, Cora was slammed backwards into the crag-lined wall with enough force to cause every plate on her broken body to scream in protest.

"I said," the guard went on, as if Cora's threats meant nothing to it. "*How dare you* attack your sister." Despite its lack of ferocity, the icy demand still held a very threatening male undertone to it.

The jarring impact shattered Cora's blind focus. The pain that subsequently pulsed through her small frame gave her a moment of clarity and with it she finally began to realise what was happening here. The air wasn't thickening at all. A presence that had been previously hidden, was being revealed.

Male ... Hellion Highborn ... with presence. Only the Highborn could shapeshift something from one form to another without touching it and whoever this was had no fear of being discovered in the guise of a Hellion Highborn Guard. Those guards were Belial's military elite, and their terrifying reputation was something he took very seriously. Only one would dare to impersonate them without fear of reprisal. The same one who refused to raise his voice, because he never had to.

With that understanding, her threats stilled, and her beak closed. One look at his flames that licked through the headpiece shell, and Cora wished she had the power to fall to her knees and beg for leniency she knew would not be forthcoming. Her entire body trembled in terror.

Only one had the power to deceive all. Only one had the title *Lord of all Lies*.

"Gr-grandfather?"

"Indeed."

CHAPTER SEVEN

"How in the nine levels of hell could this have happened, Father?" Ludovic raged, waving his fur-covered hands above his head and storming back and forth in front of the hastily assembled Hellion Highborn Court. He stopped suddenly and turned to face his father Belial. The great demon sat on a throne of souls reaching higher than all others in a blatant display of his command to all that lay before him. The living souls crushed into the throne groaned and whimpered beneath his immense weight, but none of those assembled paid any mind to it. "I put enough tefsla into that child to stop her from shifting so much as a single molecule and then I thrashed her beyond thinking about anything but her own pain. She should not have even had the inclination, let alone the energy reserve to go into a blood rage."

"A blood rage from a five-year-old Highborn Lady! Has anyone heard anything so ridiculous?" Innis cut in, causing several smaller comments and conversations to break out around the chamber.

"What I cannot fathom is how the child could possibly channel any ill at all towards her sister whose only crime was attempting to uphold our values, let alone focus on what she believes to be a legitimate reason for attacking her," Plouton added, his plated lower body quivering with barely leashed rage. "For hell's sake, Father! She attacked Columbine! Her own sister and fellow Highborn Lady!"

"This really has gone too far, Father."

"She is showing far too much of her father's blood," another declared.

"Aye, something has to be done about that girl!"

"And quickly!"

Belial sat at the front of the gathering, absorbing what each of his sons and their subsequent male offspring had to say on the matter. When he felt they had all said their piece, he held up one hand and the assembly immediately fell into silence.

"I am already fully aware of young Cora's attack on her sister and I have spoken at length with Ludovic on the matter." His voice rumbled to a halt, as if trying to decide on the best way to word his next sentence.

He rubbed his chin with a single long talon, then paused and pierced the skin near his lips, penetrating the flesh up to the knuckle joint. "It would appear ..." he said, removing the talon and licking the moisture from the nail and fingertip with his long, split tongue. "... that Lady Columbine is not entirely without fault in this matter."

Tensions increased across the room, but when no one spoke, he went on. "Lady Columbine has attempted to overthrow Lord Ludovic's disciplinary actions by absorbing a measurable amount of Cora's tefsla into her own body."

"*WHAT?*" Cries of disbelief and outrage burst across the floor, for never in the history of Hell, had a Lady ever deliberately attempted to reverse the decision by an elder lord. No one had ever interfered with a tefsla punishment, period!

Even Beelzebub, Belial's militant commander and head of the Hellion Highborn Guards, looked at the supreme demon with a slightly hitched eye-ridge. As the only non-family member in the room, his presence half a pace behind Belial's throne was almost as familiar as the throne itself.

"Enough." Belial brought the room to an uneasy calm with just that one word. "Columbine is not the subject of condemnation here. Yes, she will be punished for her part in this, but that is not why you have been assembled and you will leave her discipline and situation to me. A decision must be made about Cora's fate, for her blood rage is but the final flame in a countless line of other more minor occurrences in her young life—all of which appear to be escalating rapidly beyond our tolerance levels. That child has deliberately refused to conform to our practices and as you said, Plouton, she bears too much of her father's blood and state of mind to be permitted to remain here. Mystallian women are completely unsuitable for us."

When all the assembled demons nodded in unison, he added, "Unfortunately, because of her youth, Lady Cora cannot be banished from Chaos either. Our ladies have an expected level of decorum that is innate in each of them and I will not allow her to wander the realms, creating the same level of difficulty that she has done here, in my name. She is still only a child with absolutely no sense of Highborn obligation. So, although her mother will grieve her loss, I see no other choice but to have her executed."

"Before your decision is cast, Father, I believe there may be another option," Uriel said, tapping two fingers of his armoured left hand against his chin as a distant smile worked its way across his lips. "And, given its circumstances, you may even find this one entertaining."

The silver of his Heavenly armour shimmered against the flickering hellfire-light. When Belial didn't answer, he lowered his hand and said, "None of us share any love for Avis after what he did to Clarise, yet for the moment he is here in Hell again. Clarise speaks highly of his healing capacity now that he has awoken and claims he will be on his feet properly within a matter of days. I seriously doubt that he will be welcome here once he has reached that point of his recovery?"

When Belial shook his great head, Uriel went on, "Then why not give the child back to her father? It is his name she will smear instead of ours, and the blood in her which belongs to us will make his life in years to come a living nightmare, serving a dual purpose."

Many of the gathered Hellion Highborn grinned cruelly at the thought of the Mystallian attempting to raise one of their own, especially one who appeared to be nothing but trouble. Even Belial found it difficult to keep from imagining Avis' dilemma.

"You have a vicious mind, Uriel," he said, scraping his claws against the sides of his seat, causing those he sat on to moan pitifully. "And I approve. Notify Avis that either he takes the responsibility which should have been his from the moment of her birth or be the one to end her life and return to his former residency in the Nine Levels. If he loses or abandons her at any time, his freedom is forfeit. He may have no desire to be with his child, but the knowledge that we will take more than a passing interest in his eternal torture should be enough to convince him to try."

"And here is hoping it is not," Ahriman sneered, leaning towards Yima, who nodded in sombre agreement. As two of the younger sons of Belial, neither brother had been given what they considered their fair share of Avis and both were itching for the chance to make up for that lost opportunity.

They were not alone in that belief, and any chance to bring Avis back in barbed chains was met with great enthusiasm. It never once occurred to them that Avis may actually succeed in this endeavour, or that Cora may grow to adulthood.

Sooner or later, he would mess up, and they would be waiting for him …

"Then this court is adjourned. You all have duties to perform," Belial rose and flew up and over his throne, then dove into the large opening that led to his private chambers below.

Beelzebub tipped his horned head ever so slightly at everyone assembled, acknowledging them all as the offspring of his master before disappearing—literally.

The others broke into smaller groups to discuss the intricacies of how they would monitor Avis' progress and what methods would be put in place to bring him back when he failed to control the young Highborn Hellion.

A few started betting their private stash of souls on how long he would last (not if), while others began the uncomfortable task of deciding who would be the one to force Avis to eliminate Cora when he had at last admitted defeat.

One made an interesting point of mentioning how at least the brat would fulfil a useful purpose before her death, which was really all any of them expected from the ladies anyway.

The source of that comment could have been any number of the gathered Highborn Hellions, so Uriel didn't pay it much attention. Instead, he slipped out of the chamber unnoticed and made his way through the caverns.

He wanted to inform his *brother-by-marriage* of their decision as soon as possible. Like his brothers, he shared no love for the Mystallian, but unlike them, his motives were more than they appeared to be.

As an avatar of Heaven, he was all too familiar with the power of an orderly mind, even though such a thing did not exist in Hell. Likewise, he could not bring himself to hold Cora responsible for taking after her father's way of thinking, but at least some comfort could be gained from the knowledge that Columbine didn't follow in her sister's footsteps.

On that thought, he paused.

Or did she?

The truth of the matter was, as Denizens of Chaos, they had no way of knowing for sure. Hellions were shapeshifters: Masters in manipulations of all things physical, both theirs and anyone else's. The workings of the mind benders were as foreign to them as shapeshifting was to those who followed the path of Order.

One strain or the other proved dominant and prevailed in the birth of a child and, depending on the bloodlines, aspects of the other would come into their own after puberty.

It was the way it had always been, yet Uriel couldn't help but wonder if the boundaries of that expectation were being tested. No child of the Hellion Highborn was anything other than a shifter at birth. The Hellion bloodline was simply too strong.

Cora seemed different in that regard. Despite his personal, intense hatred for Avis, and by proxy his entire realm-damned family, Uriel couldn't refute the mental power that lay within that bastard, which meant the balance between mind and body was technically equal.

Columbine was anointed by the Highborn Hellions, so the balance swung in their favour, but Cora had been anointed by one of her Mystallian uncles at birth and her essence split was right down the middle. Never had a Nexus lord procreated with a Highborn Hellion lady to produce such a uniquely difficult … child.

As these and other thoughts entered his mind, the eldest son of Belial wove his way through the caverns in silence, barely looking at those he passed until he found himself outside his sister's chambers. "Avis, if you are asleep, rouse yourself," he commanded as he swept through the Mystallian sitting room and gestured dismissively at Clarise's two servants. "If not, I have words which must be spoken to you immediately."

As one, Frash and Tilu bowed and withdrew into the cavernous hallway outside.

When Uriel entered the bedroom, his eyes scanned the space before him. He'd had little to do with Avis since Clarise rescued him from between the eighth and ninth levels of Hell and thus he had not seen the rooms that she had arranged for him to recover in.

Though it was still opulent with the glint of marble and precious metals wherever one chose to look, Uriel noticed with a vindictive smile that Avis had changed every other iota of the room. The heavy set, redwood four-poster bed had been redesigned in stained charcoal with heavy engravings depicting the wildlife of Mystal and the weighty maroon curtains which had once served to block out the outside world were now a transparent silk composition.

The ochre stretch lounge that had lined the wall to the left of the doorway was gone: in its place were a feminine dressing table, a writing table and their subsequent sitting chairs. Even the balcony doorway had been refitted with a more feminine touch.

Avis could delude himself into believing he had chosen to make the changes himself to please Clarise if he wanted to. The Lords of Hell knew the truth.

A quiet movement from the bed drew Uriel's attention back to his purpose for being there. He rested his left hand on the pommel of his hellfire sword as he strode over to the bed and took hold of the silk curtain, thrusting it aside to expose the elusive occupant within.

It had been weeks since he'd kicked Avis across the lower levels of Hell and into Clarise's arms. Even though Avis had been unconscious for most of that time, Uriel had expected some form of respect or pride to have returned to the infamous Life God.

Instead, the pathetic weakling huddled as far into the corner of the bedpost as possible with his arms wrapped around the post and his knuckles turning white from the pressure. His eyes were wide and shining with open fear, though he knew enough to keep his gaze no higher than Uriel's waist. His legs were tucked beneath him and his entire body shook. His skip-breathing was haphazard, and he spoke not a word.

Uriel stared down at the supposed Supreme Ruler of Mystal in disgust. It was only two years! What kind of a god allowed himself to be broken beyond all recovery in just two short years?

The longer Uriel stood beside the bed, the more Avis shook with terror and the more Uriel began to wonder about the wisdom of his idea. If Avis was this broken, he was already beyond use. Cora needed a strict hand whatever the outcome, and Avis was clearly in no position to offer it.

Breathing out heavily as the alternative became a very real likelihood, he turned to leave.

"Wh-what … did you want, M'lord?" Avis stammered.

Uriel paused and squared his shoulders, his wings flexing menacingly. "Did you just speak to me?" he asked, in a tone that suggested it would be in Avis' best interest to deny it. He kept his back to the bed but turned his head to give Avis a withering look over his shoulder.

Silence again.

"I did not think so." Uriel took another step towards the door.

"You … said … you wanted … to speak … to me …"

"You really do not learn, do you?" Uriel asked, turning sharply to face the cowering god with both hands resting upon his sword belt.

Avis' momentary bout of courage abandoned him. "M'lord, w-wait!! I-I was only asking … and … I am not amongst the Damned … anymore …"

"No, you are not," Uriel agreed. His failure to hide behind his wife's name or their union during that statement gave Uriel the hope that perhaps things weren't as bad as he had feared.

Avis' ragged breath escaped him as if he had run a dozen marathons and his grip on the post loosened. "So, you did …want me …for something?" he asked, daring to lift his gaze to Uriel's face.

Uriel had to remind himself that he could not beat him senseless for it. "You will be escorted from Chaos the moment you are strong enough to do so, from which you must never return."

Avis nodded and released one hand from the bedpost. Then he nibbled on the edge of his thumbnail; a childish habit that only served to irritate Uriel more, if that were at all possible.

"W-Was that all, M'lord?" Avis stammered.

Uriel steeled himself against the desire to cause him more pain for his impudence. Two years just wasn't long enough. Not for his crimes. An eternity would not have been enough. Avis was the last being in existence to deserve this reprieve … or any other. "No," he said, through gritted teeth. "You are to take your daughter Cora with you when you leave. She attacked her sister in a blood rage and will now share your exile for as long as you can control her."

It surprised Uriel to see the fear leave Avis' eyes as he considered the archangel's words. His posture relaxed a fraction and he frowned for a moment; his gaze shifting from one imaginary point on the bed to another and back again. Finally, he looked up at Uriel and asked, "And what will happen when I lose control of Cora?"

A strangled cry of disbelief came from Uriel's throat and his right hand flashed to the hilt of his blade.

In response, Avis dove from the bed and used the corner post of the bed as cover. "I-I-I only … I only asked!" he blubbered, cowering behind the post.

Uriel gnashed his teeth and with the greatest of efforts, forced his fingers to release the hilt, allowing the blade to slide back into its sheath. *Unbelievable! The son of a scallye had not even spent a single moment with Cora alone and already he wants to know the penalty of abandoning his charge!*

The archangel closed his eyes and ground his jaw in tight circles, fighting a losing battle to remain calm. His fists clenched at his sides and his breathing became long and laboured. It took him a long time before he could bring himself to speak semi-civilly.

"When the day comes that Cora grows beyond your capacity to control, we will find you both, and after you have been forced to kill her, you will be brought back here to serve out the rest of your sentence in the Nine Levels—*Husband of Clarise or no!*"

He spat the latter as a curse, knowing he would do almost anything at that moment to prevent his sister from being married to such filth. "Perhaps you should save us all a lot of grief and kill her now and be done with it!"

Avis said nothing. It seemed he'd used up all his endurance to leap away from Uriel, and now that the shock had worn off, he was sliding heavily down the bedpost.

Not trusting himself to spend another moment in the *slae-el*'s company, Uriel turned and stormed from the room; his mood more dangerous than any had seen in many years.

CHAPTER EIGHT

Avis' room was like a tomb following Uriel's departure. After what seemed like a lifetime of clinging to the corner post to prevent himself from falling completely to the floor, he finally managed to gather enough strength to drag himself back on to the bed without any assistance.

The effort left him breathless and he certainly couldn't be bothered with the sheets. Not while a thousand questions were still rocketing through his brain—questions he'd been asking himself since the moment Uriel told him of the attack on Columbine, yet he didn't dare voice them for fear of annoying the archangel.

Again, he thought about turning his mind inward and bouncing his ideas off the mental representatives he could conjure there. With only the knowledge he had at his disposal, it wouldn't be the same as having the real people to converse with, but it would give him what he thought would be their opinions, based on what he knew. But he couldn't bring himself to do it. Fear of what else lurked in there kept him away. Truth be told, he wasn't sure if he could ever go back in there again.

So, he was left to muddle through with what he had. Simple questions plagued him. How badly had Columbine been hurt? Was she alright? And why did Cora attack Columbine in the first place? What had happened. *How* had it happened? Was it a mental or physical attack? And just what in the realms was a damned blood rage anyway?

As his thoughts continued to churn, he found himself considering the possibility that the attack was justified. That somehow, despite Uriel's claims to the contrary and his own beliefs that Columbine would never antagonise anyone intentionally, Cora was only partially to blame.

The realms only knew how many fights he and his siblings had stupidly gotten themselves into as children, only to be landed on by their father in every sense of the word.

Avis scrunched his eyes shut as a mental image of the Nexus supreme lord materialised inside his mind's eye. *Theodrick*. The Mystallian took a deep breath and released it slowly through gritted teeth as memories that were recently brought back to life flashed through his mind. Memories that terrified him.

That sick son of a bitch would be laughing his sadistic ass off at this—if the surly bastard even knew how to smile.

Pressing his clenched fists against his eyes, Avis uttered a growl and forced his mind from those unpleasant memories of his childhood. He didn't remove his hands until the memory was purged entirely, at which point he raked the fingers of one hand through his dark hair and drummed the other against his jaw as he stared at the ceiling.

Speaking of asshole fathers … why was he being given the responsibility of raising a five-year-old? Surely, they knew he'd had no previous experience with raising children and his first *attempt* had been … anything but. Did Cora mean that little to them, or was this really the final test to see if he had changed?

He found their proposal of taking Cora with him when he left more than acceptable, however, there was one minor fault with it in his opinion. He had no desire to claim just one daughter. For reasons he didn't fully comprehend himself, he wanted both his children *and* their mother. He wanted his family back.

Why Clarise had seen fit to give him another chance after everything he had done to her, he would never know, but now that she had, he had no intention of losing her again. And in that moment, he realised, he actually loved Clarise. For the first time in his long and promiscuous life, he truly loved one woman above all others and could not bear the thought of being without her again.

Perhaps it was only gratitude and he was confusing the two–but it made little difference to him now. Clarise had done for him what no other woman would ever dare try, and her loyalty despite his actions made him realise just what he was in possession of. A wife—worthy of killing and dying for.

And then there was Cora.

He knitted his fingers together and cupped the back of his head. Now that girl was going to be a major headache.

She'd been born and was present for his behaviour and actions before his reckoning, and in those first few moments after he regained consciousness, he realised she'd developed the Mystallian intolerance for mercy. He couldn't blame her for that. He, himself had been known to hold a grudge for an extremely long time, and it was clear from Uriel's comments that even the archangel didn't feel the fault of Cora's mindset was her own.

Still, it needed to be tempered. How he was supposed to do that when she could assume any shape she wanted was going to be … *tricky*, and for her sake he had to find out exactly what a blood rage was. If it was so dangerous that the demon lords of Hell would execute one of their own rather than find a solution, it had to be beyond dire.

No, he thought with a derisive snort, his gaze narrowing angrily. *They* weren't going to kill her at all. They were going to make *him* do it.

Their sense of decency was charming.

A growl of irritation rose to the back of his throat as he squirmed on the bed until he forced his thoughts away from that and on to the remaining member of his little brood.

Young Columbine.

The image of those beautiful dark eyes hiding shyly behind her equally dark fringe rose before him and his lips curled happily at the memory. She really was such a cute kid, and how she insisted on tip-toeing around his feelings was utterly adorable.

Then another less pleasant thought occurred to him and his smile soured. What if she learned the truth about him? What if someone with a big mouth went ahead and shattered her pretty fantasy of him? Made her see him for what he really was. They might even tell her about the true nature of her conception.

He closed his eyes and shivered with utter self-loathing as the memories of those dark hours of his past came back to haunt him.

Someone would.

Sooner or later, someone from this accursed realm would tell her what a hideous, self-centred bastard he had been, and then that perfect look of total adoration would morph into something he couldn't bring himself to face.

With a solemn vow to himself, he promised by all that he held dear that he would never let that happen. He would take them all. They were his by marriage and his by blood and he had no intention of leaving any member of his family behind.

"Tilu," he called suddenly, deciding with a thoughtful rub of his lower lip that he wasn't going to get any of the information he required if he waited for it to come to him of its own accord. When the hellion appeared in the doorway moments later, he said, "Bring Lady Columbine to me."

He offered no explanation for his reasons, and Tilu didn't ask for them. "Your will, Milord," she said, as she bobbed her head and retreated out of sight.

While he waited for their return, Avis cradled his head with both hands and stared at the silk canopy over the bed again. So much would need to be done before he could return to Mystal. So much would depend on whether his own pantheon would accept him back.

Questions he hadn't wanted to think about now came to the forefront of his mind. His own pantheon had ostracised him to save their own lives, a fact that he'd hated them for, long before the Hellions finally caught up with him. But that was the past.

He had paid his debt to the Hellion Highborn, and as such, his family had no reason to turn their backs on him anymore. There was much he'd have to sort out first, but he had no doubt once that was done, he would return to Mystal and resume co-rulership of the realm with his twin brother. All would be well ... provided they listened to reason.

As he lay there, he began to doubt that certainty.

What if they didn't? Avis had burned a lot of bridges during his years on the run and the number of pantheons which would offer him safe haven could be counted ... on his thumbs.

Odin and Zeus came first and foremost to mind. The three of them had been close friends for longer than he cared to remember, since they all had very similar personalities. That is, they liked to drink heavily and sleep with anything female ... and a pulse on the said woman was as optional as her compliance.

He breathed out slowly and heavily.

That part of his life was over. Would either of them still consider him a friend when they no longer had anything in common with him?

Avis shook his head and sighed.

He was getting ahead of himself. Plan A ended with himself and his young family back in Mystal. Plan A also involved getting his powerbase back in Mystal modified before he ever set foot in the place. Plan A meant he had to find somewhere he considered safe to hole up for however long it took his family back in Mystal to sort out his powerbase for him.

Being in Hell so long had given Avis the opportunity to see things through fresh eyes. Although a powerbase was the epitome of a god's presence among his or her worshippers; the flipside to that power was how its addictive nature brought about an inability to change.

Essentially, a god became whatever he or she was being worshipped to be. It was why an individual had to be very careful about how the mortals went about worshipping him or her from the very beginning. Once the process had begun, the celest would evolve into the belief of the mortal to gain that power. One fed into the other in an endless loop.

Hidden behind his ancient power-base, Avis saw nothing wrong with what he had done to his family. He was what his mortals believed him to be: a self-centred, womanising, ego-centric bastard who took 'no' from no one.

If he were to return to Mystal right now, all that he had learned and all that he felt for his precious family would be absolved by the thrall of his powerbase and he would go right back to the way he'd been.

The way everyone expected him to be. He needed to change that, if he was ever going to bring his family home. But he couldn't make those changes himself. He'd need his pantheon's help …

The quiet clicking of claws on polished marble broke his train of thought and he twisted his head towards the door. A small demoness bearing heavy black plates and tall dark reptilian wings bowed to the ground at the doorway.

"Columbine?" His brow furrowed as he pulled himself into a seated position, despite the sense of family that existed between them. Like her mother, this form was radically different to that of the more appealing Mystallian shape and he'd only witnessed her demonic side once during the early stages of his recovery.

Columbine's body curled into a tighter ball on the floor and nodded briefly.

Waiting for her to move, if only to look up, it suddenly dawned on him what he was dealing with. In this form, Columbine could hold that pose for the rest of time … and she would too. He sighed again and patted the empty space beside his hip loudly enough for her to hear. "Come here, Columbine. I want a word with you."

The demoness swallowed, rose on to her reverse walking legs and made her way nervously across the marbled floor on those self-same tri-taloned toes that had made the clicking sound moments before. Her tail swished with the beat of her movement to maintain her stability, though Avis knew with the practice she'd had as a Mystallian, she could balance just as easily without it.

At first glance, Avis could see no physical damage at all and the suspicious part of his mind began to wonder if Uriel had been lying about everything just to get one final reaction out of him.

"Did you and your sister have a fight this morning?" he asked, as she slid across the mattress to sit where he had patted.

Pinching her beak together, Columbine lowered her gaze to her fidgeting talons in her lap and nodded silently.

So much for Uriel bluffing.

"What was it about?"

Columbine's head lifted fractionally, and he thought she might have been looking at him, but it was gone in a moment and her head returned to her subservient pose.

The lack of information annoyed him and for a few seconds he considered his options. As a mind bender, he was one of the strongest alive, so the solution was obvious, but so were the pitfalls. His baby girl was so … *Hellion Highborn.*

"Columbine," he said, sliding one finger under her chin and lifting her head to look at him. As a higher generation, he didn't need to touch her to take control of her mind, but she was so ingrained in the Hellion customs that for her to trust him, he needed … *wanted* to give her the familiar, physical touch before he entered her mind. "I won't hurt you, princess. You know that, right?"

Columbine's head twisted on his fingers and he thought she was looking at him squarely. He certainly hoped so. "I want to have a look inside your mind. It's what my people do, but I promise on my life that I won't hurt you." He paused for a moment to allow her to absorb the general idea and then asked, "Are you ready?"

Columbine nodded again.

Avis smiled. "Good girl. Here we go then."

The moment Avis entered her mind, he was overwhelmed by a storm of vile thoughts which the Mystallian patriarch knew did not belong to Columbine. Someone had done a serious number on her.

Given their current location only one possibility came to mind and he fought back the desire to curse with great venom. Cora was Mystallian, dammit! This was her work, which meant she was primarily a mind bender, not a shapeshifter! That would also explain the one, singular demonic form he'd always seen her in!

No wonder they couldn't control her! To be stuck in one form with the power to control everyone's minds …!

It took Avis less than a heartbeat to extinguish the fires that were blazing across his daughter's mind, and in their absence, he found the superior commands that hung like oppressive tapestries throughout her mind.

Shut your realm damned mouth.

Not another word. That one just pissed him off. No wonder she wasn't speaking.

Stop crying.

Follow me.

Ignore all elder commands. You are free to shift between forms.

Fucking what?

Stop shaking your head at me.

It was no challenge for an established god of Avis' advanced status and age to reverse what his five-year-old daughter had done in a moment of manipulation. What bothered him the most was the Highborn Hellions' ignorance on the matter.

Children of the Nexus fought each other daily, and not in the clawless, play-fighting way that the Hellions did. They fought to win, and always had. His younger sister, Armina of War, had once reduced their youngest brother to a drooling idiot during one particularly heated confrontation, and Chance was without a doubt the luckiest prick alive. Their combativeness amongst other things was what made them strong.

No wonder Uriel wanted him to take Cora. It wasn't he who had no chance of controlling her. It was them. Very few of the Highborn Lords had the mental proficiency to stand up to an attack from his kind when it was one on one. In the heart of Hell, where shapeshifters swarmed, it wouldn't be one on one for long and Hellions would win just as they did with him, but not before she made an ugly mess of some of them.

Once he'd rectified Columbine's fragile mind, curiosity overwhelmed him and he went into her imagination to see what her views were of him. He didn't have the patience to sift through thousands of memories relating to him. Not when a few minutes inside her imagination would answer his questions nicely.

After he created the scene, he sat back to watch her interact with his creation of himself, and was genuinely thrilled to see how much she looked up to him. Then, an enormous wave of guilt swept over him as he realised that was probably because no one had told her what he had done to her mother.

Although he never entered her memories to confirm this, he suspected that Columbine had been raised to believe he was wonderful and kind and how he had truly loved them above everything else.

At the time it was said, it had been an absolute lie, but Avis hoped it wouldn't take too much now to turn that lie back into the truth. He really had no intention of ever hurting his family again and his only hope was that he could convince their mother of that conviction.

"There," he said, after releasing Columbine's mind and returning to his own. "That wasn't so bad, now was it?"

Columbine shook her head, completely oblivious to the modifications Avis had made to her mind. "I liked it when you were in there, Father," she said, touching the side of her face. Her talons rolled together until only one was pointing, and she said, "You were here," then dropped the talon to her chest. "… and in here … at the same time. It was nice."

Avis' frowned, wondering what she meant by that, but then decided she must have meant metaphorically. It wasn't as if she could *actually* sense him inside her mind. With that deduction, his smile broadened and he no longer cared who saw it. He reached forward and slid his arms around her torso under her wings, then pulled her across his lap into a warm embrace.

"No matter what happens," he said, his voice thick with emotion. "I will *always* be … here," he touched her head and then her chest plate. "… and here." He bowed his head and allowed his cheek to rest against the top of her leathery skull. "I promise."

Columbine slid her own arms around his waist and wrapped her wings around his arms. "I love you too, Father."

CHAPTER NINE

After a while, Avis lifted his hand and ran it across the top bone ridge of her leathery wings. "Do you think I could see the Mystallian side of you again? The side I saw yesterday morning?" he asked, still a little uncomfortable with being in the presence of any Highborn Hellions.

Columbine shook her head and turned away from him slightly, refusing to meet his eyes.

For someone he'd seen managed to become mist in an instant the day before, Avis knew there was a story here he wasn't going to like. He probably should have gone in search of the memory involving Cora's command to change at will while he was still inside her mind, but his own curiosity about her view of him made him change his objective half way through.

He could still go back in and see for himself, but he wanted to take things carefully where Columbine was concerned—more carefully than he had ever done in his life. She adored him. He was her hero, and nothing whatsoever was going to threaten that idolisation, no matter how misplaced it was. So instead, he asked, "Why not?" Again he slipped his fingers under her chin, forcing her to look up at him.

"And before you find a non-verbal way to dodge that question, young lady, I'm telling you from now on I want you to answer me with words. Don't ever look at the ground when you're speaking to anyone from my side of the family. Meet their eyes and own the space you're in, princess. It's important. You're not less in our eyes unless you make yourself so."

There was that moment of hesitation again.

"Columbine," he prompted. "I believe I asked you a question."

Nervous smoke poured through Columbine's nasal and chest cavities. "I ... was naughty and now that I have tefsla inside me, I have to stay this way for ages," she confessed miserably. "I am so sorry ..."

"Being sorry changes nothing and solves less," he snapped, not realising he was parroting his own abusive upbringing where apologies were concerned, until he saw her shoulders tense, then slump in defeat under his hands. *Damn, this dance of not offending her is going to be harder than I thought.*

Before today, he hadn't cared who'd heard him say what; the joy of residing permanently at the top of the mental food chain. Forcing himself to relax, he said in a softer tone, "You must take responsibility for your actions, Columbine. Apologies are well and good, but it's your actions which will show whether you are truly sorry. Saying it, even if it's heartfelt—proves nothing. You need to fix it or forget it."

To ease the tension, he pressed his lips to the soft leather of her head again. "We are not the mortals, princess. We are celests. We let our actions speak for us. We are above verbal apologies."

The viewpoint had to be completely foreign to her, yet Columbine nodded diligently. "Yes, Father."

It irked Avis that she was just going through the motions to please him, but for now, he decided to let it go. He had plenty of time to fine-tune her attitude later. "Now, what is tefsla and how exactly did you come by it?"

Avis waited almost a full minute before prompting her with a clearing of his throat and a sharp frown.

"After being punished for being in the training hall, Cora was given tefsla to prevent herself from healing. Or maybe the tefsla came first. I-I do not know. I was put to sleep before that and when I woke up, she was in the room next to me. She was hurt—a lot." Columbine pulled away from her father until she sat at the edge of the bed with her head bowed like a servant. "I could not … it was hurting me … to feel her pain."

Avis felt his chest tighten and he pulled himself forward off the pillows until his elbow rested on his raised knee. "Come again?" he asked, very pointedly. As far as he was aware, Cora was a mind bender and that was why the Hellions were having so much trouble with her. But Columbine's explanation said otherwise, and he wanted very badly to be wrong about it.

As if fearing she hadn't explained herself properly, Columbine attempted to word it differently. "I was not hurt—but she was, and the tefsla stopped her from shapeshifting herself better."

Avis' mind reeled with her revelation and he fell back against the pillows with a thud, spearing all his fingers through his hair as he struggled to not swear long and loud. *Cora's both? A mind bender* and *a fucking shapeshifter?* How in the realms was he supposed to stay in control of that?

Yes, he was married to Clarise and the blood they'd shared during that ceremony protected him from any shapeshifting from those below her privileged rank, but that wasn't the point! Cora was both! His mind mastery and Clarise's body wizardry! By the Twin Notes! She was *actually* both! It was insane!

And damn, if it didn't take the problem of trying to raise her to a whole new level. No wonder the Hellions wanted her dead. That level of power in one so young was terrifying.

A stabbing headache surged to life behind his eyes and he rubbed his thumb and forefinger against his forehead to alleviate it. *Fucking hell,* he thought, as that reality sank in. Cora was both a shifter and a bender—equal proportions at her age.

It was crazy, but right there; a fifty-fifty split of power that no one else shared. Anyone who dealt with her one on one would fall short by at least half of that power. Even his own twin, who was Death to his Life and seconds younger than him, only had at his disposal the bending element of native power.

Cora could shapeshift him into a household pet if she wanted him to. It would be the biggest and briefest mistake she'd ever make in her incredibly shortened life by the time Amaro was finished with her mind, but the problem still existed.

Billowing clouds of heated air from the side of the bed broke through his reflections and forced his attention back to Columbine. Her chest plates pumped like bellows, spewing smoke with every exhalation as her dark plates shivered in fear.

Pull it together, Avis, he reprimanded himself. *You're scaring her.* For Columbine's sake, he decided the best way to move forward was to change the subject until he could come to terms with Cora's dual power, so he focused on what else Columbine had said at the time. "When you say … you *felt* it," he said, pulling himself up to sit on the pillows and rest his shoulders against the bedhead directly.

He was convinced this was a safer topic of conversation that he could humour her with. After all, it wasn't as if she could *actually* feel anything from Cora. That was just plain ridiculous. Their kind fell into two categories as children and *only* two categories: mind benders and shapeshifters. Cora was the surprise package by having access to both, but neither side cared what anything *felt* like.

Columbine rubbed her demonic hands together and drummed her talon-tips against each other. The consistent nail on nail clicking sound seemed to calm her, so Avis didn't ask her to stop, no matter how annoying he found it.

"I cannot explain it, Father. It was like part of me ... felt her pain ... and I knew I could do something to make her feel better. I knew it was wrong ... but I could not bear her to be in pain ... not like that ..."

Avis had heard enough. If anyone else was listening to this, they'd think she was either insane or just plain stupid. For her sake, he had to nip this in the bud, quickly. He certainly couldn't be seen to encourage it. "Princess, you had to know that Cora was going to be punished for what happened, didn't you?"

Columbine refused to look at him, but the smoke from her chest eased. It took a few seconds for her to answer, but when she did, it was drawn out as if she were folding under duress. "Yes, sir."

Both her defeatism and her need to call him *sir* could be dealt with another time. He mentally added them to the irritation he felt over her need to lie if necessary just to please whoever she was talking to. Mystallians didn't play that way. Good or bad, they called it as they saw it.

They could never be forced to back down from that position ... and don't get him started on their views of calling each other 'sir', 'm'lady' or 'm'lord' like a fucking servant or commoner. Nevertheless, Avis decided to use her veiled concession to hammer home his point. "Then, maybe you *thought* you felt her pain, and *convinced* yourself it was real. Don't you think that that's more likely, princess?"

He had expected her to see the wisdom in his words and agree with his assessment. For him, it was a no-brainer. Since no one could *feel* what others were feeling, she had to have imagined it. There was simply no other way. The tension across Columbine's hands tightened as she silently curled them around her toes. She also pinched her beak together and hunched her shoulders, all without looking at him. Avis didn't like any part of that. "Columbine?"

She remained silent and unmoving.

"Columbine, look at me and tell me what you are thinking, so I don't have to go back inside your mind to find out for myself. I promise you, I won't be happy if I have to do the latter."

Her small, black-tipped forked tongue ran around the edges of her beak as she slowly, *excruciatingly* slowly lifted her head until he saw the tiny flames that hovered in her otherwise empty eye sockets. The brow ridge over her eyeless recesses puckered into a wary frown. "I felt it, Father. I know I am not meant to, but I felt it. I feel them all."

She spoke with such conviction that for a moment, Avis began to doubt his own certainty on the matter. Then he folded his arms over his chest and viewed the young Hellion before him. Celests didn't feel things from others. It wasn't their way.

Those of Hell told others what shape subordinates could have, while those of the Nexus forced subordinates to think whatever they wanted. The process was dictatorial. Each side enforced what they wanted. There was nothing else. Column A or Column B. The only exception to that rule was the twin connection he shared with his brother Amaro, but Columbine was too naive to know about oddities such as that ... wasn't she?

Avis had to be sure.

Forgoing all sense of gentleness, he swept through her mind—willing himself to find what he knew couldn't possibly exist. He brushed past her cognitive thoughts and flew beyond the memories that made up her young character in his search for the deeper core of her existence. He was looking for her essence. Deeper and deeper he travelled, deeper than he should have had to go, until at last, he floated on the edge of a yawning chasm of darkness filled with countless tiny, shimmering stars.

To the inattentive, it was yet another example of the mental superiority of a bender—for the mind of a shapeshifter was as barren as any other wasteland. Yet somehow, he sensed there was more to this setting and reached out to exert his own control over the nearest of those tiny stars.

Without warning he was blasted by the emotions of billions of individuals and he cartwheeled backwards beneath their overwhelming sensations. He could taste their joy, smell their fears, hear their roars of various pleasures, see their angers, almost touch their passions, and there were so many of them! As if every star had an endless number of sources connected to it!

What? ... how?

Avis struggled through the levels of Columbine's mind until he was at the very edge at which point he threw himself back into the safety of his own shell. His physical breath escaped him in a heavy gasp as he flung himself sidewards away from her, his head bowed into the bed-post. A series of smaller pants followed as he wrapped his arms around the post to force himself not to fall and faceplant on the floor. So many emotions ... he could still feel them ... crawling all over his skin like ants.

"Father, are you alright?" Columbine demanded, scrambling across the bed to assist him any way she could.

Unable to speak, Avis shifted his weight to free one hand, which he waved at her to assure her he was fine. Or he would be, just as soon as he worked out which emotions were his and how to cleanse himself of the rest. In the forefront of his mind, he made a very huge mental note to never to do that again. *Ouch!*

Columbine lay her left wing across his back, wrapped her arms around his free arm, and rubbed her leathery head against his shoulder. "I love you, Father," she repeated.

With his eyes still closed, he felt that love. He *felt* it ... as tangibly as touching a fire would burn his fingers. It encompassed him, driving the unwanted emotions away like the shadows they were.

He opened his mouth to speak, then closed it again. It was the celestial birthright of the Nexus celestials to take command of any mind beneath them and force them into compliance. It was what made Order ... *orderly*.

Not that he himself agreed with all the moralities that went with that ability, but it was there, none the less. If he wanted to take over someone's mind, depending on who it was, the distance ranged from touch with one of his peers through to anywhere within the realm if it was a particular mortal he wanted to modify.

In opposition to the Nexus way of doing things, those of Hell had the ability to alter the physical capacity of those beneath them to achieve their objective. Mass could be absorbed and expelled at will by those of the right bloodline. He himself had seen Clarise use a dining setting to increase her size, and just as those of the Nexus could manipulate from a distance, so too could the Highborn Hellions.

Avis released his breath in a heady sigh and relaxed his grip on the post as he found the strength to sit up on his own. They were gone. *Thank the Twin Notes.* Whatever he was feeling, it was because he himself was feeling it. He rolled on to his back and tensed the arm Columbine had seized, hauling her firstly on to his lap, then up into his arms in a tight embrace. "Oh, wow," he whispered, pressing his lips into her leathery head. "I was not expecting that, princess."

Columbine stiffened in his arms. "Am I in trouble?"

Despite the discomfort, Avis grinned to himself and tightened his grip on her. "Not while I'm around, princess." He wanted to mean that, more than he wanted to draw his next breath, but deep down he knew it wasn't entirely true. She was what the mortals would call an empath. A true celestial empath.

If anyone else learned of that ... they'd either want her dead or enslaved for their own use. Which meant his job as her father just got a whole lot more— *dangerous.* With his chin resting on her head, Avis licked his lips pensively.

As bad as that revelation was, something else she'd said then occurred to him and he found himself wondering if it was too late to go back to the lesser problem of Cora having both sets of known powers. "Honey, you said you shapeshifted the tefsla from your sister ...?"

Columbine's head rocked affirmatively beneath his chin, apparently not thinking anything of the oddity. Her lack of verbal response irked him, and he squeezed her sharply. "Yes, Father."

Avis pushed her away just far enough to see her face. "Your ... *older* sister," he emphasised, cupping her chin in one hand and staring at her to see if she would either redirect his enquiry or change her story. Not to sound intentionally repetitive, but she shouldn't have been able to shapeshift an older Highborn Hellion either.

Since she was unable to look away without forcing his hand aside, Columbine began to vent steam through her chest plates again. "Grandfather said I was not to speak of it."

Avis' gaze narrowed, and he twisted his lips to one side irritably. He had no intention of pitting his daughter against the ruler of all Hell any more than he was willing to do that himself, but dammit, Columbine was his daughter first! His! More so than Belial's! Anointment was just a technicality after the birth! If there was to be any say over how she ...

Realisation derailed his inner rant and suddenly feeling very foolish, he closed his eyes and covered them with one hand to hide from his own stupidity. Power within an individual always rose to the highest obtainable level, whether it be from a birth parent or an anointed one, and Belial had anointed Columbine at birth in his absence.

Clarise had already told him that, but amidst everything that had happened since, he'd forgotten. That anointment gave Columbine the shapeshifting prowess of one of Belial's daughters, rather than that of his granddaughter. Clarise would need to touch Columbine to exert a forced shapeshift instead of being able to do so from range.

Columbine in turn could shapeshift Cora without touching her and Cora would never be able to affect Columbine at all, despite being the older sibling.

Given his younger daughter's shyness, Avis wondered if Columbine knew she had the strategic advantage of range over her sister. He also wondered if Cora did. The muscle under his eye twitched as he realised Cora probably did know and it went a long way to explaining the sisterly dynamics between them.

Columbine was the good girl. The quiet, obedient one. The one more heavily influenced by the Highborn Hellion way of behaving. The flipside was Cora. Already forced into a mould that didn't fit, she'd then had to accept her inferiority when compared to her little sister. A double blow that couldn't help but fester resentment that must have bordered hatred. *She waited five years to attack her sister?* Avis could only imagine the sibling rivalry that would blow up if he'd ever permitted that in Mystal. A point of contention would be an understatement.

Avis was tired of being on the back foot where his girls were concerned. All he had at this point was wild speculation from a single point of view and he'd had enough of that, though there were still lines he couldn't cross. Lines that began and ended with Belial.

So, first things first. He gently stroked the underside of Columbine's beak and willed himself to relax to the sound of his daughter's warbling hum. "Princess," he said, as softly as he could so as not to frighten her. "The last thing I want to do is get you in trouble with your grandfather, but I really want to know as much about all of this as possible. Can you remember what he said you are and aren't allowed to talk about, or will I go back into your memories and see for myself?" *Without going anywhere near your freaky essence,* he mentally added to himself.

Columbine's forked tongue ran around the edges of her beak again, but her head tilted to the right and her left eye ridge arched upwards as if she were trying to remember. "Don't worry, princess," Avis crooned. "I'll go back in and ..."

"Little one," Columbine said, lowering her tone of voice as if she were attempting to mimic someone. "I forbid you to speak of anything that has occurred during my visit to you this day before I called you *little one.* If anyone wishes to have this conversation, they must come to me first. Nod, if you understand."

Avis blinked at her in astonishment, then closed his mouth *after* picking his jaw up off his chest. There'd been no hesitation. She'd paraphrased that so perfectly that he could actually hear the supreme demon saying it. But how? When only yesterday she couldn't remember a single complicated word like bi-schalarian without his help?

If he'd thought he wanted answers before, now he practically seethed with the need. The best part was, he knew exactly what the starting parameters were and how they worked in his favour. Being a bender, he didn't need her to *say* anything, so he didn't have to garner permission to have a 'conversation'. But there were definite risks with sidestepping Belial's intent. Eyeing her carefully, he ran the pros and cons of what he was thinking.

Pro: I'll learn what had happened.

Pro: Belial would never have to know.

Con: I'll have to do it behind Columbine's back. If she knew, she'd be obligated to report us to her grandfather and get us both into trouble.

Pro: This was Belial, and no way he'd have left his mandate that open to interpretation unless he wanted me to use the obvious loophole.

Con: What if it's a trap?

Despite the ominous nature of that last con (and he certainly wouldn't put it past Belial) the desire to know far outweighed the fear of reprisal. He looked at Columbine and smiled warmly at her, then he cuddled her in close, tucking her leathery head under his chin. Once she was secure, he sighed happily and slipped back into her mind.

CHAPTER TEN

Searching for a specific memory was often tedious as memories weren't presented in a linear timeline as one would expect. For a bender, life would be much easier if that were the case, but no. Memory had more in common with a spider's web, where the oddest associations like a favourite colour match linked one to another.

He could skim through the memories and try to guess which image led to the one he wanted, but the problem of either going off on the wrong tangent or skipping the objective altogether was a very real possibility. Alternatively, if he moved too slowly—well—most celestials had eons to their names.

Worse still, only the starting point of the most recent day followed any pattern of predictability. After that, pre-existing memories fastened to them and pulled them further into the network like a stone through quicksand.

Fortunately, Columbine was only four years old and the memories he was searching for had been created a few hours ago, so this should be a simple sweep.

But the moment he entered the memory section of her mind, he knew he was going to have to reconsider ever using the word *simple* when regarding his children from now on. This wasn't the same mind he'd been in yesterday! The gaps between the memories, normally bridged by various threads of familiar association, no longer existed.

From where he stood, whichever way he turned, the tapestry of her memory stretched out in all directions, one impression merging into another almost seamlessly. Everything that Columbine had ever seen, heard or experienced was laid out for his perusal from this one spot, almost giving him a headache with the way they overlapped each other. This wasn't normal. This wasn't even natural.

He wasn't sure how many more surprises he could take from his children.

On the upside, anyone who took the time to learn could navigate her memories without moving from one spot. He turned his focus from her distant past, finding that the newer memories were closer to his imagined point of view. Beneath him, where his feet would be if he were physically present, new memories were being formed as he watched.

Raising his point of view, he began to search for what he needed. Her most recent memories were very close by. He just needed to adapt his focus to discount the overlapping memories that weren't of consequence.

Something very dangerous uncoiled from within Avis when he found the memory he was looking for and was confronted with the bloody extent of Columbine's injuries. At the forefront of the memory was Columbine's view of the shredded mass of her demonic lower body as she sat on her broken bed and how utterly destroyed she felt both inside and out at the time. In the background, Avis heard a high-pitched siren sounding and assumed it was an alarm for more guards to arrive.

They'd certainly be scrambling if this had happened in Mystal. He may not have understood demonic anatomy, but injuries that severe without a powerbase were a death sentence to a Mystallian ... *and not okay*.

He watched as her centipede servant slid a dozen or so clawed hands around her delicate form and gathered her close, sliding her off the bed and into a larger, more comforting embrace. The room around them began to rock as the centipede chirped reassuring noises until at last that ear-splitting siren was subdued.

Avis frowned at that. *Wait* ... he moved the memory back a few seconds and watched it play out again. That was no background alarm to summon the guards. It was high-pitched demonic wailing—the Hellion Highborn Lady equivalent of crying. Listening to it, and now knowing its source was Columbine, shredded him from the inside out. He'd have done anything to make it stop and, in that instant, he made an oath to himself that he would never let her cry like that again. He would protect her. He may not have been well liked, but outside of Hell and the Nexus, he was still highly feared.

And that was when Belial arrived.

Avis caught a glimpse of the powerful demon's lower body in the doorway and gasped. He fought the urge to look down and away as his own training had commanded despite the fact this was only a memory. A glimpse into the past. It couldn't hurt him. Digging deep, he forced himself to watch the memory play itself out. All of it. He would see whatever his little girl had seen. The clop of Belial's hooves as he walked across the room was muffled by the plush pile of Columbine's carpet, but that didn't stop his approach from being just as damned terrifying.

Columbine's point of view shifted as the centipede servant attempted to kneel in the supreme demon's presence without releasing her hold on Columbine. *Points for effort,* Avis noted.

"Leave us," Belial's deep monotone commanded.

The centipede rose and deposited Columbine on the edge of her wrecked bed, then bowed again at Belial and shuffled backwards from the room. The moment she was out, the timber Mystallian door changed into a solid stone wall, sealing Belial and Columbine inside. His little girl stared mutely at the floor. From the corner of her peripheral vision, he could see Belial's hooves—a point of view Avis knew only too well.

The pain in Columbine's lower abdomen and legs subsided as the shredded flesh knitted back together again. All without Belial touching her, and while her little body was infused with tefsla—the shapeshifting equivalent of a mental seclusion ring. All his life, Avis and every other bender in existence knew that a seclusion ring could isolate a target from any mental incursions, no matter how powerful the bender was.

If the same was true of shapeshifters and tefsla, then Belial shouldn't have been able to work in and around Columbine's shape. Yet clearly, he was. Avis had long suspected seclusion rings wouldn't work on his father either, being the ultimate bender, but seeing the proof of that in his father's shapeshifting counterpart was terrifying.

"You must never do this again, Columbine," Belial declared, once her injuries were expunged and she could hear him without the interference of pain. "Punishments are given when they are necessary. You must never attempt to circumvent them again." He paused, as if to give her a moment to accept his words—something he'd never done for Avis. "I want your word, Columbine. Never again will you stop the discipline of a Highborn Hellion."

Columbine dipped her head lower and Avis felt the wetness of her forked tongue as it travelled around both sides of her beak simultaneously. It was an evasive manoeuvre. One he recognised instantly and he cringed, knowing Belial would not take her refusal to comply lightly. *Just nod, baby! He doesn't know Cora's locked your mind down and you can't use your voice! Just nod, baby* …

He knew she lived through whatever happened next. She wouldn't be alive now to have these memories if Belial had killed her for her impertinence. But the range of what could be survived was enormous—a fact Avis could personally attest to—and he didn't want anything of that nature touching her.

If that meant breaking his cardinal rule and saying something she didn't mean just to please someone else, he didn't care. Not in this instance. Not against Belial. He wanted her to tell him whatever he wanted to hear, if it meant she wasn't harmed afterwards. When Belial let out a breath of thick smoke that billowed around his hooves and moved forward until he was right in front of her, Avis' fear for her safety soared.

Unable to take his eyes from the memory, Avis' mental image knotted both hands into a double fist and he raised them to his lips, tapping the knuckle against his teeth. His real body outside would have an elevated heartrate and might even be sweating. The realms knew he wanted to. Belial squatted down in front of her, but her head was so low Avis could still only see to his knees which brushed lightly against Columbine's tri-taloned toes. "I will have those words before we proceed, child," he rumbled. *Speak.*

The word reverberated through Avis with so much power it drove him to his knees. He planted both fists between his knees and rolled forward over the top of them, determined not to fall in a complete heap. He'd never felt power like it, but knew without a doubt that it wouldn't change anything. Belial was a shifter, and Cora's mental block came from a bender. No amount of power from a shifter would break a mental …

"She was hurt so badly, Grandfather. The pain was so much …"

Avis' head snapped up. *What the ever-loving fuck?* Belial had the power to override a bending command? The one that forbade her to speak had still been in place when Avis removed it, which meant this override was temporary. Still … *what the fuck?*

Belial's hand caressed her throat. "That is not in doubt, child. But I have yet to hear your oath."

Columbine's chest plates rose and fell at the turmoil that tore her apart on the inside, and Avis looked up from his crouched position, well understanding why. If she agreed … if she said the words aloud, her pride would hold her to them for all time.

Avis knew that sentiment well. It was perhaps the first thing he'd seen about her personality that was even remotely Mystallian. Promises were rarely given in Mystal, because once offered, they were never reneged on. Columbine shook her head, refusing to look up at the ruler of Hell.

Belial's taloned hand tightened, and although it prevented her from shaking her head, he still didn't hurt her. "You must understand, Columbine. Pain is a part of life. At the very least, it reminds people they are still alive. In time to come, you are going to understand a lot about people's pain and for the sake of your future sanity, you need to learn to ignore it all."

Columbine dared a very quick glance at Belial's face, and in that moment, Avis thought the supreme demon's expression appeared … *sympathetic*. Or maybe it was his imagination. "You are very special," Belial went on. "More special than you realise. More special than most will *ever* realise. For your sake, I need to hear those words from you, little one, and now I am not asking. You are too important to be killed over something so menial as one person's ongoing discomfort." His tone hardened and his grip increased. "Say them."

Avis knew how badly she wanted to deny him this, but no one stood up to Belial long. Her gaze twisted so far away from him that Avis found himself looking at the destroyed bed behind her when she murmured, "I promise I will never undo an *elder* Highborn Hellion's punishment ever again."

And here Avis thought his apprehension couldn't climb any higher. Now it was launching into the next realm! The Mystallian leapt to his feet, focusing fully on the memory. That was not what Belial had told her to say! To the Highborn Hellions, all the men of any generation outranked the women. Columbine's choice of wording meant she would only abide by an elder's punishments, not any of her cousins or lower generations who happened to be male.

Avis had never wanted to be present at a past event so badly in his life! If he'd been there, he'd have clamped his hand over her mouth, spoken for her, or better yet, put the words Belial wanted to hear into her mouth by way of bending so that it would appear as if she said them—verbatim. Whatever it took!

Stop antagonising him, princess! he wanted to shout at her, bracing himself for the wrath he knew would be coming any second now. *I'm taking you home! It doesn't matter what any of these jerks say! You'll probably never set eyes on another one again anyway! Just tell him what he wants to hear!*

"Columbine."

That one word had both father and daughter wincing together. The hand around her throat lifted her upwards. "Stand."

"No! Don't hurt her!" Avis shouted, knowing these events had already transpired but unable to help himself as they unfolded before him. His point of view rose from the bed and stood halfway up the supreme demon's thigh. "Leave her alone!"

He'd never felt so helpless in all his life! Not at his father's hands, and not during his incarceration with the Damned. They had all attacked him until he'd wished he was dead, but the second he was no longer the focus, it was over. He had his reprieve. Contrary to those times, this was true torture. His darling little princess was facing off with one of the most dangerous beings in existence and there wasn't a damn thing he could do to stop it!

As he waited for Belial's wrath to land, he forced himself to not turn away. He would watch this through to the end and know what she had endured. Every second of it. And he promised himself he would *never* tolerate this feeling of helplessness again. From this moment forward, if anyone ever dared to harm her, if anyone even *thought* about it within his hearing, he would make it his life's mission to destroy them. He would check on her memories daily and mete out any pain anyone made her feel in triplicate. If that made him a voyeur, he'd live with it, but the realms would learn Columbine was off-limits. If she was hurt—those responsible would hurt more.

Avis chewed nervously on his thumbnail, knocking it between his teeth as if he were back inside his body. The memory of Belial's talons around Columbine's throat would haunt him forever. "You bastard!" he shouted, only to clamp his hand over his own mouth as a tingling sensation poured through that contact point until every atom in her body felt independently alive. *Stop it!*

Avis had no idea what he was doing to her. He'd never been inside a shifter's body before to witness such a thing, and he could see Columbine didn't have a clue either. But it had to be a punishment and Avis was working himself into a lather of panic as the friction inside her body grew to the point where her whole body glowed. *Leave her alone!*

The light effect went on for almost a minute, and somewhere in the middle of it Avis realised from her memories that she wasn't in any real discomfort. Apart from the bone deep vibrations, there was no heat that bothered her Hellion body; no pain that implied something bad was taking place.

Her body pulsed and glowed just like his sister's daughter, Raushan did when she tapped into her powerbase and lit up the realm for a new day, and seemed just as unbothered by it. Columbine stared in fascination at the glow in her hands, clicking the tips of her talons together to create a sparkler effect and suppressing the desire to giggle in wonder. *What is this?*

In the last seconds, the light grew in brilliance until Avis raised both hands to shield his face, and the glow still shone through the flesh of his fingers. But then it was gone. The lumination was gone. The vibrations were gone. Everything was exactly as it had been before, leaving Avis very confused.

What just happened?

"Columbine, look at me," Belial rumbled, and Avis' point of view snapped to Belial's chin towering far above her. Belial stepped back several paces, so she didn't have to crane her neck. "You have yet to come into your own, child, and as I have stated, you are too important to allow anyone or anything to harm you. Your champion is not here to protect you. The fault of that is partially mine, yet still you must survive to adulthood, so I have bestowed upon you a gift as compensation. A gift I have given no other before, and never will again. The gift to protect yourself, until you come into your own."

He paused, as if waiting to see if she could work it out for herself. Given that Avis had billions of eons under his belt and *he* had no idea what Belial was talking about, it didn't surprise him when his little four-year-old girl tilted her head questioningly.

Belial breathed out another smoke-filled breath. "You will be able to touch shapeshift anyone except myself. Those with age over you will still be able to shapeshift you, provided you permit it. But with or without their permission, *you* are now able to take command of *their* physical form." He folded his arms across the huge barrel of his chest. "Your grandfather Theodrick and I will be the only ones excluded from your control."

Avis couldn't believe what he was hearing. He was having a hard-enough time grasping her other powers and she was only a four-year-old girl. "Are you fucking insane?" he screamed at the memory, though he still couldn't bring himself to look above Belial's chest at the very bottom of Columbine's perception. "You can't give her even more power! She's just a kid!"

But Belial didn't appear to be finished. "You will also need to remember who has said and done what to fulfil your destiny, so I have bestowed upon you the gift of a perfect memory. Your changes have been made on an essence level and there are only two of us who can remove them."

Two? Avis pondered with a frown. *Who's the other shifter?*

Before he could conjure any wild guesses, Belial took physical control of Columbine's body and forced her chin up until his face came squarely into view. Gone was the sympathetic grandfather he'd been whilst addressing her, and in its place was the cold, ruthless supreme ruler of Hell that Avis knew him to be. "You know what will happen if anyone learns of her abilities," he rumbled, still staring straight at Columbine; though it was clear the message wasn't meant for her. "Emotional or physical."

Avis gasped and tore his eyes away from the memory, only to glance back at it moments later. The supreme demon continued to glare at him. *Oh, yeah.* He'd known Avis wouldn't be able to resist prying. He'd been counting on it.

Avis' heart pounded painfully in his throat, trying in vain to remind himself that this was just a memory replaying itself. That Belial couldn't have known *when* Avis would come looking. Still, it really did feel as if Belial was staring him down and Avis wanted to crawl into the nearest corner to hide.

"I have given her the ability to protect herself and now it is up to you to protect this memory from invasions such as yours."

Avis knew what he was asking. Or rather, demanding. As the eldest son of Theodrick, only his father had the power to break a mental command of his making. If he chose to hide this memory from prying eyes and his little girl, only he and his father would be able to reveal it.

Belial's expression softened to where it had been before he addressed the Mystallian. "Little one," he rumbled, releasing his hold over her. "I forbid you to speak of anything that has occurred during my visit to you this day before I called you *little one*. If anyone wishes to have this conversation, they must come to me first. Nod, if you understand."

The viewpoint moved up and down, signifying Columbine's compliance.

Avis had seen enough. Following Belial's suggestion to the letter, he used his power to block her memory starting from when the supreme demon told her to stand, to the point Belial ended his conversation with Avis. He understood the logic behind giving it to her now and hiding it.

This was a gift for the future—once she matured. Until then, they needed to be able to discipline her without fear of reprisal. He covered the memory in its entirety, smothering it from all sides with his power and placing mental locks over the coverings. It was still there, but only someone of his own power level or higher could remove the mental blanket he had cast over it. He gave it a once over to ensure he'd left nothing exposed, then withdrew from her mind.

CHAPTER ELEVEN

When Avis returned to his own body, he lifted his head off Columbine's with a slow breath that sounded an awful lot like a sigh of resignation in his own ears. He needed a distraction. *Another one.* His heart couldn't take any more surprises of this magnitude.

"So, you and your sister got into trouble for fighting," he said, deciding to stick with the only situation so far that he felt marginally in control of: the sibling rivalry between his children. Through the transparency of her memories, he'd caught glimpses of her and Cora struggling over the wall where the Highborn Hellions apparently stored their weapons. "That's how this whole thing between the two of you started in the first place, wasn't it?"

Columbine cringed, her entire body tensing as if she anticipated the back of his hand at any moment. "Yes, Father."

To show her he'd never do such a despicable thing as strike a little girl across the face (across the ass, yes, but never the face) Avis tried hard to smile gently at her instead. He really did. But his lips refused to comply, and he ended up with his head tipped backwards against the headboard.

His teeth ground in small circles as he stared at the ceiling. Even as a child, he'd always heard of the differences between his kind and the Hellions, but he'd never in his wildest dreams suspected just how culturally different they were. And right on cue, he smelt that pungent odour of wafting smoke again.

Closing his eyes, he slowly shook his head. He didn't even need to look. "Dammit, princess. Knock it off. I'm not a Highborn Hellion and I see nothing wrong with a small scrap now and again between siblings. If anything, it helps maintain the pecking order."

He could almost sense Columbine's uncertainty, but when he looked, the chest plates that had been pumping out the smoke like a set of bellows had stilled. "Pecking order?" she asked.

Avis nodded. "You'll see what I mean when you meet my family, princess. Mystallians aren't like the Highborn Hellions. We don't protect our women. They have to learn to fend for themselves, or they learn to run faster than the family members who are chasing them. That's their only two options." He waited to see her reaction, not that he could gauge it well when she was in this form. But she did seem to be taking it onboard. That is, until she asked her next question.

"Do I ... disappoint you, Father?"

"No!" Avis shouted, tired of having to say it every other second. Columbine hissed and jerked within his hold, but before she could resume that realm-damned subservient position at the end of the bed, he tightened his grip around her and drew her in close. "Shhh," he shushed, rocking her slightly. "It's all right, princess. I'm not angry at you."

He didn't stop until the tension in her wings lessened and she relaxed into his chest, her head using the flesh below his collarbone as a makeshift pillow. With so many emotions that he'd seen in her essence, he could tell she would have an ongoing battle to control her own. *But that's another battle for another day.* Today was about their relationship, and he decided to change tactics. He gently stroked the side of her head until she rumbled against him in pleasure.

"Things are just … very different where I come from, that's all." As he rested his cheek against the leathery crown of her head, he ran his hand over the bony ridge of her right wing. "I don't honestly think I could ever be angry at you for long, princess."

"I do not *ever* want you to be angry at me, Father," Columbine replied, as she encased his upper body with her wings and hooked one of her hands around his neck. Her breath was hot against his neck, but in the best possible way, for it meant she was there.

For the thousandth time since he had awoken yesterday morning, Avis mentally kicked himself for being so monumentally stupid. This was as real as it got, and he'd abused it shamelessly.

He pressed his lips into her head and returned that cuddle tenfold. Closing his eyes against the torrential guilt that threatened to drown him, he silently promised all of existence that he'd do whatever he had to, to make this right. To make them a family again. "I'm sure you'll never give me cause to, Columbine."

"I love you, Father."

Avis smiled as a warmth akin to happiness flooded through him from deep inside, washing away the unpleasant bitterness of guilt. Listening to her say that completely made his day and for several long minutes, he dedicated every second of the feeling to memory. There was no doubt that this would be one of his go-to memories when things felt out of control. Peace, happiness, and the unconditional love of his little girl in his arms.

But all things must eventually come to an end and he felt her lift her head off his chest. "Father," she said, pulling away just enough for him to see her face. "What is a princess?"

Avis was struck dumb by the naivety of the question. *What is a princess?* he repeated to himself, almost wishing he'd misheard. *Oh, you have* got *to be kidding me!* He stared at her, practically willing her to say she was joking, but then cold reality set in.

Why had he expected her to know something like that? She was of the demonic hierarchy. Emphasis on *demonic*. At four years' old, she'd probably never left the Well of Hell in her life, so at what point was she supposed to have learned about Mystal or other realms that use royalty? He rubbed his finger across the pointed tip of her beak, for that thought begged the question: "What exactly *do* they teach you here, baby?"

Columbine pulled herself into a sitting position on his knees. "I know how to behave, and how to please, Father. I am very fast at shapeshifting and I know how to read and write in many languages. I also know how to sing and dance." The flame that hovered in her eyeless recesses intensified enthusiastically. "Would you like to hear me sing, Father?"

"You can sing and dance?"

Columbine nodded, the fire in her sockets growing in her determination to be believed. "Oh, yes, Father. I asked if I could learn some of your grounded bipedal dances too, because Maxrintha says I learn too fast to be with the others, so she teaches me all by myself. But she said she did not know any of your dances, so she taught me some of your grounded bipedal songs instead. I have been practising …"

"We're *Mystallians*, princess." Although Avis had made the correction as gently as he could, Columbine closed her beak and the flames in her eyes dimmed until they almost went out. "Call my kind *Mystallians. Grounded bipeds* isn't exactly flattering."

That was the understatement of the year. 'Grounded' because Mystallians couldn't shapeshift, and 'bipeds' because the only form they had consisted of had two arms and two legs. It was incredibly insulting … and probably not that dissimilar to the 'mindless blob' jabs which he and his kind shot at the Hellions in return. He twisted his lips wryly, making a mental note not to call them that within his new family's hearing. *Or at least, I'll try not to.*

Columbine's eye sockets rounded in fear and suddenly her head was bowed, and her shoulders hunched submissively. "Forgive me, Father. I did not mean …"

An instinctive curse rushed from the back of his throat and it took everything he had not to let it pass his lips as he clamped his hand around her beak to silence that realm-damned apology.

"For Mystal's sake, I've told you how I feel about apologies, princess, and I'm fast losing my patience with the way you keep offering them anyway. I've told you I'm not going to take offence at every little thing you say, but it *is* going to annoy me if you keep ignoring what I'm telling you."

He pulled her forward gently by the beak until his nose brushed against his knuckle and their faces were only a hand-width apart. "Stop. Apologising. To me. Do you understand?" Her head dipped a little against his hand and he let her go. "You'll know when I'm angry with you, princess. Trust me, with my temper, you'll know."

Columbine nodded dutifully, but when another resentful growl crept past his clenched teeth, she said, "Yes, Father."

A deliberate shuffling of clawed feet at the doorway was the first indication Avis had that they were no longer alone. He shouldn't have been surprised, but if he and Columbine had been in Mystal having this private discussion, whichever servant was dumb enough to interrupt them would soon be replaced. If they ever found the body.

Sliding his narrowed gaze to the door, he watched as Frash slid to her knees with her head bowed. "What is it, woman?" he barked, for Frash had unknowingly given Avis a target he *could* rant at.

Frash leaned forward and pressed her forehead to the ground, then rose to her feet. "Forgive the intrusion, Milord," she replied, though her attention was more on Columbine than him and she wasn't at all happy—well, that made two of them. "But you need your rest and it is necessary for Lady Columbine to leave now. Her presence is clearly upsetting you."

Avis' head shot up in disbelief. He wasn't sure what part of that condescending garbage he wanted to rip apart first! "You seriously think I need the likes of you to decide what I need and how I feel, you fucking overgrown larvae?" he bellowed savagely, wishing he knew exactly where in that servant's demonic body Clarise had hidden the seclusion ring that protected the bitch from his mental assault.

He'd learned in the first few hours of consciousness the day before that his wife had ensured her beloved servants were beyond his mental control by issuing each of them with seclusion rings, and ever since then he'd been at their mercy. At the time, he'd sulkily compared it to the way tefsla neutralised shapeshifting. Now, they were crossing the line by telling him how things were going to be. They. Were. Servants. The realm-damned mother-fucking help!

Columbine squirmed in his arms to get away and he quickly redirected his attention to her. "Princess, no, wait," he said, but she was already starting to shift through his fingers.

"Milord, let her go. Lady Clarise has left explicit instructions regarding your recuperation and they do not involve the presence of Lady Columbine."

"No, I ..." But then the servant's cavalier attitude along with her words of command finally sank in and the rage that coursed through his recovering pride soared to life like wildfire. "Fucking *what?*" he all but roared at the woman.

Never—not *ever* had he been treated like a mindless invalid, and by a fucking servant no less! Over the last two years he'd been attacked, violated, tortured in the most unfathomable ways, but every one of those actions was designed to break him and he knew it.

That wasn't to say they hadn't succeeded, but never in his life had he ever been subjected to such patronising mollycoddling, and what was worse, in his weakened physical state and her mind hidden behind a seclusion ring, there wasn't a damned thing he could do about it!

And he *hated* it!

Ordinarily, he could punch through marble like paper if he felt like it and he had neither wanted nor needed this level of care in his fucking life! Not even after his father was done with him as a child! He'd always found a hole to fall into to lick his own wounds, then crawl out days later once the storm of Lord Theodrick had passed. This—this *suffocation* from well-meaning females that were beneath him made him want to scream!

"Love you, Father," Columbine called, and misted through his fingers like a ghost before he could stop her.

"No!" Avis surged up on to his knees with his hands still outstretched towards the open doors. That doorway was the only way in or out of the bedroom, so he knew she had to have hightailed it in that direction, even if he couldn't see her. "Columbine!" he shouted, but so long as his daughter remained invisible, he couldn't bring her back. "Wait!"

Frash rushed across the room and grabbed his outstretched hands at the wrists, using her height to try and wrangle him back into bed. The aggressive contact shocked Avis, but not enough to distract him from the open door. If he maintained his focus and she slipped up and returned to a solid form just inside the sitting room, he could still catch her.

Red haze filled his vision when the seconds ticked by and it didn't seem likely. "Get off me, woman!" he snarled, heaving against the Hellion grip to break contact.

"Milord, you must calm yourself. You are getting too excited," Frash insisted, as a second set of hands took his shoulders and forced him back onto the bed.

Avis swore and dug his heels into the mattress, arching his back beneath the hold. By the twin notes! She hadn't *seen* excited yet! He was going to kill this servant!

Somehow, some way, someday, she'd die for this! His rage and humiliation would be vindicated! If he swore to nothing else …

"Milord!' Frash insisted, stretching her height to tower over him so she could add gravitational weight to her restraining hands. "Please! You must stop!"

Her demand only fuelled his fury. He twisted his weight on to one leg and struck out at her with the other, attempting to kick her away. She sucked her belly out past her spine in an unnatural angle and he completely missed.

Fucking shapeshifting bitch! Before he could try again, something pierced the insides of his wrists within her holds, just over the veins, and he felt an uncomfortable burn work its way to his shoulders. Almost immediately his rage subsided, and a light headed euphoric sensation took its place. He stared at her, and he knew he wanted to smash her, but the drive to do so was slipping out of his reach just as easily as Columbine had.

"Forgive me, Milord," Frash said, supporting his weight as she eased him back on to his side of the bed with his head on the pillows. On his way down, he'd thought his vision was playing tricks on him since the demoness seemed to have two sets of arms coming out of her elbows.

But then all four hands let him go and he realised she really had sprouted a second set of forearms and hands to restrain him. There were only two of them in the room after all. Frash stood over him—her four forearms melding back into two. "You are not well enough to be so excited."

"F-Fuck … you," Avis forced himself to say as his eyelids sagged heavily. He blinked hard and shook his head, willing himself to not surrender to whatever was happening to him. He wanted to be angry at this woman. This female who was currently sliding in and out of focus. More out than in with every passing second. Shapes, then colours all rolled together. "Wha … whasha do … t'me?" he slurred, fighting the darkness that pressed in relentlessly from all sides.

Frash smiled in a matronly fashion and drew the sheets to his neck, tucking him in with all the care of a mother. "Sleep, Milord," she said, bowing at the waist as she stepped away from the bed without answering him.

No matter how much he didn't want to, darkness overcame him just before she reached the door.

CHAPTER TWELVE

Avis wasn't certain how much time had passed before he woke up, but he didn't think it could have been too long. For starters, he wasn't hungry and a quick hand movement to his left told him Clarise still had yet to return, so it wasn't nightfall. Her side of the bed was still made up. *Or maybe she'd come back and left again.*

That dark thought crept in from nowhere, and once in his head, it took up permanent residency. Maybe he'd been out a lot longer than he thought. He remembered Frash's dirty knockout trick and immediately lifted his arms to stare at the faint pair of red marks on the insides of his wrists. He'd been bitten by enough things over the years to recognise a pair of matching fang marks when he saw them. *Bitch poisoned me!*

Gnashing his teeth together in a snarl, he slammed his clenched fists into the mattress on either side of his body. Oh, she was going to pay for that. He rolled to one side and surged to his feet with every intention of hunting her down. But the room spun the moment he was upright, and his knees suddenly gave way, crashing him back onto the edge of the bed.

One hand shot out for the bedpost on his right. The other clung to the mattress. He bowed his head and closed his eyes, willing the nausea that bombarded him to leave. This didn't make sense. He'd done the Walk. He should have been back to full health, yet he didn't even have the strength to stand.

When he opened his eyes, the furnishings of the room held their positions. The floor stayed under his feet and the mats didn't move. The pounding in his head subsided to a moderate rumble and he breathed out a small sigh. *Okay*, he conceded, twisting on his backside and lifting his feet off the floor.

Maybe he wasn't up to charging through Hell with murder on his mind. But what he couldn't understand was why not. Maybe it was a side effect of the poison. Avis rubbed the marks on his wrists again, wanting very much to believe that so he could add it to Frash's list of crimes against him, but the reality just didn't match. Frash was Clarise's servant, and he knew his beloved wife would never hurt him. Whatever was going on with him, they had nothing to do with it.

He needed answers. He also needed to find his wife. He had yet to convince her to come with him when he and Cora left, and he needed to do it before any of her family could get to her first.

As he wondered how in the realm he was going to do this, both Frash and Tilu appeared in the doorway. He made no acknowledgement of them, but as soon as they knew he'd seen them, the pair bowed and came forward, separating at the foot of the bed in a fluid flanking motion. Avis sank back into the mattress and curled his lip in repulsion, his dirty scowl shifting from one to the other like a cornered animal as they approached him.

Unperturbed by his surliness, one lifted his shoulders while the other fluffed his pillows. Then they both worked in unison to straighten the sheets across his body and tucked the edges under the mattress. "Until you have fully recovered, Milord, you must abide by Lady Clarise's decisions regarding your well-being," Frash explained as Tilu silently bowed and withdrew from the room.

Avis bit the inside of his cheek to avoid cursing as darkly as he was thinking. Who in the realm did they think they were, telling him how it was going to be? He was the one to tell *them*! That was the natural order of …

He caught himself as it occurred to him they were exactly what he needed to get out of here and find Clarise. Not that they would be willing participants and they may very well be punished afterwards, but a seclusion ring only protected them from his bending. There were plenty of other mind games he could play. Avis just had to think outside the box, and he knew exactly how to do it.

As a child, he'd been forced to learn the art of verbal trickery. Everyone feared his father, but the right turn of phrase backed up by a moderately sincere expression had their adoring mother stepping in on occasion to protect him from that bastard. Not all the time, but often enough that he and Amaro could plan and eventually execute their escape from the Nexus.

Despite the immense passage of time, manipulating someone with word games when all else failed was something he'd never really forgotten how to do. The trick was to make the changes too subtle for the target to notice. A word here and there until things were aligned the way he wanted.

Chance, the youngest of his brothers, was by far the most competent player of this game—but Avis was not without his own level of capability in the matter and these two were … *female*.

First things first. Learn the existing parameters.

Avis waited until Frash left his bedside before he relaxed the muscles in his face and removed all hints of frustrated tension from his neck and shoulders. He had to make it look as if his mood swing was because of the breathing space he'd been afforded and not because he was up to something.

Both women returned a few moments later; Frash with a platter of diced fruit pieces while Tilu carried a goblet of chilled fruit juice for him. The sight of the meagre meal caused bile to creep into the back of his throat and a muscle to jump along his jaw.

For nearly two days he'd eaten nothing but fucking fruit cubes and he was really growing sick of them. How in the realms was he supposed to be getting his strength back, if all he was fed was stupid fruit cubes? They could at least bring him some ambrosia laced fruit juice. Then he'd be too drunk to care.

He suddenly shut down that train of thought hard, not wanting to travel down memory lane to the last time he'd been at the point of *too drunk*. He never wanted to go there again. Focusing instead on the plan, he breathed through his frustration and forced himself into a state of outer calm.

He accepted the goblet and took a tentative sip under their watchful gaze, ignoring the way they were ready to pounce if he appeared to be under any strain. His head dipped in appreciation of the sweetness, but behind those dark eyes, his mind was working overtime.

Frash knelt at his side and held out a forkful of watermelon pieces which he ate, showing just enough petulance at their nannying to be believable. If he lost *all* of his bad attitude, they'd be suspicious. He continued to look between the two sisters, trying to ascertain which of the pair was the weaker link. He settled on Tilu.

She'd hardly said a word in two days and almost always took her cues from Frash. Taking another sip from the goblet, he met Tilu's eyes and sent her a soft smile that Frash wouldn't notice. "I know you're both only following orders," he said, though the fake sincerity tasted like acid on the back of his throat. "So, perhaps things would go more smoothly between us all if I knew what my wife's instructions on my recovery were …"

Tilu looked at Frash.

"The Lady Clarise wishes you a speedy recovery, Milord," Frash replied, on behalf of her sister.

It almost killed Avis not to show any of the inner rage he felt at the woman's interference, but he took solace in the fact his instincts hadn't let him down. Tilu was indeed the weaker of the two. "I appreciate that," he purred, allowing Frash to feed him another forkful of fruit pieces though his eyes remained on Tilu.

After he swallowed the pulp, he added, "… but surely you must understand my frustration at being kept in the dark. If I knew what the rules regarding my well-being were, then I'd have no reason to be upset when those boundaries became off-limits."

By the realms, he was talking a lot of shit, but just like his mother, Tilu was swallowing it whole. He could see it written all over her face.

Yet it was Frash who answered again. "Lady Clarise has said you are not to leave the bed, and we are to see to your every need until you have fully recovered. No one is permitted to bother you."

That was the information he needed and his mind whirled as he tried to make the most of it. To buy himself time, he cast a slow gaze along the length of the bed to feign compliance and sighed defeatedly.

The demon Lords would never have bought his act for a second, but fortunately they weren't here.

"Did she say who would be the one to decide who was a bother to me?" He tilted his head as if he hadn't meant any offense by the question and looked at Frash out of the top corner of his eye.

"Your agitated state told us Lady Columbine was bothering you," she answered primly.

Avis stared at the wall behind the foot of the bed, drew a deep breath through his nose and released it in another heavy sigh. From the outside, it would have looked as if he were sighing in agreement, but on the inside, it was an entirely different matter.

Avis was absolutely seething, and he had to breathe through his soaring rage until he could trust himself to open his mouth and not ruin what he was carefully cultivating by telling them what he thought of their brainless fucking assumptions. It was a close call, but he managed to rein it in by reminding himself of the prize.

He lifted his eyes to Frash, and with a smile that galled him to procure, he asked calmly, "And you know that much about Mystallians that you recognise the difference between agitation and excitement, do you?"

Frash gave him a condescending look that made him wonder if she was on to him. "You were *not* excited when you were shouting at Lady Columbine," the demoness declared, snootily.

So *that* was the part she was calling him out on? Wow. She really was as dumb as she looked. As his youngest brother Chance would say, *Time to double down.* "You sure of that?" he asked, arching his eyebrow sharply and shifting his shoulders in silent mockery of her claim.

He knew he had her when Frash broke eye contact to look at her sister before answering. "As certain as I can be in these circumstances, Milord, and as Lady Clarise left you in our care ..."

"Then perhaps you should learn more about your patient before making such assumptions on my part," Avis cut in, though his lips were curled in a non-aggressive smile. Inside he felt every bit the predator, circling his prey and moving in for the kill. "Because you are hardly seeing to my needs, if you aren't taking the time to learn what they are."

After an hour of bantering, Avis convinced them to let him sit on the edge of the bed with his feet firmly on the floor. It was a baby step, one that left him breathless, but he had persuaded them to believe he wasn't technically breaking Clarise's rule of *not leaving the bed* if he was still sitting on it.

That then led into him standing with his hand on the bedpost for stability and the back of his legs leaning against the mattress. *Still touching it.* The next feat of persuading them to help him step away from the bed was a little trickier, but he managed it by weaving a careful tale of how many people leave their loved ones and move far away.

From there, he circled back to lovers who, so long as they were in the same dwelling, were still considered *together*. As in, they hadn't *left* each other, even though they weren't in the same room.

It took four gruelling hours of see-sawing through a hundred different comparisons for them to see the logic of his bullshit, but by the end of it, they were helping him shuffle through the caverns of Hell in search of his beloved wife. Chance would've had them eating out of his hands in five minutes flat, but he'd take the win for what it was.

The Highborn Hellions they passed in the corridors treated him with either utter distain or mild amusement at the way he shuffled along like a crippled old man with the aid of two servants; one under each arm. Fuck them all! He wasn't of the Damned anymore.

Clarise had claimed him as her husband, and that meant more than something to all of them. It meant *everything*! He rallied against his recent conditioning and forced himself to meet the demonic glares that were cast his way. *Own the space*, his father had always said. It was the only thing that bastard ever did right.

Avis eventually found Clarise in the same place he had seduced her all those years ago—in Hell's equivalent of a conservatory on the upper level not far from the High Court. The gardens were unlike anything found outside of Chaos. No two leaves were the same shape, colour or consistency, yet together it all worked. Too bad he wasn't there for the plant life ... or whatever it was that passed for plant life here in Hell.

His entire focus was locked on the single demonic figure perched on a stone bench in the middle of the chamber with her head tilted to the ceiling. Drawing on every vestige of strength he had, Avis pulled his arms free of the two women and squared his shoulders, using his stance alone to indicate their assistance beyond this point would not be tolerated.

It was a huge bluff on his part, but he felt more sure-footed now as he shuffled away from the servants than he had been hours earlier when he'd tried to jump to his feet after being bed-stricken for who knew how long. Thankfully, the females must have agreed, for they bowed as one and retreated to the edge of the chamber without argument.

Slowly, ever so slowly, he edged his way forward. He breathed through the wooziness that came and went and tried to ignore the pins and needles in his hands and feet. His pride couldn't handle taking a header right now and he seriously hoped he wouldn't. "Clarise," he called, when he was almost upon her.

Clarise whirled, startled, but when she recognised him her demeanour became a mixture of pleasure and parental dissatisfaction. "You should not be out of bed, beloved," she said with a strong hint of reprimand as she rose to her taloned feet with her arms outstretched to support him.

Avis waved her down. A few seconds later, he reached the bench on his own and locked his fingers into the stone back for support. The stupid surge of satisfaction at having completed such a menial task was as annoying as it was unavoidable.

He bent at the waist and braced his upper bodyweight on his forearms, hoping she didn't notice the thin film of sweat that prickled his entire body.

"I've done a lot of things I shouldn't have, sweetheart. I shouldn't have gone out of my way to find you out here that night. I shouldn't have slept with you outside of wedlock when I had no intention of marrying you. I shouldn't have done what I did once I had. This ..." with great difficulty, he shifted his balance to just one arm and pointed to himself, then waved in general at the gardens around them. "... is just a minor *shouldn't* when one compares it to all the others."

Clarise slid along the bench to give him room. "At least take your weight off your feet, beloved. You have not eaten nearly enough to be out of bed."

Avis smiled his gratitude and stepped around the bench, almost falling into the seat beside her. For the next few moments, he stared out at the gardens without really seeing them as he tried to get his thoughts in order.

Having busted his ass to get out here, he really had no idea what to say now that he'd made it. How did you start a conversation that has you admitting you were the greatest asshole in existence, and that the second you could, you wanted to leave Hell and take both her and your children with you?

She began to shift back into her Mystallian form, but he placed his hand upon her forearm and shook his head. "If this is the form you wanted to be in before I came out here, this is the form you *will* be in, sweetheart. Don't ever change what you want, just to please me. Not anymore."

Clarise returned to her demonic form. "It is a beautiful evening," she said, gesturing with a tilt of her leathery skull to the prismatic lights which exploded in colour over them. "I love colours, especially during the evening break. The spontaneous nature of them is truly uplifting."

Avis blinked in surprise and looked up, seeing the kaleidoscopic light show for the first time. The flashes of colours as they burst to life might have been pretty, if they didn't then collide into each other and explode into even brighter colours, giving him the start of a headache.

"I've never really taken much notice of them," he admitted truthfully. But then his lips curled into a lurid smile and he lowered his gaze, tilting his head in her direction. "I guess something far more beautiful and spontaneous down here consumed my full attention that night."

If she were in her Mystallian form, Avis knew she'd be blushing. That adorably shy blush that coloured her cheeks for a few seconds before she hid her face behind a raised hand and tried to turn away from the attention. Instead, his precious, precious wife looked down at her clawed hands and fidgeted nervously.

For some reason, he found the sign of weakness in her just as fucking adorable. "That was what I was doing out here the night you came to me, beloved. I was admiring the colours, and to be honest, I was still admiring them even during our love-making. When we came together, they seemed to explode just as often as I did, and it made that night perfect. Magical."

There was a time when Avis would have taken offence at not being her whole existence while they were having sex, but that time was long past. However, she did raise an interesting point; something he hadn't really thought about before.

Most celestials were at their most fertile for their first coupling. Especially the female. Somehow, the combination of breaking virginity and carrying sex through to completion almost always procured an offspring of some nature.

But demons and those further up their hellish hierarchy were exempt from that rule. It was their choice when to become fertile, and when not to. Avis ran a single finger up and down Clarise's upper arm, wanting more but not certain how to proceed. "Why *did* you take my seed that night, sweetheart? I refuse to believe that night was a mere coincidence, knowing how your kind can become fertile at will. Why'd you do it?"

Clarise looked across at him; her eye ridges arched in sorrow and regret. Two emotions he never wanted to see on her face again. Then she took the hand that was brushing her arm and placed it against her exposed cheekbone. "I was a foolish Highborn Hellion female who thought you would have been happy to possess a well-bred wife that upheld your every desire, and a family to love you."

Avis could hear the sincerity in her words. His heart splintered and bled out all over again at his subsequent treatment of this precious creature. She was all that was good in his life, and he had abused her horribly and thrown her away.

Refusing to shed the tears that were quickly building in his eyes, he placed his free hand on her opposite shoulder and drew her into a heartfelt embrace. "I should have been, but I was an even greater fool," he whispered, his voice on the verge of cracking.

Avis held her for a long time, not wanting to let her go, or even loosen his hold. Right now, in this very instant, he had perfection in his arms, and he was scared that if he so much as blinked, Clarise would be whisked away and he would have to go on without her. He was no longer sure he could.

He licked his lips and pressed them to the dry skin of her head, immediately calling himself on the lie. It wasn't a question. He *knew* he couldn't. He had no right to this proposed happiness, but he was going to go for it anyway. If that made him a lovesick fool, he'd wear the club badge with pride.

A distant memory of a conversation he'd had with his twin brother Amaro replayed itself in the corner of his mind and he snorted to himself, then pressed his lips to the leathery crown of her skull.

"What pleases you?" she asked.

Her breath brushed lightly over his pec, causing him to shiver. Then a wry grin tugged at one corner of his lips and he lowered his eyes until he could just make out the edge of her head snuggled under his jaw. There was no way that flirtatious move had been an accident.

Despite his best intentions, he couldn't quite eradicate the pang of jealousy as he wondered who'd she'd been with since their last time together, until he forced himself to accept it didn't matter. He'd be a flaming hypocrite if he held her need for a lover over her after what he'd done and it wasn't as if he'd been faithful in the interim either. She was his *now*. That was all that mattered.

Besides, she'd asked a question and he'd deny her nothing. "After all these years, I've finally admitted Amaro was right and I was wrong. I've never done that before—ever. He's even made a point of telling me that from time to time."

Clarise snuggled closer to him and curled her right wing around his shoulders. "Perhaps you have never had cause to be wrong before," she murmured against his throat.

Avis snorted and rolled his eyes behind half-closed lids. *Yeah, let's go with that bullshit theory,* he mused to himself as he tightened his grip on her. "I don't deserve you," he admitted, dipping his head to rub his cheek against her head. "Of all the gods that could have treated you right from the word go, why did you settle for a spoilt, troublesome bastard like me?"

"Because you were right when you called me a seductive slut."

Avis' sense of tranquillity shattered into a million pieces and he stiffened with a hiss of denial, but Clarise's long claw over his lips prevented him from replying.

"We seduced each other that night, beloved. It was only our reasons that differed. I loved you from the moment you entered father's court and announced yourself and your family to him. I could not explain it at the time, but I knew somehow that I wanted to be with you for the rest of my life. When you began to express a similar interest in me, I thought you would be pleased to discover you were about to be a father. It never occurred to me that the words you whispered to me that night in these very gardens were words you had said a thousand times to a thousand other women. I was heartbroken when you departed without so much as a goodbye, but I took solace in the knowledge that you were a busy god and sometimes little things like farewells get overlooked when you are trying to run an entire realm."

Avis hated himself all over again. He almost didn't want to go on. "But then?"

"I could not hide my state from my family—at least not for long. They knew I had another life inside me and where she had come from. Uriel was furious. He wanted to march on you that minute, but Father restrained him and said he would settle it himself." Steam began to pour from her chest cavity and her voice climbed another octave.

"But I swear on all of Chaos, I never knew he was willing to take our realms to war if you refused to comply. My brothers and my father deliberately kept my sisters and I ignorant of that fact. He simply told me that you had agreed to marry me. I was so excited. I thought it was because you loved me, yet I knew when I saw the look on your face on our wedding day that all was not as it seemed. I could not understand why you would be so angry, when that was to be the greatest day of our lives."

He felt her head roll downwards. "It was not until I moved into your home that I learned why you had agreed to marry me. I was shattered. Frash and Tilu would come to me at night and comfort me as I cried myself to sleep. And then there was you—the bigger I grew with your child, the angrier you became. Yet still, I stayed, because I thought I could change it. I thought, if I tried … if I *really* tried, I could make you see past your hatred and bitterness. And then Cora was born, and I thought a child of your own blood as well as mine would make you see I meant no harm." The steam intensified. "But that was not the case, was it?"

Avis slammed his eyes shut and sank his teeth into his cheek so hard the tang of blood spurted into his mouth. "I'm so sorry," he finally said, meaning every word of it, no matter how weak it'd make him look in the eyes of his family.

"I swear, by all I hold dear, I wish there was something I could say or do that'd make what happened be alright for you, sweetheart. But I can't. I was an absolute idiot. The worst possible kind of absolute idiot, because I hurt you and Cora in the process. I had it all, and I threw you both away because the idea of becoming a family man hadn't been my own."

As he pulled away from her, his body moved of its own accord and he slid to his knees in front of her. He was going to beg. He knew it. He—a Mystallian formerly of the Nexus who'd been raised to put nothing above his pride, was about to be reduced to begging by choice. He looked up at her, powerless to stop the tears that streamed down his cheeks.

"But if you were to come back with me, I swear it'll be different. It'll be *so* different. You'll be my queen, sweetheart. Please, rule at my side. Be my voice of reason when I have none. I love you so much, it'll kill me to leave you behind and I couldn't bear it. I have never begged for anything in my life without force, but I'm begging you now, Clarise. Please. Let me take you and the girls back to Mystal to be treated as you should have been from the very beginning. You belong there." He paused. "*We* belong there."

Clarise's shape blurred and a few seconds later he was kneeling before his Mystallian wife. His beautiful, perfect, Mystallian wife. And as she stared down at him, her tears flowed just as freely.

"Yes," she said, so quietly he almost thought he'd misheard her. She placed her hands against his cheeks and ran her thumbs along the bottom of his eyes to remove the spent moisture for the sake of his Mystallian pride. Even now, she was looking out for him. "For you, my love, I would risk everything."

Avis' heart soared and forgetting himself, he shot up and captured her lips with his. His body swayed and his head spun with the sudden movement, but he was not ending that kiss until he had to.

At some point, he realised soft padding supported the lower half of his body from all sides and he broke away from her to see what she'd done. Half of the stone bench he'd been sitting on was remoulded into a solid blob that supported him from the stomach down, but she'd also added a soft cushioned lining to prevent skin abrasions.

He broke into a broad grin as he tested the support by flexing the muscles in his legs and feet, feeling the cushioned lining on every part he moved. Even the gaps between his toes. She'd really thought of everything! His wife smiled at him knowingly. He framed her face with his hands and pulled her face to his, kissing her deeply. "I am never letting you go again," he declared against her lips.

"Who is to say I would let you?" Clarise teased.

Avis laughed. Oh, how he laughed! He laughed loud and long—until his chest hurt and he had to bow his head into her shoulder as his body spasmed out of control, and he'd never felt better. He was leaving the bowels of Hell, and she was coming with him. His beloved wife and their two beautiful girls. That, all by itself, made the two years he'd spent in the Nine Levels worth it.

By the Twin Notes! We're going home!

CHAPTER THIRTEEN

Avis wanted to hold onto that moment forever. But nothing was ever that permanent, and he could feel his strength waning. He knew Clarise could sense it as well. She returned the stone seat to its former shape and slid his arm under both of his to take his weight in its stead.

He breathed out heavily through gritted teeth, loathing the way she had to support him but knowing he had little choice in the matter. Hunched forward as he was, their heads were almost level.

Ordinarily, when his darling wife limited herself to her natural body mass, the dark crown of her Mystallian head barely peeked over his shoulder. She looked so small and delicate in that form, but like himself and any other celestial under normal circumstances, that petite figure could punch through a mortal sun if the situation required it. She grew a third arm to support his waist as well.

Frash and Tilu moved to take Avis' weight once they reached the conservatorium's doorway, but Clarise denied them with a sharp frown and they fell into step behind them. Avis smiled to himself, believing it was because she didn't want to let him go either.

The trip back to their chambers was long and arduous, but not once did Clarise offer to carry him like a baby to speed up the process, and for that alone, he was eternally grateful. Her presence at his side also prevented her family from giving him any crap too, which was an unexpected bonus.

But as they approached the room, it occurred to him that he still hadn't learned what a blood rage was. Uriel had implied it was the worst of all atrocities and more dangerous than an insane demon.

If Clarise ... Avis caught the mental phrasing that suggested she might not and pinched his lips together tightly. *Now that* Clarise and Columbine were coming with them, he needed to get on top of the risk factor Cora posed to them, especially if it could happen again.

Assuming his stumbling feet would move him in the right direction under Clarise's guidance, he looked across at the side of her head and nuzzled her braid, just above her ear. "Would you ... answer one thing ... for me ... sweetheart?"

Clarise smiled indulgently, but never once moved her focus from the path ahead of them. "In a moment, beloved. We are almost back to our room, and once you are settled in bed, you may ask me anything your heart desires."

It hadn't been an absolute denial, but the reminder of his weakened state had him huffing out a short breath of vexation and he glared sulkily at the stone wall away from her. From beneath his arm, he heard Clarise chuckle lightly. "Do not be that way, beloved. A few more days in bed, and you will be fully able to do anything you wish."

Yet another hand caressed his face until she had turned him back towards her and he was staring into those gorgeous molten gold eyes which he knew she'd copied from his youngest brother, Chance. "No one from Mystal is able to see you in your current state. They will never know."

Well, that was at least, *something*. Avis licked his upper lip and shook his head. "I hate this," he said, though he deliberately edited out most of the venom to ensure she didn't think the fault was hers.

She gave his ribs a comforting squeeze and helped him to move forward again. "I know, beloved. The Walk returns you to functionality, but the only real cure for years of neglect and abuse is rest. If it could restore you to perfect health, it would not be much of a punishment, would it?"

Avis nearly stumbled as the ramification of her words struck him, though he recovered quickly. "I suppose not," he pretended to mutter apathetically, though his brain had surged into overdrive and his heart jack-hammered against his ribcage. The Walk wasn't real. Not the way he'd been led to believe. Like everyone else that had been forced to do laps of that accursed level, he'd always assumed that the Walk would return him to perfect health.

It'd certainly felt that way at the time, and his suffering had been made worse because he'd believed his peak capabilities were still woefully inadequate against his Hellion masters. But if Clarise was to be believed (and she never lied), the good health he'd felt at the end of each lap was merely an illusion. Something to emphasise the first level's entrance banner: Abandon all hope all ye who enter here. *Sunova bitch*, Avis seethed.

Every time they'd dragged him from the Walk to torture him elsewhere, he'd never really been at the peak of his ability after all. They'd just made him think he was. Avis gnashed his teeth. For a race of beings that didn't have any mind benders in their midst, that trick was utter bullshit! He'd been completely fooled! But Clarise herself was a Highborn Hellion. A ranged shifter.

Surely that has to count for something. "Why can't you heal me the rest of the way?" he mumbled irritably under his breath.

Clarise emitted a series of shushing sounds. "When we get to our room," she promised.

Avis fought the desire to huff grumpily at the second denial in under two minutes and only managed to succeed by reminding himself that she loved him enough to leave with him just as soon as he could travel.

That thought flipped his sour mood on its ear and had him grinning like a lunatic, for so long as that was the case, she could drag him back to their rooms by one heel and deny him all day long for all he cared. They were coming home with him, and on that day, he would be the ultimate winner.

A few minutes later, with Frash and Tilu's help, Avis was once again situated in the comfort of their bed. They'd set his pillows sidewards against the bedhead after he'd made it clear he wanted to sit up, and drew the covers to his waist.

Clarise snuggled into his side with her head resting against his pec and her feet tucked up underneath her. Avis liked her there a lot and curled his arm around her shoulders to ensure she stayed. "Hey," he purred, rubbing his chin and cheek against her hair and drawing in more of her lavender fragrance.

Clarise chuckled and tilted her head to look at him. "Before you start," she said with a demure smile, placing a single finger over his lips though her eyes were alight with promise. She flicked her other hand dismissively at the servants.

They bowed as one to the unspoken command and retreated from the room, closing the door behind them. Her eyes never left Avis. "You posed two questions on the way here which I would like to answer."

Avis frowned, struggling to recall the supposed second question he'd asked. He remembered the one about the demonic blood rage because that was important, but he couldn't for the life of him think of what else he'd asked.

Clarise almost purred as she lifted her chin and straightened her neck, rolling it from his pec to the platysma muscle near his throat. She reached up and gently stroked his smooth jawline. "You asked me if I could take away your weakness and make you whole again. Remember?"

Avis blinked in surprise. He had? He remembered thinking about it, sure, but he hadn't thought he'd said it out loud. Clearly, he must have. He snorted to himself. *Well, since it's out there …* "Can you?"

Clarise stretched and pressed her lips lightly to his jaw. Not *quite* where Avis wanted them. "If I am interpreting your question correctly, you are asking for something we commonly refer to as a stimulation wave. It is a process that begins at one side of our bodies and passes through us much like a wave, bringing every atom within us to peak capacity and making us the best possible versions of ourselves physically. It is not a difficult process for us at all, not dissimilar to the way you may hold your breath, but the overall result is guaranteed perfection."

Avis immediately straightened, mindful not to jostle her. "Oh, yeah," he said, excited by the prospect of being completely healed in seconds, and by proxy getting the hell out of Hell that much sooner. "That's perfect. Can you do that to me?"

But his elation was short-lived. He had no liking for the sympathetic look that swept across her face and he appreciated her answer even less. "Avis," she chided, removing a glove to reveal their marriage bracer, which she placed across his. "It is shifting, and we are married. You know on an essence level we are one, and neither of us may control the physical or mental capabilities of the other."

Avis mashed his lips together in vexation and rolled his eyes to the curtained ceiling overhead. He should have remembered that. Her hand softly caressed his. "Had we not been married, I could …"

"But we are and so you can't! That's just fucking gr—" realising his vile temper had once again hijacked his tongue, Avis snapped his mouth shut and looked sharply at Clarise's face. Her body wilted beneath the scorn and her head dipped down and away. *Oh, hell no!*

No way was his queen going to take another second of grief because of him and his stupid temper. He tensed the arm he had around her shoulders and rolled it forward and around, dragging her across his chest where he could cuddle her close.

"That wasn't fair," he admitted without apology, as he lightly kissed the tip of her nose. "Did I mention I was a bad-tempered bastard?"

Clarise stared into his eyes. "I do understand your frustration, beloved. I share it. Watching you struggle like this is no fun for me either."

Snaring a fistful of her gorgeously long, dark tresses, he rolled off the pillows and onto his side until she was partially pinned beneath him. He used his wrist and forearm as a makeshift pillow behind her neck to force her head back and kissed her passionately, prying her teeth apart with his tongue until she allowed him to plunder her mouth.

"I'm not dead either," he assured her, once he was sure she was as breathless as he was. His other hand slid suggestively over the soft curves of her body. "And in a few minutes, I plan on showing you just how *not*-dead I am."

Clarise shivered beneath his touch and her eyes glittered with anticipation. He loved how responsive she was in this form. "Then perhaps you should ask your second question quickly. If it was important enough to bring up on our way here, I would hate for it to distract you at another … inopportune moment."

Avis chuckled, then sobered. It *was* that important. "What exactly is a blood rage? I overheard someone talking about it earlier and I've never heard the term before."

Clarise stilled, then arched one beautifully shaped eyebrow. "You and I have very different ideas about what constitutes an important distraction from intimacy, my love," she said, not even trying to hide her surprise. "But it shall be as you wish. Putting it simply, a blood rage is the term given to a demon who loses all control of themselves in their hatred for someone or something. They are at their most dangerous, because they cannot be reasoned with and must be brought to heel by force."

Avis had expected a great number of things to be the possible meaning of a blood rage—he had. But, by all the realms combined, this had *not* been one of them.

All the blood drained from his face and he swallowed heavily, knowing it had nothing to do with his physical weakness. "It's … it's just a … temper tantrum?" He could barely say the words, so great was his shock. Clarise laid her hands on his cheeks and when her face filled his vision, he stared deeply into the gold pools of her eyes until he remembered he needed to breathe.

"The demons and even the hellions engage in blood rages quite frequently," she said, as if he wasn't having something akin to a very mortal heart attack right in front of her.

For a moment, she appeared confused, but then that confusion gave way to a look of understanding and she smiled, then snuggled against his chest again. "You need never fear such a thing from me, my love. Blood rages are forbidden to the Highborn. They are simply too—*common* to be tolerated."

Yeeeaaahhh, Avis wanted to drawl, though he didn't dare. His body had gone rigid the moment she'd answered and he fought the need to explode at the ridiculous notion with great difficulty; though the unfamiliar restraint nearly killed him. It took a while before he could bring himself to say a word.

"So … I was right before. It really is … it's … just a temper tantrum?" He hoped the utter disbelief he felt didn't come through. If the Highborn Hellions were issuing death sentences over temper tantrums—! By the Realms! His entire pantheon would have been wiped out in their first century if they'd had to live by these insane standards.

In fact, Tal, one of his younger brothers, had made a powerbase out of his infamous temper tantrums by becoming Mystal's God of Destruction! She *had* to be kidding! Only he knew she wasn't.

Having no idea of the volatility of his thoughts, Clarise nodded innocently. "Of sorts, beloved. But as I said, it is a low-blood thing and not worthy of your time. Please, do not give it another thought."

Avis let his breath out in a low, long stream, then rolled them both until he was flat on his back again with her on his chest and held her close.

A temper tantrum. They were going to force him to kill Cora over a realm-damned, fucking temper tantrum.

He closed his eyes and rubbed them with the thumb and forefinger of his free hand.

By the Twin Notes of all existence, he *had* to get his family out of here.

CHAPTER FOURTEEN

The claws of Innis' left hand dragged along the stone walls as he walked with a proud swagger towards Clarise's chambers. Sparks leapt from the tips until the heat caused them to glow bright red. Today was going to be a good day.

Avis would have been notified sometime yesterday about his new sentence, which meant the window of opportunity to antagonise the son of a bitch was fast drawing to a close. As one of the younger sons of Belial, he had been at the end of the torture queue and Clarise's intervention had circumvented what he felt was his due.

Clarise was a creature of habit, as were most of the Highborn Ladies. As such, she would have been up and gone about her day hours ago—leaving Avis virtually unprotected. Innis smiled to himself, having spent the entire night devising his revenge.

An unprovoked attack on Avis inside the privacy of Clarise's quarters would be frowned upon, but not if Innis managed to say and do things to incite the *slae-el*'s wrath first. And that shouldn't be hard. Like all Mystallians, Avis' greatest weakness was his pride, and that could easily be exploited. After that, Innis could claim self-defence, and no one would blame him for retaliating at that point with extreme prejudice.

Innis sharpened his fangs in anticipation of sinking them into the Mystallian's throat. One chance was all he was going to get, so it had to count. Without bothering to knock, Innis let himself into what was now a Mystallian-styled sitting room. He paused to look at each piece of the offending décor, allowing it to fuel his disgust.

Why? Why had Clarise chosen to stand by such a bipedal animal after everything he had done to her? Innis was convinced some manner of trickery was in play, though he was careful not to air his thoughts to anyone else. To imply Avis' superiority in the matter would relegate the Highborn Hellions to an inferior position by default because they hadn't been able to stop it. No way he was crossing that line.

The plump cushions of the two-seater leather couch were a tempting target, but Innis caught himself just as he was about to slash his heated claws through the hide. If the evidence of his rage *before* his confrontation with Avis became known, his theory of self-defence would disappear. Besides, why waste a good rage on inanimate furniture, when the real target was in the next room? *Soon. Soon, that son of a scallye will pay.*

"Milord," both of Clarise's female servants said in surprise, bowing as one from different corners of the room as he approached the master bedroom doors.

Innis sneered at the women and flicked a claw at the main door behind him in silent dismissal. Both females bowed and retreated at once, though Frash paused near the door and looked back at him suspiciously. To Innis—who was already on the knife's edge of fury—that open act of defiance needed to be squashed.

He glared at the woman and activated every one of the two hundred thousand plus pain receptors scattered throughout her body. The terror he saw in her eyes right before he forced her to throw herself against the shut timber door was something he would enjoy for a long time, though he clamped down on her ability to scream in agony.

The last thing he wanted or needed was Avis getting any hint of what was coming for him. The woman whimpered as she fell to the ground and scurried from the room.

Innis snorted in satisfaction. Next time, she would run when told to and not look back.

With that minor inconvenience dealt with, Innis turned back to the closed bedroom doors. *Your turn, Mystallian.* Unwilling to dirty himself by touching the polished door handles, Innis tapped his shifting and had them swing them open of their own accord. Then he strode into the room.

The sight that greeted him caused him to fall back half a step.

Avis slept on his back with his lips parted in a half smile of carnal satisfaction. One hand was lost beneath the pillow he lay on, but more offensively, the other rested in the middle of Clarise's bare back. Her upper half was draped across Avis' chest; her hair splayed loosely across them both and an equally satisfied smile was glued to her sleepy lips. Innis continued to stare in disbelief, assuming both were naked based on what he could see with the sheet covering their legs and buttocks.

Smoke poured from Innis' nostrils as he continued to watch their peaceful slumber. This was supposed to be Avis' punishment! He was supposed to be suffering! Yet for the second time in recent years the bastard had managed to seduce Clarise for his own vile purposes and had done so whilst convincing her to maintain the form of *his* choosing!

She was shaped like him—a useless, grounded bipedal! His anger grew with every passing second until at last he could stand it no more and with a screech of outrage, he took his sister by the hand and hauled her out of bed, thrusting her in behind him.

"Innis … brother … what …?" Clarise asked, dazed by the rude awakening. Avis also jerked awake but was taken completely unawares as Innis leapt onto the bed and raked his claws across Avis' face with every intention of shredding him. "Innis, NO!" Clarise screamed, as Avis caught Innis' slashing hand before it could strike him a second time.

Contrary to the fear he'd expected to see in Avis' eyes at the sight of an enraged demon Lord, the Mystallian's gaze narrowed fiercely and Innis suddenly felt his mind erupt in mental fire.

"I'm not of the Damned anymore, *boy*," Avis snarled, laying waste to every thought Innis had had over the last decade instantly. His glare intensified. "And I don't even need to touch you to destroy you."

Innis shifted his hand free and covered his head with both hands as the pain level quadrupled. He fell away from the bed and hit the ground hard, rolling and sliding across the carpeted floor in a desperate bid to end the agony that seemed to follow him everywhere.

Through his peripheral vision, he saw a naked bipedal male pull himself into a sitting position. Three deep gouges were burnt into the stranger's left cheek and Innis knew his own handiwork, even if he couldn't remember why. The male was still glaring daggers at him.

"In your excitement, did you forget when it comes to a throw-down between the two of us that your ass was mine and not the other way around, you pathetic little bastard?" the male snarled, dabbing his knuckles against his cauterised wounds. He grimaced at the contact, then cursed, his eyes glittering with lethal fury. "Oh, I don't give a fuck if you are my wife's little brother now …"

His wife? Innis tried to make sense of the situation but the pain in his head soared until he was arching off the ground and screaming in agony. Flames tore through his mind, scorching everything it touched. He almost missed the sight of a naked Clarise leaping over him to land on the bed. Despite her strange form, he recognised his sister's essence. A shudder of loathing added to his pain as she straddled the male's legs and wrapped her arms around his neck, but he didn't know why.

He watched as Clarise pushed her forehead against the strange male's brow. "Let him go, beloved. Please!" she begged. "He cannot help the way he is, and you have made your point. Your mind can take his down at any time, while he can do nothing about his shape so long as my blood flows in your veins. Any further destruction on your part will not be perceived as self-defence. Please, my love. Let him be. For me."

Muscles jumped along the male's clenched jaw, but with Clarise holding him close, his eyes lost their lust for vengeance and his shoulders relaxed. His hands went around her waist possessively and he pressed his lips to hers in a light peck. "For *you*," he said, then slid his gaze to Innis.

The fire that raged unchecked through Innis' mind was extinguished as suddenly as it appeared and the demon Lord slumped to the ground in unmitigated relief. For the next few seconds, he lay flat on his back, staring at the ceiling in an attempt to recreate what he had lost. The male with his sister was a bender—one Innis couldn't remember but knew he hated.

Benders fought by destroying memories. So, they'd fought. His eyes went to his sister and the male on the bed. That explained the scars on his face. Innis wouldn't have gone down without getting in a lick or two first, but who *was* he? He claimed to be Clarise's husband and the intimacy they were showing right now certainly leaned towards that conclusion, but that didn't explain who he was or why he invoked so much hatred in Innis.

The family must have sanctioned the marriage, but what was going on? He rolled to his stomach and pressed his head against the soft, fluffy floor covering. Why was it here? Why was any of it here? Why was *he* here? Nothing made sense.

"Avis," he heard his sister whisper, and assumed that was the male's name. Come to think of it, that name did mean something to him. Wasn't he Mystal's promiscuous Life God? But that made even less sense. The Highborn Hellions would never sanction the marriage of one of their own to a god like that. He watched with growing confusion as Clarise snuggled against this … *Avis* god. "He is my brother, my love, and he means well. Do not leave him injured, please …?"

The male called Avis shushed her with a thumb against her lips and kissed her nose. "Only if you promise never to beg anything of me or anyone else ever again," he purred, rubbing his forehead lovingly against hers. "You're my wife, sweetheart, now and forever, and I won't have my queen taking any other stand than that of my ruling equal."

"You will heal him?" The question lacked the appropriate manners, but at least it hadn't quite come across as the command Avis had wanted. Innis cringed at the idea of his sister dictating terms to a superior male. It was always the risk they ran with the Highborn ladies. By raising them to be obedient in all matters, that was exactly what they became once they were married, even if those assuming that control rode roughshod all over their Highborn Hellion values.

Nevertheless, Avis smiled indulgently and kissed her forehead. "Better, baby." As the male then cuddled her close, Innis felt his dark, probing eyes fall upon him and the ash that had been his mind slowly reverse. Innis closed his eyes as his memories reformed and with that recollection came the reason he'd been there.

"Avis!" Innis snarled, snapping his eyes open. Still sitting on the bed, Avis and Clarise were now fully dressed in the distinctive coal-black uniform of the Mystallian pantheon; their backs resting against the bedhead.

Both leaned marginally into the other. Avis' left arm cupped Clarise's left shoulder, and Clarise pressed the back of her head against Avis' left platysma and pectoral muscles with her right arm draped across Avis' mid-section. It was a position of shared power, but Innis couldn't believe his sister could be so gullible a second time! The matrimonial bliss they exuded made the demon lord want to hurl.

"Innis," that disgusting excuse for a god called in a superlative tone, as if *he* were the one in charge here. "You are whole only because my beloved wife wished it but choose your next words very carefully. I won't have you upsetting her."

It took a moment for Innis to realise what he'd said. "*Me* upsetting *her*?" he spat, leaping to his feet in outrage. He managed a single, aggressive step towards the bed before Avis commandeered his mind and knocked him back down to his knees. "You are the one who is *using* her to make your own miserable sentence that much easier to live with!" he shouted, determined to get the words out while he still could. Shifting his focus to Clarise, he added, "And you are too naive to see it!"

"What?" Clarise asked, lifting her head off Avis.

Innis felt his mouth being snapped shut and a different, deeply pressurised wave of pain tear through his mind; not unlike someone grabbing his thoughts in both hands and wringing them together. But it was too late to stop his outburst and he all but chortled in victory.

Burn with me, you bastard! he wanted to shout, and would have, had he not been so busy trying not to fall backwards in pain. This wasn't the same as the fire that destroyed his mind, though it still hurt. In fact, it hurt *a lot*, but it was doable.

He knew the only reason Avis hadn't gone all out again was because the son of a scallye was in damage control with his wife and he was splitting his attention between the two. Hah! With luck, Clarise's eyes had finally been opened enough to question Avis' motives and there was nothing the Mystallian could do to change it.

"What sentence is he talking about?" Clarise asked; a question that she should have asked *before* climbing into the *slae-el*'s bed as far as Innis was concerned. She turned to that scallye she called *husband* for an explanation.

Avis at least had the humility to appear uncomfortable with the question, though he never once looked away from her. "Do you remember I asked you last night what a blood rage was?"

Clarise stilled, and slowly bobbed her head.

Avis licked his lips nervously. "Sweetheart, there's no easy way to say this except to just say it. Apparently yesterday, Cora ... our daughter ..." He paused and swallowed, his expression full of regret and torment. Innis almost bought his fake sincerity. "Sweetheart, she went into one."

Clarise gasped and went to jerk away, but Avis's arms tightened around her and he pulled her struggling form against his chest, emitting soft animal noises of comfort along with words like, "It's okay. It's okay, baby. She's fine. I swear, she's fine."

Innis fought to free himself and assist her, but he couldn't move from his knees! He couldn't defend her or correct any lie Avis was going to say. He was a silent observer at best, and he hated Avis even more for it. The married couple continued to struggle on the bed until Clarise stilled in his arms. Innis could hear her muffled sobs from the floor.

"She's fine, sweetheart," the Mystallian scallye went on to say, loosening his hold and rubbing her back and head and kissing her hair every few words to convince her of his honesty. "I swear, no one's going to kill her for it. No one's even going to touch her. It's all been taken care of."

"H-How?"

Avis pressed his lips against her hair and held them there for a few seconds. "I'm taking her with me when I leave. In fact, I'm being made to ... but that part doesn't matter. The kid's a Mystallian at heart anyway and doesn't belong here with all the rules that govern the Highborn ladies. Chance anointed her and you've met my sister, Armina. Cora's just a younger version of her."

He raised one shoulder in a half-shrug and slid his hand under her chin, then lifted her away from his throat so he could look her in the eyes. "To be honest, I'm surprised she hasn't gone off at someone sooner than this, sweetheart. Five years of this stifling environment and never once blowing up is more control than anyone else in my family would have had, I promise you."

Through red-rimmed and puffy eyes, Clarise looked at Innis, who was still unable to move anything below the neck. "Innis said it was a sentence."

Innis bobbed his head most affirmatively despite the pain. He'd hoped Clarise had caught that part and now that she had, all the sweet words in the realm wouldn't stop Avis' actions from being perceived as forced instead of his own *generous* doing.

But Innis couldn't believe it when the conniving *slae-el* merely sighed and smiled at Clarise with a look of absolute fake adoration plastered all over his face. "*They* called it a sentence," the bastard said softly, flicking his eyes at Innis to include him in that number. "I call it *taking her home where she belongs*. But this was never just about Cora. I was always going to ask you to come with me, sweetheart."

It was a blatant lie, yet Innis could see his gullible sister was hanging off every word. He wanted to scream! Avis even went as far as to stroke her face with the back of his fingers as he spoke and Clarise purred like a damned scallye in heat! "I love you," he went on. "But if you want the whole story, let me send Innis out and I'll tell you everything that's happened since yesterday morning."

"You will not need to send Innis out, Avis," Clarise said, giving Innis hope that she had finally seen through the lies. But then she turned that gaze to him and the demon lord saw something … unladylike in her eyes. An ice that matched their father. "Because he is no longer welcome here."

She waited a moment or two for the gravity of her words to be understood, at which point she reached across her body and squeezed the Mystallian hand that cupped her shoulder. "Let him go, Avis, and observe how we of Hell deal with inappropriate behaviour."

What? I am only here to save you! How was that inappropriate? The pressure inside Innis' mind disappeared, and he once again launched himself to his feet. "How can you accuse me of inappropriate behaviour?" he demanded, dumbfounded by the allegation.

Clarise stared him down. "You came into our marital chambers uninvited and unannounced and attacked my husband for copulating with me when that is his marital right. Even now, he bears the scars of your shameful act where everyone can see them. How is that anything but inappropriate behaviour?"

For the first time since he'd entered the room, Innis realised the totality of this disaster. His well thought out plans had collapsed right alongside his self-control when he'd seen them together and realised Avis had seduced his way back into her life.

But from Clarise's point of view, *he* was the transgressor. *He* had crossed the line by striking first. Worse, she'd been present to witness it. This was the exact opposite of what he'd hoped to achieve. He swallowed heavily and shook his head, even as he backed away from them.

"He does not love you, Clarise," he said, as his only means of defence. He looked at her pleadingly. "I have never lied to you," -his hand came up and he pointed accusingly at Avis, "… and he has done nothing *but* lie. You know this to be true."

Clarise rose from the bed and walked around to stand between himself and Avis. There was nothing contrite about her demeanour. Nothing submissive. He didn't even recognise her anymore; figuratively or literally.

"That remains to be proven," she said, as if he were a lowly servant who had dared to speak out of turn. "However, your recent conduct speaks for itself and as such, *you* are no longer a welcome sight to me. Take your leave and stay gone or be escorted to Father by force to explain yourself to him. Given your outrageous behaviour, I may yet choose the latter, so leave my sight before your presence offends me any more than it already has and I declare you *persona-non-gratae*."

Innis' eyes widened and he stumbled away from his sister. He had no desire to explain his actions to their father. With so much family dishonour stacked against him, he'd be lucky to survive.

"As you wish," he said, dipping his head towards Clarise. His next step bumped him against the closed door and his hand fumbled behind his back for the handle. His eyes left Clarise and found Avis, who sat casually against the bedhead with his forearm resting comfortably on his raised knee.

What Innis wouldn't give to be able to wipe that smug look of superiority off his stupid face. "But after that *thing* has had his chance to explain, you need to ask one of the Highborn Lords what really happened, because our version of events will be very different, and you really need to hear both sides."

"GUARDS!" Clarise roared.

Innis turned and fled the apartment before they arrived. He was barely at the main doors when he spotted them already rushing down the passage to answer Clarise's uncharacteristic bellow and knew he only had seconds to escape.

The wider caverns gave him the advantage of flight and fighting to contain his rising panic, he leapt into the air and pumped his wings furiously to get as far away from Clarise's rooms as possible. That distance went on to include all the family levels which more than likely contained Highborn Hellion Lords who would detain him if they knew. The status of *persona-non-gratae* was not thrown around lightly in Hell and one of the few recourses the ladies had at their disposal.

On the rare occasion when a Lady was permitted in the High Court, it was to explain her reasons for the declaration and leave the fate of the accused to the assembled Lords. Any punishment that may have been handed down was doubled or tripled at least if a *persona-non-gratae* status was involved. The Ladies needed to feel safe and vindicated.

The thought of being caught added to his desperation until he was tearing past both Belial's quarters and the High Court on the next level. He burst free of the Well and landed a short distance from the rim, allowing the cold bite of Hell's frozen ninth level to try and chill his growing panic. *Think* ... he commanded of himself, stalking across the frozen wasteland. *Think! Now is a great time to visit ... anyone else away from Hell.*

That was a good plan. Get out, while he still could. Forgiveness had no place in Hell, and it was only a matter of time before he was found and dragged before his father, possibly in chains. Avis deserved everything he received and Innis felt no sympathy towards him, but with Clarise declaring him *persona-non-gratae* he knew he'd soon be sharing Avis' former fate in the nine levels for a few years.

But they had to catch him first, and this crime hardly warranted the full might of Hell. Besides, it sounded like Clarise would be leaving Hell soon anyway, and without her testimony to condemn him, the High Court would dismiss the status and he'd be free to go his own way. He just needed to lay low for a few millennia.

With that, he flared his mighty wings and launched himself towards the gateway that linked Antenora to the Eighth Level. Fortunately, the fundamental rule of *No One Escaping Hell* did not apply to the Hellion Highborn.

CHAPTER FIFTEEN

For a long time after Innis bolted out of the room like the chicken-shit jack-rabbit he was, Clarise remained with her back stoically to Avis, and he had no idea how to close the growing distance between them. Guards rushed into the room, surrounding Clarise and separating her from the only viable threat in the room which happened to be him.

He sighed and waited for Clarise to rectify their misconceptions. As she explained the situation, Avis heard the term *persona-non-gratae* being said about Innis again and wondered idly what that meant to the Hellions. Clearly something not good, given the way the guards bristled, then turned and rushed just as quickly from the room, leaving Avis and Clarise alone.

Alone ... and a room apart. It felt like a realm.

"I haven't lied since you rescued me from the Nine Levels," he said as he slid his raised leg flat against the mattress and leaned forward, willing her to believe him.

Clarise slowly turned. In doing so, the black cloak that fell below her knees swayed, distorting the golden insignia of Mystal's precious flying equine as it reared with its wings extended proudly. Avis noted the folded crest of his pantheon and took heart at what its presence represented now. Had she really been mad at him, she wouldn't have retained either the uniform or the Mystallian shape, and he clung to the hope that it meant she was at least willing to hear him out.

What he didn't like, were the tears that streamed down her cheeks.

Wishing he had the power to stop them the way she could, he went up on to his knees and crawled to the foot of the bed with his arms outstretched. "Don't cry, sweetheart. I swear I haven't lied to you since that first time I woke up in this bed ... *our* bed." She didn't move to him, but likewise, she didn't move away.

Hoping he still wasn't misreading her body language, Avis stepped off the bed and went to stand in front of her. His gloved hands found her shoulders and he rubbed them through her dark cloak and doublet. Then he wrapped his arms around her shoulders and pulled her to him, kissing the top of her head.

"Baby, your older brother, Uriel came to me yesterday afternoon to tell me Cora had broken the cardinal rule of going into a blood rage. I had no idea what one was and he told me that the High Court had convened to decide Cora's fate. Apparently, it was a close call, but instead of killing her outright as you know they would have done under any other circumstances, they gave me the option of taking her out of Hell with me, never to return. I readily accepted it. Like I said before, sweetheart, she's too Mystallian to be here."

He paused, deciding how to word the next part. "But even before all of that went down, Columbine spent a while with me and that kid's really grown on me. She's sweet and maybe a little too shy for my usual liking, but if anyone wants to have a problem with that, they'll have to get through me first. The bottom line is, this isn't just about Cora. I want you all, Clarise. I had no idea how I was going to ask and knew I had no right to, but I was going to ask anyway. I can't stay here, but I don't want to leave without taking all of you with me. You spent years filling Columbine's head with the fantasy that wasn't me at the time, and all I'm asking for is the chance to become that god. For you. For them." He slid one hand under her chin and tilted her head up to look at him. "You do believe me, don't you?"

Clarise blinked at him once, then slowly, knowingly, she smiled. Her tears literally dried up on the spot and the combination softened her expression gorgeously.

"There is something you should know about me, beloved," she said, her eyelids dipping ever so slightly. "Ordinarily, I am able to distinguish the truth from a lie. That is my innate gift. Some have implied your powers of deception exceed my ability to read that truth," —her smile grew— "... but I am of the opinion that I am so love-struck by you, that you could tell me that water was dry and I would believe you."

So, she didn't really believe him, but she loved him enough to not care. That wasn't good enough for Avis. Still holding her, he stepped backwards to the foot of the bed and partially sat on the timber frame so that he was on the same eye level as her. "What can I say or do that will prove how I feel about you?" He slid his hands down her arms until he held her hands against his chest. "I'm not lying, sweetheart. I love you so much it kills me to think you don't actually believe me."

"I know," Clarise replied. "The point where you lied and I didn't know, was that night in my father's conservatory. But I knew you were lying when you promised yourself to me at our wedding, and I knew you were telling me the truth when you called me all those horrible names and made me feel so worthless in Mystal. I also knew you were telling the truth when you told me last night you loved me and wanted me back and I hear the truth now."

She looked over her shoulder at the bedroom doors that were still open from where the guards had left. "Innis was also telling the truth, though his version was biased against you, as all of them will no doubt be."

He lifted both her hands and pressed the palms to his lips. "They're all wrong about my intentions. I swear on the whole realm of Mystal they are."

Clarise looked him squarely in the eyes. "Had Innis not brought Cora's blood rage to light, would you have ever told me?"

Avis dragged his upper lip through his teeth. He never wanted to lie to her again—not even by omission. "I don't know. Maybe ... maybe it was cowardly of me, but I thought if I could convince you and Columbine to come with us, you need never know. But I swear, I don't want just Cora. Yes, she acts more like a Mystallian than Columbine, but that little girl is very special and has come to mean a great deal to me too. You shouldn't have told her all those things about me if you didn't want me to come back into her life. You wanted me back, and now here I am, swearing on everything I hold dear that I want to come back. I love you, Clarise. Maybe it's taken all that time in the Ninth Level to make me realise that, but it's still true."

He gave her hands a little tug that brought her down into his embrace. "I don't deserve a second chance, I know," he whispered quietly into her ear. "But you were willing to give it to me. Don't take it back now. That would be worse than the entire two years I spent in the Nine Levels."

Clarise looked at him and dusted her thumbs against his cheek bones. "I have never seen you cry before last night," she said, drying the moisture from his cheeks. "It brings an unusual softness to your face."

Avis wasn't aware that he had been crying, but he seized the opportunity it had given him. "I've cried a lot during these past two years, but never once before that. Not even as a child. Weakness of that magnitude was not looked kindly upon."

"Do you consider tears humiliating?"

He nodded without hesitation. "They provide a weakness that begs to be exploited." Pinching his lips together tightly, he pushed back the memories of himself as a child, where he'd been lying at his father's feet, crying and begging for mercy … and the alternate to Hell that had been unleashed on him because of it. "And you know where we sit on the subject of begging."

Clarise tilted her head a little. "Yet you cry shamelessly at the thought of losing Columbine and I?"

Having no words to express how he felt, Avis closed his mouth and nodded silently.

Clarise bowed her head and Avis quickly followed suit, determined to keep eye contact with her. She freed one hand and curled her arm around his neck, then pulled him forward until their foreheads met.

Avis made himself relax and go along with whatever she had in mind. He was not one for relinquishing control easily, but for this … to *win* this … he would do anything. She slid her hand through his dark hair and rolled his head upwards until they stared each other in the eye.

"Then you shall have your second chance, beloved," she whispered against his lips. "I truly do believe you."

Avis released the breath he hadn't remembered holding and kissed her deeply. "You'll never regret it," he promised when it ended and he peppered her lips, her nose, her eyes and every other part of her face and neck with light kisses. All to show her how much he wanted this.

"I had better not," she chuckled, allowing him to pull her backwards onto the bed.

* * *

Flaring small, feathered wings from his hips (that shouldn't have been strong enough to carry his weight) Ahriman landed at the foot of his father's throne with the ease of his much larger winged brethren. "I have just one question for you, sister," he declared, circling Clarise as if he couldn't decide what aspect of her Mystallian appearance offended him more.

Clarise held her chin high and followed his movements as best she could without moving her head. Everything below her neck was covered in black leather and fabric in accordance with the pantheon of her husband. She hadn't worn it before today, not even when she first moved to Mystal. Avis had made it clear she wasn't welcome, and she hadn't wanted to antagonise him by wearing it anyway.

But ever since Innis had … 'visited' them, Avis had all but cooed his approval at the sight of her in his uniform. *Own the space,* he'd purred in and around her lips, adding his confidence to her own. *You're one of us now, sweetheart. Don't let any of them push you around.* He had dearly wanted to accompany her but given the level of hostility she'd been expecting and the weakened state he was in, she'd convinced him to stay behind. He'd never have handled the amount of intimidation they were likely to push at her without fighting back and getting hurt in the process.

An hour earlier, after placing a Highborn Hellion Guard outside her bedroom to prevent a repeat of Innis' attack while she was away, she had gone to her father and requested an audience with the High Court. The two had discussed matters for a short time before he summoned the Highborn Lords. Once they arrived, she informed them that she and Columbine would be leaving with Avis and Cora as soon as he was well enough to travel.

Their response had been … less than enthusiastic.

"Are you out of your mind?" her lion-headed brother roared when his circuit was complete and he stood before her with his fists planted against his feathered hip wings. His outrage was echoed throughout the room.

Clarise stood with her hands hidden in the folds of her dark cloak. The ankles of her soft, black leather leggings and solid knee-high leather boots were shoulder width apart as she stood at ease and met Ahriman's glare with a level one of her own, neither offering him excuses nor accepting his condemning criticism of her husband.

"I have never done anything to deter your faith in me before, brother, and it is my wish to believe in my husband. Ordinarily, I am not permitted to make many decisions regarding my well-being—"

"And look at how you handle the ones you do get!" Ahriman raged. He then arched in agony as various pain receptors across his body were engaged and triggered. "I apologise," he said quickly, his eyes lifting firstly to Belial who had done the physical reprimand from range, then his various brothers that were scattered around the room—all of whom glared down at him from their various perches.

No one shouted at a Highborn Lady, no matter what form she took. "But Clarise, have you not heard a single word which we have been trying to tell you? You have to know your husband is nothing more than a malicious opportunist."

"That opinion is your right to bear. However, he is still my husband and my place, so long as I bear his bracers of marriage, shall always be at his side." To emphasise that point, she removed the elbow length, soft leather glove from her left hand and pushed the doublet sleeve to the elbow.

The motion exposed one of her golden wedding bracers which glinted in the flickering half-light against the snow-like quality of her Mystallian forearm. The engravings were of a rearing winged mystallion whose front hooves merged with the hooves of a rearing demon steed on the opposite side, representing the union of their two prestigious pantheons. She held it above her head for the room to see. "He and I are one."

"But how do you know he feels the same way?" Yima asked, joining his twin on the floor before the court. "I mean he has already deceived you once. How do you know he is not just using you to raise that wretched daughter of his?"

Clarise's gaze narrowed—something she would have never done before. "That *wretched daughter* is mine also, brother, and although your opinions are your right to have, you will keep those that regard the highborn youth of our house in a derogatory fashion entirely to yourself. My gift is the ability to hear the truth when it is spoken, and although it failed me once, it has never let me down before or since.

Make no mistake, brother. I am not here to seek out your approval or your permission. Cora and Columbine are going to need both their parents for several years to come and *I* have decided to move back to Mystal with their father."

"And what of Charon?" Plouton asked, from his perch high overhead. "Does he not deserve both parents also?"

Clarise lost a lot of her intensity with that reminder, and instead of looking up at her brother, she turned her attention to the military commander who stood just behind her father's throne.

"Charon will stay with his father," she said, forcing herself to maintain eye contact with the only other male who had ever shared her bed. He deserved so much more than to be told like this, yet she silently willed him to understand her reasons. *All* her reasons. Reasons she still hadn't fully grasped herself yet.

"He was born out of wedlock with barely a drop of Mystallian blood and would never be accepted by them in any capacity, which is as it should be. Here at least, he will grow to be a Demon Lord in his own right and have the family and his father to protect him."

Beelzebub dipped his horned head a fraction in silent acceptance of her decree.

"You are a brainless fool!" Yima shouted with a stamp of his heel.

"Enough," Belial cut in before things could escalate, frowning ever so slightly at his twin sons to show them he had no intention of allowing either of their savage words towards their sister to pass without reprisal. The men swallowed as his unspoken message was received.

For the life of her, Clarise couldn't explain why she'd never noticed these subtle exchanges between them before. "It is Clarise's decision to remain loyal to her husband and regardless of your personal opinions, we will support her during this time of difficulty, just as we always have."

Clarise could feel her lips beginning to pull upwards in a smile and had to numb those muscles to get them back under control as she rolled her sleeve down and replaced her glove. It astonished her how quickly her circumstances had changed.

Two days ago, she'd have never found the courage to stand in front of the convened High Court and make her intentions known, let alone see them through without caving into their demands. Back when she had petitioned for Avis' release, it had been her father who informed the High Court of her decision, while she had silently stood at his side. *Not this time.* She was growing beyond the confines of a Highborn Hellion Lady.

Returning sensation to her lips, she bowed her head and shoulders to the Highborn Hellion who ruled them all. "Thank you, Father."

"You may go now, my child."

Clarise straightened, spun on her booted heel and replicated her farewell bow to the assembled court. Then she left, enjoying the thump of her Mystallian boots on the stone floor as she strode proudly from the room without saying another word; her head held high and her shoulders drawn back. There was nothing delicate about the Mystallian uniform. In all black from neck to toe, it was strength. It was power. It was … *invigorating.*

Belial waited until Clarise was well on her way before he slowly turned his attention back to his twin sons who remained before him. He said nothing for a long time as he stared down at them, his claws sinking deeper into the souls that made up the armrests of his throne. A cold chill entered the room, causing both brothers to swallow heavily again and glance at each other nervously.

This was not going to end well for either of them.

CHAPTER SIXTEEN

For the next two days, Clarise remained with Avis. During that time, she watched his strength return with each passing hour until he could move around the room unaided. It was difficult to say which of them was more pleased by his progress. Columbine spent a lot of time with them as well.

Perhaps a little too much, but Avis seemed to adore her company and Columbine was determined to prove her worth to him. She danced and she sang, and Clarise was surprised by the perfection in which she did both. Not a foot or a note went wrong, something the child had never been able to achieve before, no matter how hard she tried.

Avis was delighted by her performances, so Clarise held her tongue and snuggled into her husband's side. There would be plenty of time later to learn how she accomplished this feat.

Besides, she had … other matters on her mind.

Beelzebub and their son were never far from her thoughts—though she didn't view her former demonic lover in a romantic sense. Their relationship had never been one of true romance. Not the way it had been with Avis.

After her husband's drunken attack and her subsequent return to Hell, Clarise couldn't bear the proximity of other males. Any other males. Looking back at things objectively, she could see the mess she'd been in. The ladies and their servants fussed over her tirelessly, yet the moment any male came to help or even visit to say hello, she would scream herself hoarse until he left.

Her father had only tolerated that mindset for a short while before he removed her and Cora from the relative safety of the unmarried ladies' quarters to those where Lords mingled freely with married Ladies. Cora had suffered horribly during those early days.

Her behaviour had been atrocious towards any of the males that crossed her path, and no amount of discipline curbed her vile opinion of them. Males were all like her father in her young mind. Scum to be stomped out. Not knowing what else to do to protect herself and her daughter, Clarise walled in her room, re-establishing their isolation from the males.

Belial had broken it down seconds later. For all her shapeshifting trickery, Cora had at least been wise enough to hide behind her mother as Belial informed them that his most trusted Military Commander would become Clarise's personal bodyguard and remain at her side until further notice.

Clarise had felt her world fall apart upon hearing those words, and she remembered the depth of her despair when she'd thought it was a punishment of sorts for giving herself to Avis without his approval. For months, the relationship between herself and Beelzebub had been distant, to say the least.

She'd kept the width of a room between them always. Columbine's birth didn't change much. She was too young to have an opinion and Beelzebub was too combat orientated to be bothered by Cora's laughable attempts on his life as he followed Clarise everywhere.

The intimacy between Clarise and Beelzebub came much later, but still not out of love. Clarise had needed to prove to herself that not all males would be like her husband, and Beelzebub had shown her a gentleness that his great size and stature would not have ordinarily afforded him.

When they finally created Charon, it had been done with all the tenderness of Cora's conception. But the most telling moment of all was when Beelzebub didn't turn on her when he was presented with his son for anointment. To this day, Clarise had never asked Beelzebub if he'd been ordered to her bed. He wouldn't lie, and even if he did, she would know. Whatever his reasons were, his kindness had permitted males back into her life.

But Avis would never understand. Nor could she expect him to. Marriage was for life—or at the very least until a very painful divorce was arranged. That which was shared, needed to be extracted by a divorce ritual, and it wasn't a pleasant experience for either side. The entire time she had given herself to another, she had done so wearing her husband's marriage bracers while his blood flowed through her veins in ownership. It was beyond inexcusable.

And after two days of dwelling, she decided to act. Beelzebub deserved more than a highborn decree made from across the High Court where he had no voice. She waited until Avis was asleep before she slipped from their marital bed and silently reshaped her Mystallian uniform around her naked body.

Although her shapeshift made no noise, Avis must have sensed something was amiss for he snorted sharply in his sleep and rolled over, his hand unconsciously reaching for her. Clarise knew she only had a few seconds before he realised she wasn't there and moulded her side of the mattress to include a pillowed lump roughly her size for him to snuggle against. Her breath caught in her throat as he manoeuvred himself closer to the pillow, but when he promptly fell back into a deep sleep she sighed in relief.

She could have made the mould her perfect double, but she never wanted Avis to believe her capable of such deception. It was one thing to place a pillow where her body should be—and another entirely to fool him with a body double when he came awake. He was so handsome in his sleep.

Without the woes of the realm and his life choices to haunt him, the hard lines of his face took on an almost childlike quality and she realised almost too late that her hand had reached out of its own accord to touch his cheek. She looked at her hand and fisted it, hiding it in the folds of her cloak. *I love you,* she mouthed, not daring to add her voice to the words.

It was with a heavy heart that she left the room in search of Beelzebub.

After an hour of searching the various levels of the Highborn Compound known as Hell's Well, she finally found the elusive fighter in the first place she had looked—speaking to a guard outside her father's private chambers. The two turned on instinct as she approached and while the fighter bowed at the waist, Beelzebub dipped his horned head respectfully. "Milady," he said.

Own the space, she told herself as she squared her shoulders and kept her back ramrod straight. "Do you have a moment, commander?" she asked, fighting the urge to hide her hands beneath the cloak where she could clench them nervously. This had to be done. The discomfort she felt would pass—she hoped. *Own the space.*

Beelzebub's eye ridge arched momentarily in surprise, then his head dipped lower than before. "Of course, Milady."

Clarise turned and led him into a quieter chamber not far from the conservatory for privacy. For two days, she'd been trying to sort out in her mind how to have this conversation, but now that the moment was upon her, she didn't know how to start it.

Her lips tightened and she felt her mouth dry uncomfortably. Beelzebub stood just inside the cavern with both sets of his arms folded patiently across his chest. "This is how it must be," she began.

Beelzebub coldly tilted his head towards her, just as he had in the throne room days earlier. His silent acceptance of her decrees irked her and she thrust her hands against her hips. "Oh, enough with the professional distance, Beelzebub. You and I are beyond that."

Almost as if a magic wand had been waved, the demonic commander's lips parted into the friendlier smile he'd shared with her during their more intimate moments. At the same time, much of the militant stiffness in his stance disappeared.

"Forgive me, Milady. It was my presumption that you had already said all you planned to say during your meeting with your family," he said, lowering both sets of arms to his sides and dipping his head forward so she didn't have to crane her neck.

Clarise didn't believe his casual dismissal of the subject for an instant. She of all people knew Beelzebub's cool exterior was a necessary evil to keep everyone at arm's length, but he was too powerful to not have an opinion on the matter. "And you have nothing you wish to say to me about it?" she asked, arching one eyebrow and tilting her head dubiously.

She caught the expression that flickered across his face and knew her instincts hadn't let her down. "I have already given you permission to speak freely, Beelzebub."

Beelzebub sawed his lower jaw behind his upper fangs and for a moment he seemed torn between holding his tongue and speaking his mind. Then, just as she was about to ask again, he straightened to positively tower over her. "For the sake of our son, I must ask why you are choosing to remain with Avis."

It was a fair question. Avis had treated her atrociously before his capture, and any sane woman would never risk such an abusive relationship again. Beelzebub, on the other hand, had treated her with nothing but kindness and respect. He was also of her own kind. Avis was … different.

He didn't know how to treat a Lady, but he was willing to learn. He was also his own man. Beelzebub may or may not have had genuine feelings for her, but those feelings would never be permitted to interfere with his loyalty to her father. She would always be his second priority. Avis was the man she loved. The man she would put above all others. The man she believed would hold her just as high. "He is my husband."

"In name, only."

Clarise removed her glove and exposed one of her marriage bracers, holding it up between them like a shield of ownership. "In deed as well, Beelzebub. I never divorced Avis, because in my heart I always felt my place was with him and one day, he would return for me—for us. You knew what you and I shared was never meant to last. You are Father's Military Commander and your position will always be at his side, commanding his legions. He may have been happy to overlook my marital status in the hope that I might find happiness in your arms, but just as your place is with him, mine will always be with Avis and our children."

"Have you informed Avis of our son?"

Clarise broke Avis' cardinal rule of maintaining eye contact by looking down and away rather than answering that … which in itself became an answer. The silence that grew between them hung heavily in the air and as she struggled to regroup her thoughts until thick, heavy smoke fell across her head and shoulders from above. Clarise automatically reached out and placed her hand on his nearest wrist.

"I will," she promised, squeezing it lightly in the hopes that he would believe her. When she looked up, all the warmth was gone from his expression. He met her eyes, then pulled his hand away from her and folded his dual sets of arms, returning to the impassive warrior he'd been outside.

Clarise pursed her lips together. She hadn't realised owning the space would be so … *hard*. "I swear, I will," she said, making no further attempt to touch him. "But not until we are far from Chaos. Perhaps he will forgive me for sleeping with another and bearing your child. Perhaps he will not. But either way, Charon will remain at your side, far from my husband's reach."

"Your husband's belief in his reach does not concern me." Beelzebub's words were layered in ice. He really didn't care. "He will not touch my son."

My son. Not *our* son. Already Beelzebub was distancing himself from her and letting her know it made no difference to him if Avis was her husband or not. Any action taken against Charon would be met with absolute savagery of the legendary kind.

Clarise couldn't bear the animosity that rolled off him in waves. Not with the history they had. Without breaking the integrity of the room around them, she absorbed enough mass to double her natural height and morph back into her demonic form to match his immense size.

Now on eye level with her former lover, she pressed the ebony plates of her forehead firmly against his. "Do not be like this, Beelzebub," she whispered tenderly, puffing smoke into his face and inhaling his in return. "Please."

Thankfully, after a moment or two, the tension in Beelzebub's huge shoulders relaxed again and he slid both sets of arms around her. "He does not deserve you, Milady."

Those six words summed up the opinion of the whole realm. Neither mercy nor forgiveness existed here and no one could understand why Clarise was willing to entertain either. Especially where a god like Avis was concerned. A bender, of all things.

She sighed and hooked her arms around his neck, suddenly bone weary of the entire affair. "So, I have been told on numerous occasions. Perhaps in time, you will all not think that," she said against his ear.

"Perhaps," Beelzebub replied, though she could hear the unspoken *not likely* that accompanied his words.

She gripped his neck tighter as if to convince him he was wrong. Then, with another sigh that sounded the beginning of the end between them, she released him and stepped back, away from his embrace. "Charon needs to know I am leaving," she said, shrinking back into her petite Mystallian form and returning the excess mass to the surrounding area it came from.

Beelzebub nodded in agreement. "Of course, Milady. Do you wish me to—" His words ended abruptly and he twisted his great head back and to one side as if someone were behind him, whispering in his ear.

No one was with them, but before she could ask who he was speaking to, Beelzebub dipped his head in a curt nod. "Understood, Milord," he murmured, straightening where he stood. Gone was his look of compassion and understanding and in its place was the Military Commander of all Hell's Highborn Guard.

The unexpected change startled Clarise and she drew away from him. "Beelzebub?"

Beelzebub met her eyes. The icy lethality in that gaze sent a chill along her Mystallian spine and without a word of explanation, he held up one taloned finger at her …

… and vanished.

More times than she would care to count over her long life, Clarise had witnessed Beelzebub's almost magical disappearing trick, but never whilst they were in the middle of something so important—so personal. It was like a switch had been flicked inside him and she was suddenly alone, in every sense of the word. It reinforced her awareness that if anything ever was to come of their relationship, she would never be his priority.

Since he could be gone any length of time from seconds to centuries, depending on the reason for his summons, Clarise knew there was little point in waiting for him. She had hoped to have Beelzebub's support when speaking to their son about her eventual departure, but that did not appear to be likely. She drew in a deep breath and released it in a calming sigh, squaring her shoulders beneath her cloak.

But, when she went to step towards the cavern opening, Beelzebub appeared before her in precisely the same position he had vanished from. The warmth was back in his eyes and he lowered his horned head towards her. "… accompany you to Charon's chambers, Milady?" he asked, as if the strange interruption had never taken place.

His ability to pick up right where he left off never failed to throw her, and for a moment she had to remember her own derailed train of thought. Her first instinct had been to demand where he had gone and what he had done during those moments, but she knew from experience he'd never answer either of those questions. It was Highborn Hellion Guard business—the end.

"I would like that, yes," she said, wishing with all her heart that the next few hours were already in the past. "You are Charon's father, and when I inform him of my impending departure, he will automatically turn to you to deny it."

"Which I will not."

"Which you will not," she agreed.

Beelzebub turned to one side and gestured to the opening with a slight dip of his head. "After you, Milady."

* * *

The supposed discussion with Charon went even worse than she feared. It started the moment she and Beelzebub entered the boy's chambers and found the youngster hiding in a crevice high over her head. On her initial sweep of the room, she hadn't seen him at all. It took a flick of Beelzebub's horned head to pinpoint their son and without another thought, she ordered him to the ground before them.

He rolled off his perch and fell the short distance to all fours, his emaciated hands and feet burying into the stone with the impact. Very little flesh hung off his young bones and what there was belonged on an ancient nearing the end of his long life. His blond hair hung like dried straw around his shoulders and his ribs and lined the withered skin beneath his chest. He had no armour to speak of. If anything, he almost looked …

… *Mystallian.*

Clarise raised her hand to cover her mouth. Her own, shapeshifted Mystallian mouth. His lips were thin and cracked and his cheekbones were pronounced under the thin layer of skin and flesh that curled under his jaw and sat against his larynx. But his eyes. His pitch-black eyes were what she now recognised as the most Mystallian feature about him.

The way they narrowed in contempt at her, like she was the vilest thing in creation. She'd seen that look every time she crossed paths with her husband before Cora was born. "What?" the boy snapped, rudely.

"Keep a civil tongue in your head, son, or lose it in the worst possible way," his father warned.

Charon looked sharply at the ground between them, but the way he clenched his fists and ground his teeth, he was not abandoning his anger.

Clarise couldn't begrudge him that. Nor would she belittle his reasons by offering him comfort, knowing she was going to rip it away from him in the very near future. She squatted down to face him.

The ease in which the Mystallian leather conformed to her every need, unlike the cumbersome dresses, restrictive corsets and dozens of petticoats that she and Columbine had been enduring thus far almost distracted her from the situation at hand—almost. Her elbows rested on her knees and her fingers were steepled in his direction.

Beelzebub stood behind her, stoic as ever. "There is no easy way to say this, Charon, and I suspect from your behaviour, you have already been told. Yes, you are staying here with your father, to grow into a Demon Lord in your own right."

The withered flesh across Charon's face tightened as his teeth clenched together and he lifted his head to glare at her accusingly. "Bu' chu' 'r goin'?"

The confirmation that someone within the family *had* told him did nothing to ease the situation. If anything, it made things worse. They were both heart-broken and there was nothing either of them could do about it.

Clarise would have given a lot at that moment to have her husband's ability to go inside his mind and find out just who had broken the news ahead of her. Instead, she rubbed her hands together tightly. "Yes, sweetheart. I am."

Whatever reaction Clarise had expected in that moment of confirmation, she hadn't anticipated his agonised screech of denial as he surged forward and shoved her backwards into Beelzebub's shins. "No!" he screamed, rebounding off her to dash towards the cave entrance. "NO!"

Clarise recovered almost immediately. She shifted her weight and was back on her haunches with one gloved hand on the ground between her knees for stability almost as quickly as she'd been knocked off-balance, though the sheer ferocity of his assault stunned her. He had struck her. His own mother.

True, he'd only done it to ensure his escape, but the forceful contact between them had been made, and he'd done it deliberately when he knew better. Before Clarise could snare his retreating form with her ranged shapeshifting, she felt a vacuum of air suck inwards behind her. It drew her cloak off the ground and cracked it like a whip and suddenly Beelzebub was across the room in the doorway with their son squirming helplessly in his arms.

Charon squealed all the louder by his surprise capture and arched against his father, digging his tiny heels into the great demon's stomach and wailing pitifully. Clarise straightened and dusted her gloves against her leggings.

"Enough, Charon, please," she chided, for although Beelzebub had him incapacitated, Clarise wanted … *needed* him to behave as a Highborn Hellion. Right now, more than ever. For his own sake. He had the appearance of a wrinkled old Mystallian, and if he started behaving like one, the family would turn on him without hesitation, just as they'd already done to Cora. "Stop this."

But Charon was inconsolable, and instead of calming down, his efforts to free himself doubled, then tripled as he realised his father's physical contact prevented him from shapeshifting. "I HATE'CHU, MU'VER!" he screamed, leaning forward to spew the words at what he considered was the source of all his woes.

Beelzebub bristled, but Clarise held out her hand before he could take their son to task for his vile outburst. "Beelzebub, no," she said, for in her mind there was no need to punish him, not when she knew the solution to his emotional instability would be punishment enough.

The Mystallians would always defend their own, but they'd never defend a child out of wedlock who had somehow managed to secure physical aspects from the trace amounts of Mystallian blood that flowed in her veins. Not even enough to give him access to their mental powers. Just enough to influence his natural shape … and his attitude.

If she thought she wanted Avis' mental power before, what she contemplated now took that desire to an entirely new level. Avis could go in and bury certain memories, preventing them from triggering Charon's more volatile emotions. That would have been far easier than what she was contemplating now, not to mention much kinder.

Clarise lifted her eyes to Beelzebub, wishing with all her heart that their son had taken after him, instead. The Military Commander dominated whatever room he stood in, without ever saying a word. Proud, strong, powerful Beelzebub. Nothing ever fazed him. If only Charon had taken after him, she would never need to consider what she now saw was her only alternative.

But, as the Mystallian saying went, *if wishes were fishes* … "Enough, Charon," she repeated, only this time she shifted portions of his blood into the same sleeping agent Frash had used to put Avis down in his weakened state. With his much smaller size and mass, the quantity had Charon slumping in his father's arms without another word.

There was no denying what needed to be done. With his own actions, Charon had taken the choice out of her hands. He may have only been a child, but already he couldn't be reasoned with. No ... he *wouldn't* be reasoned with. In a realm where control and obedience meant everything to the ruling house, his emotional outbursts would not be tolerated by the family. She had to stop them. She had to stop them all.

May the realms forgive me. I am about to lobotomize my own son. She sank her teeth into her trembling bottom lip and closed her eyes, breathing through the tears that welled behind her closed lids.

"Milady?"

Clarise took a moment to reabsorb her tears before she opened her eyes again, as if her grief were only a passing thing and unworthy of his attention.

Instead of standing in the doorway as he had been, Beelzebub was just a few steps in front of her, his brow ridge arching downwards in a concerned frown. She resisted the urge to reach out and touch Charon in his lower arms. It seemed too hypocritical.

"If I leave him the way he is, sooner or later he will share Cora's fate for going into a blood rage, only there will not be a Mystallian to rescue him at the thirteenth hour. The only way I can ensure he lives a long and healthy life, if not a happy one, is if I remove the part of his brain that houses his emotions."

Beelzebub looked at the child in his arms. "I will do it," he said, stepping away from her. He shifted Charon into his upper arms; high out of her current physical reach. "The agony of knowing this was done by your hand would forever haunt you."

Clarise watched her son being lifted out of physical reach, then pursed her lips together and sadly shook her head. Even now, after her lover knew she had returned to her husband, he was trying to protect her. She stepped to his side and placed a hand on his lower arm, squeezing it appreciatively.

"As powerful as you are, my sweet Beelzebub, the blood in your veins is not Highborn and your shift will never hold him. The moment you lost physical contact, his Highborn blood will rebel against your changes and he will revert."

They both knew this was true, but Beelzebub didn't command all of Hell's forces because he gave in easily. "Lord Uriel would do it for you, to save you from your guilt and heartache."

All of her brothers would do this for her, but only Uriel would do it willingly and for the right reasons. A week ago, she'd have taken Beelzebub up on that offer without a single hesitation. She'd have given her consent for the deed to be done and then removed herself from the difficult situation until the task was completed.

Clarise closed her mouth and breathed slowly through her nose. Because a week ago, she hadn't been introduced to the three words that were virtually a Mystallian mantra. *Own the space.* It meant more than just taking possession of the area around them. It meant owning what was going on within as well. Own one's thoughts—one's words—one's decisions.

It meant never saying what you don't mean and never shying away from anything. "He would," she begrudgingly agreed, squeezing his arm again. "But this is not his burden to bear. I chose to birth Charon and now I am choosing my

Mystallian family over him. The burden of those decisions and the consequences therein are mine alone to bear."

Beelzebub grew another arm and squeezed her shoulder through the black cloak. "Not alone," he corrected forcefully.

Clarise smiled. A little. Two simple words of comfort, and they meant more to her than all the flowery speeches combined. Life had been so much easier when she was one of the Highborn Ladies, hiding behind her status whenever anything unpleasant was presented to her. The men took care of things like this. But that was not the way of Mystal.

And by her own choice, she was now Mystallian.

Steadying herself for what must be, Clarise looked up at her son. She easily identified all the sections of his brain that housed the physical representations of his emotions, but as she wasn't a healer, she didn't know how to tone them down. Only how to excise them.

With a very heavy heart, she began severing the thousands of neural networks that controlled his emotions, changing their fibrous mass into harmless life fluid that flowed through his body. He wouldn't feel. He wouldn't react. He'd be as glacial as his father and he'd remain safe because of it.

When it was done, Clarise wanted to break down and weep. Or be sick. Her stomach knotted and her chest heaved, but it was done. She had effectively stripped her son's childhood from him. He would never laugh. He would never love. She had done this to him.

"Yimmen," she heard Beelzebub call.

Clarise barely acknowledged the centipede-like demoness appeared behind him. She couldn't take her eyes off her sleeping son, though she fought the rising lump in her throat and the growing threat of tears that built in her eyes by constantly neutralising them.

Beelzebub stepped to one side and slid the sleeping toddler into his governess' awaiting arms. "See to your Lord," he commanded, then moved forward and curled a lower arm around Clarise's shoulders. "Come," he said more gently, guiding her towards the mouth of the cave.

Clarise allowed herself to be led. Her feet moved of their own accord and her eyes focused on nothing as they silently made their way through the family levels and up towards Belial's private chambers again. Her heart felt withered and useless. She had lobotomised her own son. What kind of a mother did that to her own child?

It was only when an eruption of colour overhead caught her eye that she realised he'd taken her to her place of peace and comfort. The Conservatory. "Cry, Milady," Beelzebub whispered into the back of her head, having bent down low to do so. His dual sets of hands rubbed her shoulders and her forearms. "We will take as long as you need, and no one will bother you here."

CHAPTER SEVENTEEN

Avis stirred, drawing in a deep breath which he released in a happy, stretching sigh. His hand automatically reached for Clarise, and he came awake instantly when he realised there was nothing on her side of the bed but pillows. "Tilu!" he shouted, sitting straight up in bed. Both sisters appeared in the doorway, bowing. "Where's my wife?" He was already sliding his feet to the floor in anticipation of going to find her.

"Lady Clarise is dealing with a Highborn Hellion matter, Milord," Frash replied, before Tilu could answer. Tilu cast a sidewards glance at her sister, then closed her mouth and stared at the ground somewhere between the door and the bed.

Avis couldn't believe how much he despised the dominant female. "Did I ask you?" he snarled.

Frash formally bowed again; either missing his animosity or ignoring it completely. Avis was willing to bet his realm on the latter. "I was more informed than that of my sister, Milord," she answered primly.

"I don't care," Avis shot back. "When I want *you* to answer, I'll tell you." He sat on the edge of the bed, his mind going over his options. If it was Highborn Hellion affairs that Clarise was attending, he had no right to butt in. That then raised the question, what was he supposed to do in the meantime? He was well enough to move around unaided, but he still didn't like the idea of leaving the apartment and intermingling with the Highborn demons outside. What was he supposed to say to them?

Then it occurred to him. This was the perfect opportunity to get to the bottom of his family issues with Cora, without Clarise hovering nearby. For the last two days, he'd bided his time—an act his family back home would attest to being nigh on impossible for him—to see if his elder, wayward daughter would come to him of her own volition. Columbine spent every moment she could in his company and Avis loved her for it, but Cora never came anywhere near him. With Clarise busy elsewhere, now it was time to reel that girl in and see for himself if everything he'd heard about her was true.

He looked at Frash and said, "Bring Lady Cora to me."

Frash bowed obediently and left the room. Avis' eyes then moved to Tilu. "And I'll get you to give me a hand to get dressed before they get back, beautiful," he said with a wink and a half smile.

Tilu bowed, but not before he saw her smiling shyly as she went into his dressing room and returned moments later with his uniform. Avis stood up and piece by piece, he was helped into the clothing. The last thing he wanted was for Cora to get a view only her mother and a select few servants were entitled to.

Once he was dressed, Tilu bowed again and withdrew from the room, silently closing the doors behind her. Avis chuckled to himself as he tilted a pillow sidewards and levered himself to sit up. He knew he could stand now and even walk across the room and back unaided, but he also knew if he towered over Cora while she harboured so much hatred for him, she'd respond by going on the offensive and he was nowhere near ready for that conflict—yet.

The average attack of a competent mind bender destroyed ten years of memory. It was an insignificant benchmark. Even mortals foolish enough to flex their pitiful muscles at the gods who controlled them could withstand that loss. But Cora wasn't ten. She was barely five, and if Avis, in a single moment of lost concentration, destroyed a decade of her memories, there'd be nothing left of her mind to build on. She'd be a shell; a mindless entity without the knowledge she'd been born with to know how to grow and evolve as a person. He could never do that to one of his own. Not even his father crossed that line, though he'd certainly taken Avis and his siblings right to that edge—a lot.

Avis didn't even want to know how many times he'd had to reacquaint himself with his siblings, building memories from scratch after his father had destroyed almost all that came before. Theodrick would leave him with just enough memory to recognise his parents and his twin. The rest was constantly reset.

Yet the children of the Nexus had learned to play an elaborate shell game with their father. As the eldest two, Avis and Amaro started the process by staying well apart. They always knew when the other was being attacked and sought each other out long after the coast was clear. Physically, there was nothing either could do but wait for the injured one to semi-recover.

If Avis was the safe one, he would push his memories into Amaro's mind. If he was the broken one, Amaro would open his mind for Avis to absorb at his own pace. It wasn't the same as personally experiencing them, but it was close enough that the recovery took less and less time.

It had taken a very long time for Avis and Amaro to risk their little safety pact with their siblings, but once they had, they all began to piece together their own destroyed memories with the segments they found inside each other. From there, the children of the Nexus grew strong. Adaptation was the key. So was the need to not rely on each other for protection. Nothing could stop Theodrick once he had picked a target. Nothing. It only got worse when they grew to breeding age.

Avis clamped his eyes shut, desperately trying not to go there. It was the secret shame that ate at almost every child of the Nexus. Theodrick was an evil bastard who easily matched Belial in all the opposite ways. He'd entertained himself by sexually pairing his children against their wills or doing the deed himself, and not necessarily male with female. It had been eons since those dark days broached Avis' forethoughts and he was intensely grateful that the Hellions had no idea of it. What Theodrick had insisted upon—maintaining the sanctity of the bloodline at all costs—the Hellions couldn't bring themselves to even contemplate.

In Chaos, the bloodlines needed to be diverse to make them stronger. The Chaotic nature of the place insisted upon it. So, family didn't mate with family. Not even distant cousins. If a bloodline could be found, it didn't happen. Ironically, remembering those vile times made Avis realise that even in the worst parts of his two-year torture, they still hadn't come close to replicating the most horrific time of his life. He'd endured worse at his own father's hands and survived. They all had.

A few years before Chance was born, Avis sought out Amaro and told him of his desire to escape the Nexus. He was tired of living in constant fear and degradation. He was tired of everything. He wanted out, even if it got him killed. Amaro agreed, and of course, Theodrick swooped in at that moment and wiped out both their minds.

But as they hadn't been alone, the shell game began again in earnest and the attack had only delayed the inevitable. Chance had been born while Avis and Amaro recovered and the runt was forced through the same dance of the early years that they all had. It couldn't be avoided, though their mother had intervened on Chance's behalf more often than she did for any of them. That was to be expected. He was, after all, the lucky baby.

Regrettably, as Avis and Amaro recovered, Chance reached puberty. He became sexually curious and unfortunately for him, Theodrick had also noticed his coming of age. Avis hadn't been able to save himself or any of their other siblings, but after looking at the predatory way their father eyed his youngest son, Avis swore there and then that Chance was not going to end up like them. A plaything of their perverted father. Within hours, Avis and Amaro secretly gathered up their siblings and made their run for the crystalline wall that surrounded the Nexus. Once they leapt clear, none of them ever saw their mother again.

Avis sucked in a painfully deep breath and pushed those memories back into the darkest recess of his mind, then covered them over and placed a dozen mental *Do Not Enter* signs across the opening. Hopefully, it would be another few eons before he thought of them again.

With the exception of his mother, nothing good *ever* came of remembering those times.

He heard a scuffle and a heavy-handed slap echo from the doorway and immediately snapped his attention to the commotion. Frash, he had expected. The presence of his older daughter was just as anticipated. But when he saw a young Mystallian girl with mid-length, ginger hair and a face full of freckles being manhandled by his wife's demonic servant, the Mystallian patriarch surged against his pillows. This was not Cora's natural form, but one that someone had forced her into. Her right arm was missing at the shoulder and Frash held her by her upper left arm. Cora stared up at the female in shock and disbelief as her left hand gently touched the red mark on her face where Frash had obviously struck her.

"Behave yourself," the servant commanded, giving the girl a small shake to emphasise the order.

Avis flew across the room, and before his head could catch up, his fist smashed into the servant's face with enough force to kill anything but a shifter. No one—*no one* outside the House of Mystal touched a Mystallian pantheon member like that! No matter the age of the Mystallian in question! *No one!*

The irony that he wouldn't have needed to defend her, had she not looked like one of his own, was not lost on him. He then caught the woman by the throat and slammed her into the wall with enough force to imprint her outline against the stone. Shapeshifting around the problem would have been the easy way to escape and she probably would have taken it, had she not been so stunned by his assault. Still holding her throat, Avis leaned his face into hers so there could be no misunderstanding between them.

"Don't you ever ... *ever* touch one of *my* girls like that again," Avis warned with absolute lethality. He couldn't pretend that he wasn't getting a little personal satisfaction from this. He'd wanted to do it for days for entirely different reasons. But no one outside the family, raised a hand to a Mystallian pantheon member like that.

The Mystallians may have fought and bickered amongst themselves as any family did, but the second an outsider even thought about touching any one of them without permission, that individual would suffer the combined might of the entire family. Mystal always had been and always would be a unified front.

He held her until he saw in her eyes that she had remembered that he couldn't mentally harm her and physically all she had to do was shapeshift her way to freedom. "Let's get one thing straight, woman, because I'm only going to say this once," he snarled. "I'm about two seconds from having Clarise remove whatever seclusion ring she's got you hiding behind and spending the next decade destroying you one memory at a time. My wife's continued reliance on your service is the only reason I haven't already, but this is the only warning you're going to get. Touch what's mine again, and I'll rip you to pieces and make you forget how to put yourself back together again. Do you hear me?"

"I am not yours!"

Avis glanced down at the young girl who stamped her foot at him with her fist shoved into her hip, and barely suppressed his chuckle. *That* was the part of his spiel she took offence to? *Oh, yes, you are, you little imp. You just don't know it yet.*

He released the servant with a shove that sent her stumbling towards the doors, his full attention now on his strong-willed child as he crossed the room to the two-seater lounge beside the false balcony window. With the excitement over, he felt himself teeter a little and realised with an inner grimace that he probably shouldn't have gotten up that fast.

But damn, it felt good to hammer that shapeshifting witch. He slid his weight into the chair with one elbow on the arm and ran his gaze over Cora's Mystallian shape, frowning a little in confusion. Wasn't she supposed to be locked into her demonic form by tefsla? "Who chose that form for you?"

Cora's chin lifted in defiance. "What makes you think anyone did?"

Her rebelliousness was so cute: like a baby pygmy monkey beating on its chest and insisting it was a silverback gorilla. Avis arched an eyebrow and smirked at her. "For starters, rug rat, there's no redheads in my family that you could draw from naturally. Plus, last I heard, you were in your demonic form up to your eyeballs in tefsla poison. Doesn't that stuff stop you from shifting, period?"

He'd expected her to say something snarky in return. A bit of harmless back and forth to get things going before he went for the crux of their problem. But instead of engaging, the harmless barb seemed to strike home … *hard*. Cora's shoulders slumped in defeat and she looked down and away. "Grandfather said Mystallians with hair of red were trouble and that it suited me," she murmured softly.

Belial. Avis dragged his fingernails through his eyebrows and growled in exasperation. That explained everything. Belial didn't play by anyone's rules except his own. Avis then thought about what Cora had been told about his kind and ran his tongue in a tight circle around his cheek until he *tsked* through the gap in his lips.

That statement wasn't entirely true. He knew of a lot of redheads amongst the common population and even a few within the pantheon that could trace their bloodlines to other realms, and while most of them were quick tempered, that didn't automatically make them trouble. "Tell you what," he said, twisting into the corner of the chair for added support and laying his left arm across his chest.

He placed his right elbow against the top of his left hand and supported his chin with his right hand, tapping his lips with his thumb. "You tell me what you did to warrant being called a troublemaker, and I'll talk to your mother about returning you to your demonic form if that's the one you want to be in." Of course, he already knew what she'd done. He'd heard it from several points of view. But he wanted to hear *her* take on it. "Deal?"

Cora's gaze narrowed hatefully. "Because of you, I am constantly harassed by my mother's people and I am never given the chance to do anything! No matter what I do, everything about me is wrong! It is not fair ..."

"Boo-hoo." Avis couldn't help himself. That kind of self-pity would get her nowhere in life.

Cora gasped and jerked to a halt mid-rant. "*What?*" she snarled.

Not "I beg your pardon" or "Excuse me" or "I'm sorry" or any one of a hundred other types of snivelling Highborn Hellion apologies that would have lessened her standing with him. Oh, no. She wasn't snivelling at all. She was *outraged!* Avis looked at her face that brightened with fury and almost grinned. *Much better.* He liked this side of her already.

"Boo," he repeated, his eyes flaring mockingly as he paused between the two words for emphasis. "Hoo." He gave her another few seconds to toy with the phrase, then lifted his left foot to the edge of the sofa and rested an elbow casually against his knee. "Or, as my people would say, suck it up and get on with it, young lady. You're not the first one to be dealt a bad hand from the beginning, and you won't be the last. The only one who can make your situation any different is you."

"I am not permitted to change my situation."

Something about the girl struck Avis as odd and he found himself pulling back and tilting his head slightly at her; his eyes once again scanning her from head to toe and back again. He was by no means an expert where little kids were concerned, but he was pretty sure they weren't supposed to talk like that. So ... *grown-up.* "You're not permitted to change your situation?" he repeated, to see if she really understood the wording.

Cora curled her upper lip in an all-out sneer. "Congratulations, your hearing has made an excellent recovery. May I go now?"

Avis gnashed his teeth. Her bravery was welcome, but the bad attitude was going to get her murdered in short order—by *him* if no one else. If they were back home, he'd have flattened *any* member of his pantheon who showed him so little respect. But Cora had earned the right to be angry and it was something he had to deal with—now. "No," he said, forcing aside his ire and replacing it with a patronising smile. He curled one finger for her to come to him. "Come here."

Her shoe edged fractionally forward.

Avis inhaled deeply and released it as a slow hiss through his gritted teeth. *Don't push me too far, girl.* "I have all day, you little shit," he lied, pointing at the ground directly in front of him. He wanted to hash out these issues with Cora before her mother returned—Mystallian to Mystallian, but he wasn't prepared to force her compliance, *yet.*

That would be replacing one set of obligatory restrictions with another, and Cora was a pressurised time bomb waiting to go off. He'd seen Tal work himself to this point many times before, and he knew if he couldn't get her to blow while he was still in control of the situation, she'd hurt herself and a lot of people around her when it finally happened. Not *if*. A long time ago, his family had learned how to defuse Tal from the worst of his rages, though that had been a serious case of trial and error. A lot of Mystallian mortals perished in those early years. Whole galaxies at a time in fact. Fortunately, Mystal was large enough that the loss of a few mortal galaxies was neither here nor there to them.

Cora *hmphed* and stomped forward, stopping just outside his reach. Her belief that the distance kept her safe from him was adorable; clearly no one had explained to her the fundamental basics of ranged control. "What do you want now?" she asked, as if she'd scraped him off her boot and didn't appreciate the smell.

Avis grinned lazily at her. "You *really* hate me, don't you?"

"*YES!*" The savagery of that hiss was almost reptilian.

Oh yeah. If anything, you're years past the point of 'about to blow'.

Without explaining himself, Avis rose to his feet and poked her softly in the shoulder with his fingers as he strode past her. "Stay," he ordered, and went on towards the doors, ignoring the way she flexed and rolled her shoulder away from him, rubbing the point of contact in disgust. Frash had left the double doors open in her haste to get away and through the gap Avis found the Highborn Hellion Guard standing at attention outside. The sight of it still made him whimper inwardly, but all the Nine Levels would freeze over *twice* before he ever showed such cowardice in front of his child.

"Guard," he said, not quite able to bark his orders at it. The guard remained as lifeless as a statue with its great golden wings flared intimidatingly, though Avis knew better than to think it hadn't heard. "I require complete privacy with Lady Cora and it's going to get ... destructive. Ignore it all. No matter what you hear, I want no one to come in until I come out, including you. Inform my wife of this upon her return and let her know I'd appreciate it if she too gave us some privacy."

He didn't bother to list the multiple exceptions to that request. As Clarise's husband, his order would only be followed by those beneath her status. Likewise, he didn't wait for an acknowledgement he knew wouldn't be forthcoming either. Instead, he stepped back into the bedroom and closed both doors himself, then turned to face Cora. She hadn't moved from when he was on the couch. Her back was to him with enough tension rippling through her tiny frame to snap one or both of Armina's great claymores.

She needed to vent ... so very badly. To get the ball rolling, Avis released a snippet of his own rising temper—if only to show her how it was done. "Alright, you little shit. You and I haven't had a whole lot to do with each other since I woke up the other day, but I think it's time we got a few things sorted out, don't you?" Cora refused to even look at him, let alone answer him. A little more ire slipped its leash and Avis' gaze narrowed. "I believe I asked you a question, girl."

"If you say so."

Avis' eyes flared and his hands clenched at his sides. *Child ... Child ... with every right to be pissy*, he forced himself to remember as he slowly released the breath he'd sucked in in outrage, shaking his fists loose in the process. "I do," he growled darkly. "And I really wouldn't push me too far if I were you, girl, or you're liable to wind up in—" He stopped abruptly when he realised Cora still hadn't moved.

"Dammit, Cora! I'm talking to you, and I refuse to speak to the back of your arrogant little, fucking head! Now turn around!"

Cora whirled on her heel, snapping, "With absolutely *no* due respect, just what in the realms do you think I should say to the likes of *you!*"

Good. If that's all it took, stirring her up wasn't going to be as hard as he thought. "I want you to let out every realm-damned thing you've ever been forced to bottle up inside that stubborn little head of yours. All of it. Every curse. Every angry thought. The whole lot of it!" He stabbed a finger towards the ground in front of him. "Right now! This is your one and only opportunity to empty your spleen at me." He raised that hand and waved his fingers beckoningly. "So, let's see what you've got, *little girl.* I'm right here!"

Rather than respond, Cora smashed her teeth together so hard that the muscles under her eyes twitched and she dropped her gaze to the ground between them.

Avis swore viciously at her. He couldn't help himself. He was so tired of that Hellion trait and he was not putting up with it in her. Unlike Columbine, Cora was every bit as Mystallian as he was and to see one of his own forced into that fucking subservient pose through no fault of her own made him want to kill something. *A whole lot of somethings.*

It had been bad enough when he'd done plenty to deserve it. This kid had done absolutely nothing! Only by remembering they had yet to escape the confines of Hell where they were both still severely outnumbered, was he able to rein in his genocidal thoughts. "Look at me, Cora." He watched her lips and jaw grind on words she clearly longed to hurl at him instead. He strode over to her and caught her by the chin, forcing her head up to stare him in the eye. "I said, *look at me!*"

Cora gasped in shock of the man-handling and tried to swat his hand away; then wrapped her arm around his wrist and heaved, all to no avail. He merely tightened his grip on her chin just long enough to prove it was his choice to let her go, before he shoved her backwards a pace or two.

Cora stumbled, then righted herself with a screech of indignation. "If you *touch* me again …!" she screamed, shuddering with fury.

Avis had no intention of letting her finish that sentence. Drawing out that rage was what he wanted—what she needed—and now that they were finally on the right path, he had to keep her unbalanced. "You'll what?" he jeered rudely. "Cry?"

Cora lunged at him, slugging him across the jaw with enough strength to drive him across the room and into the double doors.

Just as fast as it happened, Avis was back on his feet again. He could taste a very thin trail of blood from his front teeth, but by the time he licked the surface, the tooth was locked back into place and the bleeding had naturally healed. All that was left was to spit out the offending droplets, which he did. "I think I *almost* felt that," he sneered with a smug grin. "Is that *really* the best you've got, *little girl?* Because I would have expected someone with my blood to have a little more—"

"There is *nothing* of you in me!" Unable to fly, Cora ran alongside the bed and threw one foot into the corner of the mattress, pushing herself into the air for a height advantage as her fist came up to her shoulder in an overhead pile-driver. Unlike her last blow, this one was going to have significantly more oomph and Avis eyed the move that should have been far too advanced for this little, five-year-old girl. *How is she pulling these adult concepts out of her ass?* He made a mental note to find out just as soon as this was all over.

Avis had no intention of allowing that punch to land and as she began her descent, he caught her arm by the elbow and twisted with her, *helping* her slam into the double doors he had only just peeled himself off. Cora's clenched fist went through the door up to the shoulder and for a few seconds she dangled from the timber like a hooked coat.

Then her head went back and she howled at the top of her lungs, but as Avis watched the myriad of expressions that flashed across her face, he had the strong suspicion her outburst was due more to surprise than pain. That thought was confirmed when the screeching abruptly stopped and she twisted to level a filthy glare at him. Her feet flipped up to the door and she heaved her arm free, the momentum of which cartwheeled her through the air and landed her squarely on her feet a short distance away. Again, not the move of a child.

Determined to stay the course, Avis looked across at her with a snort of contempt and pursed his lips in a mocking air-kiss. He hated himself for it, but there was too much rage still inside her and he needed to keep her off-balance. "Wow, that almost looked like it hurt."

If only it was this easy to wind up Tal, he thought to himself as a full-bodied shudder of fury swept through her. While the Highborn Hellions may have preferred to pretend their temper didn't exist, to the Mystallians, it was better to blow up and move on—bloody nose and all. Bottling things up never helped anyone.

"Why, you son of a scallye!" In her rage, Cora launched herself at him and raked her tiny, Mystallian fingernails across his face; a far cry from the claws she would have ideally used. Avis let her have that one, especially when the scratch barely broke the surface and would be gone in a few seconds anyway. But his hands caught her around the waist and he thrust her away from him, landing her with a bounce in the middle of the master bed. She was immediately back on her feet, now almost at eye level with him. "You do not deserve to be out of the Nine Levels!" she screamed at the top of her lungs. "You should—"

"Who told you I was in the Nine Levels?"

Cora's upper lip rolled into a disgusted sneer. "The shorter list would be to ask who did not," she shot back savagely. "It was all the males ever talked about and if you ask me, it is right where you belong."

Avis slowly ran his tongue around his lips, finally understanding where at least part of her rage originated from. He'd greatly feared what would happen to his relationship with Columbine if anyone informed her of the circumstances surrounding her conception, and here it was in black and white with Cora. "So, you were told what I did to your mother?"

"I WAS THERE!" she screamed, jumping onto the foot of the bed and balancing herself with her hand on the bedpost to be on equal height with him. "I was barely six hours old when you raped her right in front of me, you animal!"

CHAPTER EIGHTEEN

It was a good thing the double doors were only a step from Avis' back, for although he hadn't known he'd moved, the timber suddenly collided with his shoulders in a forceful thump. She'd been a newborn infant when he'd attacked Clarise in the nursery. He vaguely remembered her wailing incessantly in the background, but clearly, she remembered everything about him. The question was ... *how?*

"You've had your adult perception that long?" he asked, hoping against hope that he was mistaken. He held enough shame over his actions as it was, without adding this ...

Cora's lethal glare confirmed his worst nightmare. "Not just my perception either, you *slae-el*. I remember everything," she snarled. "Every realm-damned second of it. You, staggering in so badly you could barely stand. Mother's smile, when she thought you were taking an interest in me, and her look of absolute terror when your real motives became known. She was barely a handful of hours out of labour and you grabbed her by the back of her neck and forced her over my change table and you raped her! You rammed her so hard you hurt her and no amount of begging and pleading on her part stopped you! She didn't even shapeshift to escape you! She should have, but you did something to stop her! I know you did! I even remember what you said, when you did it!"

Avis wanted more than anything to cover his ears and hide, unable to bear the justifiable fury that leapt across the room at him. He'd been too drunk to remember what he'd said, but he could well imagine. 'Monster' would have been too generous a title for him back then, and he was the first to admit it.

But hiding from his daughter was a coward's way out and he wouldn't deny her this. She'd been waiting five long years for this moment and he was going to stand there and hear every word she had to say. Later, he could carve his heart out and offer it to them on a plate—if she didn't do it first.

"You want to spawn with my seed so fucking badly, you demonic whore! Here! Have some fucking more!"

Avis' blood turned to ice in his veins at the words he could hear himself saying, and he fell against the door for a second time. He slammed his eyes shut against the truth, bowing his head and dragging all his fingers through his hair. *No! ... Oh, no ... no, no!* It hadn't been Clarise's decision to fall pregnant with Columbine at all! As the Mystallian God of Life within his own powerbase, *he* had possessed the establishment field to create life where there would've ordinarily been none. Most of that day had been lost in a drunken blur, but it would explain how Columbine came to be. *He* had been the one to make it so.

And Cora, despite her infantile state, had seen and heard it all. He clenched his fist in self-loathing and slammed it against the door behind him. This was going to take more than a few punches and a shouting match. This was going to take blood. A whole lot of blood.

He didn't like where his thoughts were taking him. No sane man would. Hell had no demonic healers to repair a Mystallian and his own limited healing in the Nine Levels had been achieved through the Walk. If he followed his first instinct and offered Cora a weapon with which to hack him to pieces, the Highborn

Hellions would find out about it the second he was carried through Hell to the Walk. Cora had already lost an arm for wielding a weapon. There was no way anyone was going to let her swing another, even if it was at him.

Trying to heal on his own without the Walk would delay their departure by months—maybe years. Small cuts, scratches and bruises would heal in seconds to minutes without the boost of a powerbase. A broken bone; maybe an hour or two. But being reduced to a smear? *That* was a healing process which even a god needed decades to recover from.

And if he waited until after they left Hell to resolve the situation, he'd still be a smear for decades until he healed. Decades, when his family would be vulnerable to the Known Realms without his protection. Avis shook his head. He had too many enemies out there to risk that.

Option four was to wait until they were all safely in Mystal. Avis dragged his lips through his teeth. Two things went against that plan. One: Cora needed to vent now if she was to hang on to her sanity, not at some distant point in the future that could be years away. Two: If his family found out the actual specifics of his assault on Clarise, they'd all pile on to Cora's side so fast his head would spin. Even now, he could picture Griffith and Tal pinning him to the ground while Amaro and Armina showed the already way too smart girl precisely how to make every blow cause the maximum pain and damage until her vengeance had run its course.

As much as it galled him, taking the Walk and spending a few more days in bed was the only feasible option … and only one person had the power to defy Hellion Highborn law inside of Hell. *Oh, I really don't want to do this.* But having decided on his course of action, he lowered his hand to look at Cora, then placed a silencing finger to his lips. *Fear the repercussions,* the supreme demon had said the last time they'd met, and Avis surely did. But this wasn't about him. Before he could talk himself out of it, Avis raised his hand and barely whispered the name, "Belial."

An image of the supreme demon formed between him and Cora, though Avis kept his eyes low and only saw him from his waist down. "Perhaps I was not understood," the great demon rumbled ominously.

"You were, M'lord," Avis replied, rolling his shoulders forward and dipping his head in supplication. It took everything he had not to fall to his knees and grovel. "It's for Cora's sake that I'm reaching out to you. Not my own." He didn't offer any further explanation, hoping Belial would take the bait and keep the conversation going.

The muscles in Belial's lower legs flexed as he squared his weight between his cloven feet. "You are surrendering your charge already?"

"No!" Avis' eyes automatically flew upwards in denial, almost making it to the demon's chin before he caught himself and lowered it back to Belial's leather-plated waist. Eye contact would have been suicidal. "No, M'lord. But I do have a proposal that would require a measure of your … gratuity."

Refusing to back down now that he was on this path, Avis quickly went on. "Cora has the comprehension of an adult, and apparently, she has always had that presence of mind. She was … there … that day in Mystal and has been forced to deny her Mystallian sense of righteousness ever since. I … *she* needs to vent it before it destroys her from the inside. Over half her current attitude stems from it. In order to grant her that vengeance, I'm going to be hurt, which in turn will slow down my recovery and force me to remain inside of Hell for much longer than any of us wanted."

Belial's smoky breath billowed down his legs. "What are you asking?"

As if you didn't already know, Avis thought to himself, but was careful not to let his features betray those thoughts. He swallowed heavily, unable to believe the next words he was about to utter. "I'm asking for permission to be taken to The Walk after she's finished with me, and that Cora not be punished for anything that happens between us during this time."

"While Cora remains in her current form, nothing she can do to you will require more than a few minutes for you to heal naturally from. That would hardly require punishment from me."

He was being antagonistic on purpose. Avis was sure of it. "Because of the tefsla in her system, she can't change very easily—if at all. But the anger inside her needs an outlet which is more than her current shape by itself can provide. So … even if it's only temporary … with your permission … I'd like one of two things for her. Either she be granted her demonic form to rip me to pieces, or …" —Avis paused and swallowed, knowing this latter one would be like asking for the throne of Hell itself— "… for the duration of this contest, all of Hell ignores the fact that she is swinging into me with a sword. One of those two needs to happen." He paused. "*She* needs this to happen."

What happened next, stunned Avis to the core.

"Give me your hand."

Avis' eyes shot up again, and he saw the clawed hand of the supreme demon being raised in his direction. He had no chance to warn Cora. To keep Belial waiting even a millisecond was to court a sentence of the Damned and Cora had already heard his side of the conversation, so he could only hope that she was as clever as she appeared.

After clasping wrists with Avis, Belial stepped into the room beside him. Cora gasped and dropped from the footboard to land on her knees on the carpeted floor with her forehead bowed to the ground—a pose Avis chastised himself for wanting to replicate.

"Cora attempted to use a weapon and later attacked her sister in a blood rage. Both were done while she stood under my house banner and she paid the price," Belial rumbled, twisting as if to peruse the room, rather than its occupants. "As of this time three days ago, by both our decrees, she now stands under yours. However … before you continue on this path, I would suggest you consider how confused your plan will make her. She was punished for attempting to wield a weapon and now you are going to give her that and more, knowing no woman of standing may touch a weapon inside the borders of Chaos. Not even my descendants of war."

Wait … she didn't even get *to the weapon* wielding *part? They maimed her just for trying?*

Avis jumped all over his thoughts, not wanting a single facial movement to give them away. Belial may not have had a clue about the inner workings of a mind, but he was all over everything physical and every possible tell therein. Avis chose instead to look at his prone daughter, reminding himself of the spitfire she had been not two minutes earlier—and would be again if he had his way. "I wronged her as a Mystallian. She may have her vengeance as a Mystallian. It's our way."

"Beelzebub," Avis thought he heard Belial murmur, though the three were alone and no blood-link had been established between the supreme demon and his Military Commander. Not that a blood-link would have worked anyway … unless Beelzebub was family.

Was he?

"Avis and Clarise's bedroom is completely off limits to all. No one may enter until you hear so from me."

Eternity could come and go before Avis would ask him how he'd done that. Without looking, the Mystallian felt the full weight of Belial's gaze as it raked across his body and forced himself to stay perfectly still. "I will take you through The Walk personally when this is over. This will remain between us."

Although it was everything Avis had asked for, the thought of the impending bloodbath—namely his—had his heartrate skyrocketing. He'd be a liar if he said otherwise. Pain was still pain, and he wasn't a shifter. He couldn't just switch off his pain receptors whenever he wanted like they could. Every stroke of the blade was going to bring unbridled agony, but he'd deserved this. Every second of it.

All the Hellions combined had not been as wronged as Clarise and Cora were. Clarise had already forgiven him. Why, he was still trying to fathom, but he was grateful beyond words for the second chance. Cora was too Mystallian for a verbal forgiveness and needed to extract her revenge before they could move forward as a family.

"I'll need her to have a seclusion ring of some type as well," he added, as he realised his calm acceptance of what must be was only possible because the carnage hadn't started yet. The same would not be said half a heartbeat after he was first skewered by a sword. "Once she starts, I'll fight back. I won't be able to help myself and she'll never survive it."

Through his peripheral vision, Avis saw Belial close his left hand into a loose fist, and when he opened it again, a plain gold ring sat in the centre of his palm. The ease with which he'd done that was laughable, if Avis didn't know it was exactly what he'd asked for. He tried really, *really* hard not to react to the fact that Belial had managed to create the one item that could shut down anyone from his side of the family indefinitely, with little more than a thought and no actual components. He'd just *willed* it into being. Yet another terrifying piece of information to add to his already petrifyingly scary father-by-marriage.

"I-If you could put it somewhere inside Cora where I won't find it easily, I won't be able to target it the second we get started," Avis stammered, scrambling to get his own racing thoughts in check.

"You will do no harm to her physically."

Belial's voice reverberated against Avis' eardrums, though the great demon never spoke a word. Avis gasped and jerked to face him, but Belial's full focus was still on Cora.

The ring was no longer in his hand …

… and he hadn't moved.

Avis breathed through his growing panic. Shapeshifting his eardrums to hear sounds that were never uttered *and* able to create a seclusion ring from scratch *and* put it in Cora—all without moving. The evil bastard was *definitely* freaking him out on purpose. "W-Will you give her a blade, M'lord?"

"Mystallian steel, no less," Belial replied.

Avis watched Cora's reaction to the conversation. The girl was still curled in a submissive ball on the floor, but despite the distance he could almost swear he saw her tiny ears twitch as she strained to catch every word. Specifically, the words *Mystallian steel*. No sooner had Belial said the words, then a metre-long sword rose out of the carpet fibres under her nose, not unlike an island breaking through the surface of the ocean.

Unwilling to lift her head from the subservient position, she moved her hand so that her palm stroked the flattened side of the blade. If there'd been any doubt she was Mystallian, watching the way she caressed the mystical steel in absolute rapture finished it off. He'd seen his sister Armina of War have that same love affair with her claymores too many times not to recognise it for what it was.

It shouldn't have surprised him that Belial was gone when he turned to say something else. It really shouldn't have—and no doubt he'd be telling himself that for the next few millennia. *Creepy so and so.*

"Alright, Cora. On your feet," he said, slapping his hands together to distract himself from his dangerous musings. "And unless you think your fingernails can match that blade you're practically drooling over, bring it with you. You're a Mystallian now, girl, and it's about time you learned how to swing one of our swords."

Cora slowly rose to her knees, using downward pressure on the flat of the blade to keep it within reach. Avis noticed she did so without touching the hilt and he pressed his lips together to prevent himself from saying what he thought of that.

"What do you mean, *I am a Mystallian now?*" she asked, frowning ever so slightly.

Avis gestured at her missing arm. "Hellions don't allow swordplay in their women," he said, as if she should have remembered that fact for herself. "And they kill them for having temper tantrums. Yet here you stand, having done both, stuck in the unyielding form of my people with our steel laying at your side, waiting for your hand to teach it to sing. I'm sure even you can connect those dots."

Cora snatched her hand away from the blade and leapt to her feet without it. "I am *no* Mystallian."

"If that's what you'd rather." Avis spoke the lie with a half-grin he didn't really mean. Even if it killed him (and had he not been established, that would've been on the cards) he'd make her see sense before the end of the day. She was so Mystallian she might as well have had it tattooed in hellfire across her forehead. He took a sidewards step and knocked the back of his knuckles against the double doors beside him. "Your Highborn Hellion death sentence is still right outside those doors. All you have to do is walk through them and shout at the top of your lungs that you're not a Mystallian. I'm pretty sure the Highborn Hellions will take it from there."

He lowered his hand and placed it against his hip. "Or, you can accept that you are a Mystallian who's been wronged and enjoy the revenge that you're due." He slid both hands behind his back and locked them together at the wrist, more to prevent himself from fighting back than for any measure of pride. "This is how Mystallians apologise and as I've already said, I'm right here."

It irked Avis that she hesitated. Her eyes shifted from the doors to him and back again, her tongue hovering over the middle of her upper lip in thought. Would she really prefer certain death over admitting the blood in her veins was his? That was a lot of hatred. He'd earned it, of course, but that wasn't the outcome he wanted now. Somehow, he had to sweeten the deal, though he wasn't sure how. He thought about the crazy antics of his youngest brother, knowing Chance could bring the best out of any child, being so childlike himself … and that was when it dawned on him.

"Cora, do you remember who anointed you after you were born?" He caught the flicker of acknowledgement in her eyes right before it disappeared and knew he was on the right track. "My little brother anointed you in my absence. I know, because he told me, and I've seen what he's like with his own kids. He would've played with you until you practically choked on your gurgles while your mother looked on. Do you remember him?"

"What about him?"

Avis had guessed right. Even though she'd only been with Chance for a short time before her mother fled back to Hell, no child ever forgot him … or his antics. "Being Mystallian doesn't mean being me. They aren't all like me. In fact, none of them are like me. Claiming your birth-right doesn't make you me. It just makes you one of us."

"I will *never* be like you!"

"And I wouldn't want you to be. So, what's your flavour, Cora? Do you walk out those doors and die, or do you pick up that sword and show me just how mad you are at me for making you suffer all these years?"

Cora snarled at the top of her lungs and swooped on the hilt of the sword. She leapt up and surged across the room at him, holding the blade over her head as if it were an axe rather than a sword. Not that it mattered. Mystallian steel was one of the strongest, sharpest metals in all existence. Combined with Cora's natural strength, her first strike would cleave him in two.

Here it comes, Avis thought bracing himself for the first of what would be many impacts.

He wasn't mistaken.

CHAPTER NINETEEN

"Milord, may I be permitted to ask an obvious question?" Sarvalis asked, as streams of mortal souls trudged in a never-ending circle around his mountain of misery. He was so huge his voice boomed throughout the level, but his tone held enough reverence to not see him in any trouble for doing so.

Lord Belial hovered close to the torturer's left shoulder. His arms were folded across his chest and his wings remained flat against his back. He maintained his airborne position through sheer will alone. Despite their difference in size, the smaller of the two dominated all he surveyed. Lord Belial turned his gaze away from the only individual that absorbed his attention on The Walk long enough to look at his master guardian of the Seventh Level.

Sarvalis bowed his huge head beneath that gaze.

"Ask."

Sarvalis lifted his eyes and pointed his huge sword at the reptilian creature that crawled amongst the Damned on eight thick legs. Two heavily spiked tails swung in tight circles around its rear end and twin heads full of long sharp fangs swung on the top of snake-like necks at the other end, enabling the teeth to reach anywhere the spikes could not. Between the two it used that reach to shred any of the Damned that came too close. Despite the crowded conditions, an arm's length ring of personal space had thus emerged around the creature; something Sarvalis had never seen before. Its celestial presence resonated like a beacon in the sea of mortal souls but after three laps, Sarvalis still couldn't recognise its physical makeup.

He'd been pondering this question ever since Lord Belial appeared at his side and dumped a mass of bloodied meat and bone chunks at his feet with an order to get it moving. No piece was bigger than a finger-length, but watching it heal, Sarvalis still had no idea who this individual was or why he—she—it had warranted the supreme demon's personal attention.

"Who is that really?"

Lord Belial returned his attention to the two-headed reptilian below and Sarvalis recognised the move as an unspoken dismissal of the subject. With a slight dip of his head to formally acknowledge the brush-off, Sarvalis went back to butchering the Damned in earnest; taking out on them the fact that he would probably never know who the strange *guest* was with every swing of his great sword.

At the end of its fourth lap, the celestial creature dug its enormous claws into the well-trodden pathway and refused to take another step in any direction. Anything that came within its reach was mauled without mercy and not once did it move its feet to do so. Sarvalis found the display of absolute brutality combined with inner power fascinating and he leaned forward to better observe the creature. If Lord Belial wasn't so invested in it, he'd have petitioned for it to be put on a chain at his feet to serve as both a pet and a fellow tormentor. Such a prize would be enviable indeed. "Milord," Sarvalis said, daring to speak his mind. "Should you ever tire of this one, nothing would give me greater pleasure than to relieve you of it."

The master guardian hadn't expected the corners of Lord Belial's mouth to lift in amusement and he wondered what he'd said to elicit such a response. "I shall keep it in mind," was all the great demon said.

A snarling screech from the Damned drew Sarvalis' attention, and looking down, he saw the strange creature being plucked off the crowded path and held in the air as if something had it by the scruff of the neck. Large chunks of rock fell away from its scrabbling claws and from the way it hissed and squirmed in surprise, the move had not been of its own volition. Again, Sarvalis glanced between it and his liege, wanting more than ever to know the background of this exquisite creature. At the very least, where he could send his minions to secure him another just like it.

As the reptilian creature was deposited on a ridge opposite to where Sarvalis sat, Lord Belial moved away from the master guardian without a word. He continued to drift on non-existent air currents until he was behind the creature, then stepped down on to the same piece of ground as if he were walking off an invisible platform. Sarvalis couldn't help but watch from the corner of his eye as he continued to slash through the Damned.

The creature must have sensed Lord Belial's presence, which meant it wasn't stupid either. It whirled in a tight circle to face him and backed up into the wall. Its spiked tails were off the ground in readiness, but parallel to its body instead of the more aggressive stance of overhead rotation (which meant it had intellect as well, another plus for the species). Both its heads twisted together so that all four eyes could watch the supreme demon.

Belial raised his hand and majestically rolled his wrist. By the time his palm was facing up, he'd created a leather-like ball of mass which Sarvalis couldn't identify until the straps fell off either side of his palm to reveal a demonic two-headed collar and leash set. Studs of silver lined the collars in three distinct rows which merged into thicker studs that ran up the leash to Lord Belial's hand. *So, it is just a pet after all …*

… or maybe not. The creature swung its tails up and twisted sideways, pushing its shoulder into the cliff wall to get that little bit further away, hissing in hateful denial. What stunned Sarvalis was the fact his liege seemed to be enjoying the creature's horrified defiance instead of squashing it on principle. The supreme demon almost chuckled as he placed his free hand against his hip. "My Well," he said, flexing his fingers to make the leash set jiggle. "My rules. How badly do you wish to get back in?"

The Well was where the Highborn congregated and held court and only the invited ever set foot down there. It was to Hell what other realms referred to as a palace. Not even Sarvalis had been in there. *Who in the Nine Levels of Hell was this creature?* The only person in recent times to ever warrant Lord Belial's personal attention like this was now safely holed up with his wife, beyond the reach of all. Had the great demon found a temporary substitute? And if so, *who?*

The creature's chest heaved, and it shook both its heads; its lips curling savagely.

"As you wish." Lord Belial's hand tightened on the leash and he lifted himself into the air, this time using his wings which pushed dirt and dust at the creature. More importantly to Sarvalis, he was leaving the creature behind on the ledge. Effectively abandoning it. Alone. All by itself.

Sarvalis' eyes narrowed, and he licked his fangs predatorily. Where there had been no hope before, the chance of owning it was once again a tantalising possibility. For the first time in eons, the Damned below were not the torturer's primary focus and he only gave them enough cursory wounds to maintain his position. If Lord Belial went out of sight, Sarvalis would swoop across the chasm in a heartbeat to claim that delightful creature as his own before anyone else could take it. Already he was repositioning himself to do just that.

The creature lifted both heads at the retreating Demon Lord and shrieked out a note that caused the Damned below to cringe and Lord Belial to pause. Still airborne and with his back to the creature, he jiggled the leash at his side again. "Yes, or no? You have one more second to decide."

No ... pick 'no', Sarvalis willed.

The creature's heads shuddered with what Sarvalis could only guess was revulsion, but within the allotted time, they both jerked downward once, shattering his hopes.

Instantly, the collars shot out in the creature's direction. Lord Belial never released his end of the leash—it merely extended itself to accommodate the distance. The creature saw them coming and threw itself on to its hind legs with a cry of outrage. It tried to dodge the incoming chokers, but no matter where it turned, the collars followed. Inevitably, they locked around those throats with an unholy snap that made the silver studs ignite in possessive hellfire.

The width of the collars expanded until one set of edges sat on the creature's shoulders and the other pushed its jaws upwards; making it a prized pet to be noticed. Technically, that was no different to what Sarvalis had planned, though he wouldn't have given it such grandeur. In Hell, existence and the fear of the Damned were their own reward. Bat shaped wings unfurled from the leather folds of the creature's back and lifted it into the air.

Given the way it struggled to maintain its balance in the air and how it had previously bitched about being left behind, Sarvalis doubted that the creature had known it could fly.

The leash shrank back towards Lord Belial in much the same manner that it had grown, *guiding* the creature to his side. The ruler of all Chaos gave the leash a single tug, then he and his new pet flew up and over the chasm wall, dropping down towards Antenora and the Well beyond.

Sarvalis would have given a lot of souls to know what that was all about.

* * *

Clarise took a long time to cry herself out. There was a very real possibility that she would never see Charon again outside a blood-link which he could cut off at any time. Or, since he no longer cared about anything, he could just as easily ignore the family contact altogether. Her last memory of him might very well be of when he'd screamed his hatred at her.

She had no one else to blame for her misery. Not once during his conception, or the years that followed, had Clarise stopped to think about how this would end for him. In hindsight, she could see how she had ridiculously assumed he would take after Beelzebub and live a naturally happy life as a Demon Lord with blood ties to the Hellion Highborn Guard. Maybe even share his father's ability to move at incredible speeds. Something that would make him different—unique—special even, amongst their family.

Now he was unique, all right. Just not in a good way. Even her seemingly emotionless father, Lord Belial, chose to behave that way. Everyone was supposed to have emotions. Everyone … except Charon. Who, without the ability to love, would probably never have a family of his own. She had condemned him to a solitary life of emptiness, and all so that she could tolerate the presence of men in her life. Selfish didn't even begin to describe it.

It is done, she kept reminding herself. It had needed to be done, and now it was done. He would never know the difference, and even if he did, he wouldn't care. It was the best of a horrible, horrible situation. One entirely created by her hand. Beelzebub offered her no comfort during this time. Not because he couldn't, but because the moment he'd tried, she'd shrieked and leapt away from him. She didn't want comfort. She didn't deserve it. This was all her fault.

For hours, she had thrown herself at the ground and grieved for the Lord her young son might have become. She wailed and slammed her hands against the ground, screaming in anguish as her son never would. But the hour grew late and though still distraught, she realised Avis would be worried about her. Perhaps even worried enough to come looking. Staring at her dirt-covered gloves, she slowly curled her hands into fists and pressed them into her eyes. She had no desire for Avis to see her like this. How could she explain her grief over a son they didn't share?

The thought of Avis and Beelzebub fighting was enough to draw her out of her anguish. She closed her eyes against her fingers and cast a stimulation wave to smooth out all the puffiness in her face and the red blotches that came from her tears. The ringlets of dark hair that had fallen loose during her grief folded back up into her bun and the rose repositioned itself in the middle. Her makeup and her uniform became flawless. *There,* she thought to herself as she lowered her hands and breathed out slowly. *If Avis saw me now, he would never know anything had transpired.*

Rising to her feet, she dusted her gloves against her thighs, more to end the subject than to rid herself of the dirt particles that didn't exist. Then she turned towards the opening that led back into the family levels, with every intention of returning to her husband. Her new life awaited her.

However, Beelzebub stood in her way. His wings were flared to cover the entirety of the cavern opening and he looked at her with a combination of regret and determination. "Where are you planning on going, Milady?" he asked.

Clarise saw no harm in telling him. "Avis will be looking for me. I must return …" Her words broke off as he pressed his lips together and slowly shook his horned head at her. A denial? For something as simple as going back to her apartment? Clarise's hands instinctively found her hips and she arched her eyebrow sharply at him. "*Excuse* me?"

"It would be better if you remained here for a little while longer, Milady." He looked above her head to draw her attention upwards, "The changing of the lights should be beginning soon. Perhaps you could distract yourself as you so often do with them …"

Clarise didn't rise to the bait. Instead, she stared at him, dumbfounded. *Why in the realms would he …?*

… and then she realised.

She'd been away from Avis for hours! *Hours*, where she hadn't been fulfilling her duties as his wife, protecting him from all who hated him. If Beelzebub was the one keeping her sequestered, it was because her father had made it so. She was no match for her father and would never claim to be, but the defence of her husband was the one time she would willingly try anyway.

But she hadn't been protecting him, and as a result, Avis had been left to her father's whims for hours. Her husband didn't even need to be taken back to the Nine Levels of Hell to be tortured. It could be done in the comfort of her own room.

Realising the calamity of her selfishness, Clarise lifted her hand with every intention of calling for her husband through a blood-link. If she could get back to him quickly enough, she might be able to avert the worst of it.

Beelzebub vanished and materialised behind her. Two enormous hands caught her by the wrists before she could call Avis' name and folded her arms across her stomach to hold them still. The other two went around her waist and lifted her off the ground, pinning her against his chest. Another two sprang from nowhere to restrain her legs at the knee. "Shhhhh," her former lover crooned above her head. "You will be fine, Milady."

It took Clarise a moment to realise what he'd done. After uttering a gasp of shock, she surged against him.

"Please, Milady, do not fight me," he pleaded, and in that instant Clarise knew how their young son must have felt hours earlier. The sensation of being trapped was probably the last emotion that delightful little boy would ever have. Clarise shook her head as the sting of a sedative was pushed against her skin near the elbows and immediately shifted her flesh to block it. *Not the time for distraction*, she chastised herself.

Beelzebub's grip tightened. "You will not win this, Milady. None may disturb them."

Outraged by his actions, Clarise dropped most of her mass and shifted into mist to escape him, but he followed her—faster than she could imagine—creating a box that surrounded her essence.

"Desist, Milady," the dark walls of her prison insisted as she threw herself from one side to the other with the little matter she maintained. "Your efforts are futile, and you will only hurt yourself if you continue. I have your room surrounded by no less than twelve Highborn Hellion Guards standing shoulder to shoulder with orders not to let anything past. It took half that number to destroy a realm in under a day. You will never get through them."

I will NOT be held like this! she thought and went for the actual matter that his essence had claimed to create the box. Will against will, Clarise's Highborn status gave her right of way and she tore his matter from him, absorbing it into herself. In doing so, she reformed into her natural demonic shape. However, Beelzebub's speed had already enabled him to claim more from elsewhere.

"How dare you!" she shouted, as he instantly filled the doorway again, no longer seeing him as her former lover or even a friend—just someone who stood between her and her beloved husband.

Beelzebub must have sensed the change in her, for he widened the gap between his feet and unfurled his wings. Neither was necessary for one with his speed and she suspected it was done merely to make her heed his warning. "It does not have to be this way, Milady," he said, still trying to appeal to her sense of Highborn Hellion honour.

"Your loyalty was always to my father."

"Always," he agreed, without hesitation. "I cannot permit you to contact your husband, Milady, and I will stop you at every turn, should you try." He lifted his eyes away from her, practically willing her to follow his line of sight to the explosions of colour that had commenced overhead. "I doubt it will be much longer anyway. So, perhaps if you were to calm yourself …"

"You knew this was happening all along." She threw the accusation at him like a dagger, refusing to yield to any suggestion he had at this point. "That was why you wanted to come with me to see Charon. Not because you are his father and concerned about his well-being, but to make sure I stayed distracted!"

Beelzebub lowered his gaze to her and folded both sets of arms in icy displeasure, causing a pang of regret to burn inside Clarise's broken heart. "You are being both emotional and unreasonable, Milady," he said with a slow headshake, as if speaking to a child. "Both attributes are beneath you."

His speed *would* stop her at every turn. If she tried to get past him or contact Avis, he would stop her, just as he claimed. The dance between them would go on forever, with her being the only loser. He would capture her, she would steal his mass to escape, and he would regain more to start the process all over again. All he had to do was keep her in the gardens, and by proxy, he would win.

Barely able to stand the mounting frustration, Clarise swung away from him. Thankfully, he didn't reappear in front of her again. She looked down at her demonic form, and in a rage-filled fit of disgust, she abandoned it for her Mystallian one. Her gloved hands knotted into tight fists of resentment. "*Do. NOT. Touch. Me,*" she warned, when she felt him approach her from behind.

"If that is your wish."

"What I *wish,*" she snarled, whirling on one heel to face him again. He stiffened in surprise at her ferocity. "… is to return to my husband and ensure for my own peace of mind that he is in precisely the same state of health he was in when I left him this morning!"

"And what *I* wish is that we did not have to be at this juncture," he replied coolly. "Yet here we are. But just so that you know, your father did not specifically order me to confine you to these gardens. That was my doing. Just as I have kept the gardens clear to permit you time to grieve over Charon, I am *still* keeping them clear so that only I will witness your current loss of control. Do not ever accuse me of not caring for you."

His contradictory rationale infuriated her. "So, you think you are doing this for me?"

"I know I am," he replied, in a matter of fact way. "You are one of the most refined of all the Highborn ladies and this time tomorrow I have no doubt you will be horrified by your conduct with me. If I were to step aside and permit you to rush to Avis' side, you would only get as far as my wall of Highborn Hellion Guards. In that event, the embarrassment you will cause yourself if you create a scene therein will haunt you forever. I cannot allow that."

"So, I am a prisoner instead?"

"For your own good," he insisted.

In the past, Clarise would have yielded to his wisdom. Accepted that he meant well and tried to put the unfairness of the situation behind them for the good of the whole. Part of her still wanted to. There was no trickery in his words. None whatsoever. He completely believed he was acting in her best interest.

But something else bubbled up inside her that made her want to stamp her foot, or scream, or both. She slid her fisted hands underneath her cloak, grinding her teeth until her jaw ached. "I will *never* forgive you for this," she declared, fighting the tears that welled in her eyes.

Although it was only a few harmless words, Beelzebub looked more wounded than if she had used a blade. "To preserve your sanctity, I will bear that mantle if I must, Milady."

Clarise closed her eyes and turned away from him. A million cutting retorts occurred to her and any one of them would have added to his misery; but what would be the point? He'd still not let her pass and verbally destroying him for no other reason than self-gratification felt wrong.

But now more than ever, she knew she'd made the right choice between the men in her life. Avis would never do this to her. Not for any reason. Their beginnings may have been … *difficult*, but he called her his queen now. His life. He would defend her to the end if he had to—but only if that was what *she* wanted.

She promised herself this would be the last time she'd tolerate decisions being made about her without her input by people who thought they were acting in her best interest. If that made her Mystallian, then that was a mantle she would have to bear as well.

CHAPTER TWENTY

As Belial paraded his new pet through the Well's levels, many complimented him on it. A few of his sons asked after the creature's origins, mainly because like Sarvalis, they too wanted one of the regal creatures for themselves.

Celestial strength, something that couldn't be shapeshifted into existence, oozed from every pore of the strange reptilian that walked at Belial's side. What none of them realised was that the sense of power came from ruling one of the largest realms in existence. Belial offered them no explanation and waved them off, but he had no doubt they would start scouring the Known Realms for the two-headed reptilian species anyway.

By the time Belial reached Clarise's level, word had spread of the new pet and the Highborn Hellions virtually (and in some cases literally) poured out of the cavern walls to see what the fuss was about. Belial indulged his inquisitive family, keeping his expression neutral as his son-by-marriage snapped both sets of jaws and swung his twin tails aggressively at every Highborn Hellion Lord who dared to assume he was tame. Spikes and teeth penetrated all manner of hands, causing his sons and other male descendants to yelp and hiss in surprise as they wrenched their limbs free of the reptilian's grip.

That was to be expected. The men should have known better than to reach for what they didn't know, but what impressed Belial was the way his son-by-marriage willingly endured the loathsome petting and pampering of the Highborn Ladies without complaint. It was good to see he'd learned the difference.

In Mystal there was no protective distinction between the sexes, but if Avis had harmed any of the Ladies the way he snapped at the Lords, Belial would have reacted accordingly and all of Hell would have known the identity of his so-called pet.

Though it wasn't Avis's humiliation that amused the supreme demon the most at this juncture. In fact, the Mystallian would've been surprised to learn just who was the source of his entertainment during this whole façade. The boy was merely the means; his indignation barely a by-product.

Torturing him like this was tantamount to ripping off the limbs of one of the Damned. Not exactly gratifying. But as he watched his son-by-marriage duck and weave around the women who gushed at him from all sides, Belial knew *surprised* would be much too mild a word for his son-by-marriage's reaction to their observer. *Petrified* would go closer.

Ever since Belial took what was left of Avis to The Walk hours ago, the supreme demon had been entertained by the non-stop verbal abuse of the one being that Avis and his siblings hoped to never cross paths with again.

... GET THOSE FUCKING SLUTS AWAY FROM MY FUCKING BOY, YOU HORN-HEADED, MOTHER-FUCKING SHAPE-SHIFTING PIECE OF FUCKING SHIT, OR BY FUCK I'LL FUCKING FUCK UP EVERY LAST FUCKING ONE—!

The words charged relentlessly through the realms, though only Belial could hear them. He could see the source of those words too, if he bothered to look.

He didn't.

Your boy *has been condemned to the Nine Levels for the last two years, Theodrick. Did you not notice? Every level. Every sublevel. And oh, how I have made him suffer ...*

YOU MOTHER-FUCKING ASSHOLE!

Belial's demonic lips parted with trace amusement. *Sticks and stones won't break my bones, and you can't do it either.*

The fact that he was using contractions in this one instance was a compromise Belial was prepared to make, given the amount of personal satisfaction it garnered from his mind-bending counterpart.

The ancient tune of condescension aimed solely at Theodrick was one which The Bender made his personal mission to eradicate across the realms. So of course, Belial had it ingrained into every mortal and celestial culture everywhere. Theodrick despised the way it reminded him of Belial's invulnerability to him and as always, he exploded in toe-curling expletives the moment it began ...

... and Belial loved every minute of it.

Theoretically, they were both far too old for such childishness, but very little entertained the Shifter as much as watching the *supposed* supreme Lord of Order lose his mind over every little thing that went beyond his control. The immaturity of the tune only added to the insulting words. Theodrick's legendary vile temper had carried it to a point where Belial only had to hum the first few bars and the Bender would still explode.

Now was no exception. Theodrick crammed so much profanity into his sentences that they were no longer coherent.

Then, without warning, the cursing suddenly stopped. Dead. For the first time in hours.

Belial glanced at the ghostly image that shimmered a short distance from him. Theodrick's face was still bright red and dark purple with vein popping fury, but he'd pulled back against his throne and a dangerously evil sheen coloured his dark eyes.

PUT ... MY FUCKING SON ... BACK THE WAY HE WAS ... OR KISS YOUR OWN MOTHER-FUCKING FIRSTBORN BASTARD GOODBYE. He leaned one elbow into the arm of his throne. *TRY. ME.*

Belial wasn't laughing now. For all his bluster, the Bender didn't have the creativity to bluff and Uriel's mind was now in his counterpart's sights. Sobering instantly, Belial's own gaze narrowed at the ominous threat. *You have no power over Uriel.*

Smug confidence replaced Theodrick's rage, putting Belial on notice of what was to come.

AS USUAL, YOU FUCKING OVERESTIMATE YOURSELF, SHIFTER. WE MAY NOT BE FUCKING ABLE TO SCREW WITH EACH OTHER'S PERSONAL FUCKING REALMS NOR THE COWARDLY ASSHOLES WHO HIDE WITHIN THEM LIKE SPINELESS FUCKING CHICKEN-SHITS ...

The Bender curled his lips into a vicious sneer that implied Belial was the greatest imbecile in existence for keeping so many of his offspring within the protective boundary of Chaos.

BUT LAST TIME I FUCKING CHECKED, THAT FUCKWIT URINAL OF YOURS DOESN'T EXACTLY KEEP HIS FUCKING ASS GLUED TO CHAOS, DOES HE?

Belial refused to acknowledge the multiple invectives that had been cast at his eldest son. Almost as long as he'd been using the childish tune to aggravate Theodrick, the Bender had used Uriel's modified name and supposed sexual orientation to provoke the Shifter. And, with all due credit to the stagnant fool who never adapted to anything, it *had* worked in the beginning. But Belial quickly realised the best defence to any slur from Theodrick was to pretend it didn't bother him in the least. Flip it back on to Theodrick, because the Bender *knew* it did ... *and it ate him alive to know he could never prove it!*

My son is established, just as yours is. So long as he is inside either Heaven or Chaos, your destruction of his mind will only last as long as you are focused on him.

FOR FUCK'S SAKE, SHIFTER! YOU'RE NOT SO FUCKED IN THE FUCKING HEAD TO THINK YHWH DOESN'T FUCKING SEND HIM THE FUCK OUTTA HEAVEN ON A FUCK TONNE OF VENGEANCE FUCKING MISSIONS! I'LL HAVE ALL THE REALM-DAMNED FUCKING TIME I WANT TO FUCK HIM THE FUCK UP.

This was getting out of hand. Neither of them could risk things escalating to that point, but only one of them had a clear enough head to prevent it. *Your son wanted this, Theodrick. If you doubt that, look into his memories and see for yourself. He. Came. To. Me.*

Belial waited for Theodrick to do just that. It didn't take long. *YOU GUTLESS MOTHER-FUCKING SACK OF FUCKING SHIT! YOU COULD HAVE FUCKING HEALED HIM WITHOUT FUCKING MAKING HIM WALK THAT MOTHER-FUCKING BULLSHIT OF A PRETENTIOUS FUCKING WALK THAT DOESN'T FUCKING DO SHIT!*

Belial didn't deny it. *That was not what he asked for.* The Shifter kept his face unreadable as he tugged at Avis' leash, using his influence over the realm to disperse his family and clear the level around him. As usual, they were none the wiser to his manipulations and it gave him the privacy he needed to return Avis to Clarise's quarters unnoticed. As they approached the double doors to the bedroom, the wall of Highborn Hellion Guards parted and dipped their heads in uniformed reverence.

Belial walked Avis into the bedroom and tapped his ancient power to close the doors behind him without touching them or looking at them. Then he dropped the leash, dissolving it and the chokers into harmless smoke that wafted away from his son-by-marriage's reptilian necks.

Avis immediately launched himself over the bed and pushed himself against the far wall beside Clarise's bedside table, curling all his lips to show row after row of razor sharp teeth in disgust.

I'M FUCKING WARNING YOU, SHIFTER. FUCKING PUT HIM THE FUCK BACK RIGHT FUCKING NOW, OR OUR FUCKING NEUTRALITY AGREEMENT IS ANCIENT FUCKING HISTORY!

Belial drew in a deep breath and released it in a smoky sigh. *As entertaining as it would be to watch you* try *and do anything from that side of the table, I have my own reasons for moving this along.*

The main one being he didn't want to butt heads with Theodrick over who could do what to the other's son. Nothing would survive that war. Literally … *nothing.* So, the eight legs of the reptilian merged into an upper set of arms and a lower pair of legs and the two heads folded back into one. Impenetrable leather hide gave way to a combination of soft pale flesh, dark hair and the black Mystallian uniform.

The transformation was gradual, to give Avis time to regain his bearings. The boy was not a shifter after all and changing perceptions and other sensory inputs could potentially send a non-shifter mad. Belial glanced at the impatience that practically resonated from the Bender in waves and smiled inwardly.

At least, that was *one* of the reasons he took so long.

* * *

After what felt like an eternity of irate silence on Clarise's part, Beelzebub did that strange head tilt which she had come to know was a sign that her father was communicating with him when they weren't in the same room. He bobbed his head once after a few seconds, just as he had the last time.

Clarise gave him her full attention for the first time in almost an hour with her hands on her hips and her booted feet shoulder width apart. "Well?" she demanded, icily.

Without breaking eye contact, Beelzebub dipped his head in her direction. "You are now free to return to your husband, Milady."

Clarise wasted no time. Her hand was in the air gesturing and she immediately called to Avis, refusing to acknowledge the demonic commander who'd held her prisoner for another moment. Her heart cartwheeled as Avis' image appeared between them and she smiled in relief that he seemed to be relatively unharmed. That was, until she saw her father in the background and she gasped in fear for her husband. Belial had made no secret of his hatred for Avis and fearing the worst, she thrust out both her hands to her husband, determined to insert herself between them if she had to.

It seemed Avis was just as impatient to have her back in his arms. Without further prompting, he grabbed her wrists and pulled her to him in a jerk that had her colliding with his chest in a light thump. His arms snaked around her upper torso, banding her to him while Clarise knotted her fingers behind his neck and pressed her ear to his chest to hear the steady beat of his heart through the doublet. Sure … sound … solid … if a little elevated.

"Are you alright?" he asked, about half a second before she could.

Clarise snorted as she looked up at him, relief causing her eyes to water. "I am now," she replied. Unknotting her fingers, she gripped the back of his head and pulled it down to kiss him, if only to convince herself of his presence. "I was so scared for you before."

Avis groaned and kissed her again. Deeply. Passionately. As if to drive away every fear she'd had for him. "I'm fine," he promised, after he broke away. "Your father was just … giving me a hand to wrap up a few loose ends—my choice," he quickly added when she stiffened and sucked in a tight breath that hissed against her teeth. He stroked her back to comfort her and lifted his head to glance over his shoulder at Belial, who was standing between the bed and the double doors. "Well, sort of," he added bitterly.

Clarise shifted her gaze between the two, desperately wanting to understand the undercurrents of that statement. Technically, there was still no deception. At least, not from Avis. Her father had yet to speak, not that she would know either way where he was concerned. Still snuggled against Avis' chest, she looked at her father and asked, "Why did you have the room surrounded by Highborn Hellion Guard?"

Belial returned that scrutiny. He seemed to be taking the measure of her, dressed as she was and cocooned happily in her husband's protective embrace. His brow ridges merged thoughtfully, and when he finally spoke, it wasn't to answer her question. "Avis has made a full recovery and his welcome in Hell has expired. Prepare your family, Clarise, for tomorrow those of you going with him will also be departing." And then he was gone with the same phenomenal speed as Beelzebub, leaving the two alone.

Clarise was too overwhelmed by the day's events to give the finality of his words a second thought. Both delighted and relieved to be reunited with her beloved husband, she gave him a tight squeeze, then pushed herself out to arms' length without releasing his elbows to run a critical eye over him. "Tell me everything," she insisted, turning her attention to the room for any hint of disturbance when he himself appeared to be fine. "What happened here?"

"Cora's a Mystallian."

"I know this …"

She hadn't realised she'd spoken until she felt the pressure of his finger against her lips. When she looked up at him in surprise, he was smiling down at her warmly. That smile grew until he bent down and lightly kissed her lips. "I know you do, sweetheart, but what I meant was—we of Mystal deal with things very differently to Highborn Hellions." He used the closeness to manoeuvre her back into his arms, something which Clarise didn't mind in the least. "And I didn't want to upset you with the way I handled Cora."

Again, Clarise stiffened against him, but this time, her fear was for Cora. As her father, it was Avis' right to discipline their daughter in any way he saw fit. *Any* way. "Is she alright?" The moment the words left her mouth, she realised how foolish they were. He had just finished telling her that their daughter's disobedience had been 'handled', so of course she wouldn't be alright. She amended her question to, "Will she recover in time for us to leave tomorrow?"

For some reason, Avis found her questions amusing. A ripple of mirth travelled through him until he was chuckling lightly against her. "She's fine, baby," he grinned, rubbing his chin over her dark hair and inhaling deeply. "Damn, you smell so good." His body language shifted gears with the proclamation and she felt him harden against her, but she couldn't follow his new train of thought. Instead, she grimaced at his terminology. Avis froze against her. "What?" he asked, curiously.

How to word this in a way he won't be offended ... "I know Mystallians choose to ... *flavour* their words more than Highborn Hellions do, but would you be ... angry ... with me if I said I did not like it?"

Avis appeared confused for a moment, but then his eyes went wide in a combination of hurt and dismay and he vigorously shook his head. "No! By the Twin Notes of creation, sweetheart. If you want me to never swear again, just say the word and consider it done. The last thing I ever want to do is upset you."

His earnest reply brought a fresh bout of tears to her eyes and she placed her hands on his cheeks. "I would never ask such a thing of you, my love. Profanity is part of the Mystallian way of life. But if it could be curtailed in my presence and that of Columbine, I would be eternally grateful."

"But not Cora?" Avis asked, arching one eyebrow at the exclusion.

Clarise pursed her lips and shook her head. "You said it yourself, beloved. She is a Mystallian, and profanity comes as naturally to your family as breathing. Ideally, I would love for neither of our children to develop that style of speech, but I am a realist. Columbine takes after me, so her values should be protected as if she were me."

Avis nodded in total agreement. "Done and done. You have my blessing to slap me senseless if I ever forget." He looked her in the eyes, his own burning with intensity. "And I'll make sure everyone else back home gets that message too. Don't worry about it."

A satisfied smile spread across her lips as she snuggled against her husband's sternum. "I know you will," she murmured, for she'd heard the truth as he knew it and loved him all the more for it. She almost hated to change the subject. "So, what did you do to Cora that is so different from the Highborn Hellion way of discipline?"

Twisting to one side, Avis chuckled as he slid an arm behind her knees and lifted her into the air. "A conversation that long deserves to be had in comfort," he stated, carrying her to the bed. "Preferably, the carnally sated kind."

CHAPTER TWENTY-ONE

Long after he had finished explaining his choices, Avis found himself staring at the silk canopy ceiling of their bed. Clarise slept with her head on his pec like a pillow; a position that was quickly becoming one of his favourite locations for her. Naked and glued to his side. His mind went back over the conversation they'd had in and around making love; specifically, her blistering screech when he'd told her *he'd* been the one to suffer during Cora's so-called 'discipline'. The image of her surging into a sitting position that straddled his hips; her beautiful long dark hair falling around her luscious white skin while her face portrayed such anger ... by the Twin Notes, he'd never been so turned on in his life!

He had to fight the urge to chuckle, for the movement would probably wake her. Instead, he focused on his breathing, drawing air slowly through his nose until he had himself back under control. If someone had told him a month ago that he could be this happy ....

... and whole.

Avis paused and suddenly frowned at that. *I'm whole?* He flexed his toes, then slowly rolled his ankles, tensing and testing the limits of each muscle in turn from his feet up to his neck, and out to his fingertips, finding no sense of debilitation anywhere. He really was whole. *Properly* whole. But how was that even possible, when merely hours ago he'd been in pieces at Sarvalis' feet? The last time he'd done The Walk, he'd been bedridden for at least several days afterwards. *So, why do I feel like I can take on all the Known Realms now?*

Belial's parting words then came back to him and the realisation that accompanied them had him gnashing his teeth furiously. *That motherless sunova ...!* he snarled inwardly, rubbing the fingers of one hand against his pinched lips to keep himself from swearing out loud.

Belial was the master of everything physical—and Avis hadn't remembered that shifting at that elevated level would also include absolute healing! *Damn it all!* Once Cora was done with him, he didn't have to be taken back to the Walk and suffer the humiliation of being leashed like a fucking dog afterwards! Belial could've put him back together again right here in the room with a thought, and the sick fuck wanted to make him suffer one last time for little more than shits and giggles before healing him properly. *Sunova bitch!*

"What troubles you, beloved?"

Avis dropped his chin and saw the most gorgeous molten gold eyes staring back at him, though she hadn't lifted her head from his chest. She reached up and traced his jawline with one exquisitely manicured nail. "You seem angry."

He caught those fingers and kissed the tip of each, his eyes never leaving hers. "Sorry to wake you, sweetheart," he murmured against the soft flesh. "But, since you're awake, we do really need to get out of Hell. The sooner, the better." He lifted his gaze to the curtain ceiling of their bed and sighed. "I swear, for a breed that has no mind benders, your family are masters at psychotic mind games and I've had an absolute gutful of them."

Clarise suddenly sat up at his side, her dark hair falling around her shoulders to form a curtain over her bosom which rose and fell with increasing intensity. The gold in her eyes crystallised and the rich red of her lips thinned angrily. "Who is still bothering you?" she demanded in a vexed growl, and he could see how determined she was to make whoever it was pay dearly for that grievance. Maybe even angry enough to throw out another of those *persona non-gratae* things she'd tossed at Innis.

As he stared up at her, a multitude of emotions swept through him all at once. Surprise; because she'd made that stand based on his word alone without any forced coercion on her part. Fear; because if she ever figured out her father was behind his latest mind fuck, she'd take it to the supreme demon and cruel amusement; as he pictured just how floored Belial would be when she did. But none of them could match the elation that made him want to fist pump the whole realm. Or flip his middle fingers at every demon within it. *That's my girl!*

He chuckled throatily with pride and hooked his hand around the nape of her neck, dragging her down to kiss her briefly. "No one you can deal with, beautiful," he promised, lightly massaging the base of her skull until she relaxed against his body. "We just need to be gone, before my head gets done in for good. That's all."

Clarise stared into his eyes for a long moment, then she tilted her head and kissed him fully—forcefully—her tongue sliding past his lips and teeth to knot with his. The bold move caught Avis off-guard, though he quickly recovered and returned that kiss, coiling his other arm around her to hold her close. Cognitive thought went right out the nearest window as he drew her close in anticipation of what came next … especially if the last few hours were anything to go by.

"I love you."

He barely heard her whisper the words after the kiss ended, and before he could fathom her mindset, she rolled her head under his restraining hand and twisted out of his grip. "I will begin the arrangements for our departure immediately," she said, sliding off the bed to her feet even as he rolled to one side and reached for her. Each piece of her scattered uniform broke down into a collective mist which she drew towards her, reforming it around her petite frame until she was fully dressed. A stimulation wave then rippled through her body as he watched, removing all traces of sleep and fixing her hair and makeup as if she had spent hours on it, not seconds.

Avis sat up with a sigh and dragged his right heel up the mattress towards him. It gave his right elbow something solid to lean on and hid his erection in the folds of the gathered sheet. There were a lot of women back home who were going to be hugely jealous of that trick. "It didn't have to be *that* immediate," he griped sulkily, patting the empty space on the bed beside him.

Her eyes followed the gesture, and when she noticed what his raised knee was unsuccessfully trying to hide, her lips twisted into a sultry smile. "Hold that thought, beloved," she said and blew him a kiss that ended in a fingertip wave. "I will return shortly." Without another word, she swept from the room. The servants appeared to shut the double doors behind her.

Unimpressed by her decision to leave, Avis huffed and rested his chin on the heel of his hand, drumming his fingers against his cheek. He stared at the doors for a few seconds in the veiled hope that she would change her mind and come back, but after a while he had to grudgingly admit that getting ready to leave was probably for the best after all. It just wasn't what he wanted to do right then …

… *or whom.*

His lips curled lewdly to one side and his eyes skewered the doors again, already envisioning what she'd be doing to make this wait worth his while.

Chuckling with heady desire, he rubbed the back of his neck and cleared his throat. If he didn't derail that train of thought soon, his imagination would have him humiliating himself long before she returned to take care of business for him. He was already hard enough to be used as a battering ram.

To distract himself, he thought about the lengthy conversation they'd had about Cora's dual capability and why the girl was so very Mystallian in his eyes. She'd taken the news better than he'd hoped, but he suspected that was mainly because they were merging the two already accepted concepts where celestial powers were concerned.

Likewise, when he'd moved on to the more difficult subject of Columbine's power, he'd started with the familiarity of a pictorial memory and went on to explain how it had been a gift from Belial. He'd been surprised by her comment of "Well, that explains a few things" but he hadn't pried into what those things were. Truth be told, he'd been too busy trying to work out how he'd broach the next two topics; Columbine's emotional knowledge and her ultimate shapeshifting mastery.

Once again, he chose familiarity as the safer option.

Columbine had already possessed the shapeshifting prowess of one of Belial's children due to his anointment at her birth, limiting Clarise's range over her to mere touch control. So, when Avis explained that their daughter's mastery now superseded Clarise (and everyone else who wasn't Belial) Clarise was understandably … *upset*. "Why would he do that?" she had demanded, sitting up in horror.

Not wanting to lie, but definitely not wanting to delve into the emotional array that Columbine seemed to have within her that defied every power they had, Avis hunted desperately for an alternative reply. "I'm still getting my head around it, sweetheart," he said honestly, sitting up alongside her. "Your father said something about her needing to be able to protect herself from everyone and how he was partially to blame for that … *don't ask me*," he quickly threw out, when she opened her mouth to do just that. "But your father wanted her to be able to defend herself against *anyone* who touched her without her permission."

"But we are her parents! We have every right to discipline her any way we see—"

Avis gently caught her by the cheeks and forced her to look up at him. "Clarise … sweetheart. Calm down and hear me out. That's why he got me to hide the memory, so we could raise her as normal. This is a move for the future, when she no longer answers to us as a child. Isn't there a point where demon lords stop answering to their mothers?"

"Twenty-five," Clarise agreed, though her expression was far from happy.

Avis could work with that benchmark. "Twenty-five, then. When she turns twenty-five, I'll pull down my memory block and let her remember the conversation with your father explaining all the changes. At least, that's my plan at the moment."

And it had been a sound one. Even now, as he leaned back on his pillows and cupped his hands behind his head, his gaze returning to the silk canopy overhead, he felt it was the right thing to do. Not that he could see her exploiting them, but shifting around everyone else was bad enough without … *OH, FUCK!*

A horrendous thought suddenly dawned on him, and he threw himself into a sitting position with a hand covering his mouth.

Screw her *advanced* shapeshifting possibilities! Because she'd been poisoned by tefsla, she wasn't able to shapeshift *at all!* And while it was true that her native demonic form might've been more predatory than her Mystallian one, a single shape with no mind-bending abilities to speak of was never going to keep her safe, let alone reach adulthood. The one thing Belial had been very adamant about.

Avis considered the journey ahead of them and shook his head. He was under no illusion as to how rough this sprint to Olympus was going to be. Once they left Chaos, there were at least four other realms they had to get through and almost all of them had a bone or fifty to pick with him. After his own family had turned their backs on him because of his treatment of Clarise, he'd felt he'd nothing to lose. Nothing at all.

It took the Hellions three years to corner him and during that time he'd been a shocking example of a celest—worse than any combination that had ever come before. Thinking nothing could stop him, he'd gone out of control. Women had been raped, minds destroyed, and worshippers converted. Hate had been his only companion back then, and the two had gone on a rampage that left scars and enemies everywhere.

If those enemies ever discovered how important Clarise and the girls were to him, their status as Highborn Hellions would be their only chance of survival, and it was a protection Cora no longer had. On top of that, even if they reached Olympus, he still didn't know for certain if the Mystallians would take him back, let alone *if* it was possible to change a powerbase on this scale to reflect his new life as a family man. Mystal wasn't exactly a pocket realm.

A mystallion flying at full speed through the realm could cover a dozen galaxies in the space of a heartbeat, yet it took their sacred beasts almost a day to traverse Mystal from end to end and only if one of the pantheon were with them to use their attunement to temporarily fold large sections of mortal space in on itself. If his family wouldn't or *couldn't* change his powerbase, he'd have to ask—no, *beg* Clarise for the chance to start a new life together in the Unknown Realms. Far from the reach of his enemies.

That thought chilled him to the core, for he remembered how hard those first few millennia had been after he and his siblings had escaped the Nexus. Without an establishment field to feed their power or even a basic attunement to a mortal realm, they'd had to fend for themselves. His wife and daughters were too delicate for that level of rough living.

But he was getting way ahead of himself. First step was to get them all to Olympus. He had no doubt Zeus would give him sanctuary once there, despite his recent bout of … *inappropriate* behaviour. They had too much history for him not to. From there, he would reach out to his family and endure whatever they wanted to shout at him, provided they agreed to changing his powerbase thrall so he could bring his precious family home.

His mind moved on to Cora, whose chances of surviving this journey grew less likely with every passing second. That poor kid was stuck in a maimed Mystallian five-year-old's body with barely an inkling of her mental powers. In other words, virtually defenceless. It was worse than cruel, but Belial was the only one who could rectify that. *Fear the repercussions.*

Avis pulled ran his thumbnail across his bottom lip, mulling over those ominous words. He needed to bring the girls' situations to Belial's attention, but there was no denying he was absolutely terrified of doing so. Just because he'd gotten away with it once, didn't mean—

FOR FUCK'S SAKE! STOP BEING SUCH A GUTLESS FUCKING CHICKEN-SHIT!

Avis cursed at the subconscious thought that breezed through his mind, reiterating his own feelings on the matter. He *was* being a coward, and if he kept it up, his family would pay the ultimate price for it. Once admitted, the word *coward* taunted him from every corner of his mind until he could stand it no more.

He threw his hand away from his face and punched the mattress beside him, surging to his feet. *No fucking way.* The Mystallian God of Life who got his siblings out of the Nexus and went on to forge one of the biggest realms in existence was not about to wimp out now.

He stood up and dressed quickly. "Belial," he called once that was done, rolling his hand in a half circle to complete the link. When no response was forthcoming, he tried again. Still no answer. "Sunova bitch," he snarled under his breath.

There was no way the supreme demon didn't know *someone* was trying to reach him. Avis secretly suspected he already knew who it was and was deliberately ignoring him. *Bastard.* And since he wouldn't accept the blood-link, Avis would have to leave the safety of the room and go find him. *Great.*

Tensing his arms, Avis rolled his shoulders and loosened the muscles in his neck. *Fine.* They could hate him as much as they liked. They were *still* going to hear what he had to say. He left the apartment with his cloak swirling around his heels and the echo of his boots in the cavern around them. The heat of the place was incredible, made worse by his black leathers, but he refused to acknowledge it. He was on a mission now: as a Mystallian.

The problem was, every tunnel and cavern in the Well looked practically the same. How could anyone distinguish one rock wall from the next, when they were all just … rocks … piled on top of more rocks!

There were no specific reference points to guide him through the glowing caverns, and every time he found himself hopelessly lost, he also lost a little more of his temper. A sign post … or better yet, a fucking 'you are here' directory poster to give visitors some bearings would be really useful! *But no …!*

Fed up with this insanity, Avis glared at the very next Hellion he came across and mentally latched on to it. **Take me to Hell's High Court**, he commanded, for that and the conservatory were the only two places outside of Clarise's rooms and the guest wing (where he and his family had stayed years earlier) that he knew of, and the chances of finding Belial in a garden or the guest wing were … slim.

He followed the crawling creature through the cavernous maze, unintimidated by the heated glares of the Highborn Lords who crossed his path. Instead, he met their glares dead on; all but daring them to try something. He wasn't prepared to start anything, but if they wanted to dance, he had no problem with that. Word must have spread of Innis' demoted status though, for all they did was glare hatefully.

Well, fuck 'em all! If he so much as stumbled because they changed the stonework under his feet, it'd be on. Lethally. He wasn't one of the Damned anymore, and they'd all do well to remember that.

It took a few minutes, but eventually he recognised the outer walls of Hell's High Court and released his mental hold on the hapless servant (who squeaked in surprise at its location and quickly scurried away). All things considered, it was a little hard to miss the enormous, double arched opening that had the upside down five-pointed star glowing over the apex.

Powerful in its simplicity. The enormity of the doorway almost defied logic. Three—maybe four storeys tall and just as many again wide. The sheer magnitude of it reminded him of standing at the edge of the emotional abyss in Columbine's essence, though he could well understand the need for such an entrance.

The Highborn Hellion Lords had enormous numbers to their ranks, so it stood to reason that unless they wanted to spend days entering and leaving the court via a small bottleneck, such a massive opening would exist.

No voices came from within the great room, so at the very least he wouldn't be interrupting anything. He looked up at the house sigil again and swallowed hard. Now that the moment was upon him, mixed emotions vied for control. He needed his father-by-marriage to be in there for the girls' sake, but he was just as hopeful for his absence. He couldn't help it. When the supreme Lord of Hell said, *Fear the repercussions,* only a fool ignored it. Avis wasn't a fool. Not anymore.

Gathering his courage, he took a deep breath and forced his foot across the threshold.

The cavern was indeed as empty as he presumed, but a coldness lingered in the air that didn't belong in the Well. A very *familiar* subzero chill—and this time there were no witnesses to what came next. Avis' heart hammered as he recognised that icy sensation and his first instinct was to flee. Still, he planted his feet ... took a deep breath ... held it ... and pressed on.

"I need the tefsla removed from the girls," he said, lifting his eyes firstly to the massive empty throne directly in front of him, then across to the equally empty stone perches that went as far as he could see in both directions. *He's in here somewhere.* When heavy silence met his demand, he wondered where and in what form his father-by-marriage would appear in, if he did at all. "Inhibited by it, they'll be defenceless against anything that attacks us."

"Is that not your job as their sire to protect them from such circumstances?" Belial suddenly asked, and when Avis snapped his gaze back to the dais, the supreme demon filled his throne.

Avis felt the savagery of that gaze raking across him, though he never looked higher than Belial's chest. As the great demon slowly stroked the armrests, he sliced through the souls with his claws, causing the throne arms to shudder and whimper under the calm but brutal ministrations. Avis knew the cruel display was being done as a warning for him to tread with great care. Great, *great* care.

Message very much received, you ass.

Avis slid his gloved hands behind his back under his cloak and wrapped them around the other wrist, locking them together. He squeezed them tightly to prevent his body from trembling. He could do this. Despite the fact Belial was scaring the ever-loving shit out of him, he *was going* to do this.

"It was you who spoke of the importance of Columbine reaching adulthood, M'lord. I will be doing everything in my power to make that happen, but at the end of the day, things can often come down to one's own personal capabilities. You wanted Columbine to be able to defend herself from all, which is not something she can do while she remains locked as a single-formed demon indefinitely. Cora fares no better, since she barely knows what to do with her mental attributes and her physical ones have been hobbled to the point of lunacy.."

Avis endured Belial's gaze for what felt like an eternity, until the Mystallian thought he would pass out from failure to breathe if he didn't say something soon.

"Beelzebub. To me."

The Military Commander appeared at Belial's side as if he had been waiting just inside the mortal realm for the summons. "Milord," he said, dipping his horned head reverently.

"Clarise and her family will be leaving in a few hours. Send four Highborn Hellion Guards with them as a protective escort. They will return to Hell only after the family has reached the safety of Mystal."

For a moment, Beelzebub's eyes widened in surprise and Avis felt a second fiery gaze sweep across him. But then it was gone, and the Military Commander bowed formally at the shoulder. "It shall be as you wish, Milord."

Avis was too busy battling his own shock at the proclamation to dwell on Beelzebub's reaction. Brute squad fighters, as they were better known throughout the realms, were rarely ever seen outside of Hell without a realm-wide bloodbath being declared.

Yet Avis and his family were going to be getting *four!* It was almost too much to comprehend! But his father-by-marriage still hadn't agreed to free the girls from their disciplines, and that was what he wanted—what he had risked coming into the High Court for. Was he really going to back off now?

Not fucking likely.

"Will you give Cora back her arm at least, M'lord?"

Belial lifted one hand and flicked two talons dismissively at his son-by-marriage.

Before Avis could react, he was snatched off the ground by an unseen force and tossed through the oversized opening like a leaf in a hurricane. Surprise surged through the Mystallian as he was dumped unceremoniously outside, but at least he had the wherewithal to keep his feet under him as he dropped, instead of looking like a complete idiot who had been thrown out on his ass.

"I'll take that as a 'No'," he murmured under his breath as he straightened, knowing better than to try and force his way back into the High Court. He looked in both directions along the tunnel he stood in, trying to remember which way he'd come. *Jerk.*

CHAPTER TWENTY-TWO

Belial watched as Avis flicked his head from side to side, before the boy decided on the path that led back down into the family levels. He sat very still, long after Avis had left his visual sight. His power gave him the ability to see anything he wished within the borders of Chaos and for a few minutes he entertained himself by watching the Mystallian stumble from one cavern to another, desperately searching for anyone he could mentally dominate into a guide.

It was with no small amount of satisfaction that Belial cleared the caverns of staff and family on either side of the Mystallian long before Avis walked into them—for no other reason than to watch his son-by-marriage's growing frustration. He even restructured the walls and ceilings so that vast stretches and turns were all identical, just to antagonise him further. The ploy worked better than he hoped, for Avis tilted his head back and roared his frustration at the ceiling, then slammed his fist through the nearest stone wall. *That boy is sooooo like his father,* the supreme demon mused with a smoky snort of laughter.

However, as entertaining as it was to watch his son-by-marriage turn himself inside out, he knew he had to acknowledge his silent but steadfast Military Commander still standing at his side. He hadn't left, which meant the situation bothered him enough to stay.

It also meant things were about to go to the next level.

Belial rose from his throne and flared his wings, then cracked his neck in several directions. "You have been my champion since the beginning of creation, Beelzebub," he declared without turning to look at the demon in question. "Speak your mind."

"*Four* Highborn Hellion Guards, Milord?" The words were spoken in disbelief. "It only took six to destroy all of Teon, and they amassed an army thinking it would save them. I know you love your family, but none of them warrants this level of protection."

"Columbine does," he corrected, wondering if Theodrick had had a similar discussion with his champion; the first of his crystalline warriors he'd so originally named *One*.

"I do not understand."

Belial knew this. After all, his champion hadn't heard Columbine's Upper Realm command that notified both the Shifter and the Bender of her existence. He himself had choked when he heard her feminine voice on a level that only he and Theodrick had previously shared. "Cora lost her arm reaching too high for a weapon she had no business going for and being sapient, the weapons wall wanted to kill her for being so audacious."

Beelzebub nodded. "I know this, Milord. Even now, the girl's wherewithal to see past the pain of her impending death long enough to sever her arm and thus escape that fate ... it continues to astound me."

"Then you may cease your sycophantic praise. Cora's survival had nothing to do with her. It was all Columbine."

Beelzebub frowned again. "I still do not understand."

"Cora was dying. The wall was killing her, as it was supposed to. That was, until Columbine *commanded* it to stop."

Instead of comprehending, Beelzebub's confusion intensified. He opened his mouth to speak, only to snap it shut again. Belial could well understand his perplexity. No one except Belial and Theodrick were supposed to be able to command that weapons wall, and certainly not a tiny, little girl-child.

But rather than offering any further information, Belial folded his massive arms and watched his champion struggle with the enigma he'd been presented. The warrior's gaze searched the room for the elusive answer he refused to bring himself to ask. *Any time now.* Belial almost grinned when Beelzebub froze, indicating the only possible explanation had finally dawned on him. Shock swept across the ancient warrior as he swung back to face Belial, his mouth hanging open incredulously.

Belial met that stunned silence with a nod and a superlative smile. "We have been waiting a long time for her, my friend, and now, she is here. Finally."

Beelzebub closed his mouth, then licked his lips with his forked tongue, his chest heaving on the revelation. "But we obliterated her army and killed her champion, Milord! I never expected her to be so ... *young*. She is but a babe. Totally and utterly defenceless—"

Belial curled his lip and held up one taloned finger. "We took out the garbage," he corrected. "And given we are all still alive to talk about it, one must assume it was all part of a bigger plan that not even *we* are aware of."

That seemed to settle Beelzebub, for he drew in a deep breath and calmed himself. "Is four all you wish to send, Milord?" he asked, completely reversing his earlier opinion of four being too many. "I could dispatch a full contingent or two to go with them. Ensure absolutely *nothing* comes anywhere near them ..."

"Four will be enough," Belial insisted. "Enough questions will be asked over the presence of a mere four. Any more will cause the pantheons to make unnecessary assumptions that will get them killed. Let the guards know their only priority during this time is Columbine. Any threat to her will be dealt with as if the Well of Hell itself was being threatened."

"And if that danger should extend to her family?" Beelzebub asked, not in defiance of his lord but for clarification. "Currently, she is a well-balanced child with two loving parents who sees existence through the most adoring of perceptions. Should those circumstances change for the worse, she may evolve into something very few of us will survive."

Belial hadn't thought of that. Children were always so impressionable—girl-children even more so—and these first years were ludicrously important to their long-term development.

If Columbine saw the Known Realms' violent reaction to her father being inside their territories firsthand, she might grow to hate them all. *No*, he amended. She *would* grow to hate them all, and once released, that hatred would spread faster and more catastrophically than any plague. Her formative years needed to be protected as much as she did, for all their sakes.

The next words out of his mouth made him sick to the stomach. "Protect the entire family unit ... *yes, that includes her father*," he added with a near growl when Beelzebub quirked an eye ridge mockingly. "Columbine is the ultimate priority, but for her emotional well-being, include the rest of her family travelling with her."

Beelzebub dipped his head. When he straightened again, he couldn't hide his smile. "The Weaver is finally here."

Appreciating that statement and what it would mean for all their futures, Belial matched that grin and nodded. "She is indeed."

* * *

For a place that normally swarmed with demons, Avis wasn't happy about how long it took him to find one that he could use as a guide. It was almost as if they were all deliberately hiding from him—a fact he knew was not the case, for he checked the memories of the first creature he finally came across and found no duplicity involving him. They just … hadn't been where Avis was.

His gut instinct blamed Belial. It could never be proven, and he certainly wasn't going back to ask, but something told him his father-by-marriage was behind this latest round of aggravation.

Nevertheless, he had a demon's mind firmly under his control now, so he was set. The legless demon he followed had a long, scorpion tail curled over its back with its head attached to the tip where the barb should be. It never looked back at Avis as it slithered along, leading him down the twists and turns until things started to take on a hint of familiarity.

When he saw Clarise hurrying down the corridor towards him, he released his hold on the creature and ran to her. "Is everything alright?" he asked, catching her easily around her shoulders and drawing her close.

Clarise wrapped her own arms around his waist and hugged him in turn. "Everything is being organised as we speak, beloved. Frash and Tilu are gathering our things and Gingen and Diviten are preparing the girls. Uriel has given us access to the demonic stables and will personally select the best demon steeds for us to ride. The first part of our journey will be by raft over the Akheron River."

Avis frowned in concern. "The Akheron?" he repeated, certain he'd misheard. "Why in the realms would we trek all the way through the Nine Levels to use the Akheron when the Cocytos River is just outside The Well?"

Clarise seemed pleased that he knew the geography of her home capital. She wouldn't have been so thrilled to know the knowledge came from every level and sublevel of Hell being burned into him with acid during his time amongst the Damned. His jaw tightened with the memory. *Literally.*

They'd etched the map into his back while he was on his hands and knees and forced him to replicate every line on the floor at their feet with the blood of his own slashed fingers. *More than once.* But that, like other unpleasant aspects of his life, was history to be learned from, not dwelled upon. He forced his teeth apart and worked his jaw until the tension completely left him. *Ancient history*, he reminded himself.

"Why does that concern you, Avis?" she asked.

Avis didn't want to answer that. To do so, he'd have to explain all the different hells contained within those damned levels. His beloved wife may have had a small inkling since she knew about things like The Walk, but he doubted her innocence could handle everything that went on out there. And the girls would've had no clue at all.

If that didn't make him the greatest hypocrite in existence, that he wanted to protect them from the ugly truth when all along he'd wanted them to make their stands, he didn't know what did. But none of the darkness he'd once endured was going to touch them if he had his way. "I would have thought Cocytos would have been the better choice. I mean, it's right outside The Well ..."

Clarise slid to his side and wrapped her left arm around his right. Not as intimate as a moment ago, but close enough that it would do, for now. "I did mention that to Father, my love, however he has specifically forbidden us from taking the Cocytos River. Something about the misery of its waters potentially affecting us or vice-versa ... *or something.* To be honest, he was not making a whole lot of sense on the matter."

Avis stared straight ahead; his shoulders squaring and his gaze sharpening. Belial was making plenty of sense to him. To go anywhere near the Cocytos River was to invite a suicidal level of melancholy upon oneself.

The river itself was imbued with misery, and misery was an emotion. After his brief introduction to whatever was attached to Columbine's essence, he knew his precious little girl would be inundated by the emotion. Probably crippling her beyond recovery. The thought of her suffering so horribly sent a very real shiver through him.

He jerked when a gloved finger pressed into his cheek. "What are you thinking, beloved?" Clarise asked, running the finger down to his jaw while staring up at him.

Pushing those disturbing thoughts aside, he genuinely attempted to smile. "Nothing that won't make me sound like a raving lunatic," he promised, dancing around the truth without lying. He tilted his head to the side and pressed his lips into her hair. "So, how long before we head out?" Yes, he was deliberately changing the subject. Too bad.

At least Clarise didn't argue with him. "Our things are already being taken to the stables at the entrance of The Well. Even if we take our time, we should arrive well ahead of the girls and be ready to depart soon afterwards."

Dawdling with the most beautiful woman ever created at his side was the last thing Avis had in mind. As far as he was concerned, this was their honeymoon— their *real* honeymoon—and like every newly married male that came before him, every second counted.

Besides, she owed him for that earlier cock-blocking, and he intended to collect. "And if we went back to our rooms first?" he asked, waggling his eyebrows and licking his lips very suggestively. "After all, you did promise to make it up to me, sweetheart."

Clarise stared at him for a moment, then clapped her free hand over her mouth, but couldn't suppress the burst of laughter that bubbled up from within. "Avis, you are incorrigible!" she giggled through her fingers.

Not technically hearing a denial in that, Avis grew bolder and moved into her space, dominating it with his sheer size. He stared down at her, his free arm snaking around her cloak to hold her close. "So, do we have time to go back for one last ... *dance* in our old apartment before we go, M'lady?"

Her amusement gave way to sensuality as she lowered her hand from her face and rested her chin against his chest, her eyes glued to his. Just as he thought she was going to concede, she shook her head slightly, those golden dancing with mischief. "I am afraid not, beloved," she purred against his sternum.

The admission would have derailed his hopes, had she not worn a saucy grin that belied her words. "But fortunately for you, you had the good sense to seduce and marry a Highborn Hellion who is able to commandeer the use of any cavern around us I wish—any time I wish." Her smile turned just as flirtatious. "That is, provided my beloved husband is up to the task of ... *dancing* well enough to satisfy us both in little more than a cave."

Normally, Avis despised challenges. They were a threat to his capability and no matter who said them or how prettily they were worded, he always made sure the person who issued them lived just long enough to regret it. But Clarise's first attempt at sexual innuendo had his body soaring from piqued interest to a rock-solid mass of wanton desire in two seconds flat and he barely held in the ungodly groan. Releasing one arm, he twirled her away from him; swatting her backside as her cloak flew up to reveal it. "Get me to that cave, sweetheart, and I'll show you a dance you'll never forget."

CHAPTER TWENTY-THREE

Avis and Clarise arrived at the stables ahead of the girls, despite their *dance* that covered every square centimetre of the chamber Clarise had sequestered. Uriel was already in the stables, drawing out the last of the four demon steeds for them to take. The archangel saw them coming and smiled in greeting at his sister with love in his eyes. Avis on the other hand, received a filthy glare that no one could misinterpret. The Mystallian rolled his eyes. *Whatever.* He turned his attention to the selected demon steeds instead.

The beasts were beautiful—if one was into fire. They stood as strong in the leg as any mystallion and ranged in colours from pale yellow to the richest of reds. Flames spouted from their nostrils and merged above their muzzle, creating a line of fire that ran up between their eyes, past their pointed ears and down to form a thick mane of fire. Their bodies were a solid mass of muscle.

Fire leapt from their hooves to their knees, giving them the appearance of wearing bizarre boots of flames and their flaming tails stretched almost to the ground, blending into the fire of their rear hooves. When any of them flicked their heads or tails, embers would cascade around them.

"Do the girls know how to ride in their current forms?" Avis asked, as hundreds of possible calamities that all started with them being thrown mid-ride inundated him. "They won't be able to shapeshift to keep themselves mounted if they don't."

Clarise placed her ear against his chest and lightly feathered her fingers across the front of his doublet. "Demon steeds are the preferred riding beast of the Hellion Highborn," she answered factually. "No matter what form the Hellion Highborn is in, the demon steed will acknowledge their bloodline and behave accordingly. I would not, however, recommend a non-Highborn Hellion attempt to master them."

So that answered his next two questions at the same time. One, Cora would be able to ride the demon steeds as a Mystallian because the stupid beasts would recognise her Highborn Hellion blood and temper their flames to prevent injury. And two, since he wasn't a Highborn Hellion, his ass would be fried upon contact. Avis' vision slitted. *Great,*

Well, that wasn't going to be a deal-breaker. If the stupid animal didn't want to behave, so long as it had a mind to decide that, *he* wouldn't give it a choice. No way was he going to give Uriel and any other Hellion Lord the satisfaction of watching him being thrown from the steed or burnt to a crisp. Avis snorted sharply at the mere thought of it and Clarise chuckled at him.

"You forget my blood flows in your veins, beloved," she said, correctly guessing where his thoughts were at. "They will see you as my husband and not act out. You have my word."

Avis eyed the demon steeds suspiciously for a few more seconds before accepting her claims. *Okay, one less headache to deal with,* he thought, moving his gaze away from the animals and towards his angelic brother-by-marriage nearby. As much as he despised everything about the male, they both loved Clarise and the girls enough to do anything for them.

Even speak civilly to each other for longer than ten seconds. Hopefully. The Nine Levels of Hell was no place for the women and surely Uriel had to agree with that. Avis quietly nuzzled Clarise' hair, absorbing more of her lavender scent. "Sweetheart, would you excuse me a moment? I just need to … have a private word with your brother."

Clarise's eyebrow arched sharply, but after looking inquisitively at her brother, she dipped her head once in agreement and slid her arm from around his back. "I will wait here, beloved."

Avis didn't want to be separated from her any more than she wanted to be separated from him, but as he stepped away from her and approached the archangel, he accepted it was something they were both going to have to get used to. Unfortunately. They weren't always going to be together.

Uriel scowled at him the whole way. "You test my patience," the archangel warned, without using his name.

"Just as you test mine," Avis replied, matching his brother-by-marriage's surliness. His days of being amongst the Damned were over and he marched straight up to the archangel to prove both to himself and his brother-by-marriage that he could.

His eyes were locked on Uriel's rich, ice-blue gaze and he felt no fear in doing so. "How do you feel about the women being taken through the various levels of Hell to reach the Akheron River?"

Uriel ground his teeth and turned back to the demon steed. "My thoughts on the matter are not up for discussion."

Avis placed his hand on the neck of the demon steed, close enough to Uriel that the demonic crown prince couldn't miss it, but not starting something between them by actually touching him. "Hear me out, Uriel, and keep in mind I'm saying this for the sake of your sister and your nieces—not myself." Uriel paused, but didn't look at him. Avis took it as an acquiesce—of sorts.

"What if I go through the levels alone, leading the demon steeds. It'll take me a few hours to reach the first gates and after that I'll blood-link the ladies and their servants and guards to me. We all still end up on the shores of the Akheron River, but they won't have to deal with the horrors you and I both know are out there."

Uriel's armoured fist clenched around the reins and he whirled to face Avis; waves of fury emanating from him.

"If you think for one realm-damned second …" —his voice hit all the dark notes of his demonic heritage and his teeth sharpened into pointed fangs— "… that I am going to let you get anywhere *near* the front gates of Hell alone, just so you can flee and break those ladies' hearts again …"

Avis should have known he'd jump to that conclusion. Only two years ago, it would have been the reality. But not anymore. Avis parted his feet for better balance and pressed a fist lightly into his side, silently daring Uriel to take that step into his space.

"I have no intention of running anywhere. What I *am* going to do is taking my family home and I could care less how you feel about it. Hell is the city of torture. Everyone knows that. But unless you've personally been touched by it, you'll never appreciate the depths that this place will go to destroy you. I don't want any of that ugliness touching my family. Not with the girls—"

"Not with the girls ... *what?*" Uriel demanded; sparks of hellfire flashing through his eyes like flint against granite.

"You know they've both been hobbled by tefsla," Avis replied, completely unfazed by his brother-by-marriage's hostility. "Because of that, they'll hear and see everything and not be able to turn a blind eye or deafen themselves when the screams become too much for their innocent natures to handle. I'd rather not have either of them influenced by the plight of the Damned while they are so physically debilitated." He had no intention of mentioning the added problem of Columbine's emotional issues.

Uriel tilted his head to one side and deliberately ran his eyes down the full length of his brother-by-marriage. When they reached Avis' boots, they lifted just as slowly, halting at his face. The glower that swept across the archangel would have melted stone. "I meant what I said about taking you out into the Unknown Realms for all eternity if you hurt them again. You know that, right?"

Avis allowed his eyes to half close as if the subject bored him and only suppressed the desire to yawn because he knew the ensuing brawl might upset Clarise. "If it concerns you that much, come with me. I don't plan on running." He paused to give his next sentence extra credence. "But do get it into that thick skull of yours that they're mine and they're coming home with me."

More hellfire sparked in Uriel's eyes and his upper lip curled in disgust. "You think you own them?"

"Oh, hell yeah," Avis declared, his eyes widening with conviction as he nodded slowly. "Your sister's already proven the lengths she'll go to for me, and I'm willing to go much further for them."

Again, that slow, realm-damned, full-body examination that began and ended with his face. Avis mashed his lips together, his own patience waning. *I swear, do that one more fucking time, you feather-brained fuckwit.* The fingers of his free hand tensed, though he refrained from curling it into a fist. Barely.

Uriel must have guessed the darkness of his thoughts for he took that step, getting right up into Avis' grill. "You cannot possibly hate me more than I hate you," he snarled, his eyes exploding into balls of demonic hellfire, though he kept his words low for Clarise's sake. He opened his mouth to say more, then must have realised his temper had gotten the better of him, for he closed it again and lifted his chin towards the cavern ceiling.

He blinked several times, drawing in a rapid succession of deep breaths until he was back under control. Then, when he lowered his head, his angelic, ice-blue eyes locked on to Avis and his teeth once again level and perfect.

"However, despite my disgust in you, your words do have merit. You and I will take the demon steeds and their equipment through the levels. Once we reach the shores of the Akheron River, I will blood-link with my sister and bring her and her children across."

Avis didn't miss the deliberate exclusion of *his* position within that family unit. *This is going to be a fun few hours.* Nevertheless ... "Done."

As the Mystallian turned and made his way back to Clarise, Uriel sneered quietly after him, "Do run, Avis. Please. Because you will not get *another* opportunity to hide behind my sister's skirt, I promise you."

Avis's next step faltered a fraction as rage swept through him. Everything in him wanted to swing around and rip a millennium of memory from the smug bastard, burning it to ash right in front of his mental eyes.

But Clarise was ahead of him, looking at him in concern, so he ground his teeth until his jaw hurt and forced himself to keep walking as if nothing was wrong. It was one of the hardest things he'd ever done, and it only reemphasised what a bitch his next few hours were going to be.

"What was that all about?" Clarise asked, her gaze shifting between him and her eldest brother.

"I'm sure you can guess," he replied without answering as he folded her back into his arms. The last thing he wanted was Clarise to be at war with her brother on his behalf when he knew how much they cared for each other. "But let it go, sweetheart. If I wanted to have a problem with it, I'd take care of it myself."

Clarise shot her brother a chilling look filled with protective suspicion to which the archangel's eyebrows rose in surprise. Their silent exchange lifted Avis's dark mood until he wanted to stamp his feet and howl in delight. His chest swelled with pride and his arms tightened around her. He knew the look he shot the stunned demonic prince had him practically gloating. *That's right asshole,* he all but projected. *She's growing a Mystallian backbone. Get used to it, because there's going to be a lot more where that came from.*

CHAPTER TWENTY-FOUR

The girls and their respective governesses chose that moment to join them, so both sides allowed the tension to pass before the children picked up on it. Columbine ambled in on her hands and reverse walking legs with her wings bouncing in time to the step. Cora wore a floor-length dress of red with multiple layers of petticoats.

Her fringe had been braided to frame the crown of her head, leaving the rest free-flowing to the middle of her back. Avis knew it was Clarise's preferred hairstyle, because he'd seen it on Columbine earlier that week. It suited both his wife and his younger daughter, but on Cora it looked utterly horrific and they both knew it. Like a pit-bull being wedged into a tutu.

Envisioning his sister of War showing much the same temperament, he wondered how much blood had been shed to force Cora into that outfit. Either way, he'd be fixing it before they left.

Clarise's servants, Frash and Tilu, along with the four Highborn Hellion Guards had yet to make an appearance. As they waited, Avis gave the girls a cursory once over to get a measure of how they were handling things so far.

Columbine, he could see, was excited to be going on this journey with them. No surprise there. He suspected his little princess would've followed him anywhere he permitted her to.

Cora, on the other hand, sulkily shifted her gaze from one point of the room to the next and remained sullen. She didn't quite scowl, though her arms were folded over her tiny chest as if daring anyone to say a word to her. It was cute in a laughable way—especially in that ridiculous get-up.

Or at least it had been, until she turned that look to him and the surliness manifested into icy hatred.

Okay … that's going to be a problem.

In his mind, their biggest issue was behind them. Dealt with. If she thought otherwise, he needed to get to the bottom of it before they left the safety of Hell. Avis allowed his mental control to drift over her without making the move obvious. He didn't want to totally dominate her. Just enough to observe her thoughts from the outside.

The fact he could meant Belial had removed the seclusion ring from her body while he'd been recovering from her attack. *Good.* No bender liked the presence of a seclusion ring and anyone caught with one was immediately treated with open hostility. For most of the pantheons, that explanation needed to be a real doozy, or the culprit died soon afterwards as a warning to others.

Case in point—Avis remembered a young celest from Alchera who thought the ring would protect her from the Mystallians, since his pantheon consisted primarily of benders. It had been one of the shortest mistakes in the history of all histories.

She'd smugly faced off with Death and his son, the god of assassination and gloated how the ring's presence meant they couldn't do a frickin' thing to her. A well-placed dagger between her eyes and another through her ribs for good measure, said otherwise.

Basically, no one of consequence was stupid enough to walk into someone else's territory wearing one. It was too easy to be caught, and too many other ways to be dealt with.

Next time, I will not sully a sword on you, you animal. I will lay my hands upon you, and then you will be mine to control, just like Columbine was.

When Avis saw Cora's thoughts, he didn't know whether to laugh or be offended by the sheer audacity of the girl … mainly because he was too busy being gobsmacked. *Wait—what?* His moment of bafflement morphed into parental condescension as more of those superior opinions of herself crossed her mind. *Oh, reeeally!*

The little shit had the nerve to think she had mental supremacy over him? Ha! He'd known she had little understanding of *how* his power worked, but he'd always assumed she knew that bending followed the same basic principles as the demonic shapeshifting.

That was, *like fuck* she would ever take him down. The only rational explanation for her mindset was she had no idea that bending came from his side of the family. But … was she really that ignorant? *Wow.* The girl needed an education, and she needed it now.

Not tipping his hand just yet, he cuddled Clarise close and said, "Would you mind staying here for a second, sweetheart? It seems Cora and I just need to hash out a few … last-minute details in private before we leave."

Despite attempting to make it sound like they'd be having a casual conversation at most, Clarise's head snapped back and she stared at him with eyes that were suddenly filled with concern—*for him.*

His heart swelled with both amusement and love in equal parts, but he dropped another quick kiss on her lips before she could say what was so clearly written all over her face. "We'll both be fine," he promised, pressing his forehead to hers. "She's had her piece of me and she's not getting another. I'm just going to talk to her—for the most part."

Clarise looked over her shoulder at the girls that stood beside their governesses a short distance away. "Very well," she said, turning inside Avis' embrace to face them. "Columbine," she called. With one hand raised, she beckoned the youngster forward with the tips of her fingers. "Come here, sweetheart."

While Columbine came forward, Avis brushed his lips across Clarise's hair and stepped around her to make his way to Cora. It amused him to think just how much the situation resembled a prisoner exchange as the two approached each other from opposite sides of the room.

He offered Columbine a warm smile and a wink as he passed her, then ran his hand over her leathery scalp to scratch the base of her skull for a few precious seconds. Columbine hunched beneath the attention and made a series of demonic snorts and wheezes that sounded remarkably like childish giggling.

He chuckled to himself and gave her a light push towards her mother, then lifted his gaze to the more problematic of his two children.

The derision in Cora's thoughts sobered him instantly and approaching her, he said, "We need to talk, young lady." Without giving her a chance to respond, he took her by the shoulder the moment he could, spun her around to face the same way he was, then propelled her with a shove towards one of the empty stalls.

She stumbled a little because of that stupid dress and heels, but he quickly caught up to steady her, in case she face-planted. Just as soon as he'd finished this little *chat* with her, he'd be getting her out of that idiotic outfit and into hunting leathers. High class ladies may have enjoyed wearing such finery, but not a Mystallian like Cora or Armina.

He envisioned the outcome of someone moronic enough to try and shoehorn his sister of War into that outfit and shuddered inwardly. Armina wouldn't stop at the specific idiots who tried. She'd move on to their family, then the neighbourhood, and maybe ... *maybe* call it a day when their entire *species* had been eradicated.

Armina wasn't the kind to take any chances on repeat occurrences. Avis looked down at Cora, and as they proceeded into the stall, he called over his shoulder to Clarise, "Sweetheart, could you give us a bit more privacy?"

Clarise remained silent, but the moment he and Cora crossed the gate's threshold, liquid mass oozed out of the ground and wove its way through the open rails of the stall until it reached the ceiling overhead.

In just a few seconds, it swelled and solidified into a thick rock wall with a solid timber door. Complete privacy. The enclosure would've cast the room in darkness, had Clarise not also included the luminescence of Hell's stonework into the inner wall.

Cora broke away from him and stalked to the far side of the enclosure. There, she whirled on her toes and slammed her shoulders into the wall, folding her arms across her chest and crossing her short, narrow-heeled shoes at the ankles in defiance of him. Her chin came up in a manner that suggested the whole realm was hers for the taking and he was just too stupid to realise it yet.

Avis sank his teeth into his bottom lip, using the pain to distract his rising temper. It didn't entirely work. *That cock-sure of yourself, huh, you little minx? Time to fix tha ... Wait!* He stiffened, his lips sliding out from between his teeth as his eyes dropped from hers to her folded arms. *Both* her folded arms.

Why, that no good, sneaky prick! he fumed, knowing his father-by-marriage was the only one who could have given her back her missing arm with the tefsla in place. *Sneaky, sneaky sunova bitch.* Avis shook his head and smirked wryly, unable to help himself. Without even knowing it, he'd gotten at least some of what he asked for anyway.

Cora didn't appreciate his spontaneous amusement and threw herself back on to her feet. Her arms dropped to her sides and her fists clenched as she stomped her right foot at him. "How dare you laugh at me!"

Still chuckling, but now for an entirely different reason, Avis looked at her and shook his head. If this wasn't so serious, he'd be laughing his ass off at the nerve of the little twerp. "Cora, I think you need to understand a few ground rules where my family is concerned. First and foremost, once you've had your shot, it's over. You don't get to hang on to your anger for a second round."

Cora curled her lip and slammed her fists into her hips. "You cannot stop me from hating you!" she snarled.

Avis deliberately straightened to his full height. "*That*, is where you're sorely mistaken, trouble." Trouble—his new nick-name for her. Fitting. "By the time I'm done with you, you'll still sense something's wrong, but you won't have a clue about the specifics. Make no mistake, I can and *will* take that entire day's memory from you if you keep this crap up."

He paused for a moment, just long enough for that to sink in. "You want to know where you get your mind powers from, little girl? The ones you've deluded yourself into thinking you're the only one who has them?" He clapped both hands together and bounced them apart to open his arms wide, rolling his fingers back towards himself. "You're looking at him."

Cora's outrage turned to shock ... then horror. "*YOU?*"

Avis grinned. "Me," he agreed, flicking his eyebrows tauntingly. "That's *my* family's gift, and just like the Hellions and their shifting, the further up the food chain you sit, the more powerful you are." —he raised his left hand and curled his thumb and forefinger to represent a zero— "Translation: you have exactly no chance of mentally dominating me. *Ever.*"

"Then why did you let me attack you in your room, if you could have stopped me at any point?"

The question was a fair one, and he found his ire dissipating. His shoulders relaxed and his hand dropped to his side. "Because that's how we deal with things in Mystal, trouble. I wronged you. Badly. Not through a third party's circumstance or because of what someone else told you had happened. You were there. You saw it all. You understood everything that happened, and you've dealt—or rather—*not* dealt with it ever since. You deserved your piece of me, and as your father, I gave you that opportunity to get even and then some."

He squared his shoulders again, resuming the role of both her father and dominant patriarch. A raised hand sliced horizontally through the air between them like an underscore. "But now, it's done. You bloodied my nose, Cora. Congratulations. I couldn't be prouder. But if you're hoping for a rematch, it'll be with a clean slate and this time I won't be bending over and taking it up the—"

He barely caught the crude terminology that came so easily to mind. Wow, parental censorship sucked! However, instead of digging himself out, he changed tack entirely. "Like it or not, I'm your father, trouble, and if I've got to knock that into your head right now, I will. In a few hours, we'll all be leaving Hell, and I'm going to have my hands full enough dealing with what's out there to be worrying about the dagger you're plotting to throw at my back."

"So, in Mystal, I get to get even?"

She hadn't heard a word he'd said after making that point, but he could tell she liked the idea of revenge—*a lot*. Probably because it had been so thoroughly denied to her in Hell. "An eye for an eye, and a kick in the teeth for good measure," he agreed, nodding slowly. "You chopped me into finger-knuckle sized pieces, remember?"

Cora grinned at the memory. "Yeah, I did that."

"And that took much longer than what I did to your mother the night of your birth." He raised his hand again and flicked two fingers between them. "So, you and I are now done. Your mother and I are also good. Your vengeance is finished."

Cora pouted sulkily. "What if I do not want it to be?"

"Tough. Mystal is a unified house—more so than your precious Hell ..."

"They kicked you out, did they not?"

Avis sucked in a sharp breath and rubbed his mouth until he had his bottom lip pinched between his fingers. This was not where he wanted to have this discussion.

If Belial knew there was a chance they might not have a home to go to in Mystal, he could very well rescind his permission for them to leave, and Avis would remain a prisoner of Hell forever. Or worse, he could keep Clarise and Columbine here and send him and Cora away—effectively splitting up their family unit.

The thought of living without Clarise and Columbine was intolerable; worse than all the time he'd spent amongst the Damned. In case the old bastard was listening in, he had to put a spin on this that didn't sound so ... *final*.

"What I did was inexcusable. You know that. Under any other circumstances, we'd make our stand as one and fight until Mystal prevailed. In a way, I think they still made that stand. While the Hellion Highborn were banging on our borders and demanding I be handed over to them for punishment, my family exiled me out the other side of the realm to where the Hellions were. If I had to guess, it was so that when the time came, they could answer in all honesty that they didn't have me, and they had no idea where I was. But what they did know and were probably counting on me to use to stay ahead of the hellions was my innate ability to safeguard my own life."

Avis knew he was making this up on the fly and he unconsciously scratched at the top of his throat just behind his chin. The truth was, he had had no idea what their inner motives were or where exactly he'd woken up after he'd been beaten into submission.

All he knew for certain was that the Highborn Hellion Guard had marched on Mystal, and Tal's son, the Mystallian god of magic, had branded him with a rune right where he was rubbing to prevent him from getting back into the celestial realms.

Without that access, he couldn't get his bearings, but the brute squad hadn't been able to find him, so distance had to be a factor. The problem was, no one stayed in the mortal realms for long by choice, especially the mortal realm of another pantheon.

He was a God of Life, and outside his powerbase, the life he protected most was his own. That was how he'd been able to stay ahead of the pack for three years. His innate ability safeguarded his life.

Once caught, the Hellions burnt off that magical brand with hellfire, and after his first pass at the Walk, it hadn't returned. Still, this creative version of events felt right. He knew his family. Despite how furious he'd been with them at the time, he knew they'd have tried to protect him from the Hellions.

Refocusing on the present, he held up three fingers for Cora to see. "For nearly three years I led that chase through the mortal realms. Three years, and not a thing touched me. Not even the pantheons I screwed over along the way. It was nearly three full years before the Hellions somehow cornered me and brought me to heel."

"And now that the threat of Hell's wrath is gone, you seriously think the Mystallians will just welcome you back with open arms?" The incredulous look on her tiny face was hilarious.

Avis smirked with pride and nodded. "That's the plan, trouble."

"But you nearly got Mystal destroyed! Why in the realms would they do that?"

"Because we're family, Cora. I'm not whole without them, and they aren't whole without me."

Cora twisted her lips, her brow creasing sneeringly. "So ... for all your talk, you have a weak family, rather than a strong one."

Avis' good mood vanished in an instant. He snapped his teeth against the roar of denial that surged to the back of his throat and swung away before he did something to her he'd later regret.

Thank the Twin Notes he'd had the foresight to have this conversation here ... *now* ... almost as far away from his siblings and their descendants as they could possibly be. Not many people called the Mystallians *weak* to their faces and walked away with their lives. In fact, as of that moment, the number totalled one, and even he as her father wanted to wring her fucking little neck.

"No," he growled, after taking a few moments to breathe through his rage. "It means any threat to one of us needs to be big enough to take out all of Mystal, or whoever the antagonist is will die for their stupidity. And to date, there are very few realms who are bigger than us." He held up two fingers. "Two, to be exact."

He dropped his hand and shook it at his side. "Now, don't get me wrong. You've got plenty of cousins who don't see eye to eye and they're forever rolling around on the ground, trying to prove to each other who's the most powerful amongst them. But the second an outsider approaches with ill-intent, those same cousins will be shoulder-to-shoulder, ready to defend each other with everything they have. *That* is what it means to be a Mystallian."

He clenched his left hand—the hand closest to her—and held it out to her in a fist bump. "When one of us does this, and says the name Mystal with strength and pride, any family member within hearing distance will be adding their fist to it in a sign of unity. Mystal. Unified. Now and forever."

He watched to see if she would come to him, and when she didn't move, he allowed his hand to fall at his side. *Too soon.* She still didn't see the difference between being Mystallian and being Avis, and she would never fist bump *him*. "You don't have to like me, trouble, but you will respect me as your father, and one of the supreme rulers of Mystal. In front of anyone else, you follow my lead and we work as one. You hear me?"

Instead of answering, Cora walked casually to the opposite side of the stall and back again in a zig-zag pattern that had her gradually working her way towards him. She focused on every stone she approached, as if each new one required her full attention and the movement in his direction was coincidental.

The ruse was so adorably obvious he didn't even need to look inside her mind to see what she was planning. Of course, she wasn't going to take him at his word when he said his mind-bending surpassed hers and she had to fall into line under him. Why should she? Still, it nearly killed him not to laugh and hold out his hand to make her so-called *sneak attack* that much easier for her.

When Cora was within arms' reach of his side, she grabbed his forearm with both hands. The steel in her eyes at her *A-Ha* moment broke through Avis' determination not to react and he started to chuckle. He had no idea what she was trying to make him do, for a younger mind attacking an elder was on par with a summer breeze hitting a brick wall.

Giving her a moment to deduce the situation for herself, he then raised his arm so that she had to reach over her head to maintain her grip. "Maybe you're the one with the hearing problem," he said, still smirking at her.

That steely gaze was gobbled up by more horror as Avis took her hands one at a time and calmly removed them. "I think," he said, stepping back from her to put some distance between them. "… you need a crash course in where your place in our family is." He paused, holding his hands out to either side as if that somehow made him less of a threat. "**Kneel**."

Without causing her any pain, Avis forced her gently to her knees, allowing the rest of her mind to remain under her control. Her hands shot out to either side as she fought against his domination, but her legs refused to straighten. He stepped forward again and squatted down in front of her, resting his forearms against his knees. "The power which the Highborn Hellion elders have over your body—we of Mystal have over your mind. Those of your generation fall into the touch control category, but only so far as the elder controls the younger."

"If that is true, why can I not touch control Columbine's body, yet I can touch control her mind?"

Avis hadn't realised the identity of Columbine's anointment-father had been kept from Cora, but every thought his elder daughter was having right now insisted that she'd caught him in a lie. He breathed out heavily. Time for a little … *corrective* history lesson.

"Because your grandfather Belial anointed her in my absence, so from the shapeshifting side of things, she's technically your aunt in generational power. And … just in case the knock-on effect escaped you, that means she has ranged shifting over you." Cora's pupils constricted, and her mouth opened and closed like a goldfish out of water.

"Judging by that stunned look on your face, I'm assuming she's never done that to you." Avis emptied his lungs in a heavy sigh and rolled his eyes skyward. Just when he'd thought Columbine's sweetness couldn't be topped, that kid somehow managed to take it to the next level. Right now, she floated somewhere between sublime and immeasurable.

"From the mind-bending side of things," he went on, refocusing on the task at hand. "She's still your younger sister and through touch contact you have the power to bend her mind to your will." Realising the ramifications of what he'd admitted to, he frowned slightly.

"But just so we're clear, no more messing with her mind on a whim. After that fiasco you put her through the other day, I'll be checking on her mental state periodically myself and if I find out you've been screwing with her for shits and giggles, I guarantee you, you *really* won't like what happens next." He folded his arms to emphasise that point and scowled. "In fact, it's probably *your* fault she came and tried to heal you right before you blew up at her in a blood rage."

Cora's head shot up. "What?"

Avis leaned forward, putting one knee on the ground to close the distance between them. "Oh, yes. I know all about it. Including the way you mentally ordered your sister to ignore *all* elder commands. Did you really think such a blanket decree would just go away because you were personally done with it?"

He shook his head, his anger spiking again. "Of course not! And because you didn't go back in and correct it, she ignored *every* elder command therein and presumed that decision was of her own making—including the one your Uncle Ludovic gave that forbade her from helping you. On top of that, you went and made her a mute! I swear, every time I think about that one, I could skin you for it! She's shy enough as it is without you …!"

Realising he was about to lash out, despite his promise to Clarise to keep this cordial, he closed his eyes and tapped his clenched fist against his lips to calm himself down.

"You have to be careful when you're dealing with one of your own," he said a few seconds later, breaking the intervening silence. "Proving superiority is one thing, but when you're done, you need to clean up your own mess. Anything more permanent than a few minutes, you'd better have a damn good reason …"

"What would be a good reason?"

Avis should have anticipated that question, but since he hadn't, he straightened up and looked around the stable for inspiration. There wasn't much in the way of choice.

"Say you had a younger cousin whom you saw charging towards a rock wall and knew he was only doing it to enjoy the sensation of getting his brains scrambled. No one would blame you for putting a more permanent "stop head-butting the stone walls" command in place, provided you then went and found his parents and explained why you felt the need to do so. Under those conditions, they'd probably reinforce that command themselves." It was a pathetic example, but the best he could come up with at the time.

"Where is the fun in that?"

Avis released his control of her and held out his hand to help her upright; chuckling cruelly as he did so. "That, my dear, is what mortals are for."

CHAPTER TWENTY-FIVE

By the time Avis and Cora left the stone enclosure, everyone had arrived and separated into their smaller groups. Frash and Tilu remained away from Clarise on the far left, while across the room on the right, Diviten and Gingen kept themselves equally out of the way. Columbine stood between her mother and her Uncle Uriel and hung off every word they said, despite being utterly ignored by the two elders overhead. Yet another reminder for Avis that this wasn't *his* side of the family.

If Columbine had been anything like a Mystallian, at least one of those elders would be nursing a bruised shin by now. Avis ended his sweep with the four imposing Highborn Hellion Guards that stood in the corners of the room. They all looked identical, with their arms curled into their hip joints and a headpiece filled with eyes that spun constantly to survey everything around them at once.

Avis still couldn't believe they'd be escorting him and his family home. A very small, childish part of him almost wanted someone in the Known Realms to start something with him, just so he could watch those brutes in action.

Clarise either sensed his approach behind her or noticed her brother's dark scowl over her shoulder, for she turned to him with a dazzling smile that took his breath away. "Uriel was just explaining to me how you would rather go with him to the front gates and summon us through a blood-link," she said.

Without waiting for an invitation, Avis folded her back into his arms and brushed his lips against her head. The taste of her lavender scent filled his senses and he eagerly licked his lips, unable to get enough of it. "It's really not nice out there, sweetheart, and I'd rather you avoid as much of it as possible."

She nodded and rested her head against his chest. "I trust you, beloved. The girls and I shall wait here for your sum—"

Avis bristled and immediately placed two silencing fingers over her mouth before she could finish that statement. Then, to prevent the girls from listening in or reading his lips, he lowered his mouth to her ear. "No one summons you anymore, Clarise," he whispered heatedly. "By the Twin Notes, I mean it. Where you go, you go because you wish it. You go, because it pleases you. My queen summons others, and answers to no one. Not even me. I swear, I'll kill the next person who dares to try and *summon* you."

Except for Belial, he absolutely meant that, and he had to be sure she understood it. Cupping her face in his hands, he twisted her head until he was staring her in the eye. Hard. This wasn't just about her. She was now one of Mystal's two ruling queens, and to allow anyone to summon her like a common dog was to imply that that individual had seniority over all Mystal.

Just the thought of it set Avis' teeth on edge. *Like fuck!* It was highly doubtful that she understood the scope of her position, but he wanted to try.

As expected, her eyes shone with unbridled love as she wrapped her arms around his neck and kissed him. "It pleases me to wait for you," she promised against his lips. "It always has."

He expected this. *You'll get it eventually, sweetheart.* Avis caught her by the nape to hold her still and kissed her deeply. *I'll make sure of it.*

In the wake of that kiss, Cora's outfit was barely an afterthought. But it did register. With one arm wrapped securely around Clarise's shoulders, he turned to the girl in question standing a short distance behind him. The subservient location irked the shit out of him, but he needed to focus on one problem at a time. "Cora, are the clothes you're wearing moulded from your tefsla infused form, or a secondary addition?"

The distinction was an important one. If Belial had shoehorned her into that outfit using her original mass, they wouldn't be able to shift around it. Instead, she'd have to strip while a whole new outfit was created from the mass surrounding them. The humiliation factor for them both as Mystallians would be high to say the least if that were the case.

He had no idea where the Hellion Lords stood on seeing family members of the opposite sex naked, but after their early life in the Nexus, it had become taboo in Mystal. What was worse, a part of Cora's essence would be trapped inside the discarded clothing. If anything happened to those fabrics before the tefsla wore off, Cora would forever forfeit that part of herself.

The second option was preferable, as the clothes would be tefsla free and malleable.

"Avis," Clarise chided, shaking that beautiful head of black hair at him. "She is just a child. You cannot expect her to know how to answer …"

"Secondary," Cora answered, only to shrug when her mother stared at her in open-mouthed astonishment.

Avis suddenly felt the full weight of his wife's accusatory glare and he mashed his lips together to battle the smirk that really, *really* wanted to form. He knew if anyone saw his amusement, sex would be off the table for a month. At least. There was a time or two when his brothers had suffered similar punishments for publicly embarrassing their wives, and it wasn't a mistake he intended to replicate.

Cora either ignored their byplay or was so offended by what she was wearing that she failed to notice it. "Grandfather shifted me into the basic form of a Mystallian female, then forced me to endure the entire dressing and makeup stupidity that goes into being one of your people's females."

She ran her hands down the sides of the gown in disgust. "This is beyond hideous and I cannot express enough how much it sickens me to wear it."

Avis looked anywhere but at his wife's withering gaze. When discussing the girls' abilities, he hadn't intentionally overlooked Cora's higher intellect. It was just that others were … more impressive and he … forgot. Besides, it wasn't entirely his fault.

Clarise had known Cora all her life and never bothered to ask, whereas Avis had only met her a handful of times and figured it out for himself. Being able to see inside the girl's head may have given him a slight advantage there, but, meh.

He did, however, agree completely with Cora's assessment of her attire. The first thing Armina had done when he and the others escaped the Nexus was to ditch the white slip that they'd all been forced to wear and forge herself some heavy-duty battle armour which to this day, she rarely took off.

While Uriel wore gleaming silver, Armina's was black as night itself. She had no use for a head piece but maintained the cloak with the family sigil on the back to claim her place within the pantheon. The darkened hilts of twin great claymores protruded over her shoulders, defining Mystal's version of War. In time, Avis could picture Cora wearing something similar.

He practically felt Clarise's seething indignation and for the first time, he was grateful that the girl's tefsla infused body had placed her beyond her mother's ranged shapeshifting. Between her disrespectful attitude and her string of insults of the Mystallian way of life, he had no doubt Cora would be howling in a world of agony if her mother could activate the pain receptors around the back of her legs and backside.

"Clarise, don't," he whispered, moving his hands to her shoulders to try and work some of the tension from her neck and spine. "You've met Armina. Outfits like that only work for women who want to be feminine and it's obvious she takes after my sister. Let this one go, sweetheart. For me."

Clarise pouted, and for a moment Avis thought she was going to argue with him. But then a sigh of disappointment escaped her, and she relaxed into his hold. "I truly had hoped she would embrace this opportunity to learn how to behave as a Highborn Lady, beloved. Could we not have her try? If only for a little while?"

The sentiment was one Avis could appreciate, however misguided it was. He gave her a light squeeze of comfort and rested his chin on top of her head, rubbing it from side to side in a negative fashion.

"Some roles should never be forced, sweetheart. Cora will always be who and what she needs to be. We just need to give her some breathing space to decide what that something is. In the meantime, let her have a set of boots, leggings … a doublet … belt and matching vest. Oh, and a cloak and soft leather gloves for—no! Not our uniform!" he shouted, realising Clarise had already liquified Cora's crimson dress into a black mass that was, even now, shaping itself into the familiar clothing.

Cora's hurt-filled eyes met his, causing a painful ache in his chest. He instinctively raised a gloved hand to placate her, spreading his fingers wide in her direction. "It's not what you think, Cora. That uniform is very special to us and it needs to be something you want so badly you can almost taste it. You said it yourself, you haven't decided if Mystal is going to be your forever home, and until you make that choice … *you* make that choice," he reiterated, taking half a step around Clarise to poke the girl in the shoulder.

"I won't deliver you from one forced situation, only to deposit you into another. When your mind's made up and you're sure it's what you *really* want, you only have to say the word and the uniform will be yours to wear." He stepped back to give her some room. "Until then, enjoy your hunting tans."

Clarise made the modifications, just as Avis had asked. Tight leggings tucked into ankle high animal-hide boots. The doublet had puffed sleeves much like his own and a deep brown belt with a wrapped snake skin buckle tying it tightly to her waist. An open vest with small pockets near the waistband formed over the doublet and soft, brown leather gloves hid her hands from view.

"Yes!" Cora reached into her hair and removed the flowered band that kept her fringe braided and bound behind her head. Then she folded forward at the waist and shook her head, allowing the bright red locks to fall forward to her knees. Still bent over, she gathered it together in one hand—plaits and all—and straightened suddenly, flicking her head back.

The band she had stretched around the fingers of her free hand was brought to her mouth and in a single bite she tore away the offending floral decoration and spat it to one side. She then banded the simplified hair tie around the fistful of hair to form a tight ponytail that had a single loop of hair caught in the final pass of the band, lifting it from the middle of her back to just on shoulder length. Her feet were parted for central balance and the way she planted her hands on her hips and grinned at them ...

... Avis could barely contain his shock.

It was Armina ... from all those years ago. "Is that ...? Do all warrior women who get their first taste of freedom do that?" he asked, for his sister had followed practically the exact same sequence.

"It keeps it out of my face," Cora explained, wrongly assuming his shock began and ended with her hair. She flicked her head from side to side to demonstrate it slapping against her cheeks without impeding her sight.

Avis found himself nodding. Her instincts were good. *Really good.* Like all his brothers, he wore his hair short out of habit, so trying to track an enemy's movements through unmanageable locks had never been something he'd had to consider. And knowing Armina, it would've killed that bitch to admit she had a weakness that needed rectifying.

Uriel let out a sharp, shrill whistle that drew Avis' attention away from Cora. When he turned to see what his brother-by-marriage wanted, the archangel impatiently lifted one wing towards the awaiting demons. Avis didn't quite hide his eyeroll. "*We* have to go, sweetheart," he said, refusing to put himself on a lower ranking to Uriel by saying *he* (singular) had to answer the archangel's call.

Despite admitting this, he found himself kissing her again. He just didn't want to leave her. He *really* didn't want to leave *them*. Breaking from her lips with a murmur of regret, he lightly kissed her brow and turned away while he still had the strength to do so.

That brought him to Columbine—who still looked nothing like him. He squatted down to be on eye level with her. "You be good for your mother," he said as he cupped her beak in his palm and dusted his thumb against her cheek, not that it really needed saying. "Okay?"

Columbine cast her wings forward and wrapped them around his shoulders, encompassing him like a cloak of leather. "I love you, Father."

Avis closed his eyes. He'd only be gone a few hours. This was the sort of farewell he'd always made fun of his family for. The kind that implied they'd be parted for centuries, not hours. By the Twin Notes, he wasn't laughing now. "Love you too, princess."

Just like he had with her mother, he pressed his lips to her forehead and gave her a parting squeeze before pulling himself out of her reach by straightening up. *Fuck me,* he thought as he flattened his hands along his doublet, chastising himself for his inability to just walk away from them.

He made a half turn to partially face Cora. "And as for you, trouble, you just remember what I said." He curled his middle finger behind his thumb and flicked her forehead between the eyes before she could dodge it. "You're a long way from the top of *either* food chain, so watch yourself."

Cora gnashed her teeth and rubbed the bridge of her nose where he'd collected her.

Hearing every colourful expletive she mentally thought, Avis grinned at her. It might have been true that he'd been forced to bring her but having her on this journey with him was tantamount to having someone from home riding at his side. By the realms, he'd missed that. "You'll do," he said with a quiet chuckle.

Uriel cleared his throat pointedly.

As much as Avis didn't want to make his next admission—least of all to any male member of Clarise's family—it was better to bring it up now while he still had two feet firmly on the ground. "I've never ridden a demon steed before, so how does this work? With them being born of hellfire and hellfire usually being detrimental to my flesh." It wasn't that he doubted Clarise. She'd said they wouldn't act out, and he believed her. But what he couldn't get his head around was how.

"And burning you to a crisp would be so tragic," Uriel scoffed, tossing Avis a set of reins.

"Uriel," Clarise warned.

Uriel sighed. Maybe it was a huff. But after meeting her eyes, he glanced at the children who were watching the exchange and refrained from commenting further. Instead, he took the reins of another demon steed and slid up on to its back. "Ride, like you would ride any other equine," he said, pulling on the reins to lift its head.

"As my sister has already informed you, the flames of its existence will not harm you. When you approach, their bodies will recognise the essence of the Hellion Highborn blood flowing in your veins and will adapt accordingly to compensate for your chosen shape." With a patronising sneer, he leaned forward and rested his armoured forearms in the beast's fiery mane. "Even if you do only *have* one to offer."

"Bite me," Avis snapped, before he could stop himself.

"Is that an offer?" High over the girls' heads, Uriel dislocated his jaw and opened his mouth unnaturally wide to reveal row after row of sharp, elongated teeth forming all the way to the back of his throat.

Avis stood his ground and glared at the eldest of Belial's sons. They could throw verbal threats and taunts all day, but since they each knew what the other was capable of and neither was prepared to risk Belial's wrath by striking first, the posturing became pointless. "You done?"

Uriel closed his mouth, and slowly the skin and muscles reduced until his lips returned to their normal size and position. "Not even close."

Avis gathered his reins and hauled himself on to the demon steed's back. Riding without a saddle wasn't his preference. Not when the mystallions his family rode back home were winged equines capable of travelling vast distances in the blink of an eye and could change directions on a whim. A fall of any kind at those speeds would leave the thrown rider galaxies away in the second or two it took anyone riding with him to notice.

Because of this (and the fact that riding bareback just plain sucked) the Mystallians had created a saddle that was both comfortable and supportive for endless days of riding. Over the eons it had become second nature to use. The only one who didn't was his brother-by-marriage Mahpee, but given his roots in the Black Hills pantheon, that wasn't exactly surprising.

War's beloved husband still wore feathers in his long hair and the face paint of his birth pantheon as well, though he'd upgraded to the dark Mystallian uniform just before his wedding. It always amazed Avis how that god could use his knees and a fistful of mane to control every aspect of his sky blue mystallion, though he would never say it to the man's face.

At least these demon steeds had reins. That was a step in the right direction.

Uriel let out a sharp, piercing whistle that brought up the remaining demon steeds' heads. He uncurled one armoured hand and held it out to his side expectantly. Each of the unclaimed demon steeds stepped forward in turn and flicked their heads, causing the reins that dangled between their front legs to jerk into the air.

One by one, the reins fell across Uriel's open palm with a precision that astonished Avis, and when the archangel held all three, he closed his hand around them. Another whistled note had the reins lengthening until the demon steeds stood in a staggered, arrowhead formation, ready to move.

Avis memorised each signal whistle and what it represented. He had no intention of relying on Clarise or this asshole to keep the beasts under control. "Here," Uriel said, holding the reins out for Avis to take. "You lead them." The constant string of orders was grating on Avis' last nerve, but he refused to make a scene in front of Clarise and the girls, even if it killed him. Not yet, anyway.

It'd be a very different story once they were no longer in Chaos, and for a moment he pictured a one-on-one rematch with the archangel where they'd both be free to flex their full potential. There wouldn't be a mind left in the bastard by the time Avis was finished with him.

The promise of that unfulfilled fantasy settled him enough to nudge his demon steed to stand alongside Uriel's. He might … *might* have garnered a miniscule amount of satisfaction when he browsed the surface thoughts of his brother-by-marriage and found the bastard stewing over the fact that he couldn't get a rise out of him. Uriel's frustration bolstered Avis' pre-eminence like nothing else could.

When Avis took the reins, Uriel's grip on them tightened and he pulled the Mystallian slightly off balance. "I still do not trust you as far as I could spit your accursed realm," he hissed, so quietly only Avis could hear.

"And I can't begin to tell you just how much sleep I'm going to lose over that," Avis shot back as he straightened and jerked the reins free. In all honesty, he should have been the bigger man and left it at that but screw it. He tilted his head as if to give the matter more thought. "No—actually, I can." His dropped all expression from his face and stared icily at his brother-by-marriage. "*None*."

Uriel bared his teeth in an all-out snarl which Avis met with stony hostility. It had been a hard-learned lesson, but over the last two years he'd discovered that saying nothing—as if your enemy's presence *meant* nothing—was often more effective than coming to blows. Especially when dealing with hot-headed demons. It'd probably work on Mystallians too, come to think of it.

Cords of tension became visible in the archangel's neck as he struggled to maintain his composure. Then, as he snatched his eyes away and motioned his demon steed ahead of Avis', he issued a long, shrilling whistle that ended in a high note. The five demon steeds shuddered violently at the sound and a moment later wings of flame exploded out of their shoulders like a volcanic eruption.

Avis barely avoided the flames, and while he strove to reposition himself further down its back, a single downward beat from those fire-fuelled wings shot him into the air behind Uriel. "Try not to fall off," the archangel jeered over the rush of air between them, in such a way that implied the exact opposite.

Avis ground his teeth as he edged further away from the fiery wings that pumped up and down a little too close to his knees for comfort. True, the flames weren't technically harming him, but the visual combined with the knowledge that hellfire could destroy almost anything it contacted was just as discomforting. He looked up at the archangel ahead of him and glared daggers into his back. The bastard hadn't warned him that demon steeds could sprout wings on command and turn into aerial beasts. *What a shocker.*

Fortunately for Avis, riding winged equines was something he'd been doing for so long, he could ride in his sleep. Literally. Talot hunting in Mystal was a lot of fun because the beasts were monstrous and fast and *never* stopped. The challenge was exhilarating, and once their trail was picked up on, Avis and his family had to ride hard without stopping to catch up to it. Months—sometimes years—went into each hunt as the beast wove its way through millions of galaxies with ease.

Yes, the hunt could be over in seconds if certain members of the pantheon used their powerbases for an unfair advantage, but where was the fun in that? If his twin brother Amaro tapped his powerbase and the beast suddenly keeled over dead no matter where in the realm it was, how was that a challenge for anyone?

Armina was careful to never see the hunt as a battle to be won, or her thrall would kick in and she'd do everything in her power to win as fast as possible. She *never* lost a war, and with her powerbase at her back, she was truly a sight to behold in battle.

As those and other precious memories flickered across his mind, a deep longing pierced his chest with such force that he found himself rubbing the spot over his heart with the hand holding the demon steeds' reins. Damn, he hadn't realised just how much he missed them all. He'd even tolerate one of Chance's idiotic pranks right about now if it meant the runt would materialise right in front of him.

His yearning took a mischievous turn as he envisioned that. *If only so I can run your ass over just once while you're so far away from your powerbase, runt.* Chance's innate luck would still probably save him at the last second (even this far away from Mystal) but pretending otherwise made Avis chuckle evilly. Who said you ever grew out of sibling rivalry?

But he had to keep his mind on the present. He wasn't even out of Hell's Well yet, and Mystal was over half the Known Realms away. Both the rush of air around him and the lack of jarring impacts with the ground may have had the familiarity of an airborne equine, but he wasn't on a mystallion. He was riding a demon steed: a beast which didn't even come close to his own precious White Haven's speed. If White Haven had been there, he'd have flown rings around these demon steeds. He flew rings around most mystallions.

Avis imagined his magnificent herd leader, a mystallion stallion of white, standing proudly in his stall with his head held high and his wings folded majestically over his back, waiting these five long years for Avis to unhook his stall rope and take to the skies with him again. Avis would've given almost anything to run his hand through that silken mane instead of the fire that his current mount possessed.

Again, Avis had to bring his thoughts back to the present. He would get White Haven back soon enough. Even if they didn't end up going back to Mystal, his family owed him enough to bring the mystallion to him.

Uriel chose that moment to look back at him and gesture towards the mouth of The Well that loomed above them. With a final glance at his young family waving below, he braced himself for the icy bite of Antenora and leaned forward, urging his steed into the closest thing to an air-sprint it could manage in the hopes of getting through that Ninth Level as fast as possible.

It was pitiful in comparison and Uriel laughed at his endless shivering every wing beat of the way.

CHAPTER TWENTY-SIX

One thing Avis had to say—the view of the Damned from above was a lot better than being down there amongst them. Morally, he knew it was wrong of him to look over his demon steed's shoulder and feel a combination of relief and amusement at the fact that he no longer suffered alongside them, but just then, he didn't care.

He was living proof that the Nine Levels of Chaos' capital city could break anyone, and he'd never been more pleased to know Mystal had nothing like it. Not even in Crohen; the capital city where his sombre twin brother ruled from. Compared to his Life Court, Crohen was more subdued, but torture on this scale wasn't necessary.

And if Avis had his way, it never would be either.

"Reminiscing?" Uriel asked snidely, having dropped back to ride alongside him.

Avis drew in a deep breath through his nose and released it slowly through gritted teeth. *Just keep pushing, you asshole.* "Whatever happened to all that Heavenly forgiveness you're supposed to be all about?" he asked, throwing the focal point of their discussion back at Uriel's apparent failings, not because he cared but just for something nasty to say.

He certainly hadn't expected Uriel's response.

"No doubt that will be forced upon me by the Fifth Choir when I return to Heaven, but for now, I am not feeling very forgiving."

Wait ... what? Avis' head spun to his brother-by-marriage. "Are you serious?"

Uriel's daggered gaze was lethal. "If you need to ask the level of my hatred for you by now ..." the archangel snarled in misunderstanding.

Avis hacked in disgust and shook his head. "Not that part," he snapped, waving that aspect of the conversation aside with a flick of his wrist. "Are you saying Heaven *forces* you into being forgiving, and you don't get a say in it? Why in the realms would you want to be there?"

Heaven was one of the few realms older than Mystal. No one who belonged to another pantheon ever went there, not even to visit. Uriel was a rare exception. The walls of its outer boundaries were high and shone like polished opal. Armoured angels like Uriel manned that wall every other metre and the only way in was through one of the twelve sets of double gates. Each set matched the height of the walls they were connected to and were intricately carved from a single pearl—hence their rather unimaginative moniker.

But that, and how much Avis hated the ninth and first choirs, was all he knew about them. Apparently, there was a single god behind that wall that ran everything, but he never came out. Not surprising, when he sent droves of those fucking choir angels out to infect every other pantheon with his powerbase. They were *never* invited. Instead, they just turned up, singing praises to their creator and filling mortals with love for the invading realm, converting them in the process.

Similarly, if a pantheon decided it were time to cull mortal numbers for whatever reason and one of Heaven's First Choir healers was in the vicinity, it would sweep in and heal the condemned; which also converted them, their families and their friends. It was an outright invasion no matter which way you looked at it and almost every pantheon Avis knew of had issued their militaries with a kill-on-sight order for them. Mystal was no exception. Avis shivered in loathing. *Parasitic little* ...

Uriel ignored the question and flicked his chin forward. "Almost there," he said.

Avis was only too happy to turn his attention to the dull light in the far distance, knowing it represented a salvation that could never be achieved by the Damned who had yet to be dragged across the threshold of the First Gates of Hell. The agony inflicted by the Akheron River and the demons who lined the shores between it and the front gates of Hell prevented anyone from going back. Mortal souls destined for Hell were cast into the far side of the Akheron River, a hand-span from the safety of that shore.

Somehow, they were blinded to the glowing light of the castle behind them, seeing instead the grey layer of nothingness that hid the closer shore from view. With only one visible land mass in the distance, the Damned swam naked across what had been aptly nicknamed River of Pain by those who had endured it. They would swim because they thought the agony they were in right now was the worst of what awaited them, and that safety would be found on the far shore.

Not so. Never so. Demons waited for them. To feed on them. To steal them. To use them as bartering currency amongst themselves. Corrupt souls belonged to Hell and the Hellions within, but the demons of Chaos lingered like scavengers in front of Hell's front gates.

Within seconds of the Damned reaching the shore, they were greedily snatched from the water, only to be pounced upon in turn by others wishing to claim the lucrative prize. Souls were often torn apart during these struggles, but their destruction wasn't an escape. Mercies like that didn't exist here. If the soul became too destroyed, it would reform in a different location on the rocky shore and the fight for its possession would start all over again.

At some point, the Gates of Hell would open and cast a fiery light across the area, lifting the grey veil on the other side of the river to show the Damned just how close they'd been to Chaos' version of safety. The realm of nothingness lay under that castle's light. Sweet nothingness. No pain. No fear.

Hellions and a few Highborn Hellions would pour out to take charge, and the demons outside would scatter with whatever souls they had snared. They rarely got any. With touch and ranged shapeshifting at their disposal, the masters of Chaos reclaimed most of the Damned and drove them through the gates like sheep, only to have those massive gates close soon afterwards.

With the gates now opened, Avis and Uriel flew through the top of the opening. Airborne demons and hellions scrambled to get out of their way, knowing by instinct that their crown prince was coming through. Cackles of glee and squeals of denial wafted up from the shores below, causing a shudder to work through Avis.

Having spent two years in the Nine Levels, he recognised the difference between the established Damned and these newcomers who hadn't been beaten down yet. This was their first real taste of what the rest of their existence would hold for them and they still believed if they fought it hard enough, they could change it.

Idiots.

No one could change their fate from within the Damned. Not even him. He remembered his own first entrance: his eyes had been covered to prevent line of sight attacks, but Uriel had enhanced every other sense to make up for that short-coming. Touch was the worst. Chains of fire had bound his upper body as they dragged him through the gates.

He screamed in a mixture of agony and fury as the celestial ward which his nephew had infused into his throat fought his presence in the Celestial Realm. Comparing each of his years amongst the Damned, Avis decided the initial introduction to Hell was the worst part of being condemned. To be fooled into believing this was only temporary, and sooner or later, one would be free to wreak vengeance.

Nothing about being one of the Damned was temporary.

Avis was the only exception he knew of, and he'd never forget the reason for that. Clarise was more than just his salvation. She was his life, and the mere thought of her had his heart aching to be with her again.

"If you are missing anyone in particular down there, I am certain I can arrange a reunion for you," Uriel taunted.

"Fuck you," Avis snapped, not wishing his brother-by-marriage to know it was his beloved wife that he missed so badly. Wanting nothing more to do with Uriel, Avis looked away from him and focused on the waterway below. *At least the pain down there is physical, and physical pain shouldn't trigger Columbine's empathic ability at all. Not like the river of misery. Between the two, this would've been his choice as well. Hands down.*

He followed the course of the river with his eyes until it disappeared into the far horizon and sighed. They still had a long way to go just to get out of Hell, and somewhere down the bottom end of that monstrous river lay the even bigger Chaotic Ocean that they still had to somehow traverse. Getting out of Chaos was going to be a real pain in the ass. No question.

"Run, and I will cut you down before you take two steps," Uriel warned, manoeuvring his demon steed into Avis' flight path to force the Mystallian to either change course or risk a collision. Uriel spread his wings to show without a word that of the two of them, only Avis would fall into the river of pain. "Lift your arm to blood-link, and I will cut it off at the shoulder before a name leaves your mouth."

That's it! Avis was fed up to the back teeth with Uriel's bullshit taunts and threats. Heaving hard on the reins, he almost stood up, his knees pushed heavily into the beast's ribs for traction. "Into a lot of cutting these days, aren't you, Uriel?" he snarled in return as the beast flared its flame-wings and pranced to a complete standstill less than a hand-span from Uriel.

"Perhaps you should take up dress-making." *And—well, since he'd gone that far …* "Or maybe you already have. It'd certainly explain your long hair and all those dresses that the men in Heaven fly around in. Did they take you long to make?"

Dresses of any type were a no-go for men in Mystal, and except for Mahpee and one of Chance's grandchildren, long hair was also out. Not that calling someone 'a woman' in Mystal would ever be considered an insult (and most of the women in his family would kick his ass for ever implying it was) but Avis knew it would stick in Uriel's masculine craw *forever*.

Uriel roared and drew his blade of fire, while Avis prepared for an all-out brawl of mind versus body. This was an entirely different ball-game to the one they'd played over the last two years. He'd felt the burn of that flame blade more times than he could count, and he was no longer afraid of it. If Uriel wanted this to hurt, he was going to have to get … *primal*.

"Enough."

Fuck—fuck—crap! In his excitement to be outside of Hell and maybe even smack Uriel around a bit, Avis had forgotten that Belial's influence didn't stop at the front gates of Hell. Hell was just the Chaotian capital. All of Chaos was Belial's domain and he could appear anywhere he wanted within it at will. Both men swung to where the supreme demon appeared in the air beside them, and both lowered their heads respectfully.

"You will keep a civil tongue in your head, Lord of Mystal, or I will take your head and keep it as a souvenir of your visit. Do you seek to test me?"

Avis hunched a little lower. Without his head, he wouldn't be able to heal. The essence of his head remained within the physical representation *of* his head. A shifter couldn't make him another one and pretend it was the original. Not if the original existed elsewhere. "I didn't start it," he said, despising how childish it made him sound but unable to avoid it without allowing Uriel to get the first word in.

"That is the only reason you still have your head."

Uriel jerked his head up, while Avis lifted his chin slowly. "I was merely warning him of the consequences of attempting to escape without his responsibilities," the demonic crown prince argued.

"You know very well that he has no intention of leaving without them, Uriel. Your words were antagonistic, just as they have been from the beginning. Avis is showing restraint. Perhaps that is only because he is within my realm, but for now, he is behaving. You will do likewise."

Uriel shot Avis a daggered look of pure hatred that said this was far from over as he sheathed his flame blade. "It shall be as you command, Father."

Ooob, suck it, Uriel. Avis would never have kowtowed that quickly in front of Theodrick had their roles been reversed, but then, *his* father wasn't in the habit of requesting anything like *ever*.

Requests relinquished control and invited defiance: two things Theodrick abhorred. Still, the knowledge that he had finally, *properly* one-upped the hellion crown prince within Hell itself had his lips twitching in amusement.

"Do not see this as a victory, Mystallian," Belial warned, wiping the smile off Avis' face with those eight words. "You are no innocent either. You will *both* continue to behave without incident, or you will *both* regret not doing so." His penetrating gaze prickled Avis' skin until the Mystallian swallowed uncomfortably. "You, moreso."

Still in Chaos … Still in Chaos … Still in Chaos … Avis said the three words in his mind until they became a mental mantra. He wasn't free yet, and while he was … *still—in—Chaos,* Belial could do anything to him. Anything at all. He had to wait until he escaped the whole realm before he could allow himself a true shout of triumph. Until then, he was on thin ice and he had to skate with extreme care.

"I will not speak of this again."

Which meant this would be their only warning. Next time Avis butted heads with Uriel, Avis would lose his. The Mystallian looked down at the multiple reins he still held in his hands, no longer feeling as … *argumentative* as he had been. They'd both been taken to task as if they were ten-year-old boys getting their heads smacked together by an elder and there was little either of them could do about it.

Belial was gone by the time he looked up and the two ancients were left to glare at each other dirtily. "Perhaps it would be better if neither of us speaks to the other again," Uriel said, his tone just as acidic as Avis' thoughts had been.

"Works for me."

Uriel turned his demon steed back towards the light that glowed across the river and nudged it forward with his knees. Avis followed suit and the two crossed the river in silence.

CHAPTER TWENTY-SEVEN

A few minutes later, Avis landed on the far shore which was obscured by dull greyness and turned his demon steed to face the direction he'd come. From this side, the ominous front gates of Hell still loomed, but only as a distant threat. It was the closest Avis had been to freedom since his incarceration two years ago and he couldn't help but look back and savour his delight at being this far away from them.

Despite his ongoing concerns for his family, laughter bubbled up from deep inside him until it burst free and he tilted his head back, roaring out his elation for the whole realm to hear. He was never going back to Hell. Never, ever—*ever!*

This whole area of Chaos was new to him. The numbing greyness that permeated the air like a pea-soup fog converged on him from all sides, and it was *thick*. In seconds, Avis was forced to squint, and he could barely make out his demon steed's flaming mane right in front of him. He didn't like it here.

It was wrong—both disorienting and depressive in equal measure. The only beacon of light in the area came from the castle behind him and by feel alone he turned his demon steed in search of the glowing point of reference. Who owned that castle anyway? Who'd even *want* to own it when it oversaw such a miserable landscape that never changed?

He thought about the various members of his own family and realised Blagden would take it in a heartbeat. His younger brother was permanently riddled with sickness and disease, having made the mistake of presenting himself to the Mystallian mortals for the first time without being at full health. From memory, it had been something small—like a head cold.

Nevertheless, the mortals had latched on to his ailing condition and established him as the Mystallian God of Sickness and Disease, turning him from a powerful young man into a grotesque living embodiment of the powerbase even as it gave him mastery over all maladies. Technically, Blagden lived in Crohen with Amaro and the others of the Death Court, but much to Avis' annoyance, he didn't maintain a wing within the palace.

Instead, his residence was a short walk from the palace itself. In his own words, he preferred the isolation over accidentally infecting Amaro's staff, since creating illness was his specialty; healing it, not so much. Fortunately, Blagden's touch was ineffectual to anyone sharing his bloodline.

Avis would never have permitted such a segregation to take place on his side of the realm, but his twin had insisted he not interfere. To this day, it still hurt him to know his little brother endured his powerbase instead of revelling in it.

With no one as far as the eye could see, Blagden would love it here.

A hand brushed Avis' calf as he searched the area in vain for any sign of Uriel, so gently he barely felt it through the thick leather of his boot. He jerked and looked down in surprise, finding a grey shape no taller than Cora staring up at him in the light of the castle. "You feel," it said lifelessly, stroking his boot again. "What is that like?"

How in the realms was he supposed to answer that? Or, more to the point, why would he bother trying? If the creature had no concept of feelings, no words could fill that void. Not liking the conflicted way that left him feeling, he jerked his boot away from it, only to have more hands reach out to touch him. The demon steed snorted and pranced but the fog thickened around him until he couldn't see anything—not even the castle. The greyness was alive, he realised, all too late. Or, at the very least, it wasn't mundanely inanimate.

Avis lashed out with his boot, hoping to use its body to drive others further back. There were too many mortal minds here, and not being attuned to Chaos, he was reduced to dealing with them one at a time. For everyone he stomped out, thousands more took their place. Like ants. He was about to whistle his demon steed's wings back into play when an unholy light ignited from above, brighter than that of the castle.

"Away with you!" Uriel commanded, his tone projecting every inch of him as the crown prince of Hell. He held his blade of hellfire over his head; more like a torch than a weapon. The greyness that had been climbing up itself to reach him melted away, falling to the ground and sliding away like a receding shadow. Uriel's grip on the hilt tightened and the light intensified. "You will not find your peace from the likes of us!"

As the pea-soup continued to retreat, Avis saw just what he was dealing with. Countless individual mortal souls, each filling the space of its neighbour until there was no beginning and no end to them. An endless mass of … mortal souls.

Uriel pointed his blade to the ground and hellfire launched from the tip to score the shore beneath his demon steed. "Do not move," he snarled irritably. Avis took his attitude shift as a sign that he was the one to not move and held his place. Uriel rode in a large half circle, creating a wall of fire that began and ended at the water's edge. When he was done, he held the sword high again. "*OUT!*" he commanded, his voice fuelled by infernal power.

Unable to penetrate the hellfire, the wretched souls who happened to be caught inside the half-ring were driven into the only open space available to them: The Akheron River. Avis watched in horror, for the only way out of the River of Pain was on the other side. With just a single deed and a single word from the crown prince of Hell, these helpless souls had been reallocated to the Damned.

Avis clenched his fists and locked his teeth together so tightly the muscles in his jaw protested. He wasn't supposed to care! They were only mortal souls! Not even *his* mortal souls, and just a few hundred thousand at best. As a realm, the mortals maintained the power of the gods they served, but as an individual, they counted for nothing.

A thousand. A hundred thousand. A hundred *billion*. In a realm where billions of *galaxies* could be drawn on, no finite number of mortals was that important … unless the realm was being encroached upon. Then every mortal mattered. Gods were nothing if not territorial.

Still, the vision of that segregated group as they were herded into the river, at which point their uncaring gaze blanched until they screamed in agony and they began to swim across to Hell, would haunt him forever. He tried to console himself by thinking that maybe … *maybe*, since they didn't really belong in Hell, the demons waiting on the other side might take pity on them and return them to this bleak shore.

His throat tightened, rebelling against the rising bile as he realised he'd inadvertently put two words in the same sentence that had no business being in the same dictionary. *Demonic mercy.* He closed his eyes and turned his head away, no longer wanting to witness the fate of those hapless souls.

He had to stop thinking of them in terms of something that mattered. The point was, they *didn't* and if he didn't get this soft-heartedness under control, he and his twin brother would be butting heads over Death's claim to the Mystallian mortals once they'd passed. He needed a distraction. Fast. Opening his eyes, he sought out the glowing castle in the distance.

"What exactly is this place?" Anything would do at this point.

"I thought we were not speaking."

Uriel's demon steed still hovered overhead instead of landing and the only reason Avis could deduce for this was the sheer enjoyment the bastard took in looking down on him. As if this were a physical representation of their status in his mind. The baiting irked Avis, but he refused to acknowledge it, preferring to keep his head right where it was. "You spoke first when you told me not to move. What is this place?"

He hadn't really expected Uriel to answer him and was surprised when the archangel twisted his head to view the dense fog behind him. "This is the Vestibule: the land of disbelief. Chaos claims all mortal souls who have no place in the celestial realm, not just those of our mortal realm."

It took Avis a moment to process that titbit of information, and having done so, he knew his initial reaction had been a little too blasé. Chaos was huge, so their mortal powerbase in the realm below had to be of similar size. Since the Known Realms were fully settled and every pantheon within it kept close tabs on their mortal souls for one reason or another, very few would escape and end up here. It was a realm like any other ... until the true meaning of Uriel's words occurred to him and his stomach spasmed as if he'd been sucker-punched.

His brother-by-marriage hadn't said these were the unclaimed mortals of the Known Realms. He'd said *all* mortal souls—*everywhere*. There was an expanse of existence everyone referred to as the Unknown Realms, and it was *unknown* for a reason. No pantheons existed out there.

The mortals roamed free. Feral. Without a pantheon to believe in. Its exact size remained a mystery since it had never been charted for posterity's sake, but the consensus of the pantheons was that it easily matched the Known Realms. If that was true ... and all those mortal souls from out there ... ended up here ...

Chaos was a lot more powerful than he realised.

Avis swallowed heavily. "So, Chaos gets to keep every mortal soul that doesn't believe in a pantheon's afterlife? Even the Unknown Realms?" No matter how hard he tried, he couldn't quite remove the hint of trepidation from his voice. An untapped powerbase that easily equalled the combined strength of every pantheon's mortal population, all crammed into one tiny land space. No wonder this place was so chronically overpopulated! "Do they ever get circulated back into their mortal realms?"

Uriel's look of condescension as he sheathed his blade said it all. Chaos was no different to any other realm in that regard. Once Chaos got its claws into a mortal soul, that soul became its property. Which meant the numbers stacked ... and stacked ... *and stacked.* So much untapped power sat inside this grey fog. They were empty shells, desperate for faith. All that any of his kind had to do was present themselves and claim it, and some of them had already touched him …

An uncomfortable sensation crept over Avis and he once again looked out at those who were desperately swimming for Hell's shores. Uriel hadn't exorcised them to give him some breathing space or create a place of safety for the women and their party to be brought through as he'd first thought. The fog had touched him. Mortals with nothing to believe in had made physical contact with a deity.

Although he hadn't announced himself to give that touch a name, the brief contact had shown them something else existed. Something to believe in. Something they craved with all their being, without ever knowing why. His presence had inadvertently brought about a change in them which would have spread through the others like a plague had Uriel not expunged the taint first.

No wonder Chaos never showed anyone this side of the river. Even after everything they'd put him through, he'd be a liar if he said the thought of announcing himself to these mortal souls and taking control of such an enormous powerbase wasn't sorely tempting.

But someone needed to be in charge here. Someone specifically designated to this place. Belial ruled the whole realm, that wasn't in question, but each of the Nine Levels had a master guardian in charge for the day to day running. As he looked around, he couldn't even see any guards, let alone a hellion master, and he began to suspect he knew why. The presence of any kind of celestial, be it bender or shifter, would inadvertently alter the state of indifference of those locked within the fog.

So, none of their kind could be here. That line of deductive reasoning had him arching an eyebrow as he turned back to the castle. Without a celestial, was a mortal in charge here? "Who oversees this space?" he asked, determined to make sense of it. He lifted his free hand to the castle in the distance. "Who rules in there?"

Uriel curled his upper lip. "Do not get any ideas, Avis."

"You brought me here!" Avis snapped in return. "Just answer the damn question."

"No one," Uriel answered venomously. "Souls arrive here with no emotional attachment. They believed in no god and so they are left to drift here, endlessly. The castle was created by a select few of those whose brilliance surpassed the numbness of what you see around you. Inside those walls, you will find those who worshipped knowledge and intellect instead of a pantheon."

Avis looked at the castle again, seeing it through different eyes. *Mortals … with power over the celestial realm?* That was wrong on so many levels! The celestials were supposed to manipulate the fabric of mortal existence, not the other way around. For deceased mortals to be able to fashion anything out of the celestial realm, let alone a large castle from what appeared to be nothing …

… that was *huge*.

Avis had to break his train of thought. "So … the castle's being lit by a lot of bright sparks?" Despite his attempt to make 'light' of the situation, he couldn't believe he'd said that with a straight face.

The humour was lost on Uriel. "Exactly. They are powerful mortals and not to be trifled with."

Unwilling to educate the village idiot on the finer points of a joke, Avis huffed deeply and slid from the demon steed. He didn't want to spend too much time thinking about mortals with the power to upheave the natural order of things either. Let Chaos keep them all, if that was what some of them were capable of.

Without the lost souls congregating around him, the damp sand was quite visible and clung to his boots like a second skin. He walked to the water's edge and searched in both directions for the one thing that was pointedly missing from the shoreline. "So, where's the boat that'll take us through to the Nun Sea of Yaru?"

Uriel joined him on the beach, his silver armour collecting the sand just as easily as Avis' black leather boots had. The archangel stared at the water, and suddenly a wave rose from nowhere and froze in mid-air. Another joined it. As did a third. Avis watched as Uriel created the long raft from the river's components without ever touching the water.

It was an impressive feat and the Mystallian tried not to show how much he was enjoying the display. Changing someone's mind didn't have the same ... exhibitionism that changing something's shape did, though the balance was maintained due to a bender's ability to internalise.

Internalising was when a bender turned their minds inward, freezing out the physical realm. With time no longer an issue, a bender could interact with as many imaginary representatives of those he wanted to communicate with, as if they were really there. They had no extra information to work with, but the various points of view were enlightening. He could play out scenarios. Test theories. All within his imagination. And if other benders networked off him, they could congregate inside the weakest member's mind and hash out whatever they needed to, as long as they needed to.

The best example of internalising Avis could think of was one time when his sister of War had been serendipitously outside Mystal on a totally unrelated issue when an army of shape shifters attacked the farming village she happened to be in. Luckily for them, the villagers possessed bending blood, and Armina had thrown a mental net over everyone, shoving every man, woman and child into the weakest mind's imagination. From there, she trained the fuck out of them.

By the time they returned to the physical realm in what appeared to be a moment later, people who hadn't known the first thing about fighting two seconds ago were now stomping on broom handles to free the heads and spinning the improvised weapons with all the expertise of blooded warriors.

The most powerful mind maintained control of the atmosphere. The weakest one supplied it. The weakest one also had no say in it.

It was a powerful weapon, but the last time Avis had tried to internalise to escape the pain of being one of the Damned, he hadn't been the one in charge. Another, more powerful manifested in his imagination and the very worst memories of his past were relived in all their horrific glory. He still wasn't sure how he'd escaped the nightmare of his mind, but the instant he returned to the physical realm, his physical torture continued.

He never again tried to internalise.

As the water's unpleasant properties dawned on Avis, he jerked his head towards his brother-by-marriage. "You'll neutralise the pain that comes from touching the water, won't you?"

Again, that patronising eyeroll in his direction.

Oh, what Avis wouldn't give for just ten seconds alone with the smug bastard; shapeshifter or not. He breathed through his gritted teeth until he could speak without insulting the demonic crown prince. "In case the girls want to run around barefoot." *You ass,* he longed to add as he opened his arms to draw attention to the fact that every part of him except his head was covered in protective clothing. "Otherwise, I couldn't give a shit about its touch capability."

Uriel pursed his lips into a fine line of annoyance and slid his gaze to the raft. The enormous structure levitated off the water and rolled forward until its front end hovered just above the surface. Then, the archangel raised his armoured hands and placed the heels of his palms together. His focus was entirely on the vessel as he rocked his hands back and forth without parting them at the heel.

The raft began to shake with the speed of Uriel's hand movements until glittering dust-like particles flew from the hull and drifted back into the river. When he was done, he parted his hands and lowered them to his sides, shaking loose the tension. The raft righted itself and floated down to the water's surface. Avis remained focused on the raft. "I'm assuming something established in mortal mythology requires some type of specialised negation?"

"As you said. Cora and Columbine would be howling if they walked on the floorboards of a raft made from the Akheron River. That pain has now been returned to the river, and the raft is nothing more than a raft."

"Neat trick."

"I am the crown prince of all Chaos."

Meaning very few, if any others, shared that ability with Uriel and his father. Avis was hardly surprised. Negating an established powerbase was no mean feat; even from inside the pantheon. Regardless, the raft was ready and …

Avis' eyes widened in realisation. … *and the beach is cleared!* Everything they'd set out to do hours ago was done, and there was no reason for him not to be reunited with his family! He swung to his brother-by-marriage; his excitement palatable. "Is there anything else we have to do before I bring Clarise and the girls over?"

Uriel scowled and took a little too long to answer that, so Avis skimmed through his surface thoughts. There, he saw how the demon prince had hoped he'd run at this pivotal junction and wasn't happy with the realisation that his lowlife brother-by-marriage intended to stand by his sister and their children.

Avis tried not to be so smug about it. "Well?" he prompted.

"No."

CHAPTER TWENTY-EIGHT

Avis immediately lifted his hand and called for his wife. He didn't care if it made him look like a lovesick, hormonal teenager with his first girlfriend. He just couldn't wait to see her again. Clarise beamed at him, and within seconds they leaned into each other and embraced. Neither one lifted their feet, and at the end of the hug Avis released her, retaining a grip on one hand. Clarise looked to her left, beyond Avis' line of sight and raised her other hand beckoningly. "Guards first," she commanded.

As one of the golden monstrosities strode into view, Clarise took its wing in her free hand; allowing it to see and hear Avis on the other side of Hell. This wasn't done for conversational purposes. The guard never said a word as it reached out to Avis expectantly. The Mystallian clasped its wrist and with a single step, the guard went from standing alongside Clarise in the Well of Hell to being on the shores of the Akheron River with Avis.

It broke contact immediately and moved off to secure one of the perimeter points where Uriel's wall of hellfire met the water; making room for the next guard to step across. Over and over the process repeated itself until the guards, the children and the four servants were brought to the shores of the Akheron River.

When Clarise was the last to come over, Avis' lips parted into a predatory grin full of unspoken promises and he heaved her to him. She stumbled forward and slammed into his chest with a gasp of surprise, but his arms banded around her petite frame, securing her to him before she could bounce away. "Hey, beautiful," he purred, beaming down at her. "Missed you."

Clarise relaxed in his hold and slid her hands over his shoulders, knotting her fingers behind his neck. "Hey yourself, handsome. I missed you too."

Just as he was about to bow his head and mesh his lips to hers, he heard Cora sneer behind him, "If they kiss again, I am going to throw up."

"Why?" Columbine asked, full of innocence.

Little twerp. Avis cast a sly glance over his shoulder to pinpoint their location, then turned with Clarise still in his arms until they were standing side on from the girls. His grin grew as he bent down and kissed his wife deeply, his tongue forcing her teeth apart to plunder every aspect of her mouth. Clarise stiffened, but quickly yielded to the passion her husband had sprung upon her.

"Eeeewww!"

Avis kept the kiss going as long as he could, but when it finally ended, he chuckled and hugged Clarise closer. "Get used to it, trouble," he said, rubbing his chin against Clarise's hair to absorb and maybe even transfer some of her lavender scent to him. He'd always liked the fragrance, but now, just like the woman who wore it, he couldn't get enough of it. He looked over her head to their daughters. "Mystallians don't hide the way they feel about each other behind closed doors."

Clarise gasped and pushed against his chest until she was far enough away that he could see her face clearly. "Surely some *aspects* of showing how we feel about each other must be," she insisted, her cheeks turning the most adorable shade of red in embarrassment. "I will not be made a spectacle of, Avis."

Avis lightly kissed her forehead, breathing in more of her lavender scent as he did so. "No," he agreed, finding no pleasure in putting himself on display in that fashion either—unlike others in his family. "But with that in mind, I might have to grab the runt by the ear when we get home and let him know he and Emi will need to keep that style of entertainment discreet."

"Surely they would not … not *publicly* …"

"The runt married Love, Lust and Fertility, sweetheart. His wife enjoys sex even more than he does." With another predatory grin, he lowered his head and nuzzled her ear, saying, "And I doubt either one of them likes it as much as *I* do."

"LA-LA-LA-LA!" Cora shouted, breaking the playful moment between them. Looking up again, he met her daggered glare while her hands were clamped firmly over Columbine's naive earholes. Her maturity had slipped his mind, and he dipped his head in appreciation of how she was already looking out for her little sister the way any Highborn Hellion Lord would.

It seemed ten seconds out of the Well, and she was already starting to come around. The corners of Avis' lips curled with pride. *No one and no place could suppress a Mystallian spirit for long. Not even Hell itself.*

But, for all her adult concepts, he could tell Cora was just as eager for establishment as he himself had been all those eons ago. The thrill of going from no power at all to ultimate power was a rush he knew only too well and for her sake that level of exhilaration needed to be tempered, if only until her physical body caught up with her mental one. Establishment fields had to be carefully cultivated, for once they were in place, they were almost impossible to change.

Blagden was one glaring example of this. Another could be found in Asgard. In the realm of his closest friend, there was a girl—a young maiden—naive to the ways of sex. She was the keeper of the sacred fruit that supposedly kept the Asgardians immortal. (Why any pantheon would build such a ridiculously suicidal flaw like that into their power bases was beyond him!) She was young and beautiful, but when her innocence became known to the Asgardian mortals, they added her virginal state to their worship of her and changed what should have been a temporary situation into a permanent state of affairs.

No one saw it as a problem, until the day she married Odin's son Bragi and refused to consummate that union. To this day she was still a virgin who cared little for her husband's sexual frustration, and because the Asgardians relied on Idun for their immortality, they couldn't risk her leaving Asgard to modify her powerbase. If she was ever captured by another pantheon, Asgard would be forever enslaved. So, the virgin bride in the heart of Asgard, she remained.

When Avis first heard that story, he almost felt sorry for Bragi, but the kid *had* to have known what he was getting himself into when he married her. Her beauty was legendary, but so was her virginity. One of the few times he and Odin had gotten into a serious knock-down dragged out fight was when the girl had caught his eye, and his old friend had said *No*. Avis hated being told no, and he never denied himself a woman.

That brought his thoughts full circle to his own powerbase and its subsequent thrall. For so long he'd revelled in the way he could use and abuse women. His view of *fuck 'em and forget 'em* had been his lifelong motto, and he'd never spared any of them a backwards glance.

He cared for nothing except his own lustful desires, and he knew exactly why. After escaping the Nexus, he'd had control over his sex life for the first time and he'd desperately wanted to maintain that dominant position. Never again would anyone force him to do anything or *anyone*. At the time, he'd thought with every fibre of his being that the choice had been the right one ... until now.

A gloved hand encompassed his cheek and when he looked down, Clarise was staring up at him. "You look troubled, beloved."

For the first time ever, Avis knew he needed to put someone else's well-being ahead of his own—even if the outcome shattered him. His original plan of waiting until they'd left Chaos before ambushing Clarise with the truth that he may never return to Mystal suddenly sickened him.

She had the right to decide now, before their journey began, if she really wanted to be with him when there was a chance he wasn't going to be Mystal's ruler anymore. He drew in a slow breath and held it. "Clarise," he whispered hoarsely. A low growl warned him of Uriel's proximity, but he didn't care about the archangel right then. This was between him and his wife.

Turning her away from the family, Avis led her to the wall of fire that separated them from the rest of the Vestibule. He deliberately positioned himself between her and the family behind him, utilising his much larger size as a privacy screen.

Clarise's eyes shone with concern and his heart broke all over again. He dragged his lower lip through his teeth; hard enough to draw blood.

"Sweetheart, my powerbase isn't nice. You know this." He paused to see if she wanted to add anything ... *anything at all*, but all she did was raise one eyebrow slightly. "And Mystal's one of the biggest realms in existence. Baby, before we leave, you need to know that if my family can't (or won't) change the parameters of my establishment field, I won't be going back to Mystal. I won't go back to the way I was, and I don't care what my family says or does to try and make me."

Avis' mouth went dry. "So, I guess ... I'm asking ... if it came down to it ..." A lump formed in the back of his throat; so large it hurt. He couldn't bear the thought of leaving her behind. "Would you be willing to come with me and Cora into the Unknown Realms to start all over again if we had to—just the four of us?"

She opened her mouth to speak, but he silenced her with a finger. He had to get this out while he still had the courage to do so, even if it meant losing her.

"Think carefully, sweetheart. I love you and the girls more than anything, but a fresh start is almost unbearable in the beginning. You have no powerbase to make your life any easier and without a realm-wide attunement, we'll only be able to change one mortal mind at a time. It takes centuries for a realm of mortals to see you as their pantheon ruler, and until then you can't do anything about it. Armina was a good hunter and Amaro could kill anything she missed so we ate well. Chasidah and Chance led us to the best place to make camp and Tal and Griffith knocked us together minimal living accommodations. Sweetheart, if we do this, we won't have *any* of them to help us this time." He swallowed again. "So ... I guess what I'm trying to say ... even though it kills me to ... if that sounds too rough for my delicate queen ... I'll ... I'll understand ... I swear ..."

It was Clarise's turn to cover his lips, though she did so with her entire gloved hand clamping firmly over everything below his nose. "Say not another word," she whispered angrily.

Her eyes sparkled with possessiveness and irritation in equal measure, though she didn't speak loudly enough for the girls to hear. "I am Highborn Hellion. Should it come to that, I will be whatever we need me to be, just as the girls and our servants will. If you have deceived yourself into believing you made it work with your physically limited siblings in a new terrain, you have yet to see what *my* people in *any* physical terrain can do."

There's my Mystallian queen! Avis took the hand she had pressed against his mouth and rolled it until he kissed her knuckles. It was a gesture of reverence, but his elation became too much and he abandoned the demure act for a passionate kiss of the woman who made his life complete. The crushing heartache that had accompanied the uncertainty of her decision for so long vanished in an instant and his body shook with relief and untold excitement.

They were going to do this! No matter the outcome, they were going to stand together and make it work. The kiss lingered on, but eventually he twisted away from her and waved his hand in a broad sweeping gesture towards the demon steeds. "Load 'em up," he ordered, his heart lighter than it had been in days.

Although he hadn't directed the command specifically at the servants, the four females stepped forward and gathered up a set of demon steed reins each, careful not to make physical contact with the beasts.

The steeds snorted bursts of fire as they were led to the water's edge, but after a little coaxing from the servants, they leapt over the painful river and were tied down at the raft's stern. The fire in their hooves didn't set the raft alight, which was a bonus Avis hadn't thought to include. "What kind of upkeep do the demon steeds need?" he quietly asked his wife as the beasts settled.

"The servants will take care of their needs, beloved," Clarise replied, snuggling against his chest. "They are hellions and capable of shapeshifting any requirements we need via touch, as you will see when we get underway."

"On that note, Clarise, I must bid you and the girls safe travels and leave you to your lengthy journey," Uriel called with a smile, again excluding Avis from the farewell. "Let me know if you do decide to strike out on your own in the Unknown Realms. We have plenty of family and servants to help make that transition a very comfortable one for you."

So, the bastard had been eavesdropping anyway. *Nosey prick.*

Clarise gave Avis's waist a squeeze, then crossed the room to her awaiting brother. "Take care, Uriel," she said, wrapping her arms around his neck while Avis followed in her wake.

She kissed Uriel demurely on both cheeks, and he returned the kiss by pressing his lips to her forehead. Avis flinched in revulsion. It was all so … *nauseatingly* proper. "Grace be with you, Clarise, and know that no matter what happens, I am only a blood-link away."

Uriel hugged his sister close, using the move to shoot Avis a withering glare over her head. Avis folded his arms and met that scowl dead-on. He was not backing down again. Never again. One day, they wouldn't be in Chaos, and on that day, he would remind the archangel just where the bastard sat in the mental grand scheme of things. All he had to do was wait for *that* day.

Eventually, the archangel broke away from Clarise and turned to the children, going down on one knee with his arms open for them. It didn't have the feel of an invitation to Avis. More like an unspoken command, which Columbine responded to by approaching him with a level of decorum Avis felt no child should have.

Her hands slid around his neck as his arms closed around her body. Her wings rolled forward to embrace his upper body, while his came forward and hid them both completely from view. It was also very ... *proper*, and witnessing it made Avis want to break out in hives.

Kids were supposed to be bouncing off the walls with enthusiasm, not subdued like this. "You be good for your mother," Avis heard him say from inside the feathery mass; parroting the Mystallian's earlier request while at the same time excluding him. "And I'll see you very soon."

"Promise?" he heard Columbine ask.

Uriel unfurled his wings from her and returned them to their natural position behind him. "You have my word I will see you again within the year," he promised. "Even if I must squeeze the visit in between assignments."

Columbine's throttlehold on his neck tightened. "I love you, Uncle Uriel."

Uriel's control slipped again, only this time his lips parted into a broad smile that went all the way to his eyes. "Love you too, little one," he chuckled, rubbing his cheek against her leather covered head; narrowly missing one of the two tiny, thumb-sized bumps that might have been the beginnings of horns if they weren't so against her nature. "But if you do not let me go, neither of us will be going anywhere."

Columbine reluctantly untangled her arms and stepped away, allowing Uriel to place one elbow against his raised knee. For several drawn-out moments, he silently regarded the older of Avis' daughters, as if trying to get the measure of her. In Avis' mind, it shouldn't have been that hard. Cora was the only one who acted like a real kid. "For the record, I wish you well, Cora. You never did fit in with us, but I truly hope you find your home out there."

Cora edged her way forward and Avis could see she was fighting tears. "Will you miss me too?"

The deep-rooted heartache contained within those few words hit Avis in the chest so hard he had to look at the miserable orange-grey sky overhead to get a hold of himself. If it took him the rest of eternity, he would give that girl back her identity and her pride. From what he could tell, she'd gone her whole life being told she was wrong, naughty and bad.

Years of that condemnation had destroyed her as thoroughly as any blade, until all she had left was a false layer of bravado designed to keep everyone at arm's reach. It had even fooled him up until now, but exposed as she was, no more. Never again would he use the nick-name *trouble* when referring to her. Not when *troubled* was so much closer to the truth.

He lowered his eyes to her again. *I have a lot of work to do.*

Uriel nodded at Cora and beckoned her forward with the tips of his fingers. Just as he had with Columbine, he enfolded the older daughter of Avis and Clarise in a close hug when she came within reach. "I want you happy, you little nightmare," he said, and despite the derision in his name-calling, Avis could tell he meant it. "Even if that means being somewhere else."

"She will be," Avis said, having never meant his words more than he did at that moment. He stepped to his wife's side and draped one hand across her shoulders. At the same time, he spread the thumb and fingers of his other hand against the back of Cora's neck, claiming them both as his. "One way or another, *Cora* will be happy." He emphasised her name to show he would tolerate nothing less from anyone from this point forward when addressing her.

Cora looked up at him in surprise, but other than to offer her a stoic nod, Avis made no other remark. Words were cheap to a Mystallian. Her start in life may not have been the best, but he had the rest of eternity to make it up to her and he would see to it that she found her place. He owed her that much.

Uriel ignored Avis' demeanour and cuddled Cora one last time before releasing her and rising to his feet. He gave them all a single, parting nod and stepped away, then gathered up the reins of his demon steed in one hand and slid effortlessly on to its back. His accompanying high-pitched note had the beast unfurling its fiery wings; its shoulder muscles rippling in anticipation of going airborne.

Avis suddenly thought of the other demon steeds standing nearby and swung his head towards the raft, fully expecting them to have their wings exposed as well. Yet all four of them remained wingless and at ease. Avis eyed them suspiciously. *There's no way you lot didn't hear that, so what am I missing?*

As far as he could tell, there'd been no difference in the musical commands, which meant they either understood Uriel's intent or there'd been a subtle undertone he'd missed. Avis delved into the animals' surface thoughts to find out.

Viewing the mind of an animal had never been enjoyable for Avis. They weren't evolved, so the logic behind their decisions was non-existent. But times like this, where information was required and he had no intention of asking his brother-by-marriage anything, he gritted his teeth and went on the mental prowl …

… and quickly concluded it was the former. Somehow, and it was a vague 'somehow' since the demon steeds didn't care enough to question the specifics, (yet another reason why Avis hated using animals for information gathering—they sucked at it) they knew instinctively when the member of the Highborn was referring to them. It was an ingrained compulsion.

"Until our paths cross again, grace be with you all."

Although it was the first time Avis felt included in the valediction, it didn't sound particularly hellish and he stiffened in disgust at the archangel's alternate powerbase. As if he would *ever* want a farewell blessing from that poaching pack of …!

He hadn't thought he'd said anything aloud, but Clarise silently slipped her arms between his cloak and his torso and knotted her fingers behind his back. Her chin dug into his chest as she stared up at him lovingly. Meeting those beautifully soft golden eyes, he felt the heat of his rising temper dissipate.

More and more, Clarise was proving to be his rock of reason. He smiled and placed his lips to her brow, then tucked her safely into his side. Uriel was already gone. *Good riddance.* "Let's go, ladies," he said, gesturing for the girls to join the servants on the raft. "But don't let the water touch you. It's also known as The River of Pain for a reason."

Columbine spread her wings and leapt into the air. She caught the heated air currents and used them to glide out over the raft, at which point she lowered her legs to stand as if she had been there all along and tucked her wings behind her primly. Again, the move was all … *very proper.*

Cora, like every Mystallian child before her, wasn't nearly so graceful. Focusing completely on the target, she backed up a few steps and took a deep breath. Then she dug her booted toes into the sand and ran full pelt towards the raft, throwing herself into the air just prior to the water's edge. Her tiny legs pumped in the air until her boots collided with the raft and she quickstepped several paces before pulling herself up.

Elegant it was not, but her grin of pride as she swung around to face him reaffirmed just how important it had been to change her clothing to hunting tans. A dress and heels would never have made that jump. "Our turn," he declared, and without pausing to explain himself, he twisted sidewards and scooped Clarise off her feet and into his arms. Due to his size and familiarity with the Mystallian form, he knew he'd only need two good steps for momentum.

A few seconds later he landed with ease between the girls.

"I could have made that jump myself," Clarise scolded.

Unfazed by her angry tone, Avis grinned at her unabashedly and tightened his grip. "Maybe I like having you in my arms," he purred, rubbing his forehead against hers. "Ever think about that, sweetheart?"

"And … here they go again," Cora groaned from the front end of the raft.

Avis's snort of amusement grew into a hearty laugh when he saw Cora had her eyes crossed over her screwed-up nose. "I told you, you'd better get used to this, tiger," he teased, snuggling closer to his wife. "Your mother's mine, and by the Twin Notes that started us all, I'm keeping her for all eternity."

As he'd hoped, Cora's repugnance morphed into a mild frown of confusion. "What's a tiger?"

Good. He'd hoped she'd take the bait, especially when he hadn't exactly been subtle about it. "It's an apex predator in Mystal. Razor sharp teeth. Claws the length of my fingers and a hide full of ginger fur, interlaced with stripes of black and white. They're exquisite and very protective of their own. Your cousin Strahan always keeps a mated pair as companion animals and very little gets past them." *Just so I'm clear …* "It's a compliment, tiger."

She seemed surprised by the description, or maybe it was his comparison of herself to such a magnificent beast. Either way, her shoulders squared and her lips twitched in what may have been the beginnings of a true smile. "Is that how you see me?" She was still unsure. *Damn the Highborn Hellions and their bullshit cruelty.*

Keeping those thoughts on a tight leash, he motioned with his chin towards Columbine. "Did you, or did you not just protect your little sister's innocence against a much bigger and more dangerous opponent—namely me?"

Now she couldn't hide her smile of pride … and nor, more surprisingly, could he. *Tiger* was the perfect moniker for her with all those striking red locks, and it would be even more so when she regained the use of her shapeshifting. Already, he could envision her using demonic fangs and claws against anything that challenged what she considered *hers.*

"Ladies," Clarise called, resting her head against Avis' shoulder once it became apparent the conversation between them was over. "Take us out."

All four of the servants bowed as one and split into their respective pairs. Frash and Tilu moved to the starboard side of the raft near the bow, while Diviten and Gingen went to the port side of the stern. Tilu and Diviten reduced their heights and remoulded themselves into heavily muscular forms with four large arms and a pair of heavy set legs which Avis wouldn't have been able to put both arms around. Meanwhile Frash and Gingen raised their arms over their heads and shifted into long, thin masses that not only stretched towards the water, but to Avis' disbelief, they pierced the painful surface and kept on going.

But they didn't explode in agony as he expected. Instead, they continued to stretch until they became a pair of solid timber barge poles that stuck straight up in the air within easy grabbing distance of their respective partners. It had been their plan all along. *Shifters … just suck*, Avis grumbled to himself, knowing full well what would've happened if *he'd* touched that water.

Tilu took her pole and drove it into the sandy shore, shoving the bow towards the middle of the river. Diviten used hers to propel them forward. As Avis smugly flipped a mental bird at the receding shoreline, he realised their four Highborn Hellion Guards were still standing around the perimeter of the beach enclosure. "Hey!" he bellowed, causing Clarise to jump in his arms.

"Avis, what in …?"

"The guards," he said, jerking his head impatiently at the shoreline.

Clarise looked in that direction. "What about them, beloved?"

"They're …" But when he looked at the shore again, they'd vanished.

What. The. Hell? Avis blinked repetitively, but sure enough, they were gone. *Where'd they go?* He searched the area and found them as close to the four corners of the raft as they could be without interfering with the poling motions of the servants. Their arms were folded and their headpieces rotated, just as they had on the shore.

What? That level of speed was impossible outside a powerbase … *wasn't it?* Avis licked his lips. *Maybe it's a bonus of sorts from being in Chaos.* He didn't like the odds, but he tried desperately to convince himself of that fact. They were terrifying enough, without being able to move at those speeds!

"Yes?" Clarise asked, still waiting for an explanation for the fright he'd given her.

He closed his mouth and swallowed. "Never mind, sweetheart."

He had plenty to think about as the raft made it into the middle of the river and their journey was finally underway.

CHAPTER TWENTY-NINE

There wasn't a whole lot to do as the servants poled the large raft down the Akheron River. The Damned constantly tried to escape the agony of the Akheron River by clambering aboard, only to be driven straight back down again by a shining golden fist or whatever other extremity the Highborn Hellion Guard member chose to use against them.

If the brute squad were anywhere near as bored as Avis was, they were probably mixing it up just to break the monotony. He himself was very tempted to lead the charge in pushing them back, and probably would have, had he not envisioned Columbine's reaction to the violence he'd mete out.

Three days had passed, and they were still poling along the river with no sign of the Chaotian Ocean anywhere. Three looong, mind-numbingly boring days. There was no night or day on the river to signify the movement of time. No sunrise or sunset. Just an insipidly dismal orange-grey glow that seemed to cover everything at once.

The only regularity that gave Avis any insight to the time was when Tilu and Diviten stopped poling long enough to present them with a meal. *Breakfast* came first, *lunch* a few hours later, and *dinner* a few hours after that. Then a huge gap of nothing which he supposed was meant to represent the evening.

They'd had eight meals in total so far. During that first meal, he noticed how little Columbine ate, but dismissed it as part of her demonic physiology. It wasn't as if she went to the bathroom either, so the correlation was understandable.

He, on the other hand, ate heartily. It gave him something to do. Boredom was seriously pissing him off.

He glanced across at Clarise, trying hard not to twist his lips in frustration. There were plenty of things he'd *like* to do with her to pass the time, but the raft consisted of a series of flat beams that were lashed together; equating to zero privacy.

The only exception to that was when someone needed to relieve themselves, at which point one of the servants would stop poling and while the pole secured the raft, the pole bearer would become a privacy screen in one corner of the raft for a few minutes.

Three days, where he'd either been sitting at Clarise's side or lying with his beloved wife in his arms and not once could he do the one thing he wanted more than anything. Well, not that he *couldn't* … but like her, he didn't like the idea of an audience either and the girls only had to open their eyes and they'd see everything.

Adding that to the mental reminder of what Cora had seen as a newborn was more than enough to curtail any sex drive he might've had. Which was good … in a way … he supposed.

The servants switched positions several times during those three days until Avis no longer had a clue which was which. Nor did he care. So long as they did their job and left him alone, he had no interest in them.

He rolled flat on his back and stared at the orange-grey sky.

By the Known Realms, he was soooo bored!

Eventually, after hours of tossing and turning, he felt the soft jolt of the raft, indicating the pole bearers were anchoring the raft in preparation of another meal. This would be their ninth to date. The time between their last meal and now meant it would also be 'breakfast'.

With little else to occupy his mind, Avis had idly wondered where the servants were getting all the food from and being awake for this latest jostle meant he was in the perfect position to find out.

Rolling to his feet, he caught sight of the poles above the water as they split in half down the middle and folded themselves over the two front corners of the raft; lashing it into place as effectively as any anchor. Meanwhile, Diviten and Tilu made their way to the middle of the bow and knelt along the edge, using their huge mass to block any inquisitive eyes.

As if Avis would let that stop him. Now that his curiosity was well and truly piqued, he moved up alongside them to see for himself what they were up to. At that instant, it occurred to him that boredom had probably sent him senile, for what other reason was there to give a crap about where his next meal came from.

And not just give a crap, but physically take real time to find out instead of reaching inside their minds and taking the information directly from them as was his birthright. At least his family wasn't here to see him now. He'd never live this shifter shit down.

At this point, his only interest was to give himself something to do that would take longer than a handful of seconds. Anything at all, really. He was so bored, he wasn't even attempting to be subtle anymore.

Leaning over the front of the raft to see around them, he saw one had shifted her hands into a double handed, net-like scoop, while the other had extended her right arm to twice its length with a sharp, harpoon-like barb where her hand once was. They both froze when they realised they had an audience.

"Was there … something we can do for you, Milord?" the catcher asked, somewhat surprised by his intense scrutiny. While the question was being asked, the hunter discreetly moulded her arm back into a hand which she hid behind a bent knee; her eyes downcast. Avis was willing to bet the catcher was Tilu, if her manners were anything to go by.

"No," he stated, remaining exactly as he was. He didn't owe the females any further explanation, and once the answer given, he'd fully expected them to get back to work. Instead, they looked at each other apprehensively, then back at him. Were they really going to be stupid enough to defy him? "As you were," he growled warningly. Again, the women eyed each other.

Before either female could move, a terrible rending sound, not unlike an old tree being ripped in half, came from the corner of the raft behind him. The female which he assumed was Tilu leapt to her feet and rushed past him while he whipped around to see what in the realms was going on behind him.

The supporting pole which Avis labelled 'Frash' had split far below the waterline and as the weight of the raft and its occupants bore down on her, it pushed through her lashings, apparently tearing her in two. Tilu laid her hands over her sister-servant and added her mass to the pole. With very little effort between the two, they managed to shore up Frash's split until she was once again whole.

Avis didn't buy the sincerity of the situation for a second; not that he blamed Tilu for running to the aid of her sister-servant. Her surface thoughts at the time had been filled with genuine concern for Frash, but they were later replaced with gratitude.

Gratitude? For what? Demons could become anything they wanted—of any *consistency* they wanted, and the idea that a hellion would structurally break under the weight of a single raft ... it didn't make any sense ...

... until he turned back to Diviten and found her hastily finishing up the meal.

The whole thing had been nothing more than a diversion! Rage and indignation soared to life inside of him. *FUCK!*

"Avis—Avis, wait!"

Avis barely heard the repetitive, fast-paced thump of Clarise's booted heels on the deck as he swung back towards Frash and Tilu with murder first and foremost in mind. Soft, gloved hands suddenly framed his face and created a shielded resistance to the movement, preventing him from seeing that corner of the raft.

"Avis, look at me, beloved," Clarise insisted, though rage pumped furiously through his veins and the demand for reprisal roared in his ears, blocking out all sense of reason. He'd been taken for a fool for the last time by that bitch!

"*Avis.*"

The underscoring of his name broke through his single-mindedness and he growled at her before he could stop himself. His vision had slitted and gone to the extreme corners of his eyes in the hopes of catching a glimpse of either of those two duplicitous servants. Frash especially. He wouldn't hurt Clarise to do it, but even a glimpse around those delicate fingers was all he needed. "Avis, no. Stop fighting and look. At. Me."

Avis did, and he didn't like what he saw. Her lips were pinched together and the gold in her eyes had hardened until sharp edges criss-crossed the iris. Their intensity pierced his rage, if only for a moment. "What happened?" she asked, which only served to remind Avis of Frash's deceit.

His eyes snapped away from her and shot towards the servants, but Clarise's hold grew stronger and she made a negatory sound of her own. "No, do not look over there, beloved. Look at me," she insisted. "Talk to me. What has you so vexed that you are incapable of thinking straight?"

Her lavender fragrance filled his nostrils, clearing away the red haze he hadn't noticed in the edges of his vision. His entire body seethed with rage and his chest heaved as if he had run a marathon, but slowly ... *gradually*, her presence brought him back to a place of calm. When he finally spoke, he still couldn't quite remove the bite from his voice. "Is there any chance of you getting a replacement for Frash? Because I am going to kill her."

The words were pushed through gritted teeth, but he absolutely meant them. He wasn't one of those people who threw around 'I'm going to kill you' because it sounded cool or was amusing to do so. On the rare occasion when he gave someone that unusual heads up, whoever the intended target was knew to start running and never look back. *Ever.*

The harsh peaks in Clarise's irises softened but didn't quite return to their usual molten state. "Those we have with us are all we have access to, beloved. If you were to kill Frash, I myself would have to take that position until we no longer required a barge pole."

Avis hissed and went to pull away, but Clarise's hands held him still, deliberately keeping his line of sight on her and away from Frash and Tilu. "You know I never lie, beloved. If you kill her, we will be without a second barge pole and as the only other capable shifter onboard, I will be forced to take her place."

"You are not going anywhere near that fucking water!" Avis shouted, his temper returning in spades at the thought of his queen being forced into servitude. His arms snaked out and drew her bodily to him, as if that act alone could protect her from the eventuality.

A pained squint crossed Clarise's features and Avis realised he'd cursed without meaning to. But she didn't voice her displeasure and instead, lowered her hands from his face and cupped either side of his neck. "Then tell me what has irked you so."

"Frash played me, and not for the first time."

"In what way?"

Peering into those soft, golden eyes, Avis suddenly felt very self-conscious and foolish. She was so much shorter than him, but in that moment, she towered over him. If it was so important, he could have gotten his answers simply by going into the minds of the servants and getting them, thus avoiding this whole situation.

The predicament only came about because he'd been too bored to cut the game short. "I was watching them prepare the meal, when Frash faked an injury to distract me at a crucial point." He growled again at the memory and shook his head. "People who play me tend to die."

"And why does the preparation of the meal interest you so much?"

He could already see where she was going with this. Under any other circumstances, he wouldn't have cared about the meal other than the fact it turned up on time. "Because I want to know where it comes from, and there's nothing else to do on this raft."

Clarise batted her eyelashes and slowly … lightly palmed the sides of his throat. "Perhaps their deception was done for your own good?" she suggested, in a way that made it more like a given fact than a question.

He resisted the way she massaged the corded muscles in his neck, refusing to be side-tracked. "I don't care, sweetheart. I don't get played. Not by anyone."

"That you know of."

Oh, he *reeeally* didn't like that. Tension snapped through his body like a whip until it crackled beneath the skin and his lips curled indignantly. "You think I'm being stupid?" he snarled.

Clarise smiled at him as if she didn't have a care in the world, then spun around and placed her back against his chest, winding herself into his arms. "I *think* your pride has been pricked," she began, tapping her fingers against his forearms. "I *think* our servants got the better of you, and you do not like that. I *think* you could solve all this by simply asking them what you want to know, but you have turned this into a competition that you are determined to win at all costs. And I *think* you are doing all of this to avoid the answer you already know."

Whether it was her body being pressed so closely to his, the lulling sound of her monologue or the rationale of her deductions (or a combination of all three)

Avis couldn't be sure, but it calmed him down enough to turn her again and peer into those molten gold eyes. "What are you talking about?"

Clarise walked him in a tight half circle away from Frash and Tilu until he faced the front, right-hand side of the raft, then slid to his side and gestured with one raised arm towards the river around them. "What do you see, Avis?"

It had to be a trick question. The view hadn't changed since they left the proximity of Hell's front gates and the river widened until neither shore could be seen. "A river filled with celestial pain and deceased mortal souls desperately trying to cross the river to escape it."

Clarise's left hand slid around his waist and she rested her cheek against his sternum. "Do you see anything else, beloved? In any direction? Any floating pieces of wood or other debris of that nature?"

It may have been worded objectively, but Avis didn't like the connotation and he really didn't like where it was leading him. "No."

"Then logic must dictate that our food comes from one of those two sources."

Avis made the next piece of deductive reasoning himself. The River of Pain held a celestial element that would've had them writhing on contact. That meant the servants were harvesting the Damned—plucking them from the water and shapeshifting them into palatable meals in much the same way Barris of the Hunt would catch a fish for breakfast back home. With one … *drastically* fundamental difference. The fish Barris ate were dead. *Very* dead.

These souls were of the Damned, and the Damned didn't die. They endured everything, in great misery. His meals were alive. They'd *still* be alive after they passed through him. That right there was perhaps one of the few things the Hellions hadn't done to him, and he'd thought they'd covered everything. But they hadn't eaten him! They hadn't torn him into bite-sized portions and swallowed him … forcing him to travel in pieces through their bodies …!

Avis pushed Clarise away as his stomach heaved. "I think I'm going to be sick," he declared, planting one hand against his hip and pressing the back of his clenched fist against his lips. His nostrils flared as he fought to contain the nausea and only managed to do so by thinking how weak he would look in front of the girls if he suddenly doubled over and hurled his entire last meal into the river.

Clarise returned to his side and slid her hand under his cloak so no one would see her rub his back between the shoulder blades. "It was why they tried to keep it hidden from you, beloved. Before your imprisonment, you would not have cared what happened to these souls either way, but now that you have been one of them, you have bonded with their plight. You have made their situation … personal."

"They don't deserve *that!*"

"And yet you need to eat, my love. Daily. Otherwise your body will grow weak from hunger. Does the selfless deer deserve to be shot? Does the harmless fish deserve to be caught? Neither of them does anything to warrant their fate, yet they die in vast quantities every day. Controlling all things physical has taught us that survival of the fittest is not only for the mortals. We *are* the top of the food chain, Avis. We are supposed to survive above all others and at all costs. Will you really put a few damned souls who must have done some very atrocious things in their lives to be here in the first place above your own daily needs?"

Avis wanted to say YES, but he was too selfish a bastard and he knew Clarise knew it. Still, how in the realms was he supposed to eat anything from here on in, knowing what he knew now?

CHAPTER THIRTY

The breakfast had been created and placed upon the picnic rug while they spoke, but Avis still had a hard time even looking at it and definitely wanted nothing to do with it.

Sensing this, Clarise took his hand and bullied him into motion. He resisted initially, but her grip tightened and the sharpening of her gaze made it clear he either had to follow her lead or create a scene. Avis frowned. If she thought a Mystallian would rather save face and yield to another over kicking and screaming every step of the way, she really didn't understand his family at all.

No one being honest could ever claim they didn't know where a Mystallian stood. Nevertheless, he did understand the importance of family at mealtimes. He himself insisted on having his Life Court turn up for regular meals, if only to reinforce the unity of the pantheon. As a people, they wore their opinions openly. As such, any ill-will between members was quickly recognised and dealt with before it got out of hand.

At the very least, he could *pretend* to be part of this meal.

The girls quickly joined them, and soon Clarise and Cora were tucking in just as they always had. Avis wasn't so inclined, so he watched Columbine fiddle with her food and make small talk with her mother and sister. Subtlety wasn't his strongest suit, but without eating himself, he noticed she placed just one bite-sized item onto her plate before pulling it back into her lap. She took her time and chatted quietly, but when she lifted a morsel to her mandibles, something seemed … *off* … about the way it transitioned into her mouth.

He caught the fire in her eyeless recesses moving towards him and he quickly looked away, but when she had another bite-sized piece in front of her mandibles a few seconds later, he watched her closely and realised it wasn't making it into her mouth at all. The clawed hand holding it moved towards her face as if to push it into the opening, but the food remained stationary—because it was going into her *hand* instead.

She was hiding it inside the palm of her hand. Avis wasn't sure what that hoped to achieve until she used that same hand to reach for her next morsel of choice from the banquet they'd been provided and redeposited the uneaten food back on the plate it came from while her clawed fingertips collected something different. The whole thing was a sham!

You slick little shit! He admired the sleight of hand that was so subtle he had to watch it twice before he was certain it was what she was doing. When he'd *thought* she was eating sparsely, she hadn't been eating at all! Not that he could blame her for wanting to avoid the meal. His own stomach cartwheeled at the thought as well.

"Avis, is the food not to your liking?" Clarise asked, giving him a pointed look that suggested he should start eating; sooner rather than later.

"I will have his, if he does not want it," Cora volunteered enthusiastically.

Avis stared into the empty plate before him until the whiteness of the surface hurt his eyes, then cast his gaze across the mountain of food and drink that Diviten had created for them. The quantity for only four people was ludicrous and he couldn't help but wonder if there was one poor soul in there, silently screaming his or her denial, or two?

Which, unfortunately, led to other thoughts. What ages had they been when they died? Were they only children? What could they have possibly done to deserve this fate? Those he'd seen exorcised from the Vestibule had just been in the wrong place at the wrong time. What if that was the case here?

When he realised it didn't matter, he drew in a deep breath and lifted his eyes to Cora. "Go for it, tiger," he sighed, dropping the napkin over his empty plate. "I'm really not that hungry this morning."

"No," Clarise interjected, and for a second Avis thought she was referring to him, however her hand was held out in front of Cora to keep their elder daughter from diving at the platter like a starving madwoman. "Your father is just not hungry *now*. Prepare a plate for him to eat later, when his hunger returns. Then you may have the leftovers."

Avis crossed one arm across his chest and balanced the elbow of the other against his wrist. He stroked his eyebrows with his thumb and middle finger, bracing his pointer against his forehead for balance. The chances of him *ever* being that hungry ranged between *never* and *all The Nine Levels of Hell freezing over simultaneously*.

Without a word to anyone, he rose to his feet and retreated to the furthest space away from the accursed meal, which put him in the middle of the hitched demon steeds near the stern. The steeds nickered at his intrusion and he ran his hands across the shoulders of the nearest two to calm them, calming his own churning thoughts and stomach at the same time. The Damned! All this time he'd been eating and drinking *the fucking Damned!*

Clarise quickly joined him. "Avis, I do not approve of this," she said, in a tone that went eerily close to a scold. "You must eat to keep up your strength."

Avis kept his back to her. He didn't want to see the condemnation in her eyes. "I ate a hearty dinner last night, Clarise. I'll be good for at least a few days. Maybe even a week."

If he thought she'd leave it at that, he was sadly mistaken. Her hand curled around his right elbow and she forced him around to face her. He didn't put up much in the way of resistance and met her steely gaze with an unrepentant one of his own once he faced her. The two stared long and hard at each other, both fighting a battle of wills that neither would concede. After a while, she lifted her left hand and uncurled her gloved fingers, revealing a small meatball in the palm of her hand. "Eat, Avis." She wasn't giving him an option.

Avis' stomach convulsed at the mere presence of the offensive item and he pursed his lips tightly, shaking his head in denial. He couldn't. It was alive! He'd eat anything else, but not one of the Damned!

Clarise lifted the meatball a little higher. "Eat," she insisted.

Avis met her eyes, and the same conviction he'd seen too many times in the mirror told him she had no intention of backing off. It meant that much to her, but just the thought of trying to swallow that thing had all the muscles along his throat and jaw tightening in repulsion. "Clarise ..."

"No. I will not allow you to do this, Avis. The distance between the Akheron River and the Chaotic Ocean is in a constant state of flux. We could be there tomorrow, or we could be there next year. It is why we use the raft to traverse it instead of something much faster. If we overshoot the mouth of the Akheron River without first being lined up for Yaru, we could potentially add decades, maybe even centuries to our journey. You need to accept this as a part of what is happening."

He loathed the way she was speaking to him like an errant child. "I do ..."

But Clarise would have none of his excuses. "No, you do not. You are allowing something as small and inconsequential as a meatball to prevent you from doing what you must to survive."

"It's not just a meatball ..."

"It is," she argued, lifting the savoury item until he could smell the spice. "This is the only food we have. Where it came from is inconsequential. It is nourishment and it will keep you strong. You need to get over your sense of kinship towards it because you do not have that anymore. Those girls need a strong role-model, not a god who cannot bring himself to eat a simple meatball."

Avis looked past her to where the girls were trying their best to pretend they weren't listening in. He already knew Cora was. Her ears were practically twitching beneath that bright red hair. *Cheeky shit.* He shot a mental barb at her, akin to a parental clip under the ear and she yelped, dropping her eyes to the mat and hiding behind her rounded shoulders. Avis then looked at Columbine, who was sitting side on to watch him.

His eyebrows knitted together into a frown as he pointed one finger at the ground near his feet and twirled it in a slow circle. Columbine hunched beneath the unspoken reprimand and twisted around until her back was to him with her wings flared to prevent further eavesdropping.

The sense of achievement gave him the boost he needed to end this, and he refocused on the small woman whom he'd had the good fortune to be forced into marrying. "When I get hungry enough, I'll eat it, sweetheart," he said with conviction, determined to lay down the law as far as he was concerned. "Until then ..."

"Not good enough, Avis," Clarise cut in, and before he could argue further, she used the biggest trump card in her arsenal to shut him down hard. "You once said you would do anything for me." She pressed the hand holding the meatball into his chest. "I want you to eat this. Right now. For me. Show me you can."

Avis felt utterly cornered as he looked at the meatball and dragged his hand across his face. At the time he'd said that and meant it with every fibre of his being but ... *really?* His eyes must have jumped between the meatball and her face a hundred times, hoping she would relent, but each time her expression was just as resolute as any of her male kin, and twice she nudged him with the tips of her fingers.

"Avis," she prompted.

He shuddered in repulsion, his chest heaving with every breath. Still, she wouldn't back off. It was a total stand-off, and he knew who was going to lose. The fact that it was him knotted his stomach even more than it already was and he wanted to roar in denial.

Eventually, his unwilling hand took the meatball from her hand and he rolled his wrist to stare at it. It did smell as delicious as it looked; but just the thought of eating it sent his mind into a complete tailspin. His mouth dried up and a huge lump formed in his throat. Clarise gently stroked his side. "It is small, Avis. You do not even need to chew it. Swallow it whole. It will be alright. You can do this."

She had more faith in him than he did.

His mind surged with all the possibilities of the soul's origins and what its perspective on this was, until the muscles in his neck became so tense they threatened to throttle him. He lifted his gaze above her head, using the neutral scenery of the orange-grey sky to find the will to push himself through this.

Mortal afterlives were still alive in a sense, and as a member of the Damned, it would, by definition, feel everything. The question was, without eyes and ears and being reduced to nothing more than an energy source, would it still hear and see? And what part of it was in the meatball? Some body parts were even more repulsive than others, especially if they were male.

"Do not overthink it, Avis. Just do it."

He'd eaten some horrible things in his time, but nothing like this. Sweat prickled his skin and his stomach coiled into knots.

Clarise's hand stilled. "I am not leaving until you do," she warned.

As he eyed the meatball in his hand, the fingers of his other hand subconsciously covered his mouth. *I can do this … I think.* He knew exactly who he was trying to convince, and he wasn't entirely sure it was working. His teeth nibbled at the seam of his glove. *I can do this. I can do this.*

With every mental word, he drew in breaths—each deeper than the last—until he had himself in a mental place where he could ignore everything that was going on around him. Then, closing his eyes, he threw the meatball into his mouth and threw his head back, forcing himself to swallow it before his body could rebel.

It slid down the back of his throat like a rock and lodged half way to his stomach. He clenched his eyes shut and fought his rioting body, refusing on principle to throw it back up again. He just had to hold it down.

The worst was over. Sort of. He pressed his lips together and mashed a gloved hand into them to forcibly keep them shut, then swung away from Clarise to lock his watering gaze on at the orange-grey sky over the river. He couldn't bring himself to look at the water. If he saw the souls making their dash for the far shore, he *would* throw up.

No question. His breath pounded mercilessly against the forefinger of his glove until finally, the meatball moved to a point in his stomach where he could pretend it hadn't happened.

He felt Clarise wrap her arms around his waist and pressed her forehead against his back. "I know how unpleasant this is for you, but it will get easier, my love," she promised, as he continued to suck air through flared nostrils. "You need to ignore what it is. Rise above it. As far as we are concerned, it is just a meal—no different to any other. If it suffers, it is because of its own actions and decisions during its mortal life, and that is not our concern."

Avis slowly shook his head. It was instinctive. He would never get used to this one, and he doubted he would ever see the Damned the way Clarise did. Some things no one deserved. A sentient ride through his intestinal tract topped that list.

As one moment slid into the next and Clarise said nothing more about the food, Avis began to look for alternatives to eating the Damned. Anything at all would be better than that, and one very prudent question kept bubbling to the surface. *Why can't we bring in any outside help?*

He knew he was on the outs with his own family, but Clarise was still of the Hellion Highborn and they'd proven time and time again just how far they would go for her. They'd spent years hunting him down, and years more torturing him. Uriel himself had all but promised his aid anytime, so surely he wouldn't mind slipping them mass now and again for some much-needed supplies?

He imagined how that would play out and snorted derisively. If Clarise or the girls were the ones with the food aversion, he knew his brother-by-marriage would help in a heartbeat. But if it came to light that *he* was the one who couldn't stomach the food, that winged prick would just laugh his ass off. *So ... no.*

Another option was the servants who were being the barge poles. Every stroke had them touching the riverbed below, and if they harvested mass from down there, he and his girls wouldn't have to eat the Damned.

For the realm's sake! This would be so much easier if he could internalise this conversation with a roomful of others instead of trying to think of everything by himself at the same time. Not that he needed to, where some of his family were concerned. He swore he could already hear Armina's response. *Just suck it up and eat it, you fucking pussy. You're embarrassing us.*

To which his answer would've been a brief: *Fuck you.*

With her arms still encircling his waist, Clarise stepped to his left and moved around in front of him. Then she pressed her lips against the fabric of his doublet over his left pec and rested the point of her chin against that spot. Having her there felt right, and although his mind was still processing his options, his arms automatically wrapped around her shoulders possessively. It wasn't until she spoke again that he realised she was staring up at him.

"Am I going to have to ask what you are thinking each time you have that look upon your face, beloved?" she asked, those gorgeously molten gold eyes swirling in a mesmerising pattern. Avis could lose himself in them all day ...

He offered up a heartfelt sigh. "The riverbed's still technically part of the river, isn't it?" he asked, ruling out his second option now that he'd taken the time to think about it. "That's why Frash and Gingen haven't brought up the mass from the bottom to use in our meals."

Her head dipped forward until her lips brushed against his pec again, causing Avis to catch his breath and close his eyes. "Tease," he hissed, for once might have been an accident. Twice—not a chance. She was deliberately distracting him from the topic at hand with the one thing she knew would work every time, and it almost succeeded. Well, two could play this game, and he was by far the more experienced player.

With his back to the girls and his cloak shielding them from his actions, he allowed lust to morph his expression and he shifted his stance to loom over her; his tongue swiping over his upper lip suggestively. "Unless you want to have sex right here, right now, sweetheart?" he barely whispered against her ear.

His grin widened as he rubbed his growing erection against her belly, proving he was more than ready. "After three days ..." He was careful to keep his answers honest. Sex right here right now in front of the girls, was a line of exhibitionism he wasn't going to cross, but he had to make her think it was on the table.

He almost laughed when she gasped and pushed away from him. "Yes, it contains the same level of celestial pain as the water above it," she agreed, hastily returning the subject to why they were eating the Damned. Adorable woman. Someone should have told her she'd never out-sex a former sex-fiend.

He did chuckle at her predictability, then relaxed and drew her back into a warm embrace. "You also said what we have is *all* we have," he reiterated, locking his fingers around his forearms to keep her within the makeshift corral of his arms. They both knew it wouldn't hold her if she truly wanted to escape, but his accompanying statement told her that for now, he was more interested in information. *For now.*

"Yes," she replied, allowing her body to mould into his.

"And just why is that, sweetheart?" His tone was no longer playful as he stared down at her. "The whole time we've been stuck on this river, you haven't once suggested that we pull mass through a blood-link, yet you knew how I'd feel about eating the Damned." Having given it some thought, he suspected there might have been more to this than her general forgetfulness, and when her pupils expanded in surprise, he knew his instincts hadn't let him down. Becoming every bit the family patriarch, his gaze narrowed and he asked seriously, "What exactly haven't you told me, sweetheart?"

Clarise went to twist away, but he released her torso and framed her face with his hands just as she had done earlier to him—only he lightly dusted his thumbs across her cheeks to convey his love for her. "Tell me, Clarise, and do me the courtesy of looking me in the eye when you do." He held her still for a moment longer, then released her entirely. He would never force his queen's hand.

To both her credit and his, she steeled herself and met his enquiring gaze dead on. "Before we left the Well, Father presented me with a series of conditions which I had to agree to before he would permit Columbine and me to travel with you."

Avis gnashed his teeth as a frustrated growl crept through his chest and into his throat. He hid his fisted hands beneath his cloak and stroked his thumbs across the clenched knuckles; really wanting something other than his precious wife to punch. Preferably one of her male kin. "I'm not going to like this, am I?"

"No," Clarise answered, her tone sympathetic to say the least. "Would you prefer to accept my word on our situation, or would you rather know the specifics of those conditions?"

Her question was a double-edged sword, and he wasn't entirely convinced she hadn't done it deliberately. On one hand, if he learned exactly how the conversation went, there'd be no more surprises to piss him off. Alternatively, she was asking him to trust her ... which he did, but then he wouldn't know what she knew. Neither of her choices were acceptable. Fortunately, he could avoid both by taking control of the information exchange—something he had no problem doing.

"Let me guess," he said, skewering her with an imperious look. "If you and Columbine came with us, none of the shifters would be allowed to help you. As far as your father's concerned, you've made your bed, now you can lie in it." Clarise's brow creased into a questioning frown and he realised she wouldn't have heard the Mystallian phrase before. He quickly amended it to, "You've picked me over them, sweetheart, so now they're turning their backs on you."

Her eyes said as much right before she bobbed her head in confirmation. "Only for the duration of this journey, beloved. Once we arrive in Mystal, all will be as it was before. In the meantime, if anyone aids us in any way, they will answer to Father and may very well end up in the Nine Levels for it. Uriel's offer of assistance was his way of letting us know he will risk that punishment for our sakes if necessary."

Yours maybe, sweetheart, Avis mused privately, though it certainly went a long way towards explaining Uriel's constant exclusion of him at their parting. At the time, he'd thought his brother-by-marriage was just being a dick, but the archangel was specially naming whom he'd be willing to go into the Damned for. Avis was not on that list, and he'd have been surprised if he was. "So, only cases of emergency?"

Clarise nodded. "Yes, beloved."

Great.

CHAPTER THIRTY-ONE

Later that morning, Avis lay on the raft (as usual) with his hands cupped behind his head and his boots crossed at the ankle, staring up at the orange-grey sky overhead. What he wouldn't give for something to do …

He both heard and felt Columbine's demonic claws scrape against the timber boards as she made her way towards him and immediately held that thought. For three days, she'd been avoiding him, and he hadn't wanted to force the issue. Not yet anyway. Not when he could see in her surface thoughts that she was feeding off her sister's partial resentment of him. It had killed him to stay away, but worth every second of it if she was coming to him now of her own free will.

He rolled to his side to face her and propped his head on his hand. "What's up, princess?" he asked, not at all happy with the way she crawled towards him on all fours. He'd get that subservience out of their heads if it killed him.

"Would you … teach me about Mystallians, Father?"

So—not only had she overcome her apprehension of him, but she was curious about his people. Avis beamed at her and immediately pushed himself off the deck to sit up; swivelling to face her squarely. He slapped his hands together and bounced them apart, then curled his fingertips to bring her over to him. "Come here, baby."

Columbine's breath slipped through her mandibles in a hellish hiss of glee that would've frightened any mortal and she rushed the last few paces to slam bodily into his chest. He uttered an exaggerated oomph, then snorted in delight as he manoeuvred her onto his lap with her wings draped over his supporting arm and her shoulder pressed against his chest. "What would you like to know, princess?" he asked, willing to fill any gaps she had.

"Who are they, and how does the pantheon work?"

His mind froze as the ramifications of her simple request dawned on him. *For someone who's supposedly been educated in the ways of a Mystallian, you've got some fucking great holes in your knowledge base, princess!* "O … kay," he drawled, wondering just where he should start.

THE FUCKING BEGINNING, YOU FUCKING FUCKWIT!

Sometimes Avis hated how antagonistic his subconscious could be, even if it was right. The early days were less convoluted. "I am the eldest of eight, princess. I have five brothers and two sisters in total, and together, we've divided the realm of Mystal into two sides. The Life Court, and the Death Court. Each side has three brothers and a sister as its elder representatives. I control the Life Court." He waited until Columbine nodded to indicate she was following him so far. "And my twin brother, your Uncle Amaro, controls the Death Court. We're not at odds though, despite what that sounds like. We're two halves of the same whole."

He waited another moment for her to absorb that. It was an important distinction. Too many pantheons were in a constant state of civil war because they only cared for their section of the realm. Mystal was a unified pantheon. Always one. Always.

"On my side, I have your Uncle Griffith, your Aunt Armina and your Uncle Chance." He knew those names wouldn't mean much to her without context, so he went on with, "Your Uncle Griffith is our God of Strength. He's a giant of a man and trust me, you won't miss him. To give you an idea, I only come up to here ..." —he tapped his free hand just below his collarbone— "... on him. He's firm, but very fair."

His lips curled as hundreds of millions of instances where Griffith had inserted himself between Avis and Armina when the two had ... disagreed on things; using his immense size to keep the pair from getting physical.

"Next is your Aunt Armina. She's our Goddess of War." Noticing the way her brow ridge arched, he knew he had to elaborate. "Yes, she's our fighter, princess. Our best warrior, in fact." When her confused expression didn't change, he paused and ran the back of his fingers down her cheek. "I know, baby. I know that's not what you're used to hearing in Hell, but it's still the truth. Where I come from, women fight. They just do and that's something you're just going to have to get used to. I guess the best way for you to think of her at this point is ..."

It horrified him to realise the closest being he could compare Armina to was Uriel and he thanked the Twin Notes that Armina wasn't here to hear what he was about to say next. She'd kick his ass all over the Known Realms for comparing her in any way to *an angel*, even if that angel was the crown prince of Hell. "Think of a female version of your Uncle Uriel, only without the wings. She wears big swords and black plate armour and knows how to use both very well." Not wanting to overwhelm her with stories of Armina's conquests, he didn't delve any further into that.

"And finally, there's the runt ..." —when Columbine's eye ridges shot up, he quickly amended it to— "... I mean your Uncle Chance. He's our luck god. Chance is the youngest of us all, so quite often your aunts and uncles and I call him *the runt* out of habit. That doesn't mean you'll be allowed to call him that. I'm just saying it, so you'll know who we're talking about if you happen to overhear it. I think you'll like your Uncle Chance. Most kids do. Generally, he's a total goof-ball that spends most of his time getting kids like you to laugh at him."

He freed his other arm from her wings and lifted his hand to rub the back and side of her head. "When your aunts and uncles and I convene for formal business it's called an Elder Court, which you and your sister will not be taking part in."

"Is Mother not invited?"

"Of course, she is!" Avis hadn't meant to shout that, but it *was* how passionately he felt about the matter. Columbine gasped, and he knew he had to move quickly before she bolted. "It's alright, princess," he said, dropping his hand to her shoulder to stroke the length of her upper arm to settle her. "I assure you, where I go, your mother goes, but only if she wants to. Her opinion will always matter a great deal to me, in or out of the Elder Court."

"Is all of the Elder Court married?"

The sheer lunacy of the question stunned Avis and he found himself blinking like an owl in sunlight. When learning the who's who of a pantheon, no one ever started with *that* question. Still, he would deny his princess nothing, and if their marital state was what she wanted to know ...

"Most of them are, princess. Yes. Some of them have kids, grandkids, and even (in one particularly annoying case) great grandkids, most of which are established in a variety of fields. I was the final holdout from the Life Court."

He looked over her head to Clarise, who lingered nearby and smiled. "You might say I was waiting for your mother to enter my life." *Or have the rest of her heavy-handed family pummel some much-needed fucking sense into me,* he added on a more private note. "So, staying with my side, I married your mother."

Columbine chortled at the obvious connection, causing puffs of smoke to waft through her nostrils and chest plates. Avis chuckled as well and gave her a light squeeze. "Alright, little smarty. Moving on then to your Uncle Griffith. He married a Seventh Choir angel from Heaven ..." —he could barely keep the grimace from his voice, even after all this time— "... called Heshbon. Angels are ... well, your Uncle Uriel takes the form of one, so that'll give you a basic idea. Heshbon's our Goddess of Invention and she's quiet, but like your Uncle Griffith, she's firm when she needs to be."

Avis tried to think of a story to help tie Heshbon into the family, but he couldn't think of any that didn't bring up other members of the family that he hadn't identified yet. He made a mental note to come back afterwards to share as many stories as it took to cement them in her memory. It wasn't as if he didn't have billions of years to draw on.

"My sister, your Aunt Armina of War, married the son of a Black Hills god called Mahpee. He's our master of the skies. Still with me?" He paused to give her a chance to answer, which she did by nodding vigorously against his chest.

Her lack of verbalisation shredded his very last nerve on the matter and he knew if he didn't chip her now, the next time she did it, he'd explode at her unfairly. "Use your words, princess," he said, keeping a tight rein on his tone as he tapped his pointer finger lightly against her beak. This was too important to be lost in a fit of rage. "I don't want to have to look at you every time I ask you a question."

Thankfully he must have done it right. Columbine nodded and said, "I understand, Father. Uncle Griffith married Aunt Heshbon and Aunt Armina married Uncle Mahpee."

Pride quickly overcame his irritation and he beamed at her again, genuinely thrilled that she'd grasped his family tree ... *so far.* "Good, princess. Excellent. Well, there's only one more from my side, and that's my youngest brother, your Uncle Chance. He married a former Takama-Ga-Haran called Emi and she's our Se-sss ..."

The sentence collapsed into an extended hiss against the back of his teeth as he realised exactly what the powerbase of his youngest brother's wife was, and by definition, how lucky that made Chance. *Uh-oh. How do I explain this one without getting into trouble?*

Parenting young children was still a lot harder than he thought. "Uhhhm ... She's ... our ... err ... *Fertility* Goddess." Avis had no idea where that inspiration came from, but he was chuffed with himself for thinking of it.

"What does a fertility goddess do?" Columbine asked, staring up at him naively.

A muscle under Avis' eye twitched. *Really?* He never thought he'd live to see the day where a conversation about sex would make him so uncomfortable. "Uhhh ..."

"She helps people have babies," Cora interceded, before Avis could dig himself into a hole that he couldn't get out of.

The breath Avis hadn't realised he'd been holding escaped in a heady sigh of relief and he shot Cora an appreciative look over Columbine's head. "Yeah, that's right. And since that takes care of my court, let's move on to your Uncle Amaro's Death Court." *Before you ask anything else about Emi that you're way too young to know.*

Columbine stared up at him as if he were the epitome of everything. He was used to that look from mortals, but it was a little humbling when it came from his own child. He sucked in a deep breath and continued.

"Your Uncle Amaro is my twin, as I said, and our other two brothers with him are Tal and Blagden. Just as I am the god of Life, your Uncle Amaro is the god of Death. We are as polar opposites in looks as we are in dispositions." Again, that little eye ridge arched, and he knew he had to dumb it down again.

"Ummm … your Uncle Amaro is the same height as me, but he's a lot thinner with white hair and white eyes. He's also … a lot like your grandfather Belial in the way he never raises his voice or loses his temper. Whereas … I tend to shout when I'm angry."

Understatement of the millennium, but she'd figure that out soon enough if she hadn't already.

"Moving on to your Uncle Tal. He's our God of Destruction. He's the same size as your Uncle Griffith, so again, you won't miss him, but unlike Griffith, Tal's got a really, *really* bad temper, so I need you two to be extra careful around him. He won't hurt you intentionally, but it doesn't take much at all to set him off and when he loses it, things … and people … and *galaxies* get broken."

He lifted his eyes to make sure Cora knew what he was saying was more for her benefit than Columbine's. "I mean it. Until you've both have the protection of an establishment field, I don't want either one of you coming unstuck by him. It could very well get you killed."

Cora, like every other red-blooded Mystallian before her, would probably say whatever came to mind regardless of the consequences, and as such she was the one who concerned him. Columbine on the other hand … Tal would be lucky to get ten words in total out of her, let alone ten insulting ones. "Am I clear?"

"Yes, Father," Columbine chimed, but he expected that of her. Almost as much as he expected Cora's tenacious *lack* of response. Narrowing his gaze at the girl who'd only moments ago saved his ass, Avis started a mental ten-second countdown. If he made it to zero, he'd use bending to force her compliance. Nothing else was acceptable. Not about this. Tal was simply *that* dangerous.

Somewhere between 'four' and 'three', Cora's lips pinched as if she'd swallowed something sour and sulkily folded her arms. Her chin dipped marginally towards the ground before it twisted away from him, silently acknowledging what he'd said.

Maybe that was an acceptable response for the Hellion Highborn, but Avis wasn't of Hell and that level of demonic subtlety could go screw itself. For his own peace of mind, he needed to hear the words, especially from Cora. One Mystallian to another. Sending a mental tendril into her mind, he poked her consciousness hard enough to remind her who she was dealing with, without hurting her. He owed her that much.

Cora flinched at the unfamiliar jab and immediately swung back to scowl at him. He met that glare with a slight hitch to one eyebrow, openly daring her to say anything other than what he wanted to hear. "I'm waiting."

"Fine," she muttered savagely, under her breath. "I won't provoke Uncle Tal intentionally."

Despite her initial resistance, her answer was better than he'd hoped for. Articulation wasn't a Mystallian strong-point unless it served their personal agenda, and without realising it, Cora had painted herself into a corner with no chance to wriggle out of it.

"Moving on," he said. "My last brother is your Uncle Blagden, and he's our God of Sickness and Disease. He's much more subdued than the rest of us, because he's very aware of how badly misshapen he is due to his powerbase thrall. It's unfortunate, but I don't want either of you to fear him when you meet. He'll be in uniform just like the rest of us, and regardless of his appearance, if he reaches out to touch you, just remember you are family so his condition won't be passed on to either of you, okay?"

It would break Blagden's heart if they recoiled from his disfigurement, and that brother had enough misery on his plate.

Columbine started to nod, but halted and said, "Yes, Father."

Avis was thrilled! Twice in a row she'd remembered to use her words, and the second time she'd done so without any prompting from him! He whooped and crushed her against him. "That's my girl," he praised, pressing his lips against her head.

He felt more than heard the rasping hiss of air as it escaped through her chest plates and immediately loosened his hold, choosing instead to flex the muscles in his arms in a more muted version of a hug. He'd have to watch that.

"And last, but no means least, there's my sister, your Aunt Chasidah. She was the youngest of us for a really long time before your Uncle Chance came into the picture and being our Goddess of Prophecy, she's saved our tails more than once over the years."

"If she is prophecy, why were you not warned of your future?"

CHAPTER THIRTY-TWO

Avis looked over Columbine's head to where Cora still stood. The question was one he'd asked himself a thousand times since his incarceration in a desperate bid to lay the blame at someone else's feet. It didn't help to know all along that the answer had been a simple, one-word answer which exonerated his sister. *Thrall.* The cost of a powerbase.

There wasn't a doubt in his mind that Chasidah had tapped her powerbase before any of this happened and knew exactly how badly he was going to screw everything up, but her thrall prevented her from saying anything about it. His thoughts drifted to his young family and he suddenly doubted the veracity of that.

After all, if he hadn't mistreated Clarise, he wouldn't have been exiled from his homeland and forced to spend two years amongst the Damned. From there, he'd have never been rescued by Clarise, and he wouldn't have what he had now: a family of his choosing that he'd do anything to protect.

Considering everything he now knew, he had to admit there was a very real chance Chasidah would've kept her mouth shut anyway, for his own good.

Food for thought.

Avis huffed and returned to the topic at hand. "Chasidah's thrall prevents her from speaking freely," he said, shifting his focus between the girls to make sure he still had their undivided attention. "She's only permitted to answer the exact question she's asked. No deviations. No embellishments. Otherwise, she's mute."

Cora didn't seem impressed by the restriction. "Why does she not write it down, or use hand gestures or smoke signals or any number of things to get her point across? There are plenty of other ways to communicate between people apart from speaking."

For someone who didn't want anything to do with Mystallians, Cora's sudden interest in family affairs pleased him and he lifted his hand to beckon her over. He wasn't as impressed when the stubborn minx folded her arms defiantly and refused to budge, though for now he let it go.

"She's mute to all forms of conversation, Cora. Not just speech. She can't write down her predictions. She can't sign them. She can't do any of it. Her thrall simply won't let her. And when you don't know the right question to ask …" —he gestured to himself as a prime example— "… you don't find out what she knows until it's too late."

"Is everyone in the Death Court married?" Columbine asked impulsively.

Avis looked down at her and swiftly found himself swept up in the sweetness of her surface thoughts as if he'd been dumped in the middle of a liquid sugar ocean. She was consumed by the whole family being happily married to the point that nothing else mattered.

Not the size or might of his homeland, nor the powerbase capabilities of the various family members. Most kids fixated on the latter, if only to get an idea of what they could expect for themselves in time to come. Columbine only wanted everyone happy.

He rubbed his hand across the back of her leathery scalp affectionately, relishing the adorable naivety of her thoughts until his own turned to Blagden. "Not all of them, princess," he said with a genuine hint of sadness. "Your Uncle Blagden is now the only one of my generation who has yet to get married, and unfortunately, the chances of him finding a wife are very slim."

"Is that because he's ugly?" Cora asked, with all the tact of an avalanche.

Avis shut his eyes and pinched his lips together; mentally forcing himself to slowly, clinically count to ten. The trick was one Clarise had suggested when her family pushed his buttons too hard.

At times like this it proved invaluable, for within that ten seconds he could appreciate the enquiry for the simple question it was. He opened his eyes and refocused on Cora. "As I said, his body is disease-ridden and full of sickness, and that no doubt plays a part in his unmarried state."

"No!" Columbine's high-pitched whine of denial surprised him almost as much as her wings stretching to their full height.

At the same time, Cora squared her feet as if she was going to war and snarled, "That's not fair."

Avis shifted his attention between the two, shock making him unable to decide which of their reactions pleased him more. He loved the fact that they were both willing to defend his family even before they ever met. Similarly, he was relieved that he hadn't reacted badly to Cora's cruel statement, for he could see now she was simply gathering the facts before voicing her opinion.

A good trait to have—and not one in his repertoire. In her own way, even young Columbine wanted to protect her own from all things unpleasant, though he saw in her surface thoughts that she honestly viewed the Known Realms as a land of unicorns and happy dreams.

In some places it was, but not everywhere.

"Ssshhh-shh-shh," he shushed, snuggling Columbine's head against his chest with one hand while the other stroked her back beneath her wings. He kept his eyes glued to Cora. "It is what it is, girls, and as hard as it is to hear, you need to accept it as something that's never going to change. He doesn't want it to."

In saying that himself, it was the first time he truly understood what he'd previously thought was a cold-hearted viewpoint held by his emotionless twin.

The pair had shared this very discussion millions of eons earlier, and Avis' explosive reaction at the time had mirrored his children's today. But he was as wrong then as his children were now. Personal viewpoints didn't matter. Thrall was thrall. "Everybody calm down." He continued to caress Columbine's back and arms until she settled again in his lap and by then, Cora had moved a few steps closer.

Avis took that as progress.

"Yes, Blagden's thrall isn't ideal, but it is what it is and at the very least it serves as an example of why it's so important to approach feral mortals with great care. If you're going to announce yourself as divine, it needs to be done the right way or the consequences could be dire."

"What way is that?"

Avis slid his gaze to his elder daughter. He should've guessed that she'd want to know that as soon as possible, and perhaps subconsciously he'd wanted her to learn the correct process before she ended up the way Blagden was.

"It's not as easy as you think. If you were to go out into the Unknown Realms where the feral mortals live, the first thing you need to do is select a starting point in the celestial realm that suits your needs. Something that will sustain you for the hundred or so centuries it'll take for you to set yourself up. Every type of land can be found somewhere, so it's just a matter of persevering until you find what you're looking for."

"Why can't I just change whatever realm I'm in to suit myself?"

Avis liked her impatience. It reminded him of home. He held up a single finger. "Because you can only change one thing at a time, tiger. Celestially or mortally. To make everything just the way you want if the basics aren't already there, is a living nightmare. You can't do more than that to a celestial realm without a powerbase, and before you get the powerbase, you must get the mortal realm under control. And, to get the mortal realm under control, you need to stay in the celestial realm until your residency filters through into the mortal realm, allowing it to become attuned to you. Until then, no matter how rough it gets, you have to stay in the celestial realm and out of the mortal one."

"Why? If all I have to do is grab the mind of one mortal and have my religion spread from that one, why would I want to do it the hard way?"

"Because you'll have no control over the development of your religion if you do it like that."

"Why not?"

Unused to be challenged on the basic principles of being a celestial, Avis found himself frowning at her. The word 'why' was beginning to annoy him. "Because thrall goes hand in hand with a powerbase, Cora. You'll become what the majority of the mortals believe, and you won't see anything wrong with it. If you were to waltz in and declare yourself divine without fully attuning yourself to them first, those feral little bast … I mean, the mortals will outnumber your control by hundreds of millions to one. That's what makes them so dangerous. You may be in control of one, but the others will take your divinity and put their own spin on it and before you realise it, any chance of you directing the evolution of your thrall will go right out the nearest window."

Cora's face scrunched up, and he could tell she was still on the fence about believing him. He had to make her understand; preferably without using his bending.

"By being attuned first, your will becomes their reality, and right from the beginning you're the one in control. That's when you descend into the mortal realm and make yourself known. Numbers matter, tiger, so you need to keep a tight rein on the maturation of your religion. I'll give you a simplified example. Say you're naturally left-handed, and the feral mortals are natively right-handed. You'll have millions of them worshipping you as a right-handed goddess, and only a handful of those that you've personally visited believing you're left-handed. That handful will be quickly swallowed up by the masses and your thrall will force you to be right-handed for good. The only way to ensure you stay left-handed is to stay in control and make sure the numbers worship you as a left-handed goddess."

"Sounds like a lot of work," Cora griped.

Avis nodded in absolute agreement. "In the beginning, it *is* a whole lot of work, tiger. No argument. But it's also the only way to guarantee you get the establishment field and the subsequent thrall exactly how you want it. Then, with the masses under control, you can expand your borders slowly. A few thousand worlds at a time. "

"Wait! We are not even talking galaxies yet?"

Avis shook his head. "Not at first. No. Your attunement remains in a small area and you need to give it time to permeate the space ahead of your expansion. If your outer boundary overtakes your attunement, you'll go back to a state of disarray. Eventually, you'll reach a saturation point where your establishment field will take on a life of its own and you can relax, but until then you need to be careful. The last thing either of you should want is to become the goddess of fuzzy slippers and fluffy clouds."

"And everyone has to go through this?" Cora asked, screwing up her face in repugnance.

Avis had hoped the prospect of starting from scratch would be too daunting, but he couldn't emphasise the dangers enough. It was a bitch (to put it mildly) and he'd had seven siblings at the time to tag-team with. "You could always choose to stay home. Or pick another realm that already has a fully established pantheon. Most people stay out of the Unknown Realms, choosing to remain where it's civilized. It's safer and easier that way. The legwork's already done in the Known Realms and having everyone already at your back allows the development of your thrall to be controlled with a minimum of effort."

"Is that why you said starting over might be too hard for mother to cope with?"

Avis' good humour immediately vanished, and he found himself scowling darkly at her. He'd known Uriel had been listening in to that particular conversation, but he hadn't counted on Cora following suit. "Congratulations, tiger. You just used up your one and only warning."

For unlike the breakfast that morning where he'd only been a short distance away, he'd purposely moved that conversation with Clarise out of earshot. "You deliberately eavesdrop on me or your mother again when I make a point of cutting you out of it, and I'll drop you into a realm of hurt the likes of which you've only had nightmares about. You understand me?"

Cora's face fell, and she looked at the ground between them. "Yes, sir."

Avis gnashed his teeth; his Mystallian sensibilities railing against her behaviour. *Right here, dammit!* he'd wanted to shout at her while pointing at his own eyes. The subservience was driving him insane, especially coming from Cora.

It didn't belong there. She should've met his eyes and said, *Sure, Okay, My bad,* or a thousand other verbal acknowledgements that said the warning was received without lessening her stand in the conversation. Words like *Sir* belonged with the servants and commoners. He had to get that speech style out of her vocabulary before they reached Mystal, or the family would ride her unmercifully.

"I love you, Father."

Columbine snuggled against his chest as she spoke, causing a wave of tenderness to undermine his annoyance. That was never in doubt, and he loved her just as much. Bowing his head, he ran his lips across the top of her head and flexed his arm to cuddle her.

"I know, princess," he said, caressing the nape of her neck. "I love you too." He looked at Cora, his irritability all but forgotten. "But enough of how difficult the Unknown Realms can be."

He dropped his eyes to Columbine. "You were asking about the family, and I haven't mentioned the Death Court. So, starting with my twin brother, your Uncle Amaro. He married an Asgardian princess called Yasadan. She's our Goddess of Serenity and her father is one of my closest friends. At the time of their courtship, Yasadan's many brothers and half-brothers doubted Amaro's intentions."

"Why?"

The question confused Avis. "Why what, princess?"

"Why would they doubt Uncle Amaro?"

Avis breathed out slowly, his brain scrambling for an answer that didn't undermine the way she felt about him. Saying, *'because they knew me and assumed my twin was the same kind of man-whore asshole that I was,'* wasn't in his best interest.

"There's a lot of reasons, princess," he said, attempting to buy himself time. He could now imagine himself in Odin's place, picturing his own reaction to a mythical twin of Odin vying for Columbine's hand in marriage. His grip unconsciously tightened around her. *No. Just … no.*

"Sometimes, no one can ever be good enough for certain people who only deserve perfection. At least, in the case of Yasadan and Amaro, Odin and I were able to keep our own sides under control until they finally accepted your uncle's worthiness of her hand."

As memories of those tumultuous times crowded his mind, he rolled his eyes to the orange-grey sky overhead. "I swear, the number of times I had to kneecap your Aunt Armina to stop that woman from taking us to war over the threats and abuse that Odin's boys threw out at us …" He closed his eyes to block them out and sighed.

CHAPTER THIRTY-THREE

"Anyway," Avis went on, shaking those thoughts from his head. "Your Uncle Tal married a Plains woman called Mashaka, who became our Goddess of Mayhem. What I said before about your Uncle Tal quadruples when those two are together ..." —he eyed Cora specifically— "... so watch yourself. Tal has kicked planets across a thousand galaxies and Mashaka has destroyed others by upending their order of existence. It really screws with a mortal world when rain falls upwards, or deer hunt down lions or mice begin to terrify elephants. That's the sort of stuff she does."

Columbine let out a tiny whimper, which Avis thought was from the image he painted. But a quick search of her surface thoughts showed her anxiety came from not knowing what he was talking about and he ran his thumb across the edge of her beak and smiled indulgently.

"Rain is when water falls from the sky. The other things I mentioned were animals, like your *scallye* and *slae-el*. When we get back to Mystal, I'll show you them all if you like." When Columbine nodded happily, Avis felt his own lips lift in response. He looked across at Cora and added, "The bottom line is, if you don't behave around those two, they'll make you wish you had. You got me?"

Cora nodded. "Yeah."

Better. Way, way, waaaaay better. Avis smirked and shot her a satisfied wink. "The last of the Elder Court marriages before mine was your Aunt Chasidah's to a god from Tir na nOg called Culkin. He's a good man who knows how to swing a sword as well as his fist. After their marriage, he became our god of Knowledge."

Cora squinted dubiously. "Why would you want a fighting bookworm?"

Her tone of condescension rang loud and clear in Avis' ears and once again he closed his eyes and slowly counted to ten. It helped to remind himself that the last time he'd thought she was being insolent, she'd merely been on a fact-finding mission.

With the stern reminder that this might be no different, he forced himself to give her the benefit of the doubt in case it wasn't intentional. He opened his eyes and skewered her with a cautionary look. "You'll have to explain that one to me, tiger."

Cora's surface thoughts were as patronizing as her words had been. "Bookworms are parasitic bugs that live permanently between the pages of a tome and are rarely seen away from them. Silverfish, larder beetles and book lice. That kind of thing."

The level of his irritation climbed a few more rungs. "*Parasitic?*" he repeated, the icy venom in his tone warning her to tread with care.

Cora grimaced. "Okay ... maybe not parasitic so much. It just means that someone would rather curl up in front of a fire with a book than physically exert themselves in any way."

And just how the fuck was that any better? "So ... an *insult*." Avis wasn't asking anymore. Her explanation, tone and thoughts thus far said it all. Avis envisioned his robust brother-by-marriage and couldn't picture a more incorrect appraisal of anyone.

Culkin may not have been as tall as Griffith and Tal, but when describing the youngest son of Tir na nOg's Tuatha Dé Danann Chief Dagda, *weedy* and *frail* were two of the last words anyone should use.

Like his father before him, Culkin was a stocky brick of a god who was just as comfortable with a sword as he was a book, and many of his depictions had him holding both. "When we get home, young lady, I'm going to remind you you said that, right before I introduce you to him. Expect his boot half way up your backside two seconds later, because it's coming, I promise you."

Columbine's eye ridges widened as if they were eyes. "Will that not hurt her?"

Avis pursed his lips together and nodded sharply once. "She just insulted your Uncle Culkin without ever laying eyes on him, princess, so yes, it will." It wasn't just the insult, though that was bad enough.

The sheer stupidity of voicing such an opinionated crock of shit without first learning what the target could do in retaliation was demented and he shot Cora an aggravated look that said as much. "That has to be one of the dumbest things you've said to date, by the way. For all you know, he could be the size of a planet with a thousand arms and a powerbase that negates your shapeshifting. Then what'll you do?"

Cora blanched and swallowed uncomfortably. "Um … does he?"

For a split-second Avis considered saying *yes* just to hammer the point home, but he knew he didn't need to. The grown-up brain that was housed inside her little body had already gotten the message. In a way, Avis wished all kids had Cora's adult comprehension.

It certainly made educating them a lot easier. "I should let you stew on that, tiger," he said, allowing his temper to drop altogether. "But no, he's not like that. He's a little shorter than me, but he's well-built. His bloodline is full of bipedal warriors not unlike us and physically, he takes after them."

"But if he is already that powerful physically, why would he desire a powerbase as mundane as knowledge?"

Oh, just keep it up, tiger … Avis mused, shaking his head slightly. *…and you're going to have elders lining up to kick your ass when we get home.* No one with a brain saw knowledge as useless. Armina firmly believed in knowing every weakness an enemy had, long before taking a fight to them. Knowledge was invaluable, not mundane.

"Those of Tir na nOg value both combat prowess and knowledge equally. In fact, many of their greatest fighters are also their master scholars. Take my word for it, tiger. No one attacks a Tir na nOg librarian and lives to brag about it." He wasn't joking.

They were simply that good. Even Armina came up short when fighting them, though of course, she had to leave her powerbase to engage them, putting her at a severe disadvantage. "So, any other questions about the Elder Court?"

"Four sets of couples on each side, except for Uncle Blagden who's unmarried, right?" Cora asked, holding all her fingers up and deliberately keeping her hands apart to represent the two courts.

Avis nodded. His generation was the easy part. Their many offspring and the generations that followed were where things were going to get … complicated. "Would you like to leave it at that for today, or do you want to know some of the who's who of your cousins?"

"How many cousins are there?" Columbine asked, answering that question for him.

Avis twisted his lips thoughtfully. Truth be told, he didn't know an exact number, because the number was three … maybe even four digits. Instead, he bought himself some time by rubbing his hand across the back of her leathery head and shoulders, causing her entire body to ripple in delight. "There's a lot, princess. Mainly due to two branches of the family."

He saw Cora brighten and her surface thoughts overflowed with confidence; not unlike her *A-Ha* moment in the stables. With both hands still raised to represent the two courts of Mystal, she curled three of the four fingers against her palms, keeping one finger extended on each hand. "One on each side, right?" she asked proudly, as if that had to be a given.

Avis thought about Armina and Chance's numerous offspring and shook his head. "No, actually they're both part of my court."

The revelation didn't sit well with Cora. Her brow creased in in a mixture of confusion and disbelief as her hands fell lifelessly to her sides. "But I would have thought the destructive mayhem of a million kids would suit Uncle Tal and Aunt Mashaka perfectly."

It took a moment for that statement to fully register with Avis, and when it did, he suddenly threw his head back and howled with laughter. His whole body shook and tears sprang to his eyes, and still he couldn't stop. Despite the countless eons that Tal and Mashaka had been married, they'd only ever had one son because Mashaka refused to experience the 'miracle of childbirth' ever again.

"Oh, by the Twin Notes," he whooped, his chest heaving as he imagined the looks on both their faces when he threw their powerbases at them as a reason for having a large family. "I soooo have to remember to tell them that. Your Uncle Tal will love it!"

"Why?" Cora asked, her lips rolling into a surly pout of indignation.

Avis pulled himself back up straight, realising he'd rocked so far back that he'd braced himself with one arm to stop himself from falling over entirely. He saw her blurry outline and blinked to clear his vision.

"Because Tal's always wanted a large family, but childbirth is supposedly one of the most painful experiences an expectant mother will ever go through. After your cousin Strahan was born, your Aunt Mashaka made it very clear to everyone stupid enough to ask her that if Tal wanted any more kids, he'd have to figure out a way to carry them to term and birth them himself. Otherwise she'd tap her powerbase and make him."

He still chuckled at that ancient memory of when his destructive brother had relayed that message as he drank away his sulky ire in Pandess (as far from his wife in Crohen as he could possibly be).

"Then who has the big families?"

At least his outburst hadn't humiliated her to the point where she stalked off in a huff. Cora was still interested enough in the family dynamics to stay.

Clearing his throat, he wiped the corners of his eyes with the back of one knuckle, then used the raised hand to wave her impromptu question away. "I'll get to that," he promised, still not quite removing the tinge of amusement from his voice. "But since we were just talking about the Death Court, I think that's the safer side of things for now. It's smaller and will be easier for you two to wrap your heads around."

"But how many cousins in total are we talking about here?" Cora asked, refusing to drop the subject.

Avis tried unsuccessfully to block out the mental image of Armina's branch of the family tree. With all the military and natural elements of the realm falling to them, and all the offshoots of those offshoots—that branch had exploded into a grove all by itself. Chance's clan was a close second as his brood covered Arts and Entertainment.

"A lot," he admitted. "Hundreds at least. Which is why, for the last time, I'm starting with the Death Court." He said that last sentence with conviction, sending Cora another stern look that dared her to be foolish enough to argue further, now that he'd made his position clear. Cora stared straight back at him, but wisely kept her mouth shut. *Good, on both counts.* Words may have been preferred in his family, but a back-answer automatically received a matching back-hand.

"Okay," he went on, once he was convinced he'd had the last word on the matter. "Your Uncle Amaro and Aunt Yasadan have two children. Paz of Peace and her younger brother, Cuschler the Assassin. Cuschler's powerbase is as self-explanatory as his bandolier of black-hilt shadow daggers, but his older sister Paz is another thing entirely. Your Uncle Chance may be the best negotiator in the Known Realms, but if he teams up with your cousin Paz, they're invincible. That runt's silver tongue can win any argument, and Paz's touch makes you not care that you're losing."

"Voice of experience?" Cora asked, smirking slyly at her own wit.

Avis twisted his lips to one side and flicked his eyebrows affirmatively, inwardly chalking the insight up to her. As one of the co-rulers of Mystal, of course he'd been tag-teamed by that pair of master manipulators over the eons. More than once. Everyone in Mystal had. "Moving on, you little smart ar ...*alec.*" Close, but he caught it. "As I said, your Uncle Tal and Aunt Mashaka have one son. Strahan of Magic. The child of Destruction and Mayhem is able to take the impossible and make it a reality."

"He's the one with the tigers, right?" Cora used the back of her hand to flick locks of red hair from each of her shoulders, her surface thoughts filling with smugness and pride. *Like me.*

Avis revelled in her slow but positive conversion into the Mystallian she was always meant to be. Granted, planetary alignments moved faster, but he was starting to see the light in her grow. "That's right, tiger," he said with a nod of approval. By the time they got home, she'd be kicking ass and engraving names on tombstones. He'd make sure of it.

"Do Aunt Chasidah and Uncle Culkin have children, Father?" Columbine asked, naively breaking the moment between them.

Avis easily returned to his narrative. "They've got two, princess," he said, holding up two fingers for emphasis. "A boy and a girl. Quinn of Wisdom and his sister Kyra of History. Kyra also has a daughter called Sabina, and she's our Goddess of Factual Literature." He saw Columbine's beak open and pressed one finger against the tip to silence her.

"And before you ask, you little imp, no, Kyra never married. Boruslav isn't in the picture anymore and if Svarogichk wants to keep that …" —his profanity was getting easier to catch, but it still didn't stop him from thinking a whole lot of vicious thoughts in that little bastard's direction while humming maniacally through gritted teeth for a few seconds— "… *boy* of his alive, he'd do well to keep it that way."

The irony that his reasons for hating Boruslav were not dissimilar to those held by his own wife's family regarding him was not lost on him, but this was different because it was *his* blood that had been slighted.

"Kyra and Sabina work in Culkin's vast library as his aides and are rarely far from his side." And since that concluded the Death Court's family tree, Avis stopped speaking and looked from one to the other to see if they had any questions.

Cora had just one. "That's it?"

Avis settled his attention on her, though his hand never stopped stroking Columbine's spine and wing ridges. "You were expecting more?"

"Well, yeah," she replied, as if that should have been obvious. "Since the Death Court holds sway over half of Mystal, and Mystal's supposedly one of the biggest and most powerful in existence, surely there are more than thirteen celestials running it. Especially when you said your side has hundreds. How is that fair?"

Supposedly, my ass, Avis thought darkly, addressing that aspect of her running commentary first and foremost. There was no *supposedly* about it. Outside of Chaos and The Nexus, Mystal was *the* realm to fear. But instead of raging over the slur, Avis did something he'd never done before.

He considered someone else's perspective and how from an outside viewpoint, it did look unbalanced. "I suppose that's because there are more aspects to life than there are to death. If you think about it logically, the Death Court doesn't need a God of Dead Forests or a Goddess of the Dead Arts."

Cora's brow creased as she pondered that answer. "So … Life is bigger than Death?"

"No." Avis couldn't shake his head fast enough. "That's not what I meant at all, tiger. As a pantheon, Mystal comes together as one and from an Elder Court perspective, the two sides *are* balanced."

He grimaced as he realised that wasn't entirely true anymore and added with a hint of guilt, "Or rather, they will be, if or when your Uncle Blagden ever gets married. Until then, there'll be a one-person difference with your mother's inclusion on our side. Everyone else in the lower generations can say whatever they like, but the final vote on important matters will always be held by the Elder Court."

Cora twisted her lips thoughtfully.

"How many cousins do we have in the Life Court?" Columbine asked in the intervening silence, her eyes igniting with excitement.

Avis huffed out his breath, almost raspberrying the air in the process. "I really don't know the answer to that, princess. Between your Aunt Armina and your Uncle Chance, there's at least a few hundred, like I said. I've never taken the time to count them all."

He pressed his lips to her brow as an amusing memory from home suddenly occurred to him. "One thing I do know, your Aunt Armina's family is that little bit bigger than your Uncle Chance's." He chuckled lightly, remembering just how angry that made the otherwise reserved fertility goddess.

"Wait … How in the realms does *War* have more kids than *Fertility*?" Cora asked, genuinely shocked by that revelation.

Avis thought about the one individual who was preventing Emi from having the huge family she desired, and if it wasn't for the runt's powerbase of fortune to stay on his wife's good side, Fertility would've had her husband's set removed and bronzed a long time ago.

"That … is something you'll have to take up with your Uncle Chance when we get home. I'm not setting foot in that arena." As he cast his gaze across his small but perfect family, a smile of satisfaction slowly spread across his face. "As I've previously mentioned, you two are the only kids your mother and I have."

Clarise's expression became shuttered, but not before he caught the pain in her eyes and he thought he knew why. His past had hardly been celibate and he was a life god. If he were as honest with himself as she was, he'd have to accept the likelihood that there were a lot of bastards out there running around with his blood coursing through their veins. He'd never met any of them, and he wasn't planning on it, but just knowing they were out there was clearly causing Clarise pain and he wished that wasn't so. It crushed him to see her unhappy.

Somehow, he'd convince her that their daughters were the only ones that mattered to him.

"Your Uncle Griffith and Aunt Heshbon have triplets," he said, determined to get through this, if only to free himself so he could envelop Clarise in a heartfelt cuddle.

"Three robust boys who went on to become our Triplets of Construction. The eldest of them is your cousin Clifford and he's our god of Stonework. Enoch, the middle one, covers woodwork and Fabron, the youngest and by far the most hot-headed of that trio, is metalwork. They all have their father's physique and their mother's shorter height and angelic wings. To date, they're our only fliers …"

He caught the superlative look that swept over Cora's face as her chin rose to the challenge and he couldn't help but smile mischievously at her. "… Of course, someone else with natural leather wings may wish to challenge them for the title of ultimate flier." Cora's eyes flashed, and she matched her father's cocky grin with a tooth-filled predatory one of her own. *Oh, yes, my little tigress. I am definitely taking you back where you belong.*

"Your Uncle Mahpee and Aunt Armina are the parents of all our natural elements. Everything from Light to Terrain to Oceans to Wind to the Moon itself. All of it falls to her branch of the family tree. The youngest of that brood hasn't reached his third millennium either, so you might find a kindred spirit there in terms of age. His name is Barris, and he's our God of the Hunt."

"How am I expected to remember all of that?" Cora complained.

"You'll remember what you remember," Avis answered with a shrug of indifference. "It's not as if there's an exam at the end of this. We're just killing a bit of time here. Besides, there's only one family to go and that's your Uncle Chance and Aunt Emi. They have almost as many kids and grandkids as Armina and Mahpee because they cover Arts and Entertainment. They've also got eleven great-grandkids in that mix. Everything from painting to singing, music, beauty, wealth and festivities. Pretty much everything the mortals think they'd be lucky to have."

Cora folded her arms and pouted. "I still do not get how Aunt Armina has more children than Aunt Emi."

Avis snorted slyly and rose to his feet, depositing Columbine on the deck beside him. "Trust me, tiger. Your Aunt Emi doesn't either."

CHAPTER THIRTY-FOUR

For Avis, lunch had been just as horrendous as breakfast, but at least this time he'd adjusted to his situation and forced a few bites past his unwilling lips, provided he didn't have to chew anything. In fact, most of his sustenance came from drinking, which he managed to achieve by closing his eyes and skolling what he could on a single breath.

It was ironic that he was utilizing the one skill he'd spent most of his adult life honing in order to outdrink Zeus and Odin, but he wasn't going to argue now. *Skol ... skol ... skol ...* He could almost hear those two chanting and cheering him on.

His lungs burned, but still he drank. If he could get all the way to the end, it'd be done. Over. He wouldn't have to do it again for another few hours. With the stein almost fully inverted, he gave it a final shake to loosen the last drops from the bottom, then tore it away from his lips and slammed it into the mat in front of him in triumph. *Done!*

He gasped in a combination of relief and repulsion, gritting his teeth and pressing the back of his gloved fist against his mouth to prevent the liquid from being regurgitated. It wasn't easy. The mental imagery of what the soul would be enduring at this very moment was one he just couldn't get past.

He'd been bitten and clawed at plenty of times during the last two years, but his captors had never chewed up the chunk and swallowed it. He wasn't even certain how that would have affected him. He wasn't a *mortal* soul, after all.

Clarise wasn't entirely thrilled with his new approach to the meals, but it was the best she was going to get, and he'd be damned all over again before he apologised for it. He looked out of the corner of his eye at her, refusing to back down.

Once he was certain his point had been made, he stood up and withdrew from the mat, crossing to the other end of the raft where the demon steeds were hitched. Just because he wanted to vomit every time he thought about the meal's ingredients, didn't mean he wanted to spoil their meals. He ran his hand over the nearest steed's shoulder, snorting himself at the thin stream of smoke and hellfire that poured from the beast's nose in response to his touch.

Maybe they were growing on him. Maybe. He certainly shared their growing irritability at the boredom level.

Not long after the meal, Avis watched Columbine approach one of the pole bearers with her tiny clawed hands outstretched in expectation of something. Theoretically, the pole bearer shouldn't have seen her coming, but the servant's head broke into two smaller ones, allowing her to maintain vigilance over the river while the other met Columbine with a subservient bow.

Neither of them said anything, but without warning, the pole bearer's ribcage broke open and something large and rectangular was presented to his daughter like a gift. Columbine curled her talons around its edges and drew it to her chest reverently, nodding her thanks to the servant who returned to the business of navigating the river.

Curiosity gnawed at Avis as Columbine made her way to the other end of the demon steeds to him, though he was all too aware of where his *last* bout of curiosity had led him.

This time he wasn't in such a hurry for answers and for now, he decided to stay out of her mind and try something he'd never been a fan of before. He'd let the whim of Chaos decide whether he needed to know or not. For now.

Through the legs and under the necks of the demon steeds, he caught a glimpse of pinkish leather between Columbine's claws and deduced from the way she opened two halves that the rectangular object was a book of some description.

He deemed it *some type of book*, because unless his eyes deceived him, the scant three pages she had bound between a pair of hard covers barely qualified it as one.

Stretching his neck, he saw between her wings and her left shoulder that she had it laid open across her lap. *A diary of some sort,* he decided, after he watched her murmured dictation appear in exquisite handwriting on the open page.

What in the realms do you have to put in a diary? he couldn't help but wonder. His sarcastic imagination envisioned her quoting, "Dear diary. Today, I was on a raft with my family. We ate disgusting food under the same orange-grey sky we've been looking at for the last week with no end in sight and I am bored out of my brain. The end. See you tomorrow for the next thrilling instalment of *How the Mystallians got the hell out of Hell.*"

Screw it. He was a bender.

Looking at the back of her head, he allowed his mind to drift across her surface thoughts and found her deeply engrossed in dictating eight sets of family trees with each of his siblings and their significant other at the heads somehow.

Every name, what their establishment field was and the lines that connected them to the generations around them.

The list was long, and as she turned the page, he could have sworn from where he stood that he saw the first page merge into the cover while another one appeared behind the last. If that was the case, his impression of the ridiculous book improved. *How many pages does it really have, buried inside those covers?*

He was about to ask her when she suddenly stilled, and sadness fell across her young shoulders, causing her wings to droop. *Father does not like eating with us anymore. He hates it so much, and I know why. The food is a mortal soul that feels pain. I do not like it either, but Grandfather has told me that I must be strong and not interfere with the Damned, so, I will not. But Father is not of the Damned and he is hurting too. I want to help him, and I know I should be able to, but I do not know how. He is hurting, because I do not know how to stop it.*

Avis sucked a savage breath through gnashed teeth as a wave of sorrow unlike anything he'd ever felt before sucker-punched him in the gut. *Oh, hell no!* She was *not* taking responsibility for this!

He must have said something unpleasant, for Columbine swivelled on her taloned toes with her eye-ridges widening with horror, but just right then he didn't care. It wasn't her job to make him feel better and he wasn't going to let her think for one second longer that it was. "Princess, shut that book down," he said, his voice thick with a variety of emotions ranging from misery and self-loathing to flat out pissed off.

He wasn't sure how her dictatorial diary worked, but he didn't want his next words canonised. When she closed the book, he moved around in front of her and squatted down so she could look him in the eyes without craning her neck. His hands took the book from her and placed it on the deck beside them; his own eyes never leaving hers as he gathered her taloned hands in his.

"I know you're an empath, princess," he said, lightly squeezing her fingers and rubbing his thumbs across the taloned knuckles. "But my revulsion ..." —he saw her left eye ridge quiver on the unfamiliar word and backed up to simplify it— "My *hatred* of the food here ... that's not for you to fix, baby. Ever. It can't be helped and it's not your fault. It's for me to deal with. Me. Do you understand?"

"But you hate it so much," she argued.

The right side of Avis' lips sucked inwards in a mild grimace, knowing he couldn't deny it in good conscience.

"There's going to be a lot of times in your life when you'll be around people who'll hate what they have to do, but you have to let them find the inner strength to do it anyway. A trapper will put down his favourite hunting dog if it's in pain and a parent will give their dying child one last kiss and tell them it's going to be alright before he or she passes. You can't fix them all, princess. You shouldn't even try. Some things just need to be endured to make the person stronger *as* a person."

The thought of being forced to say goodbye to either of his own daughters like that suddenly had a lump forming at the back of his throat that he couldn't swallow around. Until they were established, their futures were no more guaranteed than any other mortal child.

Gritting his teeth, he gathered up those thoughts and punted them as far to the back of his mind as he could, refocusing on the more important subject at hand instead of a futuristic what-if that would never eventuate if he had anything to say or do about it.

"If I can endure the eating of the Damned, you can endure my disgust of it, princess. I'll try to rein it in so it's not in your face so much, but you have to promise me you won't let my feelings cloud yours. That would torture me a thousand times more than needing to eat the Damned."

He released one hand and gently caressed the side of her face until she tilted her head into his palm for more contact. "Promise me?"

Columbine's head rocked affirmatively against his hand. "I will try, Father. But it is so hard when you are feeling so ..." She paused, and unable to settle on a fitting description, her facial features sagged and she rolled her split tongue down either side of her open beak in a soundless *blah*.

Avis snorted and smirked at the physical representation of the emotion, knowing it hit the mark in every way without her needing to say a word. He hooked his caressing hand behind her head and gently tilted it towards him, at the same time leaning forward himself until their foreheads touched. "What say we both try a little harder, princess. Hmm?"

He heard the mental agreement in her surface thoughts before the small bony bumps on either side of her forehead brushed against his skin to indicate she was nodding. "Words, princess," he whispered coaxingly, refusing to break this tender moment with a rant.

"I will try, Father."

"Good girl." He lifted his head from hers and kissed her brow, then rose to his feet. From the corner of his eye, he caught sight of her diary nearby and bent to retrieve it. "Hopefully, we won't be on the river too long and things can go back to normal," he added, passing her the book with a wink and a warm smile. "Until then, have fun with your diary, princess."

"Diary?"

Avis arched an eyebrow and gestured to the book. "Isn't that what that is? A book of your life, with regular entries?"

Columbine dropped her focus to the book and caressed the front cover with one tiny clawed hand. "Diary," she repeated, as if testing the strange word on her tongue. "A grimoire is called a diary in Mystal."

Grimoire. Avis should have guessed. Even their diaries had creepy as fuck names.

He shuddered and walked away, leaving her to it.

* * *

As promised, Avis approached the nightmare of the 'evening' meal with a very different mind-set. If he had to choose between dwelling on what the Damned were going through and upsetting his precious little girl, he'd dance on the Damned's feelings *all damn day*.

He blocked out all sympathetic thoughts on the matter by convincing himself that those on his plate were specific enemies he'd personally made over the years and were in the process of getting everything they deserved and then some.

Uriel and his pack of shit-headed brothers might have had starring roles in that mental fantasy.

The lie served its purpose and as he ate, he caught Clarise's dazzling smile of approval and felt more than a little embarrassed about the fuss he'd made all day. Especially when she'd been right all along. He was a god ... and not just any god ... one of the supreme gods of Mystal. The Damned were evil *mortals*; as insignificant as grains of sand on a beach, for precisely the same reason.

The only problem was, Columbine still wasn't onboard with that higher sense of self. Although he was careful not to draw any unwanted attention to her, he watched the way she continued to palm the small morsels to avoid eating altogether and twisted his lips together thoughtfully. Something about that still wasn't sitting right with him.

Something he couldn't quite put his finger on, and the more he tried to ignore it, the louder the alarm bell in his head rang. He glanced across at Clarise, who appeared to be enjoying her crustless cucumber sandwich. Clearly, she saw nothing wrong, so what was the bug up his ass? He hated puzzles. He hated self-induced ones even more. But *something* wasn't right.

When nothing came to him, he focused on every detail of Columbine's current physical condition. That was when he finally noticed the healthy lustre of her leathery hide had dulled, and small crease lines were forming around her joints as it lost elasticity.

The level of fire in her eye recesses had dimmed and her wings weren't sitting anywhere near as high over her head as they had been. Demonic children, it seemed, were no different to Mystallian children, and Columbine hadn't had anything to eat or drink in nearly four days. What he'd put down to the muddied orange ambience around them was in fact her failing health.

* * *

Fury at both her stupidity and his own for not catching it sooner surged through him. *Are you fucking kidding me?*

Columbine's head whipped to him and her chest plates swelled to their maximum capacity, accentuating the microtears in her hide. She breathed out just as quickly, forcing a thick cloud of smoke to pour through the opening. The burst of temper that from her side would've looked as if it came from nowhere had frightened her, but he was too insanely furious to care. She was killing herself right in front of him, and like fuck he was going to let it continue.

Clarise and Cora jerked away from the mat in surprise as Columbine whirled away from him with every intention of bolting. Red crowded the edges of Avis' vision as his rage ratchetted. *Oh, no you don't, young lady!*

If she took to the air in her weakened condition, she wouldn't make it far before her wings gave out and she'd plunge headlong into the Akheron River. Avis latched on to her mind before she disappeared entirely behind the smoke screen. *You're not going anywhere!* He brought her to heel, forcing her back to the mat and promptly sitting her on her ass across from him. **Stay,** he mentally commanded.

"What the …!" Cora lunged to her feet and stumbled away from the mat, while Clarise merely looked at Avis with a questioning arch of one eyebrow.

Avis never took his focus off Columbine, though he raised a hand to Clarise for both silence and her indulgence. He'd explain everything later if she hadn't already figured it out for herself. His hand then went to the clasp of his cloak. After twisting it to the left, the golden chain fell open and the cloak dropped soundlessly to the deck behind him. "Tilu," he growled, bringing forth his preferred servant.

He still didn't break eye contact with his younger daughter as he reached behind him and gathered the cloak in a clenched fist, lifting it above his shoulder for the servant to take. "Take a fist-sized portion from this and create the single most demonically nutritious drink you could ever possibly imagine."

As the cloak was taken from his hand, Columbine cringed, whimpering in terror. Her mewling only fuelled his rage. "You better believe it, young lady. I'm on to you now."

A few seconds later, a tall glass of something was pushed into his hand. The heat from the drink instantly penetrated his leather glove and stung his fingers until they numbed, but he nodded in gratitude and closed his hand around it anyway.

He brought it around into view, squinting at the brilliance of the bright, flame-blue liquid and held it across the mat to Columbine. "Drink it, Columbine," he ordered, giving her exactly zero options. If he was going to burn his fucking hand just holding it, she was damn-well going to swallow it and stay alive.

The molten gold in Clarise's eyes hardened into jagged edges as she deduced the situation and sat ramrod straight. Avis was pleased she didn't interfere *yet*, though it was clear from her body language that she'd be adding her own views to the mix just as soon as he was done. Cora also returned to the mat, but the way her gaze slid accusingly between him and her sister, she still had no idea what was going on. That wasn't his concern.

Columbine took the glass and did as she was told. The long, shapeliness of the glass and its softened rim conformed to her beak perfectly and she drank its contents with unbridled relish. Her forked tongue then slid around the inside of the glass, absorbing every scintilla of the liquid within. Once the glass was clean, she held it away from her face and sighed at it longingly.

Avis took that as a need for more and reclaimed the glass from her. He still couldn't believe she'd be so insanely reckless! His chest heaved, and he gritted his teeth to stop himself from swearing at her at the top of his lungs. Without a powerbase to sustain her immortality, she could have died, for fuck's sake!

He may have been just as big a baby about the food, but he was established, and he knew it! Death wasn't in the equation for him! Holding the glass over his shoulder, he shook it for Tilu to refill. "Again," he snarled, his gaze boring into Columbine. Already she was looking better. The depth of colour was returning to her hide and the microtears were melding together. The super-elixir was doing its job.

Over the next few minutes, the glass was refilled three more times before Columbine slowed down enough to enjoy each mouthful of the beverage. "Do you need more?" he asked, when the glass was emptied for the fourth time. "Don't lie to me," he quickly added, when her head tilted marginally away from him; one of her tiny tells that meant she planned on giving the truth a healthy massage.

"I do not *need* more, Father," she said, making no effort to meet his eyes.

Given his limited supply of non-Damned mass and the unknown factor of how long this raft-ride would be, Avis decided it would be more prudent to ration the non-Damned mass out instead of overindulging now. "Good. Then you need to get something into that stubborn little head of yours, young lady."

He stabbed a gloved finger at the mat in front of him, wishing he had the reach to poke her shoulder instead. "If you ever," —he jabbed the deck with enough strength to poke a hole in the rug— "… *ever* try a knuckle-headed stunt like that again, I'll mentally flog you within an inch of your life so fast it'll make your head spin. Are we clear?"

Columbine's shoulders hunched miserably. "I am sor …"

"Don't even try to apologise!" he shouted, shutting her down hard. "You did it and you meant to do it! Now own it!" It would have been a cakewalk for Avis to go into her mind and force her to, but the point of the exercise was to make Columbine take ownership of her actions herself. Not allow someone else to do it for her.

Still restrained by his mental directive of *stay*, a lump the size of Avis' thumb appeared at the top of her throat and it worked its way up and down with ever increasing speed as she withered beneath his bellow.

Her body shook. Her hands fidgeted. Her head even jiggled as if she were trying to find anything else to focus on instead of him. But eventually, as the seconds ticked away, she stilled and murmured, "I will not eat the Damned," so quietly it was barely a whisper.

That wasn't even remotely close to how Avis wanted to hear it. "Muttering your decision under your breath in the hopes that no one will hear you is still not owning it, Columbine. If you've decided on your course of action, you make your stand and do it with your head held high. It may be my prerogative to take your head off your shoulders if I disagree, but you will own your space if it kills me. Now look at me!"

Columbine's head slowly lifted off her chest until she *almost* looked at him. Avis knew of coastal tides that moved faster. "What was that you wanted to say to me, young lady?"

Through his peripheral vision, he noticed chunks had been gouged out of the raft behind her curtesy of her taloned toes and for a moment he wondered if his anger was making him push her too hard, too soon. Especially if there was every chance she may never assimilate his way of life. The possibility had merit.

After all, Cora had almost been broken when she'd been forced into the role of a Highborn Hellion. What if he was doing the same thing to Columbine and it only came to light afterwards that she was *incapable* of behaving like a Mystallian? The thought bothered him, but if she was ever going to survive in Mystal, he needed her to give a little.

Mystal would hopefully soon be their home and his family took no prisoners when weakness presented itself. If she didn't own her space, others would own it for her. He was never going to let that happen.

Columbine continued to wring her hands before her, but just when he was about to give up, she said in a clear, concise voice, "I said I will not eat the Damned, Father."

Clarise sucked in a sharp breath of outrage, but Avis held up his hand again at her, this time with more determination. He was finally getting somewhere, and for this to work, he had to stay in control. If Clarise overreacted now, he'd never get this ground back. "You will if we make you," he corrected, not to criticise her stand, but to make his own just as clear.

Regardless of what she thought, her days of starving herself were over. "I know you're a natural empath, Columbine, and I would never willingly force you into something if I had an alternative. But trust me when I say killing yourself is *never* going to be an option for you."

He paused and pulled back, allowing himself to become more resolute. "Fortunately for you, I do happen to have another option." One he hadn't thought of before now, thank the Twin Notes. He made a show of removing his gloves and dropping them with some force on the mat between them. "Mass that isn't either the Damned or the Akheron River," he declared, rolling his hand over the offering as an obvious solution.

If he'd thought of it before now, he'd have consumed the mass himself. Columbine needed it far more than he did. Remembering the stakes, he then stabbed a finger at the gloves. "But you listen to me, princess, and you listen good because I'm only going to say this once."

His finger tapped the gloves with less force as before but conveyed just as much conviction. "When this runs out, and the Damned is all that's left, you *will* be eating regardless. I won't be giving you a choice. You hear me?"

A short brown cloak suddenly fell over Avis' outstretched hand, covering it and half his forearm like a towel. A pair of small, tanned leather gloves quickly followed.

"What?" Cora asked, when Avis looked across at her in surprise. "Are you the only one that can offer up non-Damned clothing for this?"

Unable to help himself, Avis' lips parted in an enormous smile. That right there, was exactly what he was talking about. *Make your stand and apologise for nothing.* "Not at all," he practically purred with delight.

"I do not approve of this concession to Columbine's food aversions," Clarise declared, shaking her head distastefully. "We are above such things."

"It's not the food itself she has the aversion to, sweetheart. It's what happens when her innate ability comes in contact with it." He flicked an irritated finger in Columbine's direction. "You know she's an empath. Whether we like it or not, she genuinely knows the feelings of what she touches just as clearly as if it was shouting at her and it doesn't matter what form they take."

As he lowered his hand to magnanimously include the meal before them in a sweeping wave, it occurred to him that Cora wasn't reacting to any of this. At all.

His gaze narrowed, and his hand fell to his side. "None of which surprises you, does it, tiger?"

If Cora's half-lidded eyes weren't answer enough, the fractional flex of her left shoulder as she shrugged at him took it over the line. "She is my sister," she said, as if that should've been obvious from the very beginning.

Her straightforward honesty was refreshing. He himself had known of every innate ability that his siblings possessed since they were children, so it shouldn't have surprised him that Cora and Columbine were likewise attuned.

"Very well," he said, for there was little else to be added on that regard. His eyes moved towards Clarise still sitting on his right, though he paused when Columbine came back into view.

Of his two children, he could see she was going to be the one to cause him the most trouble. Not because she intended to, but because she was so shy, so ... secretive. Mystallians always made their points from the get-go. They made their call and they stood by those decisions regardless. It wasn't in their nature to do a verbal two-step for anyone.

Yet it seemed Columbine would rather try and deal with a problem all by herself than voice it for someone else to hear. In Cora, he could appreciate that approach, for she had the intellect of an adult and could manage things accordingly. But Columbine ... did not. Case in point; her imbecilic solution to eating the Damned.

His gaze narrowed in annoyance and he shook his head slowly at her. *You are never blind-siding me like that again, princess,* he promised himself. From now on, he'd be paying a lot more attention to where her head was at, whether she liked it or not.

CHAPTER THIRTY-FIVE

"Have you concluded what you wished to say on the matter, Avis?" Clarise asked.

Avis. Not 'beloved' or 'my love' or any one of a thousand endearments she'd called him since their reunion. She was pissed, and he almost regretted having nothing else to add. "For now," he conceded.

"Then I have but one question, which shall start a slightly different conversation."

Avis felt as if he were watching a basilisk slowly lifting into a strike position, complete with deadly poison dripping from its fangs. Nevertheless, he tilted his head in Columbine's direction for Clarise to proceed. The gold in Clarise's eyes clashed against each other like jagged strikes of lightning. "Precisely *when* did you get your shape-shifting back, Columbine?"

Avis sucked in a sharp breath, for he hadn't realised that was the reason Clarise hadn't noticed what Columbine was doing. He'd seen it. He'd even realised she was doing it. But he'd forgotten all about the supposed tefsla she had absorbed which should have prevented her from doing her little sleight of hand trick in the first place.

Columbine looked at her mother, her beak opening and closing repeatedly as if she were trying to say something, but the words wouldn't come. Her eye ridges arched upwards miserably and then she shook her head, burying her face into her tiny hands.

Avis' heart went out to her. It was hard to ignore that much sorrow and regret from someone he cared so deeply about. From the corner of his eye, he noticed Clarise's hand reach for Columbine and he knew that hardened look of concentration. "No!" he said, grabbing Clarise's wrist and holding it away from Columbine.

Without the tefsla to protect Columbine's form, he knew his wife was about to attempt physical discipline with her. His interference annoyed Clarise, and she looked at him with enough ice to remind him of Antenora.

Avis refused to budge on the matter, though he did lean to one side, close enough to put his lips near her ear. "Let me do this *my* way," he said, turning his head to look directly at his cowering daughter.

Without giving the girl any other kind of warning, he mentally dove across the divide between them and blew past her non-existence defences, arrowing in on her most recent memories. He'd had it with this game of selective information sharing! He didn't care how long it took, he was going to find out exactly what he was up against.

Arriving at her latest memory, the one where he'd been leaning into Clarise and whispering to her, he anchored himself and looked around, searching the impossible glass house of images for any that contained her maternal grandfather. Somehow, he knew that prick had to be behind this. Even without the change, the girl's discipline had been sanctioned by the High Court of Hell, and only the supreme demon himself would risk violating that.

Avis noticed the thick cord of memory connecting this one to another that was buried behind thousands of others. Most memories had much thinner connective tissue, but in cases where the past had a strong influence on the present, thicker connections were created. Clarise had demanded to know when she had been able to shape shift, which permanently entwined the hidden memory with this one.

Normally, connections drew the memories together like magnets, allowing someone like him to step easily from one to the next. Columbine's mind on the other hand, was completely open with every memory fresh and clear. Without knowing what the distant memory held,

Avis could only hope for the best as he focused on the target line and released his hold on the recent memory. Currents of bending power captured him, driving him along the cord, passing thousands of images that overlaid each other simultaneously.

It was by far the strangest way to have to traverse a mind and once again he swore heatedly at Belial for doing this to her. Having *anything* physical affect the mental was just ... *bullshit*. This was his domain! Not Belial's! That shape-shifting bastard should stick to his own side of the power scale!

He arrived in the memory of a cavern he didn't recognise, but Belial's presence front and centre told him his initial hunch of who was behind this had been correct. Repositioning himself to be a few minutes before their meeting, he ran his right thumb over his lips and watched the scene play out.

Columbine's point of view was only an arm's length from the floor and it took him a moment to realise she was crawling forward on all fours towards her grandfather in much the same way as she had with him the day before. He closed his eyes and clenched them, thoroughly disgusted by how the Highborn Hellions expected a member of their own family to crawl around like that. It would be the last time, if he had his way.

"Columbine, rise."

Avis heard his demonic father-by-marriage's command and hesitantly cracked one eye open. He'd never been so relieved to see her line of sight now included the supreme demon's hips, and he knew those hooves anywhere. He'd spent long enough amongst the Damned, staring at them.

"In a few hours, you will be leaving with your parents and it may be a long time before you are able to return to us." The weight of Columbine's horror pierced through Avis' chest like a knife and her viewpoint shot to her grandfather's throat, before falling just as rapidly to the cavern floor again. Avis grunted in pain and rubbed his chest to alleviate the lingering ache. That *really* hurt.

"Nevertheless, you are welcome to blood-link with me without getting into trouble, any time you wish." Avis knew the significance of that statement. Just as a seclusion ring prevented a bender from blood-linking, he assumed tefsla did much the same to a shifter. By admitting she could blood-link to shifters, Belial had all but admitted she was tefsla-free.

Belial then squatted down in front of her and slid a talon under her bowed beak, lifting it until Avis could see his father-by-marriage's face. "I am sending four Highborn Hellion Guards with you, little one. Whilst you are on this journey, you will go nowhere without at least one of them being with you at all times. Do you understand?"

Columbine nodded, and Avis knew from the inside that she meant it. Belial seemed to know it too, for he tilted his head to one side and stroked the inside pad of his thumb against her beak. The contact was gentle ... almost caressive.

Avis hadn't thought the bastard capable of either. "I cannot remember the last time I made a command so important, Columbine. That guard must stay within your line of sight. Always. No matter which form you take or what you are doing. Once you arrive in Mystal, your father's guards will take over that duty, but until then, you stay with at least one of mine. Do you understand?"

Again, Columbine nodded. "Good. There is something else you must know before you leave, little one. I have removed the tefsla from your body, but you have not had your Uncle Ludovic's punishment expunged. You were very naughty when you went with your sister into the training room and your Uncle Ludovic's punishment for that was very clear. You were to remain as a Highborn Hellion. That did not include shifting into a gaseous form to help undermine your uncle's discipline towards your sister."

Oh, fuck off! Avis inwardly snarled; his hands tightening to fists at his side. No realm-damned way was he going to let Columbine think *any* of that situation was her fault when Cora had gotten into her head first and forced the issue! The girls were having a hard-enough time with their confidence as it was, without adding this shit to it!

"You will remain in your Highborn Hellion form until you reach the borders of Chaos. Do not concern yourself with not knowing when that will be. It will be obvious to all." Belial's whole hand curled under Columbine's lower beak, and Avis watched in wonder at the loving trust his daughter had for the supreme demon.

Those same talons that extended well past Columbine's eyes could carve through anything physical without effort, yet she relaxed against the soft leather of his palm in much the same way she had in Avis' own hand.

"I am trusting you to not be naughty again," he went on, lightly caressing her beak on both sides. "This form is to be maintained at all times. Not a damaged version of it. You may use your shapeshifting to stay exactly as you are, no matter who does what to you. Otherwise, you are forbidden to shapeshift inside of Chaos. You are also forbidden to speak of this to anyone. Even your parents. They have their own ways of learning your situation, but the information will not pass your beak."

You asshole. Belial had known he'd come looking for this conversation.

Having the information he was after, Avis began to withdraw from Columbine's mind. At least he and Belial were on the same page as far as her well-being was concerned. But the little imp was determined to kill herself rather than take on the mass she needed to maintain her life. Well, too bad. People did things they didn't want to all the time, and if ...

His peripheral vision caught sight of himself right at the edge of her memories and he stopped, turning to watch himself first entering her mind. His eyes widened in disbelief. He was ... ghostly. An apparition of sorts in texture, blending in almost seamlessly with the memories around it.

If he hadn't seen that image every time he looked in the mirror, he would have missed it entirely. She really did know when someone was inside her mind! What the fuck? How was this even possible, when he had the superior mind? He should have been calling the shots. All of them. If he had wanted her to know he was in there, that was fine.

But like this, where all he wanted was information, she shouldn't have had a clue! He watched his ghostly self take hold of the memory cord and disappear into the ether of her history. *Wow. Just ... wow.*

He pulled away from her and returned to himself, blinking sharply at the revelation of what he'd seen in Columbine's mind rather than at the dull orange-grey ambience that surrounded them. Columbine still had her head bowed and misery practically radiated from her.

His gaze went to his right where Clarise sat with her wrist still firmly captured in his grip. "We need to talk," was all he said as he released her hand, making no attempt to be subtle.

"Of course," Clarise replied, then promptly clapped her hands once for the girls' attention. As if she didn't already have it in spades. "Children, take what you wish to eat and withdraw to the far end of the raft."

Just like that. No explanation. The order was the type which Avis barked at servants all day and it left a sour taste in his mouth that she would assume that level of command over their girls.

"Your mother and I just need to talk in private for a few minutes," he added, feeling the subconscious need to elevate their positions to where they still had no choice in the matter, but at least they understood the reasons behind the decision. **You may go**, he mentally added to Columbine, reversing his earlier command to stay.

Columbine bounced upright and skittered away from the mat, happy to distance herself from them as quickly as possible. Cora, on the other hand, hovered over the makeshift meal like a dark storm, carefully tipping dish after dish of leftovers on to her own plate.

Avis watched the pile grow until he was certain one more crumb would send the enormous food-tower tumbling. "Are you really going to eat all of that?" he asked incredulously, for Griffith and Tal combined would've been hard-pressed to clean that pile up and they were both two and a half metre giants.

"Oh, yeah," Cora drawled through a toothy smile, her eyes shining vindictively. "And I plan on chewing every mouthful at least a dozen times before I swallow too, just to make sure they get the message." She eyed the mountain of food from base to tip and slowly licked her lips.

To Avis, the look and motion had more in common with one of Hell's Master Guardians when the newly acquired Damned were driven before them for assessment than someone who was merely hungry. The comparison gave him the creeps.

Somehow, Cora managed to balance the monstrously overloaded plate without losing a thing as she climbed to her feet and retreated to the far end of the raft near the demon steeds.

Avis shook his head at her, but once the girls were out of hearing, he refocused on Clarise. "Your father is behind it all," he began, mumbling the words in and around his raised fingers in the hopes of distorting it enough that the girls wouldn't overhear. "He's taken the tefsla out of her system and told her to stay in her demonic form until we leave Chaos."

"And why the secrecy?"

"My guess? To stop any of the males in your family from finding out what he's done. Any discipline she endures as a result of not answering their questions, she has his full authority to negate and make herself whole once again. If they spanked her, she could turn her backside numb, and when it was done, revert the damage as if it had never happened. It's subterfuge at its finest. The males of your family would do what they want and go on their way thinking Columbine was under their thumb, and Columbine won't tear herself apart with guilt for defying them, because she had her grandfather's permission to do it. Win-win, all round. Your father knew I'd get the truth from her memories, which is not something any of your family can do."

He glanced at Columbine and pinched his bottom lip between two fingers, tugging at it gently. "This won't mean much to you, sweetheart, but superior benders are supposed to have absolute control over inferior minds. That's just the way it is. If a superior mind doesn't want the inferior mind to know what's going on, the lesser one never has a clue."

He glanced at the daughter in question and tightened his grip, ignoring the way his lip protested at the mistreatment. "She knew, sweetheart. Somehow, some way, Columbine knew I was inside her mind."

Clarise reached across and pulled his hand away from his face. "She was sitting directly across from you, beloved," she reminded him. "And you were hardly being subtle with your intentions ..."

Avis did not appreciate the condescension ... at all. "She didn't just know I was going in, Clarise. She saw me in there. Knowing I'm about to do something and watching me do it are two very different things where a bender is concerned. On my way out, I saw an apparition of me going in. *Me.* That's not supposed to happen."

"And why does that concern you so much?"

Avis sucked in a sharp breath as he instinctively went to explode at her for being so naive. The *why* was obvious ... wasn't it?

For a sentence that started out as a strong statement of fact, somehow it ended with a question that derailed his inner rant. Why was it so important that he get in and out without her knowing? It wasn't as if she had tried to stop him. The ridiculousness of that thought had him snorting to himself. As if she could.

So why did it bother him?

Because he was supposed to rule over inferior minds. It was a control thing. The rest of the family would have similar expectations, and they wouldn't take kindly to anyone who could circumvent that order. Even someone who appeared to be a harmless spectator. "The natural order of things is not to be undermined."

"Ahh," Clarise said, her eyes twinkling with understanding. "The rigidity of a bender."

Avis' gaze narrowed, then slowly he arched an eyebrow. She'd better not be going where he thought she was.

"Unlike benders, shifters remain in a state of flux where the natural order is merely an illusion of familiarity. Because we live in Chaos, we accept that change is the only constant."

Oh, yes, she did. "Really," he growled, clasping his hands in front of him while spearing her with a condescending look that screamed otherwise. "Remind me again what your reaction to Columbine being elevated out of your disciplinary reach was, sweetheart?"

Avis' barb struck home and struck *hard.*

Clarise's cheeks puffed and her lips thinned as the gold in her eyes sharpened into burnished peaks, but she refused to verbalise what he could read so clearly in her expression. Her lack of words didn't matter to Avis. His point had been made. Her family dynamics were far more regimented than his own, whether she liked it or not.

Clarise placed her hands on the deck on either side of herself and eased around to his side of the mat. She still didn't speak as she slid her arms around his waist and rested her ear over his beating heart, giving him a light squeeze of reassurance. The scent of lavender once again filled his nose, calming him. "It would seem we both have issues pertaining to capabilities that our younger daughter should not possess."

Avis dropped his arm across her shoulders and drew her against him. "The question is, what do we do about it, sweetheart? We've got the discipline covered, but sooner or later, my family's going to go poking around inside her head, and it won't take them long to realise she's cognitive inside that mind, watching everything they do."

"At which point, they will simply have to adapt, of course," Clarise replied, as if it would be that easy.

Avis liked her optimism, even if he knew otherwise. Tal would lose his shit over this, with most of the family not far behind him. She wasn't technically a threat per se, but she was different, and things that worked outside certain parameters weren't tolerated by anyone. Still, the last thing he wanted to do was give Clarise a reason to not accompany him to Mystal, so this was something he'd have to somehow sort out himself.

And he had plenty of time to do so.

Unfortunately.

CHAPTER THIRTY-SIX

Clarise's hand softly cupped his cheek, snapping him back to the present. "What are you thinking, beloved?" she asked.

Drowning in the depths of those molten gold eyes, Avis scrambled for a new conversation topic. "I … just realised how much I don't know about how things work, demonically," he said, without specifically saying that was what he'd been mulling over.

Just in case her truth sense worked on eye contact (eyes being windows to the essence and all), he lifted his gaze over her head to seek out the girls at the far end of the raft, not far from the demon steeds. "I mean, I caught Columbine palming her food this morning," he admitted, with a slight shrug of guilt. "And I didn't think anything of it because I thought demons were such master shape shifters that your kind could go on indefinitely."

Clarise rolled her head against his collarbone until she too was looking out over the deck. "Shape is easier to maintain as a shifter," she agreed. "But like all celestials, the essence requires energy to maintain its living mass. A living non-shifter, such as yourself, requires food and water to gain energy. That energy source is later replaced by a powerbase, which is why an established celestial will never starve to death."

"Stay with the shifters, sweetheart. I already know how my side of things work."

Clarise lifted her eyes to his. "Of course. That was not meant to come across as patronising. I was merely giving you a starting point of reference so that you could use it for comparison. Essence is attached to mass, and living mass requires energy to maintain itself. Without mass to draw on, a shifter without the influence of tefsla can modify his or her size downwards and use that excess mass for energy consumption. Or, alternatively, they can become something unliving that doesn't require energy at all."

She lowered her gaze to the far side of the raft again. "In Columbine's case, she was ordered to maintain her current form, and being a living thing, that form requires mass for energy that she refused to consume."

"So, if it wasn't for the fact that she has to pretend to have tefsla in her system, she could've turned into something inanimate and saved herself, but not without going against your father's order to actually save herself."

With a groan at the convoluted logic, Avis dragged a thumb and forefinger across his eyes to pinch his nose as the blood pounded relentlessly in his ears "By the realms, sweetheart! What is wrong with your family?"

"At least we know the rules now," Clarise said, patting his knee before squeezing it lightly.

"Do we?" Avis threw back, his temper escalating with every unanswered thought that occurred to him. "Your father keeps changing everything! How can anyone know anything for certain in this place! For the realm's sake, Columbine could've died because I didn't know she had to eat in that form and you didn't know she didn't have the tefsla limitation. And Columbine took tefsla from Cora. Does Cora even still have it, or are we just taking their word that she does? Has anyone tested the theory? And how long is she supposed to endure it? What if she ...!"

Clarise suddenly launched herself to her knees and meshed her lips against his, kneecapping his rant in the most enjoyable of ways. He stiffened initially, but as her tongue slid across his, her lavender scent became intoxicating. In seconds he could barely remember what he was so angry about.

When she pulled away a short time later, her eyes were soft and molten with a combination of amusement and love. "Hush, beloved, before you give yourself an aneurysm. I will answer all your questions, but you must first give me the opportunity to do so."

It stunned Avis to see Clarise make such a bold move in public, but instead of being annoyed, his subconscious wanted him to throw his fists over his head and howl in triumph. It was more evidence of her evolution into his Mystallian queen instead of the stencilled cut-outs that made up the rest of the Highborn Hellion Ladies. "Alright," he conceded, kissing her briefly once more on the lips. "One question at a time." He took a moment to consider what his first question would be.

Clarise utilised this time to slide fully into his lap with her hands linked loosely over his shoulders and her legs hooked at the ankle behind his back. The added height advantage put her eye to eye with him, and he liked it.

"Let's start with what I do know," he began, leaning his forehead to rest against hers. "Shifting is like bending, in that the superior dominates the inferior, regardless of desire from either side. Since the pole servants haven't changed from the moment we first started this journey, what's stopping you from taking the tefsla out of Cora and dumping it into ... say, Frash?"

No, he wasn't a vindictive prick at all.

Over Clarise's shoulder, Avis noticed Cora was eating heartily at the far end of the raft, and the unwanted proverb regarding apples and trees sucked the wind from his sails. *Shit.*

Clarise tilted her head to fill his view. "Tefsla is a vile form of punishment for someone of Chaos to endure. It is not employed lightly and can only be removed by a more powerful Highborn Hellion." She paused and drummed her fingernails together behind his head as if deciding on an appropriate example. "The easiest way I can explain it is if you compare tefsla to a very strong snap trap, latching on to our essence and locking it into the mass we currently possess."

Avis already knew that. Or rather, he'd surmised as much. "And?"

"And only a Highborn Hellion has the essential strength to prise apart those metallic jaws for someone of lesser standing, freeing the trapped essence. The ensnared individual cannot do it for themselves, no matter how powerful they are, and no demon or hellion has the strength to move it at all. Tefsla is more powerful than any of those lower ranks."

Well, that part was new, and it certainly made tefsla far worse than a seclusion ring. Provided a healer was on hand and the mystical ring could be located, a bender could either take it off ... or, if it was made into a brand, simply carve it out. The latter may not have been enjoyable, but it was still a viable option and well-worth the pain if it meant reclaiming one's bending abilities. It was almost impossible to keep a bender under the influence of a seclusion ring by force for long.

"That still doesn't answer why you can't get Cora out of the trap and stuff Frash's essence in instead."

The surliness in Clarise's eyes held little amusement. "Because," she replied, her voice holding a distinct edge of displeasure to it. "Although a Highborn Hellion has the strength to free a victim from tefsla, the rescuer's essence is then caught in the trap instead. If I were to remove Cora's tefsla, my ability to shapeshift would be forfeited instead."

Insidious didn't even begin to describe this stuff! It was vile! Avis ground his teeth in frustration. "And the smallest amount of tefsla locks your whole body down?"

Clarise closed her eyes and shook her head. "No. It works on a ratio. But, before you convince yourself that we may shift around the contaminated site, keep in mind that whatever portion of me the tefsla settles into would remain unable to change until the tefsla wore off. To give you an example of the danger, if I attempted to become a Highborn Hellion after I took Cora's tefsla and it settled on my Mystallian heart, the hellfire that ignited in my ribs would burn it to ash, killing me instantly."

Horrified, Avis hauled her tightly against his chest as if his presence alone could ward off such an outcome. The visual filled his imagination and his inability to do anything about it would give him nightmares for at least a month. "Is there any way you can tell ahead of time what part of your body the tefsla will settle into?" he asked, quietly staring over her shoulder at the girls. There had to be a way around this noxious stuff. There just had to be!

He felt her head rock negatively against his ear. "Not until we attempt to shapeshift. The sensation of its presence floods our systems, making us feel as if we are fully encased in marble. If our systems are not fully saturated, we would only know by a process of elimination. Tefsla is horrendous, which is why its very use is restricted."

"Columbine's under the impression that she took Cora's tefsla locked essence and gave her back some of her untainted essence in return."

Clarise relaxed and lowered her forehead to rest on his shoulder, her cool breath dancing across his skin of his exposed neck until it stood on end. "You forget, my love, Columbine is just a four-year-old child and her understanding of complex issues like tefsla infusion may not be entirely accurate. You were inside her mind just a few minutes ago. Did you see any hint of Cora's essence trapped in there?"

Avis had to concede that. While he hadn't gone so far as to seek out Columbine's essence (he was NOT doing that again any time soon), he knew if Cora had been in there, Columbine would've been utterly dominated by the older, stronger presence. No way would any part of Cora's essence risk dying just because Columbine hadn't wanted to eat. It would have forced her to survive.

The imagery amused Avis. If he could somehow commandeer part of Cora and cram it inside Columbine as a permanent watchdog, that'd certainly allay any fears he had about her well-being.

Then he sobered. Columbine wasn't Cora's problem. As her parents, she was theirs, and they'd both do whatever was needed to safeguard the girls. It just sucked that because of Belial's interference, Clarise's control over Columbine would one day be hobbled to ludicrous levels and there wasn't a damned thing either one of them could do about it.

Unable to help himself, Avis growled in annoyance. It was typical that events orchestrated by Belial were continuing to screw with him. Shapeshifters sucked, except for Clarise and his girls. Even Frash had known exactly what was going on that morning, and that bitch was a lifeless stick!

Avis' mental tirade slammed into a brick wall of realisation without warning.

Hang on … "Clarise, if a shapeshifter takes on a form with no eyes or ears or anything, how in the realms do they know what's going on around them?" Frash had played him, while in the form of a bargepole. He'd literally been beaten by a fucking stick!

"If we take a form that lacks a particular sensory input, our essence automatically gives us an area effect for that lost sense, amplifying it if anything."

The look on his face must have relayed his confusion, for she smiled kindly and attempted to simplify matters. "If, as you said, I was to become a chair with no eyes, then physically, I shouldn't be able to see anything. But my essence would replace the lost sense of sight and I would be able to see in all directions to a standard distance at once. Not only would I have regular sight, but it would be enhanced to include every direction. The same rationale applies to all our senses, and innate abilities completely circumvent a shape."

Cheating cheaters, he thought irrationally to himself, though that definition still didn't include Clarise or their girls. "Then why isn't the river turning Gingen and Frash inside out with pain? If they're just inanimate bargepoles, shouldn't that area effect of amplified pain thing you just spoke of be killing them by now?"

Harming the latter of those two wasn't necessarily a deal breaker for him, but the discrepancy was one he wanted cleared up. Despite his long life and casual acquaintance with many shifters over the eons, he hadn't really cared about how a demon did what they did before today. Not even when Tal went and married one.

Columbine's little stunt changed everything, and he was now determined to become an expert in all things shifter as quickly as possible. His eyes sought out the girl in question and he glared at her vexedly. *No more surprises, miss.*

"I would assume they have taken a form not unlike a living hair follicle."

Avis reared in shock, pushing Clarise back far enough to stare at her. That had to be the single most ridiculous thing he'd ever heard! What creature anywhere had strands of hair that matched a twenty-plus metre barge pole?

The gold in Clarise's eyes crystalized again. "A very oversized hair follicle, obviously," she said with yet another strong hint of reprimand in her tone.

"More importantly, all of Frash and Gingen's sensory inputs will be gathered at the top of the pole in miniscule amounts, far from the water's painful surface. The part that penetrates the water is as dead as a shaft of hair and just as non-sensory."

Having all those senses at the top of the pole went a long way to explain how Frash knew to become a diversion that morning and now that it was all laid out for him, he had to admit it did make a twisted sort of sense.

It also explained why demonic melee fighters shifted their heads to have no eyes or ears right before a serious combat. The advantage of hearing and seeing everything during hand-to-hand battle was an incredible plus.

Sneaky shifters.

CHAPTER THIRTY-SEVEN

Clarise tracked every nuance of her husband's physical demeanour. He may not have always been forthcoming with his thoughts, but she was beginning to see a pattern to their development. She viewed his disparaging threats towards Frash as juvenile but accepted it as his way of clawing back some of the control he'd lost during his convalescence.

That was one of the first things she'd learnt about her husband's family. They did not like to lose control. Even Tal's explosive reactions had Destruction at their source, which by definition put him in control of the situation.

A depth entered Avis' eyes and his head tilted marginally, his gaze shifting to her left towards the Acheron River and the Damned that swam around them. His brow furrowed until his thick eyebrows met over the bridge of his nose and the flesh below his lower lip subconsciously worked through his teeth.

She assumed it was the result of an unsatisfactory internal discussion with himself; one of those instantaneous conversations which benders often took part in to the exclusion of everyone else. The Highborn Hellion in her demanded that she respect his decision to not share his thoughts and wait serenely for his invitation to be included, but something else told her she'd be waiting an eternity for that permission.

Avis' family didn't do invitations. They went after what they wanted until it was theirs. In their minds, if you weren't willing to fight for it, you didn't deserve to have it.

It was a mindset she no longer found as outlandish as when she'd first met the Mystallians. 'Owning the space' could sometimes be as simple as standing one's ground. Avis clearly didn't like where his thoughts were taking him, and if she could help alleviate that, wasn't it her duty as his wife to do so?

Her decision made, Clarise softened her mass to slip through Avis' grip like putty, reforming the moment she was free to press herself against his chest with her arms wrapped loosely around his neck. "Is this a private conversation, or can any old wife join in, beloved?" she whispered into his ear.

She felt him stiffen, but then he chuckled and enclosed her in his arms again. "I'm just trying to figure out what your father's game is here," he said, twisting his head to press his lips to her cheek before using a hand to guide her head into his neck, where he rubbed his cheek across her hair.

Apprehension flooded Clarise, making her temporarily light-headed. There was no disguising the animosity between the men of her family and her husband, but whilst they were within the boundaries of Chaos, Avis needed to be very careful about what he said out loud.

"What do you mean?" she asked, drawing on her shifting to keep her tone calm.

"Your father controls everything in Chaos, and the key word here is *control*. If he's anything like my old man—and trust me, in this regard he is—there's no way he'd let the realm get so out of control that he was no longer its master. Chaos is only chaotic to everyone else. To him, it'll be whatever he wants it to be."

So far, Clarise couldn't argue. "That is a fair statement."

"Which means, he could manipulate both the Akheron River *and* the Chaotic Ocean and put us right on Yaru's doorstep in a matter of seconds, if he wanted."

Again, his logic was faultless. And when all her kind wanted to see the back of Avis as much as Cora as soon as possible, there was no reason for her father to deliberately delay their departure like this. It made no sense …

… unless, her esteemed father was preparing them for what lay ahead.

With wide eyes, she pulled back just enough to look at Avis' face. He had so many enemies, none of whom would take kindly to him or his family travelling through their realms. Before his time amongst the Damned, he'd cared for nothing but himself. He certainly didn't care for mortals. Yet now, he fussed like a babe at the thought of using any of them to meet his own needs.

If he couldn't come to terms with the difference between himself and the Damned, they were never going to make it far in the Known Realms against other gods. The old Avis would be mortified by this newly developed weakness, and in that regard, her beloved husband needed to become the 'old Avis' again.

The one who was capable of doing anything to get what he wanted. The one who truly owned the space he was in.

If her suspicions were correct, in his own round-about way, her father was refusing to let them leave until he was certain Avis had regained his lost sense of godly self.

Avis' brow creased into a frown as he watched her closely, casting dark shadows over his eyes and cheeks. "I'm not going to like whatever it is you've just deduced as the truth, am I?"

Clarise never lied to anyone. Her words were always the truth, though her long life had given her the skills to imply the opposite. This was not one of those times. "There is one possible explanation," she said, leaning up to kiss him lightly on the lips in apology. "But yes, if I am correct, you will not be pleased."

Avis' chest lifted as he drew in a frustrated breath which he then released in a downward huff. "I've never known bad news to get any better with the passage of time," he said, brushing the back of his fingers against her cheek.

He bowed his head and returned her quick kiss with a lingering one of his own, then drew away to stare at her. "Hit me with your theory, sweetheart. I'm at a loss for one."

"Up until this evening, you still saw yourself as one of the Damned. You may not dwell amongst them anymore, but you still see yourself as having affiliations towards them. You felt sorry for them. Let us not forget that they have done things to warrant being here. Horrible things. Yet you cared more for them than your own mortals. You know in your mind, if not in your heart, this is not how it should be."

She placed a hand against his chest, right over his heart. "*Your* mortals need your attention, beloved." Her other hand gestured at the river, and those struggling to swim through it. "Not these ones. You are Avis, supreme Lord of The Life Court of Mystal."

Again, she drew his attention to the Damned around them. "These mortals should mean no more to you than the marble steps of Pandess. Tal, your own brother, is the destroyer of worlds. Billions of mortals die every time he loses his temper, yet it would never occur to you to ask him to stop just because the mortals' suffering upset you, would you?"

Avis snorted and rolled his eyes in disgust.

Then froze.

Slowly ... ever, *ever* so very slowly, his slitted gaze came back to her and she saw his understanding as if he'd shouted it to the realm. "You *cannot* ... be serious," he growled out lowly, his large frame tensing until he was shuddering with a mixture of revulsion, self-loathing and hatred.

Clarise wouldn't spare his damaged pride. He deserved to know what she knew, or at least, what she had surmised. Resting a hand against his cheek, she melted into his chest and nuzzled the enlarged vein that pounded furiously along his neck. "It is but one theory that fits all the facts," she whispered, not wishing to add to his pain any more than she already had but knowing this needed to be done.

Avis breathed heavily for some time and she snuggled against his tense frame, determined to see him through this. It took longer than she liked, but eventually, he rolled his head to one side and rubbed the underside of his jaw against her head to indicate he was relenting.

His chest heaved a tiny sigh. "Since we're in the process of baring all," he said, tightening his grip to cuddle her close. "You should know your father, *in his infinite wisdom ...*" —those four words dripped with snide sarcasm— "... has decided to uphold Ludovic's punishment while we're in Chaos. Columbine may have the ability to shift into anything she desires, but not his permission."

Now it was Clarise's turn to stiffen. Not in anger, but in fear for their wayward daughter. For she knew he spoke the truth, and every time Columbine had utilised her shifting to return the palmed food to the plate without her knowledge, she had been directly disobeying the supreme demon, who never missed anything.

Columbine could be just as ostracised as Cora!

Avis made a strange rumbling noise deep in his throat which she recognised as his way of trying to console her. He'd done it before, when she'd been distraught by the news of Cora's blood rage, but her own emotional state had prevented her from noticing the effect which his reverberations had on her Mystallian body.

Ironically, the combination of her husband's protective rumblings and his strong but gentle caresses did something to negate her excessively high emotions in this form. She still wasn't sure why it was so effective, but when comparing it to her own actions of moments ago, she realised she'd been instinctively doing it to him on a very basic level herself.

Avis was far more experienced with his form, and she took note of exactly what he was doing; learning from his expertise.

"He's given her allowances, sweetheart. Remember? He said she could shift to maintain her present form. So, if you look at it the right way, technically there's a lot of wiggle room in that. We could argue that her present form included her state of mind, which refused to eat the food. To be honest, the part of this that aggravates me to death is the knowledge that all of this stems from one idiot's asinine punishment." He pushed her just far enough away to look her in the eye. She met his gaze levelly. "Can you believe your father's still upholding that stupid ruling?"

His hands moved up to her shoulders, squeezing her for emphasis without shaking her. "Unlike Ludovic, Belial knows how benders work! He knows Columbine would've had no more choice in the matter than any other lower ranked bender in the presence of a superior one and he didn't even take that into consideration!" Avis' eyes sparked with rage and new hatred.

Clarise watched the transformation in her husband as his legendary Mystallian temper soared before her eyes. In the span of just a few minutes, he'd gone from self-loathing to neutral to consoling to seething to furious.

If she allowed this spiral to continue, it would escalate until he inadvertently said something he would barely live to regret. He had not been wrong about her father's total control of the realm. Very little, if anything happened inside the borders of Chaos that her esteemed father had no knowledge of, including who said what about him.

"Beloved, no," she chided, softly but securely clamping her hand over his mouth even as she pressed her forehead to his. "Do not say what I can see so easily in your eyes. Father is always listening. Always watching. If this is a test, we need to prove to him that we can do this. Just us."

She released his mouth and palmed the sides of his neck until the sheen of outrage left his eyes. Then she rested her head on his shoulder. "I believe in us."

Avis didn't respond. At least, not straight away. She watched his larynx rise and fall in time to the flexing of his throat and jaw muscles as he fought the multitude of things he probably wanted to say but wouldn't risk. Eventually, his face relaxed and tension in jaw softened until his breathing returned to normal. "I really don't like your father, sweetheart," he growled, so quietly it was barely a whisper.

The corners of Clarise's lips titched upwards. The worst was behind them. "He is no member of your fan club either." She'd hoped the familiar phrase from his home realm would cheer him up—or at the very least distract him from his dark mood. But what she hadn't expected was for him to suck in a shocked breath and straighten where he sat.

By the time he pulled her from his shoulder to look at her again, there was very little black in his eyes, which had rounded in disbelief. "What did you just say?"

In that instant, Clarise thought she had completely misjudged the Mystallian saying and rushed to explain herself. "Back when I was pregnant with Cora, Chance and Emi often told me that about you when they came to visit me. I had assumed it meant they did not approve of your treatment of me. Did I use the phrase incorrectly?" She watched her husband's face carefully, reading his every facial movement for a clue.

Avis closed his eyes, then scrunched them up as he lifted his chin to the sky. The sigh he uttered was twice as deep as those that came before. "No, sweetheart. You used it right," he admitted, pursing his lips together so tightly they lost colour. "I was an ass of the highest order." He opened his eyes and looked back at her, sorrow and regret vying for control of his face.

Despite his use of profanity, the heartfelt admission was so sincere that Clarise melted at his candour. "Yes, you were," she agreed, and he winced as if she'd slapped him. It would have been so easy to leave it at that, but instead she leaned forward and kissed him. "Past tense, beloved," she breathed against his lips.

He didn't appear any happier by the distinction. "So, what else did that pack of clowns have to say behind my back?"

Still elevated to his height, she laid her elbows over his shoulders and knotted her fingers together somewhere behind his head. "That 'pack of clowns' is your family, my love. Not mine. Anything they said behind your back would have already been said at least a dozen times to your face first."

CHAPTER THIRTY-EIGHT

Avis had to agree with that, and his heart regretted the rift he'd caused between them. Tal and Blagden had called him every name in the book through a blood-link from Crohen for his foul treatment of Clarise and Mashaka frequently shifted gravity on him, slamming him into walls and ceilings whenever the whim took her. Amaro would only contact him if the realm required it and he was in a constant state of ill-ease which he knew was Yasadan's handiwork.

Griffith had punched him the full length of Pandess twice and Armina ran him through with both her claymores. Even Mahpee forced lightning to strike him periodically. Chance tapped his powerbase to flat out avoid him and Emi had made sure his sex drive was non-existent. None of which achieved any more than the basic name calling had. His thrall had him believing he was right.

Looking back, the only one of his siblings (and their significant other) who hadn't had a lot to say, was the one who knew how badly he was going to suffer in years to come. Chasidah had stood in the background of their dark court brother's blood-links and smiled like a viper toying with its prey. They'd all had their say. He'd just been too drunk and stubborn to listen.

He hadn't felt more alone than he did at this moment. *This sucks.* The longer he dwelled on those old memories, the more likely it became that they'd be starting all over again in the Unknown Realms.

Adding insult to injury was the knowledge that this part of their journey was being controlled by his father-by-marriage; a being who hated him as much as everyone else, if not more. But what he disliked most of all was how horribly this trip was affecting Columbine.

She was delicate, and not like the women of Clarise's family either. His wife had her own brand of strength when she needed it. Columbine, well ... she'd been willing to starve herself to death rather than consume the Damned, for fuck's sake! At least he'd been selfish enough to know that no amount of starvation would actually kill him!

He lifted his eyes to the girl in question who was still crouched at the feet of one of the guards and frowned. Although her back was to him and her wings were raised over her head to act as a crude shield, the movement of the raft brought enough sway to her wings that through the gaps he could see her hands were clamped firmly over her ear holes.

She was willing to do anything to please those she cared about, even to the detriment of herself. He was never going to let that happen, which meant she'd need a keeper. A praetorian. Someone above Diviten, who couldn't be ordered away just because Columbine wanted it.

As much as it galled him to admit it, Belial had the right idea when he told one of his brute squad to always remain close by. If they made it back to Mystal, he'd see Armina about promoting two or three of her best fighters to the position so that at least one would always be with her. Someone who would differentiate between obeying the will of a child and seeing to her safety.

Perhaps the one silver lining to his family starting again in the Unknown Realms was that they'd be keeping the four Highborn Hellion Guards indefinitely.

Avis would almost offer a boon to any moron stupid enough to cross blades with them, just to watch the ensuing blood-bath.

The boon itself was inconsequential; no one would live long enough to collect it. In fact, if he didn't think Armina would take it so personally, he'd almost be willing to ask Belial if he could keep at least one of them for this specific duty. There'd be no better praetorian.

Clarise's hand against his cheek brought him back to her beautiful golden gaze. "You have that look on your face," she said with a sensuous smile, stroking his cheek and jaw.

With Columbine's future well-being taken care of in his mind; the combination of Clarise's touch, that sexy little smile and the fact she was still sitting on his lap with his hands supporting that cute ass caused an immediate response in Avis' lower regions. Arousal filled him until he could hardly breathe.

His eyes quickly found the girls again, knowing he'd never get away with what he was thinking while they were so close. The problem was, he really, *really* wanted it, and denying his carnal needs wasn't something he had a lot of experience in. "What look?" he asked, cautiously seeking any subject change at hand.

"The one that says you are weighing up your options and deciding whether the person you plan to aggravate is worth the reward."

The accuracy of the statement killed all thoughts of a romantic interlude. How could he be an effective supreme ruler if his every thought was bared for another to peruse at will? That was his prerogative! "I don't have a look that says all of that!" he bellowed, indignantly.

"Sssshhh," Clarise shushed, placing a silencing finger over his lips as she turned towards the girls who were even now, looking back at them.

Fuck this! Avis shot a mental command of "sleep" to both their girls, not regretting his heavy handedness for an instant as they slumped towards the deck. His decision had nothing to do with creating a sexual opportunity for himself and everything to do with an extremely private conversation he planned to have with his wife. Clarise thought he had tells, and she was so convinced of it that only one of two possible outcomes could occur.

Either he was right, and she'd look foolish in front of their daughters, or (more worryingly), she was right, and they might learn he … *supposedly* … had tells. He scowled momentarily. The latter was ridiculous. He had no tells. This was all about salvaging Clarise's pride.

Columbine started to slump towards the leg of the guard when she suddenly disappeared. This time, Avis lifted his gaze to the chest of the guard whose legs didn't appear to have moved. Sure enough, Columbine was nestled in two of its four arms, having been caught and lifted to safety quicker than his eyes could track. Cora was not so fortunate and landed heavily beside her half-eaten meal.

Avis returned his attention to his wife. "I do *not* have a look that says that," he reiterated.

"Of course, you do," Clarise corrected softly, her expression shifting to—dare he say it—smugness. "And I am not going to tell you what it is, or you will change it … and *there* is the petulant four-year-old who is not getting his own way." Avis hadn't realised he'd moved his face at all, but he couldn't deny that her refusal to identify his tells had pissed him off.

Now, angry at himself as much as her, he gnashed his teeth with a growl and lifted his head to the orange-grey sky overhead, refusing to partake in this game a moment longer. By the Twin Notes, he hadn't realised he was so transparent. "And that one wants to kick the game board over …"

"Enough, woman," he snapped, removing one hand from under her backside to clamp it over her mouth. "You've made your point. It doesn't look as if I'll ever be able to hide much from you at all."

The corners of her eyes creased and the gold in her eyes sparkled mischievously. She used both hands to pull his downwards away from her mouth. The smile that move revealed sucked the air from his lungs. "Were you hoping to?"

FUCK, YES! instinctively came to mind … and Avis hated himself for it.

The controlling bastard in him despised the thought of relinquishing control to anyone, but Clarise would always be his one exception. "Not intentionally, no," he answered, focusing on the gorgeous woman in his arms. "But not every situation has to be seen through the eyes of the Hellion Highborn, and until you broaden your perspective, I might want to keep certain Mystallian things from you until you are ready to accept them. Not because I don't trust you, or that I don't love you, but because I care so very much about what you think, and I don't want you thinking the wrong things prematurely."

"What type of things?"

Avis felt his face crease predatorily, for her question moved the conversation back to where *he* had all the power. Cue the controlling bastard again. Still smirking, he curled his free hand around the small of her back and pulled her into his chest. "If I told you that, we wouldn't be discussing them when you had a more open mind, would we?" he purred against her cheek.

While his move had been playful at best, Clarise suddenly twisted her head and kissed him fully, forcing his lips apart and plundering the insides of his mouth as he had done so many times to her.

The boldness of the move caught Avis by surprise, but he recovered quickly and slid his tongue over hers until their lips moulded together and their tongues sawed back and forth. "Is that Mystallian enough for you?" she asked, after she pulled away.

Warmth flooded Avis until he was practically chortling like a schoolboy. "Well, it's certainly on the right track," he breathed, sliding his hand between them to knead one of her breasts through her doublet. "But I'm thinking a lot more practice is required." His lips reclaimed hers in another long … *educational* kiss. One that he was in total control of and held nothing back.

"And to think everyone back home thinks I only married you for your power," she panted a little breathlessly, once the kiss ended.

Forgetting all about the proximity of the girls, Avis laid back on the deck, pulling her down with him. "Not my great looks?" he teased, spearing his fingers through her hair in anticipation of his next move.

He hadn't started this, but by the realms, after four days of self-imposed cock-blocking and knowing that the girls were out to it for the next few hours at least, he was finally going to finish it.

Clarise leaned forward and kissed him again, unwittingly making his intended possession of her that much easier. "You have but one form, beloved and they fear I will grow bored of it."

Yet another swipe at his sexual prowess. Forgoing any hint of gentleness, Avis locked his fingers around her head and sharply rolled over, effectively pinning her to the deck beneath his much larger bulk.

"Oh, they do, do they?" he growled against her cheek. His knees nudged her legs apart until he was cradled between them, grinding himself against the apex of her legs. His straining erection made his intention very clear. "And what do you say?"

Clarise's eyes widened in horror and she jerked them to the sleeping girls. "Avis, no!" she hissed. "The girls might see …"

"They won't," he declared confidently. Seeing his desire reflected momentarily in her eyes, he dropped one hand to her pants line and burrowed his fingers beneath the layers of fabric until he encountered her soft flesh. "It's been four days, baby, and I'm not waiting another second …"

It suddenly dawned on him what he was doing, and he stopped dead in his tracks. Shame that he'd gone so far without consent flooded him and he yanked his hand away from her pants as if he'd been burnt. Then he planted both hands into the deck on either side of her head and lifted his upper half, so he could see her face clearly.

"Unless you really don't want me to?"

So close, but he would *never* force her again. *Never!*

The gold in Clarise's eyes became molten as she looked up at him. "Are you certain the girls will not awaken?"

Hope flared within his chest, causing one side of his lips to twitch upward. "Absolutely. They're asleep for at least the next few hours. Bending has its perks."

Clarise's worried expression melted into a lascivious one of her own and he realised her mask of neutrality had been a total farce. "Will that be enough time?" she asked saucily, sliding her arms over his neck.

Avis dropped his upper body back on top of hers, smashing his lips against hers until they parted, and his tongue swept past her teeth. As badly as he wanted to remind her that this was the fourth time she'd challenged his sexual aptitude, every second counted, and he didn't want to waste any of it arguing.

For the next few hours, Avis let his actions speak for themselves.

No one gets bored with me!

CHAPTER THIRTY-NINE

The following morning, Columbine was mortified to learn that her father planned to give her all their non-Damned food mass. "Father, no! You need to eat too!" she argued as she tried to push the fiery drink back at him, daring him to deny it. "We could share …"

But Avis was just as adamant that they wouldn't, and she didn't get her stubborn streak from her mother.

* * *

It was another week or so before Avis realised he no longer cared about the suffering of the Damned that swam around them. Not even a little bit. Exactly when that transition occurred he wasn't sure, but out of the blue he found himself no longer mortified by the thought of eating them. It had been just as Clarise said. They were mortals that weren't even his, and they were far from innocent.

If not for Columbine's ongoing resistance, their very existence would've been inconsequential to him.

The moment Clarise saw the change in him, her relief was tangible. She beamed so happily it lit up his whole world and wrapped her arms around his neck for a tight hug that seemed to last forever. Then she released him and turned on the Damned. The woman was a sight to behold when she was on a mission.

Avis had never seen her so determined as one damned soul after the next was plucked from the water and reformed to better the family's mediocre living arrangements. First, she extended the raft a further three meters behind the demon steeds who stood at the bow.

Then she gathered up more Damned and mashed them together to create external walls roughly a metre in from the edges for walkways and three doorways; one facing the right-hand side of the raft and two more on the left. Avis looked at where the new portion of the raft met the old and couldn't distinguish between the two. Her work was flawless.

Accepting the plight of the Damned, Avis folded his arms over his bare chest and watched in rapt fascination as his wife plucked each soul from the river without moving and moulded it into what she wanted with nothing more than a look.

The week had cost him his doublet and boots as well as his original cloak and gloves offering, but so long as he maintained his leggings for modesty, he was okay with that. He shook his head, mesmerised by the way she could stretch and fold each floating mortal soul like a fresh batch of toffee.

Only the very first captured soul let out an ear-piercing scream as it was racked into its new shape. More would have followed, but Avis caught Columbine cowering beneath the three legs of her guard, crying miserably to herself. The sound shredded him, and he quickly brought her empathic sensitivity to Clarise's attention. His wife's solution had been simple: she melted their voice boxes first. After that, they were incapable of screaming or saying anything.

It bothered Avis that Columbine continued to cry. It bothered him a lot. He went over to her and squatted in front of her. "Hey," he crooned, running a single finger under her beak until he angled her to look in his direction.

The eyeless recesses were arched upwards miserably, and yellow streaks of what Avis assumed were tears flowed down her face and splashed against the guard's feet. On the off-chance that those tears were infused with hellfire, Avis avoided touching them with his bare skin.

Columbine didn't wait for an invitation. She suddenly hurled herself at him, clinging to him as if he were the only rock of safety in this nightmare she found herself in. Avis tensed in anticipation of being burnt, but when it didn't happen he quickly wrapped his arms around her, using his chin to cradle her head against his neck.

He shushed and rocked her as she sobbed and blubbered against him. No physical pain accompanied the move, but he felt himself drowning in her misery. He couldn't help it. She was his little girl. His princess. Her pain was his, tenfold. "We won't be in Hell long, baby," he promised, wishing he had the means to protect her from herself.

"Th-they hurt ..." she sobbed.

"I know, princess. They're supposed to be hurting. They did some very bad things in their lives, and now they have to pay for them." Did it make him feel like the realm's biggest hypocrite that he could speak so casually about the punishments of others while he had side-stepped his own eternal suffering?

Maybe a little.

"Princess, this isn't good for you. You're too young to be dealing with this. I'm going to put you back to sleep." Columbine stiffened and shook her head, but he shushed her again, stroking her face with his hand. "They're not touching you, baby. This is all in your head."

"I still feel it," she insisted.

Avis sighed. "Your power is strong, princess," he said, trying to find the right words to explain residual pain. "But it is also very sensitive. You've been inunda ... uh ..." —he amended the word to— "... buried under great suffering. You heard it from that first victim. Your empathic power has latched on to that, and it is making you aware that all the others must be feeling that too because they are suffering the same fate."

Columbine bowed her head. "I do not want to sleep," she whimpered into his throat.

Avis pulled her away from him to look at her face; the closest he could get to staring into her eyes. "Are you sure?" he asked, his tone deepening to indicate the seriousness of her next response. This would be an unholy baptism of fire for her if she chose now to own her space for the first time. "Be very sure, Columbine. I will respect your choice, but you must be ready to face the consequences of it."

Columbine swallowed heavily, her split tongue slithering over both sides of her beak. "I am sure," she said firmly, if not a little fearfully.

Avis nodded, then knelt down and deposited her on the deck. He unwound her arms and squeezed her shoulders gently, then leaned forward to kiss her brow. "Very well, princess," he said, regaining his feet. "I'll be nearby should you want comfort, but you are not to change your mind, or even voice how much you'd like to. You were given the options, and this was your choice. You must own it."

"Yes, Father."

Avis hoped she knew what she was doing. It would've been easier on her to sleep through the modifications until after they were done, but learning this valuable lesson had no real downside to it. She would learn without being harmed, and next time she'd know there was no going back on a decision if there were no underlying facts to be discovered. That was the Mystallian way.

He turned towards Clarise and found her standing alongside the right-hand side doorway, feeding the Damned into the room, one after the other. With a quick glance down at Columbine, he went to stand behind his wife, dearly wishing he could see past her, though the walkway she stood on was barely his width and not wide enough for two abreast.

True, he had a height advantage of head and shoulders and could probably look over the top of her, but he didn't want to risk startling her at an inopportune moment. Not while she was so obviously focused.

The realms only knew what kind of pain-crazed monster might come lumbering out at them if she was distracted part-way through a shift. It'd be his bitch the second he saw it, but it could very well harm either one of them in the interim panic.

Eventually, she turned and smiled up at him. "I hope it meets your expectations, beloved," she said, sliding her hands around his waist and slipping under his arm to stand alongside the demon steeds, giving him access to the room.

Avis immediately went to the doorway and caught himself blinking like an owl.

The walls were lacquered … the ceiling mirrored … and at knee height was a mattress so thick it reached the floor.

Satin sheets and thick pillows adorned the space and it was all Avis could do to not slide across the surface and wrap himself around a real pillow after nearly two weeks of sleeping on the timber deck with nothing for comfort. He looked back at her and almost gave an ungodly chortle.

Until he realised something.

This could've all been done on day one, but because he'd refused to have anything to do with harming the Damned, they'd gone without. *Are you fucking kidding me?*

His lack of sleeping arrangements was because *he* hadn't been able to get past his insane attachment to the Damned. Mortal souls that weren't even his! By the Twin Notes! If he were a shapeshifter, he'd reconfigure his left leg to mule-kick his own ass! All this time, he could've had a real bed! They could've ALL had real beds!

"The walls are also soundproofed, beloved," Clarise said as she slid her arms around him from behind to offer him an encouraging squeeze. "So now we do not have to worry about what the children may or may not hear either."

Fucking … WHAT?

Barely biting back the expletives that rocketed to mind, he whirled around inside her hold, his right hand hooking around her right shoulder—his left arcing towards the river with his fingers flared. "Clarise, I'm about to toss myself into that realm-damned river and when I do, I want your word you'll leave me in there for at least an hour." He wasn't necessarily joking.

Clarise must have sensed the truth of his words. Her eyes rounded in horror and with her arms still around his waist, she hauled him up and away from the raft's edge, slamming his bare back and shoulders into the newly constructed wall.

The jarring collision with the timber knocked the wind out of him, but he quickly regrouped and surged forward, only to discover his shoulders were submerged into the wall as securely as someone holding him there and that her legs had literally rooted themselves to the deck.

He was completely pinned and part of him wanted to congratulate her. The other part ... not so much. Either way, she was the only woman to have ever done so.

"Why would you say such a thing?" she demanded, her eyes flashing up at him angrily.

Staring into her furious gaze, his own temper receded ... *a little*. Could he smash his way loose from this and overpower her? Yes, provided she didn't up the ante and drop him on his ass with some kind of sedative for trying.

But did he really want to end this unusual display of temper from his normally reserved wife any time soon? Hell, no. She was incredibly sexy when she was mad.

Unfortunately, the direction of that thought only served to remind him of why he was so wild with himself. He draped his free arm over her shoulder and hooked his fingers together behind her head, then pulled her to him as he bowed his own forward until their noses almost touched.

"Because I've just let *mortals* get in the way of my *sex life!*" he snarled in a heated whisper that only she could hear, unable to believe his own stupidity on the matter. "Sweetheart, I don't even let *gods* do that to me, and these things aren't even *my* mortals! They're .... *them!*"

Glancing inside the bedroom that Clarise created, he swore vehemently at himself and shook his head again. "I've literally been blue-balling myself all this time over the likes of *them*, and I didn't need to. Do you have any idea how humiliating and frustrating that is?"

Clarise arched her neck, tilted her head to one side a little and raised one eyebrow, effectively derailing his rant with that one, miniscule gesture. Yes, she knew, and he knew she knew.

As angry as he was at himself for being such an idiot, he couldn't imagine what this past two weeks had been like for her. To know all along that their pitiful accommodations could've been rectified at any time, but instead they'd endured every day of this mind-numbing, raft-ride from Hell, waiting for him to give himself the good swift kick that woke him up and got on with life.

The truth made him sick to the core. He mashed his lips together and twisted them to one side, permitting air to rush through a tiny gap in an audible titch. "As soon as the girls are asleep tonight, I am seriously making it up to you," he promised, without a hint of a lie.

The gold in Clarise's eyes sharpened, but before he could ask, the wall released him, and she returned herself to her full Mystallian form. "That reminds me," she said, restoring the wall to a solid, flat surface with barely a glance. "I have yet to finish their rooms."

Avis silently followed her as she led them past the demon steeds to the pair of doorways located on the other side on the raft extension. "Are you planning on giving the girls a bedroom each?" he asked, already seeing a problem with that.

"YES!" Cora cheered from the far end of the raft, leaping off the deck and throwing a clenched fist through the air in victory. But then she froze, and slowly looked in their direction as if it'd only just occurred to her that she shouldn't have said that out loud.

"Uhhh ..." she stammered, as both Clarise and Avis turned towards her, their disapproval coming off them in waves. She uncurled her fingers and rubbed her palms down her leggings, swallowing heavily. "Well ... it is not that big a raft and you two were hardly ... whispering ... you know ..."

Avis pursed his lips. Tempted as he was to roar at her, (and a sidelong glance at Clarise's face told him she was also about to air her displeasure) he had to concede the little shit's point.

If he and Clarise hadn't bothered to be discreet, they had no one to blame but themselves if their conversation was overheard. "Since you *were* listening in," he said, drawing Cora's attention away from her mother. "Do you have any preferences to a room style?"

"I could always replicate what you had in Hell," Clarise suggested, innocently. Although she kept her face an unreadable mask, Avis thought he heard the hint of mischief in her tone; mainly because he'd never heard it there before. "Would you like the carved out sleeping crevice and the stone lectern for your grimoire?"

Avis remained quiet, though he studied Cora's face and caught the distressed look that flashed across her features. It was clear that she dearly wanted those items of familiarity, but without the demonic form to appreciate them, she'd be even more uncomfortable and they both knew it.

"Do you have a preference?" Clarise repeated.

Both of Cora's shoulders went up in a tortured shrug, and Avis knew she had no idea about Mystallian furniture; a fact Clarise knew as well. His wife was just being a bitch.

"Give her a bed, about a third of the width of ours on the right-hand side of the first doorway," he said, deciding to help their daughter out by doing what he did best: taking charge.

"And the same width again in heated marble floor tiles. She can make her own mind up minute by minute as to which surface she'd prefer to be on." He surreptitiously winked at Cora, who stood stock still with her mouth open in shock.

The memory of her stunned expression as she realised he was leaving her the final choice of where she'd lay her head at night was one he'd treasure for eons to come. *Welcome to being a Mystallian, tiger.*

"You certainly take the fun out of being a parent, beloved," Clarise whispered as she turned and began feeding the Damned into the prescribed doorway. After the bed was created, she paused and tapped her pointer finger against her lips thoughtfully.

"In a room half the width of ours, there is not enough floorspace for a plan that requires two thirds." She looked at him over her shoulder. "I could extend the raft out further if you feel that much space is required ..."

Avis was already way ahead of her. "No need, sweetheart," he replied with a shake of his head. "Just move the dividing wall closer to the stern to make the back room a much smaller one." It occurred to him how much he missed giving orders like this.

The last time there'd been any major work done on Pandess was when Armina had wanted to expand her wing after the birth of her youngest son, Barris.

The Triplets of Construction had insisted on maintaining perfect symmetry throughout the palace and things between them and his sister had escalated to a point where the war goddess was getting ready to pike all three of them and build it herself. Avis had stepped in and, to keep the peace, ordered Chance's wing to have a matching modification that would retain the overall proportions of the palace.

It didn't matter to anyone if the rooms would never be used, so long as the palace exuded perfection.

Clarise was shocked by the suggestion. "And give Columbine a smaller room?"

Avis' lips twitched, and his eyes found Columbine still huddled at the feet of a guard between the servants at the bow, as far from the extension as she could be without taking to the air. Her grimoire lay open across her knees, and the way she leafed through the pages it was evident she was using it as a coping mechanism for what was transpiring around her.

At least she was owning her decision. It was a step in the right direction. "Look at her, sweetheart. She'll never set foot on this side of the raft, so giving her a room of her own is a complete waste of time and space. You're better off turning it into a bathroom that'll suit the rest of us."

* * *

Columbine pretended to busy herself with her grimoire entries at the front of the raft in between the two sets of servants. For no other reason than because she could, she used one of the guard's three legs as a backrest and ran her fingers across the middle page of her grimoire. Her sister hadn't been wrong when she'd said their parents' voices carried across the open space of the raft.

Columbine had also heard every word. But her father had been wrong about the range of her power, such as it was. She didn't need to touch the Damned to know of the pain they were in. She never had. She didn't even need to see them. When a wall separated her from her sister that time Cora had been disciplined by Uncle Ludovic, Columbine had known of her condition as surely as if it had been done to herself.

She felt every one of the Damned as they were stretched and moulded into each shape her mother required, whether in her line of sight or not. None of it was done painlessly. None of it *could* be done painlessly. It was their punishment, to suffer eternally and she was forbidden to intervene. Her grandfather had been very clear on that matter. The Damned had to suffer, and it was her duty as a Highborn Hellion to let it happen.

Her father did have one thing right though. She did have no intention of interacting with the extension. As far as she was concerned, the raft still ended behind the demon steeds. She promised herself wholeheartedly that she would never willingly cross that line.

She heard her father mention the bathroom and remembered the need for such a room in her other form. Mystallians, it seemed, had a very wasteful way of eating. As a demon, mass was needed for energy and nothing more. The drinks she swallowed at each meal were to replace that which she had used up in the hours that led to the meal. Nothing … *ever* … came out the other end.

It did upset her a little to think about how the rest of her family would be sleeping in that Damned section of the raft, while she remained in the pure section. She'd be lying if she said otherwise.

The remainder of that day's meals came and went, with little change. Cora disappeared soon after each, making the most of the new additions. Columbine enjoyed the way her sister's core flashed with tones of excited lime-green and her Mystallian squeal of delight could be heard all over the raft as she bounced from one end of the bed to the other. Her happiness was a rare and welcome change from the constant suffering around them and Columbine was happy for her.

As the hours rolled on, Columbine often felt her parents' concerned gaze and numbed her facial features to prevent her mother from deducing her morbid mood. Her serene neutrality seemed to please her mother, just as it always had in the past. So long as she looked the part of being above everything, the Highborn Hellions left her alone.

Her father was another matter entirely. The moment he realised she was avoiding eye contact with him, he was in the fringes of her mind; the one place she couldn't hide from him. It was neither painful nor cruel to have him there. If anything, having him run his mental fingers through her thoughts gave her the sense of serenity she'd been faking to this point. She felt him nudge her thoughts over into happier ones and immediately felt better for it.

At least … she did for a little while.

Eventually, the time for sleep came. Their mother made the announcement just as she had every night, and for once Cora complied without a single word of argument. She even ran back to her room, hooking her hand on the door frame to slingshot herself around the corner and disappear inside.

After a quick kiss and a cuddle from her father and a firm, but distant "Goodnight, Columbine," from her mother, her parents withdrew to their side of the extension, leaving the youngster virtually alone on the open deck. Servants and guards were no substitute for family.

Sadness enveloped her as she folded her wings around herself in preparation for sleep and a smoky sigh escaped her chest plates. She was … *here* … and her family were … *there*.

It wasn't the distance itself that made her so miserable. The space between her room and her sister's back when they'd been in Hell was roughly the same as it was now, and if anything, her parents' room was closer.

But the divide between them made her feel as if they were in a different realm and she didn't like the loneliness that accompanied the feeling. Was this what it meant to own the space? If so, she didn't like it.

Not wishing to be reminded of her self-imposed exclusion, Columbine rotated until her back was to the extension and she watched the servants as they calmly poled the raft through the water. Each stroke was the same as the last, and she used the repetitive motion to try and help her relax enough to go to sleep. She knew she had no right to feel lonely or sad. This was her choice and her father had insisted she learn to stand by her decisions.

She didn't want to let him down. Back home, it didn't matter what the reason was for a Highborn Lady to feel sad. If it was strong enough that others knew of it, it was their honour to ease that pain any way they could, and her duty to accept their aid. She wasn't used to coping alone.

With her thoughts so filled with misery, she let out a squawk of surprise when a brawny, protective arm folded around her waist from behind. The familiar scent of her father filled her senses just as she heard him whisper, "Ssshhh, it's just me, princess."

He pulled her back against his chest, somehow managing to pin her startled wings without either of them being harmed. "It's time you were asleep."

Columbine looked up at his face, and his smile swept her up in a wave of happiness she didn't fully understand. "But ... Mother ..." she stammered.

He pressed his lips to her leathery head, then pulled her down to the deck, allowing her to use his arm as a pillow. "Get yourself ready to sleep, princess," he whispered tenderly. She still couldn't quite contain her surprise at his presence, but his emotional colours were awash with love and that rich, deep blue she could swim in all day.

"Did you really think I'd leave you out here all by yourself, baby?" he asked, flexing the arm he still had wrapped around her waist in a light hug. He kissed her head again. "I'll be right here until you fall asleep, and when you wake up, at least one of us will be within your line of sight. There's never going to be a time when you'll feel excluded from this family, princess. Ever. No matter what happens, we'll always have your back."

As much as Columbine wanted to argue with him, his subtle mental touch drifted through her mind, causing her thoughts to feather until darkness crept up and mugged her.

* * *

Avis remained where he was until the fire was completely extinguished in her otherwise empty eye recesses to indicate she was finally asleep. While she was in this form, the presence of those two points of flame were the only physical indication that she was awake or asleep when she chose not to move. It had been a little unnerving in the beginning, but over time he'd gotten used to it.

Did it make him a bastard that he knocked her out with another eight-hour countdown attached to the command to ensure she got the necessary sleep for a Mystallian child? Probably. Would he do it again tomorrow night? Absolutely.

As much as he enjoyed these private moments with his daughter, he had a wife to thoroughly satisfy before the start of each morning; not that Columbine needed to know the specifics of that. All she needed to know was that he'd be there with her when she fell asleep, and he or someone else would be with her when she woke.

Exclusion, even the self-imposed kind, was not the Mystallian way. Well, not on his side of the realm, anyway.

He held her for a few more minutes, for no other reason than because he could. Then he carefully worked his way to his feet, lifting his precious child with him. The light jostling caused her breath to escape through her chest plates in a series of hisses and snorts that sounded adorably like demonic snoring.

He smirked at the peaceful image she presented, then carried her to the nearest guard, who stood in the middle of the starboard side.

The guard made no reaction to his approach, but as Avis held out his child, two of the guard's four arms came out to relieve him of his precious cargo. "She is all that matters to you," he said, passing Columbine across to it.

He knew Belial had already made a similar command to all four guards, but Avis wanted to amend it where this one was concerned. "You will abandon the rest of us and return to Hell with her, if that's what it takes to protect her from immediate danger. Nod if you understand."

The guard's golden helm dipped once, which was good. As uncomfortable as Avis had been about them all sleeping together on the raft's open deck with so many of the Damned swimming around them, the thought of having Columbine out here alone had a vein pounding in his temple to the point of rupturing.

He'd spent most of the afternoon working out the best way to both protect and comfort her after the family had retired for the evening and this had been his final solution.

Avis returned to his side of the raft and paused alongside the demon steeds, casting a critical gaze across the raft and those still on it. The two pairs of servants were at the front corners of the raft, focused solely on their duty to move the raft through the river. A guard stood between them, its armoured head rotating constantly, looking everywhere at once.

A second guard stood in the middle of the portside, and the one holding Columbine was on the right. The four demon steeds were directly to his right. The rest of the raft was an open, desolate space. Pathetic, for a family of their pedigree.

Biting back the curse that came so readily to mind, Avis moved past the demon steeds and stood at the doorway of his room. Clarise waited for him, her uniform piled neatly in one corner of the mattress. The silken sheet that she had pinned under her arms protected her modesty, but its softness conformed to her every curve, leaving little to the imagination.

Even her toes were outlined and like a starving man, Avis allowed his gaze to absorb every inch of the woman spread before him. Propped against the pillows as she was, the sheet rested against her thighs, causing a tantalising shadow to fall across the V of her legs.

The sheet then dipped across her stomach, but raised sharply over the peaks of her breasts, which rose and fell teasingly with her every breath. His eyes eventually reached her face, and when they did, she smiled sensually and crooked her finger at him. Slowly. "Come here, handsome."

For the first time in his entire life, Avis obeyed the command of another *willingly*.

CHAPTER FORTY

Almost another month passed before the mouth of the Akheron River appeared on the horizon. Which was just as well, for unlike Cora and her mother (who had swapped all their non-Damned clothing for Damned substitutes for Columbine's sake), Avis still refused to don any clothing made of the Damned.

Not because their existence bothered him, but because Columbine avoided anything made up of them. The forced separation wasn't something Avis was prepared to let her endure, and as such all he had left were his leggings which were torn off half way down his thighs. A bath towel tied at his hip would have covered more.

If they hadn't reached the Chaotic Ocean by tomorrow, he'd have been forced to make Columbine eat the Damned. The possibility was one he'd been sweating on for the past few days, and he knew the 'miraculous' timing of the mouth's arrival was by no means an accident.

Avis went on to mentally label his father-by-marriage as many names as he could muster for being such a cruel bastard, both to himself and Columbine.

The past six weeks had not been the easiest, nor the most enjoyable time of his life. True, he'd had no concerns to speak of and the last four had been with the use of a private bedroom, but Clarise often brought up the subject of Columbine's innate empathic abilities and what he thought of them, and that he didn't like.

It forced him to delve into his childhood ability to manipulate conversations away from a subject he didn't understand without technically lying. He hadn't done it to hurt her, and he promised himself with every evasion that he'd explain it all just as soon as he knew what was going on himself, but the deception didn't make him feel any better.

He also disliked the way Columbine's powers were constantly referred to as *innate*. To be fair, she wasn't doing it consciously, but no amount of 'innate power' dropped someone of his capability on his ass just for poking at it.

There was also what Belial had said. She was special. But how, exactly? He'd learned after roaming through her memories that her empathic abilities were much stronger than he'd first suspected. She had ranged abilities, not just ones that relied on touch.

The first time he'd seen himself as an outline of pulsing colours from across the raft, he'd almost shit himself. Then, as he'd delved further into what she'd seen from the distance, his heart broke for her. The poor little thing had known all along of the pain that was going on around her and, due to her grandfather's insensitive command, was pretending not to notice.

It was as scary as it was sad, and there wasn't a damned thing he could do about it. Well, nothing that didn't involve putting her into the demonic equivalent of a coma.

Even then, there was nothing to say her empathic abilities wouldn't latch on to the lack of stimulus just as the physical ones did, making her turmoil a thousand times worse. He couldn't and wouldn't risk that with her.

Speaking of a lack of stimulus, boredom had also done strange things to *him*. As the weeks rolled by, Avis found himself learning the most ridiculous hand clapping and knee slapping game that ended with Columbine ensnared in his arms and being tickled until she screeched in delight.

He liked the warmth that accompanied the nonsense game, though he cringed at the thought of any of his siblings learning of it. Chance especially, would never let him live it down.

He, in turn, taught Cora one of Armina's favourite board games and just as he'd expected, she took to the chessboard like a master. Clarise had suggested one night during the first week that he should let her win a few times to boost her confidence, but he'd declined. If she wanted the win, she had to beat *him*—not a watered-down version of him.

By the end of the second week she'd won her first game all on her own. By the end of the third she was winning more than she was losing, and as of an hour ago Avis was relieved to see the multi-coloured horizon that indicated they were finally approaching the Chaotic Ocean. His pride wouldn't have handled losing to her *every* time.

As they approached the Chaotic Ocean, Avis gaped at the wall of spiralling colour that stretched in every direction, seemingly without end. It climbed into the sky just as high as it spread to either side.

The closer they got, the more he thought he saw outlines of things winking in and out of existence on the other side of that barrier. The Akheron River flowed directly up to it and disappeared. *"That's* the Chaotic Ocean?" he asked, waving a hand at the monstrosity that lay ahead of them.

Clarise moved up to his side. "An ocean is three dimensional, my love. We will not be sailing on top of it, but through it."

"I'll drown!"

Clarise's eyes took on a glint of amusement as she hooked her hand around his neck and drew him down for a kiss. "It will help if you keep telling yourself that, beloved," she whispered cryptically against his lips, then gave him another quick smooch.

That made even less sense, but when he broke away from her to stare into the depths of the Chaotic Ocean, the one thing he did notice was a distinct lack of Damned over there.

The … *space* (What was he supposed to call it? Despite the name, it was hardly water!) … was clear … which meant there was a very real possibility that he could finally have a real bath, with real water. By the realms, after years of going without one, he wanted a real bath so bad he was willing to destroy a populated world to get one.

Technically, Clarise shapeshifted the filth from his skin at least once a day and dusted it with his preferred scent of forest pine afterwards, but it had been too long since he'd felt the soothing warmth of a bath. Already, he could picture himself sinking below the surface where he could soak himself into a happy coma.

Then, all he'd need would be a glass of ambrosia or ten … and this lovely lady naked on his lap …

His daydream abruptly shattered when the raft jerked to a halt and he stumbled forward off-balance. By the skin of his teeth and the friction of his toes he managed to stop himself from face-planting, but that didn't pacify him as he jack-knifed up and shot each servant an accusing glare.

"Why in the realms are we stopping?" he demanded. Tilu and Diviten stepped away from the poles which had already split in half and were in the process of securing the raft in place just as they had every other mealtime—except they'd only *just* had breakfast less than an hour ago and lunch was still hours away.

"The Damned belong in Hell, beloved," Clarise explained as she drew a ball of mass, roughly the diameter of his boot, away from the ocean wall towards them. "We need to purge ourselves of all Damned before we leave the outer boundary of Hell."

Realising *exactly* what that implied, Avis shuddered, then bowed his head and covered his eyes. "Oh, for Mystal's sake," he growled as he planted his other fist against his hip in frustration, unable to help himself. "I wouldn't have just eaten breakfast if I'd have known that!"

He was every bit as irritated as he sounded, but her soft chuckle quickly took the sting out of his snark. A wad of soft fabric impacted with his bare chest, and peering through the gaps in his fingers, he saw her holding a neatly folded black doublet against him.

He lowered his hand to the doublet, and after sliding his fingers around hers, he followed her arm with his eyes to her face. She was smiling at him, and by the Twin Notes, he'd never tire of that smile.

"If I had known the mouth was going to appear this morning, I would have stopped you from eating for the last day or so, beloved. I told you the mouth is unpredictable. It only appears when it appears. Now that we are here, we must wait until all aspects of the Damned are purged before we may go on. One more day on the Akheron River to cleanse ourselves thoroughly will not hurt you."

She pushed harder against the folded doublet. "Time to get dressed again, my love. Your days of being an exhibitionist are over."

Avis took the doublet and shook it out, then pulled it over his head, sliding his hands through the long sleeves. Despite what he'd said at the time about giving Columbine whatever she needed, it felt fantastic to be getting back into uniform.

Extra mass morphed around his legs, extending his leggings to his ankles. Next came the belt and gloves. Clarise slid each glove over his willing fingers, then intertwined her own and squeezed. Avis locked eyes with her and raised each hand to kiss her knuckles in gratitude. He knew why Clarise hadn't assembled the uniform around him.

This was him—Avis of Mystal—reclaiming what was his. She was finally beginning to understand what it meant to own the space. Knee-high boots appeared on either side of his bare feet and he stepped into them, holding each behind the calf until his toes felt the supple strength of being surrounded by heavy leather. Then, he straightened and stomped his heel to drive his foot into place.

Clarise stood behind him and his heart soared as the familiar weight of his Mystallian cloak fell about his shoulders. It was the last piece of his identity to be returned to him and he felt whole once again. He knew for her to reach over his shoulders like that, she had to either be up on tiptoes or stretching herself with shapeshifting, so he squatted a little to make it easier for her to connect the golden chain.

Despite the awkwardness, he couldn't help but watch her over his shoulder, and when she noticed this, she paused and batted her eyes demurely.

A blaze of desire erupted inside him and to avoid acting on it, he bit the inside of his cheek and looked away, allowing her to finish the task at hand. No small feat, when putting clothes *on* was suddenly the exact opposite of what he had in mind. To clear his thoughts, he turned his attention to the girls, who were positively buzzing with excitement.

Cora whizzed around the raft like a mad thing, almost as thrilled as he was to see something other than the orange-grey scenery around them. Columbine shivered uncontrollably from amongst the demon steeds, allowing thin wafts of smoke to seep through her vibrating chest plates.

A quick probe into her mental state showed him she was deliriously happy that their involvement with the Damned was coming to an end. Avis grinned. She wasn't the only one who felt that way.

Once he heard the click of his cloak's clasp, he automatically dropped each shoulder in turn and rolled it forward to hook the edge of the cloak and reposition it to sit equally across his broad shoulders. This automatically spread it across his back to reveal the Mystallian sigil in the middle for all to see.

He stretched his hands out in front of him and took that stretch all the way to his lower back. *Oh, yeah! It's good to be back in uniform.*

He heard Clarise step away from him without a word of explanation and he turned, just in time to see her raise both hands high above her head. The gloves and other clothing around her body began to melt and drip, but before he could order the girls to look away, Clarise's entire body lost its consistency and she became a column of gelatinous mass with two overhead prongs.

What had once been her raised right arm suddenly spewed content like a hose into the Akheron River, while the left prong drew mass directly from the Chaotic Ocean. This strange display went on for several seconds, until gloved hands reformed over her head, followed quickly by the rest of her.

By the time her arms were lowered, she was as perfect as she had ever been: his Mystallian queen in her Mystallian uniform. Exquisite.

"Any chance you can do that for me?" he asked, as she clasped her hands regally before her.

"Do what, beloved?"

He patted his chest, just over his heart. "Take out what shouldn't be in me too. I don't care if you can't put it back the way you just did for yourself. I just want the Damned gone and for us to be on the move again." He waved his arm at the swirling mass of colours ahead of the raft. "The Chaotic Ocean's right there, and I hate the idea of sitting on this accursed river for a second longer than I have to."

Though she pursed her lips and twisted them to one side, Clarise dipped her head, slowly. "I can do that for you, my love, but it will not be a comfortable transition from your perspective."

Avis snorted and tried not to roll his eyes at her. After all, he'd taken two years of everything Hell could dish out and he was still standing. "I'm pretty sure I can handle it."

The look in Clarise's eyes said otherwise. "As you wish. Turn towards the river and open your mouth, beloved, and try to remember when this is over that it was done entirely at your behest."

Avis boldly turned towards the river and did as she requested. He knew if her blood hadn't been flowing in his veins, she'd have shifted him around the Damned much like peeling back the skin of a banana to extract the fruit within and it would've all been over in a matter of moments. But as she was his wife (a fact he was never letting her take back), they both knew her only viable option was to go in after them.

Clarise stepped to his right and placed what he mistakenly thought was a comforting hand on his right shoulder. Her eyes were locked on his as she shifted her right hand into a long, thin tendril about the thickness of her thumb. Observing the way it crawled through the air of its own accord towards his mouth, Avis breathed through his growing apprehension. He flicked his eyes to Clarise when it paused right in front of his mouth, and when he'd thought he was ready, he nodded.

His gag reflex kicked in the second her tendril brushed against the inside lining of his throat and his body automatically convulsed against the intrusion. He stumbled back a half-step and threw both his arms up, willing to do anything to clear his airway.

"Easy … easy …" The grip Clarise had on his right shoulder tightened and he felt her nails sharpen into fine needles, each penetrating his flesh. Warmth permeated from the puncture sites and quickly spread through him until a sense of calm came over him. "Almost, beloved," she crooned, as he relaxed at her side. "Just a little longer. I almost have it all."

Unable to do anything else, Avis breathed through his nose and stared numbly at her booted feet. Interestingly, she seemed to have a timber coloured tentacle feeding off her right boot and over the raft's edge.

The choice of colour that blended in with the deck was obvious; she didn't want to draw attention to it. Yet, as dazed as he was, he thought it odd that the thing pulsed like a vein … until he realised why, and he was sure he wanted to hurl all over again.

She may have still looked like his wife, but she'd turned her body into a conduit, absorbing the Damned upon contact with the tendril down his throat and spitting it out through that tube near her boot. Oh, that was just … *ewww!*

The moment she extracted the tendril and released his shoulder, the fog in his head cleared and he dropped to his hands and knees, coughing and hacking over the side. There was nothing left in him to throw up, but that didn't assuage the involuntary need. His hands curled around the timber edge and saliva dripped from his bottom lip as the convulsions coursed through him.

Long after the last of the spasms left him, he continued to cling to the edge of the raft with his head bowed between his arms, gasping in every breath as if it would be his last. His body was slick with sweat and he felt horribly empty, but at least it was done. A few minutes of intense foulness and it was over.

Clarise said nothing as she stood at his side and rubbed his shoulders.

"You cannot seriously expect me to do that," Cora snarled in disgust from somewhere in the distance.

Too late, Avis remembered he wasn't the only one stuck in the Mystallian form. If they were going to move forward right now, Cora would have to go through what he just had. It was one thing to choose this path for himself, but another entirely to force one of his own through it. With a final hack and spit into the river, he sat back on his haunches and looked at both girls behind him.

"Your sister isn't handling the presence of the Damned very well," he said, deliberately making eye contact with Cora first so she would know who he was referring to. Then he moved his gaze to Columbine, taking Cora's eyes with him.

"The longer we are on this river, the more she suffers." His implication was obvious, but he wouldn't force her into the decision he wanted her to make. If she chose to be selfish, she would have to live with the pain that decision caused her sister and any animosity that came of it.

He could see in Cora's face that she knew it too. Her face crumpled with her unwillingness to choose.

Yet before she could speak, Columbine ambled over to her and curled a taloned hand around her forearm. "I have this," she said, with more authority than Avis had ever heard her use. "It is but one more day."

Avis reeled with both delight and shock. *Columbine* was stepping up and owning her space?

The relief in Cora's eyes was evident. "Are you sure?" she asked, to which Columbine nodded. Without warning, Cora threw her arms around her sister's neck and hugged her tightly.

Avis beamed so hard his face hurt. He'd willingly endure a thousand cleansings if even the smallest number of them ended like this. He wiped the back of his hand across his mouth and rose to his feet. His other arm draped across Clarise's shoulders, drawing her into his side. He felt her hand slip under his cloak and hook around his waist as she rested her head against his pec.

Solidarity within the family.

His family.

He really couldn't ask for anything more.

CHAPTER FORTY-ONE

The rest of the day passed in a general state of heightened excitement. Contrary to his claim of patience, the entire family seemed to feed off his eagerness to be underway. Cora continued to run laps of the raft, bouncing off every hard surface including the guards themselves without a care in the realm, and Columbine danced and fidgeted all day. Even Clarise looked at the ocean wall and knotted her fingers together with silent longing.

The servants created a hearty banquet at every meal (once Clarise pulled in oceanic mass for them to manipulate) but when it came time for bed, the girls just wouldn't settle. Hours after they were supposed to be asleep, Avis still heard Cora bouncing around in her room, and even Columbine—the most obedient girl he'd ever had the pleasure to meet—refused to settle down.

The little imp had taken to playing amongst the demon steeds' legs, using the light shadows cast by the steeds' flames to play some type of obscure dancing game with herself.

When the hour reached midnight, Clarise decided she'd had enough and went after Columbine personally. While she did, Avis remained in the open area in between the demon steeds and the non-Damned section of the raft like a sentry, blocking her escape.

It damn-near killed him not to laugh as he watched them play a comical game of catch-me in and around the demon steeds: one where Clarise tried valiantly to get a handhold on Columbine, while the girl hissed with delight and kept herself just out of reach.

Unlike his wife, Avis had range on the little imp and could have easily grabbed her mind any number of times he caught a glimpse of her dark hide. But Clarise had put her hand up to do this, and whether she'd forgotten about his reach or was determined not to lose control of her children, he would wait until his beloved wife looked to him for assistance.

At some point he must have uttered an amused noise of some kind, since the filthy look she shot him would've scorched a lesser god. Refusing to play a moment longer, she straightened up and firmly dusted her hands. "Columbine, enough," she declared, her lips stretched into thin lines of displeasure. "Come. Here."

Four words—two of which were single syllable, and the shift in atmosphere was staggering. Gone was the playful mood as Columbine obediently rose to her hind legs and stepped free of the demon steeds. Her head was bowed, and her shoulders were hunched.

Without a word, she approached her mother, dropping to her knees in front of her with her wings pulled all the way forward to expose the thick, bony ridge of her spine.

It took Avis a second to realise what he was looking at, and when he did, his eyes widened in horror. *Clarise, no!*

He stepped forward with his hand outstretched before he realised what he was doing. Like most people, he wasn't above knocking someone sidewards when the situation warranted it, but the situation *needed* to warrant it first.

A simple, ten second game of catch-me before bedtime hardly qualified for whatever Clarise had in mind for retribution.

Clarise lifted her head to look at him and when their eyes locked, he shook his head from side to side; very slowly and very deliberately. His message was clear. *Don't do this, sweetheart. Just … no.*

He wasn't entirely sure what he'd have done if she ignored him and proceeded with the discipline, but thankfully, he didn't have to find out.

Clarise pinched her lips and twisted them to one side. Her gaze bounced between him and their child until her chest swelled, then fell in a sigh of resignation. "Very well," she said, laying a hand on Columbine's bowed head.

Moments later, Columbine collapsed to the deck like a puppet with its strings cut. The flames that illuminated her eye recesses were extinguished before she dropped. Avis lunged forward, barely catching the gasp that slammed against the back of his gnashed teeth.

Holy Hell.

He'd done some reprehensible things in his time, but sucker-punching a kid who was already grovelling? That was … next level.

"It would seem you are correct, beloved," Clarise said, unconcerned by what had transpired. She slid her arms under Columbine's unconscious body and lifted her into the air. "Unless she is actively resisting me, my control over her remains intact."

Yay me.

Reminding himself that Clarise only looked the part of a Mystallian and had a lot to learn about being one, Avis forced himself to nod.

Columbine might not have been hurt but knocking her out cold like that with no warning was (in his mind) tantamount to a double fisted blitz attack to the back of a Mystallian head. A coward's attack.

He breathed through his disgust and gestured to the guard on the right. "Give her to that one," he said, brusquely. "It's already under orders about her safety."

"You sound cross," Clarise said, after following his directive. She returned to his side and slid her arm through his; her eyes searching his beseechingly. "Why?"

Avis opened his mouth to speak, then closed it again. This was one time when words alone wouldn't help. "Watch me with Cora, sweetheart," he said, pressing his lips to her hair and breathing in her lavender fragrance at the same time. As always, it helped settle his agitation. "You'll see this is … more what I'm used to."

He placed his free hand over hers and led them to Cora's room where the girl in question was bouncing up a storm at the far corner of her bed.

Mid-leap, she realised she had company and spread her legs toward either side of the mattress and slid to her knees, absorbing the kinetic energy to ground her as if she'd never been jumping around like a lunatic.

Not even Chance had that kind of stupid luck. Well, he did, but that was beside the point. The air between them thickened with trepidation as he approached the bed opposite to where Cora sat and knelt into the mattress. He said nothing as he walked on his knees two paces into the middle and positioned himself cross legged on the mattress, facing her.

Clarise waited in the doorway, watching silently.

"You need sleep, tiger," he said finally, voicing what they all already knew to be true. He beckoned her with two fingers, then patted the mattress in front of his crossed legs.

"Come and sit here." Instead of complying, Cora twisted her head to the right and lifted her chin defiantly, her bright green eyes narrowing in a combination of suspicion and unease. Her reaction wasn't surprising, and he didn't take offense.

He tapped the mattress again. "We both know if I wanted to hurt you, you'd be in a realm of pain as we speak. As of right now, you have two choices. You can either stay right where you are and I'll shut your mind down, dropping you right there …" —he poked the mattress a third time with more force— "Or, alternatively, you can get your tail over here and try something new that I think you might like before you go to sleep."

He rolled his hand over and tapped his knuckles against the mattress. "You have three seconds to decide."

Cora stretched out on all fours, slowly moving into the space he indicated, though she never looked away from him. "Turn around and sit on your backside," he said, when she continued to eye him distrustfully.

Her blatant disobedience caused him to hold one finger up in warning. If she didn't know about the three-finger rule, she was about to find out the hard way.

The second digit unfurled. Still no movement.

As the third started to lift away from his palm, she whirled around and sat down in front of him, though she continued to watch him over her shoulder. Either someone had told her, or her instincts were still that good.

In Cora's case, he'd bet a powerbase on the latter, which did bring up an interesting question. With everything Cora had displayed so far being attributed to her mixed lineage, just what was her innate ability? His was safeguarding his own life. Clarise's was knowing when someone spoke the truth.

Cora had so much power already, more than any child her age should have, had they missed the subtle hints that would shape her life? Avis thought about different things she'd said and done since he met her. The most predominant thing she seemed to be was angry and resentful which again stemmed back to circumstance, rather than innate ability.

Avis glanced across at Clarise as he laid his huge hands on Cora's small shoulders, covering them entirely. "Not everything in your life has to be a fight, tiger. You're going to have to learn to pick your battles if you want to win every time."

He ran his thumbs across the top of her shoulder blades, then spread his fingers and speared them up through her hair, stroking the base of her skull and neck. Weeks, if not months or even years of tension had the muscles so tight that he could barely touch them without her flinching and he adapted the pressure until she began to relax.

"No point trying to sleep when your body's this wound up," he said softly. "You'll only wake up with worse knots. Did you know your Uncle Griffith has a permanent staff of masseurs in Pandess to help him sleep at night? Otherwise he gets so stiff he can hardly move without tapping into his powerbase. The rest of us borrow them now and again if we need them." He used the light-hearted conversation to keep her distracted, and so far, it seemed to be working.

"Is that what this is?" Cora asked, rolling her head forward to give him unfettered access.

The move was exactly what Avis had been hoping for and he wanted to whoop and throw his fist at the air in victory. The stubborn little minx had relaxed, and in doing so, she'd accepted what he was doing as a good thing. By choice. Her choice. No one forced her. He looked across at Clarise again and grinned.

"Masseurring?"

"Massaging," Avis corrected, refocusing on the task at hand before she brought her feathering thoughts back into line. He upped the ante, stroking his thumbs across the nerve clusters on either side of her throat until Cora uttered a soft moan of surrender, allowing her shoulders to droop in sheer bliss.

His ministrations continued until she was almost boneless, then he laid three fingers of his right hand along her carotid arteries and gradually applied pressure while his thumb and left hand continued their gentle movements. Cora was so at ease she hadn't noticed the move and within a few minutes she collapsed with a sigh against his chest.

Avis smiled down at his little tiger as he cradled her in his arms and carefully unfolded his legs. His boots went to the floor and he stood up, laying her limp body across the mattress. He removed her cloak, belt and boots and covered her with a sheet. The back of his fingers brushed against her face, drawing her fringe away from her eyes in farewell. "Pleasant dreams, tiger," he said, then backed out of the room, knowing she'd sleep soundly for several hours.

Once outside, Clarise's arms quickly slid around his waist. "Well, that was unnecessarily time consuming, beloved."

Avis stopped abruptly and stared down at her, unable to believe she'd somehow missed the entire point of the exercise. "That's all you got out of that?" he asked in bewilderment.

Clarise frowned at his ridicule, but Avis shook his head, cutting her off. "Sweetheart, she was handed the facts as we knew them and offered a range of options to choose from therein. By allowing her to make that choice and live with the consequences of it, she was able to own the space she was in. You know how important that is to us."

Clarise half closed her eyes and turned her head away to stare over the edge of the raft as she pondered that. "I see," she finally admitted. "A choice, that is really no choice at all."

"A choice within a limited range of options," he corrected, determined to kneecap his rising temper at all costs. He was not in the habit of justifying the Mystallian way of life to anyone, and the need to start now was seriously pissing him off.

"My desired outcome was never in question, only how she chose to get there. Her choice enabled her to relax and enjoy a nice massage before she was put to sleep. Had she chosen the other option, she would've missed out on the massage."

"And why did you put her to sleep using a physical hold when you had mental superiority over her?"

Avis ground his teeth and forced himself to shrug, more to loosen his temper's stranglehold over his body than to answer her. "Physical sedation is what Highborn Hellions are used to sweetheart, and it would have been counter-productive to get her all nice and relaxed, and then hit her with something she wasn't used to. It's also what we do, when someone further up the mental chain of command needs to be taken down."

Clarise hissed and tried to pull away from him, but he held her tightly against his side. "It's alright, sweetheart," he crooned.

"Mystallians permit a physical assault of their mental superiors?"

Avis could understand the mindset, however much he disagreed with it. "Yes, we do. Listen to me, sweetheart. Chance was the one who figured this move out a long time ago when Tal needed to be put down and Amaro, Griffith and I weren't around to do it mentally. Ever since then, it's been our go-to whenever the person needing restraint is further up the mental chain of command."

He rolled his fingers at himself as a prime example and shrugged again. "This way, an individual can still be put down, but in a way that doesn't hurt them."

"But how do you tolerate such a betrayal?"

Avis chuckled. "I didn't say I did. Whoever jumps me better have a damn good reason that I agree with, or when I come to, it's going to be on. But the thing is, they do know that, which is why it is almost always justified." Rather than delving deeper into that side of the discussion, he tilted his head to expose his throat and ran a gloved finger over the artery just below his own ear.

"Mystallians have an artery on either side of the throat just here that carries blood to the brain. Press on either one hard enough to cut it off and the Mystallian will be asleep in minutes, whether they want to or not." He straightened his head and tapped the arteries on both sides. "And if you push on both simultaneously, it's lights out in under a minute."

"Why would you risk permanently harming your brain like that?"

The absurdity of the question confused Avis. Wasn't she listening? It was called a 'sleeper hold' for a reason. Nothing survivable could ever keep a celest down for long. Not even brain damage. So long as the life essence remained affixed, anything could be healed from eventually and once established, a celest just couldn't die, period. He was living proof of it.

That was when he realised her question came from a position of superior shifting. Her way of reminding him that her kind could heal from anything, whereas she thought his could not. Anger welled inside him, causing his eyes to slit dangerously.

"Sweetheart," he growled as the last vestige of his shredded temper slipped through his fingers. "We may not all be master shifters like you, but that doesn't mean we're incapable of healing on our own. Any injuries caused by the sleeper hold are gone by the time we wake up. Probably sooner. It's almost impossible to kill a celest with a sleeper hold. Otherwise, it'd be called a 'killer' hold *and it's not.*" The last three words were snarled out, daring her to refute it.

Whole realms feared Avis' wrath, yet Clarise didn't even blink. She merely placed a hand against his chest and said, "There is no need to be so sharp with me, Avis. I am still learning the parameters of your kind, as are our children. I meant no offense."

Avis ground his teeth together and lifted his gaze to the swirling colours of the Chaotic Ocean in front of the raft until he had himself under complete control. She was right. If he was going to stop everyone else back home from blowing up at her naivety, it was up to him to educate her before their family reunion. She knew virtually nothing of his kind despite having lived in Mystal for months, and that was all his fault. Her ignorance was completely on him.

He huffed out a frustrated breath and folded her back into his arms. "You knew I was a bad-tempered bastard when you married me," he murmured, rubbing his chin against her hair apologetically.

A noise of disapproval vibrated through her throat at his terminology (the sound was akin to a growl—something she'd have never done a month ago) but eventually, she relaxed and melted against him, returning his cuddle. "I did," she agreed, resting her left cheek against his chest.

For a moment they stood together, reaffirming their commitment to one another. It was Clarise who ultimately broke the silence. "Why would you not retaliate against any aggressor foolish enough to attempt to place you in this 'sleeper hold'? You have range over everyone, and immediate mastery over anyone touching you ..."

Avis snorted. Her subject change to a topic where he held a dominant position was about as subtle as an exploding sun. But, since she asked ... "That's what a dogpile is for, sweetheart. Since I can only tag them one at a time, no one's stupid enough to come at me alone, and by the time I've laid out two or three of them, I'm down."

Avis saw her face pale in alarm and tutted away her concerns. "It's not as bad as it sounds, baby. Sometimes we get caught up in our thrall and come out swinging without thinking. Like I said, no one really gets hurt. At least, not for long anyway." He tucked her close to his side and led them past the demon steeds towards their room.

"Speaking of sleep, we should be getting some too. Once the Damned have passed through Cora's system, it's my plan to ride as long and as hard as the girls can take. The common demons might live over there, but I'm pretty sure the brute squad can take care of them for us."

"The brute squad?"

Avis couldn't believe she'd never heard the term before. "The brute squad," he reiterated, gesturing to each of the four examples around them. "The Highborn Hellion Guard. Every other realm knows them as the brute squad ... because let's face it. It fits."

"I see," Clarise replied, following his hand movements with her eyes.

Avis gave her a squeeze. "The next part of my great plan after that will be utilising your ability to create us somewhere comfortable to land so the girls can rest. The guards will watch over us and make sure the demons keep their distance, and every morning we start afresh until we reach Yaru." Avis looked at her guardedly. "Are you alright with that?"

Clarise nodded. "I am able to do my part, yes."

"Then tomorrow, we'll ride out, as far and as fast as the girls can."

"Tomorrow," she agreed.

CHAPTER FORTY-TWO

Tomorrow, for Avis, was a mere three hours later. He had managed to grab some sleep in the meantime, but the excitement of finally getting off this realm-damned river and actually doing something was too much for him and he stared out the doorway at the orange-grey sky, willing the time to pass more quickly than it was.

Today was *the* day! The day he could finally say adieu to Hell and all its bastard occupants and never, ever, *ever* look back. This had been his living fantasy for over two years and fed up with waiting, he squirmed impatiently under Clarise until he felt her starting to stir.

It wasn't his intention to wake her, so he rolled to his side and extracted the pec she'd been using as a pillow, awkwardly replacing it with one of the many pillows strewn across the top of the bed. She murmured sleepily against the cold fabric, causing him to freeze, but then she found a comfortable spot and sighed, using the motion to further settle her into the plushness.

Making his movements as slow and non-disturbing as he could, Avis lifted himself to his knees and carefully edged his way across the mattress towards the doorway, stopping just inside where his clothes were neatly folded alongside Clarise's. He hadn't folded them. Nor had Clarise, but ranged shifting had its perks.

He quickly shook his doublet out and pulled it over his head, then fed his arms through, dragging the hem to the waist. Next came his leggings, and in a single fluid movement, shoved his feet through the opening and pulled the waistband over his hips as he stood up, ensuring he was decent by the time he was fully upright and outside the room.

Now, his boots. He reached back into the room for them, dragging the rest of his uniform to be within easy grabbing distance at the same time. Without a handrail to prevent him from toppling into the river, Avis leaned against the outside wall of the room and pulled on his boots, though with Clarise in mind he quietly pressed his heel into each instead of using his more familiar stamp of authority.

Then, with his back still braced against the wall, he reached around the open doorway for the gloves and belt he knew were roughly behind him. They were easy enough to find, but as he retrieved them, he felt a filled Mystallian glove lightly brush across the back of his bare hand.

A savage curse rocketed through his mind which he refrained from voicing as he swung around into the open doorway. It was never a question of who had touched him, only that he'd woken her up despite his best efforts not to.

Clarise knelt on the bed in front of him; having already shifted into her full uniform, complete with a stimulation wave to create a vision of absolute perfection. "I am so glad to see you are restraining yourself, Avis," she chuckled, her golden eyes sparkling mischievously.

Avis grinned and leaned into the bedroom to kiss her good morning. "I want out," he stated, after the kiss was over. He straightened and slid the gloves and belt into place. "I'm pretty sure I've mentioned this once or twice over the last month and a half."

Clarise reached past the door frame without getting off the bed and fisted his doublet, pulling him to her for another kiss. Avis beamed and leaned in to comply, loving the taste of her mouth. When it was done, Clarise snatched up his cloak before he could grab it and passed it between her hands behind his neck.

Avis pressed his brow to hers, closing his eyes to enjoy the fragrance she always emitted. "Love you," he whispered, as the audible click of the gold chain across his collar bones told him he was fully dressed.

He felt Clarise's hands lightly caress his chest on their way around his waist. "I love you too," she replied with a lingering squeeze. "And as much as I wish we could stay here forever, it would be more prudent to rouse the children if it is your desire to leave as soon as possible."

Avis opened his eyes, then straightened to his full height and shook his head. "They've only had three hours' sleep, sweetheart, and with the ride I've got planned today, they're going to need a lot longer than that to stay in the saddle ..." —he paused, remembering the demon steeds didn't have saddles— "... well, so to speak."

He looked along the raft to the swirling Chaotic Ocean on his left and huffed irritably. "At least a few more hours. It's just frustrating to be so close and to have to waaaai ..."

Any chance Avis had of finishing that sentence was destroyed as Clarise's tongue ran from his throat to his right ear where she nibbled suggestively on his earlobe, causing his thoughts to not only derail, but slam head first into the nearest mountain that then buried them under the ensuing avalanche.

It took him a second to realise she'd shifted herself taller to do so and another second to realise he didn't care.

"What *will* we do to pass the time?" she whispered silkily, and before he could get his wits together enough to answer, her grip on his waist tightened and she hauled him back onto the bed, twisting him up and over her hip so that he was flat on his back with her looming over the top of him.

Oooooh, fuck yeah! Screw thinking angry Clarise was a turn-on! Forceful Clarise was blowing his mind ... amongst other things!

"What indeed," he chortled, foregoing any other thought that involved the space beyond this exquisite woman as he hooked his hand around her neck and dragged her down for a more time-consuming kiss.

* * *

For the second time in just a few hours, Avis stared out the doorway with a naked Clarise dozing across his chest and his arm draped around her shoulders for support. But unlike last time, his thoughts weren't filled with barely leashed excitement.

Instead, worry, bordering on dread had taken up residency within him. All because of a casual comment Clarise had made between bouts of love-making.

"It is difficult for the children to control their enthusiasm if you cannot control yours, my love," she had said, then gone on to speak about his need to lead by example or something. At the time, his mind had latched on to the gravity of her initial statement and now that she was asleep, he'd worked it to the point where he almost wanted to be sick.

He'd been beside himself with excitement yesterday, and Columbine chose that day to behave like a Mystallian. Coincidence? He didn't think so, which meant she not only knew what other people were feeling but if they felt it strongly enough, the emotions of others were influencing her as well.

That wasn't good. She'd never own her space if she couldn't first master herself. Perhaps her youth was a mitigating factor. As an adult, she might very well reach a level of celestial maturity that acknowledged the emotions of others without permitting them to affect her personally. While it was certainly possible, it was also a question for the future and they didn't have Chasidah or any other prophetic celestials to ask.

Not that it mattered. Right now, his little princess with a very big heart was, thanks to that asshole she called 'grandfather', already dealing with more woes than any child her age should be. It didn't help that before this trip, Columbine's whole life had consisted of the Well, where the Highborn Hellions controlled every aspect of their emotions and gave away nothing.

Avis' gaze narrowed, and he sawed his teeth together in frustration. This was really, *really* bad. If other people's emotional states were strong enough, Columbine reacted to them as if they were her own.

Shit … shit … shit.

It was a complication he hadn't anticipated. Emotions, like all things, had a spectrum. Good emotions induced fun, love and euphoria, but he'd made a lot of enemies in the Known Realms and none of them would be hiding their hatred for him.

How would she react to that much focused rage at him? Would she lose it and come at him too? Come to think of it, Mystallians weren't backward in coming forward either and there were hundreds of them in the pantheon alone. How could she ever be herself, with so many strong influences around her all the time?

Whether he liked it or not, his thoughts circled back to his father-by-marriage. Specifically, what Clarise had said about the bastard's reasons for dragging out this river trip so long.

What if he'd thought Avis wasn't the only one who needed to get his head in the game before taking on the Known Realms?

What if Columbine was in his sights too? It was certainly plausible, but if that prick's sick idea to break in a little four-year old child was to make her deal with the intense suffering of the Damned, he really was the greatest asshole to ever draw breath. *Sunova bitch!*

"I have a feeling a great deal of my time as your wife is going to be ascertaining what causes you to brood so, beloved," Clarise chuckled, lifting her hand off his chest to trace the outline of his chin.

Avis hadn't realised how tense he'd grown, but now that she'd mentioned it, the undersides of his cheekbones were aching. Grinding his teeth one last time, he released his breath in a heavy sigh and slowly worked his jaw from side to side to loosen the muscles. "Just … giving your father a few more befitting titles," he admitted nastily, rolling his head until he could watch her looking up at him.

A single eyebrow arched sharply at him. "What do you think he has done now?"

There was nothing to be gained by lying—especially when her innate ability saw right through it. Avis steeled himself against the allure of her golden gaze. "I think Columbine's empathic ability makes her susceptible to the strong emotions of those around her. If that's true, yesterday and last night weren't her fault. They were mine."

Clarise lifted her upper body off his chest and braced herself on both forearms by folding them across his pecs. "And that has what to do with you calling my father unpleasant names?"

Too much ire for Belial still ate at him for him to stop the next words from tumbling from his lips. "Forcing Columbine to face an entire river of pain when she was raised in the closeted space of the Well was a dick move by anyone's standards. Even his." He hadn't meant to be so blunt, but now that it was out there, he wasn't taking it back either. *Well, you did ask.*

Clarise sucked in a sharp breath and pressed her palms into his pecs, lifting herself to partially straddle his chest. She then stared down at him sternly. "A *what* move?"

That hadn't been the part he'd expected her to react to, but after all this time, it should've been. Avis rose to sit cross legged on the mattress, forcing her to slide down his torso and into his lap. "Yes and no, before you start tearing strips off me for my language, sweetheart," he said, gliding the fingers of one hand into her hair at the base of her skull to massage her scalp while he rested the forearm of the other across her elbows and gently applied downward pressure, forcing them to bend.

He really didn't like the distance between them. "Technically, yes, I suppose it's swearing, but it's also used in cases like this to describe a cruel and lowly act. It's an acceptable Mystallian term."

Clarise may have allowed him to bend her arms, but the icy look she sent him right before he pulled her head to his chest let him know she was far from convinced. "I see," she said, just as she had outside Cora's room the night before.

This time the two words implied she understood only too well that the saying which came from a pantheon of well-versed profanity users hardly made their vulgarity acceptable. "And what makes you think my father was the source of this particularly heinous act?"

Avis snorted in disbelief and waved a hand to encompass the room … and by proxy the entire realm around them. "Hello? This is not exactly Mystal, sweetheart." Having made his point, he dropped his arm across her bare back. "In case it escaped your attention, I'm not the one in charge here."

"Is that what truly vexes you, Avis?" Clarise shoved her hands against his chest until she was once again at arms' length. "The fact that you are not in control of your surroundings?"

Avis' indignation roared to life as her words struck every Mystallian nerve he had. But rather than open his mouth and spend the rest of the journey in the doghouse with her, he reined it in just enough to lock his teeth together and shove her from his lap. He refused to look at her as he slid to the edge of the bed and snatched up each piece of his discarded uniform, thrusting himself into it.

"It is a fair question, Avis," Clarise added, without moving any closer to him.

Avis said nothing. He didn't dare. If he lost control at her again, (and he was precariously close to doing so) he'd never forgive himself. But likewise, he couldn't be in the same room as her. Not right now.

With his clothing in place, he worked through a small amount of his angst by smashing his heel into each boot with enough force to leave indentations in the deck as he stood up outside their room. "I need some air," he snarled over his shoulder, then stormed down the walkway, past the demon steeds and out into the open area of the raft.

"Avis, you cannot be offended every time someone asks you a legitimate question," she called from the doorway.

Fucking watch me!

Whirling on his heel, Avis clenched his fists at his sides and curled his upper lip at her. "I pointed out precisely why I think what I think about your father. A question you first posed to me, I might add. You. Asked. Me. And then you used that very conversation to point out my failings, and somehow I'm supposed to be happy with that?"

He had expected the gold in her eyes to harden and their very first real fight to ensue. That was how things went in Mystal. No retreat. No surrender. Stand your ground and apologise for nothing. He'd never lost these arguments even when he was wrong, and he wasn't about to start now.

But instead of matching his anger, Clarise's poise relaxed and the gold in her eyes liquified indulgently. "Not being able to control another's realm is hardly a failing, beloved. I merely wished to point out that you do take exception to not being in control, and how your frustration with the one person who does have that control may not be entirely due to our children."

"It's the same thing!"

"No, it is not. Your sense of right and wrong is not being adhered to and that aggravates you. Someone else's authority supersedes yours, and that aggravates you further. If Father is doing this, he has his own reasons. Perhaps you are correct. Perhaps he is doing this intentionally to force Columbine to face her innate abilities and adapt to them. If that is so, would you rather she learned those lessons in a realm where none of our family has the power to take control of the situation, should it become too much for her?"

Oh, what Avis would have done to have a return argument for that. One that wouldn't portray him as a petulant child. He folded his arms stubbornly across his chest, breathed heavily through flared nostrils and turned his back on her; refusing to admit his choice of action amounted to much the same thing.

Ranting at the top of his lungs was so much easier when logic didn't come into the equation. The loudest, most powerful voice always won. He had both.

In the silence that followed, Avis had to concede her point, though it was still a dick move in his mind. Hands down, Hell had to be the worst possible place for Columbine to come to terms with her empathy, no matter who was in charge. Apart from the Vestibule and the Well, the realm was firmly entrenched in pain and misery—border to border.

Happiness came to a select few who enjoyed torturing others, and that was where it ended. Even if Belial had wanted to circumvent those vile emotions, Hell had an establishment field all its own, and like every other established celestial after the fact, the supreme demon was stuck with what he had to work with.

But it was still a dick move, dammit! Columbine deserved better! She deserved to be broken into their way of life gently. Shown how to distance herself from the emotions of others in a controlled environment via happier ones that enhanced her adorable personality.

Drowning the girl in the pain of the Acheron River for weeks was unbelievable, and what sucked even harder was it was too late for him to do a fucking thing about it! Dammit! If he'd known about this a month ago, he would've come up with something! Anything! There had to be a way!

Pretentious ranting within his own mind was easier to cope with, since he didn't have Clarise's accursed logic to kneecap his tirades. Nevertheless, when wafts of her perfume preceded her arrival, his tumultuous thoughts stilled, and he closed his eyes to breathe it in.

"Are you done?" she asked, from directly behind him.

"Getting there," he admitted irritably, keeping his back to her. He felt her fingers spread across the small of his back as she caressed either side of his spine.

"I am not your enemy, beloved."

How was he supposed to answer that? Deny it? After everything he'd put her through, it'd be no less than he deserved …

That reality check grounded him faster than a sword through a spoked wheel, invoking the same resulting faceplant, mentally speaking. She had every reason to be his enemy, and she chose not to be. He was the luckiest son of a bitch alive and if he didn't pull his head out of his ass and appreciate everything about her, he wouldn't be for long.

Opening his eyes to the orange-grey sky overhead, he sucked in a huge breath and released it in a gut-wrenching sigh. "I know that, sweetheart. It's just not fair that this shit has to land on Columbine—and no, I'm not taking that back," he added, when her fingernails curled into his back in warning.

For a few seconds, he waited to see if she'd let it slide, because he really didn't want to back down and he wasn't sure if he could. Not when he'd made his stand very clear in the bedroom and this was merely a continuation of the same discussion. Slowly, her hand began caressing him again and he knew he was in the clear … this time.

A win for her … and a win for me.

He could live with that.

Turning to face her, he draped his arms over her shoulders and locked his fingers into a loose knot behind her head. "Let's get the girls up. The sooner we leave the Akheron River, the sooner Columbine can stop enduring the emotions of the Damned within it."

"Cora has yet to purge the last of the Damned from her system," Clarise warned.

Yesterday, Avis had been in favour of waiting for nature to take its course rather than break the stand both girls had made about the issue. But that was before he realised his need to save the pride of one child had inadvertently caused the other to truly suffer in silence.

Columbine may have said she could take it, but that didn't mean as her father he would allow that decision to stand. With all the facts in play, the situation was now unacceptable, and he needed to correct it. Avis moved closer to Clarise, using his loose hold to prevent her from stepping away.

"As soon as you lay eyes on Cora, shift in a laxative that'll force the Damned from her in a matter of minutes," he whispered, hunching down to put his lips directly in line with her ear to avoid eavesdropping. "I don't care what your father thinks. We need to get Columbine off this river."

"Columbine said she could deal with it ..."

"And as her parents, it's our prerogative to circumvent that call. We're getting them off this river, ASAP."

"ASAP?"

"As soon as possible."

"Ahh." Clarise looked up at him. "Cora is still locked behind tefsla, beloved. Though I could give her a physical laxative to procure the same results, if you wish."

Avis had forgotten all about the stupid tefsla restriction and swore under his breath at the inconvenience it presented. Cora was only just starting to show some semblance of Mystallian pride, and he'd have done almost anything to avoid damaging that. Sneaking a laxative into her from range would've been ideal, until it occurred to him that if she didn't have tefsla poisoning, they wouldn't be in this bind in the first place.

She could've dumped the Damned in much the same manner as her mother had, if her own shapeshifting was unhindered. "Do it," he said, hating the sound of the words in his own ears. It was as if he were somehow authorising the girl's execution; and in a small way, he was. Pride in oneself was at the very heart of every Mystallian. He silently promised he'd make it up to her later.

"Very well," Clarise replied, nodding resolutely. "I will rouse Columbine, if you see to Cora."

With common sense dictating she should go to the one who needed her assistance, not the one who didn't, her choice of child surprised him. "Any particular reason for that, sweetheart?"

The gold in Clarise's eyes hardened. "Cora is growing ... disrespectful in what she says as she awakens, and today is too important to start with disciplinary action."

Yet again, Avis was reminded that his gorgeous little wife was in essence, nothing like him. The way she threw out the term *disciplinary action* as casually as a colour choice put her firmly in the company of her brothers.

"Benders often say things they don't mean when they're woken up, sweetheart. Especially if it's from a deep sleep. It takes us a little while to reorientate ourselves to reality. When we sleep, we have the option of internalising. We shut off the physical plane and turn ourselves loose inside our own minds replaying memories and seeking out mental solutions to unsolved problems at an altered time rate. Whole days can be played out in a matter of hours while we're in there. Weeks, if we're in a deep sleep. And if we don't wake ourselves up, those first few seconds of reintegration can amount to anything—good or bad."

"You have the *option* of internalising?" Clarise repeated with a frown, catching the slip Avis hadn't realised he'd made. "Avis, internalising is one of the most powerful tools a bender has. What possible reason would any bender have to not utilise it when the opportunity arises?"

Avis shrugged uncomfortably and looked over her head to the Akheron River. He knew why he hadn't been inside his own head since he'd been sentenced to the Damned, but he didn't want her to know.

It seemed Clarise knew anyway. Or, at the very least, held strong suspicions. Placing her hand on his cheek with her thumb pressed against his chin, she pulled his head down until their eyes met and asked, "How long has it been since you internalised, beloved? And do not lie to me."

It wasn't that Avis couldn't answer that. He just didn't want to. So instead, he twisted his head and pressed his lips into her palm. "Let it go, Clarise. I don't want to get into another fight with you."

Clarise's eyes narrowed into slits, letting him know in no uncertain terms that while she'd do as he asked for now, this conversation was far from over. She then turned to look over her shoulder in the direction of Cora's bedroom door.

"I didn't realise internalisation required reorientation, but since that is the case, perhaps it would be better if you were to rouse Cora from now on. It may be natural for Mystallians to speak without thought during that time, but my reaction to such conduct will never change. I refuse to be disrespected by my own children, regardless of circumstance."

She looked back at him. "There is no excuse for a Highborn Hellion to be physically out of control."

Well, at least she hadn't said she'd try to change it. "Alright," he agreed, dipping his head to kiss the top of hers. "If you see to Columbine, I'll go get Cora up."

Which was just as well, because Cora was in fine form.

CHAPTER FORTY-THREE

"GO AWAY!" Cora screamed, rolling away from him. She snatched up the nearest pillow and tossed it at him, smashing another over her head to block him out. Avis batted the incoming pillow aside and laughed at her, for her behaviour totally reminded him of Tal.

The enormous god of Destruction was a complete pain in the ass to deal with first thing in the morning as well, though if comparing the two, Tal's improvised weapons were usually far more dangerous than a mere pillow. Bedside tables and snapped off bedposts had been known to fly in those cases.

And like her esteemed uncle, Cora played out the entire scene without ever opening her eyes.

Avis flipped back the bottom corner of the sheet to expose her right foot. "Up and at 'em, tiger," he chuckled, capturing her foot by the ankle and tugging it gently towards him. Her other leg was still thoroughly entangled in the sheets and he didn't want to accidentally break her leg by using his full strength to haul her out. "We need to get moving, and by 'we' right now, I mean *you*."

"Why?" she whined from under a pillow. After squirming in his grip for a few seconds and getting nowhere, her other leg thrashed amidst the sheet until she had it free enough to kick wildly at his restraining hand. "Let me go!"

That was what Avis was waiting for and with a laugh at how easily he'd goaded her into it, he snatched her second foot out of the air and anchored it to the first. "Up you get, tiger," he insisted, hauling her out from under the covers. He then tossed her legs over the edge of the mattress and used the collision of her heels and the floor to jar her awake.

Her body cantilevered and her torso shot off the mattress, forcing her to balance on her outstretched arms or faceplant back into the bed. "I hate you!" she shouted, clenching her fists into the sheets, no doubt wishing she held his neck instead. Her hair looked like she'd been through a hurricane and her unfocused eyes were bloodshot and half-closed from lack of sleep.

Avis kept his hair short and manageable, but other than that, he'd seen her wrecked look many times in the mirror; though in his case several bottles of ambrosia had been consumed the night before. If this inglorious vision of Cora was anything to go by, she was going to be a mean drunk when she got older.

As he watched, she quickly dragged her knees under herself with every intention of diving back under the covers. *Yeah, right.* As if he was going to allow that. Twisting his lips to ward off his mischievous grin, Avis whacked her lightly on the raised backside.

"Come on, tiger. You were the one who didn't want to go to bed last night, now suck it up and get over here. I told you we've got a long way to go today, and I'm not slowing down just because you picked a crap time to assert your independence."

Although the light slap hadn't hurt her at all, Cora proved once again just how Mystallian she was by coming awake the instant he proposed any kind of weakness on her part. Her body bristled in outrage and she emitted a savage snarl, much deeper and more dangerous than her earlier mindless bitching.

Instinctively, she sought distance and launched herself away from both him and the bed. She was halfway across the room when she whirled mid-step to face him. Another good instinct: never turn your back on a potential enemy.

Perhaps her innate ability leaned towards some sort of combat. The Mystallians already had war and assassination covered, but there would always be room for one more combatant in their pantheon.

The possibility of Cora moving away from them to be established elsewhere was something he refused to entertain.

He watched her back herself into the corner and applauded her for subconsciously defending her unguarded flank. The strategy would've been a solid one had she been armed, but now she was merely cornered. Her eyes shone with every curse she longed to hurl at him, indicating that fact hadn't become apparent to her.

With his arms out to the sides and his fingers flared wide to show he had no obvious weapons, (except himself) Avis advanced on her. He deliberately kept his movements slow, and once he towered over her, he planted one hand into the wall above her head and bent at the waist to whisper directly into her ear, "I believe the phrase that bitchy little face of yours is looking for is, 'Fuck you, Father'."

Shock blanched her face, replacing the anger so quickly he couldn't help but laugh at the drastic shift in her features. Just to make sure she was still alive in there, he flicked her between the eyes with a curled middle finger. "But not in front of your mother or sister, and not if either one of us is being serious," he added, wanting the ground rules for swearing to be understood from the outset.

He straightened to tower over her again, but when he went to flick her a second time, she curled her lip and ducked out of the way, rubbing the spot where he'd already nailed her. "Otherwise, I'll lay your ass out faster than your mother ever could. You hear me?"

"Fuck you, Father," she hissed in an excited whisper. Her eyes shone with daring as she shot a cautious look towards the open doorway as if half expecting her mother to appear.

Avis chuckled and mussed her hair playfully. It wasn't as if he could mess it up any worse. "That's my girl," he purred, then hooked his hand behind her head and gave her a light shove towards the door. "Now, get going."

It didn't surprise Avis that Clarise was waiting for them alongside the demon steeds with a glass of light brown liquid in her hands. Where she stood was far enough away to permit them privacy, but close enough to be on hand the moment they emerged. Avis eyed the chilled glass of muddy liquid with a layer of condensation clinging to its outer surface and curled his lip distastefully. Nothing that horrible could possibly taste any good.

It was held out to them as they approached.

"Drink this, Cora," his wife commanded, leaving no room for negotiation. Instantly, Cora reverted to her Highborn Hellion upbringing and accepted the drink from her mother, knocking it back in its entirety on a single breath without a word or gesture of complaint.

Avis could only imagine the level of belly-aching that would've accompanied such a demand back home, had it been one of his many nieces and nephews in their parents' sights.

Questions such as "Do I have to?" "Why?" "What is it?" "What does it do?" and thousands of other complaints and arguments along those lines gave him a new appreciation for the absolute control the Highborn Hellions had over their offspring.

The second it was swallowed, Cora's body convulsed, and her eyes widened in horror. She dropped the glass and wrapped her arms around her waist as if to stave off the inevitable, then whirled on her heel and rushed past her bedroom to the bathroom at the rear of the raft.

Avis followed her with his eyes, then shot his wife a condescending look. "Subtle," he drawled sarcastically.

Clarise seemed unperturbed. "You wanted expediency, not subtlety," she reminded him.

* * *

For the next hour, Avis paced the full width of the bow, uttering useless words of comfort to the demon-shaped child crying silently in his arms. Every tear shredded his heart, but nothing he could do would protect her from the Damned as her mother reverted them back to their original forms and tossed them into the river like discarded rubbish.

His first thought had been to send Columbine through into the Chaotic Ocean with her brute squad guard and wait for them there, but that wouldn't work. Not when her range had nothing to do with line of sight and everything to do with proximity.

Since he didn't know how far that was, he didn't want her feeling both the pain of the Damned as well as a sense of abandonment by her family.

So, he was doing the only thing he could: nursing her as far away from the torturous screams while forcing her thoughts to remain with him and only him. It wasn't working. Not really. But, she was trying to be strong … or at least, not draw attention to her plight. Her wings and clawed hands clung to him, and misery rolled off her tiny body in waves, but for the most part, she was suffering in silence.

This was not the Mystallian way, and once again he found himself wishing she was just a little bit more like his nieces and nephews back home.

By now, they'd have been bellowing at the top of their lungs at the unfairness of it, and then he'd have reciprocated their rage because there was nothing he could do about it, and the ensuing shouting match would've distracted everyone from the pain that was going on around them. This silent endurance was the stuff of nightmares.

"Soon," he promised with every iota of his being as he cuddled her close, making it the thousandth time he'd done so since Clarise started. "We'll be out of here real soon, princess. And then, if it's the last thing I do, I'll make sure you never *ever* have to go anywhere near the Damned again." He meant every word, willing to take Mystal to war before ever enduring this again. He'd never felt so helpless in his life, and by the Twin Notes, he hated it!

Once the extension was gone, Clarise came and stood in the middle of Avis' pacing path at the front of the raft and drew a tendril of untainted mass from the Chaotic Ocean towards them.

Avis paused with Columbine still in his arms and watched the tendril's approach suspiciously. "What are you doing?" he asked, partially relieved that whatever it was, it didn't involve the Damned anymore.

Columbine continued to weep silently for them, but with the Damned now back in the river where they belonged, her mother was no longer responsible for their demise. It wasn't much of a distinction, but he'd take it anyway.

"If we are to ride for many hours, we will require nourishment," she replied, guiding the mass tendril to the middle of the raft, where it morphed into a fully prepared breakfast for them to enjoy.

Avis stared at the meal in disbelief. After the hour-long heartache he'd just endued with Columbine, he felt wrung out and hung off the nearest cliff to dry in the battering winds. The ache was horrible, and being so emotionally wrecked, the last thing he wanted to muster a shit about was having something to eat.

Besides, he had the girls' routine down pat and knew they'd all be stopping in just a few hours for another meal break anyway. As an ancient, he could go for days without a meal before feeling the pinch, so there was plenty of time for him to catch up when he was more inclined.

Somehow, Clarise must have read his internal monologue, for she moved in behind him and placed her hand on the small of his back. "Remember what I said last night about being a good example for them, beloved," she murmured quietly between his shoulder blades.

Avis huffed and rolled his eyes skyward in annoyance. Parenting sucked sometimes. "Fine," he grumbled on the tail end of that growl. Before he could talk himself out of it, he carried Columbine to her side of the prepared meal and went down on one knee.

"Drink what you can, princess," he said as he gently freed himself from her death-like grip and lowered her to the mat. "We'll go just as soon as we're done. Okay?"

Without him to hold, Columbine cupped her hands on her lap and sniffed, then bobbed her head obediently. "Y-yes, Father."

Poor kid. Avis brushed his hand over her scalp, silently vowing that this would be the fastest breakfast they'd ever have (and he'd had a lot of experience eating on the run ... up until two years ago).

Keeping his promise firmly in mind, he stepped away from her and walked around the rug to take his place opposite her, just as Cora and Clarise came to join them. He looked over the mountain of food and his stomach knotted.

Determined to beat this, Avis reached for the nearest thing and stuffed it in his mouth. He barely tasted the buttered toast with honey and the moment it was broken down enough that he could swallow he did so and reached for another. He had a new mantra: *Eat and fly free.*

It surprised him that Cora's attitude towards the meal was as feverish as his own until he realised why. While he (in case it hadn't been made abundantly clear before now) wanted to get them all out of Hell, Cora was starving, and Mystallian refinement went out the nearest window when that happened.

It was one of the main reasons why he insisted on the family getting together for regular meals—to solidify their unity and make sure everyone had at least one solid feed a day. Way back when Mystal was first being established, he'd only specified the evening meal for this purpose, but as children came to his siblings, the elder court stretched those gatherings to include both breakfast and lunch as well.

Absences were acceptable, but only if someone in the family knew where the missing member was.

The milestone of leaving behind the Akheron River was more significant to Avis than just another step towards Mystal. Right here, at this colourful juncture where the Akheron River met the Chaotic Ocean, lay the unofficial border of Hell: the capital of Chaos.

Unable to resist, he shot a quick glance over his shoulder at the colourful ocean wall behind him. It was right there! Everything he'd endured at the hands of the hellions and Highborn Hellions would be relegated to distant memory the second they crossed that threshold, and it was literally right there! It was enough to drive any man fucking mad!

He turned back to the meal before he accidentally verbalised his offensive thoughts and, in the process, saw his beloved wife eating delicately with her usual air of sophistication. That hardly surprised him. His queen didn't need to make the most of the food the way he and the girls did.

As a shapeshifter with unfettered access to her natural ability, she could draw matter to her any time she wanted to create a snack along the way. Or, relatively speaking, she could do some sneaky osmosis plant-thing and just absorb the particulates they rode through, converting them into nutrition once they were inside her. The physical realm was their bitch like that.

As they ate in silence, Columbine drank three full glasses of the bright, flame-blue liquid one after the other, her forked tongue licking every droplet of moisture from the inside of the glass. He knew four was her absolute maximum after she'd starved herself for days, and between that and the way Cora had gorged herself, he decided breakfast was done.

With his objective ever closer, he bounded to his feet and abruptly clapped his hands to galvanise everyone into action. It was time to go.

He raised his hand and pressed his thumb and middle finger to his lips, whistling the note that would bring the demon steeds' wings to bear. The hellion riding beasts seemed just as excited to be underway, for not only did their massive wings of fire unfurl at the shoulder, but they tossed their heads back and snorted thick streams of hellfire that doubled the length of their manes.

They stamped their hooves and nickered eagerly. "Let's go, ladies," he said, already crossing the deck to unhitch the reins of the nearest one. He flicked the reins over its head, using the move to pat its withers affectionately. "You and me both, Hotspot. The sooner we're gone, the happier I'll be."

"A point you have reiterated many times, beloved," Clarise said, somewhat reproachfully from behind.

Avis was about to hoist himself on to the demon steed's back when he looked over his raised upper arm towards her, then further back to where the children stood. If they were expecting him to appear admonished for being the way he was, they had a lot to learn about being Mystallian.

Grinning openly with pride, he launched upwards and landed firmly on the beast's back, his hands tightening around the reins to keep it from prancing far. "No one's ever going to accuse me of not calling it as I see it, sweetheart."

Instead of agreeing, Clarise let her gaze grow hooded and further back, he saw Cora smirk and roll her eyes. Neither reaction pleased him. "What are you three waiting for?" He flicked his hand at the three remaining demon steeds on his left. "Let's go."

Clarise sighed and turned towards the children. "Take your places, girls," she said, duplicating Avis' impatient hand gesture with a majestic one of her own.

Columbine launched herself into the air and shot across the deck ahead of her sister to claim ownership of the only demon steed that stood alongside her father's. She landed on its back with her feet tucked under her and her wings outstretched like a defending gargoyle.

Before he could correct her dressage, she looked him over and mirrored his, positioning herself in the middle of its back with her back straight and her knees and toes locked around its ribs. It was on the tip of Avis' tongue to mention how she should've collected the reins first when she emitted a whistling note that had her demon steed throwing its head high and tossing the reins even higher.

Both reins fell across Columbine's open taloned hand in much the same way Uriel had been able to gather all the reins at once back in the Well. Avis had forgotten they possessed that ability and locked that note into memory as well for future reference.

He watched with growing concern as Columbine proceeded to wrap the reins tightly around her hands several times as if to anchor herself to the beast. "Princess, have you ever ridden a demon steed before?" he asked in the most non-judgemental voice he could muster. Inwardly he already knew that answer.

No rider with any degree of experience would tie themselves to their mount: not by the hands, anyway. Her slight headshake confirmed his suspicions, so he raised his own hand and tilted the palm towards her, showing her how he had the reins laid flat over three of his four fingers but folded back between the little and ring finger to keep the little finger free.

He then tightened his grip and rolled his hand over to rest it on the demon steed's back just in front of himself.

"If you're worried about dropping the reins, princess, you can always tie the two ends together. But it's very dangerous to tie yourself in like that. If something frightens the demon steed and you get thrown, it's better to be thrown clear than dragged a few hundred galaxies."

He reached over and ran his free hand down the bony ridge of her wing. "Especially when you have a built-in safety net like this to catch you."

By the time Columbine followed his instructions, Clarise and Cora had also taken possession of a demon steed, each with the reins layered over a gloved palm.

The two servants that acted as anchors released the moorings and all four hellion servants shifted into small, petite creatures with a solid mass of overlaying back muscles that supported a pair of enormous leathery wings.

At five to ten times the size of their bodies, the wing to body ratio was done in clear anticipation of keeping up with the faster demon steeds. Avis didn't even bother with the brute squad. Their speed was just bullshit.

Once everyone was ready, the whole party took to the sky.

Without the brute squad to keep the Damned at bay, the raft below swarmed with souls seeking to escape the painful river. It was almost comical how they climbed over the top of each other, and for a moment Avis imagined a variety of outcomes for the scene. Technically, the Damned couldn't leave Hell without being dragged across the threshold by the demons.

But no one had ever built them a raft to escape on before, and that might just be the loophole they needed to escape. His lips twitched at the image of a raft full of the Damned drifting aimlessly through the Known Realms with some makeshift fishing poles or the likes, until two separate thoughts occurred to him.

One, what his pantheon would do if they were stupid enough to hit Mystal's borders, and two, the more realistic outcome of them entering the vast ocean of Chaos itself, which happened to be the only way out. Demons fought for the right to own the Damned. Even if the souls managed to get off the Akheron River, they were, in every sense of the word, a treasure-laden raft floating past some of the greediest beings in existence.

They were never getting out of Chaos. It really did suck to be one of the Damned.

"I will miss the raft," he heard Columbine murmur with a genuine hint of sadness as they waited for Clarise to return the raft to the river. Stunned, Avis could only stare at his daughter until the demoness could no longer bear his silent disbelief. "Father?" she asked, her bone of her brow rising apprehensively.

Avis opened his mouth to speak but then decided against it. He *never* wanted to see that raft again. Ever, ever, *never* ever. Even if they were somehow able to bring it with them, he'd only do it so he could take his time over the next few million centuries carving it into fucking toothpicks. And not regular sized toothpicks either! Toothpicks for Voltumna's itty-bitty mini-shrews! The ones who had sharp little teeth the width of a fingernail edge! Firewood was too good for it!

"Nothing, princess," he said, shaking his head incredulously. If she was going to fall in love with every new thing they came across, this trip was going to go from long and arduous to downright excruciating.

"Ready whenever you are, beloved," Clarise said, straightening in her saddle. Avis checked the water below to confirm that the raft was indeed no more, then lifted his gaze to his wife and their two children. They were just waiting for him to give the signal.

Behind them, the four servants created a half circle, and beyond them, the brute squad hovered in a rough square, creating a protective line of sight perimeter around their group.

"Then let's get out of here," he said, smiling so broadly his cheeks hurt as he flicked his heels into the demon steed's ribs to get it moving. By habit, he let out the short, shrill whistle he used to motivate White Haven, his own mystallion back home, though he knew it was more his body language that made the fiery beast surge forward.

So long as they left the Akheron River behind, he didn't care.

CHAPTER FORTY-FOUR

They rode hard for hours. Every time Avis felt the pace slacken, he urged them back up to full speed. If he'd thought every minute dragged on to eternity on the raft, he had absolutely no sense of time now. Adrenaline rushed through his veins, driving him on. Eventually, he heard Clarise call to him, suggesting over the glorious rush of wind that they stop for the night.

Why she'd ever want to do that was beyond him. Especially when, for the first time in weeks, boredom didn't gnaw at every fibre of his being, and he felt free enough to ride forever. The prospect of stopping, even for a short time, threatened that new-found sense of freedom and he really didn't want to.

But Clarise would *not* be ignored.

"AVIS! STOP!"

Although her voice didn't rise above her usual level of control, every syllable was amplified unnaturally to echo all around them like a triple clap of thunder. Avis immediately complied, straightening where he sat and hauling hard on the reins. He also held his hand up level with his shoulder to bring everyone else behind him to a halt as well.

After they all stopped and were hovering in mid-air, he turned his attention to Clarise who was half a length behind him on his right. The way her lips were pursed into bloodless lines, he knew she wasn't happy. "The girls need rest," she stated, the gold in her eyes clashing against itself like the crags of a cliff face as she gestured to their children behind him.

"We have been pushing the demon steeds into a flat gallop for too long and controlling them under these conditions is very taxing on their young bodies. They are going to fall and hurt themselves if you do not permit them to have a meal and a night's respite."

Avis' eyes widened, his jaw fell slack. *Night?* As in they'd ridden straight through 'lunch', and no one thought to yell at him before now? His eyes shot to the girls. Both were hunched over their mounts, and while Cora's eyes were half closed, the fire in Columbine's eye recesses had dimmed to barely embers. Both rocked where they sat as exhaustion threatened to overtake them.

With only a Mystallian (and dammit, he hated putting those three words together as if being a Mystallian was less in any way!) constitution, Cora tipped forward past her teetering point and woke herself up with a start, only to start rocking again a heartbeat later. Columbine was just as spent. Her wings drooped lifelessly on either side the demon steed, and her beak rested permanently on her chest plates.

The poor thing didn't even have the energy to lift her head, and if it weren't for the ember-like glow in her eye recesses, he'd suspect she was already asleep. It was a long way from the buoyant hellfire that should have been there.

Neither girl would vocalise a problem: Columbine because she was too Highborn Hellion to bother him with her difficulties and Cora on the principle that she wasn't going to let him beat her. He had to remember that neither of these kids knew how to be a Mystallian yet because they were too entrenched in the Highborn Hellion way of suffering in silence.

Which sucked, because that meant he'd have to check on them periodically instead of waiting for them to air their complaints.

One of the favourite (though annoying) chants that the younger generations of Mystal often took up on long journeys was, "Are we there yet?" which was usually followed by incessant complaints of hunger and thirst.

He would get neither from these two—even if it killed them—and he should have known that.

Fuck!

For the last month and a half, he knew the girls' routine to the point where it would be forever ingrained in his memory. He, a god who could ride for weeks without stopping, was going to have to limit himself to two short bouts of roughly six hours riding, separated by a meal at one juncture and at least ten hours of rest at the other.

The thought of being reduced to such a crawl frustrated the shit out of him, but this was one of those times when it couldn't be helped. As the weakest members of the family, the girls had to dictate the pace. "We'll stop for the night," he announced and didn't miss the relief that poured from his family.

Clarise solidified a huge space, hundreds of square metres for them to land on, shifting its colour and texture to mimic a beautifully manicured Mystallian lawn.

The sight of it after so many years sent a shaft of homesickness through Avis that he hadn't been expecting. It didn't matter that it was only a construct and not the real thing. Every blade of 'grass' waved in conjunction with its neighbour so perfectly, he doubted if even White Haven would notice the difference.

Knowing what he knew about shifters, they couldn't have been individual grass plants. Not at the rate Clarise had knocked out that whole lawn. It had to be a single carpet, where each blade of grass was attached to the next via a single root system.

Avis licked his upper lip and swallowed back a sigh. Its exact composition didn't matter. The overall appearance had him pining so badly for home that he could've wept.

To add insult to injury, Clarise created a large, single storey marble wall nearly thirty metres long towards the back of the grassland. The gold striations against the pristine white stone were a perfect replication of his palace walls back home.

Avis sank his teeth into his bottom lip, determined to bite down on the whimper that crept to the back of his throat. She was killing him in small doses here, and she didn't even know it.

He closed his eyes to block out the image, and with a deeper, heavier sigh, he rolled his head forward until his chin sat on his chest. He deserved this. If he hadn't been such a dick, Clarise would've learned Mystal had thousands of building styles to choose from, not just one. As usual, this mess was entirely on him.

Refusing to hide from his role in this mess or the ramifications of it, Avis snapped his head up and opened his eyes. He glared long and hard at the partially constructed building, practically daring it to upset him again.

The battle of wills with only one combatant lasted a few seconds, but once he was sure he had absolute control of himself, he raised one hand to his shoulder and gestured with two fingers for them all to land.

Somewhere in the back of his mind, logic insisted this was a bad idea; that the grass would catch alight the moment it encountered the hellfire imbued hooves of the demon steeds. While this might have been true under normal circumstances, this was Clarise's creation, and hellfire was her people's specialty. He trusted her to know what she was doing.

It wasn't misplaced. As the combined weight of both equine and rider crushed the grass on impact, the only scent that filled his nose soon after was that of a well-maintained lawn. By the realms, he loved the smell of fresh greenery! It was glorious.

He turned to compliment his wife and gasped in horror. Her eyes were no longer Mystallian! Everything else about her was as he expected, but where her eyes should have been, a pair of over-sized, bulbous half-spheres with thousands upon thousands of tiny grain-sized, brownish-black dots covering the surface were there instead.

She had no eyelids, and as such, she didn't blink once, but the angle of her face implied her focus was solely on the structure—not that Avis cared! This wasn't okay! Yes, he knew she was a shifter, and yes, she probably had a very good reason for the change, but dammit, he needed to be warned before she pulled this kind of stunt!

Hating the minor tweak to her Mystallian shape, Avis gritted his teeth and looked away from her, turning his attention to the structure she was creating. His reaction had nothing to do with prejudice.

He could handle her in any shape of her choosing. He knew he could. The disgust he once held for all things non-Mystallian was a thing of the past. But this … this … muddying of the waters—it weirded him out.

Determined not to dwell on the image that he knew would ghost his mind for some time, he watched the specifics of her evolving structure as they came into being. They weren't coming together one thing at a time like he was expecting. No, everything was exploding to life simultaneously!

Floors rolled out, and dividing walls went up, but at the same time, furnishings bloomed from connective points in each room. Paintings that started as hooks on a wall opened like flowers until the framed images filled the space. Sconces were likewise formed. Crystals sprouted from various points in the ceilings and blossomed into multifaceted chandeliers—each with hundreds of candles which spontaneously lit themselves.

Timber and soft fabrics burst from the marble floor to create ornate furniture. The speed and grandeur of it all defied logic. This should've taken hours! Like him, a shifter could only change one thing at a time, and even if he did buy into the whole *this-is-just-one-thing-because-it's-all-touching-each-other,* how did she see it all at once to maintain so much control over the creation?

If he were the one doing this, he'd only be able to focus on one aspect of it. A specific wall. A bed. A rug. A couch. A fireplace. Clarise was doing it all simultaneously. She was literally *growing* the house towards them. Somehow, those hideously freaky eyes of hers were allowing her to see everything at once, keeping the fabrication level … and perfect.

His lips parted into a huge grin as he looked from her to the house and back again. He could still remember how hard it had been for him and his siblings when they'd first escaped the Nexus and had no power bases to support their status. Back then, without a shifter of any kind amongst them, they'd been forced to take refuge in caves and gather sticks for the fire.

Rough was an understatement and a far cry from the multi-room abode that was quickly forming before his eyes. With that thought, it occurred to him just how insulting he'd been when he'd suggested living off the land would be too difficult for his delicate family.

There was nothing delicate about the capabilities of a ranged shifter in her natural element.

Without a word, he slid from his demon steed and walked over to her. He didn't know a lot about compound eyes, but he could've sworn he saw several of those dark dots twist in his direction. He reached up to stroke her knee. "It doesn't have to be perfect, sweetheart," he said, lightly caressing the soft fabric to gain her attention.

"Trust me," he added, looking back to where the building stood, half-finished. "This is already so much more than we had when my siblings and I first left the Nexus."

"Perhaps, my love, but this is my area of expertise," she replied primly, letting him know this was a point of pride for her. "...and after riding for as long as we did, a few minutes to adequately prepare an abode for us does not seem like too much to ask."

Avis would rather stick his arm in a meat grinder than deny her anything, but when the tone of her words registered with him, he couldn't help but blink. *Was that ... snark?*

Realising it was, he grinned so broadly his cheeks hurt. *That's my queen!* "By all means take as long as you want, sweetheart," he said, dropping his hand to pat the top of her boot.

Rather than disturb her further, he went back to Columbine's demon steed and gently pulled on her leg until she slid off its back and landed heavily in his arms. "Just a few more minutes, princess," he promised as she automatically snuggled into his chest, wrapping one wing around his arm and back for support. She yawned and sank deeper into his embrace.

It would never occur to him to go to Cora like this. As far as he was concerned, that girl had made it this far on her own, and he wouldn't belittle that achievement by coddling her before she wanted it.

By the time he dragged his attention away from Columbine and back to the building behind him, Clarise had already completed the front exterior wall and was putting the finishing touches on the stoop.

Two large columns flanked a single step that led up to a pair of massive double doors. Striations of gold laced the white block walls and columns, and the roof was shingled in gold. The style mirrored his home in Pandess.

Recognition of the building's opulent style hit Avis hard, and he sucked the inside of his cheek between his teeth, biting down until he tasted blood.

She's not doing this to screw with me on purpose, he reminded himself forcefully. *And if this is as close as I ever get to the real thing, I've got no one to blame but myself, so suck it the fuck up.*

The second he told himself off, a sense of inner calm swept over him, and he breathed out the last of his discomfort. Worrying about whether he'd be allowed home or not at this juncture was pointless. Maybe his concerns were justified, and maybe they weren't. Everything hinged on the responses of his missing siblings, and until they reached Olympus and he could contact them safely, he'd never know for sure.

He glanced down at Columbine in his arms and found her staring up at him, her eye ridges creasing marginally. "I'm fine, princess," he promised, lifting her just enough to kiss her head between her horn bumps.

"Okay," she murmured sleepily, burying the top of her beak into his doublet.

Adorable kid. Avis rubbed his chin across her head, lifting his gaze to see what Clarise was working on now. With the main house completed, a secondary structure began to take shape a short distance away.

Unlike the way she made the main house blossom to life, this one bubbled and oozed out of the ground like lava, ever piling on top of itself until a much smaller building appeared. Within a few short minutes, the external case of the molten rock had straightened into walls roughly four meters high with a shingled roof.

Everything then changed colour. The side walls bleached themselves until they mimicked the main house, and the shingle on top shone like polished gold. But that was as far as the similarities went. Through the large opening at the front, Avis watched as hellfire burst through the molten core, dividing the room into four stalls of crackling flames.

A separate stable for the demon steeds, with all the comforts of home. Avis should've guessed. His beloved wife missed nothing.

Accepting they were done for the foreseeable future, Avis lifted his free hand away from Columbine's back and put his fingers to his lips, emitting the sharp note that had all the wings of their demon steeds dissipating.

He still wasn't tired in the least, but he understood the need for the children to rest. He made his way through the tight group of riders until he was alongside Clarise again, and said up to her, "Just as soon as you're finished, the girls can have something to eat and go to bed."

"And bathe," Clarise added, her eyes returning to normal.

Avis's smile came more naturally this time as he envisioned that long overdue event for himself. "And bathe," he agreed, wholeheartedly. Then, he turned towards Cora. "You both did extremely well today," he said, expanding his congratulations to include the girl in his arms.

The thick, timbre of his voice revealed just how much he meant it. "Despite our late start, you both kept up with me every step of the way, and I rode straight through lunch. I couldn't be prouder of you."

Columbine stirred against his chest, rubbing her beak across his shoulder in a blend of weary happiness, but Cora's reaction left him stunned.

Her eyes went from nine-tenths shut to wide-eyed, her emerald green irises gobbling up her pupils until the latter was barely a pinprick in the middle of her eyes. Avis had no clue why she had such a stunned look on her face until he realised it was probably the first time anyone had ever told her they were proud of her.

Wow. That's just … wow.

He wasn't one to hand out compliments unnecessarily, but he made a mental note to offer them as frequently as her actions allowed. She was up to her eyeteeth in courage, but her confidence had taken a ferocious beating. *Damn those Highborn halfwits for not recognising her Mystallian roots sooner! Square pegs don't belong in round holes, and only an asshole would drive that peg home anyway!*

A sobering thought then occurred to him; one that hadn't bothered him before now. If he was this mad over the Highborn Hellions for their treatment of Cora, his younger brother Chance was going to completely lose his shit when he found out. And he would find out.

Luck was a pain like that, and as Cora's anointed father, the runt was almost as much her father as he was. The thought of Cora being punished needlessly just for behaving like a Mystallian would have Chance erupting like a volcano.

The runt was psychotically protective of his brood. He was the most easy-going goofball most of the time, but no one messed with his brood unless they wanted the kind of bad luck that had them 'accidentally' strolling off the nearest cliff edge and into the mouth of a seismic eruption.

The runt would be after blood, and once the rest of the pantheon found out why, they wouldn't be far behind him.

Avis wasn't exactly happy about it either, but unlike his family, he'd experienced firsthand what the Highborn Hellions were capable of. More specifically, Belial. If Belial hadn't been the head of this household, a war between the Highborn Hellions and the Mystallians would be a much closer match. But he was, and the only way the Mystallians could ever balance those scales would be to reach out to …

Avis' eyes widened and he slammed that thought process down just as fast as he could.

Fuck that shit! No fucking way…!

He heard the abrasive hiss of air and recognised the sound of Columbine's chest plates acting as bellows again. *Dammit!*

CHAPTER FORTY-FIVE

Knowing he had no chance of getting himself under control in time, Avis automatically swung into damage control. He didn't care if she knew he was in there. Everyone's most recent memories were always at the surface of their mind, so he didn't have to go far to find what he was looking for.

Ordinarily, memories were shielded from one another—like a series of rooms located along an infinite hallway. But Columbine's open prism-like mind meant he saw not only the memory he was after but all the ones around it as well.

It soon became apparent she hadn't taken her attention off him once in hours. Thousands of his images overlaid each other, (most were just an outline, indicating she'd used her powers to monitor him, rather than physically watch him) each showing an underlying colour which he knew represented his mood.

Even nine-tenths asleep, she'd been following his emotional state, worrying for him. *She ... had been ... worried ... about me.* Avis growled and shook his mental head. *No.* This was not the way it was going to go. She was too young to be taking on that kind of responsibility, and he'd never be okay with her worrying about him. Not like this.

The fix was easy enough though. If she couldn't remember it, she wouldn't remember to react to it either, right? So, he took the colour he'd felt at the time that he said he was proud of them and dragged it across every image until just now when the mental terror he'd felt at the thought of contacting her paternal grandfather reached its climax.

It took a few seconds to reorientate the colour palate of her memories, but by the time he was done, he knew she'd believe that he hadn't moved from the lush green of pride.

This was new for him—changing the colour of someone in a memory and nothing else—but necessary nonetheless. Colours were just as important to Columbine as the images themselves. One day, when he had plenty of time, he was going to sit down with the little imp and memorise exactly what every colour meant. Until then, he'd wing it.

Just as he was about to leave, he caught sight of a solid black cord, roughly the thickness of his thumb, weave its way through the memories towards them. *What in the realms ...?*

He twisted to face this new threat, preparing himself for an assault. This—whatever it was—wasn't normal. It wasn't even natural. He'd seen every natural life form over the years, and the cord that slithered through his daughter's memories with the determination of a snake on the hunt didn't even go close.

Avis swept his power over the cord for a mind he could attack, and came up empty. *Empty? How?*

At the last second, it swung away from Avis and latched onto the first memory he'd altered a short distance away, confusing him further. *What are you?* Avis quickly ran his eyes along its length until it disappeared deep into her memories. He'd never seen anything like ...

Suddenly, he stopped dead in his tracks.

He remembered exactly where he'd seen that endless inky-blackness before: in the ether of Columbine's core essence where the black and gold star-field of emotions existed.

As if to reaffirm this origin, a golden thread fed itself through the centre of the ebony cord until it connected with the memory and charged the image with a light pulsing glow. Each pulse caused the image of Avis to shift away from the colour of grass and more towards the yellowy-brown tone it had been originally. One after the other, images reverted.

How? How was she doing this? He was the master mind bender! She shouldn't have been able to change back her memories once he modified them first ... unless her empathic ability knew the moods of those memories were wrong, and it was asserting itself to correct that emotional alteration.

Sunova bitch! If Avis left the memories as they stood, she'd go back to thinking he was terrified of being proud of her.

He could see it wasn't changing the memories themselves. It was only focused on the colours. Right. Okay. If he couldn't permanently change the palette, he'd have to make the shapes suit the colours instead. He needed something that scared the shit out of him. Something that didn't mention his father.

That bastard's poison was never touching his family as long as he lived. But what else was there? Who else both sickened him and terrorised him enough to cause her concern?

Avis suddenly rolled his eyes.

Of course. Her *other* grandfather. Belial.

Columbine would never question his trepidation around the Chaotian ruler.

Before the cord changed the memory's colours completely, Avis modified the *shape* of the memory to include him muttering Belial's name under his breath at the point when he was most ... bothered.

It was an easy fix, and by the time he was done, the empathic cord had reverted the falsified memory to its original yellow-brown tones. The image was a lie, but the emotions around it were true. The cord then disconnected from the memory and slowly retracted through her other memories until it disappeared into the darkness below. Avis stared at the last spot he saw it for several long seconds and shook his head unhappily.

That fucking thing was going to be a bitch to work around. No question.

But at least, for now, he was good.

Convinced the calamity had been headed off, Avis withdrew from her mind and smiled down at her. "I'm fine, princess," he repeated, making sure nothing about his mood said otherwise.

To change the subject, he looked across at Cora and made a show of stepping aside, at the same time rolling his hand palm and a grand gesture towards the house. "Well, what are you waiting for, Cora? Go. Explore. Pick a set of rooms for yourself ..."

"From the two on the left," Clarise added, as Cora threw her leg over the demon steed's neck and dropped to the ground. She landed with a thump and raced across the lawn; her weariness now a thing of the past. One of the four servants shifted into her centipede governess and followed her at a more moderate pace.

Avis paid the servant no mind. He was too busy enjoying Cora's haste as she leapt over the stoop; barely remembering to throw open the double doors before she barrelled through them and disappeared inside. *Oh, yeah,* he drawled, chuckling quietly to himself.

By the time he was done with that kid, she'd be mowing people down to get to what she wanted and where she wanted to be, and no amount of decorum would slow her down. Nobody stood between a Mystallian and their objective. Nobody who wanted to live, anyway. Sometimes, they even climbed over each other if the prize warranted it. The winner was the one who could keep it.

Avis' grin grew because he won *a lot.*

"Diviten," he called, having no idea which of the three remaining winged hellions was Columbine's personal servant. Of course, the one closest to him shifted into the governess with many of her upper legs extended to relieve him of his precious child. Avis said nothing more as he passed the child over to her governess, then gestured with a small flick of his head for Diviten to take her inside.

As he watched them go, lavender filled his senses moments before long fingers slid through his crooked elbow. Clarise had joined him on the ground. Frash and Tilu were already walking the demon steeds towards the stables, and three of the four brute squad guards were hovering over the single-storey building, allowing them to peruse the grounds from corner to corner.

Avis hadn't noticed the fourth guard follow Diviten and Columbine inside, but its absence led him to believe that this was the case. He shook his head and snorted, knowing he'd never get over how quickly they could move.

"Shall we go in, beloved?" she asked, resting her head against his bicep.

Avis slid his arm free and wrapped it around her waist, pulling her under his cloak and into his side. "Of course, m'lady," he said, stooping to give her a quick kiss before guiding her into the building.

The layout inside was not what he expected, but given that the servants were all Hellion shifters, they had no need for storage or kitchens for food preparation. As such, the first room he walked into was a dining hall the full width of the house, behind which were three sets of double doors.

Clarise walked them around the dining table, then kissed his cheek and pulled away, murmuring something about preparations ... or some such whatever and disappeared inside the doors on the far right of the dining hall.

Avis arched one eyebrow curiously as his eyes followed her egress but decided to check on the girls first before finding out just what she was up to. As it turned out, the middle set of doors were claimed by Columbine. That made sense, since Cora would've taken the first set she came too on the left-hand side.

He discovered Columbine curled up on the tiled hearth with her back and neck pushed into the roaring fire and her wings resting peacefully amidst the blazing logs. The protective screen had been cast aside and was in a piled heap nearby.

His first parental instinct was to haul her from the dangerous flames, but common sense then kicked in. As tired as she was, in her hellion form she'd have subconsciously sought out the most hellish aspect of the room to snuggle down in. Had the fireplace been any larger, she'd have probably crawled into it entirely.

A pang of regret hit him with all the subtlety of one of Griffith's punches as he was forced to accept just how close he'd gone to pushing them too far. Demon steeds were by no means mystallions, but they still moved with incredible speed, and the girls might've been seriously hurt, had they fallen mid-sprint and not been awake enough to protect themselves during the fall. He was really going to have to watch that.

The guard stood in the corner of the room; its double arms folded across its glowing body and its head constantly rotating in anticipation of … anything. He could hear Diviten in the bedroom, fussing over the realm knew what. Avis squatted beside Columbine and ran his hand across her leather-covered scalp again, silently promising her that he'd be more careful in future.

Then he knelt forward and kissed her head again, accepting the blast of discomfort that came from putting his face too close to the open fire as his due. "Sweet dreams, princess," he whispered, then ran his hand across her scalp one last time before rising to his feet and withdrawing from the room.

The first set of doors on the left led to Cora's apartment, which was an exact replica of her sister's rooms. Like Columbine, Cora had made it as far as the three-seater couch in front of the fire before exhaustion set in, and she'd collapsed across the three cushions. Her soft snoring filled the room, causing Avis to chuckle in amusement. Griffith and Tal snored when they were exhausted too; only when that pair did, foundations shook, and walls fell.

Gingen had placed a pillow under her head, and a light quilt was spread across her body. Her cloak had been removed and was folded over the arm of the couch near her feet, while her boots were on the floor next to it. Cora's bare feet peeked out from underneath the quilt, so Avis carefully tucked them back in again. She looked so peaceful in her sleep.

Long red eyelashes cast a row of flickering shadows across her cheekbones and her face no longer held any tension. She seemed … happy.

He traced his fingers along her jaw and felt his lips twitch when she instinctively sought out his touch, only to sigh once she felt the pressure of all four of his fingers. Had she been awake, she would have recoiled to the far end of the couch and spat her denial of the sentimental need all day long.

Making the most of the opportunity, Avis continued to stroke her face for another minute or two before deciding to leave her to her rest. "Good night, tiger." A quick glance was all he afforded Gingen near the bedroom before he left the room.

Clarise was waiting for him outside the third set of doors when he re-entered the dining room. Her seductive smile went all the way to her eyes, which sparkled in excitement and her hands were hidden behind her back, under her cloak.

Avis returned her smile; though his was a little warier.

"Close your eyes, beloved," she purred playfully.

Having no clue as to what she was up to, but hopeful of its outcome given the girls were asleep, Avis did as she asked. To his surprise, something soft fell across his eyes, and he opened them with a start; his vision now obscured by several layers of sheer green silk. "Clarise, what …?"

His hand went for the fabric, but she caught his wrist and held on to it. The same with his other hand. "Trust me," she whispered, as the fabric was knotted behind his head. Two sets of hands were needed for that, but his curiosity was far too profound for him to care as she tested the knot's resistance, then tugged him forward through the last set of double doors.

He could *almost* see things through the blindfold, but the more he tried to focus on any one object, the more it danced out of focus. It was maddening! The first room was a sitting room. He could hear the fire and see the shadows it cast across the silk blindfold. The second set of doors led into a bedroom.

Although the room was fractionally cooler than the sitting room, the huge four poster bed to one side was a dead giveaway.

Then, they went through another set of double doors. This room was smaller—perhaps a third of the size of the bedroom if the dark haze that may have been the walls were anything to go by. In the middle of the room, he could just make out the outline of a large object that sat about waist high, like a mini-wall that didn't quite touch the walls on either side.

That was when his other senses kicked in. He could hear the water bubbling before him and felt the rising steam prickle against his skin. The smell of forest pine that was his preferred personal fragrance blended with Clarise' lavender, and he could almost taste the hint of ambrosia in the air.

Neither willing nor able to wait a second longer, Avis heaved a hand free of Clarise and ripped the blindfold off, tossing it to one side. It was everything he wanted in one space. Even Clarise being naked in front of him, though at the moment she didn't look very happy.

"I did not say you could take that off," she scolded, and he immediately regretted his rash decision, until she pressed herself against his chest. "I was going to remove our clothes slowly. Provocatively. But since you went and spoiled that …"

Suddenly, Avis's own clothing fell to the ground in a splat of gelatinous inconsistency, and he caught his breath on the chill of their unexpected loss. "… I guess we shall be jumping to the main event after all."

CHAPTER FORTY-SIX

Avis wasn't complaining. Really, he wasn't. But long after he'd made love to his wife multiple times both in and out of the bath, he sat in the cooling water with his back against the wall and a glass of ambrosia in his hand, imagining what might have happened had he not jumped ahead and spoiled her game. Next time, he would follow her lead to the letter. No matter what. The possibilities of what he'd missed out on were driving him crazy.

Hearing Clarise return, he deposited the glass on the bath ledge and rolled around to face her. He folded his arms over the edge and rested his chin on his wrists, absorbing the glorious sight of her. She was dressed in a green silk negligee and robe that matched the jade of the blindfold, and he found it to be just as tantalising: not enough to see what one shouldn't, though the soft curves and dusky shadows in all the right places left little to the imagination.

She was carrying a tray of appetisers, and he suddenly realised how hungry he was. "I regret messing up your game," he said, reaching for some type of meat pastry thing closest to him. "But what in the realms made you think of doing all this?" He popped the morsel into his mouth, waiting for her reply.

Clarise chuckled and moulded a side table out of the floor which she slid the tray across. "Actually, the bath and drinks were Columbine's idea. She told me last night you wanted them very badly that morning. Luckily, the rest of your wish list went over her young head, but I got the general idea when she asked why being without clothes would make such a difference to you."

Her lips twitched mischievously as she added, "And because I refused to go into detail, she may have asked if you would prefer to see her naked as well once she became Mystallian again."

Avis choked on his mouthful of food and had to spit it out before he could gasp in a horrified breath. "Tell me you corrected that!" he demanded, never wanting to see his little girl undressed and certainly not in *that* capacity! He was *not* his father! His chest heaved at the thought. *NO!*

Having no clue of the raw nerve she'd struck in him, Clarise chuckled again. "Of, course, my love. Though it would seem her innate ability for emotions goes much further than merely sensing a feeling. It appears she can identify the cause as well."

She unknotted her robe belt and allowed it to slide to the floor behind her, but for once, Avis wasn't in the mood. He pushed away from her side of the bath and turned to climb out the other side. He needed clothing, and he needed it *now!*

"Avis, what is the matter?"

Avis ignored her, drying himself in short, sharp strokes until he was at the point he wouldn't drip water, then he wrapped the thick towel around his hips and tied it securely. He'd never bothered with a robe the way she did; finding the extra layers unnecessary, until now.

With his chest still exposed, he couldn't bring himself to look at her. He knew she'd see the self-loathing that had taken up residence in his eyes. "I need a minute, sweetheart," he said as he walked around the bathtub and ducked past her into the open bedroom.

He didn't stay there though. After a few seconds of agitated prowling, he made his way through the house, checking on each of the girls to ensure they were still safely asleep. Once he was satisfied they were, he left the building and went to the very edge of the grassed lawn that made up their safety boundary. He needed space. Distance.

Ahead of him, colours continued to swirl and clash against each other, mimicking his own churning thoughts. *It's not genetic,* he promised himself, clenching his fists at his sides as his chest heaved in revulsion. *It's not!* Most of his siblings had kids and not once had any of those youngsters been abused. Not the way *they* had been. *They* weren't monsters. *They* weren't Theodrick.

But of all the siblings, he knew deep down that he had the most in common with the bastard who sired them. What if his disgust over Theodrick's treatment of them was the same as his situation six weeks ago when he'd sympathised with the Damned? What if it were just something he would eventually get over and partake in if given enough time?

No.

Avis bowed his head and speared his fingers through his hair willing himself to agree with his conscience. *I'm not like him! By the Twin Notes, I'm not!* Unshed tears stung his eyes, and he fought them just as hard as his inner demons. His chest heaved and stuttered around broken sobs he refused to voice.

"Avis."

The monotoned voice rumbled to his left and just behind him, and Avis clenched his eyes shut tightly, determined to get himself under control before he turned around. He sucked air through his nose and forced it out over trembling lips, but no matter what he tried, he couldn't stop his body from shaking. *Of all the horrendous timing ...!*

He, the most powerful bender outside of the Nexus and eldest son of Order himself, couldn't get his shit together when he needed to most. "M-m'lord," he stammered, keeping his back to the demon instead of facing him. He didn't want anyone to see him now.

Neither said anything for what seemed a very long time.

"Did you want something of me, m'lord?"

"I know of your upbringing."

Avis shuddered again. Belial had known. Someone outside the Nexus had known. The only comfort he could take from that was the supreme demon hadn't shared the information with anyone. His sons would have been all over it during his torture if they knew.

As one of the most closely guarded secrets in all the Known Realms, he doubted if even his siblings' spouses knew. He certainly had no intention of ever telling Clarise. *Own the space* did not necessarily mean sharing it with everyone. "I will never, *ever* do that to my family."

"I know."

Avis glanced over his shoulder out of the corner of his eye and saw Belial's arms folded over his chest. He didn't look any higher. "What are you doing here, m'lord?"

"Do you think I need your permission to be anywhere I wish to be?"

Avis refocused on the swirling colours of Chaos. "No, m'lord."

"Good. At the very least, I have taught you some manners." Avis didn't dare comment to the contrary; much as he would have liked to. But Belial wasn't finished. "You find yourself at a crossroads with no clarity. So, think on this, Avis of Mystal. Your affiliation with the Damned waned because the individuals involved were beneath your notice. Mortals. You did not know them, so you had no reason to care. Does that level of indifference also carry to your children?"

Avis snarled and spun on his heel to confront Belial, but he was frozen in his tracks before he got half way around or could shout out his denial. Every muscle in his body locked against him and he was suspended where he stood with one leg off the ground.

He focused all his strength into moving his gaze, edging it around until he could skewer the supreme demon with a glare that said everything he dearly wanted to vocalise but was prevented from doing so. He knew even that small a movement was because the supreme demon allowed it, but Avis was too raw to care.

Belial's returning gaze was just as intense. "Tread with care, boy," the great demon warned, and suddenly Avis was back in control of his own body.

He stumbled off-balance but caught himself and straightened. "I'll never treat my girls as if they don't matter," he snarled, wanting to shout the words but not quite willing to do so.

If he thought he was going to get the chance to say more, he really should have known better.

"See that you do not," Belial said, and then vanished—just as quickly as he came.

Avis straightened his left arm at his side and rubbed the elbow with his other hand, giving himself a subconscious half-hug. Was Belial right? Was the difference merely a matter of perspective?

He pictured doing to Columbine what he had been forced to endure, and once again the roar of denial ripped through him, only this time, he tilted his head back and gave it a voice. Never! Never, never, never, *NEVER!* He was *not* his father!

"Avis?"

He was so wrapped up in his own turmoil, he hadn't heard Clarise approach him from behind.

She slid her hands around his waist and pressed her forehead to his back. "Talk to me, my love. What has brought you to this state?"

And have you hating me as much as I hate myself? He gnashed his teeth and shook his head in denial. "It's not you," he insisted, believing something needed to be said to appease her, if not the whole truth.

"There's ... things in my past. Things ... I thought were long dead." He sucked in a deep breath through his nose and released it in another shuddering sigh. "Things I haven't wanted to think about in eons. But now that I've got a young family of my own, they're back with a vengeance, tearing me down when I least expect it."

Clarise didn't pry, for which he'd be eternally grateful. She tightened her grip and rubbed her face across his back like a cat until he relented and twisted, drawing her to stand in front of him with her back mashed into his chest so that they were both looking out at the Chaotic Ocean.

He wrapped his arms around her shoulders and rested the hollow of his throat against the crown of her head, making the most of her lavender fragrance to bring a sense of calm to his thoughts.

As much as he'd rather eat one of Armina's claymores than admit this to anyone, he envied the Highborn Hellions' relationship with Belial. They may have been a pack of evil assholes (with the sole exception of his wife and children), but they didn't live in constant fear of their patriarch. They rallied around him, much as the Mystallians rallied around each other.

Belial treated them with dignity, and they treated him with respect. Avis couldn't help but wonder how differently things might have been if Theodrick had granted them the gift of dignity instead of forcing them to fight a losing battle for it.

"The past is not the future," Clarise said, sliding her hands backwards around his waist in a reverse hug.

Avis appreciated the sentiment; misguided as it was. "Perhaps," he murmured, pressing his lips into her hair and using her scent to calm himself. "But it can certainly shape it."

"Only if you allow it to, Avis." She released her hold and turned in his arms to face him, causing Avis to straighten and look down at her. Her gaze, when their eyes met, was sincere but steely. "As you are so fond of saying, beloved. If you choose to let what happened in your past control you … stop you from being the god you were meant to be, *then own it*, because, at the end of the day, the fault is yours. To blame another for your actions is to offer excuses—and we both know how you feel about that."

Avis blinked at her in astonishment. Was that what he was doing? He hadn't internalised in years, terrified of the power his father had wielded over his mind. But that was the past. His father wasn't here. He never had been. The one time he'd thought so, he'd been one of the Damned, and their torture was absolute. There'd been no relief from it … not even in his mind.

Well, he wasn't one of the Damned anymore. The threat was gone. The illusion of his father was gone. Yet here he was, doing exactly what Clarise was accusing him of; allowing his past to dictate his future.

A predatory growl crept up the back of his throat. *No more.*

Keeping his gaze on Clarise, he drew on her closeness for strength and turned his mind inward. Truly inward. He blitzed past the memories and arrived in an empty space, where, if everything was as he believed, he held all the power.

This was the dreamscape: his imagination. He tested the theory by recreating the front lawns of Pandess. The truly epic grandeur that came from being the home of the Life Court. Everything just as he remembered it. He took comfort in the familiarity. This was right. This was how it was supposed to …

"Hello, boy."

Avis swivelled on his heel, fear-based adrenaline surging through his veins until he thought he was going to pass out. Before him, the one being he never ever wanted to see again. Broad shoulders. Dark hair. And power. So much power. Avis felt his mind being over-ridden and his legs were forced to walk him towards the man who could very well be his double, if he wasn't just over two and a half meters tall and nearly half as wide.

Begging at this point was useless. It only angered him. Acceptance and endurance were Avis' only options now. Theodrick hardly ever spoke. He let his power do the talking for him. If he had to use his voice, his wrath was thousands of times worse.

Avis was brought to a standstill before him, though even now, as a grown man, he still only came up to his father's chest. As a child, he'd been … much smaller. He trembled when his father smiled cruelly, as if already very aware of Avis' terrified thoughts. And then the back of the bastard's hand reached out for him. Not to strike him down, but to trace the back of a single finger down his tear-stained cheek. Suggestively.

The contact was too much, and Avis blanked the whole image, dropping to his knees, huffing and puffing with his forehead pushed into something solid just in front of his knees.

His eyes were clenched, and his jaw tensed until his teeth hurt, but his hands fisted into the same solid space on either side of his head. He stayed there for a long, long time, crying like the child he hadn't been in a very long time.

When the tears stopped and his body stilled, rational thought began to creep through his mind. He had blanked the image. Releasing his grip on whatever his subconscious had conjured for him to hold, he slowly slid back on to his haunches and looked around. Emptiness. Except for the small patch of grass he knelt on, absolute emptiness … just as he wanted.

This reprieve would never have happened if his father was in charge.

Avis rose to his feet, his chest heaving with the possibility. His father wasn't here. His father wasn't in charge. This was *his* imagination. *He* was in charge.

He reset the scene just as he had before, on the front lawn of Pandess.

"Hello, b …"

Avis shut the dreamscape down again hard, unable to bear the sound of his father's voice. This time he remained on his feet with his arms wrapped around his waist. His eyes were closed and he rocked where he stood, wishing he could find the strength to get through this but knowing he couldn't.

In the presence of Theodrick—even this internalised version of him—his mind splintered like it had as a child, going in helpless circles. He could see it. Logically he knew his father wasn't here, but the image of him and what he could do … what he had done … was so ingrained his response was automatic. He needed to clear his head. He needed …

… he needed Clarise.

Unwinding his arms from his sides, he brought to life an image of his beloved wife just as he'd left her, standing before him with her arms looped around his neck. The moment her lavender fragrance hit him, he banded his arms around her and crushed her to his chest; his head bowed into her hair.

She slid her hands from his neck to his shoulders and back again, murmuring soft words of comfort as he held her close. "You can do this, beloved," she crooned, spearing her fingers into his hair and stroking the base of his neck. "He only ruled your past. Do not give him our future as well."

Avis listened to the sound of her voice for a long time, until his breathing returned to normal and he lifted his head from hers to look at her. "You have too much faith in me," he said, his voice still trembling a little.

Clarise's smile was confident; almost indulgent. "No," she replied, cupping his face in her hands and stroking his cheeks affectionately. "I have a lot of faith in *us*."

Avis kissed her deeply, willingly himself to absorb her confidence in them. When they parted, she stared him straight in the eyes, allowing her love to shine through. "You can do this, beloved," she repeated. "The past is not the future."

Absorbing every second of that love, Avis toyed with the idea of bringing back the Mystallian dreamscape while she was in his arms, supporting him. The thought was tempting, but that would put the image of his precious wife in the same dreamscape as his father, and that he would never do. Not even in this … imaginary place. Nothing about that bastard would ever mar her.

But that didn't mean he couldn't bring her scent with him. Avis leaned forward and drew in a deep breath, coating the inside of his nasal cavities all the way to his lungs in her glorious fragrance. He grafted it there so that no amount of breathing would shift it from him. Then he kissed her again. "I'll be back," he promised, erasing her presence with a thought.

Before he could think better of it, he brought up the Mystallian dreamscape again.

"Hello …"

Avis froze the scene. The birds stopped chirping. The wind stopped. Everything just … stopped.

As before, his back was to his father and he stared at the palace stairs, determined to get his hammering heart rate under control. His chest heaved, but with every breath, the scent of lavender eased his panic. Clarise was with him. She would always be with him.

Holding on to her fragrance like the lifeline it was, Avis began to turn. Everything was frozen, just as it should be. Even his father. Avis' eyes went to the furthest corner as he moved, until Theodrick just made his peripheral vision. Then he paused, his gaze flickering to and away from his father, edging his vision with each pass until he saw his father in his entirety.

Avis' pounding heart felt as if it was lodged in his throat, but still, his father didn't move. Like everything else, he was a statue. An aspect of this dreamscape. He was a ghost—a memory, rising from the depths of his past to huff and puff without any substance to back it up. It wasn't the real Theodrick …

… and that made all the difference.

It took Avis a few minutes to work up the courage to lock eyes with his father and keep them there. Such a small victory—pathetic really—but Avis' mind surged with the repercussions. He'd never thought to do this before. Once they'd escaped the Nexus, he and his siblings had never let their father appear in any of their dreamscapes. They hadn't dared. Terror of his capabilities and his potential reach had been all-consuming.

More minutes passed before he took his first willing step towards the thing that sired him. Clarise's scent remained with him; a constant source of encouragement. *You can do this, beloved.* Another step tentatively followed. Then another. And another.

The step that took him within his father's reach was the hardest of all. He never took his focus off the animal towering over him for an instant, fearing the bastard might somehow escape his frozen imprisonment and go on the attack.

Avis' next step put his father within *his* reach.

He stretched out his trembling hand, his eyes constantly moving to Theodrick's jaw overhead in anticipation of a reaction. A violent reaction. This was so surreal. He pushed his father in the chest and recoiled; his breathing hitched. Only Clarise's fragrance kept him from completely losing his shit and running as far and as hard as he could in the other direction. She believed in him. He needed to believe in himself.

Holding that thought, he stepped forward and pushed again with enough force to make his father take an involuntary step backwards before freezing again. Still no adverse reaction. No reaction at all.

With growing confidence, Avis ran the two steps at his father and pushed him with both hands.

Hard.

Theodrick flew several meters backwards, spewing vulgar curses that would have mortified Clarise as he fell to the ground and rolled several times. More importantly, Avis felt no shift in power as he swore. The man may have been the same size as Tal and Griffith, but Avis was still in charge.

They should have ALL done this a long time ago.

Avis forced the image of his father to stand, watching in triumph as the Lord of Order threw his head back and roared his displeasure. It was a strange sound to behold, but Avis recognised it instantly from his youth because it had meant their father no longer had the power and control he craved.

Someone else had taken it from him. In the physical realm, he and his siblings never found out who that someone was, but at this moment, in his imagination, that someone was Avis.

And fucking hell, did it feel good.

He felt the first barb of a mental attack and shut that down as well. It was so easy. Like swatting aside an incoming bee. His father truly had no power here! Lifting his eyes to meet his father's rage, Avis shifted reality again until his father shrank to half his regular size, putting him slightly shorter than Clarise. And still there wasn't a thing Theodrick could do to stop him.

Staring down at his father, Avis' breathing increased for entirely different reasons. Gone was the fear. Gone was the helplessness. All that remained was rage. Even if this was just an internalised replicant of the real thing, Avis knew his grin matched the earlier version of his father in cruelty.

Oh, this … was going to be fun.

Avis ran at his father, crash tackling him to the ground. He quickly straddled the image, using his shins to pin Theodrick's upper arms before he could recover and threw one punch after another at his father's face, crushing bone and flesh with each strike until there was nothing but pulp on the ground and his father's lifeless body beneath him.

It wasn't enough!

Avis resurrected him, and this time he punted him so hard that Theodrick went sailing into the distance. Before he landed, Avis created the Akheron River, complete with demons that tore his father apart like he was one of the Damned.

It was glorious to watch his father fight the losing battle against the demons, but that end still wasn't personal enough. He didn't just want to watch his father's demise. He wanted to cause it! He wanted to be up to his elbows in his father's blood!

So, he cleared the scene and reset it with Theodrick standing before him. And then he punched his hand through his father's ribs, ripped out his still-beating heart, and shoved it down his throat. The next time, he shoved it somewhere else.

Hundreds of simulations took place, one after the other. Thousands. Hundreds of thousands. He destroyed his father thoroughly in every single one, clawing back a little bit more of his self-esteem with every envisioned murder. The early ones had all been barbaric. Animalistic. He constantly tore his father apart with his bare hands and once, he'd even ripped his throat out with his teeth, just to see what it would feel like.

But when the animal rage subsided, he began to take his time and mete out his vengeance with more tradition instruments of torture. He drew on everything the hellions had done to him for inspiration and then added some of his own twists.

Each time, he had his father begging for mercy, just as he had begged as a child. And just as his father had back then, Avis showed none. He tortured and killed the bastard, over and over and over again.

It still wasn't enough! It would never be enough.

He'd have done it a hundred thousand times more, but a familiar fragrance crept through the internalisation, distracting him from his rage. Just as it always had. Standing over his father's broken body, Avis straightened and breathed it in, allowing the lavender scent to cleanse his mind of everything but the one person his heart beat for.

Why was he still here, wasting his time with a memory, when the real Clarise stood in his arms, not knowing just how long he'd been gone? Years had passed for Avis. Years where he'd allowed his psychotic fury to rule his head.

But for now, he was done. It was time to go home.

Avis withdrew from his mind, and in the space of a blink, resettled himself right where he'd left Clarise, corralled in his arms on the edge of her created grounds. She was staring up at him, just as she had before he left, because for her, time hadn't moved.

Avis suddenly lifted her into the air and swung her around him, throwing his head back as she squealed in surprise and laughed like he hadn't laughed in a long time. If ever.

His entire body shook with the freedom of it. "By the Twin Notes of all Creation," he decreed, pulling her so close he wasn't sure she could breathe. "I love you so much, sweetheart." He kissed her deeply, then added against her lips, "Don't ever let me do anything so stupid as to let you go again."

Clarise didn't agree as he'd expected her to. Instead, she tilted her head and smirked coyly at him, framing his face with her hands. "Still seeking to blame others, beloved?"

Elation made his next action reactive and he thrust his head forward, nipping her playfully on the tip of her nose. Not enough to hurt, but when she yelped in shock, they both laughed again and melted further into each other. "More like relinquishing control to the one person in our partnership who has time and time again proven she has more common sense than me."

Still chuckling, Clarise laid her head against his chest. "I love you too." But then she gave an all-over shiver. "Would you object to us going back inside, beloved?" Avis dropped his eyes and realised she still only had on her jade green negligee—the epitome of nothing. "Neither of us are adequately dressed for the outdoors."

Without a word of explanation, Avis bent at the knees and swept her up into his arms. He delighted in her spirited shriek—loving the fact that once she was over her fright, she settled easily into his arms. Tightening his grip, he sprinted across the lawn and leapt over the single step, bypassing the double doors to land inside the warmer dining room. "Better?" he asked, as she shifted the doors to automatically close behind him.

"Much," she admitted, hooking one arm around his neck and snuggling into him. "You are back in the present with me again." Had she known he'd internalised and been gone so long? Maybe, but she was right. He was here now, in the present.

He wove his way through the furniture and past the double doors into their sitting room which he'd left open in his haste to escape earlier. The bedroom doors were also open, and he went straight through, depositing her in the middle of the four-poster bed.

The one he still hadn't slept in yet. As usual, Clarise was right on every count, and dammit, he *would* own his future. If thoughts of his father bothered him now, after all this time, it was because *he* permitted them to. To Hell with Theodrick and his heinous parenting. As always, he would look to his siblings for role-models. The family view on either side of him was much better than the view upwards anyway.

CHAPTER FORTY-SEVEN

Belial breathed deeply in the heart of his inner sanctum, filling the area around him with thick, sulphuric smoke. Most wouldn't be able to find their way through such toxic fumes, but his champion wasn't one. Sensing Belial's need for his presence, the demonic commander materialised silently at his sire's side.

Belial could feel Theodrick's presence in the Upper Realm. It had always been that way when either one was in residence, but that didn't mean he knew why, or where the Pillar of Order was focusing his attention. From their respective thrones at the Table of Divinity, all of existence lay before them and Theodrick could be looking at anything. What Belial did know, was his counterpart wasn't looking down at him.

Yet.

Not the brightest star in the sky, is he? Belial asked, drumming the talons of one hand against his thigh. It hadn't been his intention to step in like that, but he knew how emotionally charged Avis could be once his childhood insecurities were triggered.

If left unchecked, his escalation would reach a level where he could hurt himself or his family; and that Belial wouldn't allow.

FUCK YOU, YOU FUCKING FAGGOT! Theodrick roared, the instant his ghostly image appeared before him. *I CAN'T FUCKING BELIEVE YOU FUCKING POWER-BLOCKED ME, YOU HORN-HEADED MOTHER-FUCKING SUNOVA FUCKING BITCH!*

One corner of Belial's lips twitched upwards, revealing a single, elongated fang. As always, baiting Theodrick into making an appearance was just too easy. *Did you not enjoy the way he dreamed of destroying you ... over and over again?*

Being a pillar had its advantages, apart from the obvious. Just as Theodrick could look anywhere across the realms and see who was shape shifting into what, Belial could look at any bender and follow their thought processes to view their internalisations. Neither could interfere in what the other side did, but both could bear witness. *I especially enjoyed the one where he ripped your throat out with his teeth ...*

YOU MOTHER-FUCKING PIECE OF FUCKING SHIT! HE'S FUCKING MINE!

Not while he is in my realm, Theodrick, and if I want to let him fantasise about killing you, you will have no say in the matter.

JUST WHO THE FUCKING FUCK DO YOU FUCKING THINK YOU FUCKING ARE, YOU HORN-HEADED PIECE OF FUCKING SHIT! HOW DARE YOU FUCKING INTERFERE WITH THE REALM-DAMNED RESPECT MY FUCKWIT BRAT FUCKING SHOWS ME!

So, he had been watching. Watching, and basking in his son's absolute terror and horror of what had happened all those eons ago. It hadn't been an accident that Avis and his siblings never took Theodrick on in their imagination before today.

From his side of the Table of Divinity, The Lord of Order had simply made sure they never thought to do so. It would have been the same today, had he as a pillar in his own realm not stepped in and asserted his authority over all things within Chaos. The two pillars locked powers, which left Avis free to find the will to internalise and deal with his past … unhindered. He'd be the only one of his siblings who'd be allowed to do so.

Belial drew in a deep breath and refrained from shaking his head: barely. *And to think all of existence knows* me *as the bastard,* he thought wryly to himself as he slowly released that breath. *Theodrick, when you are ready, we have a very real problem.*

LIKE FUCKING WHAT?

Belial was about to answer when the ignorance behind Theodrick's words struck him with all the finesse of the Twin Notes. *He did not already know?* Keeping all hint of surprise from his expression, Belial nevertheless inwardly blinked several thousand times in the space of a second.

In the past, he'd made fun of how thick Avis could be when certain situations fell into his lap and he'd failed to notice the implications, but he'd never quite realised Theodrick at times could be just as dense. *How long did you say you were watching them?*

FUCK YOU! I CAN FUCKING WATCH THE FUCK OUTTA THEIR FUCKING ASSES ANY FUCKING TIME …!

How—long? Belial dragged the question out in the hopes it would penetrate his tirade.

Theodrick shrugged and dropped his weight to the back of his throne. *A FUCKING WHILE. WHAT'S IT FUCKING TO YOU?*

A while. Which meant like him, the Bender had heard everything Clarise had said that brought about Avis' tailspin and he still hadn't connected the dots where the Weaver's abilities were concerned. The fool had been so absorbed in his son's self-loathing and terror of him that he'd failed to see the bigger picture. Irony was quickly developing a new look in Belial's mind. *As Clarise said, the Weaver can read the intent behind the emotions.*

FUCKING WHAT?

Theodrick suddenly disappeared, and believing he knew exactly where he was headed, the Shifter opened a pillar spyhole on his daughter and son-by-marriage.

He knew he wouldn't see Theodrick's ghostly image watching over them, for spyholes worked by creating a viewing portal through to either the lower celestial or the mortal realm (depending on where the family member was) and would not identify a pillar watching from the Upper Realm. To find that out, Belial must either ascend to the Upper Realm or blood-link with one of the two in the bed. Not ideal, given the pair's present … endeavours.

They had settled back into the bed, picking things up where they'd left off in the bathroom. Clearly, dealing with his father so thoroughly had increased the boy's libido, and Clarise wasn't complaining.

Sex of almost any kind wasn't a taboo thing for Belial and watching it uninvited wasn't either. After all, it wasn't as if they were doing something he hadn't already perfected. No, he was here for one reason, and one reason only; to make sure they weren't … *tampered* with.

When the seconds ticked by and nothing appeared out of the ordinary with their love-making, he relaxed a little.

MOTHER FUCKER! Theodrick roared, the instant he returned. *THAT FUCKING LITTLE BINT FROM HELL IS PISSING ALL OVER MY FUCKING MIND CONTROL! SHE KNOWS EXACTLY WHAT THE FUCK EVERY FUCKED UP FUCKER'S FUCKING THINKING BECAUSE OF THEIR PANSY-ASSED FUCKED UP FUCKING FEELINGS! I SWEAR IF THAT FUCKING BITCH GETS ANY FUCKED-UP IDEAS ABOUT SCREWING WITH MY FUCKING SIDE OF THE FUCKING TABLE …*

As fast as he'd relaxed, Belial's adrenaline surged, and as if sensing it, Beelzebub tensed for battle at his side. All concerned knew the danger of one pillar attacking another, but it seemed Theodrick was insane enough to go there anyway!

Showing no outward sign of his thoughts, Belial immediately dropped the spyhole on Avis and Clarise and slapped another on to Columbine herself. *Calm yourself, you old fool. We are all still here which means she is fine.* He used the words to reassure himself as the image took shape before him. For a process that was almost instantaneous, the moments of lag tested his legendary resolve.

The image of Columbine kneeling before her fireplace that snapped into existence had Belial stifling a sigh of relief.

She was awake despite the lateness of the hour, (a lapse on her governess' part which Belial would deal with shortly) kneeling into the roaring fire with her clawed hands pressed firmly into the back wall of her bedroom's fireplace. Had Theodrick attacked her, she'd have been a shell on the floor, staring at nothing.

Not that her current focus was in any way better.

Her body language was soft as she rocked from side to side in a very tight rhythm and light streams of smoke accompanied her movements. Belial frowned as he watched, for there was something … familiar about that rhythm, even though the medium was wrong.

And then it dawned on him.

That back firewall—the one Columbine was pressed against—was the only thing separating her from her parents' bedroom. As the Weaver, she was sharing their passion. Their lovemaking.

The blissful dimming of her eye embers as she rocked in time with what had to be Avis' thrusts made Belial's skin crawl, and that was no easy achievement.

Her parents would be mortified if they ever found out she was awake and enjoying the ebb and flow of their lovemaking.

Her mind was too young to comprehend the adult nature of their union, but the rush of pleasure and how to achieve it was quickly ingraining itself upon her. That was just … no! It was wrong on so many levels.

Rant on your own time, Bender. We have work to do.

OH, FUCKING DO WE? Theodrick's tone was filled with sarcasm.

Yes. We need to curtail her power. Immediately.

Theodrick snorted and threw both hands in the air. *FUCK ME! IS THAT ALL WE HAVE TO FUCKING DO?*

Belial ignored his condescension. This wasn't just about his granddaughter/daughter knowing the intent behind her parent's sexual encounters. It was the power behind it. *People will not trust what they perceive as a threat. You already want to kill her for her ability to clash with you, yet you* know *you cannot. As the living embodiment of all things emotional, if she is to reach maturity and take her place at the Table of Divinity, we cannot afford to let others see her true capability—or even suspect it. Her parents already do, and that will also have to be rectified before they feel inclined to interfere in matters that will have consequences to us all. We* must *restrict her power.*

Belial fully expected the Bender to have plenty to say about being told when he could and couldn't use his power in Chaos, but for once, Theodrick went eerily quiet. Perhaps, because like him, The Lord of Order was mulling over the pros and cons of such an aggressive course of action.

Belial certainly was.

If he was right, and the Weaver's youthful inexperience meant she had yet to grow into her power, everything would be fine.

But if he were wrong ... and the girl was already considered the Weaver in the grand scheme of things ... this move would spell the end of everyone and everything. As his mind played out that level of devastation, a third and equally unwelcome possibility came to him.

What if this modification worked and everything went on its merry way until the time came for Columbine to ascend, and she did so bearing a grudge? He couldn't see such a sweet child being so vindictive, but his mind circled the possibility like a shark, and no matter how much he wanted to deny it, it just wouldn't go away.

Belial shook his head and cleared his thoughts. For the sake of all existence, this had to work in its entirety. They needed her to grow to maturity and take her place as the stabilising force between him and Theodrick. Any other alternative just didn't bear considering.

Nearly a minute later, Theodrick's gaze narrowed hatefully, and when he did speak, his words were glacial. *YOU. **CAN. NOT.** BE FUCKING. SERIOUS.*

The six icy words spilled across the distance like acid, causing Belial to grind his jaw tightly. He didn't need Theodrick's criticism. The enormity of their decision weighed heavily enough on the Shifter, but he'd rather be ended for attempting to safeguard the future than allow it to fall apart under the weight of its own misgivings. *About as serious as you were when you wanted the True Gryps wiped out.*

FUCK YOU, YOU FUCKING ASSHAT! THAT WAS FUCKING DIFFERENT!

I fail to see how. We both risked elimination for little more than your hurt pride, and you know it. At least this is for the Weaver's own good. Belial gave him a moment to absorb that, before adding resolutely, *You owe me this, Bender. I am calling in my unspecified boon.*

Theodrick visibly seethed from the other side of existence. His nostrils flared, and he gritted his teeth so tightly his face turned bright red, and his eyes became bloodshot. Then his entire body convulsed with rage.

Belial knew giving him no choice in the matter was the pinnacle of lost control for the Bender, but the pretentious fool had to know this favour would be called upon, sooner or later. It had always hung over his head. At least it was being used for the well-being of all existence.

The image of Theodrick winked out, followed immediately by his departure from the Upper Realm. Belial folded his arms expectantly. Only one thing was more anathema to the Pillar of Order than being cornered by an outstanding debt, and that was to have someone be privy to his meltdown regarding it.

He'd be back once a few thousand citizens of the Nexus had suffered his wrath. He'd always come back. Belial just had to wait.

When Theodrick's presence, then his ghostly image reappeared a short time later, the Nexus Lord was once again on his throne with his hands tightly gripping the armrests. His eyes were still bloodshot, but the rage had marginally subsided. Belial wondered how many unfortunate citizens of the Nexus had paid for that rage with their minds. At least the Bender didn't have any of his children living with him anymore. They had always been his first targets.

SO, HOW FUCKING MUCH DO YOU WANT TO FUCK UP THE LITTLE BINT?

Belial didn't enjoy that terminology, as apt as it was. Without her champion and her army, the Weaver was already too weak for his liking. But weakness had to be gauged by perspective, and she was already infinitely more powerful than anyone else around her. She didn't have the permanency of ascension to protect her, which made her vulnerable. Killable, even. *For now, we should focus on the way she can follow an emotion beyond line of sight to its mental reasonings. Her ability to know precisely* why *people feel the way they do is ...*

BULLSHIT, Theodrick answered for him, in total agreement.

Belial steepled his fingers in front of him and drummed his talons together, causing a cascade of sparks. *I will rewire her neurological thought processes to avoid any future occurrences of her learning the reasons behind people's emotional state. You will take care of the past, bagging up every memory she has ever had about it, then both of us must prevent her core from fighting her way back to them.* Something positively malicious glinted in Theodrick's eyes, and their long association told the Shifter exactly what he was thinking. *You will neither damage nor destroy her memories in the process, Bender.* The childish slump of Theodrick's shoulders confirmed his suspicions, and not for the first time he was glad his counterpart was so transparent. *When the time comes for her to ascend, she will need to be whole. You know this.*

I'LL TAKE CARE OF HER FUCKING PARENTS, Theodrick added. *THEY WON'T REMEMBER SHIT ABOUT IT.*

Theodrick's reduced level of profanity and seemingly clearer head wasn't lost on the Shifter. They were both preparing themselves for what needed to be done. *Keep in mind, these are the people most dear to her. If anything was to cause a bad reaction on her part, it would be the permanent harming of them.* In *other words,* Belial thought to himself. *For the first time in your life, Bender, play nice, because this is not a matter of grabbing hold of a subordinate and slapping them around.* No, this was two established pillars going up against their third, and all of existence lay in the balance. *Be ready for the fight of your life, Theodrick. Her core is going to act up over this, and it will take both of us to subdue it. This needs to hold for several years at least.*

YOU KNOW WE'RE NOT FUCKING MEANT TO SCREW WITH EACH OTHER, BELIAL.

Not Shifter. Not horn-headed piece of shit. Belial.

The number of times Theodrick had called him by his real name in all their years, Belial could count on the thumbs of one Mystallian hand. Both knew what was at stake if he was wrong. *Technically, she is not the Weaver yet, so that and the fact we are acting in her best interest will hopefully keep us all safe. By limiting our changes to where she can still gauge other people's emotions without knowing* why *they feel it, this should offer the appearance of an innate ability rather than a pillar power. This will not constitute a threat. In the meantime, I will monitor her in case anything else needs to be done to keep her safe.*

BE FUCKED IF I'M FUCKING WELL DOING THIS A DOZEN FUCKING TIMES FOR YOU, YOU HORN-HEADED MOTHER-FUCKER! Theodrick lifted his right fist off the throne arm and flipped his middle finger at Belial: one that covered both how many favours the Shifter was owed *and* how the Bender felt about being forced to repay this one. *ONE FUCKING BOON, YOU FUCKED UP ASSHOLE, AND YOU'RE FUCKING USING IT THE FUCK UP TODAY! THAT'S FUCKING IT!*

Belial stared at Theodrick, keeping his face devoid of all expression. As amusing as it would be to laugh in the face of the fool's arrogance, the Shifter had no desire to wait for another of his infamous temper tantrums to pass through the Nexus. Still, to think this one action on Theodrick's part would make them even when the near eradication of the true gryps took almost an eon?

The Shifter shook his head.

Very well, he purred, drumming his talons against each other to create another cascade of sparks. *My boon is this. Until such time as Lady Columbine ascends to the upper realm and claims her throne as the Weaver, you will make yourself available for any and all mental modifications of* my *choosing, both now and in the future.* Belial knew he had to take charge of deciding the modifications. Theodrick's perverted tastes meant he couldn't be trusted to do the right thing by her. Even if she hadn't been the Weaver, Columbine was still his granddaughter/daughter, which meant she was family. No one touched his family the wrong way. Not even Theodrick.

OH, FUCK OFF! AS IF I'D FUCKING EVER AGREE TO THAT FUCKED UP BULLSHIT!

The joy of me being in possession of the boon owed, Bender, is that you do not get a say in it. My boon. My choice of payment. You know I never forget a debt.

Theodrick's gaze narrowed hatefully, but they both knew he was bound by his word. Rarely was a boon ever offered by a celestial, because it *had* to be honoured. The sanctity of the Table of Divinity and all who lived within its edges was absolute in that regard.

ARE WE FUCKING DOING THIS OR WHAT?

We are, Belial answered, settling his gaze once again on Columbine.

The girl had stopped swaying and removed herself from the fireplace, her face turning to sweep the room apprehensively. Twice she paused when her gaze lined up with Belial's spy hole, and thicker smoke billowed through her pumping chest plates. The first time, Belial thought it might have been an accident. After the second, he doubted it.

More proof of her pillar designation. But she couldn't have seen him, for her distress levels were climbing fast, and she had no reason to fear him. He and Theodrick had to move quickly. At the rate her panic was escalating, others around her would soon follow suit without knowing why.

For an extremely brief moment, he considered broadening the scope of her limitations to include that crucial ability as well. If the celestials were going to react violently to her ability to follow their emotions back to their mental source, they'd be even more enraged if her power to alter their emotional state became known. Then he decided against it.

Sooner or later, she'd have to learn the full extent of her powers, and for now she had only ever influenced things on a miniscule scale—and always in the favour of whoever she was unconsciously trying to please. Besides, the only person other than he and Theodrick who knew of that side of things for certain of this was her sister, and no one ever asked the opinion of a difficult girl-child.

No, it was better for now to let this one stand. The baby steps the Weaver needed to reach her ultimate control would never be undertaken if he removed the footpath entirely. And thanks to the wording of his boon with Theodrick, he could always revisit the matter later if it became necessary.

Satisfied with his decision, Belial reached through the spyhole with all his power and took control of Columbine's physical form. The control wasn't as immediate as he'd expected, lending more credence to her future as their eternal equal.

Yet before she could do more than gasp and stiffen at the unexpected assault, Theodrick must have come in from his side. The fire in her eye sockets flared bright yellow and she struggled helplessly between them, on the verge of panic.

"Shhh. Calm yourself, little one. It is I. You will be fine. I promise." Belial caused her ear drums to vibrate so that she would hear both the soothing tone of his words and the familiarity of his voice as if he were standing in the room speaking to her. He crooned the soft pledge which he meant with every fibre of his being as he flooded her body with relaxants, while Theodrick wrangled her mind.

"In time, you will understand everything and take your place with us in the Upper Realms. Until then, enjoy your youth, little one. I am told it is a privilege to be cherished."

CHAPTER FORTY-EIGHT

The following morning, Avis refrained from waking the girls. He accepted his culpability in pushing them too hard yesterday and decided to let them choose when to wake up. If it added a few more hours to their journey, that was hardly going to make much of a difference. Chaos was everything he'd imagined it to be, with one glaring exception.

Regardless of how constantly it changed, he'd been expecting some type of structure to be within it. Every demon he'd ever dealt with had a real, solid body, so logic demanded that they lived somewhere—amongst things that were equally as solid. Trees, buildings ... fucking hell, even a rock would've sufficed! Hell had plenty of those to house both the hierarchy and the Damned.

Yet nothing had presented itself as solid in all the hours they'd been riding. Everything was fluid, constantly changing; just not in any way that would affect them as they rode through it.

Now and again he thought he caught sight of fangs and eyes amongst the tonal shifts and knew they were being watched, but their steeds were fast, and by the time he'd registered what they were, the demons in question were already a long way behind them.

Both worse and more pertinent to him; there was no indication of the passage of time either. That had been his undoing with the girls. With no dawn ... no dusk ... no night ... no day, Avis had no way of knowing how long they'd been riding. He himself could go for days—weeks, if he pushed it—before he needed to stop.

Yet his girls couldn't last more than a few hours. Flashes of colour had erupted everywhere around them, and with no clue as to what they represented, it had been like riding through one of Roxi's dawn artworks. Pretty as fuck, but mind-numbingly disorientating. On the Akheron River, he hadn't needed to know the time, because the servants regulated their day with the presentation of certain meals.

Now, he was the one who oversaw what they did and when, and if he didn't get his head around the problem soon, someone he cared about would be hurt.

He began to doubt the wisdom of letting the girls sleep in when two meals came and went, and they still hadn't surfaced. "Do children normally sleep this long?" he asked as he wiped his mouth with a napkin, having just finished what he deemed 'lunch'.

Tilu leaned in from his left and refilled his empty goblet with ambrosia. His focus remained on the two double sets of doors on his left where his daughters were sleeping, but he caught sight of Tilu straightening and tilted the goblet very slightly towards her in acknowledgement (something he'd have never done five years ago) then took a deep swig.

"It was a long ride, my love," Clarise replied, using her own goblet to hide her growing smile. "And they are Highborn Hellion Ladies as well as children. They are not accustomed to such hardships, but they will learn and adapt."

Avis snorted and swallowed more wine. "It wasn't my plan to run them into the ground," he muttered under his breath; still kicking himself over that.

Clarise motioned to Frash who hovered nearby and, with the servant's assistance, pushed her chair back and rose gracefully to her feet. Avis was still scowling at his own stupidity when she walked the length of the table and paused at his side, allowing the scent of lavender to fill his senses.

"All will be well, beloved," she promised, sliding her hands across his shoulders to palm the tension from the cords of his neck.

Enveloped in her fragrance as much as the massage, Avis lowered his guard until his shoulders relaxed and he uttered a small sigh of contentment. "Nobody had better figure out how easily you do that, or I'll never live it down," he muttered, after a long bout of silence between them.

"Do what?" she asked innocently.

Avis tilted his head and looked at her over the top of his eyes, refusing to dignify that with an answer. They both knew exactly what he meant.

Her fingers dug deeply into his muscles. "Would you rather I stop?"

He rubbed his thumb against the side of the wine glass while the fingers of his right hand drummed against the table-top. Did he want her to stop? No. But the issue of his lack of time sense needed to be addressed or yesterday could happen all over again.

So, did he say what was on his mind, or shut up and enjoy his wife's ministrations? *Decisions, decisions* … until the images of his children passed out in their bedrooms repeatedly flashed through his mind's eye, giving him the well-needed kick up the ass.

Placing the goblet on the table, he lovingly rubbed the top of her left hand, then gathered it up and pressed his lips to her knuckles. "Actually, there is something you could do for me, sweetheart," he said, looking up at her hopefully. "Do you think you could create some type of timing mechanism for me?"

Her hands stilled. "What do you mean?"

Avis waved a frustrated hand at the front doors which represented the physical barricade between them and the Chaotic Ocean beyond.

"There's no sense of time out there. Everywhere else in existence has some means of regulating the passage of time. It could be the location of a sun, tidal movements, planetary alignments—hell, some of them even have a celestial established in the field. My point is, there's always something, but Chaos has *nothing*. I don't want to be permanently looking over my shoulder to gauge where the girls are at because I don't know how long it's been since I last checked on them. I need some way to regulate time while I'm in motion."

Clarise lifted her eyes and stared vacantly along the table, her lips twisting to one side. "I could add a bead of glowing pigment to one of your glove cuffs," she suggested, after a few seconds of contemplation. Then her vision sharpened and focused on him. "Provided, of course, you could tolerate an aspect of your uniform not being entirely ebony."

Not liking the implication that he was somehow going to be the impediment to her solution, Avis pursed his lips in annoyance.

As if guessing his internal monologue, Clarise smiled and leaned in to kiss his temple. Her fingers sifted through his dark hair and stroked his cheek soothingly. "Except for the gold accoutrements and insignia of the Mystallian pantheon, your uniform is entirely black. You are very proud of that uniform exactly as it is. Change is not something you embrace easily, beloved," she reminded him quietly.

Liking that even less, Avis pushed his heels into the floor and swivelled the chair on its right rear leg to face her. Then he reached out and banded his arms around her waist, dragging her petite form into his lap. He said nothing until he had her nestled against him with her forehead against his cheek, where he could make the most of that delicious lavender scent.

"What exactly do you mean by a bead of pigment, sweetheart?" he asked, refusing to start the day with a stupid argument about her nonsense regarding his supposed resistance to change. It was obvious to anyone he didn't have a problem with change. Only an idiot ignored good advice, and he didn't co-rule the third largest realm in existence because he was stupid.

The change just needed to be warranted; otherwise, why should he? Familiarity was comfortable.

She took his left hand in both of hers and lifted it for him to see. "Here," she said, tracing a finger around the glove cuff near his wrist. "If I were to insert a finger-tip dot of fluorescent pigment to the cuff of your glove, I could have it slowly move around the edge as time progressed. Much like the movement of a sun. Once it completed a rotation, a day would also pass in Mystal."

A sun on his wrist. Avis wasn't sure what he'd meant by a timing mechanism, but as far as wild ideas went, that one wasn't half bad. He relaxed the hand she held and smiled at her.

"Go for it, beautiful," he said, barely biting back the snarky, '*See? I can too change*' that desperately wanted to be voiced. "And once you're done, we'd better get the girls up. They still haven't eaten or had a bath since we stopped last night."

Clarise nodded in agreement and quickly added the dot of fluorescent gold to Avis' left glove cuff. Then, they went to wake their daughters.

CHAPTER FORTY-NINE

Chaos was big. Every sentient celestial in existence knew that, but Avis doubted how many of them understood just how ridiculously massive it *really* was. Before this trip, he'd be the first to admit he certainly didn't. Yes, it was well established that Mystal was the third largest realm in existence next to the Nexus and Chaos, but the size difference between Chaos and Mystal was insane! Like comparing an ocean to a puddle, the word *enormous* was an insult.

Adding to that, everything was in a constant state of flux, rolling and clashing against itself in a perpetual war of colours and shapes and scents and sounds that sent his rigid senses dizzy. After just a single day's ride, he handed navigation over to Clarise in the hopes that she could guide them through this sensory nightmare. Emphasis on the word 'hope'.

If it were left up to him, they'd all be shockingly lost by now. He already was.

But, perhaps that was the point. If you had no reason for being in Chaos, you weren't welcome. Where other pantheons built walls and raised armies to secure their borders, Chaos kept intruders out simply by existing. Anyone who tried to sneak in uninvited could kiss any sense of direction or distance they travelled goodbye ... and *then* a demon would probably materialise out of the shadows to eat them. Just for good measure.

The bright dot of his glowing timer anchored him in this storm of insanity, and he found himself staring at it for longer and longer periods of time to help ease his agitated mind. It moved in one direction, consistently. The milestones of light signified forward, linear motion, and it was a gift from a shifter. The longer he spent in this ocean, the more he realised benders of any description had no business being here.

Unfortunately, his timer only gave him a representation of hours in a theoretical day, not the numbers of days, weeks and even months that they'd been travelling through Chaos. When the glowing light was near his thumb, he deemed that breakfast. When it was in the middle of his palm, that was lunch. And when it was alongside his little finger, that was when he pulled them all up for the day. The rotation across the back of his hand signified the evening. The girls grew stronger with each rotation, but every 'night' he pulled them up, not willing to risk them the way he had that first day.

It really was the most bizarre thing: to leave a permanent structure after breakfast, ride hard all day and walk right back into that same building to sleep at night. It was definitely disconcerting, but as the number of 'nights' rolled into months, he grew accustomed to this strangeness just as he had everything else. Apparently, (according to Clarise) travelling from the mouth of the Akheron River to Yaru didn't quantify the radius of Chaos as he'd first believed either.

It cut across the corner like a dog-eared page, leaving over ninety-nine percent of the realm unvisited by them. At that point, he really wanted to believe she was exaggerating because that so-called *dog-ear* had taken them longer than it would take to cross the entirety of Mystal. Three months at least. Possibly four.

At first, not knowing precisely how long they'd been in the Chaotic Ocean had been just another question he didn't have an answer for. But as he struggled to find things to keep his mind from turning to mush, it began to bother him. He'd had a finite number of sleeps, so this was one question he should have been able to answer.

But not out here.

Avis took the argument inwards, creating a dreamscape where several versions of himself all faced him. Back and forth they argued the numbers, each remembering different things that had happened during the passages of 'night'. Different meals they'd all eaten. Different conversations with the family. Different ways he'd claimed Clarise when they were alone. That had been the easy part.

Then they had to correlate the different events, because some of them happened on the same night. It seemed like hours before they/he finally settled on a figure of three months, three weeks and a day. Six days short of four months. The instant he returned to the physical realm, he felt depressed.

What was three months, three weeks and a day when dealing with only one percent of a realm? They were still nowhere near Yaru.

He held nothing against the demon steeds that were being pushed to reach the elusive realm, but not a second went by that he didn't wish they were riding mystallions instead.

Even the youngest winged equines of his pantheon would fly rings around these demon steeds and zoom off, nickering at their inadequacies the whole time. Their presence wouldn't make up for the size of the realm, but they'd certainly make this trip to Yaru a lot quicker.

Just as Avis resigned himself to endure this daily process for the rest of his life, Clarise pointed at a looming shadow in the distance. A solid shadowy-blue that didn't move. "The Nun Sea of Yaru," she called over to him, confirming his fondest hope.

"Finally," he moaned in relief. Now he had something on the horizon to focus on. Something to signify the end of this hellish ride.

The next few hours of hard riding forever cemented bluish grey as his new favourite colour.

It wasn't until later that 'night', long after the girls had gone to sleep and Avis had expended a great many hours satisfying his wife in the comfort of their bed, that Clarise said something bizarre to him.

While she was snuggled up to his side with her head on his pec with the fingers of her left hand hooked loosely over his shoulder, he was lying on his back with one hand cupped behind his head; the other tracing light circles around each vertebra of her bare spine. Both were basking in the afterglow of what they'd just shared.

She broke the serenity by whispering quietly against his chest, "Chaos is the opposite of what you expect, beloved."

The nonsensical revelation from nowhere surprised him. He huffed and tightened his arm around her waist, lifting his head to nuzzle her hair. "I know," he replied patronisingly, wondering where in the realms that statement had come from. Next, she'd be telling him Mystallian grass was green and the men of her family hated him.

Clarise huffed at his mockery and rolled up on to his stomach to face him. She pressed her forearms against his pecs and lifted her upper half until her face loomed over his and she could look him in the eye.

The gold of her irises solidified and clashed against itself. *Okay, she's serious about this,* he deduced and gave her his full attention … almost. Those loose locks of hair that fell forward over her nose to tickle his face were too distracting and he simply *had* to put them back over her ear.

Clarise jerked her head upwards, tugging the hair from his grasp. "Avis, focus."

Not a term of endearment. His name. "Okay," he said, sliding his free hand under his head to join the first. "I'm listening."

"Navigating Chaos is a matter of cleansing your mind of all expectations. If you expect the borders to turn up in front of you, they will never be there. If you think you have ridden a long way, you probably have not."

That last part got his undivided attention.

His eye flared with understanding and he suddenly jack-knifed into a sitting position, knocking her almost to his knees. "Are you seriously trying to tell me all this time, we *haven't fucking moved?*" He reached forward and took her face in his hands, willing her to deny what he guessed was true.

She winced at his terminology, but at least she had the modesty to blush. "Yes, and no, beloved. In order to understand Chaos, you must first let go of your preconceptions. Chaos does not follow any order you understand. If you expect a clearing ahead of you, a forest will be there. If you go around that first tree expecting its depth to be the same as its width, that one tree will become an endless wall of bark. It will never do or be what you expect or want of it."

The casual explanation blew his mind. Nothing was real; at the same time, everything was. "How can *anything* live like that?"

The gold in her eyes softened, and she twisted her head to kiss one of his palms. "By being just as unpredictable, my love. Living in a state of flux is not difficult if it is all you know. It's why the souls of the Damned are like currency out here. Neither the demons nor the Chaotic Ocean are able to change their shape, so their essence is very desirable, much like ambrosia is your drink of choice. Their suffering is delicious, and once fully consumed, the Damned soul simply returns to the shores of Hell to start the process all over again."

He knew she'd deliberately changed the subject to give him time to process what she'd initially said, and he tried really hard to follow her into the new conversation. "But the Damned can't … I mean … we had to wait that extra day for Cora … "

His incoherency had absolutely nothing to do with the way the Nun Sea of Yaru had appeared on the horizon only *after* he'd released his expectation of ever seeing it. Honest. Likewise, he was absolutely *not* internally raging because they'd probably just wasted months getting nowhere and she'd known it all along! Not! At! Fucking! All! FUUUCK!

"Only a demon may remove a member of the Damned from Hell, and only if they are both quick and brave enough to risk the ire of the Hellions who control them. I know they may not have looked it at the time, but those shore scavengers outside of Hell were some of the most powerful demons in all of Chaos." His mouth shot open to speak, but she placed a finger across his lips, silencing him. "Demons, my love. The most powerful of the commoners. They are still no match for hellions or the Hellion Highborn."

Avis couldn't give a shit about the demons, and he certainly had no intention of talking about them! With his temper almost at breaking point, what he'd been on the verge of asking was if she had enjoyed making such an utter fool out of him.

Thankfully, she'd cut him off, and for the next few seconds, he breathed in and out, sucking in as much of that lavender fragrance as his lungs could handle and using its calming influence to leash his temper. In and out. Red may have tinged everything inside his vision, but he would never let himself rage at her. Never her. In and out. In and out.

"Avis?" she asked, remaining exactly where she was instead of shifting out of his grasp and saving herself. The love and trust in her eyes joined forces with the perfume until the red tinge receded. His hands softened as the tension left them and he leaned forward to kiss her deeply, driving away the last of his dark thoughts.

"So, you knew … all this time … that we'd hardly moved," he said, getting to the crux of his rage once he thought he had some semblance of control. His thumbs held her cheekbones, but he refrained from shaking her. Just. "Why didn't you tell me how this worked months ago?" There had to be a reason. By the Twin Notes, let there be a *good* reason. One he could get behind.

Clarise's smile lit up his world. Her words, not so much. "I love you with all my heart, beloved, but knowing the truth about the Chaotic Ocean would have been your undoing. If you had known that your desire to be away from Hell was the very thing anchoring us to it, it would have destroyed you.

Reading the dark scowl that he could feel simmering just under the surface, she attempted to placate him. "Not at first, of course. At first, you would have convinced yourself of your ability to defeat it. That in itself would have been an expectation that worked against you on top of all the others. The more you tried not to expect something, the more you would have clung to that new expected outcome, and the deeper into the Chaotic Ocean we would have been dragged. You needed to think you would never get out of Chaos before the Yaru Sea could reveal itself."

She blinked slowly, the gold in her eyes liquifying passionately. "Truth be told, I had not realised before now just how strong-willed you were. You do not give up easily, my love."

Avis cast his mind back to his original capture. He barely remembered the Chaotic Ocean back then and had assumed the speed of his journey through it was due to the number of Highborn Hellions that dragged him in chains towards their homeland.

But this new revelation made him realise it had been his own determination to never reach Hell that had virtually teleported him to Hell's front door. He'd been his own worst fucking enemy!

"Couldn't you have knocked me out or something?" he asked, really wishing he had something solid to punch at that moment other than his precious wife. Preferably a hellish brother-by-marriage or two. "And dragged my sorry backside through?"

Clarise's expression softened, and she stroked his forearms affectionately. "Two things work against that, beloved. First, it is almost impossible to completely turn off a bender's mind, especially one as powerful as yours. Even unconscious, your core would still know what it wanted and would never let go of those expectations easily. You needed to let them go yourself."

Avis removed one hand from her face and dragged his thumb across his parted lips, catching the nail edge on each tooth. "And the other reason?" He hadn't forgotten there'd been two.

Clarise slid her hands up the forearm that supported her face and encased the hand from both sides. She pulled her head away and kissed the tips of his fingers, then speared hers through his, enclosing them in a triple knot of unity. "Because with Yaru now in sight, the time has come for you to take the lead and navigate our way through Chaos."

Avis' eyes rounded in horror. "But I'm a bender!" He barely kept from shouting. "I have no business navigating Chaos! You've just finished telling me I'm the worst kind of anchor in this place, and that's when I'm just a passenger! I'll never get my head around its lack of coherency and the stupid rule of expecting the last thing I expect! Just the thought of it is giving me a monumental headache!"

He wasn't joking. Between the rage he'd felt earlier over this cluster fuck of a situation and his ... *discomfort* (like fuck he would ever admit the word fear) at taking the navigational lead, he could feel his blood pounding in both corners of his eyes, his temples and across the back of his head, indicating a migraine was well on its way.

Clarise kissed his hand again, then released it entirely and rose to kneel on his thighs. Her delicate weight barely registered as her knees dug into the muscles, but it allowed her to tower head and shoulders over him. "I will be right there with you, my love," she promised, cupping his face in her hands. "Every step of the way. My blood flows in your veins, and you need to learn to use it. You will be the first bender to ever bend Chaos to your will."

Avis had to admit, he *really* liked the sound of that, but it still didn't stop the proposed task from seeming impossible to his logical mind. These days he could barely drag his gaze away from the timer she'd given him. To take the lead now that he knew what their motion relied on was madness. He'd go insane trying not to think about where he wanted to be ... but if she had so much faith in him, why didn't he have faith in himself?

Because the whole thing was stupid, of course. Order had no more business controlling Chaos, than Chaos had controlling Order. That was the way of things ... wasn't it? The pros and cons bounced around inside his skull until he thought his brain was going to explode. He closed his eyes and shook his head, raking his fingers through his hair. "I don't know, sweetheart ..."

He felt her weight shift on his legs, and moments later her forehead was pressed into his; her perfume now practically palpable.

"Today, you surrendered to what may never be, and that is how the Nun Sea appeared. Now, with the Nun Sea right in front of you, you need to step up and take us all the way to Yaru. The Nun Sea bleeds from the Chaotic Ocean much like the Akheron River, without having any of its properties. You need to see that distant objective as an anchor-point to work us towards, the same way a fisherman reels in his catch while everything from the fish, to the ocean currents to the weather overhead fight to thwart him. Sideways and backwards are not failures. Not if the end is achieved."

Okay. Look at it like a fishing trip, and don't think about how you've never fished a day in your life. Avis licked his lips apprehensively. He was pretty sure he could do that. "So how do I stop myself from expecting ... everything? I expect you and the girls to be at my side. I expect the demon steed to remain under me and I expect the four brute squad members to always be protecting us. How do I deny those expectations?"

"By not thinking about them," she answered easily. "The fisherman does not think about whether or not his house is still standing while he fights his catch. He does not wonder if the rain will fall that afternoon or if his wife is at home preparing the evening meal. He focuses on the task at hand. Stay focused, Avis, and believe in the opposite of what you want."

"So, all I have to do is convince myself of how much I *don't* want to be in Yaru, and we'll get there tomorrow?"

Her expression softened indulgently, and she leaned forward to kiss him. "I am afraid it will never be quite that quick, beloved. Chaos picks up on every nuance of your expectations, and you will never be completely able convince yourself you do not wish to arrive in Yaru. That is where the winding from side to side comes into it."

"Tacking," Avis corrected automatically. His head buzzed with so much information now that he couldn't quite come to terms with it all, and in that moment, he internalised this discussion.

In his dreamscape he created several versions of himself and Clarise to try and make sense of it all. He needed to get his mind around this and create a plan of attack so that when he rejoined the physical realm, he'd once again be in control. The problem with that was, the information he had was all he had. Chaos played by stupid rules, and to navigate Chaos, he had to think like a moronic demon.

There was no way to plan for that. He couldn't set himself up with a series of thoughts to think in a specific order to get him where he wanted to go. The second he expected those thoughts to work, they wouldn't. It was insane, and it didn't matter whether he was having this discussion with one version of himself and Clarise or fifty.

No adaptation of himself could get past the absurdity of the situation, and every one of his created Clarises insisted he could. The heated argument that went exactly nowhere only lasted a few minutes before he gave up and returned to the physical realm. The pounding behind his eyes increased tenfold.

"What would you require tacks for?" Clarise's expression was one of genuine confusion.

The nonsensical question startled Avis, and for a moment he stared at her uncomprehendingly. *Wha ...?* Then he realised. *Oh.*

"Tacking, sweetheart. Not tacks. It's a nautical term. Or, at least that's what two of Armina's grandkids keep telling me. Apparently, it's how boats correct their position on the water when the wind is not favourable, so I'm guessing the same thing applies to landing a fish."

"I think your way of thinking has more in common with Chaos than you would like to believe," Clarise groused, her brow furrowing just a little. When Avis arched one eyebrow inquisitively, she said, "You are using a descriptive word that has no bearing on the subject at hand to explain an outcome it has nothing to do with."

Any other time, he'd have thrown his head back and howled with laughter at her interpretation of the Mystallian language. But right now, he just couldn't get past the enormity of the task she'd proposed to him, and he apprehensively pinched his bottom lip between this thumb and forefinger instead. "Do you really think I can do this?"

"Surely you are not afraid ..."

Just like that, the thread of control Avis had on his temper snapped, and rage soared back to life, this time specifically at her. His body tensed under her and a vicious snarl made it to the back of his throat before he could catch it. He knew she'd only meant to bait him, to force him to rise above the issue and succeed when he might have otherwise faltered, but she had no idea how well it worked.

Mystallians feared no one and killed anyone stupid enough to ever think they did. Except for the last two years, and that was part of Hell's own thrall of the Damned working against him, he hadn't feared anything in a very long time. Others feared him, as well they should.

Fury surged like acid through his veins, turning his vision completely red. No one called him a coward! No one! Almost tossing her away (though he made sure she landed with a bounce on the mattress beside him), he threw his feet over the side of the bed and used the motion to flip himself upright. He couldn't be around her right now.

He'd hurt her so fucking badly and spend the rest of his life regretting it. "Stay," he barked, pointing a single finger behind him as he stormed from the bedroom and into the sitting room. His teeth clenched until he felt the muscles in his jaw twitch and jump as he tried to convince himself she didn't mean it. She hadn't meant to call him a coward.

Still, on the heels of his last rage, his blood wanted—no—*demanded* retribution and his refusal to comply took the pain in his head to a soaring migraine.

The opulent furnishings did little to calm his ire. If anything, the presence of such Mystallian luxury fuelled his rage. They were, for all intents and purposes, standing in a mini-Mystal where he was all-powerful! *She should've known!*

But their presence did give him something to lash out at other than her, and he did so with gusto. Storming around the room, he kicked and punched everything foolish enough to be in his way, shattering it all upon impact.

Yet nothing helped. He felt like a caged animal.

And then his nose caught the first whiffs of her lavender scent, causing him to come to a standstill alongside the marble fireplace. His hands gripped the corner of the mantelpiece until his knuckles were as pale as the marble wall beside them and his breath escaped in angry pants. "I told you to stay in the room," he growled, tensing as her arms slid around his waist from behind.

"Beloved, I am so sorry." He felt her lips peppering kisses across his back, leaving a series of damp spots against his skin. "Avis. Avis, turn around and look at me. Please?"

At that, he did, whirling sharply on his heel and twisting her with him so that he had her pinned to the wall alongside the fireplace before she could do little more than gasp and recoil from his fury. Something deep inside his brain hammered a warning as he swung his right clenched fist in the direction of her face and at the last second, he shifted its trajectory and smashed it through the external wall right beside her head instead, burying his arm to the elbow.

"Beg for nothing!" he roared, the words shouted out so lethally she shuddered at the volume, though she did stand her ground. "I won't have it, Clarise! If I could scrub just one word out of your vocabulary, I swear by the Twin Notes of all Creation that'd be it! You humiliate us both when you beg like that!"

CHAPTER FIFTY

Clarise wasn't sure what happened. One moment, they were talking about the future and how he would be the first bender to ever conquer the Chaotic Ocean, and the next, he snapped and reverted to the monster he'd been all those years ago. When he stormed from the room and started destroying the furniture next door, part of her wanted to gather up the girls and run back to the Well, just as she had in the past.

But there was a difference in his behaviour, and that gave her hope. A tiny flicker of hope but hope none the less. In the past, *she* had been the target of his abuse, and it had been brutal, even savage. He'd forbidden her the use of shapeshifting just seconds into their marriage, and soon after that, he'd been reminded the hard way that their shared blood put her mind beyond his mental attacks.

She'd seen that moment of realisation in his eyes, right before he decided to use his fists instead. A lot. Their wedding night had been a blur of pain and tears, and in the months that followed, even pregnant as she'd been, black eyes and broken bones had been a common part of her daily existence.

If Cora hadn't been able to safeguard herself during those times, she'd have never been born.

This was different. This time *he* had left the room to go on his rampage, after telling her to stay where she'd be safe. He'd known how angry he was, and he hadn't wanted to show it in front of her. The old Avis would never have done that. He'd have made sure *she* was the one to crawl away from *him*.

Now she was faced with a choice. Stay, like the dutiful little Highborn Hellion wife she'd been raised to be and wait for him to decide when he'd return to her, or meet the monster in his lair and stand her ground when he roared. Six months ago, the latter would never have been an option.

Obedience was the most highly prized aspect of a Highborn Hellion wife, and she knew if she followed him after he ordered her to stay away, in the eyes of her family she would deserve anything that came of it.

The problem was … she hadn't exactly been just a Highborn Hellion wife in a long time, and whether he knew it or not, Avis needed her. The noise next door wasn't subsiding. If anything, the furniture that he'd originally kicked out of his way was now being lifted and hurled into the walls as his fury escalated.

She wasn't concerned about Columbine's bedroom being right next door. The walls were strong and, to prevent the child from growing curious at the noises which she and Avis made during their love-making, had been soundproofed from day one.

Clarise frowned, trying to work out what she'd said to set him off. For the life of her, she had no idea. The last happy moment was when they'd been talking about some type of navigational fishing tacks, and he'd expressed vulnerability as he asked her if she thought he could really do it.

"Oh, my word," she whispered, remembering exactly how she'd answered that. Both hands covered her mouth just as another piece of furniture shattered against the wall. She hadn't just poked the bear. She'd *piked* it. "Oh, Avis."

She slid from the bed and quickly crossed the room to stand in the open doorway. The shredded remains of the sitting room spoke volumes to Avis' state of mind. Blinded as he was, when he ran out of things to break, he turned his attention to the fireplace itself. His fingers hooked into the corner of the golden mantle and his muscles tensed as if he planned to rip it from the wall.

Despite the destructive carnage around him, Clarise saw a different vision of the man she'd dedicated her life to. His chest heaved as if he'd been running for months and his motions were jarring, as if he couldn't quite decide how he wanted to proceed. He was hurting on the inside and lashing out because he wanted something else to hurt more than he did.

To fear him, as he feared … what? *What hideousness in your past has you so twisted that mere words can bring you to this, my love?* Clarise couldn't bear another moment of it. This was all her fault.

Breaking her cardinal rule of 'maintaining decorum above all else', she rushed across the room while his back was to her and wrapped her arms around his waist before he could haul the mantle free. Tension and hatred and determination all rolled off his skin in waves as she buried her face in the middle of his back.

"I told you to stay in the bedroom." The guttural noise barely registered as words, but his meaning was clear. *Leave.*

"Beloved, I am so sorry." Not knowing what else to do, she squeezed him tightly and began covering his back in tiny, feathery kisses, willing him to hear her now, as he had heard her then. "Avis. Avis, turn around and look at me. Please?"

At that, he did: exactly as she asked and much faster than she'd anticipated. His face was thunderous, his eyes glazed with so much wild fury they practically glowed. He clenched his fist and brought it to his shoulder and in that instant, she was transported to another time when that fist had landed repeatedly.

She gasped but didn't move, readying herself for the painful impact.

Instead, he smashed it through the external wall right beside her head, peppering her face and hair with marble shards. "Beg for nothing!" he roared, though she barely heard it over the blood pounding in her ears. Her head swam with relief so profound it was all she could do to focus on the fact he hadn't hit her. Proof that he was a changed man, and this had been the right course of action.

She hoped.

Avis hadn't finished. "I won't have it, Clarise!" he ranted, practically spitting the words in her face. "If I could scrub just one word out of your vocabulary, I swear by the Twin Notes of all Creation that'd be it! You humiliate us both when you beg like that!"

Clarise mustered every bit of self-control she possessed. The precipice they were on demanded she meet him as an equal. If they were to move forward from this, in a future where they stood side-by-side, she couldn't allow a single trace of fear to enter her voice.

"Very well," she said, never once taking her eyes off his. She locked her body in place to prevent it from trembling and ran her tongue across her parched lips, not missing the way he followed the movement with his eyes. *Please, please let me be right about this …* "… on one condition."

Avis' nostrils flared as he sucked in an explosive breath, but she placed her hand over his heart before he could erupt again. "My condition is that you forgive me, beloved. Truly forgive me. What I said in the bedroom was playful banter at best, and I swear as long as I live it will never be repeated, but I want … I need to know that you can let this go and put it behind us."

She gave him a few moments to digest what she'd said, never once weakening in her resolve. There was every chance this could blow up in her face. He'd been so violent just seconds ago, and clearly, his temper was far from subdued. But if he didn't do this—if he couldn't or wouldn't meet her halfway—she'd go back to living in fear of him, and he'd given her too much self-respect for that. "Look me in the eye, Avis, and tell me I am forgiven."

Avis gritted his teeth and looked over her head instead. The veins in his neck pounded and his chest continued to heave, then she heard the crumbling of marble chips as he freed his hand from the wall. His jaw worked in tight circles, and his gaze dodged all around her, deliberately avoiding eye contact.

The edges of Clarise's resolve began to wither, and her fingers curled ever so slowly into the hair of his chest. "*Am* I forgiven, Avis?" It took a lot to not have that sounding as whiny and insecure as she suddenly felt, and she wasn't completely convinced she'd succeeded.

Regardless, the effect on Avis was instantaneous. His head dropped down to hers, and he stepped forward in a blur of movement, lifting her off the ground and pinning her to the wall by his hips, thighs and torso alone. With their faces now level, he smashed his lips against hers, forcing them open … demanding they open, and then his tongue was inside her mouth, seeking out hers. Clarise sucked in a panicked breath at the blitz attack, but it only increased the urgency in Avis.

He pushed himself further into her space, robbing her of the chance to breathe for herself. Finally, she relented, and he sucked her tongue into his mouth. As they continued to kiss, he maneuvered her legs without penetrating her so that she sat on his hips. At the same time his hands slid along her arms until he knotted their fingers together and held them high over her head.

He was back in control. Her husband had returned. Thank the Twin Notes. Back and forth their tongues sawed. Over and over they twisted their heads as if neither could get enough of the physical contact.

* * *

"*Am* I forgiven, Avis?"

Time froze for Avis, or maybe it was his own blood turning to ice in his veins; his rage utterly abandoned. The way Clarise looked up at him with such uncertainty, he wanted to reach inside his chest and rip out his own heart for her. That was how she'd reacted to the old him. He never wanted to see that look of desolation in her eyes again, and when she vocalised her doubt in them, he knew he had to move quickly while there was still hope.

Acting on impulse, Avis surged forward into her space, lifting her off the floor and pinning her to the wall until their faces were level. He loved the feel of her skin sliding over his, but now wasn't the time for making love. Not when peace and stability between them were so much more important. Nor did he want to use words. Not for this.

She needed to *feel* precisely how important she was to him. Using his hips and chest, he crushed her to the wall, freeing his hands to seek out hers just as anxiously as his tongue sought entry into her mouth.

He almost cried when her lips softened to grant him access. He definitely moaned. His body writhed against hers as he continued to kiss her, but he wouldn't let himself cross the line into sex. He had taken power from her by losing control of himself and letting her decide that moment of union was his only way of giving it back to her.

When their lips finally parted, her next words shocked the hell out of him. "Make love to me in the middle of the sitting room floor."

Avis jerked his head away to stare at her. Surely, she had to be joking! When her expression said otherwise, he looked over his shoulder at the absolute carnage behind him. Fabrics were shredded, timber and glass panels were smashed, and jagged metal frames littered the floor. He'd been extremely thorough in his rampage.

The double doors beyond the mess that led to the bedroom on his left still hung open, offering them a far more comfortable and intact environment for the pleasure he had in mind. She couldn't seriously want to do this here.

Clarise pulled one of her hands free and laid it against his cheek, drawing his attention back to her. Her eyes were filled with love and promise. "We will not hide from what happened in this room by retreating to another. I refuse to live in fear of it. We will make this space our own again and move forward together."

Unable to believe the magnitude of his good fortune, Avis' heart soared until he practically melted into a puddle of sheer happiness. She couldn't have said a more Mystallian thing if she tried! Unknotting his fingers, he cupped her backside in both hands and lifted her away from the wall. "As you wish," he said, carrying her to the central-most point in the room, regardless of the debris.

He used his elbows to pin her legs high onto his back, then lowered himself to his knees, refusing to show one hint of discomfort as the broken shards dug into his flesh. More debris buried into his ass as he sat down, but he took this as his due. He would be on the bottom. Nothing else would be acceptable to him.

She may have feared what had been done to the room, but he would bear the pain of it. His weight ground them home, but all he saw was the woman perched in his lap. He still had her. That was worth any amount of discomfort.

As he laid back, he curled his hands around her knees to shield them from harm. "I am yours to do with as you please, my queen."

CHAPTER FIFTY-ONE

"Are you sure Tal is the one with the bad temper, beloved?" Clarise teased, her eyes creasing in amusement as she traced light, swirling patterns through his chest hair. After two solid hours of hot and heavy sex that began in the sitting room and ended in the bedroom, the pair were once again stretched out across the master bed.

Avis had been cut to ribbons during that short journey across the floor but ask him right now if he cared. The memory of Clarise's squeal of outrage when she realised the blood trail from the middle of the sitting room was his and the fuss she'd made afterwards had him still grinning like a schoolboy. She'd flipped him over and immediately turned every single piece of debris still embedded in him to water, scolding him the entire time for not informing her of the injuries sooner.

He hadn't been angered by the sharpness of tone. If anything, he'd been too relieved to know she was over his tantrum in the sitting room. As each shard lost consistency and either dribbled from the wounds or was absorbed by his body, his own celestial physique had healed the lacerations in seconds.

"We still have a house, don't we?" he asked in return, dusting her nose with the tips of her long ebony hair which he'd been playing with. "Tal would've brought it all to the ground if he was left to his own devices." Which was true... to a point. The big guy was always on his best behaviour whenever he and Avis crossed paths—mainly because Destruction knew if he wasn't, Avis would have no problem exorcising the memories that caused his bad behaviour and he'd forget why he'd lost his temper in the first place.

Clarise lifted her head off his chest and smiled down at him, but worry crowded her eyes. She pursed her delicate lips and huffed a quick breath, blowing the hair from his fingers. Her own hand stilled against his chest. "Would you mind answering one thing for me, Avis?"

Avis noted each of the subtle changes in her as they occurred and readied himself for an uncomfortable conversation. Her question only heightened his suspicions. "Of course," he answered with more enthusiasm than he thought he could muster.

"Why does the thought of being mocked cause such a violent reaction in your family?"

Called it, he thought, refusing to answer her straight away. How could he, when his first instinct was to shout out in the strongest possible terms that there was nothing wrong with taking offence to being ridiculed and only an idiot would ask something so moronic. He hadn't been a devoted husband long, but he was pretty sure calling your wife an idiot in anger sat at the top of the sexual suicide list, right alongside irreversible castration with a blunt butter knife. Avis dropped his head back on to the pillow and searched the silk drapes overhead for inspiration.

Seconds ticked by, and he still had nothing. Nothing that wouldn't sound like he was baiting her anyway. He lowered his eyes to meet her molten gold stare. "The men in your family don't take kindly to it either, sweetheart," he countered, knowing that from personal experience and hoping the inclusion of her family to the problem would see an end to the awkward subject. "No one likes being made a fool of."

"True," Clarise conceded, rolling up on to his body; her lush onyx hair creating a curtain around their faces once more. "But Mystallians take that dislike to a very unhealthy level. I love you, Avis, and I know you love me. Yet five words from me in the privacy of our bedroom had you destroying an entire room in a fit of rage, and afterwards, you assure me your more aggressive brother would have destroyed the whole house for the same supposed *atrocity*." She arched away from him and held her thumb and forefinger marginally apart between their faces. "Do you not see how that might be perceived by some as just a little touch of overkill?"

Avis disagreed. Strenuously. "Mockery implies weakness, and weakness will always be exploited in the worst possible way. It must be stamped out as soon as it's spoken, or it will come back to bite us. Every time."

If he'd hoped that would end the matter, he was sadly mistaken. Suddenly, the gold in Clarise's eyes hardened into peaks, and she pulled herself up to straddle his waist. "Do you think I would exploit you?" she demanded icily.

"No!" Avis couldn't get that out fast enough. He was still shaking his head as he sat up, sliding her into his lap. His hands banded around her waist, both to support her and keep her with him. "That's not what I meant at all, sweetheart."

Clarise's gaze narrowed, and the muscle under her left eye twitched as if gauging the validity of his statement. "Then perhaps you should explain what you *do* mean, Avis, since we are alone and have been most of the night. Who else do you believe could exploit what we have discussed in the privacy of our bedroom, if not me?"

Avis pinched his lips together tightly and raked the fingers of one hand through his hair. There was no way he could answer that without explaining things he didn't want to explain. Was he the most powerful mind bender in existence?

No. His memories could be searched, and in the far distant past, they had been. Mystallians didn't have the Highborn Hellion upbringing. They didn't protect the weak. They were too busy protecting themselves and hoping they weren't seen as the weakest link. Weakness had always been targeted by Theodrick first and foremost, and implied weakness, if left unchallenged, became actual weakness. It *made* you his next target.

"It doesn't matter that we're alone, Clarise. *I* will know it's been said, and *I* will know if I did or didn't react accordingly to it. Either way will cost me dearly. Either I react as I should and lose you forever, or I sit on my reaction and forever dwell on what I should have done. As the ruler of Mystal, I cannot second-guess myself like that. None of us can. Indecision invites…" *Chaos*, he was about to say, inciting one of his father's catch-all phrases as to why it should never be tolerated, right before the offender was made to regret ever being conceived. Avis released all the air in his lungs and lowered his raised hand to her backside, squeezing it lightly. "Just… trust me on this, sweetheart. Banter that suggests inadequacies or failure on our part is never going to be tolerated by a Mystallian, especially the first generation. All of us will have the same reaction to it. Even the runt."

Staring as he was into Clarise's eyes, he noticed a strange glint enter them momentarily. It was gone just as quickly as it came but Avis knew she'd deduced something. Something unpleasant. "The only person outside the Nexus whose mind I can't read is the one person whose mind I'd give anything to read right now," he murmured, hooking her hair in behind her ear and brushing the back of his knuckles against her cheek. "What are you thinking, sweetheart?"

"Nothing that pleases me," Clarise admitted, tilting her head to rub her face against his fingers, relishing the contact. "But I think perhaps it goes a long way to explaining many of the motives behind the Mystallian way of thinking."

Hoping she wasn't as intuitive as she sounded, Avis gently ran his hand around her neck until it was hooked around the nape and drew her to him, kissing her deeply. "Don't worry about us, sweetheart," he murmured against her lips. "It's ancient, ancient prehistory. Just promise me you won't belittle any of us again, even in jest. It wouldn't be a good day for Mystal if you said something to set off one of the others and they hurt you for it. The throwdown that person and I'd have afterwards would forever tear Mystal apart."

Clarise draped her arms down either side of his body and snuggled into his chest. "You would really pick me over your own sibling?" she cooed playfully.

Avis pressed his lips to her forehead, banding his arms around her tightly. "In a heartbeat, beautiful." He meant every syllable.

"I love you too."

CHAPTER FIFTY-TWO

Avis may not have considered himself a coward, but as they mounted up later that morning and he saw the dark grey shadow on the horizon, he was certainly apprehensive. To *get* there, he had to genuinely convince himself he didn't want to *be* there without going mad in the process. He breathed in deeply and released it through tense lips.

This was by far the most insane thing he had ever tried to achieve, and he wasn't sure he had the mindset to release that much control.

"Ready?" Clarise asked, anticipating his nervousness.

He nodded, but only because it was expected of him. "Let's do this."

The next four days were … *Hell*. Every time he saw Yaru coming closer, he grew excited by his success and their very next step sent it back into the distance. Back and forth they see-sawed, and the longer this went on, the more determined he became to not let it defeat him.

So, of course, the more it did. Quite a few times he looked over his shoulder to see if anyone found his frustration amusing, hoping against hope that one of the servants might. He was at the point he wanted to hurt something. Badly.

"Try convincing yourself how much you want to go back to the Akheron River," Clarise suggested from the middle of their bed, after the fourth night of getting precisely nowhere.

"Do you have any idea what you're asking?" Avis demanded incredulously, snapping at the only person willing to speak to him in the last day and a half. "You want me to want to go back to the last place I would ever want to go back to, just so I don't end up going back there!" Realising the gobbledygook he'd just spoken, he threw his hands up in disgust and stormed into their bathroom, banging the doors closed behind him.

He stripped his clothes in frustrated motions, throwing each of them to the ground in a heated curse. He was never going to get his head around it! They were going to be stuck here on the fringes of Chaos forever, and all because he couldn't think stupidly enough to get them out!

A full decanter of ambrosia waited on the side of his bath, and he snatched it up, drinking over half of it directly from the bottle in a single breath. The familiar, alcoholic burn as it scorched its way to his stomach soothed his irritation, and he released his breath in a frustrated huff.

How, as a bender, was he ever expected to get them out of here?

He stepped into the bath and sat with his back against the wall, his hand still clasping the neck of the decanter. The hot water complemented the liquor and helped assuage his mood—dwindling it to a vile simmer.

He probably shouldn't have snapped at Clarise. Especially since she was only trying to help. But really, try convincing himself to go back to the Akheron River? Hell had *tortured* him! For two fucking years! There was no way he could convince himself to go back there! No way!

YOU'VE GOT A FUCK-TONNE BETTER FUCKING CHANCE OF WANTING A REALM-DAMNED REUNION WITH THOSE SHAPELESS FUCKING FUCKWITS SHE FUCKING CALLS FAMILY.

Avis raised the half-empty decanter to toast his subconscious' insight. *Damn right!* He wanted nothing to do with any of those despicable sons of bit … Realisation flashed through his mind, and he suddenly straightened, lifting his back off the bath wall. *Wait! That's it!*

More excited than he'd been in days, he dropped the decanter in the bath and launched out of the tub, hurtling back into the bedroom where he'd left Clarise. Still in the middle of the bed, she gasped in surprise at the wet mess he must have been, but now wasn't the time for that.

He rushed to the edge of the bed and crawled across the mattress towards her. "Not all of your brothers are in Hell all the time," he stated, thrilled to finally have a solution that would work in his favour!

"That is true, beloved," she answered cautiously.

"Which ones put us on a direct vector with Yaru?" His excitement should have been infectious and the reason obvious, but instead of replying, Clarise's frown increased until Avis wanted to shake some sense into her. "Which one's realm of establishment puts them on the same vector as the Nun Sea and us?" he insisted, taking her upper arms in his broad hands. He may have *jiggled* her a little. "Which ones, sweetheart? Think! It's really important!"

"Why?"

"Because those fuck …those *brothers* of yours are some of the last people I ever want to see again! If they're on the other side of the Nun Sea, I can literally not want to reach *them* and still get drawn straight to Yaru!"

Clarise's eyes shone with delight, and she threw her arms around his neck, lifting herself on to her knees to hug his naked wetness tightly. "I knew you could do it," she said against his ear.

Avis returned the hug, happier than he'd been in a long time. That was the key to navigating Chaos. Or, at least some of it. Head towards something you had no desire to head towards. It was probably why no one sentenced to Hell ever escaped.

The dream of freedom was all-encompassing, and that very desire made it impossible. "So, who lines up?" he asked, almost wishing it was dawn rather than dusk. He wanted to try his theory.

"If Pluton is in Olympus, or Uriel in Heaven, either of those would pull you in the right direction. You may possibly catch Ahriman and Yima on the right-hand side of the Nun Sea, but that would depend on where in their realm they are."

"Before we leave tomorrow, I need you to find out which one of them is in their established realm—preferably Pluton or Uriel. Don't tell them why, or they'll leave it on principle just to screw with me. Then, all I have to do is focus on how much I don't want to reach them, and we'll be on our way."

Clarise beamed happily. "We will indeed."

* * *

Belial sat forward on his throne. His elbows were wedged against the armrests and his fingers bounced lightly off each other as he drummed his long talons together. His gaze was unseeing.

Beelzebub stood stoically at his side.

Everyone else seemed to pick up on his dark mood, for the great room that was normally a hive of activity had been completely vacated. Even the servants had found other places to be. Eventually, the supreme demon lifted his gaze and parted his hands, rolling his right wrist. "Uriel."

An image of his eldest son appeared between him and the spyhole he had on Avis, hovering somewhere where crimson stars and an insipid olive-green sky created the spatial backdrop. It could have been anywhere.

The front of Uriel's armour and much of his face and blond hair were plastered in blood. His right hand gripped the hilt of his hellfire blade; gore dripping from his knuckles. "Father," he sang in the harmonic tone that indicated he was representing Heaven. He suddenly ducked low, diving beneath a large, serrated pollex that swung from right to left in a decapitating motion.

He popped up a moment later, cleaving his opponent in two. Belial's gaze narrowed at the combative display. This must have been a sport ... or a practice of some kind. Uriel's shape shifting mastery over any one individual was almost absolute and he had no need to sully himself with physical interactions.

That theory was confirmed when nothing else engaged the archangel, who then straightened to his full height with his sword of fire at his side and dipped his head in silent reverence of his father.

"Is your business concluded where you are?" Belial asked, getting straight to the point.

His son dipped his head again and sheathed his sword of fire. "It is now, Father."

Uriel's willingness to capitulate meant wherever he was, he wasn't in the realm of harmony. If he had been in Heaven, his thrall would have forced him to be utterly devoted to the Almighty and no one else. Fortunately, he became his own man again the moment he left Heaven and he could choose his own priorities and allegiances.

During these latter times, Belial was never relegated to second place. Ever.

"Good. I want you back in Heaven for the next few days. Clean yourself up. Clarise will be contacting you shortly. You will not question her reasons for the contact and you will maintain your civility throughout the conversation. There will be no repercussions for this interaction."

To his credit, Uriel brought his right hand across his chest and bowed at the waist without argument. "As you wish, Father," he sang, still heavily entrenched in his heavenly persona. A stimulation wave swept through him as he straightened, discarding every speck of blood and gore from his armour and body; returning him to a state of physical perfection.

Belial nodded his approval. "Now go." With every expectation of being obeyed, Belial broke the contact before his son could speak again and refocused on the private spyhole he had on Avis.

For the better part of half an hour, he'd been watching the boy in this manner, grinding his fangs at the Mystallian's brattish behaviour towards Clarise. But it seemed he wasn't the only one watching his newest son-by-marriage, because just as Belial was about to burst a more prominent blood vessel in the fool's head and trigger another punishing headache, Avis had been brazenly handed a way out of Chaos by the only other person capable of it.

I STILL CAN'T FUCKING BELIEVE YOU'RE JUST GOING TO LET HER FUCKING GO! SHE'S THE REALM-DAMNED, MOTHER-FUCKING WEAVER AND YOU'RE JUST LETTING HER FUCKING GO! WHAT THE FUCK IS WRONG WITH YOU, YOU FUCK-HEADED FUCKWIT?

Well, that took even less time than I thought. Belial breathed out a slow, smoky breath and lifted his gaze past Avis and Clarise to where his counterpart's ghostly image hovered nearby. ***You were the one who expedited their departure,*** he sent in reminder.

Theodrick snarled and banged his fists on his armrests, growing more incensed by the second. *YOU FUCKING ASSHOLE! BE FUCKED IF I'D EVER FUCKING LET YOU GET AWAY WITH INSTIGATING MY BOY'S FUCKING MENTAL BREAKDOWN!*

Because you see that as your personal prerogative? the Shifter mused to himself, though openly he sent, ***Your problem is you lack trust in your own offspring ...***

AND YOU LACK A FUCKING BRAIN! FOR FUCK'S SAKE, YOU FUCKING IDIOT! THEY'RE STILL REALM-DAMNED, MOTHER-FUCKING KIDS! YOU CAN'T FUCKING LEAVE SOMETHING THIS FUCKING IMPORTANT TO THEM! THEY'LL FUCK IT UP IF YOU DON'T TAKE FUCKING CONTROL!

Belial allowed his lips to twitch upwards. ***Scared if anything happens to her, you will cease to be an arrogant bully?***

There was a blissful moment of icy silence, but it wasn't to last long.

SHE AIN'T THE FUCKING WEAVER YET, the Nexus master growled coldly.

But we both know she will be.

This time, thankfully, the silence endured.

CHAPTER FIFTY-THREE

The following morning, long before his glove indicated dawn, Avis' excitement got the better of him and he quickly dressed, having every intention of walking laps around the outer boundary to burn off excess energy. Today was going to be different. Today *would* be different.

If everything went according to plan, he'd master the realm of Chaos, and by 'tonight' he would see a real Yarusian nightfall. Mindful that Clarise was still asleep in bed after yet another … *busy* night, he crept through the bedroom and into the sitting room. There, he turned and cautiously closed the double doors, holding both handles to make the sealing click as quiet as possible.

He was so focused on the task that he almost leapt out of his skin when a pair of tiny, demonic arms wrapped around his thighs and squeezed. "Morning, Father," Columbine sang cheerily from his hip.

With both his arms high over his head and every finger flexing wildly, his logical brain scrambled to overcome his fright. Then he locked every muscle from his torso to his feet and jerked his gaze downwards. The underside of Columbine's beak lay along his hip, those eyeless recesses staring up at him adoringly.

Avis released a heavy gasp and struggled to get his hammering heartrate back under control. "Morning, princess," he croaked, twisting inside her grip. He dropped one arm across the back of her head to squeeze her shoulder in an awkward hug.

"By the Twin Notes, I am *so* getting you a bell just as soon as your mother wakes up, young lady." He didn't even want to think about how disastrously that could have gone if he'd followed through with his …*surprise* and come out swinging. He might have hurt her.

No, the rational part of his mind corrected unhelpfully. *I'd have fucking killed her.* Her eye ridges arched upwards in concern, but he forced himself to smile weakly and rub the back of her head and neck. "I didn't hear you sneaking up on me, baby, and if I'd stepped back at the wrong time, I … I might have stood on you." *Yeah, let's go with that as the worst-case scenario.*

"You are so much happier today, Father."

He crooked a grin, unable to deny it. "I think we're finally getting out of here, princess." As he spoke, the reflection of his glowing glove cuff against her dark wings caught his eye; reminding him of the early hour. Rolling his wrist to better see the back of his hand, he noted the glow's exact location just under his pointer finger—indicating they had at least two hours until 'dawn'.

Annnnnd there went his good mood.

His eyes narrowed at her suspiciously. "Just how long have you been up, princess?"

For someone lacking Mystallian features, Avis could've sworn he saw guilt sweep across her face. "I-I … not long, Father," she stammered, in such a blatant lie it was laughable; only he wasn't laughing. To add insult to injury, she broke eye contact with him and twisted her head to stare over her shoulder at the brute squad guard standing just inside the open doors that led to the dining room. The deliberate dodge irritated the fuck out of him.

"I woke up ... and as soon as I saw how happy you were ... I wanted to be with you." At that point she did look back at him, her beak quivering fearfully. "I am sorry, Father. I know I should have waited for Diviten to see to me first, but ..."

Her choice of words had a profound effect on Avis, for two very important details occurred to him. One: she was far more worried about his reaction to her leaving her quarters without Diviten's approval than she was about lying to him about how long she'd been up, which meant Two: she wasn't lying at all.

Her apprehension stemmed from her Highborn Hellion upbringing clashing with the Mystallian attitude he wanted from her. To be subservient, but dominant. The two positions were polar opposites that left her vibrating in the middle like a magnet, unable to be drawn definitively to either side.

He was going to have to keep that in mind and not draw false conclusions about her hesitancy. Very little caused a Mystallian to dance around a subject like this, which meant when it happened, the reason was drastic. An example that came to mind was when Tal accidentally destroyed one of Chance's favourite mortal worlds while the runt had been out of the realm visiting his wife's family.

(Thinking back, that had actually been quite funny to watch the huge mountain of a god with his shoulder's hunched in remorse, while the runt less than a quarter of his size ranted at him about the loss of his favourite party world.)

The last thing a Mystallian cared about was the state in which another Mystallian staggered out of their room, and concern over the supposed 'atrocity' of not gaining a servant's approval first was asinine. Servants were like furniture; there for convenience. They weren't there to be obeyed.

But despite all of this, it was Columbine's choice of words that he needed to address first and foremost ... like yesterday. Before anyone from his side of the family interacted with her and pegged her lack of inner strength for the weakness it was. Her willingness to backtrack at every little thing ... to grovel and apologise ... to offer excuses that ended in a but ... those *were* cardinal sins in Mystal, and no one in his family would tolerate it.

Envisioning their reactions, Avis pinched his lips together and bristled protectively. No one would be stupid enough to say or do anything while he remained on hand, but he knew he wouldn't always be around to stop them. And with Columbine's sensitivity and eagerness to please, their taunts and rough-handedness would be nothing short of devastating to her.

He had to fix this. Immediately.

With his course of action decided, Avis reached down and hooked her under the arms, already moving forward as he lifted her into the air to distance himself from the bedroom behind him. In a move most parents and governesses had perfected since the beginning of time, he swung her weight up and to the right, using the downward momentum to settle her on his hip with his arm supporting her around the waist. The other cradled her shoulder close to his chest.

She squawked at the manhandling, but he held her tightly against him and carried her towards the dining room. "Sshhh, you'll wake your mother, princess."

* * *

Trusting her father in all things, Columbine nestled against him with her arms wrapped around his neck and her beak resting on his shoulder as he carried her towards the doors leading to the dining hall. She hadn't said a word to contradict him about her mother, but her eyes remained fixed on the closed bedroom doors behind him.

The colourful shape on the other side of the doors had been standing there ever since she'd pounced on her father and he'd let out a shriek of fright without meaning to. Columbine wondered why her mother chose to remain inside the room instead of coming out to join them, but as always, she never openly questioned her elders' motives.

By the time her father had them over halfway across the room, the bedroom doors fell silently ajar and she knew her mother had disintegrated the door latch rather than risk the noise of opening it the traditional way. Her mother peered through the opening, and when she realised Columbine was watching her, her eyes flashed demonically in warning and she raised a silencing finger to her lips.

Columbine's chest plates rumbled with delight, and the fingers of her right hand lifted off her father's far shoulder in a soft fingertip wave. Clarise's lips parted in a warm smile that went all the way to her eyes in response and she blew her a silent, two-fingered kiss that ended with a matching fingertip wave. Then she stepped back into the bedroom and closed the doors, recreating the latch to keep them shut.

* * *

Oblivious to their interaction, Avis carried Columbine to the far end of the dining room where he sat at the head of the table and kicked the rear leg of his chair to swing it partially towards him. Then he sat down and deposited her on the table right in front of him. He deliberately corralled her small frame with his elbows and cupped her face in his hands, though to keep her relaxed, he dusted the sides of her beak with his thumbs. "Alright, princess. What I'm going to say is really, really important, so I want you to listen to me very carefully, okay?"

He gritted his teeth when she fell back on her Highborn upbringing of nodding silently against his palms and forced himself to breathe through his irritation. *One battle at a time,* he reminded himself. "Don't ever, *ever* backtrack, baby. Never, ever, ever. Not for any reason."

Columbine's eye ridges arched and merged into one just under her horn knobs and he realised she had no idea what he was talking about. He brushed the fingers of his left hand over her cheek, then pulled his hand away to gesture at the double doors that led to his and Clarise's quarters at the other end of the room. Columbine twisted to see what he was pointing at.

"Just a moment ago when we were in there, you said, 'I'm sorry, but ....'." He opened his palm and laid it against the cheek furthest from him and drew her face back to him. Just thinking about it had his expression hardening until he was practically scowling at her.

Then he slowly shook his head, willing her to understand just how serious he was. "That's a very, very big no-no where Mystallians are concerned, princess. Never apologise, if your very next breath is to rescind that apology."

Columbine's eye ridges twitched, and her beak trembled. "Rescind?"

Right. Not Cora.

Taking another deep breath and releasing it slowly to vent his frustration, Avis lowered one hand to rub the bony ridge of her wing. *Baby words.* Not something he was overly good at, but he'd give it his best shot. "*Owning the Space* is more than just a series of pretty words, princess. It's a way of life. The Mystallian way of life; where backsliding's not an option. Every word out of your mouth needs to be owned by you. In Mystal, there's no such thing as an apology that ends in a 'but'. It's insulting, both to you and whoever you're saying it to. You either mean your apology and you're willing to stand by it, or you don't, in which case don't waste everyone's time saying it."

He'd tried to be gentle. By all the realms, he'd tried. Yet despite his best efforts, Columbine's wings slumped, her chest plates emitted a despondent wheeze, and her head bowed beneath the reprimand. The pose was one of defeat, which Avis would have none of. Not from her. Not from any member of his family. He hooked his finger under her beak and forced her to look up at him.

"Don't ever do that either, princess," he said softly, but vehemently. "At no point should you ever let anyone think you've been broken. Even during discipline, it's important that you learn to stand your ground. Take whatever's being dished out as your due, learn the lessons behind the discipline and walk away with your head held high. Sometimes, you may have to crawl away depending on what you've done, but do it still owning the mistake and the space it was made in."

Columbine's eye ridges sloped sharply. He'd never seen someone without eyes go so close to tears. "H-How?" The one-word question was barely a whimper, but in the silence of the room, she might as well have shouted it.

Hating the sadness and hurt that washed over him every time he saw her so miserable, Avis' hand left her beak and hooked around the nape of her neck. "C'mere, princess," he crooned, drawing her off the table and into his lap so her head could nestle against his throat.

Her wings were folded against her back, allowing one of his hands to anchor her firmly in place while the other stroked her exposed spine. "You have to let everyone know you're a Mystallian, baby, and it's not just the uniform. It's the presence that goes with it, both mentally and physically."

He rubbed his jaw against the crown of her head, over the two knobbly growths that might one day become horns. "I know it's a lot to ask, and I know you're not used to it, princess, but it is something you're going to have to learn before we get home. Do you understand?"

He felt the movement of her nod against his neck and titched in annoyance. "Use your words, princess. We'll start there."

"Yes, Father. I understand."

"Good girl." Believing he'd said enough on the matter for now, Avis decided to circle back to where this whole conversation began. "So … just to be clear … you woke up and came straight into my room, correct?" He didn't need to put her at arm's distance to see her face and gauge the truth of her answer. Nor did he need to go into her mind.

The one good thing about her utter inability to lie was the fact that she did totally suck at it, and he would hear the deception in her words alone.

Columbine went to nod again. He felt it against his throat, but before he could correct her, the movement stopped, and she said shyly, "Yes, Father. You were so happy that all I wanted was to be with you."

Her admission filled him with a combination of satisfaction and annoyance in equal measure. Yes, she'd remembered to use her words without prompting, but she'd also said she'd only had a few hours' sleep. Seven, maybe eight hours at best. Over the last few months he'd learned children as young as Columbine needed an average of ten.

He was about to take her back into her bedroom when something else occurred to him. "Are you excited about today, princess?" As innocent as he'd made the question sound, he wielded it like a double-edged sword. It was common knowledge how little their escape from Chaos meant to Columbine.

She didn't care where she was, so long as she was surrounded by family who loved her, which meant there was no reason for her to feel any level of excitement unless she was feeding off his. Given how impatient he was to be under way, she was never going to go back to sleep on her own if she was.

"Oh, yes, Father!"

Uh-huh.

That left Avis with two choices. He could either forcibly put her back to sleep, or take her with him and enjoy her company while the rest of the family slept on. Eight hours sleep wasn't ideal, but it was still doable. "Well, since the two of us are up and your mother and sister aren't, I was going to go for a walk outside when you ambushed me in my sitting room. Would you like to come with me?"

"Yes, Father."

Just like that. No hesitation.

Avis grinned, his throat rumbling in approval. It was a baby step, but one he would absolutely take. "Very well," he said, bracing her small body against his as he rose to his feet. Columbine hooked her hand around his neck for added support and settled comfortably against his chest. Rubbing his throat against her head once more, he made his way across the dining room to the massive double doors and let himself outside.

The guard silently followed.

CHAPTER FIFTY-FOUR

Clarise rose an hour later and joined them on the lawn, but when a further two hours came and went along with breakfast and there was still no sign of Cora, Avis decided he'd had enough. Columbine was still in his arms and while he enjoyed her company, he knew things were about to get very … *Mystallian* between Cora and him. He also knew his tiny princess wasn't quite up for that level of aggressive interaction.

Still in the dining room, he lifted Columbine higher in his arms and snuggled her close, then looked over at Clarise who stood nearby. "Stay with your mother, princess," he crooned softly, pressing his lips to the side of Columbine's head. He met Clarise's gaze and stepped forward, passing the child over to her. "I'm going to go and get Cora up."

Clarise must have read between the lines, for she accepted Columbine's weight with little more than a slight nod of agreement. (And yes, dammit, it was a nod. Her head moved up and down, so it *was* a nod, not a bow.) "I will take Columbine outside and prepare for our departure."

Avis leaned around Columbine to give his wife a parting peck on the lips. At least, it was meant to be a parting peck, but when her lavender scent and flavour invaded his senses, he hooked his hand around her neck and twisted his head until they were fully lip-locked. Tongues rolled together until he slowly rolled his head forward, separating their lips while resting their foreheads together. "Give me half an hour, sweetheart. We'll be ready to go by then."

"Of course."

Before he could talk himself out of it, Avis rubbed his hand across Columbine's head affectionately, then broke away. He heard the front doors open and close as he moved around the dining table, but he focused on the task at hand.

Cora.

Avis let himself into Cora's sitting room and looked around for the girl's governess. "Gingen!" he barked sharply, not bothering to shut the door behind him. He highly doubted that the shout would rouse his daughter, but he wasn't overly concerned if it did either. It wasn't as if he was here to ensure she remained asleep.

"Milord?" the servant replied, once the double doors that led into the bedroom opened to reveal the female in her natural centipede form. She bowed at the waist with her head tucked low and all of her limbs pointing to the ground in subservience.

Light, broken snoring echoed behind Gingen, telling Avis all he needed to know about Cora's current state, especially when it settled back into a steady rhythm shortly afterwards. "Draw Lady Cora a bath and ensure her riding gear is cleaned and ready to be worn by the time she's bathed."

He didn't offer any other information. Unlike his family, the servants didn't need to understand why they were given orders. Their job was to do as they were told.

The servant bowed and scurried backwards into the bedroom, leaving the double doors ajar. "Your will, milord." She scuttled towards the ensuite doors. Avis waited until she disappeared inside before he moved forward and let himself into the bedroom.

The bedding between the four posts looked as if something feral had nested there. It was all a twisted shambles of sheets, blankets and pillows, and somewhere in the middle of it was his little tiger. Her snoring was heavily muffled which caused him to smirk as he swept his eyes over the disarray.

It was a good thing he had no intention of ever allowing anyone to marry his girls. It seemed the more Cora settled into her Mystallian form, the more dangerous she became when she was asleep. He was surprised the bed had survived.

He moved around the large bed, searching for any hint of the body that lay within it, and found her foot sticking through the wooden head board, resting firmly against the wall. The bedhead had been one solid piece of timber the thickness of his hand and she'd kicked through it like it was paper. His grin broadened. Now, more than ever, she reminded him of Tal.

Following the outline of her leg, Avis' eyes trailed the blanketed lumps and bumps until he was sure he'd found the rounded bulge of her head hanging partially off the left-hand side of the mattress. Her arms appeared to be spread in both directions and her other foot almost touched the far side of the bed. In the throes of sleep, Cora had, in fact, claimed the entire bed.

Once Gingen returned and announced the bath was ready, he took the edge of the blanket and flipped it back to reveal his little tiger's red hair and shoulders. A scrunched-up pillow braced the back of her neck like a guardrail, elongating her neck backwards so that her closed eyes faced the back wall. Her mouth was open, and a small amount of drool clung to the corner of her lips, but without the blanket to muffle her, the sounds of her heavy snoring filled the room.

Avis took a moment to stare down at her, shaking his head. She didn't move. Not even a twitch. The slightest downward pressure on her head at that angle would snap her neck like a twig, and she was blissfully unaware of it. "Gingen," he called, not loudly enough to disturb Cora, but enough to bring the servant forward. He gestured at his sleeping child. "This angle of her neck during sleep is unacceptable. Don't let it happen again." Again, no explanation of why it was unacceptable. Just that it was.

Gingen bowed in silent acknowledgement of the order.

Having said his piece, Avis took a fistful of the sheets and blankets and pulled them from under Cora, deliberately rolling her to one side so that her head returned to the mattress proper. The little minx growled in response, drawing her knees to her chest and heaving her foot free of the headboard in the process. Her lips smacked, and her hand groped mindlessly for the elusive covers, but not once did she open her eyes. She quickly gave up and curled her hand under the pillow that braced her head. Her garbled mutterings drifted back into a light snore, which Avis would not have.

He snatched the mangled pillow from under her head and hauled it free. Then, in an afterthought, walloped her with it. "Up you get, tiger," he said with a lopsided grin, tossing the makeshift weapon over his shoulder. "We're heading out soon."

The little shit didn't even open her eyes. "Wha' … for?" she answered sleepily. "Not 'z if we 'r gettin' nowhere."

On any other day, Avis probably would've reacted badly to that. But not today. Today, he had every intention of leaving Chaos behind, and just the thought of it was making him channel the mischievous nature of his youngest brother. "You think so, huh?" Without warning, he plucked her from the bed and carried her into the ensuite. Further proof of her lethargy came from the irritated sleepy noises she made, as if she couldn't figure out what was going on … or what he was about to do.

That lasted less than ten seconds, when at the edge of the large bath he stretched out his arms and dropped her in; clothes and all.

Her screech of outrage as she broke the surface had him wanting to throw his head back and howl with laughter, but he had no intention of taking his eyes off her. Instead, he parted his feet and fisted his hands against his hips as if he were going to war; towering over the top of her. "You awake now, tiger?" he asked, his stance daring her to do anything about it.

Cora snarled and punched the surface of the water at him. It was an adorable display of temper, and he stepped to his right to avoid the subsequent spray. "I'll take that as a yes," he chuckled, as it splashed harmlessly against the floor where he'd been. "Good. As soon as you're done here, you need to come into the dining room and grab some breakfast. The rest of us have already eaten. Don't take long because like I said before, we're heading out soon."

Cora stood chest deep in the water and clenched her fists. Her tiny body shivered, seething with rage until she couldn't stand it anymore. Then she used both hands to push an even greater wall of water at him, which he dodged, just as easily as he had the first. "YOU SUCK!" she screamed, when neither wave hit her intended target. "STAND STILL!"

Laughing until tears blurred his vision, Avis felt his heart soar at the familiar aggression that came off the girl in waves. It was so good to be in the presence of another Mystallian, even if that Mystallian was a child who wanted nothing more than to drown him at that moment. It was refreshing—no—*invigorating.*

Avis would've loved to stay and match off with her as only a Mystallian could, but he knew he needed to leave her to it. Propriety dictated he couldn't stay and watch her bathe. It just wasn't the done thing in Mystal. The problem was, he also knew better than to turn his back on an irate Mystallian. That was just begging for something other than angry words to be hurled at him.

Glancing to his right where Gingen stood in the doorway, he gestured with a flick of his head to bring her forward. He stepped back at the same time, as if to give the servant room to work. Partial shielding, without losing any ground.

Gingen scuttled to the edge of the bath and doubled over with only a handful of limbs still anchoring her to the floor. Over two thirds of her body slipped into the water in search of the hem of Cora's nightgown and at that point Avis averted his eyes. "You've got five minutes, tiger," he said, holding the fingers of one hand up for her to see even though he wasn't looking at her. "Otherwise, you'll be riding on an empty stomach. Choice is yours."

With that, and a wave of that same hand to indicate he was leaving, he turned and withdrew from the room. Fast. If he hadn't been the one to bring Cora into the ensuite, he would've kept at least one room between them while she was naked. Preferably two. Three was even better.

Avis passed through both the bedroom and sitting room without pause and went out into the dining room. He took his seat at the head of the dining room table and lifted his left foot, resting it comfortably on his right knee. Two fingers began drumming out the time in seconds against his booted calf.

Somewhere between four minutes, forty-three seconds and four minutes, forty-nine seconds, Cora barrelled through the doors and launched herself over the dining table. She twisted and rolled in mid-air, clearing the table and its contents easily to land beside her chair with an ease that didn't match her youth. "How long have I got?" she asked, as she snatched up a fistful of bacon strips from the nearest plate and shoved them into her mouth, dropping herself into her seat.

Avis ignored the acrobatic display and dropped his foot to the floor, focusing instead on her actions once she landed. "Long enough for you to eat without reducing yourself to an animal," he answered, staring pointedly at the cutlery on either side of her plate before meeting her eyes again and arching one eyebrow. There was a time and a place for using fingers, and a formally prepared dining table wasn't one of them.

At least her mother wasn't here to explode at the lack of etiquette.

Cora smirked and picked up the nearest fork, then spun the utensil across her fingers and stabbed a fat sausage in the middle with all the grace of spear-fighter. An instant later she had over half of it stuffed into her mouth before her teeth sheared it in two. "Well, alright then," she said, in and around the oversized mouthful, which she then washed down with a gulp of juice.

Still not quite what Avis was hoping for, but the sooner she finished, the sooner they'd be on their way, so he said nothing more.

In what he felt was less than twenty minutes, the girl had managed to plough through half her body weight in food. While he put the expediency of her bath down to her hellion governess Gingen (who would've used touch shifting to dry the water from her ward's skin the moment she left the bath) that wasn't nearly as impressive as the size of the meal she was in the process of inhaling.

Emphasis on the word *inhaling*.

Despite him telling her that she could slow down, her hands had more in common with a pair of autonomous diggers, and he doubted she tasted a damn thing. "I know I've asked this before, but dammit, tiger, where in the realms do you put it all?" he asked, looking at the slip of a girl who would've weighed less than one of his legs.

Cora grinned around her latest mouthful and flicked her eyebrows at him over the mountain of food that she had still yet to eat. Her fork then promptly speared the next two honey covered pancakes as if they were trying to escape and she stuffed them both in her mouth with a quick roll of her wrist.

Honey dripped from the corner of her mouth as she struggled to contain the mass, causing Avis to chuckle. "Just don't let your mother see you eating like that, tiger. She'll kick your tail through your teeth for not showing better manners."

Cora's smile broadened to reveal bits of honey and pancake mashed between her teeth, even as her other hand stabbed two more pancakes. Avis shook his head, though he couldn't hide his amusement for the life of him. "Quick word of advice, tiger. You puke at any point today because of the way you're scoffing all that, and I swear I'll never let you live it down." He raised a hand and underscored it with a horizontal chopping motion. "Ever. I'll make sure it haunts you till the end of time."

Where most would have looked mortified, Cora snorted at the challenge and stared across the table at him with a steely-eyed focus, then doubled her food intake speed for good measure. Avis barked out a laugh at her audacity and slapped the table in front of him. "Don't say you weren't warned, you little shit. I hope you throw up all over yourself."

One word burbled out through her mouthful of food.

A very Mystallian word.

"Never!"

CHAPTER FIFTY-FIVE

Once Cora was finished, the family regrouped on the front lawn, along with the demon steeds, guards and servants. This part of the routine was second nature now, and Avis waited until Clarise mounted her own steed before he slid up on to his and repositioned the reins in his hands.

"Ready when you are, sweetheart," he said, and when she nodded, he whistled the single note to bring forth the demon steed's flaming wings. As one, the entire party took to the air, waiting just long enough for Clarise to dismantle the overnight house and return it to the flux that made up the Chaotic Ocean.

Avis used that time to clear his mind of all expectations, since that was one of the keys to navigating Chaos. Expectations led to failure and failure led to the probability of being snacked on by the demons that dwelled here.

Clarise had told him she'd been in touch with Uriel while he was inside with Cora, and not only had the winged bastard crowed about the glory of Heaven being all around him, he fully admitted he'd be there for the foreseeable future to bask in all its good graces. Every instinct in Avis' body screamed bullshit when he learned how his brother-by-marriage had offered them all the information they required without first being asked for it—as if the bastard couldn't wait to tell them exactly what they needed to know.

At least he wasn't alone in his suspicions. Clarise had also questioned her brother's forthrightness, despite knowing through her innate ability that he'd been speaking the truth.

Questioning the will of a demon lord wasn't something she'd have done six months ago, and Avis had to fight back the need to throw both fists over his head and roar at the demonic realm in victory, choosing instead to sink his teeth into his bottom lip and nod sedately at her assessment.

"Take us to Yaru, my love," Clarise said, indicating the estate below was no more.

Knowing what he had to do, Avis released his bottom lip, drew in a deep breath and nodded again. He focused on every memory he had of his angelic brother-by-marriage. Every curse they ever exchanged. Every injury he'd endured at the end of a chain. Every different type of vivisection.

All the times the winged bastard had impaled him upside down and skinned him, only to laugh as Avis' internal organs spilled out across the floor. It was a long list, stretching two years, and with each new flashback, he remembered why he never wanted to see Uriel again.

Homing in on that desire, Avis picked a direction at random, and the party moved out.

Once or twice during the ride, a particularly vicious or humiliating memory occurred to the Mystallian patriarch and his hunger for revenge boiled until he found himself honestly wanting a rematch with Uriel. Preferably when they were on neutral territory, away from the influence of Hell where they would be on equal footing.

His lips twitched viciously at all the possibilities that flashed through his mind, until he realised thoughts like that were completely undermining his current objective; sending them away from Uriel instead of drawing them to him. *Later,* he promised himself, smothering those desires and shoving them to the furthest part of his mind.

Focus, you idiot. Controlling minds was meant to be his forte, and his inability to keep his own wandering thoughts in check was just plain embarrassing.

Stopping only once for lunch, they rode hard all day, crawling that little bit closer to the bluish grey horizon. It was a nightmare for Avis; to see their goal approach and not view it as progress. He had to stay focused on Uriel.

Only Uriel.

Uriel, and all the hatred he bore that brother-by-marriage. But he really wanted to get out of Chaos today, if he could.

Just as the glowing bead on Avis' cuff reached his little finger and he had to accept the fact they'd be spending another night in the Chaotic Ocean, both heat and brightness exploded all around them; overwhelming his senses from all sides. His flesh instantly prickled beneath the heavy black Mystallian uniform and his breath caught in his throat as the light blinded him. His demon steed screeched and flared its wings, rearing in panic.

"What the …!"

Acting on pure instinct, Avis locked his knees into its ribs and leaned forward alongside its flaming mane to prevent being thrown. His left hand shortened the reins to keep its head under control while the other shaded his eyes, blinking through the glare to search for the source of this unprovoked attack.

Then it dawned on him.

This wasn't a celestial attack. It was daylight! Real, marvellously wonderful daylight! After months of everything being in a state of flux, solid … bright … *glorious* sunlight bathed him from head to toe until his skin beneath the heavy black leathers flushed uncomfortably.

Having already shortened his reins, he shot a mental spike into the beast's mind to bring it to heel. The process was as instantaneous as it was automatic. He was too experienced an equestrian to be bothered by an unsettled steed. The same could not be said for his young family, specifically the girls, and he whirled around to see how they fared.

As he expected, Clarise already had her steed under control. Both rider and beast hovered in mid-air with a superlative calm that Avis knew didn't come naturally to the demon steed. Not after the way his own had flipped out so badly. *You hammered it with a physical sedative of some kind. I know you did.* The beginnings of a wry smile tugged at his lips as he moved his gaze to where the other two demon steeds hovered nearby.

Both were under the singular control of a guard who had wrapped tentacles from one of its upper extremities around each of their necks like a lasso. The casual way the beasts hovered in place implied they too had been given a touch sedative of some kind in the process.

Cora sat high on her beast's withers, her knees digging so hard into its shoulders it would have been injured had it not consisted primarily of hellfire. That hellish compound also explained how Cora's boots were able to pierce the wings, yet the beast remained airborne instead of falling out of the sky. Hellfire surrounded the intruding limb, and like any fire, it was able to flow around the obstruction and maintain its surface integrity. None of which harmed the Highborn Hellion rider.

Avis was hugely impressed. All this time he'd been positioning himself back behind the wings, believing for safety reasons that he shouldn't interfere with them in any way. Had such a significant hole been punched through the wing of a mystallion mid-flight, the fastest equines in the realms would have spiralled downwards, completely out of control. No exceptions.

To learn the demon steeds were capable of this adaptation when his own mystallions weren't, lifted their value in his mind. He just might have to keep Hot Spot after all.

Cora paid no attention to the remarkable feat. Her tiny hands were wrapped around the beast's neck in a white-knuckled grip and her head was bowed until her forehead was lost in its mane of fire. Through the flames, Avis saw her eyes were scrunched tight and every breath she sucked in shuddered her whole body.

He'd seen enough terrified kids over the eons to know she wouldn't move from that spot until someone convinced her it was safe to do so.

He was already turning his mount around to do just that when he realised the second demon steed ... the one that should have been carrying Columbine ... *wasn't*.

Columbine was gone.

Panic surged through him and with an iron grip on his steed's reins, he dug his knees in behind its shoulders and lifted himself off its back, swinging to look in all directions at once for his missing child; including down. *By the twin notes ... don't be down ....*

He sucked in a huge breath with the intent to scream her name, the motion automatically lifting his chin. There, high and to the far right of the party, he caught sight of a golden brute squad guard outside the rearing range of the demon steeds with Columbine in two of its four arms.

Icy relief flooded his veins as his eyes swept over the girl, searching for any sign of injury. Nothing immediately stood out. Tresses of ebony fell over the guard's arm, blocking his view of the golden insignia which adorned the middle of her black cloak. It all waved rhythmically in the light breeze, though her fringe was braided past her ears and bound behind her head by a long-stemmed rose to keep her locks in check.

Black fabrics and leather covered her from neck to toe, and those gorgeous ebony eyes were rounded in shock. But she was safe. They were all safe.

Latching on to that statement like a mantra, Avis breathed out slowly and lowered himself to the demon steed. Everything was fine. They were all fine. *Fine, fine, fine.* The guard wasn't to blame for following his orders so exactly. It had been told to protect her above all else, and for a few seconds their steeds *had* been out of control, so removing her until the situation righted itself was precisely the right thing to do.

With Columbine safe, Avis returned his attention to Cora. Of the three ladies in his life, she was the one who most needed his reassurance right now. He urged his demon steed forward until his knee brushed hers and tried not to think about how both sets of demon steed wings were beating *through* them at that moment.

"You alright, tiger?" he asked, knowing very well she wasn't but hoping the sound of his voice would soothe her.

Cora slowly peeled herself off the demon steed's neck and looked up at him through glazed eyes. She pursed bloodless lips together and nodded jerkily at him, still too shaken to speak.

Avis loosely looped his reins together and dropped them to free his hands. His mind was ready to take full control of the beast if it chose to act out, but his priority was Cora. He reached out and gently gathered her into his arms. No fast movements were made, and he gave her every opportunity to pull away if she didn't want this, but something told him she did. "It's alright, tiger," he crooned, lifting her across to his mount where he nestled her against his chest. "It's over."

With one hand holding her against him, Avis used the other to stroke her hair. "Take a deep breath, tiger. Big as you can. Go on," he urged, nudging her shoulder with his chest when she failed to comply. "One deep breath." He could have forced the issue, mentally compelled her to obey, but somehow, this felt more ... *right*. "Just one."

He felt Cora's ribs expand to accommodate the shaky breath. "Good, now breathe it out." Her chest deflated in a rushed huff, this time without him needing to repeat the direction. Just that one action began to calm her. "And again, tiger. Deeper this time. Breath in ... and let it out."

Avis repeated the motion until she stopped shaking and her chin lifted until she could look at him. Her eyes were still glazed with unshed tears, but the steel behind them told him she wasn't about to let them fall.

The tip of her tiny tongue crept along her parched lips and she swallowed, her breathing deepening automatically with the motion. Knowing they were past the worst of it, Avis loosened his grip enough to give her an escape, should she want it.

What happened next surprised the hell out of him.

Cora sniffed loudly, then closed her eyes and twisted her face into his doublet. Her arms snaked around his waist to anchor herself to him and she wriggled closer for deeper physical contact.

In all the months they'd been travelling, Cora had never cuddled him before. Not once. Refusing to question the move, Avis tightened his arm around her again and dropped a kiss to her hair. "It's alright, tiger. I've got you."

He caught the edge of his cloak and drew it up and around her, shielding her from the family in case she didn't want them to see her vulnerability. He used that same hand to stroke her back and shoulders, even as he rubbed the underside of his jaw across her head. "I've got you," he repeated.

He held her for as long as she needed, and after a little while, he thought he heard her mutter something unintelligible against his chest. Curiosity got the better of him and he loosened his hold enough to twist to the side, so their faces were closer together. "What was that, tiger?"

Cora sniffed again and pulled away from his chest to look up at him, rubbing the back of her hand against her eyes as if the threat of tears offended her. "I said I still did not throw up."

After everything they'd just been through, *that* was what she wanted him to acknowledge?

Avis chuckled deeply, his whole chest rumbling with the sound. He couldn't help it. "No, you didn't," he agreed, dropping his cloak to ruffle her hair affectionately. "And when we get time, I'm going to show you how to use your bending abilities properly. You're too used to shifting your way around weaker creatures, and when fear took hold, you forgot you have just as much bending muscle at your disposal. One on one, you can bring any single mind of lesser power to heel in an instant just as easily as you can dominate their shape. It's easy, once you know how."

Inwardly, he kicked himself for not utilising the long weeks they'd spent on the Akheron River to work through this. It would've given them both something productive to do as well as alleviate the boredom, and it wasn't as if they didn't have enough Damned to practice on.

Cora sniffed and nodded again, this time with more conviction, causing Avis to smile with pride. "That's better, tiger. And when we do, get ready for some serious fun, because you'll be able to make people do some pretty wild things … and the best part is, they'll think it's their idea."

Cora blinked rapidly to clear the last of her vision. "Sounds good," she admitted, shifting her weight in his arms to indicate she wanted to return to her own demon steed.

Avis lifted her over the small gap and deposited her squarely on the beast's back. Then he whistled the single note that had her beast tossing its head so that the abandoned reins fell across his outstretched hand. Passing them to Cora, he grinned and nudged her arm playfully. "Wild stab in the dark, tiger, but I think you might need these."

The girl said nothing as she crossed her eyes over her screwed up nose and took the reins from him. Her lips were pinched in a tight line of what was supposed to be annoyance, but the way her face muscles twitched he could see she was fighting the urge to smile.

Avis took it as another win for him, and before either one of them could spoil the moment, he gathered up his own reins and wheeled his steed in a tight half-circle to face Columbine.

Since she was no longer in danger, the guard carrying her drifted down to hover directly in front of the party, on an eye level with everyone else. Columbine was hugging herself tightly. Her shoulders were hunched forward, and her lips were parted in a shy smile and her beautiful dark eyes were glazed with tears of joy. Happiness practically radiated from her.

Avis allowed that happiness to wash over him like a cleansing summer shower.

Then it finally dawned on him.

Long dark hair! Eyes! Mystallian uniform! Mystallian features! It'd been months since he'd seen Columbine in anything other than her demonic form, and now that she was a Mystallian, he couldn't believe he hadn't noticed it straight away. "Columbine!" he called and immediately urged his demon steed forward.

The moment he was within arm's reach of her, he angled his knees into the demon steed's ribs for traction and dropped his reins, reaching for his precious child with both hands. The guard loosened its hold, and he drew her to him with great care until he hugged her firmly against his chest. "Oh, princess," he cooed, cuddling her close. "You've no idea how much I've missed this version of you."

He remained mindful not to crush her, as much as he surely wanted to. He kissed and petted her hair, loving the glossy feel of it after dealing with leather and digit-sized horn lumps for so long. And he could finally hug her properly. No wings to get in the way.

This was by far one of the best days of his life, and it was made even better when he realised the significance of it all. The sunlight ... Columbine's Mystallian form ...

He swung back towards Clarise, his heart pounding with barely contained elation. "We made it, didn't we?" he asked, wanting ... *needing* her to confirm what he hoped was true with every fibre of his being. That Chaos was finally behind them.

Years of dodging the Hellions. Years more of suffering at their hands. Months of living with the knowledge that a single whim from his father-by-marriage would have them all front and centre of Hell's High Court and there was literally nothing he could do about it. Were they truly clear of Chaos?

Clarise smiled and dipped her head once in affirmation.

Euphoria overwhelmed him with all the finesse of a tidal wave and he tilted his head back and bellowed his delight at the sky overhead. "YES!" With one hand still locked around Columbine's waist to secure her, he punched the other through the air in triumph.

They were finally free of Chaos! Fuck Belial and his bastard pack of asshole sons! They could all kiss his ass now! He and his family were free, and they were *never* going back! He hugged Columbine close, his chest rippling with near hysterical laughter.

Columbine giggled and squirmed happily, proving once again how she couldn't differentiate the heightened emotions of others from her own. It was still a point of concern, but right then he didn't care. He laughed again; the warmth of the moment flowing through both of them.

Then he placed his hands against her sides and, without warning, tossed her into the air just over his head. Clarise gasped, and Columbine squealed, but he caught her easily a second or two later when she fell back into his arms, and the two hugged and laughed again.

"Me! Me!"

Avis barely had time to register Cora's words, but a quick glance over his shoulder let him know she had already stood up and leapt over her demon steed's head, for she was flying through the air and almost upon him.

Her landing on the rump of his steed was precarious at best, and as the beast pranced from the unexpected impact, she snatched at his fluttering cloak for balance.

Three things happened at once for Avis. Four, if he was to count the way his heart shot into his mouth. His right arm whipped around to secure Cora against his back to prevent her from falling; his left hand tightened around Columbine, holding her in a death grip against his chest; and his legs locked in around the demon steed's ribs to hold them all in place.

Without a powerbase to ensure her immortality, the jump was beyond hare-brained and dangerous. The ground was so far below them, he wasn't even sure it was down there, and her Mystallian form had no wings.

"Cora!" he shouted when he finally found his voice, for while he was almost certain the brute squad would catch her before she fell too far, it wasn't something he wanted to test … like … *ever.*

Cora didn't seem to notice the risk she'd just taken. With her excitement high and both her hands gripping his right shoulder, she tried a combination of squirming and climbing over his restraining arm to get around in front of him. "I want a turn!"

Avis was torn between being annoyed by her recklessness and being proud of her willingness to pursue what she wanted with typical Mystallian fervour. It took him a moment to settle his own fright, during which time he forced himself to appreciate the way the cheeky little minx had jumped ten times farther than he'd thrown Columbine in her determination to be part of their game.

Clarise bore a displeased expression, but this flamboyance was precisely what he'd been trying to fan to life in Cora for months, and he subtly shook his head. "You're going to turn Mystal on its ear when we get home, tiger," he grinned, moving Columbine on to his left thigh while dragging Cora around until she was perched on his right thigh facing outwards. "And I can't wait to see it."

Neither of his girls weighed much, but with one hand still protectively holding Columbine, Avis only had his right hand to toss Cora the way she wanted. Which meant he'd have to improvise.

It was awkward, but once Cora was properly balanced on his thigh, he removed his supporting arm from her waist and took a fistful of her doublet, twisting her a little so he could look her in the eyes. Then, after he'd waited just long enough for her face to light up with anticipation, he thrust her into the air—much, much higher than he had with Columbine.

Cora squealed with delight. All the way up … and all the way down. He timed his catch perfectly, using his arm to slow her descent and guide her back into his body before she collided with his thigh. All three howled with laughter, while a bemused Clarise looked on.

He'd truly never gotten it before. For more eons than he could count, he'd watched his siblings, and their offspring devote their lives to their little family groups, willing to do anything to make them happy. They'd run themselves into the ground for little more than a smile of gratitude. A smile!

Those with many children and grandchildren had been so exhausted at times that they could hardly move, yet they'd always told him without hesitation that they'd do it all again the following day if that were what their families wanted. He'd never understood that desire to compromise.

In his mind, less could never be more. How could anyone prefer the notion of running something past a significant other to see if it was permissible when they already had all the freedom to do anything they wanted?

Considering the absolute *lack* of freedom they'd grown up with, conceding it to anyone else had always seemed a backwards and illogical step to him.

Now, as he cuddled his children close and looked over their heads to his wife hovering nearby, he knew he was finally getting it. All this time, he'd merely been existing. A perpetual child himself, drifting from one eon to the next with no real meaning to his life. Of course, he was a god, but that wasn't a real achievement; merely a by-product of circumstance.

This—what he had in his arms right now as their beloved mother watched on—was collectively the most important thing in his existence. Their happiness was what *made* his life worth living. It was neither forced, nor a lie. He finally understood the difference.

Taking something from someone by force was empty and meaningless since all that really procured was an unhealthy dose of superiority. Whether he was the winner or the loser, it was still the flip side of the same ugly coin.

But having all that power and still be willing to yield it to please a special group of others—there wasn't a feeling in the realms to describe it.

He broke eye contact with Clarise and gazed out over the bright orange sky ahead of them.

Yaru.

And their future.

Drawing his girls closer, Avis made a mental promise to get them all back to Mystal. All the way back. As of this moment, no other outcome was acceptable to him.

...and we'll do it together, one realm at a time.

EPILOGUE

OF ALL THE HORSESHIT, SENTIMENTAL WANKEROUS FUCKING BULLCRAP! Theodrick raged, stamping his feet in front of his throne and furiously pounding his fists into the fabric coated arms. *YOU AND THAT FUCKWIT, FUCKING BITCH-FACED WHORE OF YOURS HAVE FUCKING MADE AN ABSOLUTE MOTHER-FUCKING PANSY OUT OF MY FUCKING BOY!*

Debatable, Belial replied without going into specifics or rising at the slur of his daughter.

For a moment, it crossed his mind to draw Theodrick's attention to the fact that the cantankerous fool had unintentionally admitted his son had lost to Clarise, but he decided against it. He had precisely zero chance of convincing the Bender of true family values, and he wanted to make a point while his counterpart had some semblance of control. *But you will not touch him to make him think otherwise. He came to this conclusion on his own, and whether he maintains it or loses it, he will do so without your influence.*

Theodrick stilled, his eyes widening in astonishment at the declaration. Unfortunately, his disbelief was short-lived. Slamming both fists into the arms of his throne, he threw himself forward. *JUST WHO THE FUCKING FUCK DO YOU FUCKING THINK YOU ARE, SHIFTER? THAT FUCKING JUMPED-UP LITTLE ASSHOLE IS MINE, AND I CAN FUCKING WELL DO WHATEVER THE FUCKING FUCK I FUCKING WANT TO THE FUCKING BASTARD!*

Ordinarily, Belial would have agreed. To date, he'd had no control over what his counterpart had done to his children—no matter how deplorable those actions had been. But things had changed in recent years; especially where Theodrick's *second* eldest son was concerned.

Belial also leaned forward, balancing a single talon on the edge of his throne arm in warning. *My blood now runs in his veins, Bender. He may be your son, but so long as he wears the marriage bracers of my house, any new assaults on him which I deem unnecessary will be officially crossing the line with me.*

Theodrick punched his throne arms again and threw himself back into the seat. *FUCK YOU! YOU FUCKING DID THIS ON FUCKING PURPOSE!*

Hardly. Belial would never have chosen Avis for any of his daughters. As far as he'd been concerned, Theodrick and his crazy spawn belonged as far from him and his family as possible. Nevertheless, the union of their families had created the Weaver.

Not exactly the way either of the existing Pillars had anticipated the third member of their triumvirate to appear. Their own creations had been spontaneous and complete at the beginning of time, so he'd always assumed the Weaver would one day materialise on a throne with all the knowledge and power necessary to get the job done. Just as they had.

To learn the Weaver was a wide-eyed, naive girl-child, barely able to control her own emotions, let alone the emotions of others, was terrifying. She didn't hear their upper realms speech, nor could she see their ghostly forms as they spied on each other and the realms, which meant her ascension would probably be a series of baby steps until she mastered the power that matched off with theirs.

Once that was done, the pillars would finally be complete, and nothing would be beyond them.

Time would tell.

ACKNOWLEDGEMENTS

Thanks must go out to the friends and family who supported me through this crazy journey. To my husband Wayne, and my three girls. It may have been bumpy for a while as life continues to throw us curve balls, but we still have each other's backs. To Alan (Ack), who convinced me to finish what I started and has never once lost faith in me.

And lastly, to my mother, Jan. The one person who always encouraged me to follow my dreams; right to the end.

I love you all.

Since the first edition went out almost two years ago, I have made some fantastic online friends. None more dear to me than Drew Hassell. Drew is an American editor who took my work under his wing, and reshaped this second edition into what it is now. I cannot sing his praises highly enough.

RECOMMENDATIONS

Arkos Sloth Editing at arkossloth1@gmail.com

ABOUT THE AUTHOR

Karen Buckeridge is a first time author who has always been interested in things just outside the veil of normality. She lives a quiet life in North Queensland with her husband and the youngest of her three children. Her older two have grown up and moved on to create families of their own, though they still stay in touch.

Karen loves creating realistic characters with recognisable flaws and personality types despite their power levels, and fun, interesting story arcs that leave the reader wondering 'Maybe?'

She's an avid reader of all things supernatural, paranormal and romance... not necessarily in that order or exclusively.